FALLING
WITH
FOLDED
WINGS

BOOK 2

FALLING WITH FOLDED WINGS

 BOOK 2

Plum Parrot

To Brian and Christian
for all the worlds we created together

All rights reserved. No part of this publication may be reproduced, stored in a retrieval system, or transmitted in any form or by any means electronic, mechanical, photocopying, recording, or otherwise without prior written permission from Podium Publishing.

This is a work of fiction. Names, characters, places, and incidents are either products of the author's imagination or used fictitiously. Any resemblance to actual events, locales, or persons, living, dead, or undead, is entirely coincidental.

Copyright © 2023 by Miles C. Gallup

Cover design by Podium Publishing

ISBN: 978-1-0394-2136-3

Published in 2023 by Podium Publishing, ULC
www.podiumaudio.com

FALLING WITH FOLDED WINGS

BOOK 2

⚔ MORGAN ⚔

Morgan and Issa sat on one of the new stone benches encircling the hilltop where the Colony Stone rose out of the ground. Actually, it was a Town Stone now. Arthur had explained that the colony had reached a milestone with buildings that had allowed him to expend some System credits to upgrade the stone. Morgan wasn't sure of all the benefits such an upgrade entailed, but he was glad that the settlement was making progress. There were two taverns in town now, and several aspiring merchants had purchased shop deeds from the council. The "Downtown" area around the hill was starting to flesh out.

"Well, what do you think?" Issa prodded.

"Hmm? Oh yeah, I think a bit of traveling would be nice. The town seems to be coming along nicely, and there don't seem to be any imminent threats. Especially now that that Norton guy figured out a way to make rifled barrels; the militia will be able to hold the walls even easier."

"Those weapons certainly seem deadly."

"Yeah. So, did you have any particular destination in mind?"

"Well, I want to adventure. I've always wanted to, but I don't know exactly how to go about it. I've heard stories about dungeons, far-off cities, and mysterious creatures—ever since I was a little girl, I wanted to get out into the world. That's part of the reason I went into the Crucible. I just don't know where to start." She huffed out a sigh and scuffed her feet back and forth on the cobbles.

"Well, my mysterious mentor gave me a clue about where I might find a swordmaster to learn from. He even thought I might find more information about my Fighting Crane Style. We could try to search out that place."

"Perfect! Some traveling, some new sights, a chance to learn new skills—what more could we want?" Issa smiled and leaned her head against his shoulder.

"Hmm, yeah. It'll be nice to get out on the road with our roladii and not feel like there was a deadline to worry about."

"Are you going to try another guardian before we go?"

"No, even with my new skills, Tiladia puts my chances at fifty-fifty. I think I want to learn some more before going up there."

"Good! No need to take unnecessary risks!" Issa said, squeezing his arm, and Morgan nodded. They sat for a while, enjoying the spring morning, then set off to find Arthur Ballard. Morgan wanted to let him know about their plans and ensure he didn't need anything before they left. He and Issa had already said goodbye to Bronwyn, who was out helping her Urghat followers to deal with some of the fallout resulting from the Urghat horde breaking up.

They found Arthur in the new town civic building that functioned as a meeting hall and council office. He was looking at a large map laid out on a table with Rene Bisset, who had taken Reggie's place on the council. "Arthur, may I have a word with you?"

"Of course. Just a moment, Rene." Arthur walked around the table to shake Morgan's hand. Morgan was pleased when he also shook Issa's hand. Relations between the two peoples had been good, but he always appreciated it when people went out of their way to demonstrate goodwill.

"Issa and I are going to do a bit of traveling. I have a lead I want to run down that might help me advance one of my skills, and we just want to see more of the world. I figure we can help to flesh out our maps of the surrounding areas and, if we're lucky, make contact with more of the inhabitants."

"Hmm. Yes, we need to get scouts out and start trading more information with our friends in Tarn's Crossing. I suppose it wouldn't hurt for you to make your own efforts, though it will leave us down three council members. Olivia is gone, and we don't know for how long. Bronwyn should be back soon, I'd think, though. Hmm, yes, I don't have any objections. Thank you for checking in with me, Morgan."

"Yeah, no worries." Morgan almost said that he hadn't come to ask permission but rather as a courtesy, but he didn't see any point in creating needless friction. He and Issa made their way over to his tower and spent a few minutes with their mounts. The roladii appreciated a good scratch and a fresh bucket of water. Then the two of them went into the tower to make arrangements for their departure. Morgan made sure Ykleedra had plenty of food, and he gave her the important "Mission" of helping Tiladia with her translations. Tiladia assured him that Ykleedra had been a lot of help and that she should have some results for him when he returned.

Morgan was going through his belongings, making sure he had everything he wanted to bring for the journey, when he came upon the rapier that he'd taken from the smoldering guardian he'd fought on the third floor. "Hey, Issa. I completely forgot about this rapier, but I've been holding it a long time, intending to give it to you. Do you think it's better than the one you've been using?" He handed the thin, shining sword to Issa. She took it in her hand and gave it a few swings and practice feints.

"It's a beautiful weapon, Morgan. This steel has an orange glow to it—I think it has a lot of Amber ore in the mix. Let me try bonding with it." She concentrated for a moment, and then a huge smile lit up her face. "Morgan, it has lots of enchantments! It is hardened, has a self-sharpening ability, and has a small chance to inflict burning damage to an enemy when I hit them!"

"Wow, well, happy birthday."

"Birthday?"

"Oh, yeah, my people customarily celebrate the day of their birth each year. You don't do that?"

"We have something similar. We celebrate something called a name day—it's the day you are given a name."

"You don't get a name at birth?"

"Some people do. Though most people think it's dangerous to tempt fate and wait until the infant is older and stronger before giving them their name." She smiled and reached a hand up to Morgan's arm, squeezing gently. "Thank you, Morgan, for the gift!"

"Of course!" Morgan leaned down and kissed her. "Let's get packed and get going. No sense waiting; it's not even noon."

They were mounted and riding out the western gate twenty minutes later. Morgan marveled at the freedom he felt—no job, no government thumb on his neck, and no relations to worry about other than Issa, who was with him. Sure, in the back of his mind, he had a little itching worry about Ykleedra and Bronwyn and about the colony as a whole. He'd also grown quite close to Olivia over the last few weeks, and he hoped she was doing well. Of all those, though, the only one he really felt responsible for was Ykleedra, and she should be fine with Tiladia in the tower.

Munch and Issa's roladii, Gopp, made an easy pace through the game trails in the woods. They stopped in the mid-afternoon for a late lunch of dense rye bread smeared with creamy butter, sliced apples, and cubes of cured ham. "Do you miss home yet, Issa? Do you think about your friends? What do you think they are all thinking about you now, after that duel and you leaving town?" Issa's face went from relaxed to pensive, and she gave Morgan a frown.

"Really know how to dampen the mood, don't you?" She smiled to lighten the tone of her words, but Morgan could see it took her some effort. "I do miss home, but I've always wanted to get out. I've told you that. I'm sure we'll visit again soon. As for friends, yes, I had some good ones, but you didn't see them out on that field to support us, did you? Oh, I guess you wouldn't have known if any of those spectators were my friends, but I'll tell you: no, they weren't."

"Why is that, do you think?"

"Well, I think some of them took it personally when I risked my life to go into the Crucible. My best friend, Hanni, tried desperately to talk me out of it.

Then, when I came back with an advanced class and a wild story of adventure, I think some of them felt I was putting on airs, and they slowly started to spend less time with me. When you showed up, I think it was the final straw. Anyway, who needs jealous friends?" She looked down with a frown, scuffing her foot in the dirt.

"Hey, sorry to bring it up, but I know you; you definitely aren't acting better than them! If they really are avoiding you out of jealousy, I'm sure they'll come around." Morgan reached out and held her hand, and they sat for a while, enjoying the slight spring breeze as it whispered through the tree canopy. A bird was singing a bright, trilling song, and Morgan closed his eyes, once more soaking in the unrestrained feeling of freedom.

They continued riding to the west for the rest of the afternoon and into the early evening. As the shadows lengthened and the warm spring air turned to chilly twilight, they noticed that the slope of the forest floor gradually increased. In a clearing created by a massive tree that had fallen, Morgan suggested they stop for the night. Issa, ever agreeable, nodded, and they tied their roladii to some broken branches sticking out of the felled giant. They made a small fire outside their tent, set up in the lee of the trunk. While they ate a supper similar to their lunch, Morgan asked, "Issa, how close are you to twenty? You'll get a class refinement at twenty, right?"

"Yes, our advancement seems similar to humans. I'm level fourteen, so I have a ways to go." Issa bit a large chunk out of the drumstick she was holding. It looked very much like a turkey drumstick, but Issa said it was from a bird called a pultii. When she had described it, Morgan couldn't help picturing a turkey with yellow feathers.

"Do you have any idea what sort of refinement you'll be offered? Are you hoping for anything?"

"I don't! No one from Tarn's has had the Battle Witch class, so I don't know what will come. I'm excited, though!"

"Yeah, Bronwyn said your chant was extremely helpful in the Urghat fight."

"Yes! My chant will strengthen us and weaken our enemies. I've also improved my Haste spell, and I'm hoping I'll get another unique skill soon, before level twenty." Morgan nodded, and they continued to talk a while about skills, but the conversation soon turned to food and favorite things to eat. Then Morgan asked about music, and Issa said there were ways to get music samples from around the world and perhaps other worlds through the Town Stones. Morgan had never looked that deeply through the miscellaneous categories of items for sale. Issa pulled a small marble-shaped crystal out of her bag and touched it briefly. A haunting melody played on string instruments began to emanate from the marble, and Morgan and Issa lay together in their tent, listening to it for a long time.

The next day around noon, they broke free from the dense woods and found themselves in low foothills sparsely covered in thorny thickets. "The Azure Paladin told me that the citadel was in some place called the Orangerock Hills west of the woods we just left."

"I've not heard of them, but maybe the name is a clue? Perhaps we should be looking for rocky hills with an orange tint?"

"That's what I was thinking. Let's follow these hills in a northwesterly direction and see if we get lucky. If we don't find something in a few days, we can wander back in a southerly direction." Issa nodded, and they started on their way. They had covered several miles and were ready to stop for some food when Morgan noticed some dust in the distance. He spurred Munch up the next hill to try for a better vantage. As he and Issa crowned the hilltop, clanging sounds and muffled shouts came to their ears. Over the next hill, where the cloud of dust hung, Morgan caught sight of a mounted roladii as it ran up the slope and then back down out of sight. "Was that an Ardeni riding that roladii?"

"I think not—the roladii looked too small under him. Should we lay low or investigate?"

"Well, it sounds like a fight, and someone might need help. Let's check it out." Morgan didn't have to convince Issa; she was quick to spur Gopp forward, and he hurried to catch up. When they climbed the next hill, the sounds of shouting grew louder. As they crested the top, an interesting tableau revealed itself. Down the hillside, a small, dusty valley spread out for a mile or so. In the center of the valley, several wagons circled a flock of yellow, sheep-like creatures. Standing around and on the wagons were a dozen or so Cadwalli brandishing spears and short bows, and riding around them, kicking up dust and whooping, were about twenty bright-red skinned men and women on roladii. Issa loudly hissed when she saw them.

"Shadeni!"

"Shadeni?" Morgan looked at her with an eyebrow arched.

"Yes, distant cousins of us Ardeni, but they are nomads and often turn to banditry."

"Huh," Morgan muttered, looking at the satyr-like Cadwalli trying to defend their herd. "So, they're the aggressors here? You think they'll listen to reason?"

"I don't know. Shadeni follow an honor code, not unlike the Ardeni, but if they have turned fully brigand, they might just add us to their list of targets."

"Well, let's go see if they'll talk." Morgan didn't wait for a response as he walked Munch down the hillside.

⚜ OLIVIA ⚜

Nearly as soon as her vision faded to black, a pinpoint of light appeared in Olivia's view that slowly widened to reveal a new scene. Momentary vertigo assaulted her as her body tried to make sense of the sudden change of perspective. She was no longer standing in a comfortable tavern looking into the faces of her friends. Rather, she was standing on a marble dais overlooking a smooth, stone archway stretching for a mile or more across a cloud-filled chasm. On the other side of the archway, rising into still more clouds from a rocky spire, was a walled keep with dozens of soaring towers.

The keep had to be one of the largest buildings she'd ever seen. She could imagine a professional sports arena sitting comfortably within its high, gold-speckled white walls. Pennants flew from most of the towers, all of them seemed different, but from this distance, Olivia could only make out their colors, not the devices depicted on them. As she stood, slack-jawed, staring at the building, noticing new detail after new detail, a new sight came into her peripheral vision that took her breath away.

A flying ship was approaching the wall of the keep. It looked like a seventeenth-century galleon, but in addition to its masts filled with sails, long spars ran out the sides like wings with more sails. Whatever force propelled the great ship and kept it aloft seemed to emanate from a dozen swirling golden rings that spun along its keel. Olivia watched as the ship slowly floated to a stop near the top of the keep's wall, and she could just barely make out little figures moving along the deck and ropes being tossed out to secure the ship.

Olivia looked down at the marble dais on which she stood and saw a set of steps leading down to a stone walkway. Following the walkway with her eyes, she could see that it led to the archway, and also branched off to lead around the curve of the mountaintop she was apparently standing on. At first, it seemed like she'd arrived unnoticed, for she couldn't see anyone around, but as she started down the steps, she saw a small figure slowly approaching across the great stone bridge.

Looking over her shoulder, Olivia could see the rocky peak continue for several hundred feet. She turned back toward the path and started walking to meet the advancing figure. She was about fifty feet from the archway when the figure reached the near side and stopped to wait. Olivia could see that the person was small, maybe only four feet tall, with long silvery hair. As she grew nearer, she could discern a definite feminine quality about the person. At first, Olivia thought her skin was very pale, but as she got nearer still, she saw that the woman wore thick white paint on her face and neck, with dark blue stains painted around her eyes and on her lips. "Hello!" Olivia called as she stepped onto the foot of the archway.

"Welcome! We were all surprised that the token from the Chebli Sea region was activated. I am Yunsha, and I'm pleased to be your greeter." The woman had a high but sedate voice, speaking in a steady cadence that made her diction seem very precise.

"Hello, Yunsha. I'm Olivia." Olivia continued to step forward and held out a hand to the diminutive person. Yunsha reached out with both hands to grasp Olivia's in a warm, gentle grip and squeezed, and as she pulled back her hands, Olivia noted that they were clad in white gloves.

"It's very nice to meet you, Olivia. We haven't had anyone from your region at the academy in nearly eighty years."

"Is this entire complex Fainhallow Academy or is it just one or some of those buildings?" Olivia paused to gape at the massive structure once again.

"Oh, this is all the academy. Thousands of residents practice their arts within, and each year we have a new class of students. Some remain, some head home, but our population grows steadily. Oh, that's not even taking into account the diplomats, merchants, and tradesfolk that live within the walls. Come, though, let me show you around, and you'll start to get a better picture of things." Yunsha beckoned for Olivia to walk with her and then started back across the archway.

Up close, the archway was massive; Olivia could imagine four lanes of traffic going across it back home. That being said, she didn't have to experience any vertigo looking down at the clouds—they walked toward the center, and the wide expanse made her feel like she was at ground level. "There's no traffic on the bridge?"

"Oh, not this time of year. The journey down the peninsula and up the mountain takes a month by wagon, and most people visiting via that route come with the caravans at midsummer and midwinter. The midwinter caravan is a sight to see! Huge wagons shielded from the elements and drawn by Thunderak lizards." They continued in silence until they crested the arch of the bridge, and Olivia could look down its expanse to the immense, open gates of the academy. The gates looked to be made of dark metal and were swung wide, revealing a deep arched tunnel through at least fifty feet of stone.

"That wall is truly immense!" she breathed, partly to herself.

"Oh, yes. When the first Grand Mages created this school, they had in mind to defend the students from any outside interference. If you think the physical protection is impressive, you should see the wards." They continued down the slope of the arch to the gates, and Olivia saw that only one guard was on duty at the huge gate. "Hello, Barnt," Yunsha said as they walked through the gateway into the tunnel.

"M'lady Yunsha," he replied, bowing deeply. He was nearly as round as he was tall, and Olivia was impressed by the flexibility he displayed with that bow. At first, she thought he was an Urghat, but when she looked more closely, she saw that he had whiskers, a black nose, and his fur was short and sleek. Was he some kind of otter-man? They were past him and deep in the tunnel under the wall before she could speculate more. Their steps on the smooth flagstones echoed off the stone walls of the tunnel, and then, as they grew near the far end, bustling activity came to her ears.

The tunnel opened up into a courtyard that reminded Olivia more of a bustling market square in a small city than the typical courtyard of a castle or keep. Shops and stables lined the walls, and merchant stands of all shapes and sizes competed for room in the busy space. Olivia saw all sorts of people—some that looked like they were part goat, some Ardeni, some very thin people with gossamer wings, more of the otter people like the gate guard, and even some floating, billowing creatures that emitted tiny jets of steam out of their bulbous bodies as they moved. Olivia stared, once again slack-jawed, at one of the latter, noticing that its body was partially translucent and that it had a cluster of violet eyes and several long tentacle-like limbs trailing after it as it floated past.

"Never seen an Onaghi before?" Yunsha asked quietly, prompting Olivia to stop staring.

"I'm sorry! My people are new to this world, and so much is still very new to me!"

"Oh, don't worry, dear. The Onaghi have strange sensibilities and wouldn't even notice your staring. I didn't want to be rude before, but now that you bring it up, I think I have yet to meet one of your kind. I almost assumed you were a half-blood—part Ghelli and part Ardeni or Shadeni. Your people are new here, you say?"

"Yes, we're known as humans, and we're from another world. The System captured our spacecraft and deposited us near the, um, I think they're called the Gresh Woods. I had wondered if the different peoples of this world could interbreed! How fascinating!"

"Oh, we have so much to talk about! We'll have to schedule a tea after you're settled."

"That sounds very nice; thank you, Yunsha." They continued walking past the courtyard and down the main thoroughfare that ran up the center of the academy grounds. They passed several stone buildings with tall spires, and Yunsha remarked along the way what each building was.

"Here, they study the anatomy of the creatures of Fanwath." Yunsha gestured to a wide, circular-shaped building that had a domed roof.

"Oh my goodness—is that the name of this world? Fanwath? I can't believe I never asked Issa . . ." Olivia trailed off in thought.

"I take it Issa is a native friend of yours? Yes, those of us with an education refer to this world as Fanwath. Though some peoples name this world differently, using terms passed on from their ancestors that were present on one of the four worlds before the Great Joining." She continued on, and Olivia found herself lost in thought, imagining the immense power required to combine four different worlds seamlessly. "There is my favorite building—the main library." Yunsha pointed to a vast building that almost looked like a Gothic cathedral with its elaborate stone spires and stained glass windows.

"Impressive!" Olivia nodded, smiling.

"Yes, well, more than the building, the tomes within are what I love." They continued along the cobbled street, up some stone steps, and into the yawning, open hall of the academy proper. Olivia could see that the huge, barn-sized doors were held open by chains as thick as her wrists as they walked into the high, vaulted hallway. People hurried to and fro over the marble flooring, in and out of the many arched doorways that gave egress to the concourse. High overhead, hung from polished wooden beams, three many-tiered chandeliers filled the space with light comparable to a summer's day at noon. "This is the central hall of the academy where all paths converge. From here, you can reach the dormitories, the dining hall, the stairways to the upper and lower levels, the old auditorium, the first-year library, the administration offices, and the gymnasium. As you saw on the way in, most of the academy is housed in the other buildings on the grounds these days."

"It's awe-inspiring. Nearly on a scale with some of the larger universities from my homeworld. However, none of those colleges were on the top of a mountain and surrounded by an immense stone wall. And, of course, when I attended college, it wasn't for magic!"

"I'm glad to hear you have some education, magic or not—it will aid you here. Speaking of which, follow me, and I'll lead you to the administration office where your evaluation will take place." Yunsha turned and led Olivia through the third archway on their left. They walked through a series of wide hallways, all floored in the same marble as the entry hall, with cream-colored plaster walls and lots of Energy-based globes of light to keep things bright. After a short while, they came to a room with a desk at the far end and several couches lining the walls. On either side of the desk were closed wooden doors.

A rather portly Ardeni woman sat at the desk. Her bright teal hair had lots of gray mixed in, and her green-blue eyes sparkled with wit when she greeted Olivia. "Ahh, the new arrival. Here for your evaluation so soon? You don't waste any time, Yunsha."

"Well, why bother showing her around too much or getting her a room if she's going to be sent packing? Might as well get the evaluation done." Yunsha shrugged.

"Sent packing?" Olivia couldn't hide the slight quaver in her voice.

"Oh yes, dear; we can't trust every hedge-mage that heads up a provincial office of the Guild to make good decisions about who should be coming to Fainhallow. You'll need to pass some exams first. Then we can talk about your contract."

⊛ MORGAN ⊗

Morgan and Issa were noticed almost immediately by the Shadeni riders. Several of them peeled off from around the wagons and came toward the two of them. Morgan remained calm, making sure that he didn't go too fast or make threatening movements; he wanted to give this situation a chance to resolve without him having to kill a bunch of people or die. He definitely didn't want to die. He glanced at Issa as the four riders approached, kicking dust up in their haste. She was sitting calmly on Gopp's back, rising easily in the stirrups as he stepped, keeping her ride nice and smooth. When the four Shadeni were twenty-five yards or so away, Morgan pulled on his reins and sat waiting. Issa did the same.

"Hello," Morgan called as the Shadeni pulled up a dozen feet away. The Shadeni ignored him and looked at Issa.

"What do you want here, cousin? You and your outlander should ride on." The one who spoke was taller than the others, had three black lines either painted or tattooed across his face, and brandished a long, polished white spear.

"Well met, Ban-tok," Issa said, bowing slightly at the waist.

"You presume much, naming me Ban-tok, but you are correct; I lead here. This herd is our prey, though, and I will ask you again to take your outlander and leave us to our business."

"This outlander is my mate, and his name is Morgan Hall. Please address him with respect. He wishes to speak to you, Ban-tok." Morgan felt heat rise at the back of his neck as Issa introduced him as her mate, but he managed to keep a straight face. He nodded to the tall Shadeni.

"Greetings, um, Ban-tok." He stumbled a little on the honorific and mentally chided himself for not talking to Issa before riding down the hill so impulsively; he supposed it would have been nice to learn a bit more about these people.

"Yes, large-one. What business do you have here? We are rather busy."

"My name is Morgan, and I don't mean to be the bearer of bad news, but I'm not someone who can stand idly by and watch some people be robbed."

"What?" The Shadeni Ban-tok, which Morgan imagined meant chief or leader, practically guffawed. "These are the Spinelands—the only law here is might. Those hoofed-ones should have thought of this before they drove their herd through our lands."

"Their crime, then, is that they trespassed upon your lands?" Morgan grabbed on to the only angle he could see at the moment.

"Yes, they are on our lands, with a herd of holbyis that could feed and clothe our clan."

"Is it right to take everything they own because of a simple trespass? Where is the honor in destroying the lives of those weaker than you?"

"You would challenge my honor?" The Ban-tok bristled, sitting up straighter and drawing his lips back to reveal even more sharp teeth than an Ardeni, and sporting very pronounced canines.

"I ask a simple question. Is it honorable to take from the weak?"

"Of course; there is no value in weakness. Strength must be fostered, and weakness cut away—it is the way of the Spinelands." The large Shadeni brandished his spear in the air as he spoke, and his three followers cheered their agreement with his words. Issa hissed between her teeth, clearly frustrated with the circular conversation.

"Ban-tok, where I come from, it is honorable to protect the weak and help them gain strength. You can see how my code conflicts with your goals."

"You wish to make an enemy of the Spinelands Tribe?" the Ban-tok growled.

"Is there no way to settle this without us becoming enemies? Could we not negotiate a compromise?"

"I have a solution," Issa said, before the Ban-tok could answer Morgan's question. Both men looked at her; the Shadeni jostled in their saddles in agitation. "Ban-tok, why not duel Morgan? Just a test of skill, not a death dance. If he wins, you can show honor to his strength by sparing these Cadwalli and their property."

"And if I win?"

"Then you can take our mounts, and we'll spread word of your skill among our clans."

"Hmm, a test of skill?" He looked Morgan up and down again. "Very well." He turned to his three followers and barked some commands in a language or series of signals that his System language integration didn't translate. They rode off, whooping and swinging their weapons around, yelling to their comrades that were still circling the Cadwalli wagon group. "Cousin, talk to your mate, and be sure he knows the dance." After speaking, the Ban-tok rode away up the dusty valley a short way and dismounted.

"Issa, what did you get me into?" Morgan asked quietly, a half-smile on his face.

"A test of skill is different from a full duel; you can only use your weapon skills, and you can't strike to kill or maim. If you do kill or maim him, you'll be dishonored and marked as such—Shadeni from his tribe and any affiliated tribes or allies will hunt you."

"Oh, so, I have to be careful not to cut off his limbs or kill him. With a razor-sharp sword?" Morgan grunted and frowned.

"They'll respect your strength, and things will go a lot more smoothly after you beat him." Issa shrugged. "You can beat him, Morgan. I doubt a Shadeni Ban-tok living out in the wilderness has anything like your sword forms. Just don't use your other spells—sword skills only."

"Fine. Let's do this." Morgan rode Munch forward and dismounted near the tall, red man. He was stretching, flexing with his spear behind his back, and held out in various positions that Morgan recognized from his own time using the spear. More than half the Shadeni had broken off from the circled wagons and were now circling the two combatants. Issa sat atop her roladii at the circle's edge, a faint smile on her face, watching Morgan. Morgan sighed again and pulled his sword from his ring, and whipped it into a few short cuts through the air, finishing up with a flourish. He squared off with the Shadeni leader. "Could I get your name, Ban-tok? I'd like to know the name of one who so honorable agrees to this test of skill."

"I am Tarnig; learn it well." He held his spear vertically in front of him and performed a half-bow to Morgan. Morgan nodded, similarly grabbed his sword, and bowed in the same way to Tarnig. Tarnig charged or appeared to, but he stopped halfway and unleashed a series of rapid thrusts and feints at Morgan's chest. Morgan backstepped smoothly, his sword in a middle guard position, easily batting aside the thrusts. Tarnig grunted and dove to the side, rolling over one shoulder and leaping up to try to thrust at Morgan's exposed flank.

Morgan had to hide a smile as he, again, backed up and swung his sword almost lazily to slap the spear thrust away. He'd seen the move coming a mile away, and he began to wonder if Tarnig was trying to lull him into false confidence. Morgan decided to try pushing Tarnig's guard with some offense. He lunged forward and to the side, aiming a sideways slash where he knew Tarnig would jab his spear. As he'd predicted, Tarnig's spear rose and licked out toward his midriff, but his blade caught it halfway, knocking it aside. Morgan carried his swing through, performing a complete pivot and driving his sword around in a devastating spinning slash. Tarnig's eyes opened wide when he saw the blurred line of Morgan's black-silver blade arcing toward his neck.

Morgan had a momentary panic when he realized how exposed Tarnig was, and he had to use all his muscle control to pull back on his slash, tilting the blade down to just give Tarnig an inch-long gash along the top of his shoulder.

Tarnig hissed in pain, backpedaled, and again put his spear between himself and Morgan. His eyes were narrowed, calculating, and Morgan wondered just what was going on. So far, it felt like he was fighting a novice, not the leader of a nomadic group of warriors. Tarnig locked eyes with him for a moment, and then tilted his head in a slight nod.

Morgan was just opening his mouth to say something when Tarnig's long, white spear began to hum. Morgan looked at it and saw that it was vibrating in the air where Tarnig held it leveled at his midriff. Alarm bells rang in Morgan's head, and he started to jump to the side. He'd bent his knees and began to leap when the air in front of Tarnig's spear erupted in a hazy burst of steam, and a hot blast of kinetic force slammed into Morgan's chest, lifting him off his feet and sending him flopping like a ragdoll through the air and along the dusty hard-packed ground.

Morgan felt the shock and the disorientation of flipping head over heels, then he felt the crunching impact of the ground. He didn't allow himself to lay still, gasping in pain; rather, he kept his roll going until his feet were under him, and he leapt up, despite his aching bones and the blood running freely from his nose and ears and hastily scanned for Tarnig. He saw him charging over the dusty ground, his spear leveled, moving much more nimbly than he had at the start of their match. Morgan dropped into the Crane Forages, pushing Energy into his limbs, and he glided over the ground to meet his opponent.

Tarnig's grin grew wider when he saw Morgan coming so quickly, and he pulled his spear back, and Morgan could almost feel the Energy he was trying to imbue into his next strike. Morgan didn't intend to give him the chance to deliver it, so he used all the added grace of movement that his form afforded him, and he slid around the side of Tarnig, lifting his sword into a lighting thrust that slid through the meat of Tarnig's thigh. Tarnig tried to avoid him, dancing sideways, but Morgan was too fast, and he left a deep, long gash along Tarnig's hamstring. Blood sprayed over the dusty ground, and Tarnig cried out, stumbling.

Morgan capitalized on his enemy's stumble, moving into the Crane Flutters its Wings, aiming his flurry of strikes at his opponent's exposed flank. Morgan knew he had to pull his strikes, but with his heightened agility and dexterity, it wasn't that hard to aim precise slashes along Tarnig's shoulder and ribs, just giving him long, shallow gashes. Tarnig scrambled away, trying to pull his spear into a blocking position, but he was limping and bleeding, and Morgan's swings were like a force of nature. Red splashes and droplets watered the dusty ground, and Tarnig cried out, "Yield."

His voice was muffled in Morgan's ringing ears, but he could make out the word well enough, so he backed off, whipping his sword toward the ground to remove most of the blood from the blade. Then, he locked eyes with Tarnig and bowed. Tarnig, leaning over his knees, breathing heavily and bleeding from half a dozen painful gashes, grimaced, but stood straight and gave Morgan a bow. "Well fought, outlander. My Thunder Spear Style is strong, but your styles were stronger. I have much yet to learn."

"Your spear struck me like a charging roladii. Thank you for the lesson." Morgan smiled and stepped forward, offering his hand to Tarnig. Tarnig grinned and clasped his hand in a firm handshake.

"It did, didn't it? You went flying like a bull Thunderak charged you!"

Morgan laughed, wiping blood from under his nose. "My ears will be ringing for a week." It was true; his ears were still painfully ringing, but he was glad to be able to make out the man's words—superhuman vitality had its benefits.

"Well, enjoy your victory, Morgan. My band and I will hunt elsewhere. Deliver your good news to these herders." Tarnig started walking to the edge of the ring of onlookers who were still cheering and talking to each other excitedly about the match.

"Wait, Tarnig." Morgan reached out and caught his uninjured shoulder. "Your clan's lands are not that far from my own. Perhaps you'd be interested in trading?" Tarnig stopped walking and turned around, an eyebrow arched inquisitively.

"Oh? Where are your people?"

"We have begun building a town east of here, past the Gresh Woods."

"Hmm, so long as your people don't try to hunt in our lands, we shouldn't have a problem making trades. Perhaps I'll lead a band out there to visit. Will someone be there to speak for your people?"

"Yes, we have a council of leaders. Please ask to speak to them and say that Morgan sent you. So long as you don't approach in a threatening manner, you won't have trouble with the soldiers on the gates or walls."

"Very well, Morgan. Thank you for the dance of skill." Tarnig bowed once more and turned to his men, whistling loudly and making a circling motion in the air with his good arm. The Shadeni hooted and howled, and once Tarnig was mounted and moving, they rode away up the curve of the dusty valley.

"I told you you'd be able to beat him," Issa said smugly from Gopp's back.

MORGAN

Morgan and Issa rode over to the circled wagons. The Cadwalli started to clamber out from behind their cover and gather in a group, watching the two of them approach. As Morgan and Issa neared, an older Cadwalli woman wearing a beaded leather skirt and vest strode forward, waving her hand. "Welcome, heroes! Welcome!" Her voice was a high tenor and carried over the ground like a trumpet. Morgan saw Issa wave to the woman, so he did likewise.

"Hello, friends." Morgan pulled up his roladii a few feet from the group and slid from the saddle. He walked forward to the woman with steel gray hair, large goat-like eyes, and twitching ears, reached out a hand, and she clasped it in both of hers. Morgan noted the black, hard nails on her fingers.

"We owe you everything. Please, share our camp tonight, and let us feed you and toast your victory with our finest wine!"

"We'll be happy to be your guests, but please don't feel indebted. We only did what we would for any travelers in distress. My name is Issa, and this is my mate, Morgan." Morgan looked at her askance; did she really have to introduce him that way to everyone?

"Morgan, your battle with the Shadeni Overlord was a sight to behold!" This exclamation came from a younger male Cadwalli, who strode forward to stand next to the matron.

"Hush, Gulli; that was a Ban-tok. They don't call their leaders Overlords." The matron looked back to Morgan and Issa, smiling warmly. "This is my son, Gulli. I am Hundla, the Cloudsinger of this flock, and I welcome you. Please come within our wagons, and we'll make you comfortable." The group of Cadwalli muttered, shouted, or stamped their feet in agreement, and Morgan and Issa followed them into their wagon circle.

The Cadwalli spent the next several minutes widening their circle for more comfort, staking their herd on one end of the clearing and creating a cookfire on the other. Morgan and Issa were ushered into a pair of canvas camp chairs, given a large mug of honeyed mead, something Hundla called yingberry wine.

As the sun was starting to set, the Cadwalli seemed pleased with their camp and began to relax, but Morgan noted that at least four were atop their wagons, keeping watch at all times. "They certainly seem friendly," Morgan said to Issa, while they watched the Cadwalli bustling around camp.

"Yes, Cadwalli are good folk, generally. They're people, like any race, though, and there are bad apples among them. These herders seem genuine, though. I'm looking forward to what they'll feed us!" Issa sighed contentedly and took a big drink of her mead.

"Are you getting drunk already? This stuff is pretty strong, isn't it?" Morgan chuckled. Issa nodded, her cheeks flushed to a light shade of purple, and she reached a hand over to hold onto his.

"So, I'm your mate, now, am I?" Morgan raised an eyebrow at Issa.

"Of course! You wouldn't think I'd share you with others, would you?" She squeezed his hand. Morgan smiled and kissed her on the cheek.

"No, I wouldn't. Not any more than I want to share you, which would be not at all."

"Excuse me! Do you two enjoy holbyis chops? Marna has a fantastic recipe for a jelly marinade." Morgan looked up from canoodling with Issa and saw that Hundla had approached and was putting out another chair for herself next to Issa. Several other Cadwalli were gathering around the fire.

"I've never had them, but I'm sure they'll be wonderful," Morgan said, and Issa nodded along with him.

"I love meat in general," Issa added, grinning, her full set of sharp teeth on display. Morgan chuckled and took another big pull of his mead; he had a hard time thinking of any drink not made from grapes as wine, though he figured he might have to start revising his conceptions the longer he spent in this world.

"More wine!" Hundla called out, and one of the younger Cadwalli females came around with a wineskin nearly as large as her torso to fill everyone's mugs. They laughed and talked for hours around the fire while the Cadwalli cook prepared their dinners. Morgan didn't think they made such a production of dinner every night they camped, but they were clearly trying to provide something special for him and Issa.

When the food was ready, Morgan and Issa were given ceramic plates piled high with a fruit and lettuce salad dressed in a tangy, oily sauce and a sizable chop of meat with a sweet and spicy jam slathered on it. Morgan tasted the meat and found it very similar to lamb, and he was glad of the jam sauce to counteract the strong gamey flavor. The combination truly was delicious. With full bellies and buzzing heads, the group of travelers sat around the fire, enjoying the warmth of the coals and their mutual company.

"Morgan and Issa, do you hail from far away?" Hundla asked after a while.

"Not really, no. Just a day or two's hard ride. Our community is east of here through the Gresh Woods."

"The Gresh Woods? Aren't they crawling with Yovashi?" Hundla visibly shivered at the thought.

"No, definitely not crawling with them. There may have been more at one time, but the ones that were there are mostly dead or in hiding. Our people have been hunting in those woods for a month or more. There's not much that would threaten a group like yours if you wanted to visit."

"Oh? Do your people have goods to trade?"

"Yes, we're new here, but more and more, we're learning to use our abilities to craft unique items. We have knowledge from our own world, and as we apply it to concepts using Energy, we're getting some novel projects in the works. I think it would be worth your while to drive your herd there. My people need the livestock, and I'm sure you'd find yourselves well recompensed."

"This is true! You should have seen the way they drove off an Urghat invasion!" Issa squeezed Morgan's hand and smiled at him out of the corner of her mouth. Murmurs broke out around the fire, and Morgan could see that Issa had hit the right chord—the Cadwalli apparently had little love for Urghat.

"Well, where do you and Issa travel?" Hundla's words were slightly slurred, and she leaned forward precariously in her chair as she looked into Morgan's face.

"We're trying to find an ancient citadel—a place where a swordmaster trained disciples in days long past. Supposedly, it was built in a place called the Orangerock Hills." Once again, the gathered Cadwalli murmured and spoke to each other excitedly.

"We know that place! We know that place!" This exclamation came from a large Cadwalli with black-furred legs and a long black beard. Hundla motioned for him to continue speaking while she drained the dregs at the bottom of her mug. "Just a day's ride north of here, you'll come to the Rusty Hills, er, that's our name for them. If you continue about a league to the northwest, you'll come to a huge box canyon. A winding mountain road there, built by ancients, leads to the place you're talking about. You should know, though, that the place is not what you think. There is no master there or disciples—it's a dungeon controlled by the System, and none of our people have been granted entrance."

"Really? Have you tried to enter? What do you mean by dungeon?" Morgan tried to get his questions out, but he couldn't help noticing that Issa's hand was clenching his like a vise.

"Morgan! A dungeon is a place of rich Energy where the System curates encounters and challenges for adventurers that go within. I've always wanted to find one!"

"Ahem, to answer your questions, no, most of our people would not try to go within. Our herd is more interested in crafting and gathering riches than risking our lives in places like that. I don't know anyone who tried to enter, but I've heard tales that they were simply told they didn't meet the requirements."

"Would it be like the Crucible, Issa?"

"Sort of, but not exactly. A dungeon is a static challenge in a specific location. The Crucible is sort of tailored to the individuals within it, and, as you well know, it could be placed anywhere the System has influence." Morgan nodded, thinking. He was about to ask another question when one of the Cadwalli started to sing. It wasn't long before other Cadwalli joined in, and some brought out drums and stringed instruments not unlike little guitars. The music was lively, and Morgan and Issa sat back, looking into the fire or the stars, and just enjoyed it. If he had to describe the music, Morgan would have said it was somewhat like bluegrass; he found himself tapping a foot along with the drums.

"You like this, don't you?" Issa asked, her breath hot and sweet from the wine.

"Yeah, I love it. This is a great life—something I could only dream about before I came here." Issa smiled, and then she started to sing along with the Cadwalli, and while they had pleasant voices, their range was bass to tenor. When Issa's clear soprano rose above their chorus, the Cadwalli grew more enthusiastic, and the music rose to another height of exuberance. Morgan smiled at Issa, moisture filling his eyes, and he leaned back in his chair, enjoying the moment.

All too soon, the festivities wound down, and Morgan and Issa pitched their tent near one of the big Cadwalli wagons, and then they crawled into their bedding, sleeping the deep, peaceful sleep of the truly exhausted. Morgan woke with the first light of dawn, and he found he wasn't the first one up. Many of the Cadwalli were seeing to their daily chores—feeding the animals, performing maintenance on the wagons, mending gear, and another dozen activities that Morgan didn't realize needed doing. Issa woke up shortly after he did, and they ate a quick breakfast.

They were packing up their tent when Hundla came over. "Thank you again for saving our flock, Morgan and Issa. We talked about it last night, and we've decided to take you up on your offer and make a trade run to your community."

"That's great news! I'm sure it will be profitable for both our peoples!" Morgan nodded, thinking of the possibilities. They said their farewells, then Morgan and Issa rode off in the direction the Cadwalli indicated would lead them to the Orangerock Hills. In a way, Morgan was sad to leave the happy Cadwalli. He'd enjoyed their company, and the food and singing had really made him feel at home. "You know, Issa, I had a great time with the Ardeni herders when I came to find you, too. I think I'd fit right in with a group of herders. What a nice life: travel all day, see new sights, take care of your animals, camp under the stars, sing songs, drink and eat good food—what more could you want?"

"Oh, pssh! You'd grow bored within a month. You like to fight too much, and I'm sure you'd miss the idea of adventure and exploration. Driving your herd the same route day in and day out would grow old. You like it because it's new to you, and you don't have to face the prospect of doing it for the rest of your life, you silly man." Issa laughed and slapped Gopp's rump urging him into a lumbering gallop.

"Hey, wait up!" Morgan laughed and clicked his tongue at Munch, letting him know it was okay to catch her. Munch grunted loudly and sprang after his friend. They raced, laughing, through the low gullies and hills for several minutes, and though Morgan kept catching her, Issa had a way of using the terrain to pull ahead of him again and again.

It was just a little after midday when they caught their first glimpse of the Orangerock Hills. They were riding along a gully in a northwesterly direction, when they climbed up out of it, the distinct orange-colored rocks of a craggy ridgeline came into view. "Well, they certainly are orange."

"Yeah," Issa breathed, nodding.

"Well, first one to the box canyon gets a foot rub tonight." Morgan laughed and kicked Munch into a run.

"Hey!" Issa yelled, urging her roladii to chase him, "I want a backrub! My feet aren't even sore!"

OLIVIA

"I'll be waiting here, Olivia. Just relax and follow the instructions of your evaluator." Yunsha smiled warmly, her blue-stained lips parting to reveal very human-like teeth.

"Yes, Olivia, my name is Mrs. Poyle, and you can follow me. I'll take you to your evaluator." She gestured to the door on her left and began walking. Olivia pushed down her anxiety and followed. She'd always been good at tests, and she decided to go and do her best. Magister Karn had seemed impressed by her abilities, so it wasn't like she had something to hide—she wasn't trying to sneak in here or anything. As she followed Mrs. Poyle down a long hallway past a dozen or so offices, she examined the source of her anxiety.

She'd always felt anxious during tests or when giving speeches or presentations in her past life—not because she didn't know what she was doing or because she suffered from imposter syndrome. No, it was always because she worried about meeting her parents' expectations and, later, her investors'. None of that was relevant here—she had no one to let down but herself. Sure, it would benefit the colony if she could perform well in this school and learn as much as possible about different types of magic and even about the world and the System. Still, no one back in the colony could or would fault her for not succeeding here; they hadn't even gotten an invite.

She took a deep breath and slowly released it as she followed Mrs. Poyle through a wooden door with a bronze placard in the center that read, "Gandak, Senior Evaluator." The room she walked into was the size of a large broom closet. Or maybe it just seemed small because it was so crowded: a wooden desk took up the rear half of the room, and bookcases lined every wall. The bookcases were positively overflowing with books and loose papers, and notebooks. A single wooden chair sat before the desk, and, in a sizable leather-wrapped chair behind the desk was a man that looked like a devil.

Olivia had to struggle to retain her composure as she took him in. He wore a loose black robe, belted with a silvery cord, but that isn't what stood out about him. His skin was cherry red, and, as the man smiled to greet her, he revealed the long fangs hiding behind his lips. His eyes were a bright, glittering cobalt color, and he didn't have horns, so with some effort, Olivia dismissed the idea that he was actually a devil. No, he just had bright red skin and sharp teeth—nothing to worry about.

"Welcome, prospect! I am Gan-dak, and I'll be administering your evaluation. Thank you, Mrs. Poyle. I'll take it from here."

"You're welcome, sir. Good luck, Olivia," Mrs. Poyle said, as she brushed past Olivia and out into the hallway.

"Thank you . . ." Olivia called after her, but the door clicked shut, cutting her off. She turned back to Gan-dak and cleared her throat, "Um, hello, sir. I'm Olivia Bennet."

"Yes, yes, excellent. Please sit down." He gestured to the wooden chair in front of his desk. Olivia nodded and sat down. "Now, are you familiar with the evaluation process? Did your mentors prepare you?"

"Ahem, no, sir. My people are new to this world and Energy. I don't have a mentor." Olivia consciously kept her gaze steady, meeting the eyes of Gan-dak.

"Oh, truly? Well, that may be for the best. Often, we have pupils arrive with as many misconceptions as proper preparations. You may be a clean slate, so to speak. Hmm, well, let me try to explain the process a little. First, I'm going to want to scry you to be sure you meet the level requirements and that you have at least a passable Core and pathways."

"Okay," Olivia said, breathing out a slight sigh of relief. That didn't sound hard.

"Then you and I will have a brief struggle of wills, which will help me to determine your Energy affinity and your mental fortitude. Finally, I'll have you try to complete some rather difficult channeling tasks. When I say difficult, I mean it—don't be alarmed if you can't complete all of them; few students can." Gan-dak's voice was deep, and the rhythm of his speaking was slow but steady, and it made Olivia feel relaxed. In fact, he reminded her of a teacher she'd had when she'd started at MIT when she was fifteen. He'd had a very positive impact on her career, reminding her that it was essential to enjoy life and not just try to toil for one achievement after another mindlessly. Her parents had hated him.

"Okay, sir." Olivia nodded firmly, her lips pressed into a determined line. Gan-dak smiled again and opened a drawer on his desk, pulling a baseball-sized crystal ball out of it. The ball was perfectly smooth and round, but whorls of silver and black smoke drifted in an endlessly random pattern within it. Olivia was instantly entranced by it.

"Quite something, isn't it? The Gonnarath Empire had some of the best Artificers known to our world, and this is a remnant from their time. Not that we couldn't craft something similar today, though I don't know if it would be as elegant. Now please place your hands upon my desk, palms facing upward, and I'll place the scry-orb into them. All you need do is hold onto the orb, and I'll handle the rest. Okay?" Olivia nodded and reached her arms forward, resting her knuckles on the desk. Gan-dak lifted the orb and gently placed it in her palms; the surface was cool, as she'd imagined it would be. While she held it, she looked into its depths and felt herself mesmerized by the patterns of smokey light within.

"Very good, Olivia; you can release the orb now." Gan-dak's words came to her as though muffled by a blanket. "Olivia, that's all we need from the orb. You may let go." His voice was louder and more firm this time, and Olivia blinked rapidly and swallowed. Her mouth was dry as a bone, as if she'd been holding it open for several minutes without swallowing. She realized her hands were gripping the orb in a white-knuckled clench. She relaxed them and felt some pain in her fingers as the blood started to flow into them again. "Yes, thank you, Olivia." Gan-dak quickly pulled the orb away and tucked it back into the drawer. "The orb sometimes seems to contain more wonder within it for certain people. You're apparently one of those. You were completely gone while I did your initial evaluation."

"It seemed to me like I just grasped it, and then you were asking me to let go." Olivia licked her dry lips and glanced around nervously. "Did I pass?"

"Oh yes, this stage went very well. You are not yet level nine, and your Core and pathways seem very robust. You even have a fairly rare Core. You're doing quite well for someone new to Energy." Gan-dak opened another drawer and pulled out an utterly black cube, its sides about three inches long. "This is a contest cube. I take it you haven't seen one before?" Olivia shook her head. "Nothing to worry about—it functions very simply. I will push Energy into the side facing me, and you will push Energy into your side. The goal is to get it to change to your color. I'm not sure what color you or I will have—they're based on what side you push in your Energy. It will be apparent once we start." He set the cube on the desk between them.

"So, we'll be competing? I should push as much Energy as I can?" Olivia asked, stretching forth a finger to touch the cube's side facing her. Gan-dak nodded and touched the opposite side.

"Start with just a trickle, so you can see what it's like." As he spoke, the cube started to turn green, spreading toward her from the side that he was touching. Olivia nodded and sent a trickle of Energy into the cube and saw that the face she was touching turned yellow and began to spread toward Gan-dak. "Very good! Now, gradually increase your Energy flow, and I will try to match you. Let me know when you are pushing as much as possible."

Olivia nodded again and pressed her lips together in concentration, staring at the side of the cube she was touching. Slowly she began to increase the flow of Energy from her Core. She was pushing fire Energy out toward the cube, and she saw the yellow portion of the cube surge forward to meet the line of green coming from Gan-dak. It stopped advancing, and Olivia pushed more and more Energy. She glanced at Gan-dak's face and saw that he seemed utterly relaxed.

Olivia inhaled deeply and began to channel all of her other attuned Energies out along her pathways and out into the cube. The line of yellow surged into the green, pushing it almost to the far edge of the cube. Gan-dak inhaled sharply, but then the green line stabilized and pushed back against the yellow and slowly gained ground until they were at an equilibrium again. Olivia strained with all her might, willing the Energy in her Core to flow, but she couldn't get the yellow line to move forward anymore. "That's my best, I think," she grunted through clenched teeth.

"Ahh, excellent. Now relax; you can stop pushing. You definitely passed that test, Olivia!" Gan-dak was smiling broadly. "The best contest I've had from a prospect in a long time. I would admit you based on this test alone, but I'm afraid protocol states that I must continue with the evaluation." Olivia breathed deeply and relaxed, pulling her hand back from the cube.

"Thank you, sir."

"Oh, no need to thank me for the truth. While we're alone, you may call me Gan. If other students or teachers are around, please refer to me as Professor Gan-dak." He smiled at her again, and though his voice was warm and his eyes seemed kind, Olivia still felt a twinge of panic when she saw his long, white canines hanging down to his lower gums.

"Now, Olivia, you have several Energy affinities, which is a positive and a potential negative for you. Students with no affinity are a bit more moldable by the staff here and are therefore looked at a bit more favorably by some. You, however, don't just have a random affinity; your Core is attuned to four different elements. The question is, how well can you manipulate your different attunements?" Once again, Gan reached into his desk, and this time he pulled out something that looked much like a candelabra. It had a silver base and eight different arms arching out. At the end of each silver arm was a small, golf-ball-sized crystal.

"That's lovely," Olivia said quietly.

"Oh, yes, it is. This is a relatively simple device, though—each crystal lights up based on the attunement of the Energy that is channeled into it. Allow me to demonstrate." Gan-dak held one hand out toward the device, and one of the crystals flared to life in a brilliant golden hue. A moment later, another of the crystals began to glow with a strange smokey greenish-black light. "The golden light is pure Energy. The other is my corruption-attuned Energy." He smiled, closed his hand, and the lights winked out. "Now your turn!"

Olivia thought about what he'd said. He clearly had some sort of corruption attunement, but he could still channel pure Energy. Was she able to do that also? She always just channeled one of her elementally attuned Energies. From looking at her status sheet, she knew that she still had a pure Energy affinity of 9.1, though her other affinities were higher at 9.6. Still, she knew that, relatively, her pure Energy affinity was very high. Shouldn't she still be able to channel it? She held out a hand and concentrated on the crystal device. Slowly she reached into the heart of her Core, where the unattuned Energy spun in a tight golden ball. She willed it to travel out along her pathways and pushed it forth into one of the crystals. She couldn't stop the smile that burst across her face when the crystal started to emit a pure, golden light.

"Good, Olivia, are you able to channel your attuned Energy at all while maintaining that light?" Olivia locked eyes with Gan-dak, and her grin spread even further. She carefully willed her different elemental affinities out through her pathways, maintaining their separate threads, just as she did when she made attuned Energy beads. When the four threads of Energy reached her hand, she just extended her will, pushing the different elements into different crystals. Suddenly the device lit up with green, red, blue, and bright white lights, adding to the pure golden crystal still steadily pulsing forth its glow.

"Five? At once? Hold onto that, Olivia, don't let it drop!" Gan-dak stood up and walked over to the wall on his left side, pounding on a small space between two bookshelves. "Tilia! Tilia, come here! You want to see this!" He shouted.

⊗ Morgan ⊗

The ancient road leading up the side of the box canyon had been easy for Morgan and Issa to find. When they'd ridden through the scraggy orange hills for a few miles, they started to make out the stony sides of the northern edge of the canyon. Following ridgelines from there had been easy, and soon they'd broken through some scrub into a humid valley filled with twisted little trees with fragrant, oily bark and leaves. A roadway ran in switchbacks up the southern side of the rocky box canyon. The road had been carved, blasted, or molded somehow out of the very rock of the canyon wall. While not wide by modern North American standards, it was comfortable to ride up side by side on their roladii.

Loose scree made the footing a little dangerous, but the roladii were surefooted beasts, and Morgan and Issa weren't in a rush. They took the path at the roladii's natural climbing pace, which was about twice as fast as they could've climbed on foot. Little lizards scurried in and out of their hiding spots between loose rocks, and a wren of some sort warbled from the branches of the scrub that grew tenaciously in the rocky soil. The sun was warm but not uncomfortably so, and the journey up the old road turned out to be a rather pleasant interlude.

"This road is impressive work. Do you think they used magic to make it?" Morgan asked Issa when they were about two-thirds of the way up the canyon wall.

"I'm sure some earth-attuned Energy users were responsible. How else could they carve through miles of solid granite?"

"Well, where I come from, they blast through rock with explosives to make roads in the mountains. I haven't seen anything like dynamite here, though." Morgan shrugged.

"Your world sounds fascinating, Morgan. I think I'd like to see it someday."

"Hmm, well, there are some amazing things to see in my world, but I think this world has it beat in the awesome sights department. Maybe someday we'll learn how to teleport or something, and you and I can make a quick visit for some tourism." He laughed at the notion.

"I thought you said Energy wasn't in your world? I think it would be hard to teleport there if there isn't any Energy!"

"Well, I've been thinking about that; Tiladia told me that the reason we know what dragons and fae are is that Energy might have touched our world in a stream or maybe even just a trickle. It could still be doing that, right? Maybe there's a way to get there with magic. Maybe not, though. Tiladia said that sometimes Energy flows can move."

"I didn't know that, Morgan! That's interesting," Issa said, absently rubbing Gopp's neck while she rode, lost in thought. Morgan smiled to himself, watching her ride. He leaned over and patted Munch's shoulder.

"I got pretty lucky, didn't I, boy?" He said in the roladii's ear.

"What did you say?" Issa looked back at him.

"Nothing, just talking to Munch."

"Hmm." Issa shook her head and picked up her pace a little. Just then, a raptor of some sort screeched and dove out of the sky into the canyon below them and snatched some kind of rodent in its talons, lifting it and flying off to the north.

"Poor bugger," Morgan muttered, patting Munch again.

Soon enough, the rocky road climbed up over the lip of the canyon wall, and a new scene unfolded. It seemed they'd climbed out of the box canyon valley into another, higher valley, this one surrounded on three sides by rolling orange hills. The road they'd climbed out of the canyon continued to the south through the center of the little valley toward the ruined walls of a great stone keep that sat against the southern hills. "Looks like we found it, Morgan!"

"Yep! I can't imagine there's more than one citadel in these hills. Let's feed and water the roladii, and I'll strap on my armor." While Morgan pulled his heavy scaled armor out of his storage ring and started to strap on his greaves and vambraces, Issa summoned feed bags and water buckets from one of her pouches and saw to the roladii. By the time she was finished, Morgan was ready for her to help strap his scale vest to his arm and leg armor.

"What a hassle it is to put on this heavy armor! I'm glad my chain shirt is so light." She pirouetted teasingly, demonstrating her nimble footwork.

"Well, this armor is great, though. It stopped a blow from Spineripper, and that guy was as strong as a grizzly bear."

"Is that a fabled beast from your world?"

"Well, you know what a bear is, right? Grizzlies are just really big, famously pissed off bears."

"Ahh, got it." Issa gathered the feeding supplies from the roladii when they were finished, and the two of them rode the rest of the way to the crumbling keep walls.

The keep seemed totally abandoned. Morgan had entertained ideas of skeletal guardians or trolls or something, but it was silent save for the occasional warble of the little speckled birds that called this area their home. When they came to the rotten, half-fallen gates to the courtyard, they decided to tie the roladii outside with a fresh bucket of water and some scattered feed. "They should be fine for several days, even if the water runs out; roladii are hardy beasts. If they grow desperate, they'll break their leads and find water," Issa said.

Morgan looked up to the crumbled battlements and imagined what the keep had been like in its prime. It wasn't a massive structure, but it was large, and the stonework was well done. He imagined the men and women who lived and trained here had been proud of their home. Together the two adventurers stepped through the shadowed gatehouse and into the courtyard of the ancient structure. The square was approximately fifty yards wide, and most of the stairs and doorways along the outer walls had fallen into piles of rubble. The only apparent way to advance was through the large opening leading into the main keep. The door itself had rotted to just a few pieces of hanging planks along the edges, allowing a view into the shadowy interior.

Morgan called forth his sword, and he saw Issa did the same, and they advanced up the rubble-strewn steps. The entry hall of the old keep was dappled in sunlight that came through cracks in the walls and ceiling, both large and small. Morgan could see the remains of a decayed wooden stairway off to his right, but a large opening directly in front of them led to an even larger space where some motes of blue light dancing in the air caught his attention. He activated his Azure Sight skill, and the darkened corners of the room immediately sprang into focus. Nodding to Issa, he stepped forward, eyes glowing blue, to the doorway and peered within.

The large, echoing chamber must once have been a banquet hall or something similar. The floor was laid with smooth flagstones, and the walls were decked in crumbling plaster. High beams and exposed rafters lined the ceiling, and piles of rotted and petrified wood made Morgan imagine rows of tables and benches. At the far end of the hall, a series of blue motes danced in a basketball-sized, spherical pattern. He looked at Issa, and she just nodded, and the two of them walked slowly toward the sphere of motes. When they were about fifteen feet away, the motes expanded and began to spin more quickly, and then a clear, masculine voice emanated from them, "Do you come to undertake the challenge of Swordsworn Keep?"

"Um," Morgan said, then glanced at Issa. She nodded, and he continued, "Perhaps. Can you tell us anything about the challenge?"

"I will give you more information if you prove worthy to enter." The robust, ringing voice echoed through the hall.

"How does one prove they are worthy?" Morgan pressed, and the blue motes flared more brightly and spun in a large circle around Issa and Morgan. After a few seconds, they collapsed back into a ball, and the voice rang out.

"I can see that you both value the path of the sword. To enter the Swordsworn Keep, you must prove that your ability with the blade is greater than that of a novice of Von-dak."

"That's a Shadeni name. The 'dak' part means he was a noble or knight," Issa said quietly.

"Was Von-dak the swordmaster that founded this citadel?" Morgan asked.

"That is correct, seeker. Will you undergo testing?"

"Is it dangerous?"

"All tests of the blade carry risk." Though flat in tone, the voice seemed to carry some derision in its answer. Morgan looked to Issa, and he could see some worry in her eyes.

"Give us a moment to consult." The lights didn't respond, and Morgan stepped back a few paces and looked into Issa's eyes. "If it's just me that has to take the test, I'm willing, but I doubt it will let us both go in if we don't both pass the test."

"Yes, I agree with that. It's scary, but I want to try." Issa squinted her eyes in a slight, determined scowl and nodded once while she spoke. Morgan took her hands in his and continued to stare at her for a moment, and then he nodded, turning back to the ball of lights.

"Alright, I'll take the test first."

"Very well. Madam, please step to the area behind me." It paused while Issa complied, and then the ball of motes flared brighter than ever, swirling into a large circle around Morgan. The circle of light spread down to the ground and then about fifteen feet into the air. Morgan stood in the center of the blue, radiant barrier and wondered what he'd have to do. He didn't have to wait long before a hissing stream of red smoke rose out of the ground and began to solidify into the form of a humanoid skeleton. The red skeleton wielded a two-handed sword, at least as large as Morgan's, but it was straight and double-edged. Without a word or a pause, the skeleton sprang into an attack.

Morgan parried the blow and countered with a riposte that the skeleton sidestepped. There followed a series of back and forth feints, slashes, and parries that Morgan found easy to keep up with. He allowed the match to continue without using his styles or abilities for several minutes, trying to feel out the skeleton and see if he could beat it with just his basic forms and raw speed and strength. The skeleton managed to land a few minor blows against his armor, and he returned the favor but never did enough damage to dismantle or destroy his opponent. Finally, fearing there might be a time limit or rule of strikes, Morgan began to launch his Fighting Crane attacks.

He used his flurry attack first, after parrying a savage sideways slash, and it proved effective, battering through the skeleton's guard and bashing it backward into the barrier. The skeleton stumbled but recovered its strength and charged him with a vicious flurry of its own. Morgan dropped back into the Crane Defends a Nest and easily knocked aside the skeleton's attacks. Then he pushed forward into a devastating downward thrust using the Crane Takes a Minnow. His blade slipped beneath the skeleton's sternum and sheared through its spine. It collapsed and dissipated into red steam, and the blue barrier shrank down into the ball of motes.

"You have passed the challenge and are worthy of entry to Swordsworn Keep." Morgan gave a half-bow to the ball of motes and walked to Issa.

"I had to fight a skeleton. Will you be okay? Your sword mostly does piercing damage."

"Do not question the fairness of the trial, seeker. Your comrade will have a fitting challenge." The clear tenor of the voice took on a stern tone.

"I'm ready for my challenge," Issa said, giving Morgan's arm a quick squeeze, then she stepped into the center of the room. A moment later, she was obscured from his view by a tall, glowing blue barrier. Morgan listened with every fiber of his being, but he couldn't hear any sounds of battle. He tried to see through the barrier with his Azure Sight, but again, he was thwarted. He waited nervously, pacing back and forth for what seemed like hours, but he knew it was just minutes. Finally, the barrier disappeared, and Issa strode out of a small cloud of red mist. She had a few cuts on her arms, but she was smiling in triumph. "I had to fight a clay golem with a rapier. It was almost exactly my size."

"I guess you weren't lying about being fair," Morgan said, watching the dancing blue motes warily.

"You both may proceed into Swordsworn Keep. Are you ready?"

"Hey, you said you'd tell us more after we proved ourselves," Issa said, stepping toward the lights.

"I can tell you that the Swordsworn Keep is populated by enemies meant to challenge individuals or parties that enter. Along with the battles you will undoubtedly face are other challenges intended to teach you valuable lessons of the sword. Master Von-dak put part of himself into the keep in order to pass his knowledge to worthy pupils. Should you survive, you will surely come out closer to mastery of the sword."

"Is there any way to leave?" Morgan asked.

"Of course. If you return to the entrance room at any time, you may touch the anchor stone to return to this chamber. You are only allowed one entry, however."

"Let's do it, Morgan! What is life without adventure?" Issa grabbed his hand and squeezed.

"Alright. Send us in." Morgan held on tightly to Issa's hand while the blue motes once again started to surround the two of them.

⚛ BRONWYN ⚜

Bronwyn sat down next to the fire as her followers packed up the rest of the temporary camp they had set up. She had given the two arm rings she'd taken from the dead Urghat leaders to Ironhide and instructed him and the others to find Urghat they felt were worthy of the Underclaw title, who wouldn't want to start further conflicts with the humans. She'd grown to trust her little band of Urghat during their travels on the plains, and their behavior and assistance during the brief Urghat siege had solidified that feeling.

"You sure we shouldn't just bury these things somewhere?" She asked Ironhide as he watched the others packing up camp.

"Aye, they're important to our people. If we pick the right Urghat to wear them, they'll be able to work to control the other Underclaws that still have their rings."

"And make sure they swear to suppress another Overclaw!" Bronwyn growled.

"Right."

Ironhide had explained that an Overclaw was simply an Underclaw that had coerced many other Underclaws to swear allegiance to them. He'd said the clans were likely to splinter back into their own separate groups, at least until another Urghat with enough strength or smarts came along to try and unite them again.

When they'd finished packing up, the Urghat spent some time practice-fighting before starting their march. Fangripper taught Bright-tooth a relatively simple series of sword strikes across the fire. Shadow-eye was across the fire giving lessons to Soft-fur; they shared a similar affinity for manipulating some sort of shadow Energy. Though Urghat all had extremely low affinity for Energy, some were born with a gift that allowed them to master a specific spell or skill. Shadow-eye could coalesce his shadow into various weapons and change their shape at will. During Bronwyn's duel with him, he had swiftly transformed his shadow spear into two long blades, catching her off guard. The blades had seemed to phase through most material and didn't cut her but sapped a large amount of Energy with each strike. At the end of the fight, she had been so exhausted she could barely stand. She watched now as Soft-fur formed a small flickering blade in her hand, it sputtered out quickly, but her eyes were alight with excitement. Shadow-eye smiled, looking down at her with his black orb of an eye, and grunted in encouragement.

Bronwyn was sad that they'd be leaving, but it wouldn't be for too long; she'd spoken with the council about them coming to live in the colony sometime down the road. Tensions were still high at the moment, but with a bit of time, things would calm, and she'd be able to bring them around for introductions. Her motley band of followers seemed excited by the prospect of having a permanent place to call home.

When they'd finished exercising and wolfing down some travel rations, the Urghat took turns clasping wrists with Bronwyn, and they were off, slipping into the trees without hardly a sound. She was watching the branches of a bush snap back into place in their wake when Hops came bounding out of the underbrush. She smiled and squatted down, holding out her hand while he made his way across the camp toward her. He didn't clamber onto her outstretched hand, though, stopping short of it. "Well, hey there, little guy, long time no see. Have you been off on a great adventure?" Hops nuzzled his face into her hand and then stepped back slightly, looking around almost nervously. "Everything okay?" He reached inside his shell behind his head and pulled out a tiny crystal disc, holding it out to her with both hands. The crystal was shaped like a coin and was about the size of a quarter. It glittered like a diamond, but when it caught the sunlight, it shone in a multitude of colors. Bronwyn cocked her head to the side curiously and reached out toward it with her thumb and pointer finger.

When she touched the little crystal coin, her arm and hand seemed to stretch out in front of her, and then her whole body was pulled into a spiraling rainbow vortex. She soared through a tunnel of many-colored lights, passing hundreds of portal-like openings on each side, catching just brief glimpses of what lay on the other side. She saw vast deserts, lush jungles, snowy mountains, and even a few cities with strange otherworldly architecture. She flew for only a minute or two before slowing down and coming to a stop before a golden portal. A light tugging sensation like a rope around her waist pulled her forward and into it.

Bronwyn could feel the sun's warmth on her skin as she stepped out of the portal. When her eyes adjusted, she found herself at the edge of a small glade surrounded by trees. The grass at her feet was like threads of golden silk that flowed in the breeze like water lapping in a placid pond. The trees surrounding her were as big as skyscrapers, their white, birch-like trunks soaring maybe a thousand feet into the purple sky above. The giant trees were spaced apart, allowing for plenty of sky and sunlight to come through their canopies, and no lesser trees grew in their shadows. The otherworldly forest was like a well-maintained park. Hundreds of feet above her, she saw archways of golden wood stretching between the trees to circular platforms; they looked like insects from where she stood, but Bronwyn was sure there were people up there moving about on the platforms.

She stared in wonder, watching as tiny golden motes of light weaved their way through the forest, catching her eye and drawing her attention to different flowers or little animals in every corner of the magical place. She felt like she had stepped into a fairy tale or an elven city from VR games she'd played. She was mesmerized looking up at the forest city above her when someone cleared their throat, and a small, high-pitched voice spoke up. "Greetings, friend; we've been expecting you."

Bronwyn, startled, looked down and saw what could only be a fairy hovering about a foot away at the height of her chest. She was about ten inches tall and had bright blue butterfly wings with white swirling patterns. "Oh, hello, sorry, I was just admiring your forest here. Did you say you've been expecting me?"

"Oh yes! Coraignon, or, as you call him, Hops, has been very excited for you to arrive. We've been hearing all about your adventures with him! This is one of the Fae Realms, and I'd like to take you to meet our queen." She was beaming with excitement and flitting around in little circles in front of her. "Come, come, follow me. She awaits your arrival!" The fairy started to fly off toward one of the enormous trees, looking back to make sure Bronwyn followed.

Bronwyn almost felt like she was in a dream as she followed the fairy. As she walked, she pulled herself together, not wanting to seem dazed or confused. She was glad she had taken a bath the night before and wasn't wearing all her armor. She had on a simple long-sleeve white tunic and brown leather pants, with her usual traveling boots. She didn't precisely feel fit to meet a queen, but at least she wasn't caked in dirt and wearing a spiked breastplate. It occurred to her that she'd basically been kidnaped, but she couldn't muster any outrage at the situation. It was almost like the very air in this magical forest was working to calm her nerves and make her feel relaxed.

As they got closer to the tree, Bronwyn could see a faint archway carved into the trunk, and the fairy paused for a moment in front of it. She removed a green crystal and held it up to the tree, causing a matching green light to fill the arch. "Right through here, we're almost there; hurry now, it won't stay open long!" The fairy dove into the green light disappearing with a faint pop. Bronwyn paused in front of the portal briefly, removing the tie from her hair and allowing it to fall around her shoulders. She took a deep breath and stepped through yet another portal.

Evidently, she had moved through space somehow; she was not in the trunk of a tree; however, the portal she took didn't have the usual feeling of travel or vertigo she had become used to experiencing. It was as though she'd walked through an invisible wall, and her body didn't perceive the experience at all: it was just like taking a normal step. She was in the entrance hall of a staggeringly large palace; the room had to be as large as a football field, if not larger. The floor and walls were constructed from white stone with golden flecks sparkling in the natural sunlight. Planters filled with trees, shrubs, and flowers, and water features filled the space. As Bronwyn took in the scene, she even noticed vines climbing up the walls. Small animals, butterflies, and birds scurried and flitted through the little manicured gardens.

"This way now, don't get lost; the meeting hall is just ahead." The fairy flew a quick circle around Bronwyn and then took off in front of her, flying straight through the garden with no concern that Bronwyn had to follow the paths on foot. She walked briskly, trying to keep the fairy in her sight and taking in the beauty of the space around her. Before long, she approached a set of large wooden doors; they were around twenty feet high and had intricate carvings depicting dozens of scenes. Pictured in the carved wood, she saw a crown being placed on a tall, angular man. She saw battles being fought. She saw myriad animals, birds, and plants, especially in the borders. She felt like she could stand there for days and still find something new to look at.

However, more pressing than the ornately carved doors were the two guards stationed in front of them. She knew, logically, that these were different sorts of fae, but they looked exactly how elves were often depicted in fantasy VRs. One was masculine, one was very feminine, and each wore green-scaled armor. The scales were designed to look like leaves bordered with golden filigree. They held long glaives at their sides, the edges of which gleamed in the sunlight. Most eye-catching, however, were the beings themselves. They stood around seven feet tall and could only be described as perfect. They were more beautiful than anyone Bronwyn had ever seen, and their luminescent eyes pierced through her like they were judging the worth of her very soul.

"Don't worry, you're a welcome guest, just follow me!" The fairy had flown up next to Bronwyn and whispered in her ear. She flew up to the elven guards and whispered something in the ear of the left one. He smiled briefly and looked at Bronwyn, speaking in a voice that was smooth as silk and flowed like a song. "Welcome Bronwyn, friend of Coraignon, to the Summer Court. The queen has been expecting your arrival, and you may enter." He held his open hand out to his side toward the massive doors, and Bronwyn could hear a heavy lock sliding open, and the doors silently parted.

The tiny fairy beckoned Bronwyn forward and flew through the gap. Feeling slightly unsure of how to conduct herself, Bronwyn bowed her head slightly to the guard and said, "Thank you." She stepped past him and laid her hand on the door to open the gap enough to walk through. As her hand touched the surface of the wood, visions of fairies, elves, witches in deep forest cottages, and sleeping princesses flashed through her mind. She shook her head and continued to push against the door, which opened silently and without strain.

The meeting hall, while still immense, was smaller than the entrance; tall pillars lined the left and right sides, and plants and vines filled much of the space. Though all slightly different from what she'd expect of an Earth-born animal, bigger creatures resembling elk, bears, and lions lay in the grass and meandered around the raised garden beds. There was a long carpet of soft green grass down the center of the room, leading about a hundred yards from the doorway to the dais where a glittering crystal throne, bedecked in flower-covered vines, sat.

Sitting on the throne was a being so majestic and otherworldly that Bronwyn struggled for a moment to recognize that she was a person. Even from the far end of the hall, her presence brought tears to Bronwyn's eyes and caused hope to flare in her chest. She felt her fears and worries pass from her mind, and the tension that had been subconsciously tightening her shoulders slipped away. She forgot about pain, regret, and suffering in the fae queen's presence, and Bronwyn, tears flowing freely now, slowly walked forward and fell to her knees.

❦ OLIVIA ❧

After Gan-dak showed her off to his friend Tilia, a willowy, winged Ghelli woman, he announced that she could let her concentration drop and that Olivia had passed his exams. "I'm done? So, I'm in?"

"Oh yes, you're in, more than in; I'm going to recommend you receive a full scholarship with no service indenture."

"Service indenture?"

"Yes, many students arrive without the ability to pay the exorbitant tuition, so the academy binds them in a service indenture for some time. I assume you don't have several million Energy beads on your person?" He winked at her with a crooked grin.

"Uh, no, I don't." Olivia's heart had started racing, but she tried to calm herself. He'd said she'd have a full scholarship, after all.

"Not to worry—your talent is among the top in our recruit pool. The school will want to make a friend of you. Professors will want to take you under their wings, you know, to get you to sign lifelong contracts with them. Hah. Don't fret, don't fret. Not everyone here will want to steal your freedom. But seriously," here, his face grew grave, and he leaned forward to whisper, "Don't go signing any contracts until you've learned the ins and outs!"

"Oh, I've done my share of wrangling with corporate contracts and venture capitalists. Thank you for the warning, though."

"Yes, I'm sure you're quite savvy. Now, I'll take you back to the lobby so Yunsha can get you set up with some supplies and your uniform and show you to your dorm group."

"Dorm group?"

"Yes, I'm sorry to say, but first-year students share an open dormitory, even those as talented as you." Once again, Gan-dak winked at her, and then he stood up. Olivia was impressed with his height—he'd give Morgan a run for his money. She followed him out to the lobby, where Yunsha sat scribbling in a little leather notebook. "Yunsha, here's your charge! Treat her well, now." With a short bow, Gan-dak turned and started to leave.

"Wait," Olivia said, "Thank you for your time, Professor Gan-dak." She held her hand out for him to shake. He turned back to her, his grin widening, and then he gently took her hand in his.

"I'll see you around, Miss Olivia. I'm sure you'll eventually end up in one of my lectures." With that, he turned and was gone through the door before Olivia could say any more.

"Hmm, you must have done well; he's usually a great deal more surly than that." Yunsha stood up and, with her hands on her hips, gave Olivia another good look. "Well, come on! Let's get you registered. Gan-dak will have turned in your evaluation to the registrar on his way back to his office." She walked through the door on the other side of the room, and Olivia followed. Yunsha led her a short distance down the hallway and stopped at a counter with an open window and a woman sitting on a tall stool. She was another Ghelli, with lovely, wavy copper-colored hair hanging down between her glistening wings. She wore a robe similar to Gan-Dak's, and her bright, blue eyes glittered when she greeted Yunsha with a high, trilling voice, "Yunsha! Another new student? So close to the term? You've been busy!"

"Oh, she's not a find of mine; she came in with a teleport token this morning." Yunsha gestured for Olivia to come over to the window. "This is Olivia Bennet. You should have an evaluation there, from Gan-dak."

"Pleased to meet you, Olivia! I'm Benla, and you can come to me if you ever have questions about your classes, registration, or benefits."

"Thank you, um, it's nice to meet you, also." Olivia smiled, placing her hands on the counter and twining her fingers together. Benla turned around and walked to a wooden basket where a sheaf of papers sat stacked. She took the very top sheet and walked back over to the counter.

"Here it is, hot off the presses. Hmm, looks like Professor Gan-dak has recommended a full scholarship with no service indenture. Well, with these marks, I can see why. Still, I will need to get an approval stamp on this. Give me a couple of minutes, please, ladies." Without waiting for an answer, Benla turned and walked out the door behind her.

"My, my. I'd like to get a look at that evaluation," Yunsha said. Olivia looked down at her and saw that her head barely cleared the countertop. She wondered at the difficulty of creating a comfortable space for so many species. She didn't reply to Yunsha's statement right away, unsure what to say. "What was it that impressed him? Your Core?"

"Hmm? Oh, I suppose my Core and my affinity with different attunements."

"Don't play coy, child. I've been here a very long time. I'll see the report eventually. Tut, don't worry; I'll keep an eye on you. If you make it through the first year culling, I might have an assistant position for you. We'll see." She reached up a gloved hand and gently patted Olivia's clasped hands. "Don't be nervous—the hard part is over for today." Olivia sighed and let her hands relax a little. A couple of moments later, Benla came back in, smiling and humming to herself.

"Well, that went quickly; luckily, Director Orthal had a cancellation; I got right in."

"That does sound lucky," Olivia offered.

"Mmhmm." Benla was busy stamping papers and dropping them into wooden trays, and then she lifted a smooth copper ring and a flat black stone about the size of a personal computer tablet. She set the ring on top of the flat stone and then put both onto the counter. "Okay, Olivia, when you rest your hand on this slate and send forth a trickle of your Energy, you'll be registered at Fainhallow Academy. The ring will be imprinted with your identification, permissions, and a monthly stipend. Go ahead." Olivia nodded and placed her palm on the cool stone slate. She sent out a trickle of Energy, and the stone flashed a bright magenta for a moment and then a pale blue. Before her eyes, intricate runes started to appear on the band of copper, seemingly carving themselves into the metal. When the ring was covered entirely in dimly glowing runes, it flashed, and then they faded to a darker color of copper. The slate went dark, and Benla said, "All done! You can put the ring on any finger you like."

Olivia picked up the ring and slipped it onto the ring finger of her right hand. It shrank to fit, and she became aware of it, almost like she could feel the contents of her satchel when she concentrated on it. It was also imprinted with information:

Olivia Bennet—First Year—Copper Cohort—1000 Credits.

She was immediately aware that it was a sizable dimensional container, able to hold as much if not more than her blue satchel.

"Your ring will load with one thousand credits per month. It is not possible to bank them—the upper limit is one thousand, so use them or lose them!"

"Where do I spend them?" Olivia asked, gently turning the ring on her finger.

"All of the shops on the academy grounds accept academy credits. If you don't want to venture out to the shops, you can use the credits to purchase meals and supplies here in the main academy building."

"Well, thank you very much," Olivia said, backing up from the counter and turning to Yunsha.

"Well, girl, let's go get your uniforms, and then I'll show you to your dormitory." She waved to Benla and then turned, trusting that Olivia would follow her. Of course, Olivia did follow her, and they wound their way back to the main concourse hall and into a hallway on the other side of the building. Feeling overwhelmed by the strangeness of everything, Olivia found herself looking at Yunsha's back and not making eye contact with the dozens of other students they passed by. They went down a flight of stone steps and through a series of vaulted hallways until they came to a doorway labeled "Academy Supply Dispensary."

Several Ardeni were working in the dispensary, and they gave Olivia a set of textbooks, notebooks bound in leather with beautiful cream-colored parchment within, and two pens that would have made a Manhattan banker jealous—polished wood with a silver cap and nib. The attendants assured her that they would last her for years; one had a fine point and the other a thick, reed-like tip for filling in shading. Yunsha said she should keep her school supplies in her ring because they wouldn't want her to bring her satchel to some classes. After stowing her books, the attendants measured Olivia and asked her if she preferred trousers or skirts. Olivia thought about it and then asked, "What's the trend among the students?"

"Ahh, smart—don't want to stand out, do you?" Yunsha nodded. "Most of the females among the two-legged races are wearing skirts under their robes these days." Olivia nodded to the attendant, and he hurried back to a cubby-covered wall to dig out uniforms that were approximately her size. Olivia could see several different colors in the cubbies, but the attendant brought her a stack of folded, light-gray robes, button-up shirts, skirts, and shiny black shoes. "Gray is for novices. If you make it through your courses this year, you'll be promoted to apprentice and get the blue robes."

"What's after blue?"

"Hah, worry about this year, girl." She winked at her to soften the words. "But if you must know, if you stay for a third year, you'll be wearing burgundy, and if you make it past that, you'll be studying under a master and wear black with a silver pin." She tapped her pin, which Olivia hadn't noticed until now, and she saw that it was shaped like a serpent in a figure eight and glinted with a golden luster. "Different pins for different cohorts, but gold is for masters. There, now I've given you something to dream about." She chuckled and indicated the stack of clothing. Olivia nodded and swept it into her ring.

They walked back through the cold, stone hallways of basement level one, then up to the concourse. Yunsha picked a doorway a dozen yards from the one they came in, and after following it through another short hallway, they came to a stairway leading up. "Novices dorm on the third floor." She started climbing the steps, and Olivia followed close behind. They passed the first landing without pause, and then on the third floor, they exited into a long, wide hallway with closed doors lining both sides. "Let's see; which cohort were you in again?"

"My ring says Copper cohort."

"Well, at least metallic grade, though Copper is going to be filled with scholarship recipients like you. Not that that's bad—more of them are here on merit than in Silver or Gold. The ones to really watch out for are the gemstone cohorts, though—very competitive." She emphasized "Very" with a bit of a chuckle afterward. Olivia decided not to worry about it for the moment. "Hmm, let's see here," Yunsha said, walking down the hallway and looking at the various door labels. "Yep, there it is." She stopped in front of a door, just like all the others, but it had a fancifully scripted "Copper" on the square placard. "In we go!" She twisted the handle and pushed the door open.

The door opened into a long, rectangular room with a high ceiling. Lining the walls of both sides of the room were three narrow beds and three plain wooden armoires. The room's flooring consisted of well-worn wooden planks, the walls were plastered in a creamy white, and the high ceiling bore a dozen sets of exposed beams. Light came from a high chandelier emitting warm yellow light and from a large bay window at the far end of the dorm. Two couches sat facing each other in front of the window, and a bench piled with cushions lined the short wall beneath the glass. Olivia walked into the room, stepping on a long, plush, burgundy rug that ran the length of the room. Five faces turned toward her from the far end of the room.

Two people lounged on the couches with books on their chests; two others sat under the bay window, leaning conspiratorially toward each other. The fifth was lying on the rug between the couches, his arms cradling his head, as he and all the others stared at Olivia and Yunsha. Yunsha pushed Olivia forward gently and called out, "Copper cohort! This is your sixth member, Olivia. Show her her bed, go over your schedule and welcome her!" Then Yunsha turned toward the door and said more softly, "Good luck, Olivia; I'll be watching you."

⸎ OLIVIA ⸏

Olivia watched the door click closed behind Yunsha, and then she turned back to the group of people at the far end of the room. She slowly started walking toward them, doing her best to plaster a smile on her face. She was about halfway there, in the middle of the long burgundy rug, when a small figure charged toward her from the couch. Olivia could see that it wasn't a child but rather another person of Yunsha's race. "Hello, Olivia! I'm Veena!" Exclaimed the girl, or woman—Olivia wasn't sure how to tell her age, as she also wore a smooth white stain of makeup over her exposed flesh. Her eye sockets and lips were dyed deep green, and she had straight, white-blonde hair hanging down to her hips.

"Pleased to meet you, Veena." Olivia held out a hand, and Veena took it in her gloved hand. Then Veena turned and gestured to the other four individuals still lounging at the far end of the room.

"Come, and I'll introduce the others." She pulled Olivia by the hand toward the bright window. They stopped a few feet in front of the couches, and Veena pointed to the man lounging on the rug. He was a big, red-skinned man like Gan-dak. "This is Rald." The man smiled, revealing his fangs, and turned his dark, cobalt eyes on Olivia, rubbing his hands sheepishly through his spikey, black hair.

"Hey, sorry if I don't get up; I'm lazy." Before Olivia could respond, Veena continued her introductions.

"That little Bogoli is my baby brother, Hanwol."

"Baby? We're twins!" The diminutive man was slightly smaller than Veena, and his smooth-shaven head was stained a deep blue, like the rest of his face. Three silver stripes were painted from his forehead to his jawline, and his deep red eyes stared menacingly at his sister.

"Nice to meet you, Hanwol," Olivia said, trying to head off the fraternal conflict.

"Hmmph." Hanwol flopped back onto the couch, staring at the ceiling.

"On the other couch is Adaida, sister of Shani—the one soaking in the sun, there, under the windows." Olivia smiled at the two Ghelli sisters, noting their differences; while their faces were very similar, their colorings were quite a contrast. They were both beautiful, tall, willowy women, but Shani had silvery blonde hair, and Adaida had deep chestnut curls.

"It's nice that some of you have siblings here at the academy," Olivia said, trying to break the ice a little.

"Oh, it's nice for those Ghelli girls, but I'd much rather not be here in Veena's shadow," Hanwol muttered from the couch.

"Oh, hush! He's such a moody boy." Veena laughed and sat down at the end of the couch, pushing her brother's feet off the edge. "Don't put your shoes on the furniture! Olivia, sit down; tell us about yourself. Forgive me if this is insulting, but what are your people called? I've never met anyone quite like you." The others perked up and stared at her, waiting for the answer. Olivia cleared her throat and sat down on the other couch next to Adaida.

"I'm a human. My people come from another world. We were traveling through space to find new homes for our kind when the System found us and sort of kidnapped us, placing us on this world." She shrugged.

"Well, that's interesting!" Rald said, sitting up and scooting his back against the couch opposite Olivia. "Your people can travel between stars?"

"Yes, we had a lot of advanced technology. Well, advanced in our opinion, I guess. We didn't know anything about Energy or the System, though." This caused a bit of a stir in the conversation, and Shani sat up and leaned forward from the window seat.

"So, you don't know much about Energy? Oh, dear. I'm afraid our shot at the induction prizes just went down significantly. No offense."

"Induction prizes?" Olivia looked around blankly.

"Ugh, you don't even know what we're talking about?" Adaida sat up, her four gossamer wings twitching with agitation. "We need to prepare her."

"What level are you, Olivia?" Asked Veena.

"Um, I'm level eight. Can you explain what this is about?"

"Oh, thank Nature, she's at least got some levels," Shani said, leaning further forward toward Olivia. "Do you know any spells? I'm assuming you have a fully developed Core and pathways?" Olivia was starting to get irritated by the grilling and the lack of information coming her way.

"How about you all slow down with the questions and give me a little information? Then, maybe I'll spill my guts?" Olivia sat up, pulling her shoulders back and staring around the group, her mouth set in a firm line.

"Hey, she's tough. I like it!" Rald said, chuckling.

"Alright, hush, everyone," Veena said. "Olivia, the reason you aren't allowed to take a class before you come here is that each year the new students are put into a competition for various prize packages. For some rewards, we're scored as a cohort, so we all win, or we all lose. The competition runs for the first month of school, and we're scored on some criteria individually and on how we perform in a few competitions with other cohorts. Our overall score will determine our placement after the first month."

"Thank you," Olivia smiled at Veena. "How many cohorts are there?"

"So far, there are nine this year." Hanwol sat up next to his sister, and Olivia struggled to keep a straight face seeing them sitting next to each other. He was definitely smaller than she, and his blue head with red eyes looked perpetually angry.

"There won't be any more," Rald said definitively. "Not this late—classes start in two days."

"He's right," Adaida nodded, glancing at her sister, who also nodded. "So, Olivia, what can you tell us about yourself? Do you know any spells at all? Can you channel? I mean, they put you into Copper, so I assume you had some talent with something, right?"

"Sure. I have a Core and four elemental affinities, and I seem to be talented when it comes to channeling more than one affinity at a time. And, yes, I know a few simple spells." Olivia sat back, feeling more relaxed because everyone seemed to have breathed a sigh of relief at her words.

"We can work with that." Shani nodded and once again lay back in the cushions on the window seat, soaking in the sunlight.

"Well, let me show you around, Olivia." Veena turned and gestured to a plain wooden door on the wall just a few feet past the last bed. "There's the door to the bathrooms. There's a short hallway in there and then two bathrooms. The boys have been using the one on the left, and the ladies the one on the right."

"Don't you mean the men?" Hanwol asked, his voice strained at the obvious point of contention. Rald just chuckled, and Veena ignored him.

"Anyway, nothing's stopping you from using either bathroom, but, trust me, they're slobs." She turned to the other wall of the long room and pointed to the bed closest to the entry door. "That's your bed and your closet. Sorry, you get one of the ones furthest from the window, but first come, first serve, as they say." She smiled. "That's the whole tour! Let me know if you have any questions!"

"Can anyone tell me what classes we have? Do we all have the same schedule?" Olivia looked around at the group.

"Oh yes. Come, let's go over to your bed and go over your classes and texts." Veena beckoned her, and Olivia followed to the narrow bed. They sat down, facing each other, and Olivia pulled her books out of her ring one by one. The first book was titled *Cultivation and Core Development*. "That's our fourth class of the day." Olivia nodded and pulled out the next book, *A Novice's Guide to Enchantment*. "We start the day with that class."

"Oh, that's exciting! I've been hoping to learn more about enchantment." Olivia cracked the book and thumbed through the thick, illustrated pages noting the many diagrams and runes.

"Enchantment combined with spellcraft can become a potent combination!" Veena nodded. Olivia pulled out the next book and read the title.

"Applied Alchemy for the Adventurous Soul?"

"Yes, alchemy is an extensive subject area, and the academy teaches a focused subset of it that is considered useful for cultivators trying to improve their power. That's our second class of the day." Olivia opened the book to a random page and saw that it looked a lot like a cookbook recipe.

"Hmm," she said, setting the book aside and pulling out the last one. She read the title, "Introduction to Spellcraft."

"Our third class, and probably the most important, well, maybe tied with the cultivation class. You'll learn about channeling Energy into specific patterns to create spells and improve existing spells. I'm pretty sure they'll even let us learn spells from scrolls so that we can use them as building blocks for more advanced spells."

"That sounds great!" Olivia was beaming as she thumbed through the first few pages—they were very densely covered in fine print. "I love books like this—full of information!"

"Oh, good! I was afraid you'd struggle with the texts. I'm sure some of the others will be put at ease that you're actually excited by them! Anyway, those are our four classes, and then, at the end of the day, we have combat practice and physical education."

Veena left Olivia alone for a while to read through the first few pages of each of her books. Olivia watched her walk over to the others and saw that she and her brother began playing some sort of a game. They sat cross-legged in front of each other, taking turns tossing some small objects onto the floor in front of them. The others were all napping or reading books. Olivia yawned, started reading through *Introduction to Spellcraft*, and found the first few pages very difficult and slow reading. She had to constantly backtrack to make sure she understood what she'd just read. Anyone watching her would have seen the smile on her face, though, because, if Olivia looked forward to anything, it was reading a challenging text.

That evening, the six members of Copper cohort walked through the hallways together to the cafeteria, and Olivia was introduced to academy food. The cafeteria wasn't overly crowded—apparently, there wasn't a set dinnertime but rather a dinner window. Olivia had donned her cottony pleated skirt, knee-length socks, thin, buttoned shirt, and snug outer robes, all a pale gray color. Her shiny black shoes reminded her of a pair she'd seen at a department store that had been priced way outside her comfort zone. They were very comfortable, despite their thick heels. Dressed as she was, she felt she fit in very well with the motley cohort, and it seemed she did—no one gave her a second glance in the cafeteria.

They were given plates and allowed to select from the buffet line of hot dishes. Olivia took a steaming green vegetable dish, copying Shani when she put a dollop of butter on top. Then she took a large piece of some sort of red meat and a flaky dinner roll. When they sat down to eat, she noticed that everyone had piled a lot of food on their plates, probably twice what she had. Rald's plate was stacked with the most—several types of meat and three dinner rolls, all slathered in butter. He saw Olivia looking at his plate and smiled, "You should eat more. You'll need the reserves when we start combat training in two days."

"Really? It's that intense?"

"Oh, yes," Adaida said. "You're going to sleep like the dead once that starts."

"How do you all know so much about how the academy works?"

"Our families and friends," Veena said, nudging her brother, who scowled and took another bite of food.

"Anyway, you'll get a chance to pack in some more food tomorrow after the welcome assembly."

"Oh, I'm glad I came in time to see that! The mage guild representative who gave me the token only told me to be here by the first. I'm glad I came a little early."

"We are, too!" Veena said. Some of the others nodded; Rald just grunted and ate some more.

"Is anything else happening tomorrow?"

"Just the assembly, officially. Some of the cohorts are planning some sort of informal competition in the afternoon, though." Hanwol offered.

"Hush, Han!" Veena nudged him.

"What?" Olivia asked.

"Well, we weren't going to mess around with it. Some of those cohorts are very competitive and are aiming to cause trouble," Shani replied for her.

"I don't think we should shy away from the competition. Let's see what they're made of. If we don't win, we at least get a feel for what we're up against in future competitions." Olivia looked around the table, meeting their eyes.

"I knew I liked you," Rald said, grinning with his teeth full of meat.

⚜ MORGAN ⚜

When the blue lights began to fade, allowing Morgan to see his surroundings, he found that he and Issa were standing on a stone platform on a hillside overlooking the high valley where the Citadel sat. There were some tremendous differences between what he saw in the valley now versus what had been there when he and Issa rode their roladii in earlier. The orange hillsides were decked in the same short, wiry trees, but now they were covered in bright green leaves. The valley floor was also verdant, tall green grass sprouting from the soil. However, more strange than the change in vegetation were the dozen tents and campfires surrounding the citadel.

When Morgan followed the rows of tents with his eyes, finally resting on the citadel, he took in a sharp breath. Issa followed his gaze and said, "It's new!"

"Well, if not new, it's certainly whole." The citadel was no longer a crumbling ruin—sheer walls of perfectly fitted stone blocks with individuals that patrolled the ramparts Morgan couldn't see clearly at this distance. "What the fuck is going on? Did we get sent back in time?"

"Look," Issa said, pointing to a pedestal behind them, "The stone the lights spoke of. If we touch that, we will leave this place." The stone she referred to was a smooth blue sphere that sat atop the pedestal. "I think we're in a pocket dimension. The dungeon the swordmaster created with his spirit is this place. I've only read about dungeons, but I know they are many and varied; perhaps a dungeon can look like a real place but be apart from it."

"Huh. There's a trail leading down into the valley. What do you reckon the deal is with those tents?"

"I don't know. It seems too few to be a sieging force. Shall we investigate?" Issa's eyes were bright with excitement, and Morgan couldn't blame her; what a mysterious place! He nodded, and swords in hand, they walked down the meandering gravel path to the valley floor. It had been late afternoon, judging by the sun, when they arrived; after hiking for an hour down the hillside, the sun hadn't seemed to move.

"It seems the clock is stuck in this place."

"What? Oh, the time isn't changing!" Issa squinted at the low, orange sun poking above the western hills. "How strange!"

"Yeah, it is." They continued on the path to the valley's center, where it merged with the tight stone flags of the ancient road, though it was no longer ancient. The stones were smooth and flat, and no debris marred their surface. Morgan glanced at Issa, and she nodded with a grin, and they walked forward on the road. "Get ready," he said when he saw a figure walking toward them from the nearest tent, still a few hundred yards distant. She nodded, and he felt a slight surge of her aura as she began to channel her Battle Chant. She didn't unleash her voice, but he could see that she was primed; her eyes had darkened to a smokey purple, and black wisps of steaming Energy rose into the air from her shoulders.

Morgan began to channel Energy into his limbs, ready to leap into any of his sword forms at the slightest hint of danger, but the figure stopped a good stone's throw from them and shouted, in a rough but friendly voice, "Hail, I'm no threat to you, strangers. Are you here to challenge the keep?" Morgan looked at Issa, and she raised an eyebrow and tilted her head to the side, indicating she didn't know what to say.

"Perhaps. Who are you, stranger?" Morgan asked, walking forward warily.

"I'm Yan Gronnik, and I'm waiting my turn to try the gate guardian." As he spoke, Morgan got close enough to see the details of the man. He was tall, not as tall as he was, but still big for the people of this world. His skin was red, and his hair was pulled up in a high top-knot with the sides shaved clean. He wore bronze-colored chain mail and had a heavy-looking broadsword on his hip.

"There are others in the dungeon?" Morgan asked.

"Dungeon? No, friend. It's a keep full of the undead and untold treasure." The man had a puzzled look on his face which prompted Morgan to look at Issa questioningly. She motioned for him to wait.

"Nice to meet you, Yan. I'm Issa, and this is Morgan. Yes, we're here to challenge the guardian, also."

"Ahh, well, there are twelve of us ahead of you, and he only makes an appearance every ten days at midnight. I hope you brought camping supplies." Yan walked forward toward them as he spoke and held out a hand to Issa. She kept her chant ready but reached forward to shake his hand. He smiled and reached for Morgan's hand next. Morgan took it, noting the rough calluses on his palm and his iron-like grip.

"Is there no way to get in sooner? Would anyone be willing to sell their position, do you think?" Issa asked.

"The only way is to challenge for a position, but you won't have an easy time of it. Still, the law says you have the right."

"The law?"

"The Code of the Sword, of course."

"Forgive us; we've traveled far," Morgan said, "The Code says we can challenge you for your position in line?"

"Ahh, that makes sense; you seem strange to me, indeed. Yes, the Code is clear: those waiting for the guardian must accept or refuse a challenge. To refuse is to forfeit your position."

"And what if we want to enter together?" Issa pressed.

"Well, naturally, you would. Each of us is here with our partner or squire as Thun-dak calls his second."

"You're all in groups of two?"

"Yes, of course." His voice was flat like it made perfect sense.

"Thank you, Yan. Morgan and I will set up camp shortly, but we'd like a moment alone together if you don't mind." Issa smiled her most charming smile. Yan bowed and turned to walk sedately back toward his tent. Issa pulled Morgan another thirty yards or so back down the road and turned to him. "This is all part of the dungeon, I think. It's too coincidental that they are all in pairs of two, and there's some sort of 'code' that allows us to challenge them for position. I'll wager that they are stronger, better sword fighters the further up the list we go."

"This is too weird; are these people even real?" Morgan looked around at the strange valley, frozen in time and, presumably, outside normal space.

"I don't know; it seems impossible. What if ten people came into this dungeon? Would there be groups of ten swordsmen waiting to challenge the 'guardian?' We can't be the first to ever set foot in here; I feel like the dungeon organizes itself to fit the challengers."

"He seemed very real, though. What if the dungeon captures challengers that fail and messes with their minds." Morgan's thoughts ran through various horrifying possibilities.

"Oh, Morgan; it's just as easy to imagine the System and the Swordmaster have created these swordsmen out of Energy and matter and filled them with his own will to populate this place."

"It does feel very scripted. Well, if we're going to operate on the theory that this place is tailored to the challengers, can we assume the battles, challenges, and treasures are meant to be attainable by us?"

"I hope so! If it was meant to challenge everyone in the world, there's no way we'd get very far. There are definitely some dungeons like that, though. I've heard stories of adventurers going into dungeons and getting utterly destroyed at the entrance."

"Well, shit. Let's take it slow until we find out what kind of place this is. Am I right in assuming you aren't up to camping here for four months . . ." Morgan cut himself off in thought. Issa looked at him expectantly. "Hold up.

The sun doesn't move. How are ten days supposed to pass, let alone a hundred and twenty?"

"Ahh, good point!" Issa reached out with both her hands and jostled his shoulders. "It seems we are not supposed to wait around. We need to challenge the others in order to move things forward."

"You seem pretty sure. Let's go see what things look like before we start swinging, though." Morgan took Issa's hand, and they walked, more relaxed this time, toward the cluster of tents. "If you're right, to make things move forward, I think we need to get to the front of the line. Do we start at the bottom or go straight to the top?"

"Well, as you said, we might want to take it slow until we see what sort of place this is." Issa squeezed his hand, and he nodded at her statement. Soon they were standing on the road with several tents off to each side. Morgan could see various clusters of people here and there among them. Some sat by their cookfires, some lounged on bedrolls in the grass, and some stood around talking. While they looked around, Yan walked up to them.

"Glad to see you decided to come into the camp." He had a mug of something in one hand and took a long pull.

"Yan, if we wanted to challenge someone for their spot, is there any idea who the toughest is here?" Morgan asked, putting aside pretense.

"Huh, a bit like a viper hound, aren't you? Won't let go of that snake! Well, if you want to put forth a challenge, I'd start with those in the lowest spot: Henk Thar and his brother Kell."

"Let me guess; the fighters get stronger the closer to the top spot on the waiting list?" Morgan didn't hide his wry smile.

"Hmm, funny coincidence, but, yeah, I'd say so." As Yan spoke, Morgan looked at Issa, and she winked at him with a sideways grin. Morgan couldn't imagine this was a random occurrence and was becoming more and more sure that the "Challengers" were part of the dungeon scenario.

"Please point me toward Henk and Kell, my friend." Morgan clapped a friendly hand on Yan's shoulder. Yan, for his part, smiled gamely and pointed to a large tent on the southern side of the road. Flying from the peak of the domed tent was an orange and teal pennant. Two Ardeni men sat outside the tent, one lounging back and reading a small book and the other roasting a piece of meat on a stick. "Thanks, Yan." Still holding Issa's hand, Morgan walked toward the two brothers' tent. As they drew near, Morgan let go of her hand, and he felt the weight of her aura increase as she readied her Battle Chant.

"What's this then? We've no meat to share, considering the wait ahead of us." The Ardeni by the fire cleared his throat and spat a wad of phlegm into the fire, where it sizzled. He had close-cut blonde hair and bright green eyes.

Morgan noted the eyes because, in his experience, Ardeni hair usually matched their eyes.

"Hello. Henk? Kell? I'm afraid that my partner and I would like to challenge you for your position in the queue."

"Oh?" The other Ardeni said, standing up and setting his little book down. He raised his voice in a mocking sing-song, "You're afraid you'd like to challenge?" He stepped around the fire, his bright red eyes flashing as he scowled. "Come on then, fools." He drew the broadsword at his belt and walked out to the road, his back to Morgan and Issa. His brother stood and spat again, walking after his brother. Morgan saw that he had two short, curved swords hanging from his belt, but he didn't draw them yet.

"Well, let's go." Issa nudged Morgan, and he nodded. He'd been holding his long, black-bladed sword in one hand with the curve resting on his shoulder. He took it in two hands and walked forward with the blade in a middle guard. Issa stalked behind and to his right, her rapier held ready. The two brothers stopped walking when they reached the center of the road and then turned to face Morgan and Issa as they approached. The green-eyed, spitting brother drew his two short swords and smiled crookedly, openly leering at Issa.

"Ready?" The other brother with the bright red eyes asked, shaking out his long mane of crimson hair. Morgan looked at Issa and saw her eyes' purple and black gleam and the black steam rising from her shoulders. He gripped his sword, pouring Energy into his limbs, and nodded.

The two brothers complemented each other nicely, but they were no match for Morgan and Issa. Though they did a good job protecting each others' flanks, Morgan and Issa had reach and speed on their side, not to mention Issa's battle chant. She didn't even Haste Morgan—only herself. Her discordant ringing voice rose above the clang of steel, and Morgan felt his arms grow faster and stronger, and he saw the terror in his opponents' eyes as their will was sapped. For his part, Morgan kept them at bay with quick slashes and thrusts while he reached out with his advanced Energy Drain. He felt the currents of Energy in their bodies and just started willing it to flow to him. Their faces blanched, and Morgan felt a surge of power and speed as their Energy fueled him further. He launched into the Crane Flutters its Wings, completely destroying the guard of the dual-wielding brother and tearing long deep furrows in his chest. He collapsed in a shower of blood.

While Morgan dispatched the first brother, Issa flashed in a series of zig-zagging side steps, finishing her maneuver with several quick thrusts that slipped past the other brother's weak attempts to parry, piercing him three times—once in the stomach, once between his ribs, and finally a ripping stab in the side of his neck. Issa stepped back, whipping the blood from her rapier as he fell, writhing in the dirt, his life's blood pumping and spraying forth on the gray flagstones.

Morgan stepped back to Issa's side and looked around warily. The other challengers stood watching, but no one cheered or objected; they watched impassively as the two brothers died. Golden motes rose from the two bodies and streamed into Issa and Morgan. When the flood ended and the euphoria of victory and Energy coursed through them, they saw that the bodies of their opponents had dissipated into a misty smoke that slowly dispersed in the light breeze.

Congratulations! You have achieved level 21 Vortex Duelist and have gained 8 Intelligence, 8 Agility, 6 Will, 6 Dexterity.

"Their bodies are gone," Issa said quietly, "And I leveled."

"I did, too. Does that mean they weren't real? That fight was pretty easy; I almost feel guilty."

"Well, they could have refused the challenge, and yes, I think that means they were constructs made by the dungeon." Issa wiped her blade down and stored it away, and Morgan did the same when he looked around and saw that the other challengers had silently gone back to their previous activities.

"Should we eat and rest before we challenge the next?"

OLIVIA

Olivia looked up from her bowl of hot cereal and asked her cohort, "How often will I get to visit home?" The collective chewing and crunching around the table slowed down, and then Rald swallowed loudly and answered her.

"Well, you're free on weekends. We have a week at midsummer and a week at midwinter, and, at the end of the year, you have a month free until the next session starts, but that's only if you intend to spend more than a year here." He shrugged and took another big bite of toast.

"There are a few more breaks here and there. I can show you a calendar later if you want," Veena added.

"Well, my home is a thousand miles away. How hard is it to get those teleport tokens?" This question was met with a longer silence, but then Shani cleared her throat.

"They're really expensive. The school will give you one per year, but you can try to earn others. You can do work for professors in your spare time. I suppose that's only if you aren't rich; I don't know how much money you have." She looked at Olivia with an eyebrow arched in question.

"Well, I'm not rich. I suppose that's something I'll have to figure out." Olivia bent back to her breakfast, cleaning up the warm, buttery grains.

"Anyone want this bacon?" Hanwol asked, holding up a piece of thick, peppered bacon. Olivia snatched it and took a bite, unbelievably relieved that, apparently, pigs existed in this world.

"Oh, my god. I didn't see this up there—I knew there were boar-like creatures near our settlement, but I was worried that pigs weren't a thing here." She savored the meat, chewing slowly.

"Well, remember that the System has integrated your language with ours; whatever you think of as a 'pig' was a different word for us when the System arrived, and chances are our version is a different animal but so similar that the System assigned your word to it in your mind." Hanwol spoke matter-of-factly, taking sips of fruit juice between sentences.

"Ugh, it hurts my brain. I don't care, though, because this is bacon. Now let me enjoy it!" Olivia grinned at the small man. "Hey, on another note, can I ask a question? I don't want to offend anyone, but I was wondering something about you and Veena." Olivia looked at Veena while she chewed, waiting for a response.

"Go ahead," Hanwol said before Veena could reply.

"Well, first, I'm sorry, but I haven't learned what your race is called, and I'm curious. Second, I was wondering why you paint your faces. Is that rude?" Olivia scrunched down, slightly embarrassed at such a forward question in front of everyone.

"It's only rude if you're trying to be rude, and I know you aren't," Veena replied. "We're called Bogoli; we're from the southern hemisphere of this world. Our history tells us we originated from a different world than the Ardeni and Shadeni when the System merged our worlds. As for why we paint our faces, well, it's something we've always done. It has to do with some spiritual beliefs that I won't go into, and, to be blunt, it's strange to us that none of you do it!" The Ghelli sisters laughed at that, and Rald snorted.

"Did Ghelli originate from the same world as the other races?" Olivia looked at Adaida while she asked the question.

"No, we, the Cadwalli, and the Vodkin came from yet another world. However, some of our ancient texts claim that all the intelligent races of Fanwath were born on one world and spread out in our solar system before the System came and mashed us all together. Most of the other races dispute that, though."

"We need to get going if we're going to join the tournament," Rald interrupted.

"Ugh!" Veena said. "Did you at least find out what the competition will be?"

"Yeah, push-stones." Rald drummed his fingers on the table, a frown on his face.

"Push-stones?" Olivia asked.

"It could be worse," Shani said, "They're round stones about the size of a fist, enchanted to be highly reactive to Energy. The goal is to push them past your opponent without letting them drop between you. Usually, you have your hands secured behind your back so that you have to control your Energy flow directly from your Core."

"Is it hard?" Olivia looked around at everyone's faces. Shani and Adaida looked thoughtful, Hanwol and Veena wore frowns, and Rald was grinning.

"Nah, I used to play a lot with my friends. With any luck, you guys won't even have to take a turn. The way they set it up, we have to stand in a line and face off with another team. Only the first person in the line has to go until he or she gets beaten, then the next person in the cohort steps up to face the winner. Hopefully, if I go first, I can just keep beating all the others. We'll see." He stood up and shrugged. "Only one way to find out!"

They stood up together and walked from the cafeteria out through a series of wide hallways to the large doors that opened onto the east side of the main academy building. Encroaching outbuildings had spared this side of the building by design—it housed the well-manicured, grassy commons where students gathered to get sunshine, play games, and exercise. The yard spread out all the way to the eastern curtain wall, and there, in the shadow of the massive wall, a large group of students wearing the grays of first-year cohorts were gathering.

As Olivia's cohort approached, she did her best to make an account of the other cohorts. She saw a few Ardeni, a few more Shadeni, many Ghelli and Bogoli, and even a couple of Cadwalli. It seemed that certain races were either more gifted with spellwork or more favored by those making the selection. What surprised her the most was when she saw some individuals that had to be a mixture of races. She saw a very pale-blue girl with Ghelli wings and a tall man with skin almost purple in tone. More than anything, she noticed the baleful stares some of the groups shot their way as they approached.

The light-blue Ghelli woman stepped forward as Olivia's cohort walked up. Everyone got quiet as she started to speak, "Copper, I presume?" Shani nodded, and the girl continued, "I'm Sarice of Ruby cohort. You're the last to arrive, and we've set up the ladders. Gemstones will get a bye in the first round . . ."

"How is that fair?" Rald interjected. Sarice hissed softly and glared at him for a moment.

"It's not fair. But there are nine cohorts, and with odd numbers, there will be byes. The gemstones obviously tested more highly. Why wouldn't you want to face off with a team closer to you in ability?"

"That's tremendously condescending, don't you think?" Shani asked. Sarice sighed and looked around at the other students with a pained expression.

"Look, this is what we agreed on. You can leave if it's not to your liking, and we'll give Wood cohort your forfeit."

"Whatever." Rald spat in the grass, and Sarice managed to look both offended and sorry for him at the same time.

"As I was saying, the gemstones will get a bye, and the first round will be Wood versus Copper, Bone versus Silver, and Stone versus Gold." There was minimal discussion amongst the crowd, making Olivia believe that the matches had already been discussed and decided.

"Alright, let us warm up a little before we start. Where are the stones?" Rald looked around pointedly, and the crowd parted to reveal a small wooden box with pyrographed runes on the cover. Rald stomped over and opened the lid, lifting out a dark round stone about the size of a baseball. When he brought it over, Olivia could see that it had been etched with runes, and the etchings had been filled with dark metal that reminded her of pewter. "Follow me, team; let's get used to the stone before we have to play."

They walked a dozen paces away from the others in the grass, and Rald tossed the stone down at their feet. "Most of you know how this works, but let me explain for Olivia's sake. This stone is enchanted to be very receptive to Energy. Most people struggle to tightly control their Energy when pushed out directly from their Core, so that's part of the challenge. The idea is that you need to focus a stream of Energy at the stone and lift it into the air. Then you 'push' it past your opponent. Your opponent will, of course, try to resist with their own Energy and 'push' it past you. Make sense?"

"In theory, yes," Olivia said, stepping forward toward the stone. "I've only ever tried pushing Energy out through my hands. I'll try, though."

"Put your hands behind your back. It makes it easier to focus on your Core," Veena said, a pensive look on her face. Olivia could tell that the little confrontation with Sarice had bothered some of her cohort members. She followed Veena's advice, clasping her hands behind her back and staring at the stone. She reached inward to her Core and concentrated on moving a tendril of Energy along a narrow pathway near her navel and then *pushed* it out of her body. The Energy moved out and then began to dissipate immediately. She focused her will and pushed more Energy along the same path, pressing the Energy into a condensed beam and forcing it out to the stone.

The stone lifted into the air almost immediately, and Olivia felt a surge of triumph. Relieved sighs escaped the lips of some of her teammates. "Good, hold it there!" Rald stepped around her and faced her from a few feet away. "Now, try to push it toward me gently." Olivia nodded, her brows furrowed in concentration, and nudged the stone with a bit more Energy. It shot forward toward Rald, and he grunted, taking a step back, but the stone stopped and hovered in place. Then it slowly began to shift to Olivia's left and move toward her. She realized he was pushing it against her, and suddenly the game clicked for her. She channeled forth another stream of Energy and pushed it toward the stone, catching it on the side and nudging it back toward Rald. He grinned, baring his teeth, and Olivia felt a surge of Energy begin to drive the stone ball back against her two streams of Energy. She felt like she could add a third stream and push more Energy through them, but their little contest was interrupted by a shrill whistle. Rald met her eyes, and they both let their Energy dissipate, allowing the stone to drop into the grass with a thud.

"That wasn't bad, Olivia; you're a quick study," Adaida said, as they walked back toward the crowd of other cohorts.

"Thank you." Olivia had a bounce in her step as they lined up in the grass behind Rald; she was glad she knew what to do, even if her team decided to put her at the back of the line. Rald faced off with Wood cohort's first contestant; she was a tall Ardeni woman who'd obviously managed to upgrade her race at least once—her height was the first clue, but her glistening silvery hair and bright eyes were dead giveaways. Still, when the "Judge" from the Ruby Cohort dropped the stone between the two contestants, Rald quickly took control and pushed it past her. She cursed, a word Olivia hadn't heard before, and stepped aside for the next person in her cohort.

"Going to take all the glory for your team, Rald?" The Ghelli woman from Ruby cohort asked as she picked up the stone.

"Hah, if they can't get past me, why would we let them match off against our stronger players?" He chuckled as he looked back at the rest of Copper cohort and winked. She snorted and held the stone high, waiting for a nod from each contestant, then dropped it. Rald won again, and then three more times, and Wood cohort was out.

"They only have five members?" Olivia asked Shani, who was in line before her.

"Yeah, some cohorts have five and some seven, but most have six, like us." Olivia didn't think that was exactly fair, but this world didn't really seem to operate on fairness.

The other two contests wrapped up shortly after theirs; Bone cohort bested the Silver cohort, and Gold beat Stone. Then, the gemstone cohorts entered the competition, and Olivia's Copper cohort was matched up against Garnet. Once again, Rald faced each of Garnet cohort's members, beating them all. He struggled with the first two, but the next four went down quickly. He hadn't been joking about being good.

After the second round, Copper, Jade, and Ruby were the only teams remaining. Everyone else was watching and cheering as Ruby finished mopping up Gold, and then Sarice walked over and looked at Rald. "Well, three teams means odd numbers. You'll face Jade and then Ruby."

"So, you'll give your team another bye? Figures." He spat again, and Sarice sighed heavily.

"Does anyone object? I don't see a way to solve this otherwise? I'm sorry we didn't have ten cohorts to make this easier."

"Why not have Ruby and Jade face-off, then the winner take us on?" Hanwol put forth.

"Shouldn't the last two teams be the best? Just take your medicine and let us beat you," a small Bogoli man with deep blue-dyed skin and a bright yellow swirl painted atop his bald head shouted. Rald stopped talking and stared at the diminutive figure for a moment. He didn't say anything, and the crowd grew quiet, but then he snorted and nodded, walking forward to face off with the Jade cohort. Olivia and the others lined up behind him.

This time, Sarice acted as "Judge," picking up the stone and looking from the Bogoli man to Rald, waiting for each to nod, and then she dropped the stone. Immediately, Rald grunted and took a step back, bracing himself as the stone moved swiftly toward him. He strained and managed to stop its forward momentum for several seconds, but then it jerked to the right and shot forward past him, falling to roll in the grass next to Adaida. Rald groaned and stepped aside, making room for Veena.

"What's his name," Olivia whispered to Shani.

"That's Gan. He's a prick," Shani replied.

Gan had little difficulty besting Veena, then Hanwol. Adaida put up quite a fight, doing better even than Rald, but, eventually, Gan managed to push the stone past her. Shani lost almost instantly, and then, butterflies doing backflips in her stomach, Olivia stepped up to the line. Gan grinned and cracked his knuckles, staring at her. Sarice looked at Gan, who nodded, and then at Olivia, but she paused and said, "Hmm, interesting. What's your name?" It caught Olivia off guard; she was nervous enough, but now the whole pack of cohorts was staring at her, waiting for her answer.

"Olivia." Her voice was soft but curt, and she didn't take her eyes off Gan.

"Ready, Olivia?" Sarice's voice held a hint of amusement, which irritated Olivia. She concentrated on her Core, winding three threads of Energy separately and priming them to fire out toward the stone. She quickly glanced at Sarice and nodded, staring at the stone. Sarice held the stone out and dropped it. Before it could hit the ground, Olivia fired her Energy threads, one to push it forward, another to push its side, and a third to drive it forward again. She didn't hold back, shoving all the Energy she could through the pathway under her navel, and she felt it widen in the process.

She was the first to put Energy into the stone, but she felt resistance before her second thread hit it. Gan was pushing straight forward, though, and when her second thread hit the side, his eyes widened in surprise; then, her third thread launched the stone past his head, and he stumbled backward. "What the shit?" the Ghelli woman standing behind Gan exclaimed.

"Haha, marvelous! It looks like Copper was hiding a ringer in their anchor position."

Olivia smiled and reset herself. She heard Gan mutter to his team, "Watch out; she's fast." Olivia knew that part of her victory was due to catching Gan off guard, but she hoped the rest of his team wasn't as good as he was. As the Ghelli woman stepped forward, Olivia prepared her three threads again and nodded to Sarice. Just like with Gan, she was first to hit the stone, and this time there was little resistance—the stone soared past her opponent without a hitch. Her team was cheering and clapping her back by now, and Olivia couldn't hide her smile and the excitement that flushed her cheeks. She beat two more opponents easily, and then the last Jade member stepped in front of her.

"Okay, Olivia! Beat Gwinna and your team will face Ruby!" Sarice said, and her smile seemed genuine. Olivia looked at Gwinna and saw an individual unlike any she'd seen before. Her skin was painted white like a Bogoli, but she was at least a foot taller than any Bogoli she'd yet met. Her silvery hair was so lustrous it seemed like it was spun from the precious metal. More than that, though, her blue eyes glittered like gemstones, emitting a light of their own. Like Yunsha, her eyelids and lips were stained blue.

"She's had a lot of racial upgrades. Her family is extremely wealthy—I think she's well into improved racial ranks," Shani hissed quietly into Olivia's ear.

"Are you ready, contestants?" Sarice asked, her voice rising at the end in excitement. Gwinna smirked and nodded. Olivia looked at Sarice and nodded. This time she was going to try to hit the stone with her second thread on the opposite side, hoping to catch Gwinna off guard. Sarice held the stone out, dropped it, and then Olivia sent her Energy toward it. Before her first thread could touch the stone, it seemed to be getting larger; she just managed to realize it was flying toward her face before she felt a crack, and the world went dark.

⚎ MORGAN ⚏

Morgan sat across the fire from Issa, watching her meditate. She'd gained a level and gotten a new skill called Hexing Shriek. When he asked her what it did, she had said that enemies she affected with it would feel more demoralized and suffer from reduced Energy and stamina recovery. He'd noticed that it seemed to take a while for her eyes to return to their usual bright yellow after the battle. Even when she'd dropped her Battle Chant, they'd remained dark and purple for quite a while. He wondered what effect her class was having on her. Judging by his own class, he didn't think it was anything to worry about. He had some scary abilities, but they didn't seem to affect him outside of their use.

After they'd beaten the two Ardeni brothers, Yan had approached them and said that he and his partner, his wife, would forfeit their position without a contest. They'd been the next in line if Morgan and Issa continued to challenge the assembled sword users. Morgan had walked over to Henk and Kell's tent to see if they'd left any valuables, but nothing other than blankets and an old, embroidered pillow were inside the canvas dwelling. On a whim, he'd pulled out one of the tent stakes so that he could lower the canvas side enough to take the pennant from the peak. He rolled it up and stuffed it in his pouch as a memento. "What are you thinking about?" Issa asked from across the fire.

"Oh, just about that pennant I took. I suppose I'm dwelling a bit on the fact that I didn't know those brothers weren't real people when I slaughtered that guy."

"Stop it. They were willing to fight, and if you hadn't taken them seriously, real or not, they would have killed you or me if they could've."

"Yeah, I know. Don't worry; I'm not going to start pulling punches when your neck is on the line with mine."

"Good." Issa nodded and started rooting around in her pouch, pulling out ingredients for dinner. She produced a copper pot and some raw meat wrapped in paper. She put some of the meat in the pot and then used it to shove away some of the burning logs and smooth out some of the hot coals. She set the pot onto the coals and let the meat brown, sprinkling some herbs and salt into the pot while it sizzled. While it was browning, Issa produced another paper package filled with chopped roots and vegetables. As the meat finished browning, she added some vegetables and stirred them up with the meat fat.

"Are you making stew?" Morgan's mouth was filling with saliva at the scent.

"That's right. We're going to have a hard road ahead of us, challenging these others." She gestured around at the other tents. After a few minutes, she brought out a bottle of red wine and splashed it into the pan. She took a sip of the wine and then put it away.

"Hey, what about me?"

"You want some?" Issa grinned. "I think there's still some right here." She pointed to her lower lip. Morgan laughed, moved around the fire to sit next to her, and kissed her on the spot where she'd pointed.

"Mmm, good wine." He inhaled deeply of the simmering meat and vegetables, then laid back on the blanket they'd spread over the grass. Issa kept working on their meal for a while, and Morgan thought he might have dozed off when she nudged him with a bowl. He sat up and ate ravenously. The meat was rich and fatty, and the vegetables tasted a lot like carrots and potatoes. "God, that's good."

"Thank you! Next meal is up to you." She winked at him, taking a big bite.

"Hmm, no problem. I packed some good sandwich fixings." She scoffed at his response but kept eating with a smile in her eyes. When they finished eating, they spread out their bedrolls and lay awake, talking and reminiscing for a while. Issa told Morgan more about her childhood, and he did the same. She told him about helping her father in his shop after her mother died, and he tried to explain to her what movie theaters were like. She yawned after a while, and Morgan insisted that she sleep first while he sat watch. A few hours later, the sun still hanging over the western hills, Morgan woke her and took his turn sleeping. Several hours later, they were both awake and done with breakfast.

They tracked down Yan pretty easily. He seemed to be looking out for them and made himself obvious, standing on a slight rise by the edge of the road. They walked up to him, and Morgan said, "Hey, Yan. Mind showing us who's next in line?"

"Hmm, let me think. That would be Trise and Kwilla. Those two are fast, so watch yourselves. C'mon, and I'll point 'em out for ya." Yan walked over to the road and pointed to the third tent in a row of three. The tent was low, really only comfortable for someone sitting or lying down. Morgan could see a pair of feet extending out from the open flap and a woman hunched in front of the fire stirring something in a pan. They walked over to the tent, and Issa cleared her throat. The woman turned and glared balefully at them. Her skin was a deep blue, much darker than Issa's, and her dark eyes matched her spiky black hair.

"What? You wanna challenge us, huh? Suppose you think we'll back down after what you did to those brothers? No chance. Kwilla, get up; time to fight." A loud yawn came from the tent's interior, and the feet stirred and were pulled in. A moment later, a thin, beautiful, rugged-looking Ghelli came crawling out of the tent. She stood, and was head and shoulders taller than Issa, even with her racial upgrades. Kwilla was deeply tanned and sported dozens of thin, white scars around her arms and face. Even her glistening wings were notched in places. She arched her back in a deep stretch and said, "Oh, if we must. C'mon then." She turned and walked toward the road; her long legs, clad in tight leather, moved like a dancer's over the loose rocks, scrub, and clumps of grass.

The women were both fencers, wielding rapiers similar in appearance to Issa's. At first, they seemed to be a dangerous match for him and Issa—Morgan wasn't as fast as they were, and Kwilla kept slipping his guard and putting pressure on Issa while she was already occupied with Trise. Once, Kwilla slid past him and aimed a deadly thrust at Issa's kidney. Morgan barely managed to activate Guard Ally in time, but he did, and the potentially fatal thrust skittered off his thick scale armor. In frustration, Morgan activated his Energy Drain, pulling glittering, smoky Energy lines from the two swordswomen to him. He could feel them resisting, but they were no match for his will, and he pulled with everything he had. At the same time, Issa sidestepped Trise and used her Hexing Shriek, catching both women in the cone of her shout. When Issa's discordant echoing shriek hit them, Morgan felt resistance to his Energy Drain fall away, and he pulled even harder. Trise moaned and dropped to a knee, and Issa's rapier caught her in the throat. "No!" Kwilla cried, dropping her sword and falling to her knees in front of Trise. "Yield!"

"You yield?" Issa yelled, pulling her rapier free and backing up. Morgan also backed off, dropping his Energy Drain.

"Yes, dammit!" Kwilla was holding Trise's face in her hands. "Trise, hold on, Trise." Kwilla poured a small vial of silvery liquid between Trise's lips, clasping her hand over the gaping wound in the center of her neck. "You're okay, Trise. You're going to be fine." She laid her back, and Morgan could hear Trise take a shuddering breath and cough out some blood; then Kwilla was laughing quietly and kissing Trise all over her face. "You're okay. You're okay." Morgan looked at Issa and raised an eyebrow.

"Thank you for backing off," Kwilla said, looking over her shoulder at Morgan and Issa. "I'd die a thousand times before I watched Trise die." Morgan was about to reply when Trise and Kwilla began to shimmer, their skin and garb seeming to glow from within, and then they broke apart into a cloud of silvery motes that streamed into Morgan and Issa. After absorbing the Energy, Morgan looked and saw that the two women were gone entirely.

"What the . . .? I know you said you think they're constructs of the dungeon, but they sure as hell seemed real to me."

"Yes, they did, didn't they?" Issa had a troubled look on her face. "Could they just be based on real people? Maybe these are memories of the Swordmaster?" Issa's face unclouded a little, and she looked at Morgan with a smile.

"That sounds very plausible. I was starting to worry that other souls might be trapped in here." Morgan's face paled a little.

"God, I didn't think of that. I like my idea better, though. I'd rather beat up on some old memories than on enslaved souls."

"Well, let's hope that's what it is, then."

The following two pairs of challengers forfeited their positions to Morgan and Issa without a contest. The two swordsmen in the sixth position put up a fight to the death, but they didn't seem much more difficult to vanquish than the first brothers. A brother and sister were in the seventh position, and they, too, forfeited.

After that, Morgan and Issa took a break, eating sandwiches as Morgan had promised and taking turns sleeping. Morgan was starting to think keeping watch was unnecessary—no animals ever appeared in the strange twilit valley, and the other challengers never approached their tent. Still, he knew the moment he let his guard down, something bad would probably happen.

Their next fight, for position eight, was the first one in which Morgan momentarily thought they might be in trouble. The two sisters they fought were a small race of people whom Issa called Bogoli. They wore black robes and had white-painted faces. They each wielded rapiers, but those weren't what caused trouble for Morgan and Issa—these were the first combatants they'd faced out here that used as many spells and skills as they did. They outright resisted Issa's attacks, and Morgan's Energy Drain felt like it was barely taking effect. They, in turn, threw lightning bolts that burned and stunned Morgan momentarily. While he was stunned, one of the sisters managed to put two painful holes in his butt cheek and the back of his thigh. He was leaking blood like a tapped wine barrel when he finally got around one of their guards and executed a flurry of blows that she simply couldn't stop. Once she dropped, it was only a matter of time before he and Issa wore down the other sister.

*****Congratulations! You have achieved level 22 Vortex Duelist and have gained 8 Intelligence, 8 Agility, 6 Will, 6 Dexterity.*****

"Did you level?" He looked at Issa's flushed face, noting she had a singed eyebrow and some of her hair had been burned shorter than the rest. He almost laughed, but he didn't, and he thanked all the powers in the universe for that.

"No! It's like you're cheating with that high Energy affinity!"

"Hey, congratulations, you two." Yan walked up the road whistling softly. "That was quite a show. You're really moving up the line and making it shorter for those of us that were smart enough to forfeit. Nice job!"

"Thanks, Yan," Morgan sketched a slightly mocking bow.

"Well, those sisters had a chest by their tent. It's still there and, by rights, yours. You should check it out." Yan smiled and hooked his thumbs in his belt, rocking back and forth on the balls of his feet, seemingly proud of himself. Issa grabbed Morgan's arm in excitement and pulled him off the road toward the sisters' tent.

"Hurry up! This is the first loot we've seen in this place! Imagine what it could be!" Morgan smiled and let her pull him through the partially deserted plot of tents. Presumably, their most challenging opponents were yet to come, so he hoped that the loot would be something helpful.

⁂ OLIVIA ⁂

Olivia dreamt of dark pits and mutilated corpses; she dreamt of writhing tentacles and terrible crunching bones. Often, she was running through endless winding tunnels, something close behind her, and above her terror was a terrible sadness because underneath the wails of her pursuers were the sobs and pleading cries of her tortured friends. She woke, panting and drenched in sweat, a deep, painful throbbing behind her eyes. She was in a bed in a dimly lit room, and she heard the sound of heels clicking on a tile floor as someone approached. She struggled to sit up, but another throbbing wave rolled out from behind her eyes, and she laid her head back on her pillow with a soft groan.

"She stirs! Oh, poor thing. That was a terrible knock you took to the head. My topical treatment did wonders for the injury, but you'll feel even better after you drink this syrup." The voice accompanying the clicking of heels was soft and feminine, and the thin, delicate fingers that gently touched her forehead sent cool shivers of relief into her throbbing skull. She turned into the touch and blearily saw an angelic figure leaning over her. For a moment, she thought it really was an angel, but then her eyes focused in the dim light, and she saw that it was a Ghelli woman with the largest wings she'd ever seen. They glowed luminously, and Olivia swore she could see faint sparkles of light drifting off them. "That's it, come back to me. Here, open your lips and take this spoon." Olivia felt the tip of a spoon on her lower lip, and she did as she was told, letting the woman put the spoon in her mouth and swallowing the thick, syrupy contents. Warmth flooded forth into her, and she felt the throbbing in her head recede to a very dim ache.

"Uh, that's better, thank you!" Once again, she struggled to sit up, and the woman helped her, shoving another pillow behind her shoulders.

"Poor girl! You missed all the festivities—the welcoming assembly and the new cohort mixer. Ahh, well, plenty of time to get to know the others over the next few months! Let's be glad that rock didn't spill your brains out and kill you instantly, hmm?" The woman sat at the edge of her bed, and Olivia could see that she had little antennae protruding from her beautiful chestnut hair. Her eyes were like pools of glowing honey, and Oliva felt transfixed by her beauty. "Oh, I've seen that look before! It's the side effect of improving my race so many times. Don't let it fool you; I'm ugly on the inside." She chuckled as she said the last, and Olivia didn't believe her for even a second.

"Thank you, um, miss." Olivia fumbled awkwardly, not knowing what to call the woman.

"I'm Nurse Tyliste, but just call me Tyliste; I'm not formal. I think you'll be okay to get back to your dorm. I'll have one of my aides walk with you. You'll want to head to your classes with your cohort, won't you?" Olivia just nodded at the question, and Tyliste stood, her beautiful wings bouncing with the motion, and tiny motes of golden dust showered down around them.

"Your wings. Um, your wings are beautiful," Olivia mumbled, feeling sort of light-headed.

"Hoho, thank you, sweetie. I can see my medicine has gotten you a little drunk. Don't worry; it will fade." She seemed to drift away into the dimly lit sick ward, and Olivia heard her talking to someone. A moment later, another Ghelli arrived, this one much less mythical, his wings far less luminous. Olivia smiled and scooted her legs off the side of the bed and saw her shoes resting next to it.

"Let me help you," the young man said, kneeling to push her shoes onto her still-stockinged feet. Olivia followed him out of the sick ward, noting that all the other beds were empty, and then through several hallways and one stairway to her dormitory. The whole walk seemed like a dream, and when he said goodbye and walked away, Olivia felt like the entire thing might have been some sort of drug-induced delusion. She stepped into the dorm room and was suddenly glad that her bed was so close to the door. She stumbled over to it, lay down, and was deep asleep before she could think any more about her ordeal.

"Olivia. Olivia!" She opened her eyes to see Veena standing next to her bed. "We didn't even hear you come in last night! I'm so glad you're alright! That bitch, Gwinna! She could've killed you. I think she might have tried." Veena was wringing her hands together, looking at Olivia. Some of the others started wandering over toward the two of them.

"You should have seen Rald," Shani said. "He almost attacked her. All the cohorts crowded around and kept them apart, though, and then we rushed you to the infirmary."

"That was a dirty move, for sure," Rald said with a yawn. "Better get ready for class, though." He turned and walked through the doorway to the bathrooms. Olivia sat up and looked around. Most of the others were in various states of dress; Adaida was fully dressed and sitting on the edge of her perfectly made bed, reading through a text. Hanwol was nowhere to be seen, probably in the bathroom.

"Did I miss a lot at the assembly?" She looked at Shani and Veena questioningly.

"Oh, no. It was boring. Professor Oylla-dak was impressive, though; she's a Shadeni with an advanced race. I'd never seen her before, and it was inspiring—tall, beautiful, and huge red wings she kept folded behind her back. She unfurled them when her speech was over and actually flew out of the amphitheater!" Shani spoke wistfully, her eyes glazing over as she remembered the sight.

"That's something I didn't know. Shadeni get wings when they advance their race?" Olivia stood up, relieved to see that she no longer felt dizzy or had any sort of a headache.

"Yes, lots of races start to develop different features as their race gets more and more evolved. You saw Gwinna, right? Her eyes glow and are like gemstones. If she makes it to advanced racial levels, she might begin to make her form non-corporeal for a few seconds at a time. It's always a little different based on the individual." Veena supplied this answer as the three of them walked toward the bathroom.

The cohort hurriedly finished getting ready, then made their way through the hallways, out through the main concourse to another building where their Enchantment class was. On their way outside, the cohort filled Olivia in on what she'd missed with regard to announcements. During the welcome assembly, Professor Oylla-dak, the headmistress of first-year students, had given a brief overview of the opening challenge. Each student would be evaluated in their year-one courses at the end of the first month, and their cohorts would be given a cumulative score. This score would account for half of their overall score, and the other half would come from competitions that the various course instructors would put on.

Their Enchantment class was held in a squat, gray building with a row of stained glass windows that ran the entire length of the eastern and western walls. The interior of the building was largely taken up by an instruction room with work tables that reminded Olivia of classrooms where she'd done lab work for her chemistry and biology classes in college. Her cohort wasn't the first to arrive, but they were still early, and they took two tables under the western windows. The light coming in from the eastern windows was lovely, and Olivia felt very relaxed in the room. Cabinets lined the walls, and a row of bookcases along the southern wall was filled with reference books. The teacher's exemplar table ran the length of the northern edge of the classroom, and standing behind it was another mixed-race individual; Olivia was sure of it.

Professor Brince had light pink-red skin and two short dragonfly wings extending from his upper back. He had a jovial demeanor and greeted each group of students as they came through the door. When Olivia and her cohort entered and took their table, he walked by and said, "Greetings, Copper! I've heard good things about your cohort this year. I'm looking forward to seeing what sort of wonders you'll come up with in my class." They all uttered platitudinous responses, though Rald spoke up with a grin.

"Don't expect too much from me, sir. My talents lie elsewhere."

"Don't sell yourself short—you've never had me for a teacher before!" He chuckled and walked over to greet the Wood cohort as they came through the door.

Olivia was taking out her text, a notebook, and a writing utensil when she felt a presence to her right, and her cohort grew quiet. She glanced up and saw Sarice standing next to her with her hands clasped in front of her. Olivia hadn't been this close to the girl before, and she was a little taken aback by her beauty. Unlike Professor Brince, she'd inherited full Ghelli wings, and her teal eyes and hair accented her pale blue skin very nicely; she'd apparently lucked out with the blending of her parents' heritage.

"Olivia, right?" She asked quietly, glancing nervously around at Olivia's cohort, who'd stopped what they'd been doing to stare at her.

"Yes, that's right."

"I wanted to say I'm sorry you got hurt yesterday. Gwinna shouldn't have done that, and I was responsible for judging your match, so, well, I just wanted you to know that I thought it was awful."

"Mmhmm, alright, you've said it, now get lost," Rald growled from the table in front of Olivia's.

"No, it's okay, Rald. Thanks for coming to say that, Sarice." Olivia smiled, partly because she wanted people to know she wasn't shaken by what had happened to her, but also because she did appreciate the gesture Sarice was making. Sarice nodded and, with a slightly withering glance at Rald, she walked back over to her cohort, who were sitting near the opposite wall.

"Don't trust her," Shani said, shaking her head. "She has too much money and tries to walk too many lines to be trustworthy." Olivia didn't say anything but went back to reading through the first pages of her text. The buzz in the classroom died down shortly after that, though, and Olivia looked up to see Gwinna walking in with her cohort. She looked coolly around the room, and when her eyes met Olivia's, they just kept going as though she didn't even register. Jade cohort sat in the center row of tables near the front of the room.

"Cold bitch," Veena muttered. Before Olivia could respond, Professor Brince walked to the front of the class, cleared his throat and announced that he was starting class and that they'd all best listen up.

"Before we can learn to enchant, we must learn the language of enchantment. The System has made it easy for all of us creatures living in its shadow to communicate, but that doesn't extend to the knowledge of runecraft. Before I teach you to imbue runes with Energy and tie their lines of power into complex patterns, you must learn the runes themselves. Thankfully, for me, this is the easiest part of the course—you simply need to memorize all eighty base runes, the sixteen conjunction runes, and the two-hundred-fourteen ancillary runes. You may use my class time for the next six days to study because your exam will be in one week. All the runes are listed on pages thirteen through ninety-four of your text. Good luck!" With that, he turned and walked out the door behind the exemplar table.

"I'm dead," Rald said, among the outraged thrum of conversation that broke out in the classroom.

"And I thought he seemed like a nice teacher . . ." Olivia said, her voice trailing off as she began to flip her book to page thirteen.

⚭ MORGAN ⚭

The chest the two Bogoli sisters had in their camp didn't look like a System generated treasure chest, at least not one Morgan had seen before. It was long and shallow, more like a toolbox than a chest, crafted from a shiny dark wood with bronze metal corner plates. No runes were apparent on the chest, and Issa spent a long time staring at it from all angles. Finally, she felt comfortable enough to lift it from one end and look beneath it. Not finding anything alarming, she shrugged and said, "I don't see any traps or anything."

"Alright, I'll open it. Stand back a bit."

"Wait. I think we have a smarter way of doing this kind of thing. Why not use your Guard Ability on me, and I'll open it. Then, if a dart shoots out, or it explodes, you'll take half the damage that you would have taken if you opened it yourself." After she spoke, Morgan opened his mouth to argue but couldn't think of a problem with her logic. He just nodded and backed up a step, then activated Guard Ally on her. Issa nodded and leaned forward to lift the clasp on the chest carefully. No fireballs were forthcoming, and she didn't cry out in alarm, so Morgan moved forward to see what was within.

Nestled in the burgundy-colored cloth lining of the chest was a rapier with a beautifully wrought silvery basket hilt. The silver and black leather sheath hid the blade, but Morgan could feel a wave of cold Energy emanating from the powerful weapon. Next to the sword sat a polished cherry scroll case. Finally, resting in the folds of cloth was a heavy-looking leather pouch. "Looks like you got another new sword, Issa."

"Oh, no, Morgan, I already have this nice rapier that you gave me!"

"Well, check it out; maybe it's better," Morgan said, reaching into the chest to pick up the scroll case. He opened it to see the scroll within while Issa picked up the sword. The scroll was tightly wound around a cherry scroll rod, and when he studied the header, he saw that it was written in plain text: "Whispering Death Style."

"Morgan! This sword has a spirit within it. When I sent my Energy into it, it spoke to me!" Her voice was high with excitement.

"Did you bond with it? Be careful; Tiladia told me that intelligent items with spirits might try to dominate your will."

"Yes, I felt a little struggle, but I concentrated my will and felt it calm down. It called me 'mistress' and said it was happy to have a strong new master. Morgan, it told me its name was Icicle!"

"That's cool! Hah, get it? Cool?" Issa just looked at him with an arched eyebrow. "Well, anyway, here—it's a sword style, I think. I don't want to learn another while I'm still mastering the Fighting Crane style." He handed her the scroll case and then leaned over to pick up the pouch. He felt the familiar clicking sound and the satisfying weight of lots of Energy beads. He opened the top of the pouch and saw that the beads were just standard non-attuned beads, but there had to be more than a hundred of them.

"I can't use the scroll yet. It says 'requirement not met—advanced sword mastery.' I guess I'll need to keep it for later." Issa tucked the scroll into her pouch and then went to work fitting her new sword sheath to her belt.

"Good idea—Tiladia says that intelligent items don't like being in dimensional containers." Issa nodded while she buckled her belt.

"My father taught me that. Since I'm making out like a bandit with this new sword and the potential sword style, you should keep those Energy beads."

"Alright, but it's not like I wouldn't share anything I own with you." Morgan put the beads into his ring. "What do you think? Should we go see who the next challengers are?"

Congratulations! You have achieved level 23 Vortex Duelist and have gained 8 Intelligence, 8 Agility, 6 Will, 6 Dexterity. You have learned the class spell: Vortex Lance—Basic.

Vortex Lance—Basic: Prerequisite: Vortex Class Core. You are able to project a vortex of Energy from your weapon to strike distant foes. While potentially devastating, this attack has a slow build-up and requires a sizable Energy investment. This skill scales with the rank of your Vortex Core. Energy cost: 350, Cooldown: Medium.

Morgan and Issa stood panting and covered in blood over the corpses of the eleventh pair of challengers. They'd had a relatively easy time of the ninth and tenth, mainly because they'd each been large, brutish pairs of combatants wielding deadly but slow weapons. Issa and Morgan had easily countered them with their debilitating attacks and ability to wear them down. These most recent enemies, though, had been a real challenge. One had been an Ardeni man with a sword and shield, and the other was an older Cadwalli fighting with dual slender scimitars.

In the end, though, they'd prevailed. Morgan had used Guard Ally on Issa and absorbed a dozen or so slashes from the Cadwalli on his armor. The

Ardeni had actually clinched their victory for them: he'd sucked in a tremendous breath, and Morgan had instinctively dropped into the Crane Defends the Nest. When the Ardeni belched forth a massive gout of flames, it had largely been deflected by Morgan's Energy-enhanced parry and proceeded past him to ignite the Cadwalli's fur. After that, Issa had finished the Cadwalli, then it had been a matter of mopping things up. Still, they had painted the cobbles red with blood before it was over, much of it their own.

"I leveled and got a skill. What about you?" Morgan asked Issa, still breathing deeply.

"Ancestors! I still haven't gained another level! Your damned affinity lets you apply a lot more of the Energy from your kills to your growth." Issa's face, still red with exertion, had grown clouded, her eyebrows pulled down in a glare.

"Hey, it's not fair, but we're on the same team. Don't get pissed at me!" He reached out and gently squeezed her shoulder.

"Oh, I'm not really mad, just frustrated. How can I complain? We won again, and this sword I've earned has been amazing. I feel like I'm learning a lot with each combat, and Icicle even said that she thinks I'm getting close to improving my proficiency to advanced!"

"She? Hah, I didn't know your sword was a girl. She talks to you that much, huh? Well, my sword hasn't given me any glimpses into the future since I dueled Swent, so, yeah, I'm a little jealous of your blade. Plus, you do ice damage with each stab!"

"That's true, and yes, Icicle is a girl!" She beamed, cleaning her frosty blue blade off on a piece of ragged cloth and sheathing it. "Well, should we see about the final challengers?"

"Aren't you tired?" Morgan stretched, actually feeling pretty good after the considerable influx of Energy from their victory. If only the Energy cleaned the blood off as well, he'd have nothing to complain about.

"Not really. This was our first fight of this 'day,' and I'm anxious to see what's next." As if on cue, Yan walked up from where he'd been watching the fight.

"Looks like you two are down to the final spot. Tal-dak and Shinra aren't to be trifled with. That's their tent over there." He pointed to a large blue canvas tent. Morgan and Issa had already surmised it was the campsite of the leading pair of sword wielders. It stood on its own on a slight rise in the valley floor, and the other tents had all been accounted for—they'd either defeated the occupants or met them to accept their forfeits.

"Alright, might as well strike while the iron's hot." Morgan started walking up the slope toward the high blue tent. Issa walked to his right, and they were about twenty feet away when a tall, imposing figure stepped out. He had the deep red skin of the Shadeni and wore heavy, black-plated armor. His head was helmed, but enough of his face was exposed for Morgan to see the sinister smile exposing his exceptionally long canines. Gleaming, sky-blue eyes stared out of the grill of the helm, and his voice rumbled across the hilltop.

"You should stay content to wait behind us for the guardian. No need to throw your lives away." A massive, black two-handed sword appeared in front of him, point-down, and he leaned lazily against the hilt. The sword had to be six feet long with a straight, double-edged blade that was at least as wide as Morgan's hand.

"Tal-dak, I presume?" Morgan tried to keep his voice steady, betraying none of his thoughts. Internally, he was feeling a little stressed. Tal-dak emitted a strong aura that weighed heavily on him. He decided to try to "Flex" his aura to see if it would remove some of the pressure. As he let his Energy flow into his limbs and pushed his aura out, he added all the weight of the deaths he was responsible for; he pushed into it the Yovashi Bane title and the gravity of their plight at his hands, and, above it all, he drove forward his rage at the implicit threat to Issa that Tal-dak's words carried. Suddenly Tal-dak didn't seem quite so large or imposing, and he flinched back for a moment. Morgan noticed black steam rising out of the corner of his eyes, and he saw that Issa was channeling her Battle Chant, getting it ready.

"My, my," said a sultry voice from their right, and Morgan turned to see a Shadeni woman standing there. She was tall and slender, wearing a shiny round silver shield and wielding a gleaming broadsword. "Is your bite as bad as your bark, doggy?" She walked forward to stand next to Tal-dak, and he stood up straighter, his grin widening. "Well, you don't have to answer that. We'll find out in a moment, I'm sure." She and Tal-dak walked down the gentle slope to the road, waiting for Morgan and Issa to follow.

"I didn't like her talking to you that way, Morgan!" Issa hissed as they watched the two walk away.

"They certainly seem disdainfully confident." Morgan summoned his sword and whipped it through the air a couple of times in pent-up aggression. "We need to be on our A game, Issa."

"I've never heard that term, but I know what you mean, Morgan. I'll Haste you at the start—you should try to destroy one of them as quickly as possible, and then we'll work on the second." Morgan nodded, and they began to descend the slope toward the waiting pair of Shadeni. Morgan could feel Issa's Battle Chant building, and she started to hiss a discordant, buzzing sound that made his muscles jittery and his sword feel light. Morgan, for his part, began to push Energy into his limbs, priming them to spring into any of his sword forms.

When they reached the pair, they bowed, and Morgan and Issa did the same, and then Morgan briefly felt Issa's hand on his shoulder, and a surge of Energy flowed into him. He swore he could hear everyone breathing like slow motion bellows and his singing muscles leaped into lightning action as he launched himself at Shinra while activating Guard Ally on Issa at the same time. Shinra somehow brought her shield up in time to block Morgan's first cleave, and Morgan was thrown off balance by the wave of force that reverberated out of the shiny metal. It was like his blow had been sent back at him. Distantly he heard Issa's Battle Chant rise in volume, and he heard the great whooshing sound of Tal-dak's sword as he swung it with terrible force again and again.

Morgan regained his balance and launched a flurry of blows with the Crane Flutters its Wings—with Haste and his style active, the swings were just a blur of black smoke in the air. Morgan was sure he'd get through Shinra's guard this time because her shield was low, and she moved much too slowly to get it in position to block. However, just as he was about to make contact with his first terrible slash, she seemed to waver like a mirage, and then she was twenty feet back from where she'd been. Morgan cleaved the empty air four times before he realized what had happened. He started to walk toward her, but he felt a crushing blow across his shoulder blades, and he stumbled. Tal-dak had hit Issa, but his Guard Ally had saved her. Even with only half the damage hitting him, he felt his scale armor strain to contain the blow, and the force of it nearly knocked him to his knee.

Twice more, Morgan closed in on Shinra, sure to unleash a devastating attack only to have her shimmer and appear twenty or more feet back from where she'd been. Morgan kept circling her, trying to make her stay near the other two combatants, but she was quick in her own right, and he had a hard time keeping tabs on Issa's fight while defending against her. Finally, in frustration, Morgan pushed his way close to her again and worked to set her up for another flurry from the Crane Flutters its Wings. Before he attacked, though, he activated his Circle of Combat skill. He knew it was a bit risky—he wouldn't be able to help Issa until he'd finished with Shinra, and it cost a lot of Energy, but he was tired of her cat and mouse games and was worried that Tal-dak would wear Issa down.

He'd never used the skill before, and he was almost caught off guard by it—a black whirling wall of Energy shot up around him and Shinra, leaving an open area about twenty paces across in the middle. As soon as he saw the wall come up behind Shinra, he unleashed his style, and Shinra wavered and reappeared directly against the wall of his Circle of Combat. More than that, she seemed to have slammed into it because she stumbled forward, a look of shock on her face, only to be met with Morgan's flurry of blows. She nearly recovered enough to get her shield up, but not quite, and Morgan's first cleave took her arm off at the shoulder. She screamed and flailed with her sword, but Morgan's subsequent three arcing cuts tore terrible gashes in her body and took her other hand off at the wrist. She fell to the ground, unmoving and the black walls of his circle faded away into smoky mist.

He turned quickly to where he could hear the clang of steel on steel and saw Issa circling Tal-dak, her rapier licking out and mostly being rebuffed by his armor. Morgan strode forward and pointed his sword at Tal-dak, channeling his new skill, Vortex Lance. It took a few heartbeats for the Energy to gather in his sword, but then a smoking, glowing projectile erupted from his sword, leaving a whirling pattern of force behind it. The sound it made was like a high-powered rifle round ripping through the air without the percussive blast of the explosive to launch it. A flash erupted from Tal-dak's back shoulder plate, and a wave of force visibly rippled through him. He stumbled forward onto one knee and roared in pain and rage. As he struggled to his feet, Morgan could see the deformation of his armor plate and the sheet of blood running down his back and side.

Issa didn't stand idly while her opponent stumbled; she lunged forward and gave him two painful punctures at his armor joints while he struggled to his feet. As he roared and lifted his sword, Issa used her Hexing Shriek, and he stumbled back from the sound but then swung his sword wildly at her. However, Morgan had closed the distance and smashed his sword against Tal-dak's damaged rear shoulder plate, shearing through the deformed, rippled metal. His blade sliced through muscle, tendon, and bit deeply into bone, and Morgan pulled with Energy Drain as he ripped the sword free and backed off. A torrent of shimmering Energy flowed out of Tal-dak to him, and Tal-dak roared again, flailing madly with his sword. Morgan could see that he was having trouble aiming his blows with his right shoulder so severely wounded. "Back off, Issa," Morgan called while he started channeling Azure Burst.

Issa backpedaled, and Tal-dak turned on Morgan with a furious snarl, only to be sent sprawling by a concussion of blue flames. He slid on his back toward Issa, and she neatly stepped forward and thrust her rapier between the grill on his helmet, burying it six inches into his eye. Tal-dak violently twitched once and then lay still. Dense motes of Energy accumulated on the two corpses and then flowed into Morgan and Issa.

"Finally, level!" Issa said, picking her sword up from the road where it had fallen as Tal-dak's corpse disappeared.

MORGAN

Tal-dak and Shinra were Morgan and Issa's second opponents to leave behind a chest. While Issa studied the chest, Morgan looked around at the much more sparsely populated cluster of tents. Most of the remaining challengers were sitting or standing near their tents, talking or eating, but none of them gave any attention to the victors. He also noticed that the shadows seemed longer, and he looked to the western hills, noting that the sun had begun to sink lower. Defeating the final challengers had, apparently, unstuck the clock in this place. "I don't think there's anything dangerous about this chest," Issa said, interrupting his thoughts. He looked at the large, square box, activating his Azure Sight skill, but, as usual, couldn't see anything that Issa had missed. It was another chest that didn't look like it came from the System—thick, pale planks and a bronze clasp and nails.

"Well, same as before, then. I'll guard you, and you open it."

Morgan activated Guard Ally and then backed off a good ten feet. Issa gently opened the lid, and, once again, nothing happened. She took in a hissing breath, though, and Morgan hurried to see what was in the chest that had her attention. Nestled in the folds of a rough-spun blanket were two large, faintly pulsating apples. Morgan didn't know if they were really apples, but they looked like colossal granny smiths. Next to the blanket was a shiny black scroll case with a silver crane embossed in the center. Morgan's mouth watered when he caught a whiff of the sweet, fruity aroma coming from the apples, but he couldn't take his eyes off the scroll case. "What the fuck?"

"Those fruits are calling to me!" Issa said, and Morgan glanced at her to see her mouth slightly open and drool starting to leak out of the corner of her mouth. To be fair, he would probably be in the same state if the sight of that crane scroll hadn't shocked him out of it.

"Do you see that scroll? It seems a little too coincidental, don't you think?"

"Uh," Issa licked her lips and gulped, taking a step back from the chest. "Um, you think it has to do with your sword style?"

"Do you mind if I check?" Issa shook her head, and Morgan reached past the fruit to grasp the scroll case. It had a silver clasp holding it closed, so he opened it and gently lifted the tightly bound scroll out. He unfurled it enough to see the densely packed runes and stared at them for a moment. They started to shift around, and then a message appeared in his vision:

Prerequisite for the form, the Crane Takes Flight, not met: Sword Mastery—Advanced.

Morgan, his fingers trembling, gently re-rolled the scroll and put it into his ring. "It's another form for my style, all right. I need to get my sword skill up to advanced, though."

"That's great, Morgan, but the fruit?" Issa leaned over the chest again, her eyes fixated on the apples.

"Well, if that guardian is going to appear tonight, we have until midnight. I guess we could eat them. What do you think they do? Another racial upgrade?"

"That's what my body is telling me! Oh, Morgan, I ache to eat them!" Issa leaned in closer.

"Well, you go first. Just one, though!" Morgan chuckled. He also wanted to eat the fruit, but his mind was still racing about his style scroll. This dungeon definitely seemed tailored to the two of them—all the duels with the other pairs, the difficulty level, and now treasure that seemed far too unlikely to be a coincidence. The question Morgan was struggling with was whether the System was responsible or if the spirit or "Soul fragment" of the Swordmaster that created this dungeon was. Maybe it was both? He didn't have time to worry about it anymore because Issa took up one of the apples and began to chomp away at it. She sat down abruptly, but she kept eating. She made little moaning sounds as she swallowed, and Morgan sat back from the chest to watch her.

With each bite, her eyes became more glazed, and Morgan began to notice tiny pulses of light flaring underneath her skin, flashing out from beneath her chain shirt along her arms and up her neck. As she swallowed the last bite, she moaned again, then lay back on the scrubby grass, writhing. Steam started to rise from her body; first, it was white, like water vapor, but then it began to darken. The steam quickly dissipated as it rose from her, much like Energy vapor after the System or a spell generated something temporary. He watched her steaming and flashing for a couple of long minutes, and then she arched her back and moaned again. Morgan grabbed one of her hands, and her skin was hot to the touch. He felt movement against his palm and held her hand up to see that her nails had grown longer and more pointed, almost like claws.

Starting to worry, Morgan leaned over her face to see if she seemed to be in pain, but her lips were raised at the corners in a smile, and Issa's eyes were rolled back in her head, short pants coming out of her mouth. She didn't seem to be in any pain, more the opposite. "What the hell?" Morgan's eye had been caught by how Issa's canines had grown. She'd always had several more sharp teeth in her mouth than a human, but now her canines were notably longer. Nothing terrifying or disfiguring, but definitely a change. Shortly, her muscles ceased spasming, and she lay back down, a soft purr escaping her lips as she fell into a deep sleep. Still, her body was emitting constant steam, and beneath it, Morgan could see that her skin had become more vibrant, almost glowing from within.

A good twenty minutes later, the steam ceased, and Issa stretched, yawning deeply as she lazily rolled to her side to look at Morgan. Her eyes, always a bright yellow-gold, were now glowing with their own luminosity and her hair was much more gold than yellow. All of her seemed leaner and longer, her fingers, forearms, and collar bones. "Mmm, that was incredible. Morgan, I gained three racial ranks." She arched her back, stretching her arms out above her head, taking a long, deep breath.

"No shit?" He looked at her, and while he'd always found her attractive, she was starting to become beautiful in an almost unearthly way. "Stand up for a minute." He stood and held out his hand, pulling her to her feet. She'd definitely gotten taller, but not as much as he'd imagined, based on the first time she gained racial ranks in the Crucible. "You're a little taller, but not as much as I would've thought."

"Mmm, yes, racial ranks improve your physique, basically helping you reach your body's maximum potential if you'd been raised in a perfect environment with perfect food and perfect everything else. At least that's what they do, at first. Then you start to get other benefits, like, Morgan, I can see so much better now! Even in this dim twilight, everything stands out so clearly."

"Well, you also have fangs now, and look at your nails."

"Fangs?" Issa hissed the word and held a thumb up to her teeth. "Really, Morgan? Fangs? Are you afraid I'll bite you?" She growled at him and bared her teeth.

"Hah, maybe the wrong word. Okay, okay, they're not really that big, but still, they did grow!" While he was sputtering, Issa looked at her nails and then reached up to gently scratch the back of Morgan's neck and the base of his scalp.

"These seem to work just fine," she said, pulling him down for a kiss. "Anyway," she stepped back from him and pointed at the other apple, still sitting in the chest, "It's your turn." Morgan nodded and picked up the fruit. It felt like it was alive with Energy; he could feel it vibrating almost imperceptibly.

"I'm a little nervous," he said, taking a seat in the grass. "What if I grow horns or something?" Issa laughed and punched his shoulder, and he shrugged and took a big bite of the apple. The first thing he decided was that this was most certainly not an apple. It tasted like a carrot dipped in honey, though the way it dissolved as he chewed was more like cotton candy. He could feel it tingling all the way to his stomach, and he continued to bite, chew and swallow as waves of euphoria, not unlike intoxication, began to roll out from his stomach and up into his head. His arms and hands were tingling by the time he finished eating the fruit, and the world was dancing and vibrating with yellow and blue halos around every object.

Morgan couldn't explain his feelings any other way than to say it was orgasmic. He'd never taken any opiates, but the feeling he had right now was what he imagined people meant when they talked about "Chasing the dragon." Every cell in his body was tingling, and it felt like a warm, buzzing liquid was surrounding his brain. When he looked up at the night sky, the stars seemed to be swimming in a cobalt jelly, and when he stared at any one star, it grew in size and intensity to the point where its pulsing light sent warm waves over his face. The entire time, he was dimly aware that his body was twitching and a dense fog engulfed him. Slowly, profound, healthy exhaustion seeped into his mind, and he closed his eyes to oblivion.

"Morgan?" He felt a gentle jostling of his shoulder and then, "Morgan!" Issa's voice was louder and more urgent. He opened his eyes and saw Issa leaning over him, a slight frown on her face. He smiled and stretched.

"God, that feels good."

"I was starting to worry, you oaf! You've been out for almost two hours!" She stood up and stared down at him with her hands on her hips. "Well? How do you feel?"

"I just said! I feel good! How do I look?" Morgan looked at his arms and hands, not seeing much difference.

"Well, you definitely grew a little again. Thank the ancestors I did, too! Other than that, you seem more vibrant, and almost all your scars are gone. Maybe your race doesn't show much when it comes to actual physical changes. Of course, the biggest changes come when you progress past basic into improved or even advanced, though I've never met anyone with an advanced race."

Morgan stood up, and, based on how his cloth pants and shirt felt, he had grown again, not more than an inch or so in height, but he was broader too. He took a deep breath and enjoyed the pleasing way his chest expanded with a massive inhalation. He checked his status sheet, and the only change was that he had a base-seven race now. None of his other stats were different. "It seems like my strength or vitality should have gone up with my improved body."

"Oh, they have. Not directly—but now you have a potential for far greater attributes than before. Your muscles are denser; your organs will function better, and even your brain and blood vessels are improved. Look around; I bet your vision is clearer too."

"Well, my vision was already good, thanks to my previous upgrades, but yeah, it doesn't seem as dark to me, and I can see little details even in the low light." Morgan ran a thumb over his teeth, and they all felt normal. "No fangs for me!" Issa mockingly chomped her teeth at him, and then she pulled him into a hug.

"You look good, though," she murmured into his chest, gently scratching his back through his soft, cotton shirt. "Let's go to the tent; we still have a few hours 'til midnight." Morgan couldn't argue with that.

⊚ BRONWYN ⊚

A voice came to Bronwyn, not just through her ears but filling her mind, her very being with its rich, feminine tenor, "Stand, child. Stand before me, that I may look better upon you." Struggling with the flood of emotions that had overwhelmed her, Bronwyn stood up, wiping the tears from her eyes and cheeks, only to have them replaced with more. "Why do you weep so, child?"

"I don't know. I feel overwhelmed; I feel relieved. I've never had so many emotions at once!" Her voice sounded blubbery to her, but she didn't care; shame didn't exist for her here.

"Oh, dear! It's been an age since I spoke with a young human in person. I'm sorry, child, let me pull back my aura." Suddenly Bronwyn felt the surging feelings of hope, joy, and relief start to fade, at least to the point where she could control her breathing and tears. She took several long, shaky breaths, then sighed; she still felt hopeful and at ease but no longer completely overwhelmed.

"Thank you!"

"How uncharacteristic of you, Bronwyn! We've watched you for a while now, and I was surprised you fell to your knees before me, and now you thank me?" Bronwyn wasn't sure how to take that statement. Was she being mocked? A slight tingle of her old anger tickled the back of her mind, and the tiniest of frowns touched her lips. "Oh, child! I'm not mocking you! I've simply admired your fire and didn't expect you to be so kindly disposed toward being kidnapped! I warned Coraignon that he should take his true form and speak to you first, but he, of course, was too shy."

"Coraignon. That's Hops, right?"

"Yes! Oh, how we teased Coraignon about how you dubbed him."

"Well, I've just felt really good since I got here. I've been amazed by everything I saw; I don't think I had a chance to get angry," Bronwyn laughed.

"Of course, of course, and then I hit you with my aura. I'm sorry, dear child." Bronwyn finally managed to bring her gaze up to the queen's face and noticed that her lips didn't move while she spoke. Her skin was lightly tanned with a hint of golden honey, and her eyes were brown and green, dappled with flecks of yellow-gold. Her lips and cheeks were rosy and full of vibrance, and the long, golden-brown mane of curls that hung around her shoulders had a glow all to itself. She wore a pale-green gossamer gown and a delicate crown bedecked in a rainbow of gemstones.

"You're beautiful!" The words just blurted out of her mouth, and Bronwyn looked down, heat rising in her cheeks.

"Oh, child. Don't dwell on this appearance; my form is as fickle as the seasons, though I try to maintain this summer disposition as much as possible. Do you know why you're here, Bronwyn Tallow?"

"Something to do with Hops, er, Coraignon?" Bronwyn looked up again; the rollercoaster of emotions she'd experienced was taking a toll on her; she felt like lying down right there.

"Partially correct. The truth is, you'd never have met Coraignon had I not sent him to visit your people."

"Why?"

"You're humans, and I've not had contact with humans for nigh two thousand years, not since the Winter Court pulled the Energy stream away from Earth." She looked at Bronwyn, saw the confused look on her face, and continued, "I'm the Summer Queen, dear, and my motives differ from those of the Winter Court. Did you know that humans are something of children or, more accurately, great-grandchildren of the fae?"

"Um, no. On Earth, we talk about the, um, fae, as fairy tales, stories that aren't true."

"Of course. How could you not, cut off from the Fae Realms as you are."

"So, fairies, um, the fae, used to be on Earth? For real?"

"That's right, Bronwyn, and when I felt your people reconnect to the Realms, joy filled my heart."

"Well, I don't know much about the fae, but I've really enjoyed Hops's company."

"And he yours, dear. He's shown us how brave you've been and how you've stood against darkness already in your new world."

"Are we not on Fanwath here?"

"Not exactly, though we're connected. The Realms touch many worlds."

"Well, thank you for bringing me here; I'm glad to meet you, but what can I do for you?"

"That's more like the Bronwyn I've grown fond of watching! What do your stories tell you about the fae?"

"Hmm, I remember stories about how fairies stole children out of the cribs and about how people who visited your realm sometimes never returned or returned to find that everyone they knew had grown old. Hey! Is that going to happen to me?"

"No, Bronwyn, fear not. There are places in the Realms where you could be lost in time and certain foods that could cause such to occur, but I'll keep you safe. You'll not lose any time here; it wouldn't serve my needs or yours. As for your other stories, they might have a root in truth. We used to bargain for children from some of the younger races and raise them among us. They often grew to love a fae, and children would be born. Many such children were no doubt ancestors to you, modern humans. What else do you know?"

"I think there are good and bad fairies?"

"Not precisely. There are fae of the Winter Court, and they might seem evil to you, though their designs are not rooted in malice. Their goals are in opposition to my Summer Court, and that's one of the reasons you're here." Thinking of different "Courts" of fae, Bronwyn suddenly had a thought.

"What about the System?" A pulse of irritation, almost imperceptibly quick, flared out from the queen, and Bronwyn shrank back from the deep well of power she felt behind it.

"Pardon me, child. I didn't mean to lose control of my emotions, but you surprised me with that question. I am not fond of the System. The System is younger than the fae and many other elder races, but it has proliferated and begun to feel like a thorn in my heel."

"Is the System alive?"

"Oh, you are surprising with your questions. Let's save that chat for another time; first, let me talk to you about why I've asked you to come here. Or rather, why Coraignon tricked you into coming here." Bronwyn closed her mouth and nodded. "We fae are bound by rules and cannot interfere directly with the affairs of the lesser races, though we can act through agents. There must always be a balance between the agents of the Winter Court and those of my Summer Court. The Winter Court has agents on Fanwath, and I've been taking my time in choosing a suitable counter to those forces. When you humans appeared, I became very interested in choosing one of you for that role. Can you guess whom?"

Bronwyn blushed and almost felt embarrassed, as though what she was going to say might be wrong, but she said it anyway, "Me?" Warmth radiated from the queen, and for the first time, Bronwyn saw her lips move into a smile.

"That's right, Bronwyn! Your good heart and fiery spirit first drew Coraignon to you, and then, as he showed me your actions, I became enamored of you. I want you to be my agent on Fanwath." Warmth once again flowed out of the queen, and Bronwyn felt like her heart would swell to bursting. Tears once again formed in her eyes, and she hastily wiped at them. "Sweet Bronwyn, your emotions are overwhelming you, and I'm sorry for that. I won't let you answer my request just yet. First, I'll ask that you spend an evening here, away from my direct influence, so that you can decide with a clear head. There are things

I want you to know so that you can make an informed decision, though. Does that sound reasonable?"

"Yes," Bronwyn managed to croak out, her throat feeling swollen with emotion.

"If you accept my offer and take on the mantle of a fae agent, I'll be able to grant you boons, but you'll give up some of your freedom; you'll need to adopt some of my goals as your own. I can promise you here and now that I'll never ask you to do something that makes your heart rebel. I'll never ask you to act in a way that would taint your honor. I will, however, give you secrets, and you must keep them to yourself, even holding them from those you love. Finally, my offer and your acceptance do not an agent of Summer make; you'll need to pass a trial." She stopped speaking for a moment and studied Bronwyn, perhaps waiting for some sort of response, and Bronwyn licked her lips, trying to think of what to say. "I've given you much to think about. I'll have you rest now, and on the morrow, I'll hear your questions and your response to my request."

"Thank you," Bronwyn said, still feeling overwhelmed by the warmth and love that had rolled out of the fae queen.

"You're welcome, child. Follow Lipesca, and she'll take you to a place where you can rest in peace." The queen gestured to Bronwyn's left, and when she looked, another little winged fairy fluttered next to her.

"Come with me, Lady Bronwyn!" she said in a piping, enthusiastic voice. Bronwyn nervously glanced back to the queen and sketched a rather embarrassing bow, bending at the waist and then hurriedly straightening to follow the little fairy without waiting to see how the queen responded. The fairy flitted through the throne hall, out through a side passage, and as Bronwyn followed her from the room, she started to feel the heady emotions fade, though she still felt drained from the experience. Lipesca paused at intersections so that Bronwyn wouldn't get lost but otherwise zoomed ahead of her down the hallways. She stopped in front of a rich, nut-brown door with a depiction of a mighty stag carved into it. "This is your room, Lady Bronwyn."

"Lipesca, thank you. Can I ask you a question?" The little fairy nodded eagerly. "Does your queen have that effect on everyone? Do you other fae feel overwhelmed with emotions in her presence?"

"No, not as much as you, Lady Bronwyn. Humans are more emotional than fae. I'm supposed to warn you not to wander from your room; there are places here that are dangerous to you, though not intentionally. Some things are meant for fae and not for humans. If you need something, there's a cord inside the door here. Just pull it!" She waved happily and darted away, something like a large, sparkly hummingbird. Bronwyn tried the polished bronze doorknob, and it turned easily, allowing her to pull the door open. When she stepped into the room and saw her accommodations, she breathed a happy sigh and closed the door.

The room was large, but not overly so; it was smaller than the room Morgan had given her at his tower, but that didn't detract from it. In fact, Bronwyn stood there with her mouth hanging open for a few moments while she took it in. The floor was carpeted in living, green grass. The walls were knotted wood that looked like the inside of a tree trunk. The room was circular, and she almost believed she was inside a tree. Light came out of a crystal globe that was warm and yellow and made her think of a summer day. Her bed sat snugly against the far wall, a hollowed-out log filled with another soft bed of grass. A babbling brook came in through a round knothole in the wall and pooled in a depression off to her left before flowing out through another hole. "A bath?" Bronwyn walked over to the water and felt it, smiling when she realized it was lukewarm like a shallow pool on a hot summer afternoon.

Now that she was a good way from the queen, Bronwyn started to feel embarrassed for how emotional she'd been in the throne room. Had she really been on her knees and blubbering? It all seemed almost like a dream to her. Clearly, the queen was incredibly powerful; she'd mentioned not seeing humans for thousands of years. How old was she? Could Bronwyn trust her? She felt like she would have done anything for the queen while she was in her presence, and that made her nervous. Still, she seemed so *good*, and Bronwyn really had felt the love and warmth that she projected. Could that be faked? She supposed it could; it seemed like you could do just about anything with enough Energy, and that woman had it in spades.

While she got undressed and slipped into the refreshing little pond, Bronwyn tried to remember everything she'd ever read or seen in VR about fairies and their queens and lands. She didn't know much. She had a vague notion that it was dangerous to ask them for favors, but she wasn't the one here asking for favors. "So that means I have something the Queen wants, which means I'm the one in control here. Unless I can't keep from falling on my knees and weeping." She snorted at herself and reclined in the little pool, putting her feet up on a mossy bank. She soaked for a while, mulling over what it might be like to work for someone like the Summer Queen of the fae. She was still kind of amazed by the idea that the fae were a thing and that they used to be on Earth. What had made the Energy go away from Earth? Had the queen mentioned something about the Winter Court?

"Before I agree to anything, I need to talk to her about the Winter Court and why Energy left the Earth," she said, climbing out of the pool. She let herself drip dry on the grass, standing under the warm globe in the wooden ceiling. When she was dry, she pulled on her undergarments and then curled up on the soft grass bed, perfectly warm. She'd barely thought about falling asleep when the light dimmed, and little stars appeared on the ceiling. For all the world, it looked and felt like she was sleeping outdoors on a balmy summer night. When she drifted off to sleep, she dreamed of knights and dragons. She dreamed of fairies dancing in glades and of beautiful men and women making love in beds of flowers. When she woke, she felt better and more rested than she could ever remember.

OLIVIA

Olivia did her best to tune out the chatter in the enchantment lab while she began to study the runes in her text. Many of the other students were doing the same, quietly reading through their list of runes, but many others were babbling in outraged tones about the "Absurd" way their instructor had kicked off the class. "Are you just going to read that book? Don't you have an opinion about this?" Veena asked, nudging her.

"About what?" Olivia looked up from the list of base runes.

"We think the professor will use our first exam results as part of our score for the opening challenge."

"Isn't that obvious?" Olivia looked around, puzzled by their lack of certainty. Rald snorted, and Hanwol yawned hugely.

"Well, yes, I suppose it is," Shani muttered, looking around the table. "So, who's good at memorizing things?"

"I am." Olivia shrugged and added, "I've always been good at it. It's part of the reason I finished my undergrad so early. Oh, you guys don't know what that means. Anyway, I finished schooling at age seventeen, which most people in my home country finish at age twenty-two. Unfortunately, I don't have any good tricks to help you all—it's just something I'm good at. Well, I guess that's not true. I've had plenty of instructors teach methods for studying that might help those of you that aren't good at memorizing things. We can do flashcards, mnemonic tricks, chunking, and a few others."

"Yes, please!" Rald said. "I'm not great at this stuff."

"Of course, we can start right now; let's do flashcards first. You all know what those are?" Olivia looked around, seeing most of the others nodding. Adaida even started pulling out some thick paper sheets and cutting them up into little squares with a pair of gleaming silver scissors. They spent the rest of the period making flashcards and drilling each other on the first twenty runes. It became clear during this practice that Veena and Hanwol had already learned many of the runes from lessons they'd taken before coming to the academy. Rald acted like it was cheating, but Olivia thought it made sense—why wouldn't cultures value education outside of this exclusive academy? They didn't have much time to talk about it, though; other cohorts were starting to pack up and move to the next class.

First-year alchemy was held in a large, open-air shade structure that abutted an enormous greenhouse. There were lab tables under the high, peaked roof, though none were too close to the edge. Olivia imagined that was the case to keep the elements out of a student's ingredients in case of inclement weather. Their instructor, an older Cadwalli woman, introduced herself as Professor Ghall. Though Olivia found it hard to discern emotion in the Cadwalli face, she seemed friendly enough. Her eyes didn't seem as expressive as other races, and her strange vertical pupils were a little off-putting. Additionally, the firm, leathery skin of her face didn't seem to smile as readily as other races and, in fact, seemed to be in a perpetual frown.

They spent most of their class time introducing themselves to Professor Ghall. When it was Olivia's turn, the professor walked up to her group's table and stared at her openly while she spoke. "I'm Olivia Bennet. I'm from a small community called First Landing that is quite distant from here, near the Chebli Sea."

"Is that right? Tell me, Olivia, what were the races of your parents?" Olivia was slightly taken aback by the blunt question and felt the blood rushing to her face. Everyone in the class had gotten quiet, though Adaida cleared her throat uncomfortably.

"My parents are human, as am I," she said softly, looking directly at Professor Ghall's face.

"Hmm, human, is it? I've learned all there is to know of the fauna and flora of this great world, and I have never heard of your people. How is that?" The frown lines on Professor Ghall's face deepened as she stared even more intently at Olivia.

"My people are new to this world. We arrived by traveling through the stars on a spacecraft."

"Fascinating. Are you meant to be some sort of an expeditionary force? Will there be an invasion of your kind?" A low murmur broke out among the students as they started to speculate. Some of them sounded alarmed.

"No! I mean to say, no, my people won't be invading. We didn't even know this world was inhabited when we came here, and the journey took hundreds of years. Not to mention, the System took away all of our equipment and our ship."

"Hmph. We'll have some good chats; I'm sure," the professor said, then turned to Veena, "And you? What's your name?" Olivia didn't hear any of the responses that followed hers; her ears were rushing with the heat of embarrassment and racing thoughts. As if things weren't strange enough for her being the only human here, now this professor had planted the seed that her people might be hostile. A short while later, Professor Ghall finished her interviews and moved back to the front of the class. "Well, students, I'll be teaching you four recipes over the next month. You'll be evaluated on your ability to replicate those recipes and their potency. This is the only challenge you'll have from my class with regard to the opening competition."

They spent the next hour talking about reagents and some fundamental theories of alchemy. Olivia found it interesting in that it reminded her of chemistry, but with entirely new rules. Most of it revolved around a reagent's inherent affinities and how they interacted with the Energy affinities of other reagents and the Energy of the alchemist. More than just mixing ingredients, alchemy involved active channeling from the alchemist; a person's will attribute was critical when it came to getting the most out of the reagents. Professor Ghall spoke in broad strokes and generalities that first day, but Olivia found it all very interesting and couldn't wait to start putting those theories into practice. She was disappointed when their time was up, and they had to move to their next class.

That disappointment soon faded when she met their next instructor. Professor ap'Rall was a diminutive Ardeni woman with white hair and gleaming orange-gold eyes. She had a friendly demeanor and told the students to call her Alyss. Their first lesson took place in a lecture hall on the ground floor of the main academy building, and Olivia sat near her cohort, listening with rapt attention as Alyss demonstrated the concept of spellcrafting.

"Spellcrafting is the practice of taking existing knowledge and proven technique and intuitively applying them in new constructions of Energy. The System recognizes this practice and rewards successful creation and refinement of spells." Alyss spoke clearly and methodically, and when she finished this statement, she moved around her lectern to stand in front of the class.

"Let me give you a simple example. When I first gained my class, I learned a spell called Illuminating Globe." She paused and appeared to concentrate, and then a baseball-sized ball of yellow energy appeared, floating above her palm. "This is a pure construction of Energy that simply sheds light in an area proportional to the amount of Energy I pour into it. If I wanted to make this room uncomfortably bright, I could. Now, later in my studies, I gained an affinity for water. I wondered to myself, what if I used my water-attuned Energy when I cast my Illuminating Globe? Instead of channeling pure Energy into it, I could try to channel my water-attuned Energy." Again, she paused, and the glow from her orb faded slowly, and then it took on a blue, swirling sheen, and Olivia could see that it very clearly was now an orb of swirling water.

"Not a particularly useful change, is it?" Alyss asked, smiling at the audience. "Luckily, with a water affinity comes an understanding of all the states of water." The ball in her hand started to crackle as the outside began to solidify into ice. The ball rapidly lightened in color, and then frost began to accumulate on its outer surface. Soon, vapors of cold air rose from the frozen surface of the ball, and waves of tangible cold wafted out over the rows of gathered students. The room temperature started to drop, and Olivia found herself shivering. "A new spell! Freezing Orb. The System gave me almost a full level when I figured this one out, and it wasn't even difficult." She snapped her fingers, and the ball dispersed in a puff of icy air.

Olivia thought back to when she'd made her Stunning Ice Shards spell and how she'd gained an influx of Energy. Just as she'd surmised back then, it seemed the System did actively encourage innovation with spells. She thought about her theory of the System being a parasitic entity and how this new revelation fit into that construct. She chided herself; she was trying to shoehorn data into a theory instead of looking at data and forming a hypothesis. She'd have to back up a bit and really come at the problem more scientifically.

Alyss spoke to the class about her experiences and general theories, and then she posed a question to the class, "Who among you have affinities for different types of Energy?" Olivia looked around before raising her hand, a little leery of sticking her neck out after their last class. About half the students raised their hands, though, so she joined in. She noticed that, among her cohort, Hanwol, Shani, and Adaida raised their hands. "Excellent. You'll find that more doors are open to those of you with more than one affinity, though there are still many ways to innovate even with just pure Energy. I'll teach you all, don't worry. Tomorrow, I'll be evaluating your abilities individually, and then I'll be giving you an assignment. Your performance on my assignment will be the basis on which I award points for the first month's competition." Some murmurs broke out among the students as they realized prior knowledge might mean they'd have a more challenging assignment. Alyss didn't stick around to answer questions, though, she simply dismissed the class and left through the doorway at the bottom of the auditorium. "Let's see if we can grab a bite to eat before our next class," Rald said. "We've got almost an hour."

"Can everyone afford three or four credits? I know a good sandwich place near the academy," Shani said as they all stood up.

"Oh, spirits! Not that sandwich place again," Adaida said, laughing.

"What? They're good!" Shani gave her sister a shove, but she was also laughing.

"I'll eat anything right now, so let's go. I can spot anyone the credits if you're short," Rald said as he started marching out of the building.

"Guess that's that," Olivia said, following Rald, and the others came trampling after them. They were laughing and amiably joking as they made their way down the main thoroughfare out of the academy, and Olivia enjoyed the feeling. She'd never have imagined she'd be a student again, back when she'd joined the *Pilgrim* expedition. The whole thing felt decidedly surreal.

"How old are you, Olivia?" Veena asked as she turned to wait for her; Olivia's wandering thoughts had caused her to lag a bit behind.

"Hmm, well, truthfully, I'm not really sure; I was twenty-eight when we left Earth, but the spaceflight should have taken two hundred plus years. Hah, don't look at me like that; I was asleep for the whole journey. Subjectively I'm still only twenty-eight." Her entire cohort had turned to look at her, apparently quite interested in the answer. "Well, quit staring! How old are you guys?"

"I'm nineteen," Rald said.

"I'm seventeen, and Hanwol is four minutes younger than me," Veena laughed, poking her brother.

"We're twenty," Shani and Adaida said together.

"I guess I'm a bit old to be coming here, huh?" Olivia asked, feeling a little self-conscious all of a sudden.

"Nah, everyone's different. Plus, you didn't grow up with the System and Energy—you should be proud that you're here at all! C'mon, guys; quit bugging her, and let's get some food. I'm starved!" Rald started walking faster, and everyone hurried to keep up; Olivia silently thanked him for taking the attention away from her.

OLIVIA

The sandwiches were good; Olivia couldn't argue with that—the bread had been fresh, and the meat and vegetables slathered in a rich sauce had filled her belly nicely. While they ate, the cohort continued talking about relative age, and Olivia, for the first time, was introduced to how the System calculated days and minutes. After learning about the System's twenty-hour day with seventy-five minute hours, and 375 days per year, she did some quick math and realized she wasn't quite as old when compared to the others as she'd thought. At least not, subjectively. "It's weird, though, because when I think of an hour, I still think of sixty minutes. You'd think with the System Language Integration, I'd think of the same time period that you all do."

"Hmm, yeah, maybe the concept of an hour translated, but not your exact definition," Veena mumbled around her last bite of sandwich.

"This conversation is boring. Enough about time," Adaida said. "We need to think about how we're going to beat the other cohorts, especially when it comes to spellcrafting." That got the table buzzing, and everyone started talking about their ideas for spells, but then Hanwol spoke up with a dour expression.

"Useless speculation. We'll find out tomorrow after Alyss evaluates us all. She'll tell us exactly what we'll need to do."

"Grouch," Veena said, scooting her chair away from the table.

"Yep, time to get going," Rald said.

"I'm anxious for our next class; all the cohorts have separate classrooms and instructors." Shani grabbed her sister's hand as she spoke, and they swung their clasped hands between them, walking quickly with excitement. Olivia hurried after them, and the Bogoli siblings brought up the rear.

"Why's that?" She asked.

"I'm not sure, but that's what they told us during orientation," Shani said, looking back at her.

"It's because everyone cultivates differently, and it would be too hard for one instructor to guide all the students in all the cohorts," Hanwol said.

"Goodness, you're turning into quite a know-it-all today, brother." Veena snorted when Hanwol didn't acknowledge her ribbing. Olivia tuned them out, paying attention to the winding route Rald was leading them through in the main academy building. They climbed three different sets of stairs and finally came to a long hallway with twelve doors lining the left-hand side. Rald looked at the numbers above each door and stopped by the one labeled 406.

"Here we go," he said, looking back over the cohort. Then, he turned the knob and stepped inside. The Ghelli sisters walked in after him, and Olivia followed close behind. The only way Olivia could think of to describe the room they entered was serene. A bank of pale blue stained glass windows dominated the far wall, providing the only light source in the room. Wooden flooring took up the area near the door where a shoe rack sat. Rald was already shoeless, having put his shoes on the rack, and the Ghelli were also taking their shoes off. Olivia followed suit while she looked around some more. The rest of the room's flooring was composed of a springy mat. She wondered if it was bamboo; did they have bamboo in this world? Ten different shelves lined the wall under the stained glass, and on each was a different assortment of plants, rocks, and incense. Sitting in the middle of the mat was a very lean Ardeni man. He wore a sleeveless tunic and loose pants, and he was strumming on an instrument that reminded Olivia of a harp; the tune was quite lovely.

"Welcome, Copper," he said in a smooth voice, rising to his feet in a fluid motion. "Yes, please remove your shoes and then come onto the mat. Sit here close to me, and we can talk about cultivation." He waited for them to approach and take a seat on the mat, then he walked in front of them, gently drumming his fingers on his instrument while he spoke. "I am Sange. Yes, I'm a professor, but just call me Sange. This is a rabanichord, and I think you'll find its tune helpful while we meditate here. I'll be getting to know each of you—all about your affinities, your Cores, and your cultivation drills. I'll work with each of you to improve them, and I hope you'll all come to understand the true importance of a powerful Core. Your Core is both your source of Energy and a limiting factor—unless you learn to push your Core development into advanced stages, you'll never master the most powerful of magics."

Olivia watched Sange pacing back and forth as he spoke, admiring the smooth movements and the aura of barely contained power that he presented. His head was shaved smooth, and his face sported a neatly trimmed magenta beard. The contrast of the magenta beard with his blue skin and red-purple eyes was very complimentary. She realized she'd been staring at him so intently and thinking about how interesting he looked that she hadn't heard his instructions when everyone started getting up and walking. She blushed furiously and scrambled after Veena. "What are we doing? I spaced out!" She hissed into her ear. Veena looked up at her with a grin.

"Spacing out, huh? Interesting! Well, we're all supposed to sit near a different shrine. He said to find one that 'spoke to you,' whatever that means."

"Thank you!" Olivia walked over to the far wall, where the different shelves were arrayed with plants, rocks, and unlit incense sticks. Like Veena, she didn't know what to look for, but everyone seemed to be in the same boat, just wandering up and down the row of altars. Olivia was standing by the fourth in the series of ten, and she decided to walk up to it. She knelt to sniff the incense stick and pulled back—it was something like cinnamon and bothered her nose. She stood and wandered over to the next one, where Rald had been standing but was walking away. Olivia sniffed the incense, and it wasn't unpleasant, reminding her of bergamot. She looked at the plant and saw that it had waxy round leaves growing in a clay pot of rocky, moist soil. Gently, she rubbed one of the leaves and sniffed her fingers, noting a faint tang of pine. Smiling, she picked up the large, smooth stone resting on the altar and held its cool surface to her cheek.

At first, Olivia just felt the chilly, heavy presence of the stone, but then she started to feel a stirring presence within, not necessarily a consciousness, but something was there, and it was steeped in Energy. Olivia gently set the stone back down on the altar, and then she sat in front of it on her knees, her hands resting together on her lap. She glanced to her left and right and saw Adaida seated in front of an altar, but everyone else was still moving from one to another. Slowly, the members of her cohort began to make choices, first Rald, then Veena, then Hanwol, and finally, Sheena, with a huff, just seemed to select an altar to sit at randomly.

"Good. Please begin to channel your cultivation drills, and I'll come and speak to you individually." Sange made good on his stated intention, kneeling in front of Veena and talking with her in a very low, hushed voice. Olivia closed her eyes and tried to tune out the world, concentrating on the cultivation drill that the System had awarded her when she'd developed her Prisma Core during the orientation. She pushed her Energy out along the pathways in her body, paying careful attention to all the little nooks and whirls—she hadn't even realized she had the little pathway leading out from her navel before they played that push-stone game.

More than she ever had in the past, she turned her inner eye toward the stream of Energy slowly inching through her body. Before, when she'd done this drill, she'd only ever tried to add Energy to the circulation from the Energy gateways in her hands. Now, she concentrated on finding any other external pathways, and as she uncovered them, she tried to absorb ambient Energy and add it to the circulation. She started with the one in her navel and slowly spread out from there. She found another opening near the base of her throat and two more at her knees. Finally, her circulation of Energy reached her extremities, and she absorbed even more ambient Energy through her hands and the two gateways she discovered in her feet.

"Wonderful! It looks like you're really making the most out of that simple cultivation drill!" Sange's voice was soft, but it came from right in front of her face, startling Olivia. She opened her eyes and saw him sitting cross-legged in front of her, a slight grin on his face.

"I really haven't used this drill very much. I always seem to get busy or have another priority." She looked down, her face reddening. She didn't know why, but she felt like she was back in middle school explaining why she hadn't done her homework. It's not like she'd been assigned to work on her Core, but she knew how important Sange felt it to be.

"Well, that's alright, for now. Going forward, though, you need to take Core development very seriously!" His words were stern, but he said them with a slight grin and the hint of a buried chuckle in his voice. "Now, let's see what we're dealing with; I have to confess, I haven't gotten your student file yet. Did you recently arrive at the academy?"

"Yes, just the day before yesterday. I'm Olivia."

"Excellent, Olivia. I knew your name, though—we professors talk. I just don't know the details about your Core or affinities. Care to fill me in?"

"Oh, of course. I have a Prisma class Core, and I have affinities with earth, which is funny to me because it's the name of our planet, fire, water, and air."

"That is funny. When I say 'earth,' it's synonymous with natural material. Isn't the System Language Integration fascinating? In any case, those are a lot of affinities. That Core is rather rare, as well. I'm not surprised your provincial mage representative promoted your admission here. How well can you control those differently attuned Energies? I know this is a rude question, but do you mind telling me what the System rates your affinities at?" Olivia almost answered him immediately, but something made her think twice about it. Why had he said it was a rude question? How did her affinity relate to the other people here? No one had ever asked her that question before, and she wondered if there was something taboo about revealing that aspect of yourself. "I can see the hesitation on your face. Olivia, I'm duty-bound to protect the interests of all my students. I'm not going to reveal what you tell me to anyone, just as I won't tell you anything about your cohort members' pathways or affinities. That's up to you all to share with each other if you want to."

"Well," Olivia wavered a little, but she felt like she'd have a hard enough time fitting in and succeeding in this strange place without alienating one of her professors. Still, she decided to round down and keep it simple, speaking very quietly, "My Energy affinity is nine." Sange's smile fell away, and his eyes seemed to focus on a distant point. He was quiet for a long moment, then he looked at her and spoke.

"With all of your affinities?" His voice was strangely flat. Olivia nodded. "Have you told anyone else here that?"

"No," Olivia spoke softly. Sange glanced around, ensuring that none of the other cohort members were listening.

"Listen, Olivia. That's very high. It's best you keep that number to yourself, and I'll do the same. If your cohort asks you about it, ever, simply tell them that you have a high affinity—no need for exact numbers. You see, when people hear 'high affinity,' they're going to assume something around five. I may be acting a bit overprotective, but I don't want you to become a target for jealous students or, ancestors forbid, professors. Nor do you want extreme interest and competition from professors who recruit apprentices. At least, not now. You need to develop yourself more, free from those sorts of external pressures."

"Okay, thank you for the advice." Olivia's face was solemn, but she knew all too well what it was like to have headhunters after you. True, pharmaceutical recruiters and government think tanks were probably different from power-hungry wizards, but she was happy to have the head's up about under-representing her abilities for now.

"Now, there's affinity, and then there's talent. Tell me, have you ever tried threading more than one affinity at a time through your pathways?" Olivia simply nodded to his question, and he grinned slyly at her. "And? Were you successful?" Again, Olvia nodded. "Ahh, being coy now, I see. Well, I won't press it for now, but I'm going to give you an assignment. First, answer this question: have you ever drawn differently attuned Energy into your Core while doing your cultivation drill?"

"No," Olivia said softly, trying to picture the implications.

"Excellent, then this is your assignment: today, tonight, and tomorrow, during my class, you are to concentrate on feeling, finding, and cultivating Energies that match your affinities." He grinned, winked at her, and stood, walking over to Hanwol, who was apparently next in line for his consultation.

⊱ MORGAN ⊰

The sisters were high in the sky, shedding their pale luminescence over the open cobbled roadway leading to the imposing gates. Morgan and Issa had come down the road to wait for the mysterious guardian that was supposed to make its appearance at midnight every ten days. Yan had acted as if the time had never been stuck while the two adventurers had gone through their challenges and insisted that tonight was the tenth day and the guardian's appearance was imminent. Morgan stood with his sword naked and resting on his shoulder. Issa, also with her blade drawn, stood a bit to his left. Dark, shadowy mist rose from her as she primed her battle chant. "Any minute now," Issa said, glancing over her shoulder to the watching swordsfolk.

"They make me nervous. I can't help but suspect a betrayal or something in the middle of our challenge." Morgan spoke softly, looking over the various warriors who had forfeited to them over the last couple of "Days."

"I don't think so, Morgan. If there's one thing about this strange place that seems consistent, it's the way the strange denizens follow their rules. Yan doesn't strike me as suspicious, anyway." Issa stiffened suddenly and looked back toward the gate. "It got colder. See that mist on the ground!" Morgan looked to where she was pointing, seeing a pool of white-blue mist gathering on the cobbles in front of the gate. He activated Azure Sight, and suddenly the world lit up like midday. He could see the mist gathering more and more densely, and a faint outline of a large man was standing in its center. While he watched, the mist climbed the man's silhouette, filling in his form, making him more and more solid by the second.

"Can you see that figure? Standing in the mist?" He looked at Issa and saw her shaking her head, squinting. "Well, get ready; I think the guardian has arrived." Morgan gripped his hilt and pulled his blade into a middle guard, lowering his center of gravity and priming a Vortex Lance. He channeled the Energy into his sword blade, holding it and allowing it to gather. He could feel it was ready, but still, he held it, trying to push more Energy into the spell. Issa's voice began to fill the night air with an eerie, discordant hum, and Morgan felt his sword become lighter as his arms steadied. He watched as the mist finished coursing into the spectral figure, and then, with a pulse of blue light, the mist was gone; a luminescent figure wearing shiny chain armor and holding a massive, smoldering sword stood before them. With his Azure Sight, even at this distance, Morgan could see the sword was narrow but dense, with no sharp edges but a needle-sharp point. A word came to Morgan's mind: estoc.

"Now I see him!" Issa hissed, lifting her voice louder and driving her battle chant forth. Morgan didn't respond, but he unleashed his Vortex Lance. The overcharged spell caused his sword to recoil as the bolt of Energy flashed forth, leaving a swirl of smoking air echoing its passage. Morgan caught his sword in a tighter grip before it flew from his hands, almost missing the sight of his Energy Lance ripping through the chest of the ghostly guardian. The bolt of Energy tore a hole as wide as Morgan's fist as it entered the figure, and a torrent of sizzling blue matter sprayed across the cobbles behind the guardian, causing it to hiss and snarl, staggering backward.

Issa dashed forward and to the side, her Hexing Shriek momentarily interrupting her battle chant. The shriek palpably struck the guardian, and its backward stumble became more frenetic as it wheeled its shimmering arms, finally catching its balance by dragging the tip of its estoc along the hard cobbles, leaving a fiery smoking trail. Meanwhile, Morgan had pressed his attack, using the Crane Advances to glide smoothly across the ground, his heavy, curved blade held in a middle guard, angling for an attack on the guardian's flank. In the guardian's pale, nearly translucent face, its eyes began to smolder with orange fire, and, just as Morgan launched into the Crane Flutters its Wings, it winked out of existence, leaving behind a cloud of orange embers and smoke.

Morgan scanned the area before him, only to hear Issa scream, "Morgan! Behind!" He had time to begin turning, but then pain as he'd never experienced before ripped through him as the orange-hot estoc punched a nickel-sized hole through his left rhomboid, his lung, and out through his pectoral. Helpless in pain and driven by the force of the thrust that had slipped neatly between his scaled armor, Morgan stumbled to his knees, coughing a spray of blood. He felt a heavy kick to his back, and the estoc was ripped free, and he fell forward, barely catching himself with his hands, his sword clattering on the cobbles. Morgan's vision was black at the edges, and red in the center, as he frantically grabbed his sword hilt and started to stand, but then a searing streak of orange flashed in the corner of his eye, and the round, heavy blade of the estoc smashed into his helmet just above his ear, and he fell over.

Dimly, Morgan could hear Issa screaming, and no other blows immediately hit him, so he thought maybe she had gotten the guardian's attention. With a tremendous effort of will, Morgan fought against the darkness creeping around the periphery of his vision, taking heavy, rasping, painful breaths and scrambling for his sword several inches from his right hand. He grabbed the blade and rolled to his back, trying to get eyes on the guardian. It was there, not ten feet away, punching the tip of the estoc at Issa as she valiantly dodged and tried to parry. As Morgan struggled to his feet, he saw Issa attempt a riposte, only to have her much lighter, shorter weapon batted aside as the guardian lunged and punched the estoc deep into her shoulder. She screamed and flailed backward, moving with a blur as she must have Hasted herself.

Morgan growled, reaching out with his senses, activating Energy Drain and feeling for the guardian's Energy currents. He felt them, smoldering and cold simultaneously, and he pulled them with all his will. A torrent of swirling, smokey orange and cobalt Energy flooded into him, causing the guardian to stagger and instantly filling Morgan with a surge of strength. He felt his breaths coming more easily, and the pain in his chest subsided, and then he activated Hollow Charge, flashing toward the staggering guardian and activating Azure Burst. The guardian's shimmering translucent sheen peeled away as Morgan's blue crackling fire washed over it. He followed the stumbling smoldering figure, hacking like a maniac with his sword, too distressed and undisciplined to use his forms. Still, his blade connected several times, shearing off pieces of the guardian's armor and sending splashes of blue, misty matter spraying out.

Finally, in control of the fight's momentum, Morgan started to regain his senses, and while he waited for the cooldown on Energy Drain, he began to press his attack with his sword forms. He slipped past the guardian's flailing guard with the Crane Takes a Minnow, ripping the guardian's shredded chain mail further and piercing its stomach. He pulled back his blade, parrying a counter thrust, and was about to start another attack when he felt, in the back of his mind, an attack coming from behind him. He recognized the prescience of his sword, even though it was only the second time it had ever come through for him, and he whirled around, lifting his blade into the Crane Defends the Nest. He felt a whoosh of displaced air where the guardian had been, and then it was there, launching a terrible stab at what would have been at Morgan's back had he not spun.

Morgan's defense was perfectly placed, and he knocked aside the estoc and hacked into the side of the guardian's neck on the upswing. Then, Issa was back in the fight, and she landed several lightning lunges, sinking her blade into the guardian's back. The cold Energy in her sword did something to the wet matter the guardian was composed of, freezing it and causing it to break apart. In too close now for the estoc to nimbly pierce him, Morgan kept his black blade against the guardian's neck, driving it down and to the side with all his strength. He felt it bite, deeper and deeper as he pushed the guardian down, shoving his body and weight against the guardian while it fumbled to try to hammer him with the heavy hilt of its sword. Meanwhile, Issa piled stab after stab into it, and its struggles became weaker and weaker. Finally, Morgan wrenched with all his might on his sword's handle, smashing the guardian into the cobbles.

The estoc clattered against the cobbles, and the guardian seemed to melt into mist. Meanwhile, a torrent of golden-white motes of Energy poured into Morgan and Issa. Morgan instantly felt better, his wound closing the rest of the way, and he saw Issa straighten up and take a deep, cleansing breath.

Congratulations! You have achieved level 24 Vortex Duelist and have gained 8 Intelligence, 8 Agility, 6 Will, 6 Dexterity. You have learned the skill: Hollow Charge—Improved.

Hollow Charge—Improved: Prerequisite: Vortex Class Core. You expend some Energy to sheath yourself in the currents of your Vortex Core and move with great alacrity up to 25 feet. Your Core will absorb Energy-based attacks that hit you during this charge and for several seconds after. Energy cost: 150, Cooldown: Medium.

Issa was panting heavily, leaning forward, her hands on her knees. Morgan stepped up to her and gently took her shoulders, straightening her. "Let me see," he said, pulling at the leather lacings on the side of her chain shirt. He knew she was still hurting because she didn't protest. Having undone all the lacing, he lifted the front of her chain shirt and saw that the estoc had left a weeping, blackened puncture just above her right breast. "Goddammit, I wish you healed as much from Energy as I do." He pulled one of his last two healing draughts from the Yovashi home out of his ring, popping the cork stopper. He gently dropped some into the bloody, burned wound, liberally smearing the thick liquid around the area, then handed the bottle to Issa and said, "Drink the rest." She nodded and gulped it down. "Feeling better?" He knew the answer before she spoke—her skin had regained its vibrant glow, and the pained squints around her eyes were gone.

"Yes, thank you."

While Issa worked on lacing up her chain shirt, Morgan looked around the scene of the battle and saw that the guardian's estoc was still lying on the cobbles. He also noticed that the enormous gates were slightly ajar. He walked over to the long, straight sword. Was it really a sword if it didn't have a cutting edge? He supposed so; even fencing foils were considered swords, right? The estoc had a long ivory-colored hilt with a round, silvery pommel. The guard had the shape of an X, and along each metal arm, a silver serpent was engraved. The blade itself was about six inches longer than even his two-handed sword, though it was perfectly straight and round, and, as it lay on the cobbles, it emitted vapors of black smoke. Morgan reached down and put his hand around the hilt, lifting the sword.

The first thing he noticed was the weight. He could move it easily enough, but he didn't think his old, pre-System self would have been able to swing it or hold it straight while he thrust it. It had to be over a hundred pounds. "What the hell is this thing made of?" While he was marveling at the weight of the thing, Morgan noticed how warm the handle was, and he saw an orange, flickering gleam run up and down the blade.

"You know, if that guardian had hit either of us in the heart, where I'm sure it was aiming, we'd be dead." Issa had walked up behind him and looked at the long, stabbing sword.

"Yeah, I don't think it missed my heart by much. Think about that—almost finished with one stab, despite all my Energy or skills." Morgan shuddered when he looked at Issa and the black hole in her chain mail. "This is a wicked fucking weapon. Do you think I should bond with it? What if it has a spirit within?"

"You'll know it if you start to bond and have a chance to pull back." Issa patted her rapier hilt. "At least that's how it worked for me."

"Alright," Morgan said, planting the point of the estoc on the cobbles and holding the hilt in both hands. He ran a trickle of Energy into the sword and felt an instant connection:

Heartspark: Artificed Weapon. Enchantments: 1. Hardness—This weapon has been strengthened by a master Artificer; resistance to shattering or bending is increased by a factor of one thousand. 2. Scorching—This weapon has been enchanted with elemental fire, allowing it to pierce armor and damage flesh more easily. 3. Heart seeking—This weapon is drawn to the hearts of living creatures. Thrusts aimed in the general vicinity of a creature's heart are more likely to strike the organ.

"It's not intelligent, but it's got a lot of enchantments. Let's just say we're lucky to be alive, or maybe just I am. You were moving so fast the guardian was lucky to hit you at all." Morgan described the enchantments on the sword and stowed it away in his ring. He wanted to learn to use it because it was a devastating weapon.

"Well, we did it, Morgan!" Issa forced a smile, and Morgan tried to stop dwelling on how close they'd both come to dying. He looked at the gate and smiled.

"Yeah, we sure did. I wonder what's waiting inside?"

OLIVIA

Time went by very quickly during Core development class, and it seemed like mere moments had passed after Sange spoke to her when Adaida was shaking Olivia's shoulder, letting her know it was time to move on. Olivia stood and stretched. She'd been trying to feel differently attuned currents of Energy around her, and she'd felt like she was just sensing a tickling feeling of something different when Adaida had shaken her shoulder. She honestly had to bite down to keep from saying something rude. Her exaggerated stretch was a way to push back the impulse while her rational mind resurfaced. "Uh, that feels good. Okay, thanks, Adaida." She followed the others to the shoe rack and noticed that Sange was nowhere to be seen. "Sange left?"

"Yeah, after he finished 'interviewing' us." Veena snorted.

"What? You don't like him?" Oliva looked around to gauge the sentiment of the cohort.

"Oh, he's fine. I just never liked the meditative, soft-spoken, mysterious type. It seems a bit forced." Veena grunted as she pulled on her shoe.

"Hah, true. He definitely has a way . . ." Rald trailed off. "Anyway, let's go before we're the last ones to combat training."

Olivia followed the cohort through the hallways and down two flights of stairs. They entered a long, wide hallway with big double doors at the end. One of the doors was propped open, and as they advanced, Olivia could see a brightly lit, airy room with wood plank flooring. The closer they got, the more it resembled a high school basketball gymnasium to her. When she stepped in, she saw that the roof was a good thirty feet up and had an angled slope with the high side on the west. There, a bank of windows let in the bright afternoon sun. A row of benches lined the room, and sitting and standing around them were several cohorts that had arrived before them. Olivia and the rest of Copper cohort moved to an area away from the other groups and waited.

"Cohorts! Line up, single file, at the western wall. Stand silently while I give you instructions!" The voice that shouted the instructions was loud and piercing and decidedly condescending in tone. Olivia hurriedly followed her cohort while she looked around for the speaker. She'd just started to line up when she finally saw the big otter-like person wearing a loose, flowing white robe striding toward them. "I am Commander Grobak! You will address me as Commander, Commander Grobak, or sir. Is that clear?" Many of the cohort members said yes, some nodded, and others just muttered. "What in the fates was that?" Commander Grobak screamed, his voice echoing and reverberating from the walls. "When I ask the cohorts a question, you will answer loudly and in unison. Stop fidgeting! Now, do you all understand how to address me?" In their defense, it sounded like the cohorts tried to follow his directive, but some students were loud, some were quiet, some spoke quickly, some slowly, and it all just sounded like a mess. "That's it! Run and touch the wall, and back again! Do it until I tell you to stop!" He paused to see their response, and when the cohorts looked around uncertainly and only a few students started running, he screamed again, "Go! Now, now, now! Run!"

Olivia stopped waiting and watching what others would do and started running. Commander Grobak's voice chased her as he screamed at the others to get moving or to move faster. Olivia had seen enough movies involving basic training and taken enough psychology classes to understand what was happening here: Grobak was going to spend some time breaking them down before he tried to build them up. She wasn't worried; she could play the game. She'd do what Grobak wanted, and the whole time, she'd know she was just getting through the experience. She'd had professors that hated her and tried to make her drop their courses, and she'd swallowed her pride and written some drivel to match their theories and appease their egos and finished with perfect marks.

Grobak made them sprint back and forth four times before screaming at them to line up again. "Now, let's try again! When I ask you a question, you will loudly answer in unison! Do you all understand how to address me?"

"Yes!" The students shouted, coughed, and sputtered, but the word came out mostly together.

"Better!" Grobak nodded, walking back and forth in front of the lined-up cohorts. Olivia was just happy that he didn't say they had to finish all their responses with "Sir" like in the movies about basic. She'd never had to do any military training, even for the *Pilgrim* mission. She knew most of the colonists had done so, but Director Paulson had just been happy to get her on board. A simple health evaluation, and she'd been green-lit. "Now listen up! Take a good look at me! That's right; I'm a Vodkin! I know the ideas you have about us. I know how you high-Energy races feel about us! You're right; I don't have much Energy affinity. Guess what? That means I've earned my levels a hell of a lot more than you lot ever will. I know how to fight, and I don't use fancy magic tricks to do it. If you want to learn to survive when everything's stacked against you, on your worst day ever, you'll pay attention to me. Put away your misconceptions, open your minds, and you'll leave this place better off, even if you never learn any new magic. Are we clear?" He shouted the last question with renewed ferocity and reverberating volume.

"Yes!"

"Better! Now, listen: this is the only easy day you'll ever have in my class. Today, I'm going to check out your exercise robes, and from now on, you'll arrive here wearing them. Never wear shoes in my hall again. Are we clear, cohorts?"

"Yes!" Olivia thought the cohorts were getting better; their voices were loud and almost in unison that time. Commander Grobak walked to the far wall and started producing large wicker baskets. In all, he put nine baskets on the wooden flooring, and then he started calling the cohorts over, one by one, to give them robes. Every cohort got a set of white, cottony robes and pants. In addition, they were each given a belt colored to match their cohort—brown for Wood, off-white for Bone, gray for Stone, copper for Copper, and so on.

"Now, put your robes away and line up again!" The cohorts hurried to get into their lines, stopping their hushed conversations. "Today, you only have one activity: my assessment of you. I'll stand before your row, and, one by one, you'll punch my hand as hard as you can. Are we clear?" Once again, his voice rose by several octaves and decibels as he shouted the question.

"Yes!" Olivia screamed it with the rest of the students. She watched silently as Commander Grobak stood in front of first Wood, then Bone, then Stone. He held up one meaty palm and allowed the students to punch it, one by one. Olivia never saw his palm move by so much as a centimeter, even when the bigger, more muscular students hit it. After each cohort punched his palm, he nodded and dismissed them. Soon it was Copper's turn, and Olivia watched her friends punch his hand, and then it was her turn. He looked down at her and nodded, angling his palm so that she could punch up at it. Olivia cocked her arm back and grunted, punching out at the otter-man's hand with all her might. Her fist connected with a soft thwap, and he smiled at her and nodded.

"Okay, Copper. See you tomorrow. Be sure to eat a big breakfast!" Grobak didn't wait for a response, moving over to Silver cohort's line. Olivia looked at her cohort, and they hurried from the gymnasium.

"That guy is insane," Veena huffed as they cleared the doorway.

"Yes, I've never been screamed at that much in my entire life!" Shani looked genuinely upset. Olivia walked over to her and put a hand on her shoulder.

"Don't let him get to you. That's typical military training. He must be some sort of military man back home. I'm sure that's why they chose him for this job. He'll berate us a lot while we're learning, but then when we improve, his praise will seem so much better. It's psychology 101."

"What?" Hanwol said, looking oddly at Olivia.

"Oh, nothing, just an idiom from my world. I mean, it's basic. This is how they operate. Just do what he says and try your hardest to improve, and we'll get by."

"What was the deal with us punching his hand?" Veena asked, looking around at their faces while they walked toward the cafeteria.

"I guess he's using it as a metric for our improvement," Rald ventured. "We get a score from his course as well when it comes to the competition. I bet he'll see how much we improve our punch and rate us."

"Well, I apologize in advance—I've never been much of an athlete, let alone a fighter." Olivia looked down and subconsciously touched the scar over her eye.

"Bleh, us neither," Adaida said, indicating her sister.

"Well, that might not be a bad thing," Rald said. "Think about it—it's a lot easier to improve from zero than it is to improve from an already solid position."

"Hmm, I like the way you think, Rald." Veena grinned up at him, her blue-green lips pulling back to reveal white teeth.

That evening, they all were back in their dormitory early. Olivia was reading through her list of runes when she felt a chill in the air and heard Shani grunt in frustration from her bed across the room. "What're you doing, Shani?" she called.

"I'm trying to modify a spell. I have a cold affinity, and I'm trying to do what the professor showed us in class—change my light spell to give off cold Energy instead of light. I can't get it to stick, though."

"Well, I felt the wave of cold air. It must have been a lot if I could feel it over here. Maybe try smaller at first? Aren't you worried about leveling, though?"

"Why would I be?" Shani looked at her, and Veena also looked up.

"Well, because we aren't supposed to be higher than level ten, right?"

"Only at admission. We're free to level now, but if you think you're going to win the competition, you might wait to get to level ten before it's over—the rewards might improve the classes you get offered. I'm only level seven, though, so I can mess around." Shani held out her palm and concentrated, creating a tiny point of light hovering above her palm. Olivia turned back to her book but then set it down, unable to focus. After all, she was still only level eight; it wouldn't hurt for her to do some experimenting.

She'd managed to add electricity to her Icy Shards spell, but she still didn't have any pure electricity or earth spells. She thought about how her Fiery Burst spell worked: she knew she could already modify it to send forth a tiny stream of fire or a massive torrent of fire by simply modulating the amount of Energy she fed the spell. What if she didn't let the spell automatically grab her fire-attuned Energy? What if she carefully pushed air-attuned Energy into it when it started to activate? She decided to try it, sitting up on her bed and holding her palm out toward the empty space between her sleeping area and the door. She looked inward to her Core and clamped down on all of her Energy with an effort of will. Then, she activated her Fiery Burst spell, but when she felt it start to draw on her fire-attuned Energy, she held it back and, instead, tried to push some air-attuned Energy into it.

Her first attempt failed—she hadn't gotten the air-attuned Energy flowing into the spell fast enough, and it simply faded away. She tried again; this time, she didn't clamp her air Energy at all, and as soon as she cast the spell, she sent the air-attuned Energy flowing. She felt a cool tingle in her arm, and then a blast of air flew out of her palm, kicking up motes of dust from the wooden floor.

Congratulations! You have learned the spell: Wind Gust—Basic.
Congratulations! You have achieved level 9 base human and have 5 attribute points to allocate.

Olivia flopped onto her back as the stream of Energy motes flooded into her chest. "Oh my God! I didn't realize I was that close!"

"What's going on? Adaida stood up from her bed and walked over to Olivia. "Did you just level? You bitch! Did you already make a new spell?" She was smiling, so Olivia didn't take the insult seriously.

"Yeah, I did. I'm level nine now. Do you all think I could make another spell without leveling? I don't know how much the System will reward me."

"It depends on the spell!" Shani chimed in. "You should hold off, Olivia! What if part of our test is to create a spell? You should keep working on ideas and start practicing the different steps, but don't finish a new spell until you have to for class. In fact, you should start thinking of more and more complexity—try to come up with something great!" The others generally echoed Shani's sentiment, and Olivia nodded, scooting up on her pillow. She was starting to worry that she'd made a mistake. What if she gained another level through her efforts in her classes over the next month? She might not benefit from any award she got if it had to do with class selection.

Olivia put the thought out of her mind; none of the professors had warned them about leveling or practicing what they'd shown them. She supposed that could be because the professors assumed they wouldn't do anything stupid, but what could she do? Olivia hadn't been one to cry over spilt milk, even back on Earth. She was the type of person who did her best to control what was within her control and try to let the other stuff work itself out. Smiling slyly, she pointed a finger at Shani's bed and concentrated, casting Wind Gust in a controlled burst at her silvery-blond hair where it hung down over her right shoulder. The cool flood of air Energy traveling through her arm gave her a bit of a rush, and then she saw Shani's curls fluttering in the breeze.

"Hey! Is there a window open or something?" Shani sat up and yanked her folded quilt from the foot of her bed up over her, pulling it close in around her neck. Olivia snickered, imagining the other types of spells she might come up with.

Morgan

Morgan looked at the heavy wooden gates and the human-sized gap that had opened between them. He wanted to continue, to see what he could find and learn in this strange place, but he found himself preoccupied with the idea that Issa had almost died just a few minutes ago. He looked at her, and some of his consternation must have been written on his face because she frowned at him and said, "What?"

"Nothing." He sighed heavily and looked around the area. "None of the other challengers are watching anymore. You'd think Yan would have had a few words for us, at least." He didn't know if his ploy to change topics would work, but it might at least buy him a few minutes to examine his feelings. Issa sniffed and looked around, and Morgan's heart lurched at the idea that he might never see her little nose twitch like that again. Inwardly, he told himself to get a grip while he said, "Maybe we should rest a bit before heading in."

"What if the door closes? We don't know how long our window is." She looked at him with a funny expression. "Are you scared?" Morgan smiled, pulled her into a hug, and took a long deep breath of her hair, savoring the lingering scent of the oil she used to keep fresh during travel. Was that vanilla?

"The only thing I'm scared of is life without you," he said quietly. Issa pulled back and looked at his eyes and the strain written therein.

"Didn't you ever consider I could die? We're all going to die, Morgan. This world is dangerous, and the pursuit of power makes it doubly so." She spoke softly and gently reached up to rub at the sides of his neck with her fingers.

"Maybe we should take the gains we've gotten and find a quiet place? Should we really be charging into dungeons? It's been a long time since I've had something to lose, Issa, and it hit me when that bastard almost skewered our hearts. What would I do if you died?"

"Morgan, I love you, but I don't want to be a farmer or a merchant. I don't want to be helpless if someone stronger comes along and decides they want what we have. You know we aren't the strongest people in this world, right?" Her voice was soft, but some steel had entered it as she said the last words.

"Yeah. Logically, I know all that. I know it's selfish to want to hide you away and keep you to myself. Hah, but I can't help the impulse I have right now just to snatch you up and run to a quiet town and enjoy the long lifespans we've earned." He smiled to let her know he was only half-serious. "I respect you enough to know you aren't going to go for something like that. C'mon, let's go." He grabbed her hand and started walking toward the gate.

"It bothers me, too, you know? The thought of you dying," Issa quietly said while they walked. I've thought about it a lot; I think it would ruin me, so you better not die!"

"Well," Morgan squeezed her hand, "That's kind of my plan."

When they reached the ajar gate, Morgan let go of Issa's hand, and they both drew their swords. Morgan activated Azure Sight and peered around the edge of the heavy, dry wood. A stone courtyard could be seen through the low-ceilinged gatehouse, cloaked in silvery twilight. Morgan couldn't make out any people or monsters, though he thought he saw some movement near the far end of the courtyard behind a parked cart. "I don't see anything, but I'm pretty sure things were moving on the walls when we first got here. We'll be sitting ducks in the courtyard."

"Let's move into the gatehouse and peek around the corners," Issa whispered. Morgan nodded, and he slowly slipped through the open gates, Issa right behind him. When they were within the gatehouse, he moved over to the right-hand wall and crept carefully forward, past the raised portcullis and then to the stone corner of the wall. He peered out to his right, then his left, taking stock. He could see several figures moving about on the ramparts, and he figured there might be more above their heads, patrolling over the gatehouse. He was about to turn and report what he saw to Issa when a large, armored figure strode out from behind the parked wagon into the center of the courtyard, looking straight at him.

"Students! Guards! Come down from the wall and deal with this rabble!" The man's voice rang out, and Morgan could hear shuffling steps on the ramparts and then stomping on the wooden stairs to each side of the courtyard. He looked at Issa and then back at the gate.

"Shit. Run? Or?"

"He called them students; let's see what they're made of!" Her eyes darkened, and black-purple smoke rose from her as she started up her Battle Chant. Morgan couldn't argue with that, so he gripped his sword and started reaching out with Energy Drain, feeling for his approaching opponents. "Let's keep the gatehouse to our backs!" Issa stepped forward as she spoke, taking a position on Morgan's left. They didn't have to wait long; shortly, three figures came into view from the left and four from the right. They were all Ardeni or Shadeni, and they looked like ordinary people, other than the fact that a slight luminosity surrounded them and their skin had a sheen of translucence. All wielded swords of one type or another; one had a massive two-handed greatsword, and next to him was a woman with a short stabbing sword like a gladius. Several wielded scimitar-like weapons and another had a broadsword and shield. Bringing up the rear was a robe-wearing katana wielder.

"Issa, hang back a minute—I'm going to try to give us the momentum." Morgan concentrated—he had a couple of seconds to act, and he couldn't wait for her response. He'd never tried the combination he was about to do, but he'd theorized it in his head many times, rehearsing how he'd carry it out. Morgan moved his body into the Crane Defends the Nest, pouring Energy into the enhanced parrying the form provided, then he used Hollow Charge, aiming at the shield-wearing student near the center of the pack. Before he closed the distance in a flash, he activated Azure Burst.

As he was flashing over the cobbles in the courtyard, he was aware of some offensive spells hitting him but being absorbed by his Vortex Core. In fact, whatever the students had thrown at him had refunded the full cost of his charge. Just as he was about to impact the shield-bearing student, his Azure Burst exploded outward, ripping through the converging attackers and sending several of them sprawling. Morgan brought his sword down into a middle guard and backed up a step, already reaching out with Energy Drain. He'd never tried to draw from so many targets at once, and he knew it would be costly—over a thousand Energy points. Still, that was only a third of his available Energy, and Morgan decided to go for it. He felt Issa rush up beside him as he reached out and pulled.

None of the students had recovered enough to launch a counter-attack yet. When his Core started to draw their Energy forcefully, the luminous halo that surrounded them dimmed noticeably, and they, as one, wailed in agony. One of the scimitar-wielding students was stumbling to her feet near Issa. Morgan didn't have to say anything; Issa darted forward and whipped her rapier's sharp edge through the student's throat. Luminous crimson blood splashed out over the cobbles, and the student grabbed her throat, falling backward and writhing about, choking on her blood.

Morgan drove forward at a group of three students who were burned but not down. They'd staggered with his Energy Drain but were recovered enough to get their weapons up and try to advance. Morgan decided to push a full offensive, launching into the Crane Flutters its Wings, cleaving in wide, angled slashes. He learned that the attack was effective against multiple weakened opponents, but he also found that three opponents, one of which had a greatsword, might be more than he bargained for. He bashed through the guards of the first two students with his first cleave, knocking aside their smaller blades and ripping shallow cuts across their torsos. His second cleave came up against a heavy sword wielded by a student that knew what he was doing. The student riposted his cleave, even powered by his Energy-infused form, and the long, straight edge of the greatsword slipped between his arm and side, the blade slicing upward along his vulnerable armpit.

Morgan felt the edge rub along the thick leather joint of his scale armor at first, but then, as the student drove forward, pushing the sword the whole length, he felt the leather give, and a sharp pain erupted from his armpit. Morgan grunted, releasing his sword with his right hand to pull his arm away from the greatsword. Ignoring the burning pain, he stepped forward and behind the greatsword wielder, gripped his sword, and pivoted in a downward slash, ripping a terrible wound open on the back of the student's knee. The student cried out and fell forward, his greatsword clattering on the cobbles. Morgan didn't hesitate, thrusting this sword deep into the student's lower back. He looked around and saw that during their brief scuffle Issa had dispatched another student, but was fighting a defensive battle against the shield user and the katana-wielding student.

Issa was clearly faster than the students, perhaps having Hasted herself, and was having no trouble keeping them at bay, so Morgan turned to the gladius and scimitar wielders he'd already wounded. Their luminous glow was almost gone, and their faces were haggard and wan. Shimmering crimson flowed over their torn garments, and they regarded Morgan with wary eyes as they tried to flank him. Morgan slipped into the Crane Takes a Minnow, using the Energy flowing through his legs to allow him to glide quickly to his right, flanking one of the students and keeping them both in his line of sight. The student lunged forward with her gladius, trying to steal the initiative, but Morgan was ready, and his sword flicked up like a serpent's tongue, impaling her through her stomach. Morgan tried to wrench his sword free quickly, but it wasn't fast enough. The other student charged and hacked downward with his scimitar, and Morgan was forced to release his sword and hop backward to avoid the cut. Morgan almost pulled his spear from his ring, but he held back—not because he didn't think the spear would finish this fight rather handily, but because he was in a dungeon created by a swordmaster's soul, and he was afraid some judgment might be passed on him if he were to win this fight with a spear after having his sword disarmed.

While he dodged another clumsy slash from his opponent, Morgan heard Issa shriek and spared a quick glance. She'd used her Hex attack and shaken her opponents enough for her to slip forward and lunge with her rapier, scoring a hit on the katana wielder. Morgan quickly refocused on his enemy and decided to try something he'd wondered about: could he cast Vortex Lance using his hand as a "Weapon?" Backpedaling, he held up his hand and pointed his palm at the advancing student. His opponent was tired, weakened, and shaken by the disastrous showing of his comrades, and Morgan was able to stay out of his reach for the long seconds it took to charge up his spell. When he felt it was ready, he stopped moving, allowing the student to charge forward with a wild swing, but when his sword was at the apex, Morgan released his Vortex Lance. The ripping concussive retort as the Energy projectile tore through the air and punched a fist-sized hole through the student's chest echoed through the courtyard.

Morgan strode forward, not sparing a look at the crumpled corpse of his enemy, and grabbed his sword from the body of the gladius fighter. He moved to Issa, noting that her opponents were moving sluggishly and that the cobbles were smeared with the glistening crimson blood these strange people expelled. He hesitated to jump into the fight—he could see the gleam in Issa's eyes and the grin on her face as she slowly whittled her two opponents down. Still, it was two versus one, and Morgan didn't want to play games with Issa's life. He used Hollow Charge, ripping his sword through the side of one of her opponents. He hit so hard and with such unopposed ferocity that his sword opened half the student's abdomen, allowing a flood of shimmering crimson to pour out with the unmistakable glistening shapes of entrails within. Morgan, adrenaline pouring through his veins, wasn't fazed and pivoted, lifting his sword to advance on the last enemy, the bleeding, staggering, katana-wielding student.

"Leave it, Morgan!" Issa hissed, and suddenly she blurred, flashing left then lunging forward, shedding the katana with the dull back of her blade and then burying her rapier into the exposed armpit of the student's sword arm. He crumpled, twitching, and she pulled her blade out, whipping the blood off in a flourish. She looked up at Morgan and grinned. Morgan smiled back, breathing heavily, and noticed that his armpit still throbbed. He looked around and realized none of the bodies had dissolved, nor had any Energy motes started to coalesce. He was about to say something when the tall figure that had called the students to combat strode forward out of the shadows near the keep entrance.

"So, you can bully some students? Let's see how you fare against Drillmaster Groll!"

MORGAN

Drillmaster Groll stepped forward, his heavy foot clanking against the cobbles in the courtyard. Morgan took a good look at his armor—the way it encased him from neck to toes in heavy-looking blue-gray plates. Even his joints had little articulated plates on them. Morgan knew there was a name for those armor pieces, but he didn't know it. Groll, like his students, emitted a silver-blue luminescence, and when he shifted slightly, reaching over his shoulder to unhook a massive greatsword, Morgan felt some nervousness. He hadn't had time to mess around with it, but he decided to swap his sword with the estoc he'd won from the gate guardian; he didn't fancy his odds of slashing through that armor.

He hefted the blade, admiring how the orange flicker of its internal fire surged up and down the metal while he moved it. He'd have to be careful with his forms; this sword was meant for stabbing and parrying—his most devastating form was a cleaving attack that would be ineffectual without a cutting surface. The hackles on his neck rose when he heard Issa's discordant Battle Chant start up, but he reveled in the surge of vibrancy that coursed through his limbs. Morgan lifted Heartspark into a middle guard and began to channel Vortex Lance. Groll's eyes flared with crimson fire the instant Morgan started to cast the spell, and he roared, whipping his gigantic, gleaming greatsword in an arc over his head and down toward the ground in front of him. A red glimmer erupted along the length of the blade while he swung it, and though neither Morgan nor Issa were in range of the swing, standing some twenty feet distant, they both dodged out of the way.

It was a good thing they did—as the greatsword cut the air, the red glimmer seemed to detach and ripple through the air, extending the range of the cut a dozen fold. The cobbles in front of where Morgan had been standing erupted into powdered stone fragments, and the cut continued past where he'd been. Morgan rolled to his feet, his Vortex Lance ruined by his broken concentration. Groll broke into a chuckle, and Morgan frowned, circling closer to him while Issa worked on getting to his other flank. As he got closer, Morgan could make out his features and realized that Groll was the biggest Ardeni he'd ever seen, easily as tall as Morgan but much broader in the shoulders. His blue head was shaved clean, but his bushy orange eyebrows and beard stood out starkly. Groll seemed to ignore Issa, staring at Morgan, and then he charged.

Morgan lowered his center and dropped into the Crane Defends the Nest. He poured Energy into his limbs and used his increased parrying surface to meet the tremendous blow of Groll's greatsword. It felt like trying to block a grizzly bear's swipe with a broomstick. His estoc was flung to the side, but Morgan's sword skills were improving—he didn't let the blow cleave him in half as it broke his guard; instead, he pivoted and allowed the momentum to swing him out of range of the slash. He found himself at Groll's side, with his enemy overextended. He lunged with the estoc, driving the point into the armor covering his exposed left side. The razor point flared with orange fire as it burned through the heavy plate armor, and Morgan shoved with all his might. The blade sank a foot into Groll's body, and he screamed a deafening, choking howl of disbelief and pain.

Morgan stumbled in shock as Groll collapsed, dragging Morgan with him as he clung to the estoc. The giant drillmaster coughed a gurgling torrent of blood, and then he lay still. Suddenly a dense layer of Energy motes coalesced over the fallen swordsman and all the vanquished students in the courtyard. Thick, shimmering ribbons of Energy flowed into Morgan and Issa.

Congratulations! You have achieved level 25 Vortex Duelist and have gained 8 Intelligence, 8 Agility, 6 Will, 6 Dexterity.

"Morgan! How did you do that?" Issa hurried toward him as soon as she'd recovered from the influx of Energy.

"I made a good parry, er riposte? Anyway, Heartspark is the real hero—it melted through his armor, and I'm pretty sure his heart, too. Glad I swapped out my sword for this fight!" Morgan picked up the still smoldering estoc and held it out to admire the furious orange glow that rippled up and down its length.

"Morgan! A chest!" Issa walked quickly toward the courtyard's center, where a sizable footlocker-shaped chest had appeared. "This definitely wasn't here before, but it doesn't look like a System chest."

"Well, yeah, things are different in this dungeon than in the Crucible, but I think the System still has an influence; that skill scroll I got seems too specifically perfect for me. I mean, I don't even know if my sword style is from this planet. I had a vision of a master using it, and he seemed human to me, but that might have been a mental bias—I don't think I ever saw his face. Anyway, the point I was trying to get to is that I feel like the System put that reward there for me." Morgan kind of trailed off as Issa cocked an eyebrow at him but didn't respond. Was he being crazy?

"In any case, this seems like an award for clearing the courtyard," Issa said, squatting to look at the chest more closely. It was remarkably similar in construction to the chest that had been near Tal-dak and Shinra's tent—pale planks with bronze corner plates and clasp.

"I doubt it's trapped—it looks like Tal-dak's chest, and it's an award. Why trap it?" While he spoke, Morgan looked closely at the chest with Azure Sight and noticed nothing.

"Nevertheless, let's use our strategy." Issa looked at him, waiting for Morgan to cast Guard Ally, and he did so, then backed up a few steps. She nodded and opened the chest, and nothing exploded or shot out of it. "This looks good, Morgan!" Her voice was hushed with awe as she knelt in front of the open chest. Morgan rushed over to see what she was looking at. The chest had a polished wooden insert with variously shaped holes cut into it. Each hole contained an item: there were six round holes with small, colorful, labeled vials resting in them, two rectangular cutouts held bars of gleaming amber-colored metal, and two thin oblong cutouts held gold foil-wrapped packages.

"Wow. Is that amber-ore?" He asked, leaning to look more closely. Issa nodded, lifting out one of the big rectangles of dense metal. Morgan could see by the way her tendons stood out in her forearms that it was heavy.

"It's a lot, Morgan. This is a precious prize by itself." She handed the metal bar to him, and Morgan could feel the Energy thrumming within it. Looking closely, he saw swirls of blue-gray running through the ore. He admired it for a moment more and then stowed it in his ring.

"You take the other one. What are those vials?" He reached down and plucked one of the vials out and read the label aloud while Issa hefted the other ingot out and stored it in her pouch, "Dranim's Miracle Elixir—cures most poison, disease, and mends injuries."

"They're all the same," Issa said, examining the labels. They split up the six elixirs, and then Issa asked, "What do you think is wrapped in the foil?"

"Isn't there a label?" Morgan watched as Issa gingerly lifted one of the little foil-wrapped packages out of the slot in the chest and turned it around in her hands, looking for a label. She squinted at the bottom of the package, and suddenly her face exploded with a huge smile.

"Randon's Core Cake!" She handed the golden package to Morgan, and he noted the dense but squishy consistency of the material wrapped within.

"Do you think it's meant to improve our Cores?" The idea of a food that could improve his Core seemed silly to him, but he supposed he'd seen sillier. It could be made of rare natural materials or something or baked in some sort of alchemical process.

"I don't know. I've never heard of such a thing, but the universe is a big place, Morgan. Should we try it?"

"I don't know, let's think about this—I haven't put a lot of work into cultivating my Core, and it's already base three, close to base four, I think. Maybe we should save these until we're stuck? Or until we need a boost in a hurry?" Issa frowned at his words, but she slowly nodded.

"You're right. We should be smart about it. Let's save them for now." She reached into the box and took out the other cake, putting it into her pouch. Morgan put his cake into his ring, and then he stood up and looked around the courtyard. "Well, what's next? Into the keep? Whatever's going on in this dungeon, it seems kind of scripted. I mean, if this were the real world, everyone inside would have come running to help during the battle."

"That's true. Well, I say we go in and see what the next encounter is." Issa started to walk toward the short flight of steps leading to the keep entrance, but Morgan put a hand on her shoulder.

"I knew you'd say that, but let's just think for a minute—that Drillmaster guy was pretty tough. I got a lucky kill shot on him, but we could be in trouble if things get progressively harder. That guy was cutting the cobblestones from twenty feet away!" Issa didn't reply to him; rather, she just looked back at him and stared pointedly. "Alright. I get it. No guts, no glory, eh?" She smiled and turned to keep walking, and Morgan followed after.

The stairs were clean and free of debris, and the large wooden doors looked sturdy and well-maintained. It was a stark contrast to the ruined keep they'd explored outside the pocket world of the dungeon. Before trying to open the door, he and Issa both readied their swords. Morgan wielded his Umbral Razor just because it was more familiar to him, and he didn't know what to expect. Anticipating the keep to be dark, he maintained his Azure Sight spell, and then he carefully pulled on the large brass handle of the right-side door.

The foyer of the keep was the same general shape as the ruined version in the outside world, but the flagstones were polished to a sheen, and the walls were painted and in good repair. Art hung on the walls, and the wooden stairway was oiled and reflected the flickering lights mounted on the walls in ten-foot intervals. As soon as Morgan stepped through the doorway, two individuals who had been standing to either side of the far doorway started marching toward him, drawing broadswords. They wore chain-mail shirts and walked with the grace of professional fighters. Both were Ardeni men with close-cropped colorful hair, and neither offered any conversation.

Morgan stepped to the right, making room for Issa, and he felt her hand on his shoulder. A moment later, a surge of Energy flooded him, and, not waiting for an invitation, he used Hollow Charge to launch himself at the right-hand guard. His first slash was met with a shimmering wall of Energy that seemed to be projected from the guard's sword, so he cautiously sidestepped and continued to test the guard's defenses. Issa was keeping the other guard busy, so Morgan poured everything he had into a series of feints and slashes, making the most of Issa's haste. The shimmering barrier wasn't permanent, and, after several strikes, it wavered, and the guard was forced to use his blade to parry. Morgan wanted to keep pressing with just sword strikes, rather than using his Energy abilities, as long as the fight was in control because he wanted to improve his skill level.

After watching Issa in the courtyard melee, he'd seen that she was definitely on the verge of breaking through to advanced, displaying a lot more speed and control with her sword than he did. Rather than being bothered by it, Morgan felt inspired to improve, and so he worked to beat his opponent with his blade alone. It wasn't a trivial feat—the guard was better than any of the courtyard combatants other than the Drillmaster. When his haste wore off, he had to work very hard to find an opening in the Ardeni guard, exchanging parries, feints, and maneuvering his feet in order to find a pattern to exploit. After what felt like a very long time but was probably only two minutes or so, he saw that the guard tended to over-extend when he lunged at Morgan's left side. Morgan drew him into another lunge by feigning a stumble to his right, but, just as the guard went for it, Morgan pivoted on his leading foot, swiveling his body out of the way and chopping his long blade toward the extended arms of his foe. He took the guard's hand off at the wrist, and his blade clattered to the ground amid a shower of faintly glowing crimson blood.

The eeriest thing about the whole fight had been the silence of the Ardeni guardsman, continuing even after Morgan chopped off his hand. The guard's mouth opened in a silent wail, but his remaining hand reached for a long poniard at his waist, so Morgan lunged, and the angled point of his sword split the chain mail and slipped into the guard's chest. While his opponent crumpled, Morgan quickly scanned for Issa and saw that she was, once again, proving that speed and skill trumped size. The guard she'd been fighting was sluggish and bright; luminous blood soaked the tops of his trousers, running out from beneath his chain mail; Issa must have stabbed him several times. He only watched for a couple of seconds before Issa delivered a killing blow, taking advantage of the guard's slow movements and slipping inside his guard to drive her rapier up under his chin.

The guards' bodies dissolved into mist as motes of Energy flooded into Morgan and Issa. She looked at Morgan and said, "Level!"

"Nice! Seventeen now?" She nodded, looking around the room.

"No chest this time."

"Yeah, I think we're going to have to fight harder than that for chests. Did you notice nothing came to interfere with the fight again?"

"Yes, I figured that's why you were toying with your opponent!"

"I wasn't toying with him! I was trying to improve my swordplay." Morgan walked toward the center of the room. "Well? Into the main hall or up the stairs and explore a little first?"

"Or through this door on the left?" Issa pointed, and Morgan realized there was a smaller door he'd missed between two columns.

"Let's explore. I have a feeling there's a big fight waiting in the central hall." He walked past her to the smaller door on the left side of the room, opposite the stairs, and, with the utmost care to be quiet, he pushed it open.

❦ OLIVIA ❧

The first few days of academy classes went by in a blur for Olivia. Her favorite part of the day was during the morning when she and her cohort would find a quiet place in the first-year library to study runes. The library, even the limited section for first-year students, was a magnificent place with an ambiance of gravitas that made Olivia feel special just for sitting in it. The bookcases were massive and ornate, tall rolling ladders affixed to each bank. The tables and furniture were richly stained hardwoods and leather, and fascinating artwork from portraits to battle scenes could be found in every nook and cranny.

By the third day, Olivia had made a significant dent in the runes, proving that she could both write and define more than half of them when quizzed by her classmates. None of the others could match her, though Shani came close. Adaida was miffed that Shani beat her on the practice quiz, but the most explosively frustrated reaction came from a surprising source—Veena. "This is rot! If you have a trick you're not sharing, you need to come clean with it, Olivia!"

"I don't have a trick, Veena. I've always been good at memorizing. If you think I'm bad, you should have met my sophomore student advisor—he had an eidetic memory." Veena had stared at Olivia and then packed up her books and walked out of the library. The following day, when they went to study, Veena had gone off by herself. Hanwol had laughed it off, saying that Veena was too used to being the top student. Aside from that minor conflict, Veena seemed amiable enough during their other classes and in the dormitory that afternoon, so no one pressed the issue when she said she just wanted to study runes in peace.

Olivia noticed something strange during her rune study: some of the runes looked familiar to her, though she couldn't place them. At first, she thought they were runes she'd seen on System items like the Colony Stone, reward chests, or skill scrolls. When she brought it up, her classmates said that wouldn't be possible because the System used a set of runes that were different from the ones taught at the academy. This opened a whole other can of worms—how many sets of enchanting runes existed? None of her classmates knew the answer. Olivia wracked her brain for possible sources of her sense of familiarity with some of the runes. Then a dim recollection stirred in her mind: Bronwyn handing her a tapestry with a colorful ringed design.

She'd had that thought in the middle of physical education on the fourth day. They were practicing falls; as strange as that sounded, Commander Grobak insisted that knowing how to fall without hurting yourself was vital to fighting and surviving combat. She grunted as she landed on her butt and back, slapping her free arm out to absorb the impact, Rald's firm grip on her other wrist. The memory flashed into her mind as she hit the mat, and she resolved to dig the tapestry out of her satchel when she got back to the dormitory.

After their "Combat practice," the cohort hustled to the cafeteria, grabbed a tray of hot food, and then made their way back to their dorm. They didn't stick around to eat or socialize—too many pressures were on their minds because of the competition, and they'd agreed to spend as much time as possible studying or preparing. Olivia thought over her other classes as she walked back to the dorm with the others.

Things were going very well in her spellcraft class. On her second day, Alyss spent some time evaluating each student and assigned them a first-month project that they'd be evaluated on. She'd seemed to like Olivia right away, asking her about her experience with spells and if she'd ever modified any. Olivia hadn't seen any reason to dissemble, so she'd told her about the two spells she'd created. They were talking at the front table, and Alyss had assured her that their conversation was private; even so, Olivia had looked around nervously when she finished describing her exploits. Alyss had smiled and asked her about her affinities. Then she'd assigned her what seemed like a challenging, but exciting, task: She was to read chapters twelve through fourteen of her spellcraft text about meta-elements, and then she had to create a spell that used one of them.

The class was working through the text chapter by chapter, and they were still on the first one, so Olivia had been excited to dig into something more advanced. It turned out that meta-elements existed in a state "Beyond" the primary four elements. Some were created by applying attuned Energy through a catalyst, and others were made via a combination of more than one element in a specific ratio. That was as far as Olivia had read so far; she knew she'd need to figure it out before the month was up, but she figured she had to prioritize, and some of her deadlines were coming up much more quickly.

Alchemy had been very easy so far. They were assigned some pages to read each day, professor Ghall demonstrated a simple recipe, and they had to replicate it. So far, they hadn't had to make anything with more than three ingredients, the only tricky part being the application of Energy at the correct times and in the right amounts. Olivia never had any issue with this; it surprised her that so many students did. Several gaseous expulsions had required the students to move out into the open air while it cleared. Each time this happened, Ghall looked annoyed but resigned, and made notes on her ever-present clipboard.

Her best class by far was Cultivation and Core Development. On the second day, she sat in front of an altar with burning incense that smelled vaguely like sandalwood and began channeling her cultivation drill. She remembered what Sange had told her to do, and she'd thought about it all night. While she ran through her drill this time, she let her senses drift, and she focused on the flaming tip of the incense. Ever so slowly, she became aware of the fire Energy hovering around that orange ember, and she began to pull it toward her while she ran through her drill. Soon, she had a steady, impossibly fine thread of fire-attuned Energy streaming into her through the channel at her belly button, flowing directly into her Core with each cycle. Sange had been thrilled. After that, she found it easier to notice the differently attuned Energy around her, at least those Energies that matched her affinities. On the third day of class, she'd leveled her Core, and Sange had crowed about it, resulting in Olivia receiving some glares from the other members of her cohort.

They arrived back at the dorm, cutting Olivia's reminiscing short, and she flopped down on her bed with a loud sigh. "I'm so sore! Why on earth do we need to slam each other onto the mats over and over and over?"

"If you don't learn to fall, then when we start throwing each other around for real, you're going to break something." Rald shrugged and moved to the far end of the oblong room, where he dropped down and started doing push-ups.

"Oh, Matron! Who are you trying to impress?" Shani had a look of utter disgust on her face as she watched Rald pumping up and down.

"What? Grobak, of course! I don't stand a chance to win points in most of the classes, but I know how to get stronger, and I'm going to damn well do it." Olivia laughed and looked around the dorm to see what everyone else was doing. Veena sat on her bed staring at her enchantment text, and Adaida and Hanwol had taken a seat by the window and were quizzing each other with flashcards. She shrugged and put a hand into her satchel, "Looking" around at the contents. She found the neatly folded tapestry and pulled it out.

The conversation among her peers faded into the background while she stared at the exposed flap of the folded cloth. Even on this relatively small portion of the tapestry, she could make out dozens of runes in the faded design. Some were very similar to those she'd been studying, though they were all slightly different. She wondered if this tapestry had a foreign runic language on it, but one that was close to her textbook runes. Her mind wrestled with various ideas, and the truth she had to accept was that she just knew too little about runes and enchanting to understand the implications. She'd have to set this aside for now, but something told her it was significant. Very carefully, she slipped the tapestry back into her satchel.

Laying back with a sigh on her pillow, Olivia struggled with her desire to close her eyes and get a long night of sleep; she had to get some more studying done if she was going to ace that test in a few days. She'd prioritized learning the runes because that was her first tangible assessment that she knew about. She was aware that the other professors were constantly watching her and the other students, making little evaluations day by day. Still, this test was going to be a serious score, and she'd have an honest idea of her standing with the other students after it.

Idly, Olivia rubbed at her forehead, and she thought she could feel a tiny nodule of bone that stood out from the rest of her smooth brow. An image of a stone flashing in front of her eyes and then everything going dark made her wince. She'd not said a word to Gwinna since that first day, and she didn't think the other girl even acknowledged her existence. Olivia tried to shrug it off, but she thought of that stone cracking into her head and how the nurse said she was lucky she didn't die. Had that bitch actually been trying to kill her, or was she just careless? Olivia was good at burying things, good at concentrating on other thoughts when something bothered her, but there were times when those thoughts would bubble up, and right now, she was having a hard time not feeling very alone and vulnerable.

She was the only human in a thousand miles, as far as she knew. While everyone in her cohort was friendly, they were also different and tended to do their own things when they weren't actively moving around together or studying as a group. She wished she could travel quickly and easily back to the colony. She'd love to sit in the tavern and listen to other humans gossip and maybe drink a few cups of mead with Bronwyn.

She wondered how Bronwyn was doing—had she settled things with the Urghat? Did she still have one of their Underclaw titles? Olivia felt like Bronwyn had to be doing okay—like she'd know somehow if Bronwyn weren't, but she also knew that was silly. Bronwyn could be dead for all she knew. That idea caused her heart to lurch for a moment, and Olivia had to come to grips with the notion that Bronwyn and Morgan were the only people in this world whom she'd grown really familiar with. What would she do if they were dead when she returned to the colony? Her mind kept spinning for a while, then Olivia forcefully shut down the self-destructive tailspin of emotions and pulled out her enchanting textbook.

When the group made their way to the library the next morning, Veena wandered off alone, and Olivia almost followed after her. Adaida saw her looking in the direction Veena had gone and said, "She's moody. If you go after her, you'll either irritate her or encourage this behavior. Best to just let things go; the test is Monday, and then she'll either get over it or not." Olivia almost argued with Adaida, but she just sighed and nodded. She sat in one of the luxurious leather chairs at the study table and pulled out the flashcards she'd made herself.

"Anyone wanna take turns quizzing?" She looked around the table, but Rald and Hanwol had already paired up, Shani and Adaida were slow to respond, and Olivia could take a hint. "No worries, I'll just quiz myself for a while."

"Why don't you come study with me for a while?" Olivia spun around to find the source of the invitation and saw Sarice had walked up behind her. "My cohort members aren't taking this quiz as seriously as I'd like, and I could use a partner for a while; the test is tomorrow, after all." Olivia looked back at her group: Hanwol and Rald hadn't even looked up, and Adaida and Shani shot her looks that she was having difficulty interpreting. Were they warning her off? Adaida had a raised eyebrow and a bit of a grin, and Shani just had a frown on her face. Olivia opened her mouth to speak, but Shani cut her off.

"Trying to poach one of our best?"

"What do you mean?" Sarice glared at Shani.

"For next year. Trying to get her to skip up to Gold?"

"I hadn't thought of that, no. I'm just trying to get through tomorrow. What do you care? The test is individual, not cohort-based."

"Whatever. Do what you want, Olivia." Shani turned back down to her book, dismissing the matter. Olivia had a waspish retort on her tongue, something about not asking for permission, but she bit it back. Her face red and a stormcloud behind her eyes, she stood up and nodded to Sarice. Sarice, for her part, managed to keep her smile almost imperceptible, and she turned and walked a short way to a couch situated under a tall, narrow window. She and Olivia sat down next to each other, and Olivia scooted sideways a bit so she could look at Sarice more easily.

"I don't mind studying with you on something like this, but I'm not going to do anything to harm my cohort." Olivia wanted to set the ground rules as clearly as possible.

"I know that, silly. I wouldn't expect you to. I'm not going to betray my cohort, either!" Sarice's smile was really something. Unlike the Ardeni and Shadeni, the Ghelli had very human-like teeth, and her whole face lit up with warmth when her lips curled in the friendly expression. "Tell me, Olivia, are all humans as interesting looking as you? Your dark hair and light eyes are quite a contrast. You seem a lot like us Ghelli, but you're sturdy like an Ardeni, and, of course, you don't have wings. I wonder what other differences there are?" At first, Olivia was taken aback by her forwardness, but the scientist in her was pleased.

"Oh, I'm sure there are more differences, but I'm amazed that so many races on this world are so similar to humans. Bipedal, mammalian, you get the idea. Though, I suppose, having wings sets you quite apart. Can I ask, are you able to fly with them?" Sarice stared at her for a moment before responding, and Olivia wondered if she'd gone too far. Then she wondered if it was her lack of response to the compliments that had baffled the girl or the fact that she hadn't returned them. Olivia's sense of awkwardness began to grow, and she could feel some heat in her cheeks; then, Sarice cleared her throat and spoke.

"Well, not until I evolve my race quite a lot. Then I could, yes. Right now, the best I can hope for is to slow my fall if I jump off some high point." Sarice looked over her shoulder at one of her shimmering wings with a bit of a wistful sigh.

"Well, they're beautiful, in any case." Olivia smiled at the way Sarice's face lit up at the compliment. That had definitely been the problem earlier; she'd wanted a return compliment.

"You're very sweet, Olivia. Well? Shall we see what we know about these runes? Tomorrow's the big day." Sarice gestured toward the stack of flashcards Olivia had gripped in her hand.

"Yeah, of course. Let's go." She glanced to her right at the table where her group was sitting and saw that they all seemed engrossed in their own studies, all but Shani. Shani was staring right at Olivia, and her face didn't look happy.

BRONWYN

"I will not let her manipulate me!" Bronwyn hissed to herself as she followed the little fairy guiding her back to the throne room. "I will not be emotional!" She felt very clear-headed today, and when she thought about the events that had transpired yesterday following her touching Hops's little crystal coin, it all seemed like a blurry dream. She could remember what the queen had said to her, but it didn't feel like it could have really happened the way she remembered. Still, here she was, on her way back to speak to the mystical fairy queen. She followed the little flitting, sparkling fairy, a different one from yesterday, through the hallways carpeted in soft bark and grass and through chambers with gardens and flowing streams until she saw the tall, elf-like guards, and realized the fairy had brought her to the front doors of the throne room.

The guards didn't even look at her, and the doors were already slightly open, so Bronwyn followed the fairy through the tall, narrow opening and into the big pillar-lined hall again. She zeroed in on the queen, sitting on her flower-covered throne, and started marching toward her, all the while admonishing herself to keep it together. As she drew near, she felt the queen's aura again, and the warmth and happiness that came with it. She felt her stress and worries start to drift away, and she said, perhaps a bit too loudly, "Can you please stop that?" The rush of positivity wavered and then pulled back a little as the queen leaned forward to speak.

"I'm sorry, child. I've reined in my aura now; is that better?" It was better, but it was still there. Perhaps it was the best Bronwyn could hope for. At least, she felt like she could speak her mind.

"I'm not trying to be rude, but I want to be able to think about things without breaking into tears, okay?"

"I wouldn't have it any other way. As you grow more accustomed to my presence and your own power grows, my aura will affect you less and less. Unless I want it to, that is." A slight smile touched the queen's lips. "Have you considered my proposal?"

"I have, and I'd like to talk with you a bit more before making up my mind."
"Of course; I have some time. What can I say to assuage your doubts?"
"Is there any way you can make me believe that you won't lie to me?"
"Well, I can make you believe almost anything. The fact that I don't want to do so should give you some comfort and confidence in my words. I can also tell you that the fae don't lie. We often withhold the truth or give half-answers, but we do not lie."

"Is that true? What about Hops? He pretended to be a little squirrel turtle; isn't that sort of a lie? If I knew he was a fae man, I wouldn't have taken a bath with him!"

"You make a good point, Bronwyn. Fae have some leeway involved with the truth in indirect circumstances. Coraignon didn't lie to you; he simply never showed you his true self. Had you somehow asked him if he were hiding his true form, he would have told you the truth or simply not answered."

"So, if I ask you a direct question, you won't lie to me?"
"That's right."
"Are you trying to trick me, somehow?" The queen's face remained impassive, and she didn't hesitate for even a second.
"No."
"Is it in my best interest to accept your offer?"
"I can't answer that, but not because I want to lie to you; I don't know the answer. I think what I have to offer you is to your benefit. I think you'll thrive working with the Summer Court, but even someone as old as I cannot see the future. Well, aside from glimpses that I don't necessarily ask for."
"Are you at war with the Winter Court? Will I be in danger from them?"
"Yes, I suppose our relationship could be described as a war. To me, it's more of a constant struggle, but it can and has escalated to violence many times. You certainly will become a target for their agents should you don the mantle of the Summer Court. Do you have more questions?"
"Yes, thank you for answering so many. Can you tell me how Energy was taken away from Earth?"
"I will give you a very brief primer on what is a story that could fill a hundred volumes: The Summer Court works to foster the spread of Energy, and we grow stronger, indirectly, through the people and creatures that thrive on Energy-rich worlds. The Winter Court tries to grow their power by taking the Energy directly, stealing it away from other lands, and siphoning it into their Winter Realms. We battled for tens of thousands of years on Earth, and the Winter Court won." Some sadness slipped through into the queen's aura before she caught it, and Bronwyn felt an icy grip on her heart and nearly sobbed aloud. It was gone in a second, but not before Bronwyn sensed the depth of the Queen's sorrow at the losses she suffered on Earth. Bronwyn wanted to help

her. She wanted to crawl up on that dais, wrap her arms around the queen, and swear that she'd do anything to help make things right. She even took a small step forward but shook her head and cleared her throat.

"Are you doing that on purpose? Influencing me with emotions?"

"No, Bronwyn, that was my mistake again. I've not dealt with humans in a long while, and I forget how deeply you feel. Fae are different; we have feelings, but they are things we can look at and contemplate. They don't rule us."

"If I become one of your agents, will I still be able to help my people? Will I have free will?"

"You'll most definitely be able to help your people! That's what I want for you! I want humanity to thrive on Fanwath because you're some of my favorite children and your gifts with Energy are nearly unrivaled among the younger races. I cannot properly explain my joy when I sensed you all on Fanwath. As for your free will: yes, you'll have autonomy, save for when I have given you an explicit task; you will feel pressure to complete missions for me. I promise you, though, and Bronwyn, I do not break promises, that I will never ask you to do something that causes your heart grief, and I will listen to your requests and always consider your well-being."

"I have one more question. If I agree to be your agent, will I ever be allowed to change my mind?" Bronwyn studied the queen's face as she asked her question, but the impossibly perfect visage gave nothing away.

"You will be able to remove the mantle of the Summer Court, but all that you've gained in my service will be taken from you."

"When you say 'mantle,' are you speaking figuratively, or is there something I'll actually be wearing?" The queen's lips spread into a genuine smile for the second time.

"I'm being figurative, child."

"Alright. I'm in. I like how I feel when I'm here, and I like that you want to see my people prosper. What do I need to do?" The queen stood up, her smile broadening, and she stepped down to stand in front of Bronwyn. She was imposingly tall, and the aura of power emanating from her made Bronwyn feel like she was standing next to a nuclear reactor.

"First, you must accept my mark, and then you must face the Trial of Summer, where your will and character will be tested." She reached forward and rested her right palm on top of Bronwyn's chest, over her heart. "Are you certain?" Bronwyn nodded, nervously biting her bottom lip. "Brace yourself, child." Bronwyn stiffened and stood up straight, pulling her shoulders back. She felt warmth radiate out of the queen's hand; at first, it was pleasant and even comforted Bronwyn, then it grew hotter, and she felt it spear through her like a knife. She gasped but stood still, and the pain was gone as quickly as it started.

Congratulations! You have earned the title "Agent of Summer." This is a transient title. You have the favor of the Summer Queen and access to areas of the Summer Realms where outsiders are forbidden.

The queen hissed and stepped back, "Infernal System! Even here, it puts information in your head. It rides you like a parasite, leeching some Energy from everything you do. I'd help you be rid of it, but I think we can learn from your connection to it, at least for now."

"Before the System, would I have known what you just did to me?"

"No, but I would have explained it. My mark," she pulled the collar of Bronwyn's shirt down enough to expose the flesh over her left breast. She gestured to a mark, something like a tattoo, depicting a glittering silver circle adorned with lifelike yellow and white flowers, "Will give you access to areas of the Realms that are forbidden to the non-Fae. It also serves as proof of my favor should the denizens within the Realms challenge you."

"Okay," Bronwyn looked at the mark, admiring how the silvery ring seemed to move in a circle on her flesh and how the flowers looked so real that she almost thought she could pluck one. She reluctantly pulled her collar up and fastened the button that had come loose.

"Now, are you ready to face the Trial of Summer? I know the System helped you form a Core, but I think you might find something greater if you make your way through."

"What do I need to do?"

"You'll need to earn three blessings and then make your way to one of the Summer sources. I can't tell you more, child. I'm sorry." Bronwyn just nodded, and the queen turned and held out a hand; a brilliant oval of light appeared in the air, and through it, Bronwyn could see a sunny glade. "Step through, child of Summer." Unable to think of anything else she should say, Bronwyn straightened her back and stepped through the shimmering opening. Her foot landed on soft grass, and when she set down her other foot, the portal was gone.

The glade was bright and surrounded by young, skinny trees with yellow and gray speckled bark. A small hill rose on the far side, and a lightning-struck tree stood there, still tall and mighty looking but split with a dark, black opening at its center. Something urged Bronwyn to approach the tree and examine the hollow.

She trudged up the slight slope, realizing as she went that it was further than her eyes had led her to believe. By the time she'd come to the crest, the tree had grown in her perspective to a true giant, a fallen patriarch of the forest. Whatever mighty lightning strike that had torn the trunk in two had blackened the edges and opened the earth, creating a tunnel that descended into the loamy soil. Bronwyn knew she was expected to go within, so she took out her old light stone and hung the chain around her neck, activating it so that a pool of white-yellow light moved with her into the darkness.

It smelled like bark, charcoal, and damp soil, and the ground was soft and springy under her feet. The tunnel had a gentle slope, but it meandered from side to side so that she wasn't ever able to see more than a few feet ahead of her. Just as it started to widen, Bronwyn saw a junction up ahead, and she began to hear something that reminded her of when she used to lay in her bed on a Saturday morning and the apartment maintenance crew would cut the grass and trim the hedges. It was a buzzing, droning sound, but it seemed to be getting louder. She moved to the intersection of tunnels, and the sound grew in volume and intensity. Not knowing what to expect, Bronwyn cast her Stone Warding spell, covering her arms in a thin layer of protective stone, and holding them in front of her while she slowly turned around, looking for what was creating the racket.

The buzzing and humming grew to such intensity that the ground began to vibrate and loose dirt and pebbles fell from the ceiling. Bronwyn thought about turning and running out of the tunnel when a horde of crawling and flying insects surged around the bend to her left and were upon her. They were larger than any insects she'd ever seen, from ants the size of rats to flying bees that looked like small dogs. She cried out in alarm, using her Stone Fists to strike out at the swarm, but they were innumerable, and the few she smashed were replaced by ten others.

She pushed Energy into her Stone Warding, trying to cover her entire body, and she managed to avoid their stings and bites for a while. Still, no matter how she struggled and surged, pushing and jumping, she couldn't get out of the swarm and, eventually, her Energy ran so low that she couldn't maintain her armor, and the stings started to land on her flesh. She cried out as the burning toxins from the bee-like flying creatures coursed into her veins, and she veritably vibrated with pain as the crawling, ant-like bugs began to bite her legs and then crawled upon their companions to lay into her back and arms.

Bronwyn writhed under the vibrating, poking, buzzing, biting, crawling, stinging swarm, trying to scream in agony but unable to find her voice. When the pain started to fade, and her body felt numb, she thought she had died. She lay there for a while, her face in the bark dust, moss, and dirt at the bottom of the tunnel. Then she realized the buzzing was gone; it was silent. Was she dead? She still couldn't move, but she thought she could feel herself breathing when she concentrated.

It felt like an eternity later when she felt a tingling itch at the tip of her left pinky. Ever so slowly, the tingling and itching sensation started up on her other extremities and spread through her limbs. When Bronwyn could turn her head and open her eyes, she found herself lying in the tunnel, completely alone and covered with swollen, itchy bites and stings. When she was finally able to scoot herself up onto her butt and lean against the wall, a System message appeared in her vision:

Congratulations! You have earned the feat: "Blessing of the Swarm." You are now far more resistant to natural toxins.

MORGAN

Morgan rifled through the bookcase, trying to figure out if any of the volumes were worth anything. He and Issa were in a room that must have been officer or instructor quarters. They'd had to fight a shimmering, luminescent man wearing ghostly pajamas and wielding a longsword with deadly skill. They'd been able to take him easily enough, two on one, but he'd definitely known how to fight, leaping out of his bed and striking at them with alarming deftness. Morgan and Issa had both gained another level and improved their coordination with each other a great deal over the last several hours. Morgan had switched back to his estoc once they'd gotten into closer hallways, using its piercing, thrusting nature to much greater effect in the tight spaces than he would have been able to with his long, cleaving sword.

They'd fought maybe a dozen "Students" in the hallways and barracks or dormitories, and he and Issa had put together some very effective strategies for quick victories against solo enemies, which had made up the majority of their encounters. Issa would Haste herself and take their opponent's flank, and they'd take turns punching holes in their enemies. Stronger opponents or small groups of enemies were a bit trickier, but they'd been up to the task so far; the only spell Morgan had used regularly was Vortex Lance, always saving his Energy Drain for an emergency that hadn't yet come. His Vortex Lance was getting faster and more accurate, and he wondered if it would evolve out of its basic form soon.

"These books don't seem like anything special, but I'm going to take them anyway. I have plenty of room in my pouch, and my library needs content!" He scooped the books into his pouch, and Issa snorted, digging around in the nightstand near the vanquished officer's bed.

"Nothing much here—some sort of prayer necklace, but I feel bad taking something like that. It doesn't seem valuable anyway." She closed the drawer, and they moved back into the hallway. This had been the last door in the long corridor filled with a score of doors leading to sleeping quarters. So far, they'd gotten a lot of fighting experience but very little loot—a few pouches of

Energy beads, some nice knives, books of questionable value, and quite a few pieces of art. They hadn't run into any "Boss" type foes like the drillmaster and no reward chests. "We should go back to that junction; I think the other direction leads to a mess hall and kitchen."

"Yeah, let's go." Morgan led the way back toward the hallway they hadn't explored. Issa said she remembered seeing chimneys outside in that direction and guessed that it was where the kitchens would be. The way the encounters seemed scripted, in that no reinforcements ever came, and once they cleared an area, it stayed clear, made it impossible to feel like the place was "Real" for Morgan.

The students and instructors they fought never spoke and seemed a lot less tangible than the people waiting outside the keep had been. Morgan wondered what the basis for these enemies was—did they come from the mind of the Swordmaster? What did it say about the Swordmaster that the people outside were so much more fleshed out than the students and instructors inside? He supposed that wasn't totally true—the drillmaster had been quite substantial. Morgan theorized that the more substantial "Ghosts" in this place held a more prominent spot in the Swordmaster's memories. Maybe those people outside were people he'd had duels with or known closely in his life. Perhaps these students were just some of the thousands that came through his citadel, and he didn't get to know many of them.

They walked quietly up the hallway toward the double wooden doors that they had yet to explore through. Morgan held his ear to the door, but he couldn't hear anything, which wasn't surprising. The enemies they'd managed to surprise, while they might be going through some motions of their old lives, were very quiet about it, never speaking. He gripped the door handle and gently depressed the latch, and pulled it open an inch to peek through. Six long, wooden tables filled a low-ceilinged hall. They were all empty except the farthest one from the door, where a woman sat, silently dipping a spoon into a large bowl and lifting the contents to her lips. She was a Shadeni with long black hair and dark, furrowed brows. Morgan had never seen someone look so angry while eating.

"One woman sitting at the far end of the room," he said softly, closing the door and looking at Issa. She nodded and shrugged. Morgan didn't know what he'd expected; they weren't exactly trying to sneak past encounters, so he shrugged also and pulled the door open. They stepped into the mess hall, and the Shadeni woman sat up straight, shoving her bowl away from herself, glaring at Morgan and Issa through narrowed eyes.

"Intruders? This far into the keep? So, you found the students wanting, hmm? Perhaps Swordmistress Jinna can regain the honor of the school." One moment she was sitting and speaking in clipped, sharp words, and then she was standing with two short, narrow swords in her hands. What bothered Morgan was that he hadn't seen her move or even heard the chair scoot back. Issa flinched, and he heard and felt her Battle Chant start to pour forth from her. "Two fledglings, hmm? No matter, I've faced worse odds."

The woman's swords weren't long, but her limbs were. She had to be a match for Morgan in height, though she was far more lithe. She wore a black leather vest, but her pants were as bright red as her flesh, and at first, Morgan thought she wasn't wearing any—talk about distracting. He shook his head and gripped Heartspark in a short guard, the pommel near his hip, the blade held out and up between him and the woman who'd called herself Jinna. Issa slowly circled to the left, hoping to flank Jinna, as they had so many opponents before.

Jinna glanced at Issa, then at Morgan, and then a half-smile quirked up one side of her mouth, exposing a single long canine. She hummed a strange, buzzing sound, and then Morgan was looking at three different exact copies of the original swordswoman. They all had that same smirk, and, at first, Morgan thought they were just mirror images—illusions. Then the one on the left jumped over the table and charged at Issa, and the other two darted toward him.

Morgan took several sidesteps away from Issa and began to channel Azure Burst—he wasn't going to hold back against such a foe. As the two Jinnas closed in on him, each trying to split his guard, he unleashed the burst, and they both reacted by bracing their two shortswords in front of them. Morgan's bubble of blue fire poured over and around them, upturning and blackening one of the tables, but the two swordswomen were unscathed.

"Fuck!" Morgan reached out with Energy Drain, feeling for the currents of Energy flowing within them, and almost had his body perforated by flurries of thrusts coming from both copies of Jinna. He swept his long estoc in an arc, trying to make room while grabbing hold of the Energy coursing through both of his opponents. He managed to drive the one on the left back, but the other got two hard stabs through after his sweeping parry passed her by. One sank into his side between two of his scales, and the other raked along the back of his neck. Morgan growled and yanked on the threads of Energy he'd grasped, and the two swordswomen wailed together, going pale and falling to the ground, writhing. Morgan looked to his left and saw that the other Jinna had pressed Issa back into the far corner and was landing blow after blow through her guard—she greatly outmatched even Issa's speed and skill.

Judging by the impact his Energy Drain had on the two Jinnas that had attacked him, Morgan thought they must be copies. He yanked even harder, willing his Core to spin and pull, and he felt the hot white Energy of the spell unwind and flow into him, repairing his flesh and completely dispelling the two copies. Morgan pointed his estoc at Jinna's back and began channeling

Vortex Lance as he stepped toward the two combatants. Three heartbeats later, he unleashed the spell, and the ringing, hissing report of the Energy bolt tearing through the air and slamming into her back echoed through the low-ceilinged hall. Jinna cried out and stumbled forward. Issa had seen Morgan's spell charging up, and she was ready. She stepped to the side and drove her rapier through Jinna's exposed flesh, just under her black leather vest. The blade dug a deep furrow, and as Jinna stumbled further, Issa yanked it sideways, eviscerating the swordswoman.

Issa fell back, leaning against the wall, clutching her stomach and panting. Her face was alarmingly devoid of color, her usual pale blue skin disturbingly missing the pigment. Morgan charged up to her and saw that crimson blood was leaking like a punctured soda bottle through her chain shirt and around her fingers. Just as he got there and pushed his hand against the wound, he felt the Energy stream into him from the vanquished Swordmistress. Issa exhaled heavily as the torrent of Energy poured into her. Some color came back into her cheeks, and the flow of blood slowed down.

"Fuck, Issa; I think she stabbed your abdominal artery. Drink this!" Morgan produced one of the Miracle Elixirs they'd gotten from the chest in the courtyard and pulled the cork with his teeth, putting the bottle to her lips. She drank it down, and Morgan immediately felt the heat under his palm as it went to work, finishing up the repairs to her flesh. Issa sighed heavily and relaxed against the wall.

"Morgan, everything was going black; I thought it was the end." Tears started to leak out of her eyes, and she took short, gasping breaths. Morgan pulled the bottom of her chain shirt up and looked at her stomach. She had a Y-shaped white scar, but there was no other evidence of the wound. He stood up and pulled her into a hug.

"Shh. You're alright. That was close, though—I didn't know she'd stabbed you that badly! I'm such an idiot! Why didn't I put Guard Ally on you?"

"She was so fast, Morgan! I didn't know it either. I felt a stinging punch and thought she'd just pierced my armor a little. She stabbed me a half-dozen times in a few seconds! Morgan, I was like a child before her!"

"Well, that's why we work as a team. Her copies were spell creations; when I pulled out their Energy, they just dissolved. She couldn't handle us both by herself." Morgan looked to where Jinna had fallen to see if she'd left anything behind. He was hoping to get a look at her swords, but they had disappeared along with her corpse. He walked toward the back of the room where she'd been sitting, pulling Issa along by the hand. She was still shaken but was coming back to herself. "Look, Issa! A chest on the table where she was sitting."

"Thank you, Ancestors! I didn't almost bleed out for nothing!" She managed a half-hearted smile, and Morgan squeezed her hand. They opened the chest in their usual manner; once again, there was no trap. This one was a bit smaller than the others and more square than rectangular. Otherwise, it had a similar design. Inside was a supple leather vest much like the one Swordmistress Jinna had been wearing. Morgan held it up, and though it might look alright on a man, he thought it would suit Issa more. The leather armor would fully cover her torso, with a high neck but no sleeves at all. It was wonderfully smooth and supple, and a true master had done the stitchwork. More impressive was the silky, peach-colored lining that was absolutely saturated with silvery, stitched runes.

Morgan helped Issa shrug out of her blood-stained, ripped chain-mail shirt. She made him turn around while she used a canteen and her old shirt to scrub the blood off her chest and belly. He found this rather endearing, considering he'd seen her naked plenty of times, so he dutifully studied the far wall while she cleaned up and slipped into her new vest. "Oh, this is amazing! It's so comfortable, and it has a lot of enchantments. It self-cleans and repairs; it hardens to absorb damage, and even constricts around wounds to staunch bleeding."

"Damn, almost like it was tailor-made to be exactly what you needed, eh?" Morgan looked at her in the tight leather vest, glad to see it didn't leave any vulnerable gaps at her waistline. "Well, either it's a lucky coincidence, or, like the scroll I got, it was made for you." He shrugged and looked into the chest. The only other item was a black, felt pouch about the size of his fist. Morgan lifted it out and realized it had a single heavy object within it. He opened the drawstring and revealed a crystal orb with swirling smoke and tiny specks of flickering light moving about within it. He immediately felt a pull from the orb, originating with a deep resonance in his Core. "What have we here?"

⚜ OLIVIA ⚜

Olivia's first weekend at the academy started with a tedious morning of lying in bed studying runes. When she woke up, she'd seen that Rald and the two Bogoli siblings were gone, and Shani was in the bathroom. Adaida was still breathing slow, deep breaths, even now, hours after dawn. Olivia smiled and kept writing runes over and over onto her notebook pages. She didn't know what the test would be like on Monday. Did they have such a thing as multiple-choice here? She wanted to prepare for the worst-case scenario—blank sheets of paper and a writing utensil.

She'd finished her second full run-through of all the runes when Adaida finally sat up and stretched, yawning hugely. "Where is everyone?"

"I don't know where Veena, Hanwol, and Rald are. Your sister said she was going for breakfast and shopping. I wasn't invited." Olivia cringed inwardly—why did she have to add that last bit? Even if it was true, she didn't have to let Adaida know that it bothered her that Shani hadn't asked her to come along.

"Huh, bitch could've woken me up. Is she still punishing you for fraternizing with the enemy?" Adaida sat on the edge of her bed, stretching and fluttering her dragonfly wings. Her thick hair was a tangled mess, and she smiled warmly at Olivia. "Don't let it bother you. She's always been way too competitive. She doesn't trust Sarice, though, and I have to admit, she might be right about her. Just be careful."

"Thanks. I don't know why I said that. I'm too old to be petulant. Hey, I'm ready for a break; you wanna go get some food?"

"Now you're talking! Let me run a brush through this mess and change my clothes."

"Sounds good!" Olivia sat up and got dressed while Adaida was in the bathroom. She made her bed and marveled at how easy it was to keep things clean when you had containers that could hold everything you own. When Adaida came out, dressed in her uniform gray robes with her shimmering chestnut hair pulled back into a neat plait, Olivia led the way through the hallways to the main concourse and outside the academy building. "Let's go somewhere off-campus. I'm tired of the cafeteria. I'll buy! I haven't spent hardly any of my stipend."

"I won't argue with that! I know a place you might like, an Ilyathi place near gate street."

"Um, please don't laugh, but what's an Ilyathi?" Olivia looked at Adaida with a sideways glance, hoping the question wasn't too ridiculous.

"Oh, don't worry—there aren't a lot of them around. They're another race on Fanwath. Kind of strange people, but they make good food. They're not much in the way of Energy users, though. I don't think I've seen any in the academy classes, even the second and third-year cohorts. Let's see—they're bipedal, but their skin is gray. They have black eyes, and the strangest thing is their arms—they have four, and they're more like tentacles than arms. You know what I mean?"

Olivia's face had blanched a little at the description, and she said, "Are they related to Yovashi?"

"Oh, you know about Yovashi? That's surprising—they're quite rare these days. Hmm, I don't know about related, but yes, they come from the same origin world. The Ilyathi are quite peaceful, though, so don't get worried; they're nothing like the spooky stories people tell their kids about the Yovashi."

"Okay, that's a relief." Olivia decided not to get into her story about the Yovashi she'd met; it just didn't feel right to bring it up on this sunny day walking to lunch with a new friend. If she were being honest with herself, Olivia thought, she'd admit that she just didn't want to think about it and explain her scar and everything else that came up with the topic of the Yovashi.

She followed Adaida along the busy sidewalk, marveling at the colorful crowds of various types of people. She admired the different kinds of clothing on display, the animals and carts, and the smells coming from food stands and out of homes and shops; everything seemed brighter and more vivid under the bright sun today. Perhaps it was the fact that it was Saturday and her first day at the academy without any explicit obligations. That was another odd thing she hadn't really put any thought into—the fact that there were seven days in the week, and the System had integrated her words for them seamlessly with the words the other races apparently used. It was very convenient, but it felt strange to be on an alien world with different races of people talking about weekends and a test coming up on Monday.

Adaida and Olivia sat at a small table outside the shop where a gray-skinned Ilyathi prepared several types of soup. The soup that Adaida talked Olivia into was much like a bowl of pho she'd had while attending a seminar in Seattle. The noodles were a little crunchy, and they had a green tint to them, but they were tasty. The broth was rich and aromatic, and the fresh veggies and seasoned meat settled in her stomach nicely. The Ilyathi woman who served them was a lot different from a Yovashi. Still, she shared the Yovashi's smooth, expressionless facial features, which made her seem more alien than most of the other races Olivia had met.

After they ate, they went back to the academy grounds and tracked Veena and Hanwol down in the library. They were sitting at their usual table studying their runes quietly, and didn't look up when Adaida and Olivia sat down. Olivia quietly took out her flashcards and reviewed them while waiting for the others to speak. "Glad you're allowing your brother to study with you, Veena," Adaida said, a twisted grin on her lips.

"Oh, I couldn't stop him. He followed me like a lost puppy when I left the dorm this morning." Veena spoke archly, staring at her text and not looking at Adaida when she responded.

"Someone has to keep an eye on you while you mope," Hanwol said, slapping her book closed.

"You little ass!" Veena picked up her book and moved to stand, but Olivia reached out and put a hand on her shoulder.

"Veena, stop this. Let's study together. Who cares if I'm better at memorizing runes than some of you? I'm going to be shit at other things!"

"Not so far! Practically the star of every class, aren't you?" Veena glared at Olivia, but then some shame crept into her eyes, and she looked down. "I sound like a little kid, don't I?"

"Yeah, you do. You should be glad Olivia is doing so well—she's in our cohort after all!" Adaida thumped Veena on the shoulder with the flat of her hand. Veena blew out an explosive sigh.

"Alright, let's have a practice test." And they did, drilling and practicing for the next several hours. Later in the afternoon, Rald wandered in, wearing his combat practice garb and covered with grass stains. He said he'd been practicing throws with other cohort members in the commons. Adaida acted upset that he didn't bring any of their cohort for the practice, but he shrugged, saying everyone had been asleep.

"Well, next time you plan something like that, let us know ahead of time. We need to practice as badly as anyone. Also, you might have benefited from some study with us on runes!" Adaida seemed to notice her scolding tone and looked down, trailing off her last words.

"Oh, well. Let's all agree to do some throws on the commons tomorrow morning, then study runes in the afternoon. I want our cohort to have a good showing on Monday!" Olivia hoped to steer the group into mutual cooperation, and it worked for the most part. Rald sat down, and they studied a bit more, then they made their way to the cafeteria for dinner. No one had seen Shani all day, but Adaida didn't seem worried about her. They'd finished eating and were lounging around the couches by the bay window in their dorm when she finally made an appearance.

"Where have you been all day?" Adaida asked, jumping up. Everyone else got quiet and watched for her response.

"Shopping and I met Bennis for dinner. What's it to you?"

"Well, you could let me know!" Adaida seemed a good deal more peeved than she'd let on earlier. Shani looked at Olivia and frowned.

"I told Olivia. Didn't she tell you?" Olivia sat up straighter and tried to force a smile at the mention of her name. It came out looking more crooked and strange than comfortable.

"Well, she did, but that doesn't excuse it. You should have talked to me. You know I would have liked to see Bennis." At the second mention of that name, Rald looked at the others and mouthed the word, a question mark on his face.

"He's our uncle. He works in a shop on the grounds," Shani said, looking at the rest of the group.

"Guys, please come sit down. I think we should talk," Olivia said, pointing to the couches. Shani shrugged and flopped down across from Olivia next to Hanwol, and Adaida sat down next to her. "Listen, we've been getting more and more agitated with each other and getting offended by silly, little things. Pressure does that to people, and we need to be aware of it and not let it mess with our group dynamic. We all want to succeed, right?"

"Yeah, of course," Rald said without hesitating. Most of the others nodded, though Shani had a frown on her face.

"Shani, I know I upset you when I went off to study with Sarice the other day. I'm sorry if that bothered you, but you need to trust that I wouldn't say or do anything to hurt our cohort. Don't you think I deserve the benefit of the doubt?"

"Hmm. I suppose. I think I took it out on you because I was mad at Veena for going off without us."

"Well, I'm not perfect! This whole thing is stressing me out. I not only have to take a test I'm worried about, but I have to compete with everyone." Veena crossed her arms and sat back, scowling.

"We all feel that way, Veena," Olivia said. "We *all* are figuring out how to cope with this pressure, and it's only going to get worse. Listen, I promise that I will always look out for my cohort no matter how well I do. Can we all agree that we need to help each other and stick together during these classes? I guarantee, one of the unspoken tests they are giving us is how well we deal with pressure." Olivia held her hand out, palm up. "Put your hands on mine, and let's make a vow." The other students looked at each other, perhaps taking the word "Vow" more seriously than Olivia had intended it, but then Rald reached into the circle and put his hand atop Olivia's. Then Hanwol and Adaida joined in.

Everyone looked at Shani and Veena, and Veena broke first, adding her hand to the pile. Finally, Shani sighed so heavily you'd think she had the weight of the world on her shoulders and put her hand atop Veena's. "I swear," said Olivia, "That I will always leverage my success to help my cohort and never seek personal gain if it comes to the detriment of my cohort."

"I swear the same," said Rald.

"No, say the words!" Adaida said, adding, "I swear always to work to help my cohort succeed and never seek personal gain at the expense of my cohort!" Rald nodded and repeated her words, and then the others all echoed the sentiment, some more exactly than others, but all in the right spirit. When their hands dropped, Veena sighed.

"I thought you were going to use a spell to bind us."

"No," Olivia said, "Friends shouldn't have to use spells to make promises to each other, right?" Everyone agreed, some nodding and others exclaiming, "Yeah!" They relaxed into their couches, laughing in released tension.

"We're going to make the best cohort this school has ever seen," Shani said quietly, looking directly at Olivia and smiling in a way that lit her eyes like Olivia hadn't ever noticed before.

The rest of the weekend went by very quickly. On Sunday, they did as planned—practicing their simple throws and falls on the grass in the commons and then studying runes all afternoon. Olivia had them down; she knew this, though she didn't rub it in. She took the opportunity to solidify her knowledge and make sure she could write out all of the runes from memory, defining each one. After Olivia, Veena and Shani scored the highest on their practice tests, with Adaida and Hanwol doing passably well. Rald was going to struggle to get more than half of them, though. Olivia just hoped their overall average would be high enough to keep their cohort competitive.

The morning of the test, Olivia and her cohort left early, ate a hearty breakfast, and avoided the other cohorts on their way to the Enchantment lab. They were surprised to find that Jade cohort had arrived before them and were all sitting outside the door, with noses in their texts. Professor Brince had yet to unlock the door. Olivia and her friends stood off to the side, some casting sideways dirty looks at the other cohort, especially toward Gwinna.

Olivia did her best not to look at the other girl, but it still threw her off a little. She didn't realize how much Gwinna had gotten under her skin. Was she afraid to make eye contact with her? Olivia bit the inside of her cheek and forced herself to look directly at her, staring with her icy blue and silver eyes. Gwinna's head jerked up, and she looked at Olivia, her own blue eyes glowing like dimly lit LEDs. They looked like gemstones—no whites or irises, just glowing blue gems. Olivia refused to look away, and Gwinna slowly let a smile spread on her face, and then she looked back to her book. Olivia had the distinct impression she'd just been dismissed, but she was proud of herself for not cowering and avoiding her glare.

The test was very similar to what Olivia had hypothesized as a worst-case scenario. They had to write each rune from memory, name it, and define it. They weren't writing on paper, though—they wrote their runes on a piece of slate with a delicate chalk stencil. As they finished each one, the slate seemed to absorb it, and then they'd write the next one. However, what Olivia hadn't anticipated was a brutal time limit; they had only one hour to write all the runes. The time limit was rather harsh because some of the runes were quite complex and took a while to draw perfectly. Olivia was suddenly grateful for the extra studying she'd done with her cohort, even after she'd mastered the runes.

She finished with a few minutes to spare, and Professor Brince came and collected her slate, indicating that she should leave the room. When she stood and looked around the classroom, she could see that there were a few other empty seats. She quietly walked out the door and stood in the sun, waiting for her cohort members. Olivia felt like she'd done very well. She had definitely defined and named all the runes correctly; her only doubt was whether she had been going too fast and drawn an incorrect line or swirl on the more complicated runes. She was going over them in her head when she felt a cool touch on her elbow. "Finished early, hmm?" Olivia started and looked to the familiar voice, seeing Sarice standing next to her.

"Oh, yes. How did you do?"

"Quite well, I'd say. Though the first one out was Gwinna." She gestured with her chin at a tree not far away, where Gwinna sat reading a book.

"Does speed factor into the score, you figure?"

"I don't know, to be honest." Sarice slowly pulled her hand back from Olivia's arm, and Olivia wasn't sure what to make of it. Was she flirting with her? Was she just a touchy-feely person? As she struggled to find something to say to keep the conversation flowing, the door crashed open, and a throng of students pushed out, saving Olivia from another socially awkward moment.

"Ancestors!" Rald yelled, walking up to Olivia and Sarice. "That test was roladii shit!"

"You didn't finish?" Sarice asked, looking up at the big Shadeni.

"Nah, I think I was getting close, though. Only a few of you finished! I guess we'll see soon enough; Brince said the scores would be posted within an hour before she kicked us out."

◈ OLIVIA ◈

Nervous buzzing filled the air as the students groused about the test or speculated on their possible scores. Olivia's cohort had pulled her away from Sarice when they came out; now, they stood off to the side of the building, waiting for the report. Veena had just finished a lengthy exposition about how unfair the test had been and that they should have been given more time. "How many did you finish before the time ran out?" Olivia directed her question to the group as a whole, not just Veena.

"Well over half, at least, but I already told you that. What about you others?" Rald responded loudly, not at all shy about reporting his, in Olivia's opinion, poor showing.

"I think I was nearly finished, but I lost count," Shani replied, shrugging.

"Same here," Veena sighed, a deep frown marring her smooth, white face paint.

"I finished right as she stopped us," Hanwol replied, "But I was rushing the last third or so. I think I made a lot of mistakes."

"I honestly don't know how I did," Adaida said. "It's all a blur to me. I think I did a good job on the runes I finished, but I have no idea how many I did. Didn't you all find that stencil amazingly accurate? I loved drawing with it!"

"Well, yeah, I guess so." Rald rubbed his chin contemplatively. "It would be nice to have a tool like that, wouldn't it?"

"I was going to ask you all if those types of things were rare. I'd love to have one of those slates!" Olivia looked around, but no one seemed to have an answer for her.

"Maybe we'll learn to make them." Adaida shrugged. Olivia was about to reply to her when the crowd of students nearest the door surged forward and started talking loudly. She followed closely behind Rald as he pushed his way through; even considering the gemstone cohorts, he was one of the largest students in the first-year class, and he plowed purposefully through. Soon they were standing at the front of the semi-circle of students looking at the notice hanging in the window.

	Cohorts Ranked by Average Score:
1	Jade
2	Ruby
3	Copper
4	Gold
5	Garnet
6	Silver
7	Bone
8	Stone
9	Wood

	Top Ten Ranked Students:
1	Gwinna Daneesh - 100% Olivia Bennet - 100%
3	Sarice Fwynal - 95%
4	Gan Bidash - 93%
5	Trinna ap'Ganno - 88%
6	Shani Rishal - 84%
7	Veena Fenash - 83%
8	Rolfo ap'Zahn - 80%
9	Drurl-dak - 74%
	Pirk Thillis - 71%

"Flames! Nice job, Olivia!" Rald turned and thumped her on the shoulder. Several of the students standing around also turned to look at her, and most of them didn't seem too friendly. Olivia saw another paper with a much longer list hanging beneath the first one. It had all of the other students' names and scores listed. She briefly scanned it, noting that Rald had scored a 62%, Hanwol a 68%, and Adaida had just missed the cut for the top ten at 70%. Having seen the results, Olivia started to back out of the press of students, noticing that most of her cohort were right behind her. When they got away from the main crowd, Olivia turned to see what they were saying.

"Not shabby at all! Third rank for our cohort! Bet they didn't expect that from Copper!" Rald seemed very happy.

"Yes, it puts us in a good position, competitively. Still, this is only the first test. There will be more challenges and tests in the next few weeks, so don't get too excited." Veena seemed to be handling the fact that she wasn't the top scorer much better than Olivia had expected, considering her behavior over the last few days.

"We can talk about it later, but now we have to hurry to Alchemy," Shani said, pointing to how the other cohorts were walking up the path to the main boulevard.

"Right, let's go, but congratulations, Olivia!" Adaida said, warmly squeezing Olivia's shoulder as she walked by.

"Yeah, can you believe it? First rank? Gwinna must have smoke coming out of her ears!" Hanwol was chuckling as he walked by.

"You know she does! Her family probably paid a fortune to get her that rune list outside of the Academy," Shani added, putting her arm over Olivia's shoulders and hustling her along the pathway with the others. Olivia enjoyed the camaraderie and wanted to bask in it. Still, she had a feeling in the back of her mind that reminded her all too much of college back on Earth—Now, she'd set expectations for herself, and she'd have to work very hard to keep up with them.

The rest of their classes were uneventful that day, but one exception: during Spellcrafting class, Alyss pulled Olivia aside and asked her about her progress with meta-elements. Olivia had tried to avoid mentioning her lack of progress by talking in generalities about the one chapter she'd read, but Alyss hadn't been impressed. She'd told Olivia that she expected big things from her, and she needed to remember to prioritize her strengths. "I hope you aren't wasting too much time on Enchanting and Alchemy or, stars forbid, physical education. You know that if you intend to be a master mage, Core Development and Spellcraft will be the most critical to your success. Those other pursuits are nice hobbies or good careers for the less gifted, but for you, they are distractions from the true keys to greatness," she'd said.

Olivia hadn't known how to respond, so she'd just nodded and said she'd redouble her efforts. It was true, Sange had told them all that Core Cultivation was crucial, and it made sense that Spellcrafting would be, too. However, she found it strange to learn that some professors didn't value the other classes as much. She wondered what Professor Brince would say if she asked her for an opinion. Regardless, she was done memorizing runes, for now, so she would turn to Spellcraft with more gusto.

When they finished combat training that afternoon, Olivia showered and changed back into her grays and then told her cohort that she wanted to go to the library to study Spellcraft. No one seemed interested in accompanying her. "Be sure to come back before they close the cafeteria—you don't want to be wandering the halls when there isn't any supervision," Hanwol said offhandedly, as she was getting ready to leave.

"What do you mean?"

"Well, the professors and staff are all pretty much off duty after that. Who knows what mischief someone like Gwinna might get up to if she ran into you in a dark hallway."

"Oh, hush, Hanwol!" Veena smacked him on top of his head.

"Well, he's got a point," Rald said. "That girl is a little insane."

"I'm sure I'll be fine, and I'm only going for a couple of hours. Thanks, everyone." Olivia left before more could be said on the topic. Gwinna did scare her; she couldn't deny it. The girl was freaky looking, and her personality was colder than a Noah unit. She startled herself with that thought—when was the last time she'd thought about her old life? How strange to think she used to have a Noah unit as a lab assistant on the Ark ship! The six months prior to launch, she'd spent more time with an AI bot than she had with any living person.

Her thoughts wandered while she traversed the halls, and it was with a bit of a surprise that she found herself walking into the library. There were a lot more students there in the evening than in the morning; most of the tables had at least one person sitting at them, though Olivia's favorite chair by one of the windows, a plush leather one with a footstool, was empty, so she quickly walked over to it. As she crossed the main library floor, she avoided making eye contact with the other students—she wasn't sure anyone even looked at her, but she didn't feel like having a conversation, and she also didn't want to see any hostile glares. Maybe she was being paranoid, but she definitely hadn't gotten a friendly vibe from other cohorts after the test results that morning. She sank into her chair and spared a glance around, noting, with a sigh of relief, that no one was even looking at her.

Olivia loved libraries, and she was instantly put into a studious mood when she pulled her Spellcraft text out of her ring and thumbed to one of the chapters Alyss had told her to study. She was reading a section about the combination of air-attuned Energy with water-attuned Energy when she had her first epiphany—she'd almost created a meta-element when she'd made her Stunning Ice Shards spell. She'd applied the quality of electricity from the air element to her ice spell. If she'd taken it a step further and combined the two elements with enough Energy and will, she'd have created arcfrost—a far more potent meta-element that was dozens of times faster in the air and carried a much more powerful charge.

She was reading about the methods for combining the elements, her mind racing with implications, when a man cleared his throat near her. Olivia looked up to see an individual unlike any she'd yet met. He was imposingly tall, much taller than Morgan, even—maybe seven feet tall, but narrow and all angles. His nose, brow, cheekbones, and jawline were sharp. His limbs seemed long, even for his height; his fingers, where he held them clutched in front of himself, were like jointed drumsticks—Olivia could imagine him wrapping his grip around a basketball as easily as she would a softball. His eyes were angular, and his sharp ears poked up through his thin, dark hair. When Olivia looked up at him, he smiled, revealing sharp teeth, and his dark eyes conveyed absolutely no warmth. Olivia sat up, pulling her feet off the footstool, and he gestured to it, "May I?"

"Um, sure." At first, Olivia thought he wanted to take the footstool, but he sat down on it, his long bony knees poking up almost to his chest. He was garbed in a fancy, tailored suit, not terribly different from what she'd imagine someone like Sherlock Holmes would have worn in the 1800s. It was cut from a very rich, deep navy cloth. His pale skin stood out from it in stark contrast. "May I help you?" she asked as he sat staring at her.

"Hello, Olivia. My name is Professor Somhairle. I've heard a great deal about you." His voice was deep and rich, and though his eyes were cold and deep, his smile and the warm timbre of his words put her at ease. She was about to respond with a simple hello, but then she cocked her head and thought about what he'd said.

"Hello, pardon me, but your name sounds almost like it comes from my world. It sounds almost, hmm, Irish?"

"Oh? What a fabulous coincidence. I'm afraid I'm not familiar with your world or the 'Irish,' but I can tell you that I'm part fae, and the fae are an elder race that has visited many, many worlds."

"Part fae? As in fairy?"

"Hmm, that word isn't familiar, but perhaps. My grandmother gave me this name, though I've never met her. I was raised by Ghelli relatives. Enough about me, though, Olivia. I wanted to let you know that I'm impressed by your progress so far. You've been quite the talk amongst my peers here at the academy; we're starting to expect some great things from you."

"Oh? I'm not all that special. Are you talking about the rune test? I'm just good at memorizing things."

"Oh, good, good, keep your archers hidden in the trees. I love it!" He winked knowingly at her, and Olivia felt embarrassed like he'd caught her in a lie, even though she was only trying to be modest, polite even.

"Oh, I'm not hiding anything," she said, a bit flustered by his proximity and the cloying scent of spice drifting into her nostrils from him. What was that? Rosemary and almond oil?

"Nevertheless, I've been impressed. I'm going to need a new apprentice in a year or two, and I think I'll be watching you closely. Keep it in mind, Olivia—I have a great deal that I can teach you, and I could even help you sooner if you get yourself into trouble. I'll give you one of my calling cards; simply channel some Energy into it if you'd like to chat. I'll be able to meet you here most evenings." He smiled again, and Olivia felt herself a bit more at ease as he reached two long fingers inside the breast of his beautiful vest and came out holding a dark blue paper card. It was about three inches by four and inscribed with silvery runes. He held it out to her, and Olivia reached for it instinctively, not wanting to be rude. It was cold between her fingers like she was holding a flake of ice. An involuntary shiver ran over her spine, and Professor Somhairle let a deep chuckle roll out of his chest. "Excellent. I'll leave you to study now. Do your best—you'll need to show some of these whelps who you are sooner rather than later."

"Thank you," Olivia said quietly, watching him stand to his towering height, and then he strode out of the library, gone before Olivia realized she'd been holding her breath. She let it out with a gasp and looked around the library; no one else was in sight. She looked out the window and saw that it was pitch-dark out, and no one was walking around. How long had she been studying? How long had she spoken with Professor Somhairle? She could swear there had been people sitting around when he first walked up to her, but it only felt like they'd talked for a minute or two. She put her book and the professor's card into her ring and stood up, wracking her brain to figure out if she'd lost any time. She really needed to visit the market and see if she could buy a watch.

⋰ MORGAN ⋱

Morgan held the orb at arm's length, slightly worried because he could feel his Core spinning faster and reaching out toward it. "Do you feel anything from this? Like in your Core?" He held the orb out toward Issa, and she squinted, concentrating, then shook her head.

"No. What is it?"

"I don't know, but my Core is really feeling agitated; the Energy is surging in me. I feel like I should try to cultivate from this orb."

"It's a reward, so I doubt it's dangerous. Sit down, and I'll watch over you while you do it." Issa watched him as he sat down in the empty space between the back table and the doorway they hadn't explored. Sitting in a lotus position, he placed the orb on the floor in front of him, and then he looked inward to his Core. His Core, always a spinning maelstrom, was more chaotic than usual; the tendrils of Energy were stretching and contracting and moving much more quickly than usual while at rest. He exerted his will and tried to calm it, forcing the long, thrashing tendrils of Energy back into a uniform swirl. Only when he felt he had complete control did he reach out with his senses toward the orb of swirling Energy.

His eyes were closed, but he'd grown so used to "Looking" inward at his Core that he wasn't surprised when he could see the ball of dense Energy. It was like his Core was a swirling, burning sun, and the orb was an endless well of deep, engulfing Energy—a black hole. At first, when Morgan felt the orb's power, he pulled back. What if he tried to cultivate that dark, pulling Energy, and it was stronger than his Core? What if it pulled the Energy out of him instead? Mentally he frowned and steeled himself; he imagined Issa admonishing his caution and gathered his will. Before he reached for that Energy, he would make himself ready. He turned to his Core and willed it to spin faster. He remembered how he felt when he was in the Crucible, and the Urghat had him in a death grip, and he pulled with everything he had to siphon its Energy. Morgan channeled that desperation and willed his Core to respond.

Once he had his Core moving with the frenetic Energy of a deep-sea whirlpool, he opened his channels and emptied his body of Energy, pulling it all into his Core. He was careful not to extend his pull beyond his body yet. When he'd consolidated his Energy, he reached out to the orb with his mind and, with a furious effort of will, began to siphon off the Energy within. It felt cold and empty and endless, and he felt his concentration start to slip as the vastness of it began to overwhelm his senses. A jolt of adrenaline, fueled by panic, surged through him, and he realized his Energy was leaking from his Core and flowing along his pathways toward the orb.

Morgan furrowed his brow in frustration and renewed his concentration. He pulled back from the orb and forced his Energy back into his Core. Suddenly he had a thought and almost slapped himself on the head. Why wasn't he using his cultivation drill? Morgan calmed himself and took several deep breaths to re-center. Then he began his drill, slowly cycling his Energy through his pathways, and only when he was on the return portion of his drill did he reach out and pull at the Energy around him, including the Energy in the orb. This time the vacuum created by his Vortex Core was more potent; along with the ambient Energy in the room, a tendril of the cold, empty Energy within the orb flowed toward his Core, slipping through his pathways like a rivulet of glacial water through a warm tide. Morgan felt it enter his Core, and he directed it to the very center of the vortex, allowing it to pool like a singularity at the center of a swirling galaxy.

A smile crept along Morgan's lips, and he began another round of his drill. Again, he pushed his Energy out through his pathways, and again he pulled ambient Energy in along with the Energy in the orb. His Core's dark, empty heart joined in the drawback this time, and a broader stream poured into him from the orb, joining the vacuum of Energy at his Core. Something happened then, like an engine catching and revving up after cranking the starter—his Core began to spin faster than he knew it could, and the stream of Energy from the orb widened into a torrent, flooding into his Core through his pathways at such a rate that it became painful. Morgan could feel his pathways straining to contain the surge, and he could feel the powerful, pulling Energy gathering to such a degree that it almost eclipsed the rest of the Energy swirling around it.

Morgan, at first, reveled in the feeling of power that poured through his pathways and swelled within his Core, but as his pathways began to burn and the center of his Core slowly grew more and more dense, pulling at the fringes of his vortex of normal Energy, he bit down on his teeth and clenched his fists in strain. Just as he started to feel a tickling wave of panic begin to fray at the back of his mind, the stream of Energy from the orb ceased, and his Core pulsed heavily. The Empty singularity at the center of his Core condensed, and a large portion of its Energy bled off into the spinning vortex around it, joining the pure Energy that spun there, and an equilibrium was established. Morgan sighed heavily, took a deep breath, and examined his Core.

The vortex of Energy spun more powerfully and seemed more vibrant than ever, and, as he looked to the singularity at its center, Morgan knew it consisted of void-attuned Energy. The knowledge was there as sure as he knew his opposing digits were called thumbs. His store of void-attuned Energy matched his pure Energy. The movement of his vortex balanced the pull of the void perfectly, keeping it from absorbing and converting his pure Energy. Morgan, his eyes still closed, smiled and looked at his status sheet:

Status			
Name:	Morgan Hall		
Race:	Human - Base 7		
Class:	Vortex Duelist - Epic		
Level:	26		
Core:	Vortex Class - Base 7		
Energy Affinity:	9.2, Void 9.2	Energy:	4103/4103
Strength:	65	Vitality:	60
Dexterity:	44 (66)	Agility:	93
Intelligence:	116	Will:	101
Points Available:	0		
Titles & Feats:	Human Champion, First Hollow Guard, Ardeni Friend, Mark of Loyalty, Yovashi Bane, Legacy of the Azure Paladin, First Vortex Duelist		
Skills:	• System Language Integration - Not Upgradeable • Animal Taming - Basic • Stealthy Maneuvers - Basic • Melee Weapon Mastery - Basic • Fighting Crane Style - Basic • Sword Mastery - Improved • Vortex Core Cultivation Drill - Basic	• Backstab - Basic Energy Drain - Advanced • Circle of Combat - Improved • Guard Ally - Basic Hollow Charge - Improved • Azure Burst - Basic • Azure Sight - Basic • Vortex Lance - Basic	

"Holy shit! My Core advanced four ranks!" Morgan opened his eyes and looked at Issa, or he tried to, but she wasn't standing where he'd last seen her. He stood up and looked around and saw that she was peeking through the door, out into the hallway where they'd come from.

"What? Sorry, I was checking that nothing was out there. You've been kind of out of it for a while." She gently closed the door and walked back to him. "I saw the orb dissolve as a stream of Energy flowed into you, but that was twenty minutes ago. Took you a while to process everything?"

"Well, it only seemed like a couple of minutes to me, but I guess so. I gained an affinity for Void Energy, and my Core gained a new aspect. Along with that, my pathways seem more robust, and my Core's rank went up by four!"

"Wow! Four ranks at once? That must have been quite an experience! Hmm, kind of too bad you weren't already a higher rank. I imagine such growth would be a lot more valuable for someone with an improved or advanced Core. Oh well!" She ruffled his hair playfully when his grin turned to a frown. "Don't dwell on it! You never know what tomorrow will bring, so let's be happy for your improvement!"

"So, what's the deal with affinities when it comes to spells? The only thing I know about it is that I should be able to make a void-attuned Energy bead now." Morgan stretched, looking in at his Core again, admiring the way it resembled some sort of celestial body with bright, spinning arms of Energy around a deep, resonating well of power.

"It should allow you to learn new spells that require that affinity, and maybe you can alter your existing spells by using the void Energy instead of normal Energy. You should experiment with it when we get out of here, maybe." Issa gestured to the door, "Are you feeling up to see what's beyond here? I'm guessing it's a kitchen."

"Yeah, I feel great. I'm brimming with Energy!" Morgan grinned and picked up his estoc from where it leaned against the table. They explored the kitchens, not finding any lurking cook or giant rat or anything else Morgan could imagine might be in the kitchen of a keep-dungeon. They found some pots and pans and a set of decent cooking knives. The pantry held sacks of grain, some moldy wheels of cheese, and several barrels of watery wine, but none of the foodstuffs seemed appetizing, and Issa postulated that it might not last long outside the dungeon. Morgan shrugged, and they made their way back out to the mess hall where they'd fought Jinna. "What's next? Have we missed anything? Time to check out the main hall?"

"Unless there are some secret stairs or something, I think that's all we have left."

"Alright, let's see what's in store for us—I'm assuming you want to proceed?" Morgan started walking along the wide hallway that led back to the junction.

"Yes, of course. I'm a little nervous, but we've worked so hard to get to this point, I'd hate to back out now." Issa walked just behind him, and soon, they were making the turn back to the entry hall. A few minutes later, they were standing in the hall they'd already cleared and passed through several times while exploring the keep's nooks and crannies. The only doorway they'd found and hadn't opened was before them: the large double doors leading to the main hall.

"So, if I remember right, through these doors is the big hall where we met the glowing spirit orbs that sent us into the dungeon, right? There wasn't another hallway or anything?"

"That's the way I remember it." Issa nodded.

"Well, we should be ready for a fight then." Morgan remembered the hall being a vast chamber, so he decided to swap his estoc out for his curved, long blade. He liked the estoc but still felt more comfortable with the slashing weapon. He held it in a middle guard and started channeling Vortex Lance, getting it primed and ready to fire. Issa, for her part, started humming the preamble to her Battle Chant. Morgan felt goosebumps along his neck as her strange harmony came forth, bringing with it a chilling touch of Energy that empowered his limbs. He looked into her purple-black eyes and nodded, and she stepped forward, pulling the left-hand door open with her free hand.

The inside of the great hall was similar to what they'd seen in the ruined version of the keep, but, as with the rest of this version, it was whole and clean, free from rubble and ruin. Narrow, polished wooden tables ran the length of the hall on the left and the right, embroidered runners of rich silk down the center of each table. A huge, ornate chandelier hung from the center of the tall chamber shedding bright yellow light down on the occupants.

Sitting at the table on wooden benches were dozens of individuals from the Ardeni and Shadeni races, all wielding or bearing a sword of one kind or another. They lounged, watching Morgan and Issa walk into the room with various levels of interest. Some stared raptly, others glanced at them and then back at their neighbor to continue conversations, and others turned to the far end of the hall to see the reaction of the man sitting there on a chair that more resembled a stool than a throne.

He was a man of average height, wearing naught but a loose linen shirt and brown leather pants. He held a sheathed longsword in one hand, leaning forward on it while he watched Morgan and Issa step into his audience hall. Morgan almost turned around and slammed the door when he saw all the gathered swordsmen and women, but then he noticed that all save the man at the far end were slightly translucent and shimmered in the light. They were more specters than people, and Morgan didn't feel any threat or animosity from them. Were they here to bear witness to their combat?

"Come forward and present yourselves, students. By the host gathered here, you've battled hard to face me. Stand straight and tell me your names." At those words, Morgan's breath caught, and he realized that the shimmering spectators looked familiar. In fact, sitting on the bench farthest from the door and closest to the Swordmaster were Drillmaster Groll and Swordmistress Jinna—here, sitting and watching with placid expressions, were the students and teachers that Morgan and Issa had fought and vanquished throughout the keep. Even some of the challengers from outside were present, leaning against the wall, tankards in their hands.

ᚙ MORGAN ᚙ

Morgan glanced at Issa; she nodded, and they both advanced down the center of the hall toward the man that Morgan presumed was the Swordmaster. The luminescent gallery of vanquished combatants watched them in silence, some standing behind the tables, some sitting up straight, some lounging languidly. The Swordmaster watched them, still sitting on the edge of his short wooden chair, his back straight but his face relaxed. He was a Shadeni, but one like Morgan hadn't met before. He had close-cut black hair, but actual horns poked up from the sides of his head, a good four inches, black and glossy like little bull horns. While he wasn't especially tall, there was a sense of gravity about him, almost like light bent toward him as it passed by—a shimmering, practically imperceptible veil of shadow that clung to his form.

Morgan noted the relaxed way in which the Swordmaster rested his hand on the pommel of his longsword, and then his eye drifted down to the sword. Its blade was straight with two edges and at least as long as Morgan's curved sword; the metal was black as a starless night sky, drinking the light around it. The guard and pommel were crafted of the same dark metal, but they were plain and unadorned. Morgan couldn't see much of the hilt beneath the Swordmaster's hand, but it seemed to be wrapped in sturdy leather—nothing fancy. The simple utility of that blade was frightening in its statement, "Here is a sword meant for cutting and killing, not looking pretty." As they stepped past the last table and stood before the Swordmaster, Morgan and Issa stood side by side, backs straight, but swords out and ready.

"Well? Don't be shy; name yourselves!" The Swordmaster's voice was gravelly and severe, but it had a hint of decorum in the tone. A touch of a smile scrunched the bright red skin around his eyes, but Morgan could see the Shadeni's canines were much more pronounced than those of the others he'd met.

"I'm Issa ap'Roald, pleased to meet you, sir," Issa said, catching Morgan off-guard. He glanced at her and saw that she'd even bowed slightly while speaking. The Swordmaster let out a quiet but prolonged, "Ah," then turned to Morgan expectantly.

"I'm Morgan Hall. Might I have your name, Swordmaster?" Morgan did not bow. Not because he wanted to show disrespect, but because he thought it would come off phony; he didn't even know if he'd do it right.

"You may. I am Von-dak, the Swordmaster of this keep. Welcome to my domain. I've heard tales of your exploits here from my companions. It's been a great while since we've had outsiders enter this place, the last ones being your friends Tal-dak and Shinra." He paused and gestured to the two fighters leaning against the wall. They both nodded, though neither looked happy.

"Are they . . ." Morgan started to ask, but Von-dak continued speaking.

"I exist as a fragment of my former self. With me are the memories of my friends and students, and yes, some of the adventurers that have come this way over the years have left a piece of themselves as well. I didn't make this place as a trap, though; don't fret. When I felt myself being called to another realm, I wanted to leave behind some of what I had learned. It cost me dearly, and the System has since come and bargained for some changes, but I think it was worth it in the end. Have you not learned valuable lessons? Have I not shared some of my wealth with you for your victories?"

"Yes, that's true, sir, but . . ." Again, Morgan was cut off.

"Well, I can't take all the credit for those treasures—the System has supplemented my store of rewards, though I begin to doubt the price I paid was worth it; however, that's a story not meant for your ears. So, you've found and bested most of the challenges I put in your way." He glanced around the tables and continued, "You missed a few, but I'm impressed, nevertheless. Now, I'll offer you a choice and a bargain. Are you ready to hear me?"

Morgan felt Issa's hand reach along his wrist to grab onto his hand while he held his sword. Her thin fingers wrapped around the back of his hand, and he loosened his grip to clasp onto her. "We're ready," Issa said, speaking for them both.

"Very well; I challenge you both to a duel. If you can survive my onslaught for a mere ten seconds or land a single blow with your sword against me, I will give you a personalized lesson that will complement your sword fighting style. If I slay you within those ten seconds, your soul will reside here with me for one hundred years, after which you will be permitted to leave with your life intact again. I'm sure you'll learn something during that time, eh, Shinra?" The swordswoman didn't respond, and Morgan could see by her eyes that her mind was far away.

"What if one of us should perish, and do we both have to accept the duel?" Morgan asked, glancing down at Issa.

"If one perishes, but the other survives, I will teach the survivor." Morgan noticed how the Swordmaster followed with his eyes as Morgan looked at Issa again. What's more, he saw the corner of his mouth quirk up, and his deep red and gold eyes squint slightly.

"If we refuse the duel?" Morgan pressed.

"Then I will give you a trinket and send you on your way." The Swordmaster scoffed and waved a hand dismissively at the thought.

Morgan leaned close to Issa and whispered, "I don't want you to fight him with me."

"Well, I don't want you to fight him, but I wouldn't ask you to watch me fight him alone!" She hissed back. Von-dak snorted, a smile curling his lips, but he didn't say anything. Morgan knew Issa didn't want to back down—it would eat at her that they came this far and didn't take the final challenge. He also knew that he couldn't imagine living for a hundred years outside this dungeon while she languished like Shinra and the others. He turned to the Swordmaster, still sitting placidly on his plain wooden chair.

"Are all the 'challengers' outside the gates people who have come into your dungeon and lost their duels with you?"

"That's right."

"It seems like this place has been in ruins longer than a hundred years. Shouldn't some of them have gone back into the world by now?"

"Well," Von-dak frowned, "Some have, I'm sure. Others seem to change their mind about wanting to leave over the course of their enforced time here. Perhaps they lose their will." He shrugged, and for the first time, his hand resting on his sword's pommel moved, twitching slightly. Morgan didn't know what to make of this place or his statement. He knew he couldn't let Von-dak kill Issa, though, even if he thought he could wait a hundred years to see her again.

"Is your training the only reward? Or will the System provide something as well?" Issa interjected.

Again, Von-dak scoffed, "Bah, I'm sure the trinket you'd get for leaving will also be given to you if you survive the duel. Perhaps something better."

"What if we both leave, then?" Morgan stored his sword and turned to Issa, putting his hands on either side of her face. Her eyes were full of light and fierce, and Morgan knew there was no way she'd back out unless he begged her. He couldn't do that. "Kiss me then, you stubborn woman." He forgot about Von-dak, forgot about the host of conquered ghosts, and kissed Issa fully, savoring her soft lips and the scent of her, like vanilla and sweat and everything he loved. She kissed him back, pulling hard on the back of his neck, and Morgan had to pull back before he lost himself in her. "All right, then, Swordmaster. Let's duel."

Von-dak jumped to his feet, so fluid and quick that Morgan didn't see the movement. His sword was in his hand, and he walked away from his chair into the cleared area between it and the tables. He squared off with Morgan and Issa, and then he bowed. "When you're ready."

Issa's throat began to vibrate with her Battle Chant, and Morgan readied his spells, slipping into the Crane Defends the Nest. He just had to survive for ten seconds. They should be able to do that. He felt warmth flood him as Issa put her hand on his back and pushed Energy from her Haste spell into him. His eyes dilated, and his heart quickened, and he zeroed in on the Swordmaster, ready. "Say when, Issa."

"Ready," Issa said from beside him, and then Von-dak streaked forward like a comet. Even Hasted, Morgan couldn't activate his Hollow Charge before Von-dak was on him, slapping his sword sideways and smashing into him with his shoulder. Morgan flew to the side, careening into one of the tables, forced to scramble on all fours for purchase. He'd just regained his feet when he saw that Von-dak hadn't pursued him; he was after Issa. She moved in streaks and blurs, faster than Morgan's eyes could track, trying to avoid his slashing black razor of a sword. Still, in the space of two heartbeats, he smashed aside her guard, hacked her shoulder, causing her to spin, and then he, as fast as some kind of nightmarish pneumatic machine, chopped his blade into her back and side no less than six times. Morgan fell to his knees and screamed out like something vital was being torn from him while Issa's body tumbled away from the onslaught.

Von-dak spun to face Morgan and advanced like a snake over an oily floor. He was halfway to him when he stopped, a puzzled expression on his face. Morgan had screamed not from fear or loss but because he'd taken the blows meant for Issa. At least, he'd taken half of them; his Guard Ally ability had absorbed the other half. It hadn't stopped enough damage for him to avoid having his left arm sheared through at the elbow or for the mangling slashes in his side and back to be absorbed by his armor. No, he was terribly wounded, sporting several deep gashes that had severed ribs, and partially eviscerated him. He sat, crumpled, on his knees, blood pooling around him, and smiled at Von-dak.

Von-dak's surprise turned to strain as Morgan pulled, willing his Vortex Core and the dark void at its center to yank as much of Von-dak's Energy as possible. The effect was incredible; a torrent of pure white Energy rushed out of the Swordmaster and into him, straining his pathways as it coursed through them and into his Core. Some of it spun out and into his body, staunching the torrential blood loss that was beginning to turn his vision dark.

"Uh," Von-dak grunted and staggered, but then he lifted his blade and scowled, "How?" Then comprehension dawned on him, and he spun, only to find Issa's rapier already slipping in and out of his gut, quick as a serpent's tongue.

"Hit!" She said wildly with a fierce grin; then, her eyes fell on Morgan, and the color drained from her face. Upon being stabbed, Von-dak had lowered his sword. He turned, a smile on his face, and watched as Issa ran to Morgan, hugging his still kneeling form close and talking softly into his ear, "Oh, Morgan, your arm! What about the rest of you? Can you hear me? Why aren't you speaking?"

"He'll live, I'll wager; he absorbed a considerable amount of my Energy. Quite more than I was anticipating. Won't help his arm, though. Still, there are remedies for that. I'm so pleased to have two new students! Very tricky play there!" Von-dak's entire demeanor seemed to have undergone a transformation—where before he'd been stoic and somewhat dismissive, if polite, now his voice carried a current of warmth.

"Ugh. Issa, my ring is on that hand on the ground. Can you get it for me so that I can drink a potion?" Morgan's voice was scratchy and weak. He knew he was out of the woods when it came to bleeding to death—the huge Energy Drain had seen his bleeding slow to a trickle, but he had already lost enough that he could barely focus his eyes. He wanted to drink a healing potion so he could assess his condition.

"Oh, I'm sorry, Morgan!" She produced one of her own healing potions and pulled the stopper, pouring the sweet, thick syrup into his dry, cottony mouth. Morgan let the warmth flood through him as he worked the potion around in his mouth, generating enough saliva to take a big gulp. Energy and warmth flooded through his limbs as the miracle tincture did its thing. His vision cleared, and the fogginess in his mind retreated, and he lifted his shortened arm to look at the damage. He'd lost it from the elbow down, and smooth flesh was already covering the stump; that potion worked fast, but it apparently couldn't regrow a limb.

MORGAN

Morgan stood and stretched, wincing at the sharp pains in his side and back. Even with the Energy Drain and the healing potion, his ribs were still tender, and something inside him wasn't fully healed. He coughed and moved to wipe his mouth, only to wave his stump around in front of him. "Oh, God. That's awkward."

"What?" Issa asked gently, still clinging close to him, her hands tenderly squeezing his neck and good arm.

"Huh, nothing. Gonna take a while to get used to one arm. Jesus, how am I going to buckle my pants, let alone my armor?" He looked down at the severed member, still sheathed in the ineffectual scale sleeve. It was surreal to see his own hand sticking out at the end, so far from him. "Talk about awkward," he said, leaning over to pry the storage ring off his old middle finger. He had to hold it down by putting a foot on the wrist while pulling. Issa moved to help him, but he grunted and yanked the ring off before she could intervene. He stood, red-faced, and noted that Von-dak was back on his wooden chair, quietly watching them. Morgan frowned at him, wanted to cuss him out, but held his tongue for now.

"Here, let me see that." Issa wormed her fingers into his fist, pulled the ring out, and then slipped it onto his ring finger.

"Thanks," he said softly, and then he reached down and pulled his severed arm into his ring. "I don't want to look at that anymore." He also picked up his fallen sword and slipped it into his ring. "Thank God I don't have to use two hands to access the ring, eh?" He tried to smile, but it came out crooked. Issa's face was still wan, and her eyes were brimming with tears. Morgan could tell she felt responsible for his injury, and he was trying to lighten the mood, but he was also feeling a little sorry for himself, so his efforts had a hollow ring to them.

"That was an interesting strategy. I hope your goal was to beat the parameters of the duel and not to win—because I would have killed you both eventually in a real fight. You realize this, yes?" Morgan looked over at Von-dak and frowned.

"Yeah, no shit. No, I didn't think we would kill you, but I didn't think you'd fucking ruin me with one combination. Congratulations. Now you can try to teach me some improvements to my two-handed fighting style while I only have one hand." Morgan let some of his self-pity bleed into his voice, and Issa squeezed his arm, her face falling even more. Her pity and guilt and his lack of self-control started to cascade in his mind, and the frustration built to the point where he could hear a rushing sound in his ears, and he thought he might actually break out in a sob. He gulped it down and shut his mouth, taking a deep breath through his nose.

"Good. Master your emotions; they are useful, but not if they control you. A missing arm is problematic for a swordsman, but as long as you have one, I can teach you more than you can grasp in the time you'll spend with me. After you leave, you can seek a remedy for your injury; you should know there are many. Have you yet advanced your race? I am not familiar with your kind." Issa squeezed harder on Morgan's arm as he said the last words, and her eyes brightened as she looked up at him.

"He's right, Morgan! When you advance to a new tier, your body will undergo a metamorphosis. I've never seen it in Tarn's Crossing, but I've heard stories." Almost against his will, hope blossomed in Morgan's heart. Guilt rushed through him, momentarily, as he realized how lucky they were to be in this world with these miraculous happenings. Memories of injured squad mates and dead colonists flashed through his mind, and he shook his head at his moping.

"There, see? All is not lost." Von-dak stood and twirled his sword, smoothly lifting it to his back and hooking it on something attached to the leather straps crisscrossing his torso. "Now, students, you should see what the meddling System has left for your reward before your lessons begin. When you're done collecting your trinkets, meet me in the courtyard." He didn't wait for a response, walking briskly out of the room. As Morgan watched him leave, he noticed that the audience of semi-ethereal swordsmen and women was gone.

"Morgan, I'm so sorry I didn't ask you to leave. We should have been happy with what we'd won, and we'd be outside celebrating right now." Issa's voice was soft, her eyes downcast, and Morgan hated seeing her like this.

"Issa, I love you. I love you for the way you are. If you start changing because of your worries over me, you'll grow to resent me, here," Morgan gently touched her chest over her heart. "Whether you mean to or not. Slowly, we'd start to want to be apart because of that feeling, and then that rift would grow over time. I want you to keep that spirit, that drive for adventure because it makes me a better person when I'm with you. You're right about me—I'd grow bored living life as a herder, farmer, or tradesman. I say we need to take risks and experience glory while we're able—let's save farming for when we're old!"

He kissed her forehead, and when he pulled back to look at her, she had tears running down her cheeks, but she didn't look sad.

"I love you too, Morgan. I'm sorry about your arm, but I'd love you with two arms or none. Or four, for that matter." She put her arms around his waist and squeezed him, and he leaned into it.

"That feels good." As usual, while she was hugging him, he inhaled deeply of her hair and smiled. He could almost forget about all the fights, all the danger, all the blood, and pain. Besides, there was treasure to investigate. "What did he mean by the System's trinkets. Is there a chest?" He looked around but didn't see anything at first. Issa let go of his waist and walked over to the Swordmaster's chair.

"Here!" She said, moving around behind the chair. Morgan followed and saw another chest, much like the ones before, but smaller, only about a foot square. Without saying anything, Morgan activated Guard Ally on Issa and then stepped back.

"Open it up." Issa looked at him, then frowned slightly.

"You have to stop using that ability on me all the time. You think I'll like it if this thing blows up and sends you through a wall?"

"We've always opened chests like this? What's changed? Just because I got hurt? Listen, this is still a good strategy, don't get squeamish on me." Morgan nodded to the chest, and Issa huffed, but she leaned forward and opened the lid. As usual, nothing happened—it didn't seem the System wanted its rewards to be treacherous. Golden light haloed the opening of the chest, and Morgan moved closer to see why Issa had taken a sharp inhalation. The first thing he noticed were the two golden Advancement Orbs floating near the center. However, underneath the orbs were several more items glinting in the reflected light. "Hey, at least we're getting another level out of this."

"Yeah, let's use the orbs now, so we can get at what's under them more easily." Issa looked at Morgan with an eyebrow raised, and he nodded. She reached in and touched one of the orbs, and Morgan saw the golden glow suffuse her for a moment. She closed her eyes, and her mouth parted slightly as she shivered with the sensation. She opened her eyes and blew out a deep breath a moment later.

"What a sensation! Well, one more level to my class refinement; I hope it's a good one! Your turn." She backed up a step, but Morgan didn't move forward.

"Actually, if you're one away from a refinement, maybe you should take it. You level slower than I do, anyway."

"Oh, ancestors! Are you giving up because of your arm? You can still advance, Morgan, and we'll figure out something for your arm!" She stepped toward him and poked him in the chest while speaking, her voice tinged with a slight growl. Morgan couldn't help laughing.

"No! It's not that; I'm just trying to think of the best use for our resources!"

"I don't care if it's the most logical thing—we both earned an orb, and you're taking yours!"

"Sheesh, alright! Relax!" He chuckled, pushing past her and touching the orb. A flow of golden Energy rushed into him, and he took a big, deep breath, noting that his ribs no longer ached.

Congratulations! You have achieved level 27 Vortex Duelist and have gained 8 Intelligence, 8 Agility, 6 Will, 6 Dexterity.

He checked his status page and noticed that he'd lost two points in additional dexterity—no doubt because part of his armor with the dexterity enchantment had been sheared off. Still, his dexterity was climbing steadily with his new class, enough so that he was starting to worry a bit about his vitality and strength lagging behind in a few levels. He supposed he'd worry about that when it happened, but he'd get a new refinement in two levels, so it might not become an issue. "Alright, what else do we have in there?"

"Let me look," Issa said, pushing past him and leaning over the chest. "Some silvery bracers. They're beautiful! A scroll case, a pouch, a little leather book, and a piece of horn or antler, I think."

"Well, you get the bracers." Morgan couldn't help chuckling when he said it. Issa looked up at him, saw his face, and she smiled, too.

"Oh, making jokes already? Alright, well, I wanted them anyway; look at them, Morgan!" She pulled out two silvery bracers with embossed and enameled blue and red birds in flight on their outer surface.

"Wow, those are beautiful," Morgan said, letting out a low whistle of appreciation. Issa slipped one over her wrist, and it molded itself to her arm, covering it from wrist to about two-thirds of the way to her elbow. She put the other on, and then her eyes glazed over as she read something in her System UI.

"They're enchanted to self-repair and to help deflect projectiles! They're also made of something called sun silver and very durable." She was lovingly tracing the outlines of a blue feathered bird while she spoke, and Morgan reached down to gently squeeze her shoulder. Well, he tried to reach down to squeeze her shoulder, but his left arm was gone, so he just kind of leaned over awkwardly for a moment. He grunted and shifted so he could do it with his right hand.

"More importantly, they're beautiful," he said, grinning when she looked up at him. She stood up and kissed him, then pointed at the chest.

"You see what the other stuff is." She stepped aside and continued to admire her new bracers.

Morgan knelt in front of the chest and reached in with his hand, lifting out the little pouch. It was very light, and it had a label affixed to its drawstring. He read it aloud, "Petals of the Threen Sun Rose—advanced alchemy reagent."

Morgan loosened the drawstring and was surprised when a yellow-red glow escaped the opening, and a rich, spicy odor filled the room. Not wanting to waste any potency, he pulled the string tight. He slipped the pouch into his ring and reached down to the scroll. It looked just like the one he'd gotten outside the keep, the one with the Fighting Crane Sword Style form.

Unfurling the scroll, Morgan stared at the runes on the page, and they started to shift around, but just like before, a message appeared:

*****Prerequisite for the form, the Crane Lances Forth, not met: Sword Mastery—Advanced.*****

"It's another form for my sword style. Another one I can't use yet." Issa grunted in acknowledgment, and Morgan slipped the scroll into his ring. Next, he pulled out the little leather book, and he saw that it had an embossed title along its spine, "Gaerwolt's Secret Recipes." Morgan raised an eyebrow, and then he opened the front flap and started reading the handwritten note on the first page:

Vania,

Herein I've left for you my most treasured alchemical processes. You've been such a joy to teach in the last few decades, and I'm so sorry to see you go, but the heart is a cruel taskmaster, and I know you must follow your feelings. I hope that Bareltom will treat you well and that you'll find time to open the alchemical specialty store that you've dreamt about for so long. You're more than qualified now, and I've enclosed your journeyman papers. Don't let Bareltom be stingy, now! He is well known for his business acumen, and he should see the wisdom in supplying you with the reagents you need to get started. Simply describe to him some of the wonders you can create with the enclosed recipes!

With great love and respect,

Gaerwolt the Singed

"Wow, I think Gaerwolt had a thing for Vania," Morgan absently said, while he thumbed through the complicated-looking recipes in the little book.

"What is it? A love story?" Issa leaned down, suddenly more interested.

"Sort of—it's an alchemy recipe book, but it was a gift to a woman that I think the author was in love with. I don't know; it could all be in my head. Check it out." He handed the book to Issa, and she started reading the little note while he reached into the chest and lifted out the piece of white horn. As soon as he touched the shiny, smooth surface, he felt the Energy throbbing within it. Whatever it was, this horn was probably a valuable crafting material. It was about eight inches long and mostly straight. It was about three inches wide at the base, tapering to a rounded point at the other end. Nothing happened when he tried to bond with it, and there was no label.

"He definitely loved her. Poor Gaerwolt!" Issa said, closing the book.

"Hah, yeah. Poor guy. This horn is for crafting, I think. I can't figure it out."

He handed it to her, and she studied it then also shrugged. She gave Morgan the book and the horn, and he put them into his storage ring. "Well, good chest! Shall we go see what Von-dak has in store for us? Then we can get out of this place."

Issa nodded, "Yes, let's." She took his hand, and together they walked out through the foyer they'd so recently fought in and then into the courtyard.

BRONWYN

Bronwyn stood and gingerly began to stretch out her cramped and aching muscles and joints. She may have recovered and gained the boon, but she was still feeling the effects of the toxins that had immobilized her. Her knuckles were swollen and red, and when she tried to make a fist, it felt like her hands were wearing overstuffed mittens. The rest of her joints felt similarly sore, and when she tried to take a few steps, her ankles screamed in protest. She finally decided that she'd have to sit there for a while and let the toxins run their course before continuing.

She tried to speed things along by flushing her system with lots of water, downing a full canteen and then another and peeing there in the tunnel, a few feet downslope from where she'd been resting. Bronwyn didn't know if her efforts were any help, but after an hour or so, she began to feel more like herself and she could walk without cringing in pain.

She decided to press ahead and continue with the trial. She wasn't sure if she should feel pissed at the queen for sending her in there without more warning than she had. Her experience with the swarm had been hellacious, both the physical pain and the mental torment of actually believing she was about to die. Could she have died? Did some people not survive the toxins? Had it just been a test of her vitality, or had it also been a test of will? The questions tormented Bronwyn, but she knew she'd never find the answers in her head, so she tried to focus on the situation at hand.

The tunnel from which the swarm had emerged had the steepest downward slope, so Bronwyn decided to go that way. She had a feeling that she wouldn't be running into the swarm again, so she figured it would be interesting to see what was down that path. The ground was springy, and the loamy walls drank up the sounds of her passage, so she moved forward quietly, with just the occasional soft squelch of her boot stepping on a patch of moist moss. After descending for several minutes, long enough for the stiffness to completely work out of her joints, Bronwyn stepped through an arched opening into a vaulted, circular chamber with smooth, packed-dirt walls. The room was unremarkable save for the shaft of sunlight that streamed through a gap high in the ceiling.

The light seemed to stir the dusty soil, sending motes swirling up in tiny invisible updrafts. Bronwyn's eyes followed the swirling dust, and then she was caught by surprise when she saw a dun-colored doe with little white spots dappling its coat. Its coloring so perfectly matched the environment that she'd nearly missed it. Bronwyn took one step into the room, and the doe bolted through one of the three oval tunnel entrances on the far side of the chamber. Some instinct in Bronwyn sent her running after the doe, heedless of danger. She didn't know why she was chasing it: was it to see where it went, or did she hope to catch it? She didn't think about it, she just ran.

The tunnel she chased it into was much like the one she'd come from, and it blurred by as she focused her attention downslope, where she could just catch a glimpse of the doe down the various long straight sections. Bronwyn pushed herself, enjoying the feeling of letting go of all her trepidation and worries and just running wildly through the springy, soil-scented tunnels. She passed branching tunnels here and there and crashed through a few more round, earthen chambers, but each glimpse she caught of the spotted doe reassured her that she was on the right path.

She came to a long, straight tunnel with a very gentle downward slope, and she pumped her legs, sprinting with everything she had. She could see the doe up ahead and she watched it go through another opening. When she caught up and burst through the archway, she slid to a halt to take in the scene, her lungs pumping like a bellows as she caught her breath.

She was in another dome-shaped underground chamber with a much larger aperture in the ceiling shedding sunlight down onto a patch of grass. The doe was ahead of her in the grass, pulling feebly at a leg caught in the jaws of a trap. Bronwyn glanced around the chamber but didn't see anything else. There weren't any other creatures around, and only smooth, hard-packed dirt walls surrounded the strange grassy underground meadow. Bronwyn walked slowly toward the struggling doe, and in her heart, she knew she had a choice to make. Was she a hunter? She'd chased down the creature, and now it was here—her prize. Or would she let her tender sensibilities get the better of her and try to release her?

Bronwyn wondered what the queen would want, but then she shook her head; how could she discern the machinations of a being that had been scheming and planning for thousands of years? The queen had picked Bronwyn to be her agent, not the other way around; she felt like it was stupid to act the way she thought the queen would want her to. Rather, she should act the way she wanted to because that was who she was, and the queen liked who she was. Pleased with her logic, Bronwyn continued to approach the doe, saying, "Shh, beautiful. I'm going to help you."

Bronwyn practically tiptoed; she was carefully trying not to startle the doe. It had stopped struggling and looked over one spotted shoulder at Bronwyn, big glistening black eyes unblinking. "That looks like it hurts. I'm sorry, sweetie. Hold still, and I'll get it off." Bronwyn worked to keep her voice steady and low, and she crouched as she took the last few steps to the quivering creature.

The trap was hooked to a chain that was staked into the earth. Bronwyn had seen depictions of bear traps in VR games and on the net, and this trap looked similar but with smaller teeth and springs. She slowly reached forward with both hands and grasped the two sides of the trap's jaws, pulling them apart. The doe yanked its leg free and bolted a few steps away. Then it stopped and turned back to Bronwyn. Slowly it walked back to her, not limping or quivering anymore, and Bronwyn dropped to her knee, keeping herself low as it approached.

The doe walked right up to her and pushed its moist, black nose against Bronwyn's cheek. It huffed out a breath of hot air, blowing some of Bronwyn's red hair back from her eyes, and then turned and ran from the chamber.

*****Congratulations! You have earned the feat: "Blessing of the Herd." Over grassy plains or in the shade of trees, you will move more swiftly and with less effort.*****

"Thank you!" Bronwyn called after the running doe. "That was a hell of a lot better than getting stung almost to death." She stood and stretched, looking up at the shaft of warm sunlight that illuminated the room. She wondered, briefly, if she'd have gotten a different sort of blessing for killing the doe or if she'd have failed the trial altogether. She supposed it didn't matter; she acted the way she felt she should, and she'd gotten her second blessing; all was well. Two tunnels led away from the underground meadow, and Bronwyn walked toward the one on the left, not thinking about it, but trusting her instincts.

The tunnel started out with an even slope, but soon she found herself climbing a gentle grade. She leaned into the climb, enjoying the exercise; her chase of the doe had worked out any of the residual stiffness from the swarm's toxins, and her muscles and lungs felt strong. The tunnel seemed very straight and continued at the same slope for a long time.

She felt like she'd been climbing for hours when a deep, grinding rumble echoed down the tunnel. Bronwyn paused for a moment, listening, and then she heard it again, this time with a sharp, cracking clap. "Thunder?" she asked, frowning in concentration. She continued her climb a bit more slowly now, listening and peering ahead for any signs of what was to come.

The grinding, cracking thunder continued to sound every couple of minutes, and Bronwyn noticed that the ground, still springy and firm, was more and more damp. Finally, the long sloping tunnel's end came into view, and she saw a gray sky with sheeting rain falling. A flash of lightning confirmed what she'd suspected—there was a storm raging outside.

She trudged up the increasingly damp tunnel until she was just a few paces from the gray-lit opening. The storm's sheeting rain pounded the grassy slope leading away from the tunnel, and every few breaths, a shockingly bright, jagged lightning bolt lanced through the cloudy sky, accompanied by an immediate peal of thunder that, at this distance, shook the air and had Bronwyn covering her ears and wincing.

She edged up to the opening, staying under the exposed-stone overhang, but still got splashed by the falling rain. It was warm, and its smell made Bronwyn smile as childhood memories she'd forgotten flooded into her mind. She remembered playing outside in the summer in rural San Bernardino, getting caught in a monsoon, and running through the desert scrub to her father's ranch house. She remembered the tang of ozone and the fresh scent of the palo verde trees and creosote. Most of all, she remembered how the rain wasn't cold, just refreshing. She had to fight an urge to run out into the storm; the lightning was far more violent and frequent in this storm than the ones in her memory. She peered outside to take in the view, though.

Bronwyn's cave opening provided a view of a small valley surrounded by high steep hills and stony peaks. The stormy gray clouds obscured the tops of the mountains, but she could see to the far side of the oval basin and, remarkably, could make out another cave entrance on the far side. The entire valley floor was covered in lush, green grass, with an occasional slender, broad-leafed tree bending violently in the storm's gusts. The other cave was directly across from her, a mile or, accounting for tricks of perception, maybe two away.

She stood there, watching the storm and gazing out at the little valley, and, after maybe the third time it happened, she realized her eyes kept settling on the tiny, distant cave entrance. She felt like she was supposed to go there. It was downhill and over flat, grassy ground. She felt like she could make the run in a couple of minutes. She itched to launch herself out into the storm, sprinting for everything she was worth. She realized she was grinning, almost maniacally, and that's when she knew she was going to go for it. Again, she had the faint realization that she was being tested, and there was more than one correct answer. She could wait out the storm, but she could also let herself do what she wanted. She charged out over the grass with a wild, "Whoop!"

Bronwyn bounded over the wet grass, instantly soaked by the sheeting rain. She laughed and howled up at the storm as she tore over the valley floor. She was running fast; downward momentum, strong, agile, pumping legs, and her new boon from the doe combined to allow her to cover ground like no human on Earth ever had. She was laughing, tears of joy streaming from her eyes, only a few dozen paces from the fast-approaching cave mouth when the lightning struck her. With a tremendous clap of thunder, Bronwyn's body arched through the air, her hair standing out like a great red halo, and her body rigid with electricity. It was over as quickly as it started, and she crashed to the grass, tumbling and rolling to flop just inside the cave.

Bronwyn's body twitched, and then her eyes sprang open, and despite her tingling, numb body, and the scorched, blasted boot on her left foot, she started to giggle.

Congratulations! You have earned the feat: "Blessing of the Summer Storm." In times of great need, raise your voice with the force of thunder behind it.

◈ OLIVIA ◈

Eyes closed against the bright lights, Olivia strained to tune out the murmured conversations, low humming of mantras, and the crackling, popping sounds of cantrips starting up and fizzling out. She was sitting at her table in the Spellcraft lab they'd moved to after the first day of courses. It was a wide room on the second sublevel of the main academy building with a low ceiling and lots of tables set up in clusters around the room's edges. Professor ap'Rall, Alyss, roamed the center of the room, giving pointers and observing as students tried to apply the lessons she'd given them over the last week and a half. At first, she'd wondered why they had such a wide-open noisy room when concentration was so critical. She'd come to the rather obvious conclusion that it was intentional—what good was magic if you couldn't concentrate enough in the real world to use it?

Olivia finally managed to turn her inner eye inward and study her Core, tuning out the distractions in the lab. The familiar shape filled her vision, and she admired the white center of pure Energy surrounded by the swirling rings of her various attunements. It was beautiful and growing more so with each advancement she made to her Core. That wasn't what she was doing at the moment, though. No, she was working on her first meta-element: arcfrost. Olivia had learned that her first spell creations were simplistic combinations or substitutions of attuned Energy. To make a meta-element, one must know the weave and be nimble enough with her mind to make it a reality. So far, Olivia hadn't been able to do it. Gently, she tugged a thread of water-attuned Energy out of its ring and, as she held it quivering near her Core, she pulled loose a thread of air-attuned Energy, drawing it up close to the other thread.

The first part of the weave was simple—she just had to make a basic pattern to shift the water Energy into ice and the air into electricity. She'd learned that each time she cast a spell, her Energy flowed out of her in a sort of schema that weaved it into actualization. When she cast Icy Shards, the spell automatically took her water-attuned Energy and twisted it into ice. Now that she was manually manipulating her Energy, she had to weave it herself, but it was a very simple pattern. Once she had her strands of ice and electricity, the hard part began; she had to make the arcfrost weave before pushing it through her pathways and into reality. She'd failed yesterday, which was the first time she'd tried practically applying the pattern. It was much more challenging to manipulate Energy threads than draw practice patterns on paper. She had the pattern in her mind, as solid as she could imagine the letters in the alphabet. Still, she struggled.

The tricky part was that she'd be halfway through the weave when the first threads started to unravel, and by the time she got to the end, the pattern would be half undone. Olivia was frustrated at first and almost threw her hands up; she either was doing something wrong or wasn't meant to do it. Then something happened; on about her tenth try, she realized she'd gotten a little farther on the weave than the last time. What if it wasn't a matter of her doing something wrong but not doing something fast enough? She'd come to that conclusion yesterday and then determined to repeat the weave as many times as she needed to until she got fast enough to complete it before it unraveled. And so, for nearly the full duration of her Spellcraft lab, she worked on that weave over and over. By the time someone jostled her shoulder to let her know time was up, she'd made good progress; she was more than two-thirds of the way to finishing the weave.

She cleared her mind and opened her eyes to see that it hadn't been a cohort member to jostle her but Alyss herself. "Oh, thank you, Alyss. Is it time to go?"

"Yes, Olivia, good work today; I see what you're doing, and I'm impressed, you know." Her smile was true and warm, and Olivia felt the heat from it enter her own heart, and suddenly she was very glad to be in this classroom, learning from this woman. Her cohort had come a long way in the last few days, talking, joking, and being actual friends, which had helped Olivia's sense of homesickness. Still, it was Alyss's genuine warmth and desire to see Olivia do well that really touched her. She reminded Olivia of the best parts of her mother and her favorite teacher combined.

"Thank you, Alyss! I think I'm onto something! I can't wait to show you what I come up with." Olivia stood, slipping her text into her ring, and looked around for her cohort. She saw them lingering over by the door, Adaida looking back at her expectantly.

"I'm excited to see what you do, also, Olivia. Tell me, how close do you think you are to level ten?" Alyss moved sideways, surreptitiously putting herself between Olivia and her cohort.

"I think I'm still early into nine. I haven't done anything to gain Energy since I leveled, though I have been cultivating my Core. Sange said that people can level slowly doing that also, so I'm really not sure."

"Mmhmm, listen, Olivia, I think you have a good shot at gaining at least one or two of the awards for the opening competition. It'd be best if you didn't level before then if no one has told you that already," Olivia opened her mouth to say she knew that, but Alyss kept speaking, "Let's save your project demonstration for my class until after the award, shall we? I'll let you describe your process and give you a grade based on that. Let's keep this between you and me for now, though, okay? That goes for your cohort, too." Alyss looked at her until she nodded.

"Um, sure, that's very nice of you, Alyss. I'll make sure I work hard; I really do have a good plan for what I'm going to do; it's just going to be a bit harder not to complete any of the stages before I try it out."

"Yes, of course. I'll keep that in mind when I'm considering the scores. Now hustle to your next class! See you tomorrow." Alyss waved and stepped back, motioning for Olivia to pass in front of her.

"Bye, Alyss," she said, walking quickly over to her waiting cohort.

"The flame was that about?" Rald asked as he shouldered open the door and walked through.

"She was talking to me about my project."

"Really? Doing something wrong?" Veena asked, walking just in front of Olivia.

"No, not really; she was just checking my progress." Olivia didn't like being evasive with her friends, but she didn't want to get in trouble with Alyss, so she settled on vagueness. "I think she just didn't get a chance to talk to me during class because she has to spend so much time coaching Rald." Everyone laughed at that, even Rald.

"Hey, I can't help it if she's got a thing for her favorite student." He feigned bravado, but Olivia thought that she'd be able to see him blushing if not for his already bright red skin. Alyss really did spend a lot of time with him during class, but Olivia was more inclined to believe it was because he needed the extra help. She didn't say that, though—more fun to tease him about an imagined crush.

Olivia was getting better and better at consciously cultivating variously attuned Energy rather than just blindly absorbing ambient Energy. Sange had been pleased when she'd isolated the fire-attuned Energy from the incense stick, but he'd pushed her to pull attuned Energy from water, a dense, flaky stone, and from a crystal he'd called a "Charge-sphere." When they arrived in his class that day, he'd sent them to their individual stations, and Olivia saw that her little "Altar" had the charge-sphere and a bowl of water sitting on it. "Today, you will try to pull two streams of differently attuned Energy at once while you cultivate. Moreover, when they enter your pathways, I want you to braid them so they come to your core intertwined. Do you know why I'm asking you to do this?"

Olivia thought about the question, and when she considered braiding Energy streams, her mind drifted to the patterns she had to weave to create meta-elements. "To help me get faster at weaving meta-elements?"

"Exactly. Alyss told me about your project for her class. This will be a good exercise to help you not only cultivate but gain more and faster control of your Energy weaving. Take it seriously, and don't waste your time in here—this ability will prove invaluable as you advance in the practice of magic." Sange's voice was uncharacteristically stern when he said the last statement, and it took Olivia a bit by surprise.

"Do you feel like I've been wasting my time?"

"Oh, no, not you, Olivia. I just worry because I've spoken to other Cultivation Mentors. Some students are progressing very quickly, and I feel the strain of wanting you all to be competitive."

"Well, I want to work hard, and I try, but I'm also worried about leveling. If I cultivate too much, won't I hit level ten before the challenge is over? Alyss thinks I need to be careful not to level before the awards are given out."

"Yes, that's a concern, but that's also why I'm not giving you dense Energy artifacts to use for cultivation. This is just plain water, and the charge-sphere is a very weak one. Also, when I force you to focus on only a few of your affinities, it slows down your cultivation immensely. Still, it improves your ability, and when we start pushing for growth, you're going to take off. Trust me, Olivia."

"I do trust you, Sange. Don't worry; I'm not slacking off." Olivia sat down and assumed her lotus position, and Sange nodded, moving to speak with Veena. Olivia had gathered that growth or "Leveling" at the academy was accomplished through innovation and cultivation—they weren't going to be fighting and killing each other for Energy. She was a little worried about holding back her progress in order to avoid leveling before the first month passed. Still, if she could believe Alyss and Sange, the knowledge and practice they were giving her would allow for some exponential gains as soon as she stopped holding back. With that in mind, she bent to the task that Sange had given her.

It was a very different kind of difficult to take two strands of differently attuned Energy from outside her body and pull them into her pathways while trying to braid them. She had no problem pulling the threads out of the sources, directing them into her Core with her cultivation drill. However, bending them to her will as they entered the pathway through her palm was an order of magnitude more difficult than doing the same from Energy that was already in her Core. Was this Energy less pliable because it came from outside her? She struggled, bending the threads with sheer concentration, and, as beads of sweat broke out on her forehead, she finally got them to twist together. She continued the twisting motion, pulling the threads into her pathway millimeter by millimeter in her mind's eye.

When Olivia finally pulled the braided thread through to her Core, she was drenched in sweat, though she didn't realize it yet. Her entire being was wrapped up in the arduous task of keeping the Energy moving slowly as she twisted it together. When it reached her Core, she was faced with a new problem—unwinding the braid so the differently attuned rings of Energy around her Core could receive the individual threads. Ever so carefully, she pulled the braid apart and allowed the rings to siphon off their threads, and then she opened her eyes, faint and a bit dizzy. Sange was standing in front of her, smiling. "Take a break; you've earned it."

﷽ OLIVIA ﷽

Olivia slipped her book into her ring and stood up, stretching. She, once again, had lost track of time in the library and seemed to be the only occupant still studying. She winced as she straightened her wrists over her head; they were sore from combat training. Commander Grobak had them doing grappling drills repeatedly, and Olivia's wrists and forearms were covered in bruises from yellow to purple, some being a week old and some fresh from today. Grobak didn't do anything in half measures, and just like they'd spent more than a week learning to fall, now they were learning to grab each other's wrists and break the holds, over and over and over again. Sometimes it wasn't so bad, like when Olivia was partnered with a smaller girl like Veena. Other times, she'd leave with swollen, sore skin all around her wrists from trying to break Rald's or another strong student's grip.

She lowered her arms and started walking out of the library, hoping that she wouldn't be alone in the hallways, too; the school was creepy at night when half the lights were out, and the shadows grew long. She was making good progress with her Energy braiding and had been practicing making her second meta-element when she'd lost track of time. She'd been so engrossed that she really didn't have any idea what time it was. The second meta-element she was studying was a no-brainer: earth plus fire, and it was called magma, not to be confused with naturally occurring magma, apparently. According to her text, the meta-element, magma, was far hotter and persisted in its form for a lot longer, despite external conditions. She'd made good progress, and her practice with arcfrost and braiding Energy while cultivating had made it a lot easier to pick up the pace with this new pattern.

Olivia was walking down a long hallway toward the second west-wing stairwell when she passed a junction. She almost walked right through, but a flash of light to her left caused her head to jerk, and she stared down the long, dark side corridor. "Strange that all the lights are out down there," she muttered, goosebumps starting to crawl up the back of her neck. The light flashed again, and this time she saw the source—one of the globes that normally lit up the hallways had flickered briefly to life, then gone out again. While it was lit, Olivia had seen the sprawled form of a student. Starting into the dark hallway, Olivia summoned her fire orb and let it grow to the size of a softball, floating above her palm and bathing the darkened hallway in orange light.

Something tickled in the back of her mind, urging her to turn around and hustle to her dorm, but she couldn't just leave a person lying in the middle of the hallway. What if they were hurt? She glanced up and down the dark hallway, and the light orb up above flashed again, illuminating the area briefly—nothing else was in the hallway, just her and the student on the ground. Olivia hurried up to the form, seeing that it was a girl and that she recognized her; it was Haidis, a Ghelli girl that was in Jade cohort. Olivia knelt next to her and felt for a pulse. It was there, but thready and weak. Just as she started to jostle her to see if she could wake her, a strident voice called out from behind her, "What did you do to her?" Olivia jerked around and saw, standing at the junction of hallways, Gwinna and, a moment later, a black-robed professor that Olivia didn't recognize.

"I didn't do anything! I just found her here!" Olivia hated how defensive she sounded. She motioned for them to come over. "She needs help; her pulse is really weak!"

"Stand back from the student," the tall, heavyset Ardeni man said. He was clean-shaven, including his head, but his eyes were a piercingly bright shade of yellow as he stormed down the hallway. Olivia straightened up and took a step back, watching him approach. As he neared, he seemed less tall; she was getting used to the generally smaller stature of the native races she'd met. Gwinna followed him at a respectable distance, a strange expression on her face. "Well, first-year? Care to tell me the truth of what happened here?" The professor had a sneer in his voice, and he glanced at Olivia, then snorted when she didn't respond immediately. He knelt and held a hand over Haidis, muttering to himself while an orange glow began to emit from his extended palm.

"I already said I don't know. I was walking back from the library when I saw her lying here." Olivia was feeling very uncomfortable by the shortness with which the professor had spoken to her and how Gwinna had a half-grin on her face.

"Hmm, she's been electrocuted. I'll need to take her to the infirmary . . ."

"Olivia has an air affinity!" Gwinna cut in. The professor stopped speaking and scowled at Olivia. He did something very quickly with his hands, and Olivia felt a coldness clamp down on her, starting at the edges of her skin and contracting until there was a ball of ice at her center, right where she envisioned her Core. She convulsed at the uncomfortable feeling, gasping out her breath and panting to regain it. It was like she'd swallowed a cube of dry ice and then been punched in the gut.

"She's been hobbled. Gwinna, take her to solitary detention and let Professor Thain know that I'll be there to conduct an interview soon. Olivia, is it? Do not resist Gwinna; simply walk along with her and do as you're told. Any resistance will lead to further sanctions." With that, the professor stooped and lifted Haidis, turned, and briskly walked away. Olivia could barely register his words, let alone his movements, though. Her eyes had gone blurry with tears, and she was simply struggling to breathe.

"Come on then, Olivia," Gwinna said, taking her arm. She stressed and dragged out her name like O-liv-ee-ah. She began to pull her, and Olivia couldn't muster the strength to resist. The best she could do was walk along, stooping over to try to comfort the burning, painful sensation at the center of her being.

"Wha, what did, did he do?" She managed to gasp out as she allowed Gwinna to lead her along. Gwinna looked at her and tsked, shaking her head.

"Poor thing. Someone with your affinity. It must really hurt having your Core and Energy cut off. I can't imagine it. Luckily, I'd never do anything that would warrant such treatment." Olivia groaned at these words, unable to push out a retort. She tried to turn her eye inward to see her Core, but while stumbling behind Gwinna, contorted with the uncomfortable pressure and the difficulty breathing, she couldn't concentrate enough. She lurched, moaning and gasping with every step, and the journey through the dim corridors became a blur of agony and fear.

After an indeterminate amount of time, she felt the tug on her arm lessen, and she looked up from the blurry floor to see that they were standing in a small room with a desk. Two doors led out of the room, and Gwinna walked up to one of them and knocked politely but insistently. A moment later, the door opened, and another black-robed professor poked his head out. "Yes?"

"This student attacked another student with Energy. Professor ap'Gravin wants you to put her in solitary detention until he can investigate. She's hobbled."

"Hobbled? That won't be necessary in the detention cell. I'll take it from here, student."

"I don't think Professor ap'Gravin wants you to remove her hobble until he can inves . . ."

"Nonsense. Hurry along now; I'll handle this." Olivia thought she could feel the anger radiating out of Gwinna, but the other girl simply nodded and left, not sparing Olivia another glance.

"Alright, then. Oh dear, you look like you're suffering a great deal. First time being hobbled? Well, it certainly isn't pleasant, especially if you have a lot of Energy affinity. Hmm, come on, then. Once we get you in your detention cell, I can take it off you." He took Olivia by her wrist, and she limply complied, following him through the other door and into a long hallway filled with six identical wooden doors. He stopped at the first door on the right and held his palm up to a brass plate above the doorknob. A loud click sounded, and then he opened the door and led Olivia inside the small room.

Olivia limply followed him into the room and let him steer her to the side and into a small wooden chair. Gasping, she managed to look up to see the professor and noted that he was a Cadwalli, one of very few that she'd seen at the academy so far. "There now, I'm Professor Thain, though the title is simply a formality with me; I don't teach any classes. Hmm, I wonder what you did to deserve a hobbling? Well, let me warn you before I take it off: if you manifest any Energy constructions in this room, the wards will drain you of Energy to the point where you'll be rendered insensate. Understand?" Olivia nodded weakly, and then Professor Thain held out his black-nailed hands and concentrated. Suddenly a tremendous pressure was released from Olivia's Core, and warmth spread through her body. She was able to breathe without resistance again, and she gasped, sobbing with relief. "Poor girl. What happened?"

"I didn't do anything!" Olivia sobbed. "I just found a girl unconscious, and the other professor assumed I hurt her and did that hobbling thing!" Olivia felt her frustration well up, and her helplessness overwhelmed her, and she started to sob in earnest.

"Oh, hmm. Well, Professor ap'Gravin is a strict fellow, that's for sure, but I'm sure he's doing an investigation and will clear things up. Still, it's the middle of the night, so you might be here for a while. Why not rest there on the cot, and I'm sure things will be better in the morning." Professor Thain had a pleasant yet gruff warble to his voice, and he gestured to the little wooden cot that sat opposite the chair Olivia was in. Then he turned to the door and spoke again, "Don't forget what I said about manifesting Energy. You can cultivate; just don't push any Energy out for any reason. Trust me; you don't want to experience the draining wards." Then he was gone, the door clicking shut behind him.

Olivia couldn't believe the turn of events in the last few minutes. One moment she'd been happily making progress with her studies, thinking about winning some awards in the competition, and the next, she'd been tortured and thrown into a holding cell. What kind of school was this? The shock was wearing off, and the physical relief of having her Core unblocked had subsided to the point where she was able to get a grip on her emotions, but rather than calming down, her fear and frustration had turned to anger. She'd been set up; that much was clear. Gwinna just happened to be there with a professor that would snap to judgment against her? She didn't think so. How convenient that the fallen student was in Gwinna's cohort and had been hurt by electricity. How convenient that Gwinna had been able to quickly point out Olivia's affinity!

Olivia wiped her face on her sleeve and determined not to cry anymore. This wasn't the end of the world. There was magic here, and lots of it; surely they'd have a way of proving that she wasn't lying. She'd just be patient and wait for now. If ap'Gravin didn't treat her fairly, she'd ask to speak with one of her other professors. They'd have to let her have an advocate, wouldn't they? Alyss or Sange would be able to help. Yes, that was the answer. She'd bide her time for now; her cohort would notice her absence and let their professors know something was amiss. Even if ap'Gravin was biased, he must have rules that he had to follow; it wouldn't make sense for an institution with rules about everything else not to have rules about justice.

Feeling more resolute, Olivia sat on the bed in the lotus position and took up her cultivation drill. She'd gotten so much better at drawing Energy and weaving and unweaving the various threads as she did so that it was almost second nature. She reached out, looking for differently attuned Energies but only found pure, ambient Energy at first. Then she felt a little tickle of something in the ceiling, and she explored it with her inner eye. As she pushed her senses, following the hint of strange Energy, she found within the stone little pools of all sorts of attuned Energy: fire, air, earth, water, and dozens she didn't recognize.

Some of the different Energies felt dark and cold, some were noxious and stinging, and others felt warm and cleansing. Olivia pulled back and thought about it, considering Professor Thain's words about wards. Were these little pools of Energies part of the wards? Could she actually draw Energy from them? It seemed like a fundamental design flaw if she could unless her ability was truly uncommon. Maybe others with lower affinity couldn't reach into those pools. Perhaps she couldn't, she reasoned; she hadn't tried yet. Would it set the wards off if she did?

Tentatively, Olivia reached into the little pool that felt like fire-attuned Energy and gently pulled a little thread out of it toward her. Nothing happened, and she continued, pulling it into her pathway. Then she grabbed a thread of the water-attuned Energy and pulled it. Again, nothing happened, and she repeated the process with air and earth. Soon, she was busily working on a complicated braid of four Energy types, running it through her cultivation drill and then unwinding it to pull them all into her Core. The hours slipped away, and in her concentration, Olivia didn't notice the passage of time, nor was she aware of the tiny sparks and flashing motes of light popping through the stone ceiling of her cell.

MORGAN

When they entered the courtyard, it was empty save for Von-dak, who stood idly in the center of the open space. When he saw Morgan and Issa, his expression brightened, and he waved them over. "Let's begin your lessons; my time is limited with you since you won't be staying."

"There's a limit to how long we can stay here?" Morgan asked, stepping down the short stairway to the flat flagstones of the courtyard.

"Oh, yes. Have you noticed the other inhabitants of my little domain are no longer lingering around? I, too, must drift into a sort of sleep soon; it's part of the arrangement I made with the System when it arrived and inserted itself into my affairs." Morgan started to ask for more clarity about the situation, but Von-dak held up a hand and spoke some more, "Don't try to pry for more. I can't speak about many things, and, as I said, time is short. Issa, come forward with your rapier; I'll give you some pointers first. Morgan, pay attention!"

Issa looked at Morgan as she walked past him, smiling ruefully and glancing at his shortened left arm with a pained look in her eyes. She'd be a long time getting over his injury, he figured. He didn't want her to blame herself, but it was clear that he'd been fine with skipping the final challenge; he'd probably feel guilty if the roles were reversed. Morgan determined to put her at ease as soon as possible and not whine about his, hopefully, temporary predicament. He watched as Issa drew her rapier and stood in front of Von-dak. Von-dak's long, black sword seemed to condense in a smoky blur until he held a rapier-shaped sword. "Neat trick," Morgan said, but they both ignored him.

He sat down on the steps and watched as Von-dak sparred with Issa, encouraging her to use everything in her arsenal with regard to swordwork. Issa was fast; Morgan had a hard time keeping up with her when they practiced, but Von-dak managed to match her easily, and Morgan knew from their duel that he was holding back and just operating at Issa's ability level. After they sparred for a while, Von-dak began to give her pointers on her stance, the way she moved her sword, or how she gripped it. Then, as she adjusted, he started to ask her questions about why she chose to use that attack, why she was doing a particular thing with her feet, or what she had been expecting him to do.

As Issa answered his questions and followed his instructions, Morgan began to notice a very strange thing—motes of Energy would occasionally drift from Von-dak to Issa. Were his lessons more than just lessons but a direct infusion of some sort?

After what seemed like hours of drilling, Issa let out an excited whoop and shouted, "I did it! I broke through to advanced sword mastery! Thank you, Von-dak!" Von-dak also grinned, lowering his blade and stepping back.

"I could take you further, but if Morgan is to get his fair share, I think you should sit down and meditate on what you've learned." Issa moved to sit next to Morgan, favoring him with a warm smile as she wiped the sweat from her brow. "Morgan, come forward." Morgan stood up and walked out onto the flagstones.

"I might have a problem," he said, holding out his one hand. "I don't have any one-handed swords. I guess I could use one of Issa's rapiers?" He glanced back at her, and she nodded, smiling brightly.

"That won't be necessary," Von-dak said. "I caused your injury, so perhaps one of my older blades will better serve to instruct you." He seemed to concentrate for a moment, and then a long, narrow wooden case appeared out of nowhere at Morgan's feet. Morgan was used to seeing chests coalesce out of swirling, sparkling mist, but this one just winked into existence. "Open it." Von-dak gestured to the case. Morgan knelt and felt along the long case for a clasp, but there wasn't one. Awkwardly he gripped the wooden top above the seam and lifted. The wooden lid to the case was light and slipped freely off the felt-lined lower half. Morgan set it aside, then looked upon the gleaming blade he'd exposed.

He immediately categorized the sword as being shaped like an arming sword from medieval Europe. The straight, double-edged blade was about thirty inches long and tapered to a sharp point. It was crafted from very shiny metal, similar to stainless steel to Morgan's untrained eye, but suffused with a gleaming luster that seemed to come from beneath its surface. The crossguard was carved to look like two howling wolves facing away from each other, and the grip was wrapped in silver threaded white leather. Finally, it had a pommel shaped like a third wolf's head holding a ball of red metal about the size of Morgan's thumbnail between its jaws.

"Bloodfang," Von-dak said quietly, "It served me well for quite a few years when I was young. Pick it up, Morgan."

"Alright." Morgan gripped the supple white handle of the sword and lifted it out of the case. At first, it felt cumbersome, like picking up a long lead bar, but as he lifted it, it seemed to grow lighter and more comfortable in his hand.

"It's bonding with you. Best return the favor." Von-dak chuckled as he spoke. Morgan nodded and trickled some Energy into the blade.

Bloodfang: Artificed, Conscious Weapon. Enchantments: 1. Sharpness—This weapon will maintain its unnaturally sharp edge, recovering from wear and damage over time. 2. Solar Steel—This weapon has been forged of Energy infused Solar Steel—its significant weight and hardness are offset for the wielder by the imbued Energy. 3. Wolf Soul—This weapon has been imbued with the conscious spirit of a Corran Blood Rager through the workings of a legendary artificer. The spirit will aid the owner of this sword in various ways when enough blood has been spilled.

"The scabbard is long gone, I'm afraid, but with your condition, you'll probably want to use a metal ring on your belt. Easier to slip the sword in and out of that with one hand."

"It's a beautiful weapon," Morgan said, admiring how it felt in his hand and the way its blade shimmered in the light as he moved it. "It's just that my style is focused on two-handed blades."

"So, modify it. Are you the master, or is it your sword?" Von-dak scoffed. "Show me. Let me see your style's forms as best as you can with that sword." Morgan nodded and proceeded to push his way through his forms, doing his best to keep his body positioned correctly, even though he only had one arm held out with the one-handed blade. Overall, it went a lot better than he thought it would. Imbuing his forms with Energy, he still moved quite fluidly and managed to achieve the desired effect of each of his forms, if a little sloppily.

"That went better than I thought it would," he said, catching his breath.

"I see your forms—that style is similar to one I know. Why do you back up when doing that third form?"

"The Crane Defends the Nest? I don't know; it's a defensive form, so it just felt right."

"My old master would beat me every time I backed up. He'd say, 'sword battles are won by attacking.' I don't feel as adamant about it as he did—sometimes retreat is the only option, but if you regularly use a form that has you retreating, you're setting yourself up for a real master to see the pattern and cut you apart. None of your forms require you to move in a certain direction. Many times, it's better to circle while defending. Take your mind outside of the box you've built and realize that your movements are meant to be more fluid. You aren't required to use a certain sword with these styles, either. In fact, you could use anything once you truly master them—a knife, a spear, even a club. Of course, nothing matches the elegance of the sword, but it might do you good to practice with something else so that you see the versatility of your style."

"I . . ." Morgan struggled with what to say; he'd been so focused on being like the swordsman in his vision that he really had painted himself into a box.

"Don't talk; we've spent enough time talking. Attack!" Thus began the most difficult three hours of exercise Morgan had ever spent. It was harder than basic, harder than his own drills by a massive margin, and harder even than when he and Issa had pushed themselves in the Crucible. Swordmaster Von-dak kept pushing him to run through his forms. Each time Morgan finished, with Von-dak parrying and attacking, he'd shout, "Again!"

At first, Morgan felt very awkward with the one-handed blade, his balance thrown off by his missing arm, but slowly he started to get into a rhythm. His Energy flowed freely through his body as he cycled his forms, one after the other, taking in the tips that Von-dak gave him after each one. He was so engrossed and pressed so hard by Von-dak's seemingly endless stamina that he didn't have time to wonder if he was also receiving motes of Energy from the swordmaster like Issa had. His every muscle fiber and brain synapse were absorbed by the intense back and forth of swords.

Morgan didn't hold back, trying his damnedest to hit Von-dak, but no matter how fast or how viciously he swung, Von-dak easily matched him. The swordmaster also seemed to have no problem pushing his defenses to their limit, but whenever his blade slipped past Morgan's guard, he'd just lightly tap where he could have laid a brutal cut.

Morgan was breathing heavily and sweating profusely when Von-dak finally twirled his sword and stepped back. "Morgan, you're on the cusp of advancing, but we're out of time. Keep practicing with Issa, and you'll be there soon; I already see huge improvements in your style. I think the injury I gave you might have been a blessing in disguise. Use the time you have without that arm to learn from it; keep mixing up your forms and remember to change your momentum, and never get stuck in a pattern." He turned so that his words also included Issa and continued, "It's been a pleasure to teach you both. Go forth and spread word of old Von-dak and his school for those brave enough to seek out the challenge."

Morgan and Issa both started to utter their thanks, but the world shifted suddenly, and the light went from bright afternoon to predawn gray, and the temperature dropped by several degrees. Looking around, Morgan realized that he and Issa were standing in the ruined courtyard of the swordmaster's keep, the version they'd seen when they first sought out the dungeon. "Wow, that was abrupt," Morgan said, looking over to Issa, who still sat on the steps, though these steps were crumbled and strewn with rubble.

"I guess he wanted to squeeze as much teaching in as he could in the time he had available." Issa stood up and brushed her butt off. "Too bad you didn't make it to advanced sword mastery yet."

"Yeah, but he said I'm close."

"You sure were moving a lot more smoothly and quickly toward the end there. I was impressed by how much he helped you in that short time." She walked over to Morgan and held out her hand. "That's a beautiful sword he gave you, too." Morgan gently laid the flat of the blade against her palm.

"Yeah, I was afraid it was just a loner, but here it is." Issa admired it for a moment, and then Morgan slipped it into his belt. "I have to be careful not to cut my leg off while I get used to it."

"We can try to make you a ring to hold it more securely when we make camp. Let's go see if our Roladii abandoned us. How long do you think we were in there?"

"Over a week, for sure. We rested a lot outside the keep while we dealt with the 'challengers,'" Morgan replied, resting his hand on Issa's shoulder and walking toward the shattered gates of the ruined keep. "Umm, Issa?"

"Yes?" She looked up at him sweetly.

"Can you help me with my belt and pants? I've had to take a piss since before Von-dak's lessons began!"

"Ancestors! Is this what I have in store for me from now on?"

⟨ OLIVIA ⟩

In the middle of the night, Olivia's Core leveled again. She'd been a little surprised, but not terribly so; Sange had told her that early Core levels came quickly. She wasn't too worried about hitting level ten from cultivation because she knew that only a tiny portion of the Energy she cultivated went toward her personal level; most of it went to her Core improvement and, until she started really pulling huge amounts of Energy into her Core, it wouldn't have a significant impact in that regard. Still, she was pleased with the advancement. Sometime after midnight, the differently attuned Energy sources she'd been drawing from went dry, and she had to draw pure ambient Energy. When her Core leveled, she decided to call it a night and try to sleep until morning.

Olivia lay on the little cot, noting its lack of a blanket with mixed feelings. She wasn't cold, but the idea that they wouldn't include a blanket sent disturbing messages. Did they not care about her comfort? Were they worried that a student put in here might be suicidal? Was it just an oversight? She restlessly flopped onto her back, unable to sleep, her mind racing with all the implications of her predicament. Would her being suspected of a violent attack affect her standing in the competition? Would she lose points in her classes if she was held here during the day and missed them? What if she were held even longer?

In an effort to still her mind, she closed her eyes and imagined herself flying through an imagined landscape. In the past, this activity had helped her sleep when she'd been restless with worry over a presentation, test, or project launch. She imagined gliding down a steep valley road and into a green landscape filled with colorful trees and little animals. She veered toward a small pond and noticed the deer drinking from the water. Soon she was gliding over a streambed and under a bridge, and then her consciousness slipped away, and sleep found her.

A loud knock came from the door, and Olivia was startled awake. As she blinked her eyes clear, a loud click came from the door, and then it opened a crack. A familiar voice said, "Olivia? It's Alyss. I'm coming in." The door opened a bit more, then Alyss spoke again, "You can leave us. I'm going to speak with her privately." A man's muffled reply sounded, and then Alyss was stepping into the room and closing the door behind her. "Oh, Olivia! What sort of mess are you mixed up in?"

"I'm not sure, but I'll tell you, I'm not happy about the treatment I've had!" Olivia had let her fear slip away during the night, and she was ready for some verbal sparring if that's what Alyss wanted.

"Tell me what happened." Alyss moved over to the cot, and Olivia pulled her knees up and leaned against the wall; there was no headboard.

"I'd been studying in the library, and it was getting late, so I was walking back to my dorm. I saw a student, Haidis, lying on the floor in a dark hallway. I went to investigate, and then Gwinna and some ass of a professor showed up and blamed me for attacking her."

"Right, Professor ap'Gravin. Don't let others hear you speak that way, please, Olivia. He may be lacking in manners, but he holds a lot of clout around here."

"Lacking in manners? He tortured me!" At Alyss's shocked expression, Olivia told her the details of the story, about the hobbling and being stuck in this room with no real explanation of what would happen to her. She almost started to tear up, but she swallowed the feeling and focused on her anger.

"Oh, Olivia, I'm so sorry! Hobbling is slang for a class of spells that block your Core off with another person's Energy. It's mildly irritating to someone with very low affinity and terribly uncomfortable for someone with high affinity. I'll give Professor ap'Gravin the benefit of the doubt and assume he didn't know how badly it would affect you, but people will also try to see his perspective—he may have truly believed you were dangerous. I'm sorry, Olivia," she said as Olivia opened her mouth to object, "I know this doesn't seem fair. It really isn't, and it only gets worse: Professor ap'Gravin has the right to investigate the matter, and he has a window of time to operate before any of us can interfere. The only person who could speak on your behalf immediately and put an end to the matter is Professor Oylla-dak, the head of the first-year class. Sadly, she's gone on academy business until Friday."

"So, a full week? How long until other professors can intervene?" Olivia tried to keep the panic out of her voice.

"In five days, any of your professors can demand to see Professor ap'Gravin's findings. If he has no evidence of your misdeeds by then, we can demand you be allowed to return to class." Alyss tried to sound hopeful, but Olivia could see the disappointment in her eyes.

"So, either way, I'm getting robbed of nearly a fourth of the first month's classes?" Bitterness tainted Olivia's words, and when she saw the genuine concern on Alyss's face, she felt a bit of shame. If she were honest with herself, she hadn't realized how invested she'd become in the opening competition; she'd always been competitive academically but never in a showy, in-your-face way.

She'd simply done her best and let her results speak for themselves. She'd never been framed for assault before, though, and she wasn't sure how to cope with the feeling of injustice she was currently raging against.

"It all seems rather convenient for your competition, doesn't it?" Alyss said softly, as though she wasn't sure she should be speaking out loud. "Olivia, you're going to have to rise above this. If you're truly innocent, and I believe you when you say you are, then any investigation will show that result. If Professor ap'Gravin is aiding Gwinna or others who fear your placement, then he'll just drag his feet and announce that he couldn't find any proof at the last minute. That means you're probably stuck here for five full days, in which case, you're going to have to buckle down. I can say that this won't affect your ranking in my class, provided you do as I hope you will with the meta-elements. You're going to miss some lessons, but I think it's nothing you can't pick up by reading the associated chapters a few times. Just stick with your work on the meta-elements. I'll speak to your other instructors and see if I can get you some help. Keep up with your cultivation!"

"Oh, about that . . ." Olivia paused, unsure she wanted to finish her statement, but she felt like she could trust Alyss. "Um, I was cultivating last night, and I was reaching for sources of attuned Energy, and I felt lots of differently attuned pools of Energy in the ceiling. Is it safe to cultivate from there?"

"Hmm? Let me see here." Alyss closed her eyes and concentrated for a while, and then she opened them and smiled. "I think you're feeling the Energy traps for the wards on this room. They're designed to absorb certain types of Energy, and if you found them with your inner eye, then yes, you should be fine drawing it off. It won't break the wards." In a way, Olivia was glad to hear this, but, in another, she was disappointed—she'd kind of liked the idea that she was doing something so clever or challenging that the people who'd designed the wards hadn't thought of it.

"Alyss, do you think I still have a chance in the competition?" Olivia asked quietly, as Alyss stood up and straightened her robes.

"Oh, definitely. Not overall, perhaps; you'll lose a lot of points in alchemy and enchanting and probably physical education by missing a week, but you should be able to keep up with my class and Core Cultivation. And, Olivia, the best awards come for those two classes. Don't forget; there's also an overall prize for the top-scoring cohorts. Don't give up!" With that, Alyss moved to the door and placed her hand on the brass plate. When it clicked, she opened the door and turned to Olivia, "Either I or one of your cohort members will bring you news later today. Chin up, Olivia."

Olivia sat on her narrow cot and stewed. She kept running through the events of the previous night in her mind and grew angrier and angrier each time she remembered Gwinna's rich, throaty voice saying, "Olivia has an air affinity!" Olivia was not a violent person; she'd had to act violently in this world a few times, but never toward someone as mundane as a fellow student. That being said, she was feeling very violent right now.

As she felt her heart racing and grew conscious of her murderous thoughts, Olivia clenched her fists and forced herself to take deep breaths and think about something else. She thought about when she'd been struggling to perfect her cryo-pod prototype before her presentation to Vynatek; she'd been stressing about myriad things: some bad press generated by one of the undergrads she'd let go, one of her chief investors going bankrupt, her mother's breast cancer relapsing, and her absolute lack of a love life. The pressure had mounted to the point where she'd had an actual panic attack. When she'd checked herself into the university medical center, afraid she'd had a heart attack, the old, silver-haired doctor who'd seen her had given her some excellent advice: focus on what you can control and let the rest sort itself out.

Olivia decided to follow that advice now. She couldn't control the fact that she was locked in this room. She couldn't do anything about Gwinna right now. She could, however, study her texts, work with her meta-elements, cultivate, and exercise. Speaking of exercise, she was hungry, and she needed to use the toilet. She moved to the door and banged on it, listening for a response. A few moments later, the lock clicked, and the door opened, revealing Professor Thain's weathered, bearded face. "Yes?" he asked, clearly making an effort to be patient.

"I have to go to the bathroom, and I'm hungry and thirsty." Olivia knew it wasn't his fault she was in this predicament, but she couldn't help thinking of him as a jailor.

"Of course, of course. I'm sorry; we haven't had anyone in here for a while, and my routine's a bit off. I'll take you to the bathroom, but please don't do anything to get yourself in trouble. I'd hate to hobble you again. Also, I'm sure breakfast is on its way. We tend to be pretty far down the delivery list for the cafeteria." He opened the door and pointed further down the hallway. "Bathroom's the door at the end of the hall. Go ahead; I won't follow you in. There's no other exit. Please hurry, though; I don't want to stand in this hallway all morning."

"Thank you," Olivia said, walking past him, down past the other two pairs of doorways, and then opening the door at the end of the hall. Inside was a sink and a toilet, and not much room to use them. She took care of her business, splashed some water on her face, and then walked back to her room. Professor Thain nodded with a smile on his face, then locked her back in. Olivia sat in her windowless cell and, with new determination, took out her spellcrafting book.

So far, she'd learned the patterns for two meta-elements and gotten fast enough to complete one of them before it started to decay. She knew that if she pushed the woven Energy out of her pathway, she'd create arcfrost. She just didn't want to do it yet, because she was afraid it would level her. She could use more practice with magma—she couldn't quite create the full weave before it started to decay, but right now, she wanted to expand her repertoire a little. She flipped through her text to the next meta-element: plasma. It required a mesh of air-attuned Energy and fire-attuned Energy. According to her text, it was one of the most dangerous meta-elements to create, requiring a lot of fine control to keep the product from harming unintended targets, including the caster.

Olivia started with her notebook and pencils, drawing the pattern for plasma over and over. She spent fifteen minutes on her first draft, learning all the twists and knots, then she worked to draw it faster with each successive attempt. When she could draw the whole pattern in less than a minute, she put aside her drawing tools and assumed her lotus position. She turned her mind inward and slowly drew forth a strand of air-attuned Energy, then the fire-attuned strand, and then she meticulously began to weave the pattern for plasma.

MORGAN

Morgan and Issa had found their roladii about a half-mile up the valley from where they'd tied their leads. As Issa had predicted, they'd pulled free when their supply of food had run low. Still, they hadn't wandered far, and they came running when the two adventurers whistled. Issa was hugging and scratching Gopp, and Morgan did the same, running his hand over his mount's dusty back and scratching between his feathers. "Good boy, Munch!"

"They seem fine—no scratches or cuts, and they're plenty fat still. Aren't you, boy?" Issa laughed, slapping her roladii's thick haunch. Morgan smiled at her, relieved to see she was starting to act like her old self. He hadn't liked the sadness he saw in her eyes when she looked at him and his missing arm.

"Well, there's plenty of light; should we start back? I figure we should head home for a while and take stock of things before starting another new adventure."

"Yes, definitely. We have some goods we can trade, and I think we should see about getting your race evolved as soon as possible. We might need to travel to Tarn's or even further to one of the bigger cities."

"Oh, man, for a second there, I thought you weren't going to focus on my arm." Morgan chuckled to himself, pulling his riding gear out of his pouch. "Though, I guess it's hard to forget when I need your help constantly. Let me get this tack started, then maybe you can tighten the buckles for me?" Issa didn't respond, and he knew she was trying to be tactful. He supposed he needed to let her feel how she felt for a while. It's not like they'd been dealing with his injury for a long time; it had been less than a day, really.

Having an improved body and a massive strength compared to when he'd been on Earth certainly made it easier to cope with the injury. He easily hoisted his saddle up on Munch and managed to get the straps started underneath him. He slipped his halter and reins over Munch's head, then he stepped back and smiled at Issa. "Do you mind?"

"Of course not," She replied, though the laughter she'd had with Gopp wasn't in her voice. She stepped over and quickly pulled Munch's straps tight, buckling them. While she was leaning over, Morgan slipped up behind, wrapped his arm around her waist, and pulled her backward, so they both tumbled into the grass. She laughed and feigned a struggle but turned into him, and they both lay side by side in the grass for a moment staring at each other's faces. Morgan leaned forward to kiss her, savoring the softness of her lips and caressing her hair with his hand.

"I'd give up both my arms for you, you know? It'd make touching you a little harder, but I'd try. I'd use my feet if I had to."

"Shut up, dummy. You know I feel the same, though." She kissed him back, and they lay together in the grass for a while, soaking in each other's presence and listening to the sounds of insects buzzing and birds talking and the roladii quietly munching on grass.

They camped at the top of the old stone road that led down into the box canyon that night. Morgan did his best not to act frustrated with his missing arm—he struggled to do everything from setting up the tent to fixing some food. He was starting to learn a whole new appreciation for people he'd known with missing limbs. Well, that wasn't entirely true; everyone he'd known who had lost an arm or leg in the war had been fitted with prosthetics pretty quickly. He knew there were people without resources who didn't get the high-tech prosthetics that had been available to the various militaries and more stable governments, but he hadn't known any of them. His friend, Mark Alvarez, had lost his leg from the knee down when his transport blew up. Later that year, when Morgan ran into him, he'd been fitted with a prosthetic with nerve attachments. He'd sworn he could feel it when Morgan tapped on his chrome-colored shin.

"Now that's an idea," Morgan muttered while he stirred the little pot of stew Issa had started cooking.

"What?" Issa looked up from where she sat, using an awl and some scrap leather to repair a strap on the old saddle that the herders had given Morgan.

"I was thinking about a friend of mine who lost his leg in combat back home. He got something called a prosthetic leg replacement. Basically, it's an artificial leg that allowed him to walk almost naturally. I was thinking, I mean, there's actual magic in this world. Shouldn't it be possible to get an artificial arm while I'm working to improve my race?"

"I'm sure of it, Morgan. We could look into it if we don't have any luck getting you some racial advancement treasures. You're getting close, though; aren't you up to base seven?"

"Yeah, I am. I just need three more, right? Is that what you and Von-dak meant by an evolution? Moving past base to improved?"

"Yes, each tier is an evolution. I wonder what other changes you might experience! Some Ardeni grow a tail." Her smile was mischievous, but Morgan couldn't quite tell if she was joking.

"Seriously?" He raised an eyebrow, and she just smiled some more, not answering. Did he need to be worried about his body evolving into a monkey or something? "No, that would be devolving, right?" Issa giggled as he muttered to himself, and Morgan stirred the stew.

The next day they moved quickly through the box canyon and then through the Orangerock Hills toward the Gresh Woods. They made good time and didn't encounter any Shadeni raiders or Cadwalli herders. They saw lots of wildlife, though—little rabbit-like creatures, sheep-like holbyis, deer-like huldii, something that looked like a cross between a moose and a buffalo that Issa didn't have a name for, and even a huge Thunderak lizard that hissed and scuttled away at their approach. "There's a lot of wildlife, but it doesn't seem very dangerous. Are there no big predator animals around here other than the boyii packs?"

"I'm sure there are. Maybe they were driven off by the Yeksa your people killed or by the Yovashi that used to live near here. Where there's so much life, there must be predators, though. Maybe they're avoiding us; most predators are smart enough to avoid other predators. If their bellies are full, they won't want to risk injury." Issa spoke like she knew what she was talking about, and Morgan had to remind himself that her people were primarily hunters.

They camped at the edge of the woods that night, content in the knowledge that they'd make it back to the colony the next day. Being near the dark forest and its long shadows brought a sense of danger to the night, and Morgan insisted they take turns keeping watch. Issa didn't argue, but when it came time for her to sleep, she curled up with a blanket near the fire, resting her head on Morgan's lap. "Keep watch while I use you as a pillow, then," she said, smiling to herself. Morgan chuckled, using a stick to push the coals apart and allow the fire to die down; he didn't want the light in his eyes while he watched, and it wasn't a cold night.

While he listened and scanned the darkness, his mind wandered, and he found himself performing his cultivation drill, almost by accident. He shook his head, stopping midway through a cycle because he was absolutely unaware of his surroundings or how much time had passed. He looked up at the sky and could just make out the sisters behind the tree canopy, and he realized it was past midnight. As gently as he could, he slipped out from under Issa's head, bunching a blanket up as a pillow for her. He stood and stretched, silently kicking some blood back into his leg that had fallen asleep.

The night was anything but quiet; hoots of some kind of bird echoed through the trees, wood creaked and cracked in the high branches, the wind sang through leaves, and now and then, an animal would call out in the distance like a cross between a bark and a cough. He peered into the shadows, idly wondering if any animals or monsters were watching them, ready to dismiss the notion, but then a pair of bright eyes reflecting the moonlight caught him by surprise. He stared at the eyes, peering at him from the side of a tree trunk at about the height a person might stand. Morgan didn't make any threatening movements. Instead, he carefully walked to the edge of the little patch of grass where they'd made camp, holding his hand out to show it was empty.

He didn't know why he was trying to put the watcher at ease; it would probably have been wiser to draw his sword and shout for Issa to wake. Something about the eyes, and the way they hugged the tree, though, made Morgan think whoever was watching him was frightened or curious, but not dangerous.

Slowly the eyes moved away from the tree, and a shape emerged from the shadow. It looked humanoid, but definitely not human, with long thin limbs that moved stiffly like the joints didn't match up with where a human's would be. It stepped out of a dark shadow cast by the canopy of leaves and into a ray of moonlight, and Morgan got a good look. The creature looked to be made of wood and bark, maybe five feet tall with thin limbs and three long digits on each hand. It held a hand up, and Morgan took a step forward. Just then, a shriek sounded from maybe a hundred yards behind the creature, and it shrieked in turn, opening a mouth that split the lower half of its head and revealed rows of sharp, splintery wooden teeth. It screamed again, turned, and ran into the darkness like a rabbit running into a shrub.

Morgan felt Issa's presence before she spoke, "What was that?" Her hand came to rest on his lower back, and she stood at his side, naked rapier facing the darkness.

"Some kind of tree or bark person. It didn't attack me or anything; I think it got scared." Issa laughed at his words.

"Morgan, I love how you think; you're always so willing to give the benefit of the doubt. It sounds like you met a Striksa. They're not really dangerous to people unless they find you wounded. They mainly eat carrion, but Morgan, sweetie, if a few of them came upon you lying hurt in the forest, they would eat you alive, completely oblivious to your screams. They aren't nice."

"Not a pleasant image. Well, there go my dreams of making allies of the little tree people. Are you ready to keep watch for a while?" He turned back to the camp and stooped to pick up the blanket, shaking it out. "I'm ready for some shut-eye."

"Hmm, sure. I'll wake you at dawn, and we can hurry back to First Landing and have breakfast or lunch there." She sat by the still orange coals and patted her lap. Morgan smiled and lay down, resting his head on her lap and quickly falling asleep as she caressed his brow.

Later that morning, they made good time riding their roladii through the forest toward First Landing. Morgan used his Guardian's Senses ability to make sure they were on the right path, focusing on Arthur Ballard as a guide.

At first, he'd tried to concentrate on Bronwyn but had been alarmed to find his sense of her so distant as to almost not register. It was like she was on the other side of the world somehow. He took some comfort that he could feel her at all; she wasn't dead, but she was definitely somewhere out of his reach. When he told Issa, she looked concerned also but tried to sound hopeful, saying that it could be that she'd found a way to teleport somewhere.

They rode into First Landing just before noon. The guards at the gate waved them in warmly, expressing concern about Morgan when they saw his arm. He shrugged, trying to make light of it but inwardly dreading how he'd have to explain it to everyone he knew in town; it wasn't something like a scar that he could cover with some clothing. They were coming in through the southern gate, and the houses had really multiplied in the area while they were gone. The cobbled road had branch streets now, leading down rows of little homes. There were wagons on the road, and Morgan was surprised to see quite a few people that weren't human walking around conducting business.

They passed by not one but two new taverns when they got near the central hill, and Morgan almost stopped by one of the new establishments to eat but decided he wanted to check in with Alec Green at the original tavern first to see what was new in town. When they came around the hill, he saw a new sign hanging in front of the big wooden building, "Green's Tavern and Brewery."

"I guess when you aren't the only game in town, you can't just call your place 'the tavern.'" Issa smiled, and they tied their roladii to a post near the wooden deck and then walked into the building. People moved out of Morgan's way when he walked in, and he realized he towered over pretty much everyone. He certainly had a jump on them in terms of racial levels. He wondered if anyone in town had gotten any ranks other than Bronwyn. Even Issa was taller than many of the humans, which put things into perspective for him; Morgan had gotten used to thinking of her as small and quick, but she wasn't really so small anymore.

"Morgan? Is that you? Come on up to the bar!" Alec's familiar voice cut through the din in the room, and Morgan turned to see him leaning over his bar, a grin on his ruddy face. "Jesus, man, what happened?" He asked when he saw Morgan's missing appendage.

"Ancestors! It's rude to ask questions like that, you know! Maybe he's tired of explaining to everyone!" Issa's vehemence caught Morgan by surprise, and he realized it wasn't just him that was tired of talking and thinking about his injury. He put his arm over her shoulders and pulled her close, kissing the top of her head.

"It's alright, Issa," he said quietly and then continued, more loudly, "We had a lot of success, but I didn't escape unscathed. Good news is, I'll probably find a way to recover in this world of magic. I am tired of dwelling on it, though. How about some brunch?" The wince that Alec had affected when Issa snapped at him faded, and he thumped the counter.

"Coming right up! Sit down and take a load off, friends!"

OLIVIA

Olivia was surprised when the person from her cohort who came to see her that first day was Rald. She wasn't sure why, but she had expected Veena or Adaida. Rald smiled grimly at her when Professor Thain opened the door, and then he'd come in and tried to tell her about all their classes. Unfortunately, his recall was spotty at best, and the real reason he came was revealed when he got to his summary of Physical Education and Combat Practice. "Look, I was talking to Commander Grobak; I don't know why, but he seems to like me. Anyway, he's going to be basing a huge portion of our competition score on how much our punch improves from the first day to the thirtieth. He said he'd be scoring us on all the other stuff, like falls, grappling, and general endurance, but according to him, he'll know how much we've improved based on that punch."

"It seems a bit far-fetched. He had all of us punch his hand that day, but how can he remember exactly how hard we punched?" Olivia tried to wrap her head around it and supposed he might have some sort of eidetic sensory memory in his hand, but it seemed ridiculous.

"I asked him that! He has an artificed ring that records each punch!" Rald was practically crowing.

"Oh, really? That's fascinating! I'd love to ask Professor Brince about it. I never thought artificed items could be so nuanced in their function!"

"Oh, they sure can. I've seen some very interesting enchantments around here. Look at your ring, for instance—it's a storage item, and it keeps track of your rank at the academy and your credit balance. And it's so small! Imagine all the tiny runes that must be in the metal. Veena thinks they're layered with some runes on each layer, invisible under the top layers."

"It is fascinating, Rald, but I feel like you had another point you were going to make about Grobak?"

"Oh, yeah, well, I think you should work on your punch while you're in here. I know you don't think physical combat is your thing, and that's alright, but I bet you can get a decent score if you really improve at least that one thing."

"Well, I don't have great practice facilities here." Olivia's droll tone was lost on Rald.

"Oh, I know, I know, but you can do a few simple exercises to improve your strength, and I have a present for you." He grinned and flourished one hand over his storage ring and held up two dark-brown leather gloves. "These are artificed so that you can punch the air and feel like you're hitting a practice bag. The harder you punch, the more resistance they'll give you. My dad gave them to me years ago, so I'm sorry about the sweat stains." Rald held them out, rubbing at the dark leather and darker stains. "Really, it's not all sweat; I oil them regularly."

"Um, thank you, Rald," Olivia said, taking the dark, smooth leather gloves from him. They looked like they'd be way too big for her hands, which wasn't surprising; Rald was a large man. "I don't think they'll fit, though."

"Oh, you can bond with them. They'll fit you after that. Don't worry, I don't really need them anymore, but if you want to give them back, I can rebond with them."

"Is that how it works? I always thought my items in my bound containers were safe. Can someone just take my ring from me and bond with it?"

"Oh, no. I removed my bond from these gloves. It's easy; you just reach out to an item you've bonded with and pull your Energy signature out of it." He watched while Olivia slipped one of the gloves on and briefly concentrated. The glove shrank to fit her hand perfectly. The one she wasn't wearing also shrank—they worked as a set. "Before I leave you to it, I want to give you some pointers about punching and then show you some exercises, okay?"

"Alright, worth a try. It's not like I have much else to do. Well, I do, actually. Rald, wait until I can show you guys the spellcrafting I've been working on. I'm so excited!" She'd reached out and squeezed his wrist enthusiastically, and Rald smiled at her, patting her hand.

"Uh, sure. We're all expecting something great from you. I'm going to be happy to levitate a piece of wood." He chuckled, shaking his head at himself.

"Do you have any affinities? Other than the normal Energy, I mean?"

"Nah, I don't; I have a pretty high regular affinity, though. It's why my clan sent me here. I hope to learn enough to get a good class and then help with our war efforts when I get home. I doubt I'll be here for more than a year."

"Your people are at war?"

"Oh, yeah. Always. I'm from the Ridonne Empire, and we're always struggling to hold back raiders from the Beneset Steppes." He spoke the names of those places like Olivia should know what he was talking about, and she wanted to ask him for more details, but he stood up and motioned for her to follow suit. "Let me show you what you do wrong when you punch."

Rald worked patiently with Olivia for more than an hour, showing her how to square her legs, rotate her hips and drive her punch as she pivoted on her back foot. He had to stop midway through and help her make a better fist. "You don't want any space in there, grip down tight and put your thumb outside. Your fingers will move if you have extra space there, and your hit won't be as solid."

He also took a few minutes to show her how to do push-ups. She tried to tell him she knew how, but when she showed him, he moved her hands, so they were pointed in and closer to the center of her chest. He'd said, "Your chest is stronger than your triceps. You want to build your chest muscles as much as you can and use that to power the upper portion of your punch. Of course, all your muscles are important, and most of the power will come from your lower body when you rotate your hips, but still, work on this." Olivia wasn't an athletic person, but she wasn't a klutz either. She followed Rald's instructions, and he seemed pleased with her form by the time he left. She continued to practice her punches for a while, enjoying the exercise and marveling at how the gloves worked. It felt like she was hitting a soft, unmoving bag every time she drove her fist forward.

Professor Thain brought her a sandwich and a glass of milk for dinner, and when he came back for the dishes, he let her use the bathroom to get ready for bed. He told Olivia to call for him whenever she needed to use the facilities, but she'd been okay waiting until mealtimes during that first day in the cell. That evening she wound down by reading the next chapters in her Alchemy and Enchanting texts. They were both about simple recipes, and she dearly wished she could practice them in the lab, but her imagination had to suffice for now.

Olivia wasn't sure why, but she felt exhausted that night, and she knew she was falling asleep early, but she wasn't sure how early, her cell being underground with no window. She knew the light would turn off on its own sometime during the night, but she didn't know what time. She had meant to ask Professor Thain, but had forgotten. Still, she decided to make the most of her exhaustion and enjoy a good night's sleep. Putting aside her texts, she curled up on the cot and drifted into a deep sleep.

She woke several times in the night, troubled by vague dreams that made her uneasy but unable to recall what they were about. Her cell was pitch-black, and the first time she woke, she was so disoriented that she'd almost summoned a ball of flames to take a look around. Only at the very last second did she remember about the wards and where she was; she choked back a sob and redirected the Energy she had almost manifested back to her Core.

The restless night seemed like a bad dream when she woke to the bright light that had clicked on sometime in the early morning. She called for Professor Thain to let her go to the bathroom, and then she started her morning routine: exercise and punching, break for breakfast, work through her cultivation drill, and practice her meta-element weaving. Professor Thain had arrived with her lunch by then, and he gave her another bathroom break. Then, she did the whole thing over again.

She was happy when the door clicked open unexpectedly that afternoon, and Adaida poked her head in. "Hey, criminal. Can I visit you?" The bright twinkle in her honey-colored eyes betrayed how proud of herself she was for that faux insult.

"Oh, I suppose. I have to battle with some other inmates later, but I can squeeze you in." Olivia returned the grin and sat down on her cot, patting the thin mattress next to her.

"Other inmates? Do the guards place bets on who will win the fights?" Adaida laughed and sat down next to her. The door clicked closed, and the sound of the lock clicking shut was jarring. "By the Tree, they don't want you to get out, do they? What exactly did you do? The rumors are delicious, but I'm curious about the facts."

"Oh God, there are rumors? Of course, there are. I didn't do anything!" Olivia spent the next several minutes describing what happened, in detail, to get her locked up in that room. She found it strange that Rald never asked her, but then Rald was a peculiar guy; he was always joking or very serious. She supposed it was sweet that he'd come to help her with her combat practice, and maybe he'd avoided asking her about her "Crime" out of kindness.

"That sounds absurd! Of course, Gwinna is behind it, that bitch!"

"This whole thing is absurd if you ask me. It seems a lot of power is given to that professor just because he saw me. I have to wonder if my lack of connections is part of the problem; I can't imagine this treatment happening to someone like Gwinna or Sarice!"

"Of course not! That professor, ap'Gravin, practically works for Gwinna's family! I'm sure there's some prejudice among the senior staff, too; you're definitely being singled out for your race and lack of representation. I don't know Professor Oylla-dak very well, but I hope when she gets back, she roots out the creeps responsible for this because I can guarantee ap'Gravin won't find anyone else to blame in his 'investigation window.'"

"It doesn't matter. I'm making progress on my spellcrafting and cultivating in here. I can handle three more days." Olivia was happy for Adaida's vehement defense, but she didn't want to dwell on what she couldn't control right now. There'd be time to figure out who was behind this mess sometime later when she had a bit more clout.

"Alright, well, I came to see what I could do to help. I tried to come yesterday, but Rald insisted he had to get you started on some exercises for Grobak's class. What can I tell you about the other classes? Want me to go over the lectures from today?"

"Yes, please, Adaida! Let me get my texts out!" Olivia took out her texts, and they went over the day's lessons one by one. Even with Adaida's notes, Olivia felt like she was missing a lot when it came to Enchanting and Alchemy. Still, she felt like she was far ahead of the curve on spellcrafting—Adaida described a lesson about manipulating Energy into simple patterns, exclaiming about how difficult it was, and Olivia had to bite her tongue to keep from saying something that might be taken as demeaning.

Her time with Adaida went quickly, and before she knew it, Professor Thain was knocking on her door with a simple dinner of cubed meat in a sauce with a large chunk of buttered bread. He gave her a tall tin cup filled with watery wine and then turned to Adaida and said, "I'd invite you to stay for dinner, miss, but it's time for you to clear out, I'm afraid. Visiting hours are over."

"Hmm, alright. If I don't see you tomorrow, someone will, Olivia. Hang in there." Then she leaned over and gave Olivia a very warm hug, and her usual sarcastic facade crumbled a little. "This whole thing is truly unfair, Olivia, and I'd be scared witless if I were in your shoes. I'm so impressed by you. You're going to be fine!" Then she stood and hurried out the door before Olivia could reply.

"Your cohort seems to think a lot of you," Professor Thain said as he backed out. "I'll pick up your dishes in an hour or so."

Olivia ate her food in silence, ruminating on everything. Adaida's warmth had surprised her. She got along well with her cohort, but she hadn't felt particularly close to any of them, and it felt good to think that they cared about her and not just her performance in the induction competition. Before, she'd been working hard because she wanted to do well for herself, but now she felt some investment in her friends. She wanted to help Copper beat Jade and the other higher tier cohorts because Rald and Adaida deserved it, and so did the others, probably; it wasn't their fault that only one person could visit her at a time.

After eating, she performed another set of exercises and a round of punching, noting that she had many sore muscles already. Then she broke to use the restroom one last time, and she finished the night just like the one before, reading her texts until her eyes grew too heavy, and she slept.

◈ OLIVIA ◈

The next few days ran together in Olivia's mind. She followed a simple routine of exercising, cultivating, eating, studying, eating, visiting with a cohort member, eating, cultivating, studying, and sleeping. Her studying consisted of reading texts and practicing her Energy weaving. She was pleased with her progress; so far, she'd gotten fast enough to complete three meta-element patterns before they dissipated, and she was close to mastering a fourth: pyrosteam. It was the first meta-element she'd tried to create from opposing elements, and, though it was difficult, it was supposedly, according to the text, capable of immense destruction.

She ached to let one of the meta-elements she formed in her channels pour forth into the world, but she knew the consequences might be disastrous; she was pretty sure she'd level from the creation of the spell, and she also knew that the wards in her cell would not tolerate it. Still, Olivia wanted to see what she'd created; she wanted to watch her burst of plasma rip through the door or the pyrosteam carve a runnel out of the stonework. She didn't really know if that would happen, but she fantasized.

She'd tried to make progress with her punching and push-up exercises, and she felt like she had improved, pushing herself until she was sore in her chest and triceps every morning when she woke up. She didn't have any great hopes of impressing Commander Grobak, though; she just wasn't built for fistfights. Thinking of fistfights brought her mind to Bronwyn, and she often found herself wondering how her friend was doing. Had she settled things with the Urghat? Was she getting along with the council, or was she off adventuring? She smiled, wondering what Bronwyn would have done if she'd been here when Olivia had been framed for her "Crime."

Never once did that professor that had sentenced her to this "Detention" ever come to interview her. None of her cohort members had heard anything official about what Olivia had done, only reporting rumors that were most likely spread by Gwinna and Jade cohort. Olivia found it frustrating and concentrated on the injustice whenever she practiced her punches, finding that it helped to fuel her aggression.

She spent the morning of her fifth day in the detention cell just like she had the previous four, all the while waiting and hoping for the door to open with someone telling her she could leave. When Professor Thain brought her breakfast, he claimed ignorance, saying he hadn't heard any news yet about her fate. Frustrated, she slumped onto her cot with her sandwich. She ran a hand through her greasy hair and noticed how her armpits stank. Sure, she could use the sink to rinse off a bit, but a nice bath or shower would have been a real treat. Even Shani had remarked on her appearance and ripe odor the afternoon before.

It wasn't until near dinnertime that a knock sounded on her door, and it opened to reveal Alyss. Olivia sat up from her cot where she'd been lying on her back, tossing a ball of paper up and catching it. "Professor?"

"Hi, Olivia! Come on, let's get you out of here; I'll fill you in while we walk." Olivia didn't have to be asked twice; she hopped up and followed Alyss out into the hallway. "Professor ap'Gravin made this very difficult—several of us were trying to find him all day so that we could demand the results of his investigation. It was almost as though he was avoiding us!" She looked sideways at Olivia and winked. "Professor Brince finally cornered him and secured your release! No evidence could be found to implicate you. Even the girl that was injured claimed she never saw what happened to her."

"It's Friday, right? I lost track in there." Olivia was being dramatic; her friends had given her updates, and, though she had asked for reminders, she knew it was Friday.

"That's right—one more week of the induction competition. How are you feeling about things?" They were walking up a set of steps that Olivia didn't remember at all; she'd been completely out of it when she'd followed Gwinna down to the detention rooms.

"I am extremely excited to show you what I've done with meta-elements, Alyss! I also leveled my Core twice while I was locked up!" Alyss glanced sharply at her and raised an eyebrow.

"Be careful! You must be close to ten!"

"I know, I know. I didn't think I'd get two levels in there; the Energy didn't feel very rich after I drained those pools from the wards."

"Alright," Alyss nodded, "I will give you some advice, and I want you to take me seriously, okay?"

"Yes, ok." Olivia wasn't used to Alyss sounding so somber, so she inhaled deeply, trying to calm her excitement at being out of that cell at last.

"For the next week, do not go anywhere without your cohort. I'm going to escort you all the way to your dorm, and after that, you are to be with at least two of them at all times. It's for your own good, okay?" Olivia got her meaning right away, and she nodded.

"I had a similar thought, Alyss. I don't want to put myself in a vulnerable position, especially before the induction awards are given out."

"Good, Olivia. I've lost some faith and trust in this institution over this predicament, and I'll be having a long talk with Professor Oylla-dak when she returns. Keep that between you and me, though, alright?"

"Of course, Alyss. Thank you for looking out for me." Olivia nodded solemnly as she spoke, her lips pressed into a thin, severe line.

"Next week, I'm going to have you describe to me what you're able to do with meta-elements, and I'm going to give you a preliminary score. Once the awards are given out, I'll expect you to demonstrate them to the class. I think it will be a good experience for you and also an eye-opening one for some of the other students." Olivia wasn't sure how she felt about Alyss's expectations. On the one hand, it was flattering that she felt confident enough to prepare her this way, but on the other, she didn't want to let her down.

"What if my results don't match what I'm hoping to do?"

"I'll have an idea about that after you describe your process to me. Don't worry, Olivia. Now, this is your hallway, isn't it?" She gestured with her open palm to the hallway on her left, and Olivia saw the familiar row of doors and nodded.

"Yes. Thank you again, Alyss." Alyss smiled at her and watched as she went to her cohort's door, opened it, and slipped inside. Adaida and Hanwol were the only members in the dormitory at that moment, both of them sitting on a couch with their noses buried in books. When Olivia walked in and approached them, Adaida looked up and almost dropped her book in surprise.

"Olivia! Out of prison at last!" She jumped up and hugged her, and Hanwol set his book down, observing the two.

"Welcome back, Olivia. I'm glad you didn't get expelled."

"Why would she?" Adaida bristled. "That bitch, Gwinna, made the whole thing up. I told you!" Of all her cohort members, Hanwol was the only one that hadn't visited her, and Olivia now wondered if he'd actually believed she attacked that girl.

"Right, of course," he said, picking his book up and making a show of finding his page.

"Don't worry, Hanwol. I'm not out to hurt anyone. Yet!" Olivia said, looking at Adaida and laughing as she said the "Yet." Adaida also laughed, leaving an arm draped over Olivia's shoulders, and pulled her to sit down on the couch next to her.

"Well, any tales? Anything we need to know?"

"No, not really. There was no evidence tying me to Haidis's attack. Anyway, I don't want to be caught alone until next Friday, so we should all move around together. I don't trust Gwinna not to try something else." Adaida nodded sagely, but Hanwol lowered his book and glanced at Olivia to see if she were being serious.

"I think you're being paranoid. It's not Gwinna's fault that you were standing over that girl."

"Oh, Nature!" Adaida huffed, "Ignore him! He has a massive crush on Gwinna." Hanwol snorted and looked back at his book, but he didn't deny her words. Olivia preferred to think he was acting that way because of a crush than to believe he thought she was guilty, so she smiled and stood up, extricating herself from Adaida.

"I need a bath. I'm a filthy mess; thanks for not saying anything, Adaida!" She walked toward the bathrooms but turned back to say, "Don't forget what I said! You guys can't leave me alone, so don't go disappearing while I'm in there!"

Olivia slept better than she had in a long while that night. It took her a little time to fall asleep, but as she lay there on her side, watching the moons reflected in the big bay windows and listening to the soft breathing of her cohort members, her eyes grew heavy, and the next thing she knew Veena was jostling her shoulder to wake her up. "C'mon, Olivia. Some of us want to get breakfast, and I know you don't want to get left alone."

"Right, just let me clean my face and teeth real quick," she said, stretching into a yawn.

"Hurry, I'm starving!" Adaida leaned over her, grinning madly, letting her long, thick hair hang into her face. Olivia snorted in surprise and rolled out of bed. Adaida was definitely acting a lot more friendly to her lately. It was almost strange, but she wasn't going to complain; friends were good. She hurried to get ready, and while she was scrubbing her face, she couldn't help thinking how bizarre it was that she'd basically been in prison yesterday, and now she was going off to get breakfast with her friends.

The weekend went by quickly; Olivia and her friends spent time reviewing their lessons, eating out, and exercising on the commons. They didn't particularly try to avoid the other cohorts, but it seemed like everyone was feeling the pressure of the last week of the competition and kept to themselves while they studied. Sunday evening, Olivia, Adaida, and Shani went to the library to work on memorizing the few simple Enchanting techniques they'd learned so far. They'd been at it for an hour or so when Olivia loudly exclaimed, "This isn't fair! I can't really understand how this works without having practiced scribing these runes, modulating my Energy with a stylus."

"Just use class time next week. We're going to be in the lab, and if it's anything like last week, we'll only learn one or two artifices." Shani shrugged. "You're quick; you'll pick it up."

"She is quick, isn't she?" Adaida said, grinning from across the table.

"You've been awfully friendly and complimentary this weekend, Adaida." Olivia regretted the words the moment they left her mouth. Adaida's face fell, and she scowled at her book.

"Well, why shouldn't I be? Should I be a grouch all the time?" She asked, suddenly looking up at Olivia.

"No, I didn't mean it like that . . ."

"I'm going to head back. You girls behave yourselves now," Shani said, interrupting Olivia. She made her book disappear and then strolled out of the library, a sly grin on her face.

"What's the deal with her?" Olivia asked, watching her leave.

"Don't change the subject! What's wrong with me being nice to you?" Adaida asked, her cheeks reddening, though Olivia couldn't tell if it was anger or embarrassment.

"Nothing! It's just you seem different. You weren't so friendly the first couple of weeks. I'm happy that we're getting along; that's all I meant to say. My words aren't always the best choice, and I don't notice it until they've already slipped out of my mouth. Okay? Don't worry."

"How'd you get that scar, Olivia?" Adaida asked, completely changing the subject. Olivia got quiet and reached a hand up to her eye; she hadn't thought about the scar in a long time. "I'm sorry, that was rude. I shouldn't ask." Adaida said the words, but her eyes looked at her expectantly, like she wanted an answer, despite her words.

"When we first came here, there was a quest from the System to investigate a cave. I went with some friends, and a Yovashi attacked us."

"Nature! A true Yovashi? A male?"

"Yes, I almost died. My friend survived and carried me back to town. She bought some sort of healing cream from the store on the Colony Stone and used it to mend my skin and bones. My eye was almost ruined, but the cream put it back together. I know it looks different, but I see things normally out of it." While she listened, Adaida reached over the table and took Olivia's hand.

"It looks different, sure, but it's beautiful. Don't be self-conscious, okay? I'm sorry I brought it up, but it's not because you look ugly or weird; it's because you're amazing." Now it was Olivia's turn to blush, and she looked down self-consciously.

"Stop it. See what I mean? You're being so nice!" She laughed a little and looked up, tears brimming in her eyes. "I really hated being alone in that cell. I miss my friends and family, and you don't know how much it means to have you being so kind to me."

"Ugh! Who's cutting spiceweed around here?" Adaida asked, wiping at her eyes. Olivia laughed and brushed a sleeve across her cheeks, sniffing noisily. "C'mon, let's head back to the dorm. We've a big week ahead. You're going to have to tell me about your friends and family sometime, though. It helps to share what we miss, you know; it makes them more solid in our minds."

✦ OLIVIA ✦

On Monday morning, Olivia sat next to Veena, as usual, in their Enchanting lab, and while they waited for Professor Brince to come in, she asked, "Isn't it odd that there are seven days in your week and on my planet we also have seven days in a week?"

"Yeah, that comes up quite often. You know Fanwath was formed from the merging of four other worlds by the System, right?"

"Yes." Olivia nodded.

"Well, according to the histories I've read, the peoples that came from different worlds had a lot of things in common—seven-day weeks, similar body shape, well, most of them, some of the same customs, etcetera. What's even odder is that when some of the larger cities started to develop City Stones and open up teleportation between worlds, the first high-level visitors were remarkably, oh, compatible might be the right word here."

"So, they also had seven-day weeks? What about other customs, like I've noticed dining customs and, oh, everything!"

"I don't think they all did, but many, yes. Some people claim it's the System manipulating cultures on worlds as it finds them, spending a few thousand years making them more compatible before the merger. Some say it's the elder races—that they visited thousands, maybe millions of worlds long before there was a System and that we're all kind of related through them. I'm sure people living on older worlds know more than we do. Well, I shouldn't say we; I should say I. There are plenty of people in our world who know more than my history teachers, or I do."

"Well, the System isn't present on Earth, so I think that theory must be wrong."

"As far as you know, you mean." Veena grinned as Olivia connected the dots.

"Yeah, I guess the System may be manipulating things on my planet behind the scenes. I doubt it, though—we're way past this world when it comes to tech; I don't think it would have been shaping our culture for thousands of years and then allow us to develop nukes and spaceships and AI. It seems like that would make integration harder rather than easier."

"Hmm, yeah, who knows. Maybe it's the elder races theory."

"Just who are the elder races?" Olivia asked, and Veena opened her mouth to answer, but that's when Professor Brince stepped into the room and called for quiet. Olivia turned her attention to the professor and was pleased to learn that they'd be practicing the artificing they'd done last week before moving on to the day's lesson.

By the end of the class, she felt a lot better about what she'd missed while in the detention cell. Veena helped her with a few pointers, and she was able to apply the book learning she'd done without too much difficulty; she created a rune phrase that, when etched with Energy, caused a book's pages to flip by themselves every thirty seconds. It wasn't really a wondrous enchantment, but it was a proof of concept that had Olivia's mind whirling at potential applications.

The page-turning effect was part of a generic rune-set that allowed for autonomous movement. Olivia started to imagine gears inscribed in such a way and used in a larger machine—she could already envision clockwork automobiles powered by Energy. Before they left, she gathered some little scraps of material that she could practice on, checking with Professor Brince beforehand; the last thing she wanted was to get in trouble again before Friday. Brince had okayed her request and even suggested a shop in town where she could buy some artificing equipment like etching chisels, shears, blades, and needles.

On the way to Alchemy, Olivia lagged a bit behind her cohort as she sorted through the big handful of metal scraps she'd taken, trying to organize them a little before she stuffed them into her ring. She felt a presence over her shoulder, and then Sarice's voice said, "Glad you're back, Olivia." Olivia contained the impulse to flinch away—Sarice spoke very close to her ear. Instead, she slowed down, turning so that Sarice would come up beside her.

"Thanks. I'm glad to be back too." Olivia looked around, feeling an urge to see who was watching or listening while she spoke to Sarice. Maybe she wanted to know if Gwinna was nearby, or perhaps she wanted to make sure Shani wasn't watching; she still insisted that Olivia should avoid Sarice. She didn't see anyone paying attention to them, though, so she relaxed and kept walking.

"Well, I don't think it's fair how they treated you like you were guilty. That'd never stand in Persi Gables—that's my home city."

"No, nor in my home. I could be arrested but not held without evidence. Well, at least not for very long, I don't think. My knowledge of the justice system comes from watching crime dramas."

"Oh? I love dramas! I've even visited the great Ridonne Playhouse!"

"Isn't that the empire where Rald is from?"

"Hmm, Rald? He's the big fellow in your cohort? I wouldn't be surprised; there are a lot of Shadeni living in the Ridonne Empire. They make up a large part of the military." Olivia noticed that Sarice had slowed down while she spoke and that they'd lagged further behind her cohort. She started to feel a little nervous, and though she wondered if she was just being paranoid, she decided not to take any risks.

"Thanks for the kind words, Sarice, but I need to catch up to my cohort—I have to talk to them. See you in the next class!" With that, she broke into a trot, rounded a corner, and nearly bumped into Hanwol.

"I was just coming back to check on you," he said, stumbling back.

"Oh, good, thank you! Yeah, I got distracted; let's catch up to the others." They did catch up to the others, and the rest of their classes went without incident. By the time they returned to their dormitory, Olivia felt a lot better about her standing in all of her classes except for Physical Education and Combat Training. Her physical fitness had improved a lot in the last few weeks, and she was sure she could throw a punch better than any of her friends back on Earth, but she ran slower than many of the other students, and when it came to grappling and throws, she just felt clumsy.

"Hey, don't stress out about it," Rald said as they all stretched out in the sitting area of their dorm to eat the meals they'd grabbed to go from the cafeteria. "I told you, Grobak's looking for improvement, not for you to be better than everyone else."

"Besides, for someone with real talent in channeling and spellcrafting, you shouldn't worry so much about physical combat," Shani added, munching on a piece of buttered toast.

"Yeah, I doubt you'll even need to continue that course next year," Veena said, nodding along with Shani.

"Well, I like the exercise, and what if something happened and I couldn't cast a spell for some reason? Like if someone hobbled me?"

"Oh, roots!" Adaida said, "If someone is strong enough to hobble you, then you should just comply! It takes a real power discrepancy to pull that off on someone. I've heard it's terrible! Did they hobble you, Olivia?"

"Didn't I tell you guys? Yes, they hobbled me! It was awful, like I was being held down in a cold hole, looking through a dark tunnel to see out my eyes. All my senses were dulled, and it ached like a block of ice was squeezing my Core."

"Nature!" Adaida said, scooting closer to Olivia on the couch and taking her hand. "Sorry that happened, Liv."

"Hey! You called me Liv." Olivia smiled and looked closely into Adaida's eyes, wanting to see her reaction. The Ghelli girl blushed.

"Is that okay? Is it wrong in your culture to shorten names?"

"No, it's just the only person that ever called me that was my mom. I used to love it, but I don't think my friends ever felt comfortable enough with me to try out a nickname." Olivia had never said that out loud, and it sounded pathetic to her ears, but it was true; everyone who was her "Friend" had also been competing with her, or years older than her, or, later in life, her subordinate.

"Well, you guys can call me Ra or Ald!" Rald said, grinning. Olivia looked away from Adaida and stared at Rald, then they all burst into laughter.

"That's ridiculous," Hanwol said flatly, "But, seriously, you guys should call me Han. It sounds so much more dashing than Hanwol."

"Oh, okay. Next time we're in class, I'll be sure to call you Han so Gwinna can hear it," Veena said with a wicked giggle.

"Oh, dear Ancestors! Why am I stuck in school with my sister? Why couldn't they at least put us in separate cohorts?"

"Olivia, what are you working on for Spellcrafting? Alyss dropped some hints last week that you were working on something special, but I never see you actually casting spells." Shani had laughed along with the others at Veena teasing Hanwol, but she had a straight face now, and Olivia could tell she was worried about her progress.

"I can't cast the spells I'm working on because I'm afraid it will level me. I've leveled my Core twice since I hit level nine, so I think I'm getting close to ten." She shrugged helplessly.

"Really? So, how are you going to get placed in the competition?" Veena asked.

"I have to explain precisely what I mean to do to Alyss, and she'll score me based on that. If I win, I have to prove my concept, I suppose."

"Gwinna and some of the others won't like the idea that you can win a prize before showing your spell. If you weren't in my cohort, I wouldn't like it either, if I'm being honest." Shani frowned, tracing a circle on her folded knee with her pointer finger.

"Well, that's tough for them," Rald said, and Adaida nodded along with him.

"Yeah, she can shove their noses in it when she's done processing her awards." Adaida squeezed Olivia's hand, which she still held.

"Right, well, we should all get some studying in—three more days until it's Friday." With that, Veena pulled out her big Enchanting book and began to read, utterly tuning everyone else out. Olivia stood, giving Adaida's hand one last squeeze, then she walked over to her bed and pulled out her spellcraft book. She was very confident about three of her meta-elements, but she was still having some trouble keeping the knots tight on her pyrosteam pattern. She read through the chapter again, looking for insight, and then she practiced until well past midnight. Olivia knew she almost had it, and she hated to stop, but she knew she'd be a zombie if she didn't get a few hours of sleep before class.

Going into the week, Olivia had felt like Friday was a million years away, but, as often happens when one is busy, the next three days flew by in a blur. She learned and practiced all the artificing techniques that Professor Brince expected them to know. In addition to those, she worked on a tiny model of a clockwork engine that rolled around in a circle. It had one wheel made of cork that turned around a central point. Olivia had snipped the gears out of little copper sheets she'd taken from the artificing lab, and she'd stamped her runes into the metal with a set of tools she'd purchased with her first month's credits in town. The little engine worked when she channeled a tiny bit of Energy into the runes. Her friends weren't really impressed, but Olivia was ecstatic—if she could replicate this on a much larger scale, she could easily create automobiles, a mill, or anything that required a moving part.

When she'd made the little model, she'd gotten a small influx of Energy and almost had a panic attack, afraid she'd level, but she'd managed to hang onto nine for now. Olivia was so nervous about leveling that she refused to practice making any of the recipes they learned in Alchemy. She assisted Veena to prove she knew what to do to Professor Ghall, who'd been quite understanding of Olivia's desire not to level. The same held true in their Cultivation class; Sange didn't want her to complete her drill anymore before she leveled to ten. He gave her feeble sources of her Energy affinities and made her practice braiding the different threads of Energy together but warned her not to draw the finished braid into her Core. Instead, she had to unwind it and push the Energy back out when she finished.

That left Physical Education and Combat Training and dear, old Commander Grobak, who seemed to delight in watching young men and women fall to the ground over and over. They ran, they grappled, and they threw each other onto mats. Olivia thought they might never add something new to the routine, but on Thursday, Grobak surprised them by saying they'd play a game since the big awards assembly would be on the next day. Most of the students cheered, but Olivia instantly had a flashback of the push-ball match, and she looked around nervously for Gwinna. Sure enough, the girl with the glowing cobalt eyes was staring right at her with a slight grin on her face.

"There will be no Energy use allowed in this game. Is that clear, you bunch of witches and wizards?" Grobak shouted, and Olivia felt a surge of relief.

"Yes!" the assembled cohorts shouted out of reflex. They were loud, and they spoke sharply and in unison. Grobak had done wonders with them as far as that was concerned. Grobak nodded sharply, and then he produced a large hemp sack and dumped it onto the wooden planks. Ten brown leather balls thudded and rolled around at his feet. Then, to Olivia's dismay, he led the cohorts in a dodgeball tournament. It was essentially the same game as the one on Earth, but instead of bouncy rubber balls, they were hurling five-pound leather balls stuffed with God knows what. The rules were similar, but there was no blocking or catching—the only way to get someone out was to strike them with the ball.

Olivia did what she'd always done in gym class on the very small handful of times she'd ever played—she hung in the back, behind Rald and Adaida, and tried to dodge. If a ball rolled near her, she picked it up and tossed it to Rald. Surprisingly, the tactic wasn't half bad because Rald could really throw the ball, and their cohort beat nearly all comers, finally only losing to Bone and their three big throwers. Jade had been eliminated almost immediately by Bone, so Olivia never had to square off against Gwinna, which was a relief to her. She inwardly hated the fact that Gwinna still intimidated her, but she didn't know what to do about it.

To celebrate their second-place victory, the first month of school, and the end of the induction competition, Olivia and her cohort decided to skip the cafeteria and go to the market to eat at a restaurant. "I know just the place! I've been worried about my credits, but we get them refilled this weekend, so let's splurge!" Rald said as they all hurried back to their dorm to get changed.

"Oh, please! I don't want to eat something weird, Rald. Can we just eat at a normal restaurant?" Shani grabbed him by the arm, begging like a prisoner about to be tossed in solitary.

"Relax! It's nothing weird. It's that Ardeni place, the one with the stained glass that looks like a boat. You know it?" Several of the others nodded and agreed.

"Yeah, I heard that place is good. We should definitely wear some nice clothes, though. Or should we wear our uniforms?" Hanwol asked.

"I'm sick of my uniform!" Adaida said. "I'll never buy any gray clothes for the rest of my life!"

"I wouldn't mind wearing something else for a change," Olivia added, smiling at Adaida. She knew just what she wanted to wear—her maroon coat with the mustard brocade hem. Olivia hadn't worn her shiny boots since she'd arrived, and she was looking forward to a fancy meal. She still had quite a few of her credits, and if that wasn't enough, she'd made a couple dozen quad-attuned Energy beads in the last month while she was taking breaks from studying. "This place better be good, Rald. I'm in the mood for fancy food, wine, and dessert!"

BRONWYN

Bronwyn wriggled her toes, making sure they all still worked. They were scorched and sore but otherwise whole; her boot was another matter. She took out another pair she'd picked up from the Colony Stone and stowed away her ruined pair. She scooted back against the tunnel wall, the stormy opening on her right and the descending tunnel on her left, and then she fished around in her pouch for some clean socks. Her right arm was particularly tingly and sore, and she figured the lightning must have traveled through it as either the entrance or exit; she couldn't tell which her foot had been. "Good as new," she said, tying up the laces on her new boots.

She considered the three blessings she'd earned in the trial and, not for the first time, wondered if there were different ones. Could she have taken different paths or made other choices to earn different sorts of blessings? Bronwyn couldn't think of a way she could have avoided the swarm. She supposed there could be some chance involved; if she'd waited outside the lightning-struck tree for a while or moved more quickly, could she have avoided it? Deciding she could ask the queen when she finished, Bronwyn stood up, brushed the dust off herself, and started down the tunnel. She might have gotten her three blessings, but the queen had said something about reaching one of the "Summer Sources."

Bronwyn strode down the hallway, feeling surprisingly good for someone who'd just been blasted by lightning. She supposed she could chalk up her good feelings, or at least some of them, to the fact that her vitality was something like four times as high as when she'd first woken up in this world. That had to mean something, right? It didn't explain her good mood, though. Really thinking about it, she decided she was happy that her gut instincts had paid off in this trial. She'd begun to doubt herself over the last few months, and it felt good that she was doing well and receiving "Blessings" from the Fae for her choices and behavior. "Plus, it was fun as hell racing through that storm!" She laughed and didn't try to stifle it, continuing to walk confidently down the springy, round tunnel.

She came to a junction of three tunnels and stood there for a moment. Looking in each direction, Bronwyn couldn't see anything notably different about any of them. Each tunnel was roughly oval, and they each had a slight downward slope. Due to the slope, she could only see about a hundred feet in any direction. While she stood there, contemplating her options, she decided to take a few steps in each direction.

She first walked down the right-hand tunnel, and she noticed something—Bronwyn thought she caught a brief whiff of woodsmoke. She turned and went back to the junction and tried the central tunnel. She didn't smell anything this time but noticed that the temperature dropped significantly. Turning around, she moved a short way down the last tunnel, the one on the left. This tunnel felt warm; she was sure of it, much warmer than the central tunnel. "Hmm, smoke, cold, or warm?"

She didn't bother returning to the junction; she wanted to walk down the warm tunnel. "I'm supposed to be an Agent of Summer, right?" As she walked, she felt the tunnel begin to curve to her right, and then the grade grew steeper. She continued, walking confidently, and the tunnel continued to bend to the right, more tightly now and descending even more steeply. After a few minutes of this, she found her footing growing more and more unsteady, the force of gravity pulling her down the steep, tight spiral of the passage. It reached the point where she would have to sit down and scoot or start running to avoid falling, so she chose the bolder approach, allowing gravity to pull her into a run as she rapidly descended. She was braced for the end of the spiral, so it wasn't with any great shock when, with a final stumbling step, she fell through open air to sprawl onto a soft, springy cavern floor. It was warm and bright in the room, and the ground was loamy and covered with soft green moss, so she didn't suffer any harm from the fall. She rolled over onto her rump and sat up, looking around.

The cavern wasn't huge, only about twenty paces across, and she couldn't see any other exits. The warmth and light came from an orb that hovered in the middle of the room. It was bright, yellow, and heat radiated from it like a miniature sun. It pulled at Bronwyn like a favorite friend, song, or food. It felt like a memory she cherished and wanted to savor, and it took all of her willpower to keep from rushing over to it. The orb pulsed, and another wave of heat washed over her, and she remembered lying on the beach, watching her aunt Tass chasing after her cousins while they screamed with laughter. "Holy shit," Bronwyn hadn't thought of her dad's sister in years. She stood up and slowly moved closer to the orb, and it pulsed again.

Bronwyn was sitting on a rocky outcrop, looking over the canyon she'd just hiked. Her dog, Boots, was lying on the grass nearby, tongue hanging out happily as she soaked in the sun. Bronwyn pulled her hair out of its tie and let it fall down her shoulders. Closing her eyes, she, too, bathed in the sun and relished how her muscles felt after the challenging but rewarding hike up the canyon trail. She had a big tournament on Monday, and she'd come up here to get her mind off things. She took a deep breath, savoring the dusty pine scent of the air. Boots stood up and came over to lick her face, and Bronwyn laughed, reaching into her pack to find her collapsible dish so she could give the poor girl some water.

Suddenly she was back in the cavern with the pulsing globe of summer, and Bronwyn felt a surge of loss for her old dog, and her eyes filled with water. She hadn't thought of Boots for a long time. Why? She'd loved her so much, and those hikes she'd taken with her had been some of the best times of her life. She didn't know why the bright, pulsing orb had shown her those memories, but she was grateful. It felt almost like she'd been blocking off a part of herself all these years, and she didn't know why or what it meant. Had her life just gotten too busy? Had she filled the corners of her consciousness with things she'd found more pressing? While contemplating, she'd taken two more steps toward the orb, and she could feel the potential building like it was going to pulse again, and something made her quickly step forward and put her hand into the basketball-sized orb of radiant light.

White light filled Bronwyn's vision, and she lost sense of her body. She was floating in space filled with warmth and potential, and she had the impression that she wasn't alone. She didn't know who was with her or what, but she felt as though she was under intense scrutiny. She could see nothing, or she could see everything; it was impossible to tell. She tried to imagine a way to define her surroundings, and the only thing she could come up with was that she was inside, no, not inside; she was part of the potential of Summer with a capital S. While Bronwyn struggled to perceive what was happening to her properly, a dry, deep voice rolled over her consciousness, *"Ahh, has another Child of Summer come to drink from the well?"*

"I'm trying . . ." She didn't even know what to say she was doing. She tried again, "I want to be an agent of the Summer Queen."

"So, you need a taste of Summer to carry with you, no?"

"Yes." Bronwyn thought it seemed right. She felt a prickling sensation starting at her Core and rushing through every fiber of her being, and then the voice sounded in her mind again:

"You bear the Queen's mark and three blessings of Summer. Your heart seems true, Child of Summer."

"What do I need to do?"

"Draw from me; pull me into your Core. Forsake what you've gathered thus far." Draw from it? Did it mean she should cultivate the Energy here? Bronwyn couldn't feel her body, let alone sit down with her legs crossed, so she turned her

attention inward, looked at her Core, and began the cultivation drill that the System taught her when she'd earned her Amber Core so many days ago. "*No, Child, not like that. Forget that petty knowledge. Reach out, feel the heat around you, embrace the summer Energy and pull it within. Let it course through your pathways and enrich you. Brace yourself, Child.*" Bronwyn imagined herself breathing deeply, though her lungs were not something she could feel right now. Then, she stopped thinking about the cultivation drill the System had taught her and concentrated on the warmth around her.

The Energy around here was thick, and when she stopped trying to see it and just felt it, she knew it was embracing her, pulsing against her like waves lapping at a rowboat. She concentrated on that feeling, the tingle of the Energy against her being, and she willed it to come inside; she pulled it toward her Core.

As soon as the first tendrils started to flow into her pathways, she became far more viscerally aware of the Summer Energy and pulled it through her pathways toward her Core. It flowed thickly at first, like water pushing up a sand-clogged channel but, just as water would as it soaked through the sand, the Energy started to flow more quickly, and soon it was surging through her pathways into her Core. At first, it was pleasantly warm and invigorating, but as the trickle grew to a torrent and then a tsunami of Energy, her pathways burned, and the Core at the center of her being flared with brilliant yellow-white light, pulsing and spinning rapidly.

Bronwyn did as the voice had instructed and braced herself. She wasn't going to back down now, so she just held on and let the Energy wash through and into her. In her mind, she screamed like someone riding a rocket out of the atmosphere for the first time. Just as she was beginning to wonder if she could take anymore, her Core pulsed heavily, and the earth-attuned Energy she'd held and gathered for so long surged out. It ripped through her pathways, scouring them clean, and burst out of her to be burned up and absorbed by the Summer Energy surrounding her.

Bronwyn looked at her Core, and where it had shone with a steady amber glow before, it now flared like a hot yellow sun. She followed her pathways with her mind and saw that the nodes she'd had in her hands were gone, replaced by delicate, multi-layered pathways. "*You've done well, Summer Child. Your heart is a good match for us. I hope you'll visit again with tales of what you've done for our cause.*"

"Thank you," Bronwyn said, or imagined saying, and then the white light filling her vision faded, and she was standing outside the cave, where the storm had been. The skies had cleared, and the fresh scent that always followed a summer storm hung in the air. Bronwyn took one step, and then suddenly, her vision filled with System notifications:

Notice! Your Amber Class Core has been exchanged/upgraded to a Summer Class Core.

Notice! Your earth affinity has been lost!
Notice! You have gained an affinity for solar Energy.
Notice! You no longer meet the prerequisites for your skill: Fetters of Stone - Basic. You have lost this skill.
Notice! You no longer meet the prerequisites for your skill: Stone Fists - Basic. You have lost this skill.
Notice! You no longer meet the prerequisites for your skill: Stone Warding—improved. You have lost this skill.
Notice! You no longer meet the prerequisites for your Class: Stone Pugilist. You have lost this class.
Calculating.
Congratulations! You are eligible for a Class Selection. Locate your class options via your status screen.

"Ahh, fuck!" Bronwyn smacked her hand into her palm. She'd just started to get used to her skillset and had been happy with the way things were progressing. She hoped her new Core would prove to be stronger than the old one, but right now, she was feeling cheated. She called up her status sheet, and the first thing she noticed, other than her missing class and the new description of her Core, was that her new Core was rank three, whereas her old one had been two. Her solar affinity was a full point higher than her earth affinity had been, also. "At least that's something," she muttered and tapped the button for class selection. The list was much shorter than when she'd been level ten:

Class selection option 1: Solar Monk—Advanced. Your affinity to the sun's heat and vibrance allows you to shape Energy into martial weapons and boons. Class attributes: Agility, Vitality, Intelligence, Will.

Class selection option 2: Solar Mage—Advanced. You shape solar Energy into devastating attacks and use your will to bend it to great utility. Class attributes: Intelligence, Will, and Vitality.

Warning! Not a System-curated Class ***Class selection option 3: Summer Banneret—Epic. Wield the might of Summer to spread its influence in hostile lands. Class attributes: Unbound.***

When she read the third option, Bronwyn's lips spread into a wide, toothy grin. It was almost like the System was panicking with that warning. She wanted to select it right away, but just as she was steeling her nerves for the fallout, a shimmering, orange-yellow rip in reality appeared next to her, and she could see the Queen's throne room almost like she were looking through a window. "Time for me to come back, hmm?" She figured it was for the best—it would be good to confirm with the Queen that option three was the way to go. Feeling rather triumphant, Bronwyn stepped through the portal, her mind full of questions and her heart full of heat.

✧ MORGAN ✦

Morgan sat behind the desk in the tower's study and frowned at the little alchemy book. *Gaerwolt's Secret Recipes* was half recipe book and half love letter. Each recipe was prefaced with a love poem or essay about a memory Gaerwolt had with the woman for whom he'd intended the book. Still, it was filled with a dozen or so very promising-sounding recipes, especially one near the back that purportedly created an elixir that would "Delve a person's heritage for racial advancement." Morgan cleared his throat and called, "Tiladia?"

"Yes, Morgan?" the tinkling voice responded after just a couple of heartbeats.

"Tiladia, can you please read this alchemical recipe and tell me if any of the ingredients are among the herbs, flowers, and fruits we harvested from the atrium?"

"Of course, please lay the book open on the desk there, and I'll take a look." She flared and swiftly moved to hover near the desk. Morgan put the open recipe book out before her, and she pulsed slightly, perusing the words. "Yes, Morgan, nearly all of these ingredients should be among your harvested ingredients, save some of the more common ones you can easily purchase. Also, you're missing one rare ingredient, 'Petals of a Threen Sun Rose.' I know not where to acquire such."

Morgan laughed, "Ahh, now it becomes clear. I was awarded some of those along with the book you're reading."

"Then you should be able to replicate this recipe if you have the requisite alchemy skill and equipment."

"I don't have any skill or equipment, I'm afraid." Morgan sighed—nothing was ever easy.

"Morgan, there is a very well-equipped alchemy lab on the sixth floor of this tower."

"Hmm, that's right. You did tell me that. I haven't thought about challenging guardians in a while, and it didn't occur to me. What do you think my odds are?" Morgan stood and slipped the book back into his ring.

"I sense that your overall power has increased significantly, Morgan, but I've yet to see you in action with your missing limb. If you are as nimble as you once were, judging by your increased Energy levels and new abilities, you have an excellent chance."

"Well, I seem to do fairly well with the one-handed sword, though I'm sure I'd be better off with a shield or something in my other hand. Still, maybe I'll give it a try."

"Give what a try?" Issa asked from the doorway. Morgan hadn't heard her approach and jumped a little in surprise.

"The next guardian. There's an alchemy lab up there, and . . ."

"Do you think that's a good idea right now?" Issa cut him off with a frown, looking pointedly at his arm.

"Maybe you could let me finish my thought?" Morgan sighed and walked closer to her.

"I'm sorry, Morgan." She glanced at Tiladia, almost like she blamed the spirit for Morgan's interest in the sixth floor.

"Listen, Issa. What would you do if there were no way to heal my arm?"

"There are ways to heal it, though!"

"Just answer the question, please. Also, put yourself in my shoes. How would you feel if you had my injury and I tried to talk you out of doing anything dangerous?" Issa frowned even more, and Morgan wanted to lean forward and kiss her, but he knew that would only upset her.

"Okay, I get it. Still, there are things we can do without you fighting right now, aren't there?"

"Sure, but listen: that alchemy book we got as a reward back in the dungeon? It has a recipe to advance someone's race. One ingredient is those glowing flower petals we got. Don't you think the System is trying to tell us something?"

"Yes, but do you trust the System? If you do, that still doesn't mean we need to open the alchemy lab on this tower right away. There are alchemy labs in this settlement! I don't know how well equipped they are, but there are alchemists in Tarn's Crossing. We could be there in a few days!" Morgan had to admit she had a point.

"I think that's a good point—I don't know if any of the humans have much skill with alchemy yet, anyway. Well, you were right. Isn't it nice when we talk things through?" He asked, arching an eyebrow. Her frown turned to a grin, and it was she that reached up to kiss him. After she pulled away, Morgan continued, "I don't want to waste time. Let's head out first thing?" She nodded. "That means we need to get a lot done this afternoon—Arthur wanted to meet with us, and I want to talk to Tiladia and Ykleedra about their findings. They've finished reading and translating two of those Yovashi texts, isn't that right, Tiladia?"

"That's correct, Morgan, and I think you'll be intrigued." The falling crystal sound of her voice approached as she spoke, and Morgan thought he heard a note of excitement.

"Well, I want to visit the Ardeni lodge some hunters built here. I'm excited to hear about what they've accomplished with your people. I'll go do that now, and you talk to Tiladia, okay?"

"Sure, then we can meet for dinner at the tavern and talk to Arthur." Morgan reached out and gently squeezed Issa's shoulder. "Thanks for talking a little sense into me."

"Well, that's what people do when they care about each other," she purred, nuzzling into his chest.

"Alright, just 'cause you got your way, you don't have to be all affectionate now," he chuckled, squeezing her into a hug. He felt a sharp pain on his left pectoral and realized she was biting him. "Ow! You're going to draw blood! Your teeth are sharp, you know!" Issa snarled, gripping his flesh between her teeth, but when he looked down at her, he saw the amusement in her eyes. She released him and grinned wickedly.

"You weren't complaining about them last night!"

"God! That was different!" Morgan rubbed his chest, making a show of looking under his shirt to see if he was wounded.

"Big baby! I'll see you for dinner," she spun and gracefully strode out through the foyer.

"She's a handful, Tiladia." Morgan chuckled and walked through the central chamber to the library. "Tiladia, can you give me the report on these books now? Do you need to get Ykleedra?"

"I will be able to describe what we've found with great accuracy, Morgan. Ykleedra is napping; she turned to a nocturnal schedule while you were away."

"Did she? It doesn't seem healthy—I wanted her to get to know some of the colonists. I need to remember to talk to Maria about coming to the tower and engaging her in conversation or lessons while I'm gone. I know Maria is busy, but maybe she can recommend someone else if she can't do it."

"A wonderful idea, Morgan, though I do spend a lot of time with her." Tiladia's tinkling voice followed him into the library.

"I appreciate that, Tiladia. I really do. Well, what did you find in these books?"

"Would you like me to be verbose, Morgan? Or shall I speak briefly and then answer questions?"

"Uh, well, how about you just start explaining things, and then I'll interrupt if I need more clarity?"

"That sounds fine, Morgan. One of the texts we translated was a brief history of the Yovashi on this world. We learned that the Yovashi and another race called the Ilyathi shared an origin world. Their world was combined with three others when the System came to this section of the universe. Prior to the System's arrival, the Yovashi were rather powerful Energy users, having learned to create class patterns and abilities from Energy without the System's assistance. The System offered them methods to perfect what they already knew, promising much more efficiency, power, and growth. The Yovashi refused, preferring to do things their way and refusing to subjugate themselves, as they put it. Part of their resistance was that the System taught the Ilyathi how to use Energy and helped them to free themselves from the Yovashi. Prior to that, they were treated as a race of enslaved people. According to the Yovashi text, the madness that descends on the males of their species is due to the conflict with the System. They call it a curse, though the mechanism by which each new male is infected is not known."

"So, they weren't exactly nice people before the System came and before their males were 'cursed?'"

"If you refer to their treatment of the Ilyathi, then no, they weren't very nice. They also performed ritual sacrifices."

"Jesus. Did Ykleedra read all this?"

"I'm afraid so, Morgan. I needed her help with the translation, and we'd already read a lot together before I realized the extent of the darkness contained in that history. I felt it was better to confront the facts together and for me to explain the faults with her people's history than to cut her off."

"Well, hopefully, that was wise. I'm not exactly qualified to decide. Still, I think it's more important than ever for Ykleedra to get involved in a healthy society. So, back to the text—is it really possible for people to create classes and skills and spells without the help of the System?"

"Yes, Morgan. We elder races did it also. Dragons used Energy to fly, wield powerful breath weapons, and even transform our shape. We did all this without any sort of System, so I'm not surprised to hear about the Yovashi. I must say, though, I don't think they were as mighty as we dragons. The System didn't try to assert itself on my world."

"Don't you think that it's possible the System just hadn't gotten to your world yet?"

"I suppose so," Tiladia sounded wistful, and she assumed her dragon shape, looping around the library for a moment while Morgan watched.

"Tiladia!" he called after her, "What about the second book you translated?" She swooped down and spun around him, then returned to her amorphous form.

"Oh, it was a book describing the best methods to flay and dismember a person without causing their death."

"Are you fucking serious?" Morgan looked around the tabletop for the book in question.

"I'm afraid so, Morgan. It's that one there. It has disturbing images within." Morgan picked up the book, not bothering to flip through the pages. He carried it back into the study and put it into one of the desk drawers.

"Keep Ykleedra away from that!" he said, turning to Tiladia, who had floated quietly behind him.

"Yes, Morgan. Why not destroy it?"

"I have a hard time destroying books, and who knows what in that book might be valuable to history someday."

"Wise," Tiladia tinkled, bobbing up and down.

"Are you patronizing me?" Morgan asked, arching an eyebrow at her.

"No, Morgan! I'm sorry, my thoughts are distracted, thinking about my life. We dragons were so magnificent, Morgan! I hope you can find a way to travel to one of the worlds where we dwell. I'd love to introduce you to some of my kin!" Morgan laughed, realizing, once again, that Tiladia was a person with her own feelings and thoughts.

"Thanks for all your help, Tiladia. I'm sorry I treat you like a computer sometimes."

"A computer, Morgan? I'm excellent at counting, but I never enjoyed maths."

"Just ignore me; I'm not making a lot of sense. Thanks again for your help, though. Do you think you can translate the rest of these texts without Ykleedra? I would rather she didn't read any more disturbing things about her people."

"Yes, Morgan, I have a good working knowledge of the Yovashi alphabet now. I'll continue to work on them, and when I'm spending time with Ykleedra, I'll teach her about dragon philosophy and history, if you don't mind." She spun around excitedly, again taking the form of the brightly glowing mist dragon.

"I like you, Tiladia, and you seem to have a strong grasp of right and wrong, so yes, I think that would be healthy for her." Morgan nodded, trying to see a flaw in the plan.

"Excellent! Of course, if you find her a human tutor, we can devise lessons together!" She grew even more frenetic, performing a backflip.

"I can see you're excited about this, Tiladia!" Morgan laughed, watching her performance.

"Yes! I'm beginning to think of Ykleedra as one of my nestlings. I think I can help her to find greatness!" Morgan smiled, thinking of the idea of a dragon's spirit teaching and raising one of the last of the monstrous Yovashi. It seemed insane, but it also seemed perfect.

"Alright, Tiladia, I'm heading out. I'll do a bit of shopping and touring before I meet Issa for dinner."

"Goodbye, Morgan. Pick up something tasty for Ykleedra!"

⊙ MORGAN ⊙

"Well, that's a little disturbing," Arthur said after Morgan explained that he could sense Bronwyn but that she was extremely distant and not in any clear direction that he could tell.

"You haven't heard anything from her? Or from those Urghat she had following her?" Issa asked.

"No. It's not surprising with regard to the Urghat, though. They've made themselves scarce since we repelled their invasion. I don't imagine any of them would come around without Bronwyn present to vouch for them."

"My people still hunt them on the plains. The hunters in the lodge claim that most Urghat have retreated to the Blue Spines." Issa said, a slight frown on her face. "I hope Bronwyn's followers aren't among their prey."

"Yeah, I hadn't thought of that. Hopefully, they're with her or far from here." Morgan drummed his fingers on the table. "Well, nothing we can do about it for now. Take heart that she's alive. Is there anything you need from us before we travel to Tarn's? I don't think we'll be gone more than a couple of weeks, but I can't be sure."

"If you're going to Tarn's Crossing, I have a diplomatic package I'd like you to bring to their governor—just some correspondence and some artwork that our artisans want to offer as a gesture of goodwill and thanks."

"Sure, no problem. Everything else going alright?"

"Quite well, actually. We've got a burgeoning flock of those sheep-creatures, the bolyo, or something."

"Holbyis," Issa said.

"Right, right. We've also started up some trade with a few of the local nomad bands. So far, nothing has come to threaten us. We've continued to build our arsenal of defensive weapons, though. Boris has figured out a way to make rifled cannon barrels, and they're on the verge of making Energy powered projectiles—black powder may have a very short-lived use for us."

"That's good, I suppose, though I wish it weren't necessary. Still, I'm not naive—there are a lot of hostiles out there, and as our territory expands, we might run into things much worse than Urghat." Issa nodded along with Morgan's words. "Any word from Olivia?"

"Not a peep, though she thought it might be difficult to communicate with us."

"Right, hey, hang on a second." Morgan closed his eyes and concentrated for a minute. "Yep, I can feel her. She's south and east of here, quite a lot farther than Tarn's Crossing. It's good to know she's alive, though, eh?"

"Yes, quite. That's a handy skill, Morgan."

"Well, it sounds like the council is handling things just fine, though now that we're out of any immediate crisis, maybe we should see about an election to replace me? Maybe Bronwyn and Olivia, too? I feel bad doing it while they're gone, but we did talk about it before everyone left."

"For now, the six of us in the colony aren't having any trouble organizing things. If it becomes a problem, we have a quorum and can vote to fill your seats. Your connection to the locals is valuable, though, Morgan, and I'd rather not have you leave the council for now." Arthur glanced at Issa when he said "Locals," and Morgan chuckled.

"He does have a good connection to the locals, doesn't he?" Issa grinned at Arthur, but her sharp teeth, and the squint of her eyes, didn't make the grin seem exceptionally friendly.

"Um, I didn't mean any offense," Arthur sputtered.

"Of course, Arthur. Well, if there's nothing else?" Morgan scooted back his chair.

"No, nothing else. Let me get that package for you, so you don't have to look for me in the morning before you leave." Arthur stood, and Issa and Morgan followed him out of the little meeting room and through the bustling tavern. "It's in my house on the north end, not far from your tower." They walked along the cobbled road, and Morgan noticed the new streetlights for the first time—outside buildings and at every street junction, they added a level of civilization that had been missing before. In the twilight of evening, they spread warm glows of orange-yellow comfort.

"Nice lamp posts," Morgan noted.

"Yes, the artisans completed them as one of those 'quests' from the Town Stone. Supposedly, there was quite a hefty reward for each post completed. I can't complain when the System makes managing the colony easy like that, but I must admit I balk at the loss of autonomy."

"Those sorts of things will become less common as your town develops," Issa said. "Though, we still get occasional infrastructure quests in Tarn's Crossing. My father recently picked up a quest to repair the runes on our bridge."

"Intriguing," Arthur murmured, turning down a side path toward a large, single-story home. "Please wait just a moment while I run in for the package. I'd invite you in, but I'm sorry; I wasn't expecting guests." He didn't wait for a reply, just turned and walked up the dimly lit path to his dark home. Morgan watched, lightly resting his hand on Issa's shoulder.

"I want to spar a bit before we sleep; I haven't worked with my new style nearly enough," Issa said quietly. She'd used the scroll that gave her the Whispering Death fighting style during their journey, and they'd only practiced a few times since then. It was a complex, offense-oriented style that favored quick movements and feints. It fit Issa and her rapier perfectly. She'd improved in speed and in her ability to chain attacks, parries, and dodges when her sword skill moved to "Advanced." So much so that she had little trouble besting Morgan when they limited themselves to blade work alone. Still, it was good for him—he felt like he was even more on the cusp of breaking through to advanced than he had been back in the citadel.

"Sure, I'm not tired yet, anyway." Morgan watched as lights flickered on in the windows of Arthur's home, and then, a few moments later, Arthur stepped back out through his door and approached them. He held a small leather bag out to Morgan.

"Everything is in here. Sorry to give you another bag to carry, but at least it isn't heavy. Please don't lose it, though; many of our artisans labored for the items contained within."

"I'll keep it safe. Well, Arthur, if we don't see you again before we leave, stay safe." Morgan reached out his hand and shook Arthur's. Issa surprised him by giving Arthur a quick hug.

"You're doing good work, Arthur. Thank you for befriending my people," she said as she pulled back, holding his shoulders. It hadn't really registered to Morgan until just now, but she was as tall as Arthur was and far more substantially built. She made him look frail. Having evolved his own race along with hers, she still seemed small to him, but that was far from reality.

"Well, thank you. Safe journeys, you two." Morgan thought the older man might have blushed, but it was impossible to see in the dim light. Arthur turned with one last quick wave and then walked to his home.

"That was nice, Issa," Morgan said as they walked down the cobbled lane that now ran within a few dozen paces of his tower.

"Well, it's true. The Ardeni I spoke with said that they'd been treated like heroes by the people in First Landing and that Arthur gave a speech honoring some of them for their exploits on the plains." Morgan grunted in acknowledgment, picturing the scene. He hoped things continued to go so well.

That night, they practiced together for more than two hours, and halfway through their session, Ykleedra came into the dueling hall to watch. Morgan paused their sparring long enough to give Ykleedra a small dimensional container he'd bought from the artisan hall. "It has lots of good food in it—fish, small game, birds. It's yours to keep."

"Thank you, Morgan!" Ykleedra's raspy voice rose slightly with excitement. "Did Tiladia tell you about what we learned?"

"Oh, yes. Thank you so much for helping her to learn your language, Ykleedra. You can stop working on that project for now, though. I spoke with a very nice woman in town today about you. She's going to come and visit you to get to know you a little. How do you feel about that?"

"Why, Morgan?" Her voice was quiet now, and she edged sideways so that Issa, who was working through her rapier styles a few paces away, couldn't see her face.

"Not for anything bad, Ykleedra. I want you to become part of this community, and you can't do that if you're holed up in this tower all your life. I told her that the sun bothers your eyes, so she'll come in the evening. My hope is that she'll be able to find people to be your friends and teachers." Morgan hunched down, putting his hand on his knee so that his eyes were on a level with hers.

"I didn't do anything wrong?"

"No! Of course not! Tiladia told me how much help you've been, but there's a lot more to life than just helping me, okay? I want you to learn and grow and start working toward your own goals. Tiladia will be giving you some lessons, also."

"Truly? Do you think I could learn to work magic and how to weave?" Two of her legs began to tap rapidly on the wooden floor, and Morgan took it as a sign of excitement.

"I don't see why not. You should ask Tiladia about it first; she knows a lot and can start to guide you. When Maria comes here, let her know your interests, and she'll be able to find the right tutors for you."

"I'm going to talk to Tiladia right now, Morgan. Good luck with your big knife practice! I'm sorry your mate is so hard on you." Ykleedra turned and scurried out of the hall while Morgan slowly closed his gaping mouth. Was Issa kicking his ass that badly?

The next day, Morgan and Issa loaded up their gear, packed a plethora of new travel rations, and saddled their roladii. "Looking forward to seeing your dad?" Morgan asked as they rode through town toward the south gate.

"Of course! I'm also looking forward to his cooking! He'll owe us a welcoming home meal, don't you think?"

"Hah, for sure!"

"Morgan! Jeez, buddy, what happened to you?" A friendly voice called from the walkway to their right. Morgan looked and saw Boris waving.

"Oh, hey Boris! Glad to see you before we leave again!" Morgan stopped Munch, and Boris walked over.

"Well? I don't know if I should compliment you on getting better looking, again, or if I should make you tell me what the hell happened to your arm?"

"Ahh, you see, when someone plays with sharp objects, there are bound to be accidents." Morgan laughed.

"Ancestors! It's not something to laugh about!" Issa said, slapping his shoulder.

"Uh, hmm. I wonder what kind of prosthetic I could come up with if I research the right runes." Boris's eyes started to glaze over in thought.

"Hey, man, thank you for the thought. Issa and I might have a solution, though. I just need to keep upgrading my race, and apparently, at some point, my body is going to kind of renew itself or something. I'm not really clear on it."

"At each tier, your body will go through a kind of metamorphosis," Issa supplied.

"Oh? How fascinating!"

"Hey, Boris, it's not exactly easy to get racial upgrades, though, so it wouldn't hurt to advance the prosthetics field, you know, in case of other 'accidents.'" Morgan grinned down at his friend, and Boris gave him a wink.

"I like the challenge! If you can't find a solution, maybe I'll have something for you next time you're in town."

"See you soon, Boris!" Morgan said, giving Munch a little kick. A short while later, they'd passed the main residential area of the colony and out through the gate. "Let's see if we can get to the Chebli Sea before dark. What are the odds we'll run into Teric and his crew?"

"The sea is a big place, Morgan; besides, I think their next run isn't 'til after summer."

"Huh, good points, darlin', but I'm still going to hope for it!"

MORGAN

The journey through the grasslands of the Chebli Sea went smoothly for Morgan and Issa. They didn't run into the Ardeni herders, nor did they encounter any wildlife of any size. They saw lots of birds and small animals scurrying through the grass at their approach, but, for the most part, they were alone, like two small boats on a vast ocean with wavy, red-purple water. "It smells different than last time," Morgan remarked near the end of their third day of riding.

"I think the flowers will be gone in a week or so. Their fragrance is much less noticeable this time, isn't it?" Issa replied, taking an exaggerated sniff.

"Yeah, that's it." They were, if Morgan's memory served, about half a day from the Rill Catcher, and it was getting on toward evening. "Let's set up camp. The weather's nice, the sky is clear; let's enjoy the grasslands one last night before we have to turn toward the forest."

"Oh, that sounds good. My back is tired of this saddle, anyway." Issa rubbed Gopp's shoulder and dismounted. There wasn't any point in looking for an "Ideal" campsite—it was grasslands as far as they could see in every direction. Morgan started setting up the tent while Issa cleared an area for a campfire. They let the roladii wander freely because they wouldn't go far with grass so near.

That evening they sat by the small fire, cooked some meat and veggies on kabobs, and even drank some of the cheb-cheb that Morgan had been hoarding. They curled up together in the tent, enjoying each other's company for a long while, and then Issa said she wanted to keep watch first for a change. Morgan didn't argue, he liked being the first to watch, but if she wanted to, he didn't think it was fair to always get his way. He closed his eyes while Issa slowly stroked his shaggy hair. He briefly thought about how he needed a haircut, and then he was sinking into oblivion, a dream of sitting near a placidly flowing river already overtaking his mind.

Morgan woke with the feeling of warmth on his face. He felt good, better than he had in a long while, and he stretched, enjoying how his muscles pulled taut while he took in a big lungful of fresh air. It was only when he looked around the tent and saw the yellow sunlight through the canvas fabric that he registered what was going on; he'd slept through the entire night. "Issa?" he called out, scrambling out of the warm blanket and poking his head out of the tent flap. He saw Gopp and Munch a little way's off, doing what they did best, eating grass. He saw the cold remnants of their fire, but he didn't see Issa. He stood up and looked around—everywhere was grass, a little higher than his waist, but no sign of Issa in any direction. Unless she'd fallen?

After a brief moment of panic, Morgan remembered his Guardian's Senses ability and reached out for Issa. He felt her, solid and alive but much farther than she should be. She was off to the west, a good day or two away from him at the pace they'd been keeping. "What the fuck?" Morgan pulled his tack out of his storage bag and, with only one arm, struggled to get it onto Munch's back. After sloppily yanking the leather straps through the buckles, he looped a lead over Gopp's neck and jumped onto Munch, kicking his heels and racing in the direction he could feel Issa. The tent, blankets, and cold fire sat forlornly in the middle of the sea while the two roladii tore through the grass, exuberant in their morning sprint.

Morgan had never felt panic like he felt in that moment. There was no rational explanation for how Issa had gotten so far away in the middle of the night. His mind raced with possibilities, none of them good. She had to have been taken, right? The question ran through his mind over and over. She couldn't travel so quickly, even with Gopp, and she'd left Gopp. Even if she wanted to leave, she wouldn't do so without saying anything. What could have taken her? She'd slaughter an Urghat that tried, or Yeksa, even if there were enough to overpower her, she'd have made a hell of a ruckus. What about a Yovashi? Could one still live around here? Morgan knew from experience that some Yovashi had the ability to do teleportation magic. He urged Munch to even greater speed, careless of the beast's endurance.

Hours later, Morgan was forced to allow Munch a break. The poor animal was straining to keep up the speed, but he was huffing and wheezing with effort, and foamy sweat was gathering along his shoulders and haunches. Morgan got off the roladii and gave both of them water from a bucket he kept in his storage pouch. Then, he let them eat grass while he continued jogging in Issa's direction. After the two roladii had become dots in the distance, he whistled for them to come, and they did. While they continued to eat in the new location, Morgan jogged off again. He did this four times, and by the time Munch and Gopp caught up to him that fourth time, they no longer ate grass ravenously, and Morgan jumped back onto Munch's saddle, letting him run at a more sedate pace.

He pushed Munch to keep trotting for another couple of hours, then he watered the two mounts again and continued running, leading the two of them at, what was for them, a leisurely pace. Morgan took heart by constantly feeling for Issa and feeling that he was gaining ground on her. She didn't seem to be moving any further, and Morgan felt like he'd covered more than half the distance to her by the time the sun began to sink toward the western horizon. Running into the sinking sun, he didn't notice at first but soon realized that low hills were taking shape in the distance with taller mountains behind them. He was tired, having ridden or run the entire day, but he didn't slow as twilight came over the grasslands, and the hills and mountains became deep purple bruises against the moonlit sky.

Morgan grunted, scrambling up the loose scree on a rocky hillside. The hills had grown steeper as he pushed on in the night, but Morgan refused to stop; he felt Issa closer now, but he could sense she was much higher than he was. He reasoned she had to be up in the mountains, the foothills of which he was now scrambling through. He knew he was being reckless, but he couldn't be still while she was suffering some unknown fate. He'd left Munch and Gopp back in the lower foothills in a small gully filled with grass and leafy shrubs. They weren't much help when it came to scrambling up hillsides. Morgan was feeling the loss of his arm more and more as the going grew steeper. He was forced to leverage his strength and agility; he'd grab handholds, kick himself up, and hop from perch to perch. Still, his body was exhausted, and the skin of his hand was raw and scraped, his nails chipped and filled with dirt.

At some point, in the middle of the night, Morgan could feel that Issa was mostly above him, hardly any further west. He had gained a lot of elevation already and knew that he was high on the slope of a rocky, barren mountain. The problem was that he'd worked himself up to a rather steep and stony escarpment. He'd need to find a crevasse or a path or something, or he'd have to set some sort of world record for one-handed mountain climbing. There wasn't anything Morgan wouldn't try for Issa, but he figured he'd do more for her alive than dead at the bottom of a cliff, so he started to work his way south, along the base of the rocky wall. He constantly scanned upward with his Azure Sight, looking for signs of a path, a structure, anything. Hours went by as he wended his way along the mountainside, looking for a way up. All the while, he reached out with his Guardian's Senses, making sure Issa hadn't moved and that she was still alive. Each time he felt her presence, he felt renewed strength flood his limbs, and he pushed on.

The eastern horizon was growing light when Morgan finally found what he was looking for: a narrow crack in the rocky escarpment some way south and further east of where he felt Issa's presence. It was just wide enough for him to stand in, each side of the crevice nearly touching one of his shoulders. Rocks and roots made convenient grips and steps as he wormed his way up the crevice, climbing nearly vertically toward the top of the escarpment. He could see the triangle of gray sky that signaled the end of his climb and knew he was about halfway when the jutting rock he was pulling on slipped free of the cliffside, and he fell. Stones and dirt accompanied him as he tumbled and bounced down the jagged rocky walls of the cleft. He flailed his arm, trying to get a purchase on anything, but his efforts were fruitless, and he tumbled and slammed into the ground. He felt a crunch in his chest and the world went dark.

He was sure the darkness only claimed him for a few seconds, and he gasped a lung full of dusty air and surged to his hand and knees. Morgan coughed for several long seconds, wincing at the pain in his side. He knew he'd broken or cracked at least one rib. He marveled at the fact that he'd only suffered some hurt ribs after such a fall. Truly, his improved body was a lot sturdier than a typical human's. He knelt there for a long moment, catching his breath and chuckling. "I'm losing it," he said, shaking his head. Exhaustion was becoming a real problem, but he didn't care—there was no way he would rest until he'd laid eyes on Issa and seen that she was safe.

Morgan stood and rummaged in his ring for one of the weaker healing potions he'd picked up at the Contribution Store in First Landing. He drank it and sighed loudly as relief flooded into his bruised and scraped skin, and the sharp pain in his ribs became a dull ache. He looked at his hand, whistled appreciatively at the lack of blisters, and began his ascent anew. This time he took more time, carefully testing each handhold.

As the day brightened, Morgan felt the sun's glow begin to warm his back. He had just passed the point where he'd fallen when he came to a large indentation atop a jutting boulder and decided to sit there and have a small break. He scooted his back against the crevice wall, looked out over the rolling hills to the southeast, and saw the purple-red sea of grass. From this height, he could see where the Rill Catcher cut through the grassland and even the blue-green haze of forests far to the east. It was beautiful, and if Morgan weren't constantly feeling for Issa, he might have found the view sublime enough to lull him into relaxation, but that wasn't the case. He drank a few gulps of water, scarfed down a hard biscuit, and resumed his climb.

With only one arm, Morgan had to use the sides of the aperture and his legs to wedge and push himself up. By the time he finally scrambled out onto the flat top of the escarpment, he was brown from the dirt and mud that his sweat had created. He lay flat on the ground, trying to control his breathing while taking stock. He was on top of a kind of plateau, though another escarpment led to an even higher peak in the distance. Still, on this wide ledge that spread out for about a mile, he could make out a copse of scraggly trees and the walls of some sort of tall, rectangular keep. He could feel Issa's presence coming from the keep. While he lay there watching the keep, perhaps a halfmile distant, he saw a huge, winged shape lift off from the top of the structure, swoop lazily as it caught an updraft, and then glide out over the plateau and down over the stony cliffside to the northeast. Judging by the distance, Morgan surmised the winged creature was at least as big as a horse with something like a twenty-foot wingspan.

Frantically, he felt for Issa, and when he felt her still alive and within the keep, he breathed out a sigh. The creature hadn't eaten her or taken her away, though what was its intention if it was responsible for bringing her here? Were there more of them in that keep? Was it doing someone's bidding? A million more questions rushed through Morgan's mind, but he had no answers, and there was only one way he could think of to get some: he had to get into that keep.

The copse of scraggly trees grew along the next cliff base and up against the keep. Morgan didn't know if anyone watched from the keep's walls or its tall narrow windows, so he crawled on his belly for two or three hundred yards to the edge of the little wooded area. Only when he was several body lengths into the trees and scrubs did he stand up, squatting low, and begin to work his way toward the gray walls.

He crept to the edge of the little copse, noting how quiet it was. He didn't hear a bird chirp or an animal scurry the entire time he worked his way from tree to tree. When he got to the last row of trees, before being exposed, he squatted low behind a particularly fat, gnarled trunk and studied the keep. The stones were enormous, evenly cut, and laid with the skill of an expert, but the masonry was in great disrepair. Much of the mortar was crumbling, and the stones had significant open gaps between them. Morgan could only imagine how wet it must get inside during a storm. He couldn't see the roof from his position, but he felt like he could probably scale that wall fairly easily, even one-handed. He saw several rectangular windows about twenty feet from the ground, most were unshuttered, and the shutters that covered one of the windows were hanging crookedly with a wide gap between them.

He was about to creep over the swaying, brown grass to the wall when he heard the strangest sound rippling through the air. It was like a warbling, chirping, "Cwooo, cwooo," coming from above and echoing off the stony side of the keep. Morgan crouched down behind his tree and watched as the winged creature swooped down and landed on the top of the keep's wall. It hung there, back facing Morgan, and took a couple of steps on massive taloned feet before it dropped down, either inside the keep itself or some hidden courtyard. This time, Morgan had gotten a good look at it, and he shivered at its strangeness. It had a long, flexible tail with a barb, broad wings like a moth, and a flat face with plate-sized eyes reminiscent of an owl.

Morgan felt a surge of urgency. What if that thing had taken Issa and was saving her for a meal? What if it was hungry now? He cursed his missing hand, knowing he'd never get his armor strapped on in a timely fashion, and knowing he could scale that wall ten times faster with two hands. Still, he had to get in there, so he checked that his sword was still secure in the ring on his belt, and he hurried across the yellow grass to the side of the keep. No way would he let some bird-moth eat Issa.

⊗ MORGAN ⊗

As he hurried across the twenty or so paces between the trees and the wall, Morgan tried to map out an ascent path. He saw plenty of gaps in the mortar beneath the right-hand window, so he ran that way. When he stood against the stone wall, the window suddenly seemed higher, and the stone blocks looked a lot larger. The bottom row of blocks stood as high as his knees, and he could only imagine the feat of engineering someone went through to get them up on this plateau shelf to build this keep. Or maybe they'd been quarried right here? He shook his head and concentrated on the task at hand. Morgan reached up, got a firm grip between two blocks where some mortar had crumbled away, and then jammed the toe of his boot into a gap, pulling himself up three feet.

He hugged the wall and reached for a new hold; when he felt it, he lifted his left leg, found a grip for his toe, and push-pulled himself up again. He had the stump of his left arm splayed out and his chest flat against the keep, knowing that if his foothold slipped, he'd be hanging by one hand. Gingerly, he repeated the process, and after a few more pulls, when he glanced down, the ground seemed much further away than it should. "Perspective is everything," he muttered between gritted teeth. Either by luck or skill, Morgan managed to scale far enough that when he reached his hand up for a new hold, he grabbed the lip of the stone windowsill. He stretched his hand in, grabbed the inside edge, and pulled himself, scrabbling with his feet, high enough to see through the open window.

The room beyond the window was in ruins. The wooden slats of the ceiling had collapsed in areas, and the furniture and rugs were weather-beaten and falling apart. A door hung loosely on the opposite wall, and cobwebs and dust liberally coated the space. Morgan felt safe pulling himself through, as the room looked like no one had been in it for decades. When he'd mounted the stone sill and carefully slid to the floor, he gingerly applied his weight to the creaking, dry floorboards, and they held.

Morgan carefully glided across the room to the crooked door, his ears straining for any sound that might give him a clue as to the goings-on in the keep. Only when he was standing directly against the door, his ear turned to the gap between it and the wall, did he hear the first sound that didn't originate from him: a man's distant, screaming voice. "So, it's not just Issa and the flying creature in here," Morgan whispered, easing some fingers around the edge of the crooked door and giving it a stiff yank. It pulled free of the doorjamb and slid toward him a few inches.

Morgan wished he had Issa's camouflage cloak, but simple old sneaking would have to do. He pulled his sword free and, holding it ready, slipped out through the door. He found himself in a dusty hallway that was much less damaged by the elements than the room he'd just come through. The floorboards still creaked, but less so, and the plaster still clung to the walls, mostly intact. Morgan looked left and right, noting a corner not far to the right and more doors on his left-hand side. Those doors likely led to the rooms with the other windows he'd seen outside. As he contemplated his choice, another faint, warbling scream echoed through the hallway to the right, so Morgan took that as a sign. He slunk over the floorboards and peered around the corner, hanging to the shadows.

Another short hallway ended at the head of some stone steps leading down. Morgan moved noiselessly to the steps and activated his Azure Sight, looking down into the shadowy stairwell. Nothing moved, and he could see that the dust on the steps was undisturbed. He silently began to descend the stone steps, counting out twenty-two steps by the time he came to a flat landing. A short corridor continued straight ahead about five paces and then bent to the left.

Morgan crept to the corner and peeked around, holding his breath in anticipation. He saw another battered wooden door a few paces further on, with daylight seeping through the cracks in its weathered slats. Continuing forward, Morgan held an ear to the door. Several heartbeats passed before the sound of something large shuffling around came to him, off to the right and below the door. Then he heard a strident male voice, speaking quite loudly, "Oh, that's a lovely girl, aren't you? What did you bring me this time?"

"Cwoo, Cwoo!" It was the moth-bird thing! Morgan strained to see out the gap in the boards but could only make out a continuation of the hallway and then a railing. Daylight seemed to be streaming in over the railing. Was it a central courtyard?

"Oh, a sheep, that'll be delicious, won't it, Lovely? And we can feed the pets, too." Morgan didn't like the sound of the man's voice, but then it struck him—he'd called whatever the bird-moth had brought back a sheep. There were no sheep on this world. Holbyis looked like sheep, though. Was this man calling a holbyis a sheep? Was he from Earth? Morgan tried the latch on the door and found it unlocked. He pulled it gently and steadily, gritting his teeth as it scraped along the stone floor, the hinges sagging from age and rot.

The man had begun to hum, and the giant bird creature was making that warbling sound, so the door's slow scrape seemed to go unnoticed. Just as Morgan began to creep through the gap he'd created, another shriek of abject misery echoed up from the depths of the keep, much louder here, now that he'd opened the door.

"Oh, dear! It sounds like Gunther is being a little rough with the stock. What do you think, Lovely? Should I go rescue the poor wretch?"

"Cwoo!"

"Oh, I agree, I agree. Gunther needs his pleasures, too, doesn't he? Let's instead get a start on our dinner. Keiry!" He shrieked the final word, and Morgan almost stumbled at the force of it as he was edging closer and closer to the railing, trying to stay in the shadows and as silent as possible. He had just made the corner of the wall where it met the railing when a new voice, this one feminine, spoke up.

"Yes, Lord?" Morgan peeked an eye around the corner and looked at the scene below. There was, indeed, a central courtyard in the tall, narrow keep. The courtyard was, by necessity, also tall and narrow with a railing on the second floor, where Morgan hid, fully encompassing it. Down on the first floor, piled in a corner, was a nest of branches and grass with the huge, moth-like bird nestled in its center. On the flagstones in front of the nest, a bloody holbyis lay, and standing over it was a tall, skeletal man that definitely looked human. A diminutive Ardeni woman stood before him, completely nude, her bright blue hair shorn to a stubble. The man, clothed in yellow-gold robes bearing dozens of stains, ran a hand through his long, greasy hair and looked down his nose at the Ardeni.

"Isn't it obvious? Lovely has brought you supplies for dinner! See that you prepare something delicious. He gestured to the dead holbyis.

"Yes, Lord, I shall, though I fear our herb supply grows thin."

"Nonsense! I just stocked them!"

"Lord, that was several months ago. I'll endeavor to make do, though. Might I get some assistance lifting the holbyis?"

"Holbyis! Bah, enough with the nonsense words. I've told you that animal is a sheep! Here, I'll make it easier to carry," the "Lord" said. Then, he took a step back, pointed a finger at the holbyis, and made a gesture. The dead animal's head separated as though struck by a guillotine. He gestured again, and the rear half was sectioned, spilling intestines and organs out onto the flagstones. "Be sure to scrub this mess after you've carried the meat to the kitchen."

"Yes, Lord," the woman said, bending to lift a front quarter of the dead holbyis, and that's when Morgan noticed the pale gray collar she wore. She grunted, hoisting the bloody chunk to her chest, thoroughly drenching herself in gore.

"By the way, what of Lovely's gift from last night? Has the creature woken?"

"I believe so, Lord. Gunther's put her in a cell with the other female stock."

"Excellent! I'll need to inspect her later. She seemed a promising specimen, don't you think, Keiry?"

"Oh, yes, Lord. I'd wager that she has advanced her racial traits quite a few times."

"Good, good. Now get to the kitchens!" The scarecrow-like figure cackled as Keiry turned and hustled back through the doorway that, presumably, led to the kitchens. Morgan watched him with a growing sense of disgust. He was talking about Issa; that much was clear. So she was being held with other "Stock." Morgan didn't like the sound of that at all, nor did he like the idea that a human was here and armed with some dangerous Energy abilities.

Could he be from Earth? Could humans exist on more than one planet? Morgan tried to gauge how dangerous that man's abilities were based on what he'd seen him do to that holbyis corpse. He imagined he could do some damage to a corpse with his Vortex Lance, but the man below had casually sliced through the body several times, with almost no visible effort. He was definitely dangerous.

It seemed like the woman had been enslaved to him somehow. Was it the collar? How under the man's control was she? Could Morgan approach her for help or information, or would she be compelled to expose him? Morgan was tempted to try to sneak down to the courtyard and kill him, but he didn't know if that would be suicidal or not. What if he pointed at Morgan and sliced him in half? Morgan needed more answers, and it sounded like Issa had a little more time before things got critical for her. She was being held, and this "Lord" still wanted to inspect her, so Morgan didn't think whoever Gunther was would be a threat to her just yet. That decided, he focused on gathering some more intel, which meant snooping around and hopefully getting a chance to talk to Keiry.

Morgan could see an opening on the far side of the courtyard almost directly above where Keiry had entered the keep; the walkway he was lurking on led around to it. Keeping low, and hugging the stone wall of the keep, as far from the railing as possible, Morgan crept around the courtyard, listening to the man below humming and talking in a sing-song voice to his giant moth-bird. After several tense moments, he slipped into the hallway leading away from the courtyard. He crept forward, searching the abandoned rooms and hallways on the second floor until he finally found another set of steps leading downward. Noise and heat came from the wooden door at their base, and he felt he'd finally had some good luck—he'd descended right to the kitchens.

Slowly and gently, he depressed the door latch and pulled open the door just a crack, peeking through. The kitchen was empty of people, though a glowing fire smoldered in the huge cast-iron oven. A central butcher block counter held three pieces of the dead holbyis, though Morgan thought Keiry was probably off picking up more of the dead animal. Seizing his moment, he opened the door, slipped into the kitchen, and moved to the doorway on the far side of the room. He slipped behind the door and silently waited.

Just a few moments later, he heard the slapping sound of bare feet and Keiry's grunt as she hefted a large portion of the holbyis onto her shoulder. She strode into the kitchen and slammed the hunk of meat and bone onto the butcher's counter. "Ancestors, help me!" She sobbed, bracing her hands on the countertop and shaking.

Morgan gently pushed the kitchen door closed, then he turned to the sobbing woman and said, "I'm not your ancestor, but maybe I can help."

OLIVIA

The awards assembly took place in a large auditorium that Olivia hadn't yet visited. It reminded her a lot of one of the larger lecture halls at a university, except for the aesthetics: polished wooden seats with soft cushions, warm glowing light fixtures, wooden paneling hung with elaborate tapestries to dampen the echo, and a slightly raised stage on which all the first-year professors sat in plush leather chairs. The first-year cohorts were seated in the center-front section of seats, while the second and third-year students who deigned to come to see the new class win their awards sparsely filled out the other sections of seating. All in all, Olivia would say half the seats in the auditorium were empty.

Professor Oylla-dak started the assembly off with a short speech. It was Olivia's first time seeing the evolved Shadeni, and she was both impressed and intimidated by her. She stood nearly seven feet tall, with broad red wings folded on her back. Her obsidian hair and eyes glimmered in the light from the chandeliers, and she exuded a general aura of power. She wore black robes similar to the other professors, but she also wore a sword belt with a long straight scabbard hanging at her hip. She wrapped up her speech by saying, "Fainhallow is a grand and storied institution, and all of you should be proud to have been chosen to attend. While you still have much to prove to be considered true alums, take heart in the sure knowledge that you've passed through your first hurdle. The first month of studies here is competitive and stressful. We generally lose ten percent of our new students during this month, but you all have beaten those odds—only two of your fellows fled the academy prior to this moment. Congratulations!"

The assembled students and professors clapped, but Olivia and her cohort looked at each other in puzzlement. Who had dropped out? True, they hadn't been keeping close tabs on all of the other cohorts, but they hadn't heard of any students leaving before this. Had they gotten bad news about their performance and chosen to leave before the assembly? Professor Oylla-dak continued, "Someday, you'll all remember your time here with fondness and hopefully share some of your success with the school that got you started. Because of generous alumni, we're able to offer the awards for the induction challenge—some of the items would be impossible to procure with simple financial means. We have awards won from dungeons; we have System granted boons, and, of course, we have some awards purchased from City Stones. I'm very excited to see how this year's crop of winners grow and contribute to the academy over the next few years. With that, I'll introduce your first professor to present his awards: Commander Grobak, please step forward!"

Professor Oylla-dak stepped back and to the side but remained standing. Grobak struggled to extricate himself from his chair but, with a loud grunt, popped to his feet. Some giggles broke out among the students, but when he stood at the front of the stage and cleared his throat, everyone quieted down. "Alright, students, I have four awards, as you know: top three students and top cohort. Am I clear?"

"Yes!" the assembled students shouted, including, to Olivia's amusement, most of the older students.

"Good, good. Third place in Physical Education and Combat Training goes to Tarl ap'Grund from Bone cohort! Come up to the stage, please!" Lots of cheering broke out from the Bone cohort, and they were joined by good-spirited students in nearby cohorts, clapping Tarl on the back as he hurried up to the stage. "Second place goes to Rolfo ap'Yalli from Ruby cohort!" Another Ardeni student stood and enthusiastically ran up to the stage among the cheering of his cohort. "Finally, my top student for the induction competition is Rald from Copper cohort! Get up here, Rald!" Olivia and the rest of Copper burst into cheers, thumping Rald on the back as he stood and strutted up to the stage.

Hanwol stood on his seat and howled, "Rald! You're the best!" Veena yanked his arm until he fell back into his chair, though everyone around was laughing and clapping.

"Good! Gentlemen, you've done your cohorts proud. Take a bow and then return to your seats." The three winners received another thunderous round of applause, and then they walked back to their seats, and Grobak continued, "It was difficult for me to choose the winning cohort—it was very close. I saw a lot of improvement from nearly every student, but the cohort that had the most improvement overall was Ruby! Congratulations, Ruby! Stand and receive your applause!" Ruby cohort stood, cheering for themselves, but the applause from the rest of the cohorts was a bit subdued—a lot of them had held out hope that they'd win the cohort prize, including Copper. Adaida was frowning as she clapped, and Rald cursed loud enough that he got a dirty look from one of the second-year professors. "Everyone, your prizes will be delivered to your dormitories this afternoon. Congratulations! Now, next up is my diminutive friend, Professor Ghall, with your Alchemy awards." Grobak bowed and then plopped himself back into his seat while Professor Ghall, sparing a scowl for Grobak, approached the front of the stage.

"That should have been ours! Grobak as much said so to me yesterday," Rald hissed. Shani shushed him, though, and he sat back glowering. Olivia wondered if he was overconfident or if something had happened to change Grobak's mind.

"Thank you, students! It's been a real pleasure this last month teaching you the basics of Alchemy. Some of you are shaping up to be real stars! My prizes for the top three students are all the same this year, so please come up together: Shani Rishal, Veena Fenash, and Sarice Fwynal!" Olivia and her cohort erupted in a cheer—they knew Shani and Veena were doing well, but to have them both in the top three boded well for the cohort prize.

They walked to the stage, Shani managing to saunter while also maintaining a demure expression. Veena proudly strode ahead of her, excited to be on the stage. As Shani and Veena climbed the stage from the left, Sarice stepped up from the right. She had a broad smile on her face, but her body language betrayed her anxiety. Still, everyone applauded, and Professor Ghall continued her presentation, "Thank you, ladies, and well done! Shani and Veena, you may as well stay here. Copper cohort has won the Alchemy prize!" Again, the applause was scattered and tepid around the hall, but it didn't stop Olivia and her friends from standing and cheering.

After everyone had taken their seats, Professor Ghall said, "As with the dear Commander's prizes, mine will be brought to your dormitories after lunch. Congratulations everyone! Professor Brince, please come forward."

Brince awarded three students that Olivia didn't know and gave the cohort prize to Jade. Olivia clapped as softly as possible, watching with a twinge of pure irritation as Gwinna stood with her cohort to bow like she'd done something special. She hadn't really hoped to win anything from the Enchanting professor, but it was a bit disappointing that no one in their cohort had placed in the top three. Hanwol seemed particularly upset, apparently having had high hopes for his chances. When Brince finished, she asked for Sange to step forward, and Olivia felt a little flutter of nervous anticipation in her stomach.

"Greetings, students. What a wonderful first month it's been! I'm so impressed by many of you that I had a tough time determining my top three students. That said, I had to choose, and choose, I did! In third place, please clap for Sarice Fwynal." Sarice acted surprised and smiled coquettishly as she walked to the stage. "Second place goes to Gwinna Daneesh!" Gwinna stood quickly, but, rather than pleased, she looked positively disturbed. She stalked to the stage with her lips pressed into a thin line and her back as straight as a board. "Finally, I'd like to congratulate Olivia Bennet for claiming the top spot. Come up, Olivia!"

The butterflies in her stomach began to fly in a tornado pattern as Olivia stood up to walk to the stage. Every eye was on her, and she tried to force a smile, though she knew her face was wan with anxiety. It felt like she was walking in a dimly glimpsed dream as she mounted the stage, nearly tripping over herself as her heel caught. Some giggles erupted as she caught herself, but rather than make her more self-conscious, the laughter brought her back to the moment, and she felt a wave of relief.

"Take a bow, students! Your prizes will be delivered to your dorms. Now, the cohort prize was another tough decision . . ." Olivia lost track of his words as she heard Gwinna's smooth, deep voice say, "So the alien has a talent for cultivation?"

"Hush, Gwinna, that's rude," Sarice whispered as the three of them stepped off the stage. Just then, the crowd erupted with more applause as Silver cohort stood to bow, apparently having won the cohort prize.

"Not what you said earlier, sweetie," Gwinna said, loud enough for Olivia to hear, and then stalked back to her cohort. Olivia, for her part, tried to act like she'd heard nothing as she climbed the slight ramp to her seat. She didn't glance at Sarice, not wanting to see the other woman's face. The applause had died down while she'd been walking, and Silver were retaking their seats.

"Now, students, please welcome Professor ap'Rall to present the awards for Spellcraft." Sange smoothly moved back to his seat as Alyss stood and approached the front of the stage. The chatter, laughter, and clapping died down to silence as she stood calmly, waiting for silence.

"Thank you, everyone. I'm very pleased to announce the top-scoring students in my class for the induction month. It's clear we have some rising stars this year, as I've already seen all three of these faces up here today. In third place, please welcome Sarice Fwynal!" Olivia had a sense of déjà vu, and her stomach started to flutter again. She noticed Sarice give her a quick glance with half a smile on her face, but it didn't assuage her nerves. She looked over to where Jade cohort sat and saw Gwinna staring daggers at her. When Sarice was fully on the stage, Alyss said, "In second position is Gwinna Daneesh!" Murmurs broke out in the audience as the scene from the cultivation prize replayed itself. However, this time, Gwinna didn't manage to contain her frustration with just a frown; she loudly scoffed and stared at Olivia as she stood and walked to the stage. Her cobalt blue eyes were ablaze with an inner light, and Olivia, despite the hot shame that flooded her scalp, looked away.

Alyss glanced to her left at Gwinna, a small frown tugging at the corner of her mouth as the murmurs in the crowd continued. "You may have guessed it—the first spot goes to Olivia Bennet! Come forward, Olivia!" A great stir spread through the crowd, starting with Copper cheering and pushing Olivia to her feet. She moved woodenly, dreading approaching the stage with Gwinna standing there staring at her and shrinking from the muttered outrage that seemed to be rippling through the crowd. "Come, Olivia, stand tall and claim what you've earned."

"Has she, though?" A strident voice called out from the side of the auditorium. Olivia froze and looked to see the professor that had hobbled her standing against the wall near a large contingent of second-year students.

"What do you mean, Professor ap'Gravin?" Alyss asked, standing straight and staring down her nose at the imposing man. Professor Oylla-dak, who'd remained quiet, only politely applauding for the winners thus far, stepped forward next to Alyss.

"Yes, whatever do you mean, Professor?" Her voice was strong, rich, and smooth, and the ripples of power that emanated from it were palpable. When she spoke, Olivia's limbs unlocked, and she started walking to the stage again.

"What do I mean? Why, simply that no one has witnessed this Human casting a single spell. What, pray tell, did she accomplish to beat out such talent?" He gestured to the other students.

"Is that any concern of yours? This is my class, and I award the placements!" Alyss bristled and turned to Oylla-dak. By this time, Olivia had managed to step up onto the stage, and she stood to Alyss's left, opposite Gwinna and Sarice.

"I think we can all agree that Alyss is trustworthy. She has no connection to this student nor any reason to favor her in a dishonorable way. Are you making an accusation, ap'Gravin?" Oylla-dak stepped forward again, now looming behind Olivia, her presence so palpable, it felt like she had a small volcano erupting behind her.

"Not at all. Is it some secret that we cannot know what this student has accomplished? All the students have seen what Gwinna and Sarice can do; surely it would be a learning experience for all to see what your first-place student has accomplished." He spoke calmly with a buttery drawl to his words, but Olivia and everyone else knew what he was up to. "Gwinna managed to combine her Spirit Armor spell with a Phantom Blade spell, adding an offensive component to her family's signature defense. Truly an uncommon feat for a first-year, wouldn't you say? Can you really say that this Human has accomplished something more?"

"I can say . . ." Alyss began, but Oylla-dak cut her off.

"Enough. Alyss has said that Olivia is worthy of the top spot. Tomorrow, after she has processed her induction prizes, Olivia will demonstrate what she can do for everyone. If she fails to live up to Alyss's expectations, then Alyss will furnish a new reward as compensation from her own resources. Since you so confidently accuse Alyss of favoritism, you will put a prize of equal value up as an additional award for Olivia should I deem her demonstration sufficient. In other words, Professor ap'Gravin, it's time to back up your words with some treasure." It was like a spell broke on the crowd, and they cheered loudly and raucously. Professor ap'Gravin frowned but nodded and sat down.

"Thank you, Professor," Alyss said, looking at Oylla-dak, who nodded serenely. "Students! I have one more announcement. My cohort award will go to Garnet cohort! While they didn't have any true standouts, their average ability edged out the competition. Congratulations, Garnet!" Olivia clapped and then hastily stepped off the stage, but Alyss reached forward and grabbed her wrist and said, "Olivia, don't worry! If you can pull off what you described to me, you're going to be just fine."

"Thank you, Alyss; I'll try not to let you down." Alyss smiled in an attempt, Olivia felt, to reassure her, then she turned and spoke quietly to Professor Oylla-dak. Olivia hurried back to her seat, her mind racing over what had just happened and thinking about her nascent spells that she would have to perform in front of everyone tomorrow. Her friends congratulated her and laughed about Gwinna and ap'Gravin, but it hardly registered; she was excited about her awards and stressed about having to perform, and her mind couldn't find purchase in the present. As Oylla-dak finished speaking and everyone started to applaud, though, Adaida took her hand and pulled her to her feet.

"C'mon, Liv. You're turning white on us; let's get you back to the dorm." Olivia allowed her to lead her through the crowd. All the while, she had the strangest feeling like she was dreaming, and these blue and red and winged and furry people were all figments of her imagination, and she'd wake up any moment in her lovely apartment with the chef's kitchen and get ready for another day at the institute. By the time they made it back to the dormitory, though, she'd started to regain some color, and Adaida's warm hand gripping hers helped her to find an anchor in reality. She sat on her bed and forced herself to take several deep, slow breaths. "Feeling better?" Adaida was sitting on the bed near her, and her other cohort members were standing around looking at her with concern.

"Yeah, I think I started to have a panic attack. Thank you for getting me out of there!"

"No worries, lovely," Rald said offhandedly. "We wanted to get back here to see our prizes anyway."

MORGAN

Keiry spun around with a gasp, and Morgan held his hand out palm-down, his sword tucked against his body by his shortened left arm. "Please stay quiet; like I said, I'm here to help."

"Who are you?" Keiry hissed, covering her breasts with her arms and moving around to the other side of the butcher's table. Morgan did his best to make it obvious he was looking at her face and nothing else. "You're one of Lord Blake's people?"

"No. No, I don't know who that asshole is, but he's not one of my people. He looks human, yes, but I don't know where he's from."

"He's from Uthria, or at least that's what he's fond of saying while he 'instructs' me." Keiry seemed to relax slightly now that she had the counter between herself and Morgan.

"I don't know where that is, which is fascinating, but I think we have more pressing matters. Has he enslaved you somehow?" Morgan nodded to the gray metal ring on Keiry's neck. Keiry reached a hand up to touch the collar, and the tears that had stopped when Morgan surprised her started to flow again.

"Yes! If I don't obey him, he tortures me with this collar, and it keeps me from using Energy." Her voice had gotten louder as she gasped out a despairing sob, and Morgan gestured with his hand to keep her volume down.

"Does it compel you to act in any way? Do I have to worry about you calling out for him and reporting that you saw me?" He spoke in a low voice, almost a whisper, hoping she'd follow suit.

"No, nothing like that. He has to tell me to do something," she replied, still sobbing but speaking more quietly.

"Alright, well, keep working like you would if I weren't here; I don't want to tip him off. Do you want to borrow some clothing?"

"No, if he came in here and saw me with clothes on, he'd punish me." She gave up trying to cover herself and picked up a large cleaver, turning to the meat. Morgan averted his eyes, looking pointedly to the side of her.

"What can you tell me about Blake? How long has he been here? Do you have any idea of his strengths? Any weaknesses? I'm pretty sure his bird creature kidnapped my friend, and I need to find her."

"Blake is a devil. He's been here a long time, I think, though I've only been here a couple of years. He's converted the central wing of the keep into a kind of laboratory where he experiments on us. He has several pens where he keeps different captives, and further in are maternity cells where he keeps the pregnant ones."

"What? Maternity cells?" Morgan felt heat rushing to his head, and a faint ringing had begun in his ears.

"Yes! He breeds us and experiments on the children! I think he's trying to create elixirs to improve his bloodline." Keiry saw Morgan's face and continued, speaking quickly, "Your friend just arrived, and she was paralyzed from Lovely's sting. He won't have done anything to her yet. She's probably safe for another day or so." Morgan forced himself to breathe several times, turning and leaning against the wall. He couldn't rush into this. He wanted to charge around the keep, killing anything that got in his way until he found Issa, but he wouldn't do her any good if this Blake guy killed him. He had to think this through.

"What about Blake? I get that he's an evil bastard, but how strong is he? I saw him chop that holbyis up."

"He's a powerful Energy user. He's hinted that he's coming up on his third class refinement."

"So, nearly level forty, and strong with Energy. Has he ever mentioned his race? He can't be human because the System treated us like we were new when my people got here."

"No, but he often laughs and calls us mortals when mocking us. Aren't we all mortal? Even those of us like you who have advanced their race?"

"I would think so, yeah. He sure looked human from a distance, but I wasn't close enough to be sure. It's that obvious about my racial advancement, huh? My name's Morgan, by the way. I know your name from listening to Blake yell at you. Sorry."

"Morgan, he's very dangerous, but his only helpers that aren't enslaved are Gunther and Lovely." Keiry continued to chop a large hunk of holbyis haunch into cubes, and Morgan started to get an idea.

"What are you going to cook?"

"I'm going to make a stew." She looked at Morgan's face and understanding flashed in her eyes. "He's ordered me never to poison him. I'd hate for someone to put something in the stew pot when I wasn't looking."

"Yeah, that would be bad. Does Gunther eat with him?"

"Usually, yes," she replied, then her face fell, "Also, he sometimes brings up some of his favorites to 'keep him company.'"

"Hmm, don't worry, I won't do anything to hurt any innocents." Morgan leaned back against the wall and "Looked" into his storage ring. There, just as he remembered stashing them ages ago, were the five vials of what Tiladia had called a "Powerful sedative." He had no idea what sort of dosage he'd need to add to a stew; he didn't even know if it would work after cooking. He'd add it at the last minute to minimize that, he decided. What if Blake had strong resistance? Morgan mulled it over and decided it was worth a try. If the sedative didn't affect him, he'd have to try plan B. "Hey, I'm going to wait on the other side of that door in case you get company while you're cooking. Do me a favor and give the door a knock when you're getting close to serving the stew, will you?"

"Yes, I'll need to step out to set the table; I'll tap on the door then." She smiled at Morgan, and he realized it was the first time she'd done so. She was pretty, but some of her teeth were missing, and she looked down quickly when they made eye contact. The heat that had subsided while he was planning rose again in his head, and he had to count to ten as he slipped back through the rear door to the kitchen to keep from charging off in a rage. He sat on the dusty flagstones, leaning against the crumbling plaster of the wall.

Morgan's thoughts drifted into dark passages. He'd seen horrible things before, but something about the way Keiry acted spoke to him of a cruelty that went beyond what even the Yovashi that he'd seen had done. Yeah, the Yovashi ate people alive, relishing their pain, but it was a quick, brutal sort of cruelty. Keiry had been under Blake's thumb for years now, and she was clearly traumatized. Worse yet, the things she described sounded like a new level of horror—breeding programs for enslaved people and experiments on their children? Morgan knew he had to put an end to what was happening in this keep, one way or another. He knew he was anxious for Issa when he noticed himself drumming his fingers on the cold flagstones. He hadn't heard any more screams, and he took heart in that fact. Hopefully, Issa was just waking up and would be left alone for now.

Should he go try to find her? Get eyes on her? Make sure nothing bad was happening? Or should he stick to his plan and try to take Blake and his lackey out with his methodical course of action? He itched to hurry through the shadows and see Issa, but he knew the folly of that action: if Blake saw him somehow, he could very well kill Morgan in a fight, and then Issa's fate would be sealed. He had to play it smart. He calmed himself by reaching out with his Guardian's Senses yet again and feeling her presence strong and nearby. She was so close that he swore he could almost touch her. It seemed like she was just twenty or thirty or so paces away from him, deeper in the keep. What if he could touch her, though stone separated them?

Just like he did when he reached out to drain Energy from someone, Morgan reached out his senses and tried to feel Issa's Energy. At first, there was nothing, then he felt a tickle of vibrant, earthy Energy, and he realized he was feeling Keiry. He stretched out his senses further, past the kitchen and through the void, as it appeared to his inner eye, and then he touched her. He was sure it was her, the vibrant pulsing, pure Energy of her Core. Morgan didn't want to drain her, but he gave her just a little tug to know he was there, then he pulled back.

He couldn't stop the grin spreading on his face like he'd just gotten away with cheating on a test. He supposed there was some risk in what he'd just done—what if he'd accidentally touched Blake, and the higher-level man had realized what was going on? Still, he felt good knowing Issa was so close, and he hoped she'd sensed him and taken heart.

Morgan was on his third cultivation drill cycle when a gentle knock came through the door. He stood, listening carefully, and when he heard the other door open and close, he slipped back into the kitchen. The holbyis meat had been taken away, and the butcher's block cleaned. Sitting on the freshly oiled wood was a large copper, lidded pot. Morgan quickly moved to the pot and lifted off the lid, his mouth watering at the scent of the rich stew within. He pulled a vial of the sedative from his ring, yanked the cork off with his teeth, and sprinkled it into the pot. He contemplated for a moment and then shrugged, repeating the process three more times. He decided to save one vial for future use. He picked up the ladle that sat on the wood next to the pot, stirred the stew a few times, then put everything back the way he'd found it.

Morgan moved to the kitchen door that Keiry had used and waited quietly. He wondered about the collar that Keiry wore and how thorough the compulsion to obey was. If Keiry saw Morgan dose the pot, would she have to throw it out? He glanced back at the counter and realized he'd left the ladle wet with stew, whereas it had been dry when he picked it up. Just to be sure that wouldn't trigger Keiry's collar somehow, he hurried over to the butcher's counter and pulled an old shirt out of his ring, wiping off the ladle and the drippings he'd gotten on the wooden counter. Then he rushed back to the corner behind where the door would open.

He only waited a few moments before the door opened, and Keiry walked into the kitchen. She glanced around nervously, then picked up the ladle, holding it against the pot while she lifted it by its two handles. When she turned back to the door, she spotted Morgan. She looked a little startled but nodded without saying anything and walked out the open door. Morgan followed her, silently gliding through the shadows. They took two turns, and then Keiry paused before a set of double doors. She glanced further down the hall and turned back to Morgan, nodding. Was she telling him to keep going? He nodded back to her, and she pushed through the doors, letting them swing shut behind her.

Morgan sidled up to the door, listening for a moment. He heard an indistinct male voice and some clatter of furniture sliding around. Looking down the hallway, he saw another hallway branched to the left, so he moved that way to investigate. When he turned the corner, he could see the dark hallway continued past the room where Keiry had gone, but there was another wooden door there. A servant's entrance to the dining hall, perhaps? Morgan carefully approached the door and saw that it was slightly ajar and opened inward. He inched one eye over the narrow opening and looked within when he got to the doorjamb.

He couldn't have asked for a better position. The long banquet table was directly in front of him, and at the near end, with his back to Morgan, sat Lord Blake. Seated on either side of the table were six other individuals, all completely naked, save the dark gray collars on their necks. Blake's guests were two men and four women, some Ardeni, some Shadeni, and one Ghelli. The chair at the far end of the table was empty. "Keiry, clear Gunther's place setting. He won't be joining us. He's worn himself a bit ragged with his exercise." Blake chuckled, glancing around the table to see if his remarks had amused his "Guests."

"Yes, Lord Blake," Keiry said as she finished ladling stew into the bowl in front of a tall Shadeni male. Morgan watched as she moved down the line, trying to see if Blake was eating yet. Oddly, he seemed to be waiting for everyone to be served before he started eating. Perhaps his sense of decorum at the dinner table overshadowed the fact that his guests were enslaved. Finally, Keiry finished with the final dish, and she set the pot of stew in the center of the table. As she moved to pick up the unused place setting, Blake picked up his spoon.

"Well, let's see what sort of treat you've prepared, Keiry. Eat up, guests! You'll need your strength on the morrow, as it's your turn in the rotation!" He chuckled, but none of the assembled "Guests" moved or said anything. Lord Blake took a big bite of stew, made a smacking noise with his lips, then said, "Excellent! I said eat up! Don't make me repeat myself again." He spoke smoothly, but such malevolence was carried with his words that Morgan almost felt compelled to action.

Morgan gripped the doorjamb he lurked behind until his knuckles turned white, and the wood creaked slightly. Everyone at the table was tucking into the stew now, including Blake. Morgan watched, waiting for some sign that the sedative was working, dreading that it wouldn't or that it would only work on the enslaved people. What would he do then? What would he do if Blake saw everyone pass out and attacked Keiry? Morgan knew exactly what he'd do. He let go of the doorjamb and wrapped his hand around the hilt of his sword, waiting and watching.

⊰ MORGAN ⊱

Morgan was starting to think the sedative wasn't going to work. Perhaps the dosage for such a large pot had been insufficient. Perhaps alchemical concoctions couldn't be mixed with other substances. He didn't know, but he wasn't going to let this chance slip away—it had been quite a while since he'd backstabbed anyone, but he still remembered how. Very carefully, he pulled his sword free of the ring it hung through, slowly so as not to let the steel sing out. Holding the sword firmly in his fist, he ran through it in his head: kick the door open, Hollow Charge to Blake's back, backstab as many times as he could. He debated priming a Vortex Lance and starting with that, but he didn't know what kind of defense Blake had, and he just felt like a backstab would be more devastating.

He was just steeling himself to act when one of the Ardeni women fell forward, her head clunking as it thumped into the table. Blake took another bite of stew, not even looking up until he'd swallowed it. He set his spoon down and looked at the woman. "Gods, woman. Did old Gunther keep you up all night?" He chuckled to himself, but then more of the "Guests" started to slump over, one even sliding down and slipping under the table. "What the . . ." He shook his head as though to clear it, then he braced himself against the table, his head wobbling.

Morgan didn't wait any longer. He kicked the door, charged at Blake, and felt his Backstab skill guiding his blade. He drove it home, slipping it into the flesh at the nape of Blake's neck and jamming six inches of solar steel into his brain. Morgan relaxed as Blake's body flopped onto the table. Everyone else in the room, save Keiry, was sound asleep. He breathed deeply, stilling his racing mind and planning his next move. It was a pity Gunther hadn't been at dinner, but Keiry could show him where Gunther was. "Will Gunther have any idea Blake is dead? Do you know where Gunther is?" he asked Keiry, but he stopped talking as he saw the horror on her face and felt a slight tug on his sword.

Morgan looked down and was suddenly aware that he hadn't received any Energy for slaying Blake. Additionally, there wasn't much blood seeping out around his sword blade. More worrisome than any of that, though, was that Blake's body was twitching. "Oh, fuck no," Morgan said, yanking his sword free. He stepped to the side of Blake's chair and brought Bloodfang down on Blake's exposed neck. He cut halfway through, which was remarkable because he felt like the fine blade, combined with his strength, could have cut through a small tree. Still, he lifted it and hacked down again and again until he severed the head from the twitching body.

The body still shuddered, like it didn't know it was dead, and Morgan bent to pick up Blake's head by the hair. "This motherfucker is not human." Keiry was kneeling behind the table, peeking over the top to see what had happened. "Keiry, go throw some more coals in the oven!"

He set Blake's head, purple tongue lolling out of its mouth, on the table and then threw his chair over backward, sending his twitching body sprawling. Then, as Keiry rushed from the room, Morgan went to work, hacking the limbs off the shuddering, thrashing body. It was messy, sweaty work, and it took him a lot longer than he thought it should. Once again, he lamented his missing arm. Still, after a long, laborious process, he had Blake's body, his limbs, and his head all separated. Even then, the various parts shuddered and twitched.

Morgan yanked the tablecloth off the table, piled the bloody parts of Blake on the fabric, gathered up the corners, and dragged it back toward the kitchen. At one point, he contemplated throwing Blake's body into his storage pouch, and he stopped himself for purely selfish reasons: he still hadn't gotten any Energy for killing Blake, and he was afraid he'd lose out if the creature officially "Died" in his dimensional container. So, he dragged the twitching mess along the hallway, leaving a bloody smear in his wake, to the kitchen. When he arrived, he saw that Keiry had stoked the flames in the big cast-iron double oven, and he smiled at her, his face splattered with blood.

"We'll take care of this guy, one way or another!" He couldn't help the ghoulish grin on his face, and then he opened the tablecloth, picked up Blake's head, and tossed it into the fire. The coal chamber for the big stove was in the center of the two ovens, and it was pretty large, so Morgan shoved Blake's two severed arms into the burning coals and slammed the door shut, opening the vents and flues wide. "Let's let those burn down a bit, and then I'll toss some more in there." He looked to the twitching legs and torso and shivered. Keiry had backed away from the stove into a corner and watched the scene in wide-eyed horror.

A couple of minutes passed, and Morgan was going to pop the coal chamber open to check on the process when he saw deep golden motes start to coalesce on the remaining body parts. They stopped twitching, and a stream of Energy coursed into his chest.

Congratulations! You have achieved level 28 Vortex Duelist and have gained 8 Intelligence, 8 Agility, 6 Will, 6 Dexterity.

"Alright, one down. Show me where to find Gunther, Keiry." She nodded and scooted out of the corner, moving toward the door. "Hang on a second." Morgan rummaged in his pouch for an old shirt and gave it to her. "Wear this for now; we'll find you something better soon." She smiled, the first genuinely happy expression Morgan had seen on her, and slipped the shirt over her head. She had to pull the sleeves up a dozen inches, and the shirt hung down to her knees, but at least she wasn't running around naked.

Morgan followed her through the corridors to an archway that opened onto the courtyard. Keiry turned to him and held a finger to her lips, miming a bird flapping its wings. Morgan nodded, and she tip-toed out into the courtyard and then back into the keep through a large, central doorway. Morgan followed quickly, glancing to the far corner where the giant bird's nest was. His heart almost stopped when he saw the big, saucer-like yellow eye following his movements, but then he was back inside the keep, and Keiry shut the door behind him.

They were in a wide central hallway with double doors about fifteen paces further on. One of the doors was propped open with a large piece of broken stonework. "Through there and down some steps, you'll find the main holding cells, and Gunther's room is just beyond, near the maternity cells."

"Where did Blake keep his quarters? His laboratory?"

"There's a spiral stair in the room beyond; his rooms are up there."

"Alright, do me a favor—go check on those that ate the stew, make sure they're still breathing, and burn the rest of Blake's body. Just to be sure." Keiry nodded and slipped back out the door; Morgan, sword held ready, approached the open doorway. He was just a couple of paces from the door when he heard a man's voice screaming commands.

"Yes! Like that! Line up, fools! Hold your weapons ready!"

"Fuck." Morgan strode through the doorway, walking onto a flagstone landing atop a short set of stairs leading down into a high-ceilinged grand hall. The marble floor, which once must have been host to dancing and merrymaking, was now lined with six iron cages, three to a side. The cage doors were open, and their former occupants, twenty or so naked men and women, stood at the base of the steps, pointing weapons toward Morgan. Behind them was a tall, gray-skinned man with no hair and a single eye in the center of his forehead. He wore a red enameled breastplate and wielded a heavy, spiked mace in one hand and a bronze, gem-studded rod in the other.

"Who are you? Where's Lord Blake?" he shrieked, revealing teeth that looked like he'd filed them to points.

"He's dead, asshole." Morgan scanned the throng of collared people and found what he was looking for. Rage colored his vision red when he saw Issa, naked, collared, face bruised, and blood freshly running from her nose. She held a wooden club, and Morgan could see her straining to lower it. Morgan looked back at Gunther and growled, "You fucked up."

"Stop him! Kill him!" Gunther shrieked, waving the bronze rod up in the air. Morgan didn't wait to see if the assembled mob followed the command; he took a hopping leap off the top of the steps, focusing on Gunther, and used Hollow Charge to streak through the air, over the crowd. When he was close to Gunther, he activated Circle of Combat. A black maelstrom of Energy surged up around him and Gunther, ripping through racks of equipment, wooden benches, and various other small objects that were strewn about the center of the hall.

"No, no, Gunther. This will just be you and me."

"If Blake is dead, I'm master here! I can reward you greatly to leave." Gunther licked his lips, his tongue flicking over his sharp teeth as the two circled each other.

"No, there won't be any mercy for you, Gunther. I suppose that's not true; I could make you fight Issa, and I think she'd take her time with you. I'm just going to kill you. Count your blessings."

"No, wait, you see . . ." Gunther feinted left, then tried to swing his heavy mace down on Morgan from the right. Morgan saw it coming a mile away and stepped outside the swing, using his sword to push the mace along. Gunther stumbled, losing himself in the momentum, and Morgan stepped in and thrust his sword into Gunther's side. He pulled back, noting the spurt of arterial blood that pumped out as he withdrew his blade.

"I think I hit your renal artery, Gunther. You're a dead man walking." Morgan took another step back and held his sword out, ready for another wild attack. Gunther gasped, though, and dropped the rod, reaching back and trying to push his hand against the burbling hole in his side. He groaned, spat some word Morgan didn't recognize, and then charged, swinging his mace in a furious overhand smash. Morgan instinctively slipped into the Crane Defends the Nest, but he didn't back up; he moved forward and to the side.

He easily parried Gunther's mace, then brought his sword around and sliced at the side of Gunther's neck. Just the top inch of his sword hit, but it was enough. Blood fountained out from the slash, and suddenly Morgan felt incredible strength flow out of his sword and into his limbs. Wait? Limbs? He looked to his left arm, and there, stretching out from his stump, was an ethereal red, glowing arm. He flexed the phantom fist, noting the long gleaming talons. Fury filled his mind, and he tore into Gunther with alternating hacks from his sword and swipes from the taloned ghost-arm.

When he came back to himself, he was on his knees, Gunther's mangled corpse an unrecognizable mess of flesh and bone before him. He looked up and around and saw the wide-eyed stares of the formerly enslaved people. Even Issa was hesitant at first to approach him, but when he made eye contact with her, she charged forward and flung her arms around his neck, kissing his face. "I knew you were coming! I felt you the whole time."

"Ugh, sorry. I lost myself—I think the Blood Rager's spirit came out of my sword and affected me." Morgan kissed her back but saw that he was getting blood all over her. He stood up, moving between her and the crowd of former prisoners, then he pulled a cloak from his ring and wrapped it around her. "Do you see a brass-colored rod?" He looked around, pushing aside debris with his boot. Then he saw the rod under what might have once been Gunther's arm. He bent down to pick it up. "I think this controls the collars. Any idea how to work it?"

"Bond with it," a man's voice called from the crowd. Morgan nodded and ran a trickle of Energy into the rod. It became clear to him how to use it, then, and he pointed the rod at Issa.

"Release."

⟨ OLIVIA ⟩

"You shouldn't let them get to you like that, Olivia," Veena said, taking a seat at the foot of Olivia's bed. They were all still hovering around her, some sitting on her bed, some on Veena's, and Rald reclined on the floor between them. "I know it's stressful, but you're going to be fine. Alyss wouldn't have chosen you if she weren't confident in your ability. I, for one, am excited to see that professor choke on his words."

"Thanks, Veena," Olivia said quietly. She wanted to explain that she'd been under pressure before and learned to deal with it to an extent, but this was a new level for her. She'd never felt so isolated and alone before, and the hostility that she'd felt from so many of the students staring at her in the crowd had begun to overwhelm her. Only now, sitting in the relative safety of their dormitory, was it even clear to her what had happened. She wanted to explain those things, but she didn't want to insult her friends who had been so good to her—how would they feel if she said she felt alone while sitting among them? Instead, she swallowed her feelings yet again and looked around.

"Well, when do you think they'll deliver our awards?"

"Anytime now, I'd guess. I owe you an apology, Olivia," Shani said as she sat on the edge of Veena's bed, looking intently at Olivia.

"Why?" Olivia sat up and looked more closely at her. The Ghelli woman had pulled her long white-blonde hair back in a bun and wore severe makeup that gave her face a more angular look than usual. She was beautiful but cold looking at the same time.

"When you first joined us, I thought you'd bring us down, but you've outperformed all of us. I think it was the rest of us that let the group down. All but Rald, maybe." She spoke softly, looking down. "I really thought we'd have more of a shot at some of the cohort prizes."

"It's true, I am great," Rald managed to say with a straight face, "But you all did just fine. The professors said it was a hard decision; I'm sure Copper was in the running. Too bad there's only one cohort prize per class."

"If anyone let the cohort down, it's me," Hanwol said morosely.

"Why? Because you didn't win any individual prizes? I didn't either! Still, we won the alchemy prize, which means we all did well. None of us should feel bad," Adaida said, reaching out to thump Hanwol on the head.

"Yeah, Han! Chin up!" Olivia purposefully used his nickname and, just as she'd hoped, it perked him up a little. They continued to talk about the assembly and Oylla-dak and how incredible she was, but they were cut off by a knock on the door. Rald jumped up and stepped over to the door, pulling it open. An Ardeni man stepped in carrying a large woven basket. He was wearing civilian clothes, and Olivia surmised he must be one of the administration personnel. He confirmed that he was in the Copper dormitory and then handed the basket to Rald. He left with a simple, "Congratulations."

"Well?" Shani asked, "Bring it over here!" Rald nodded and came over to sit on the floor between the two beds again. He set the basket on the ground in front of him. "Go on; you open it." Everyone nodded and uttered things like, "Yeah! Open it, Rald!" He nodded and lifted the round wicker top off the basket, revealing several individually wrapped items, varying in size but all small enough to be held in one hand. Rald reached in and picked up a package about the size of his fist, wrapped in green tissue paper and bearing a label.

"Alchemy prize—cohort," he read aloud. He reached in and pulled out five more packages just like it and lined them up on the floor near the basket. "Should we open these first?" Everyone answered in the affirmative, and he passed them out. Olivia took hers and carefully untied the ribbon, pulling the tissue away and revealing a small vial filled with brilliant orange liquid. The vial bore a label that said, "Radasheen's Hereditary Delver."

"What the heck is this?" Olivia asked.

"Just a minute," Veena replied, already thumbing through a thick volume that Olivia hadn't seen her read before.

"What's that book?" Rald asked, but it was Hanwol who answered:

"That's her alchemical catalog. She's been obsessed with alchemy since she was little."

"Got it! It's a rare and potent racial elixir. It unlocks racial advancements by opening new pathways and triggering evolutions. Anecdotes indicate that it can lead to as many as four racial ranks." This elicited some excited chatter among her cohort members, and Olivia was thrilled, too—she'd seen what racial enhancements had done for Morgan and Bronwyn.

"Will advancing our race help with class options?"

"Most people think so, yes," Hanwol said, carefully studying his elixir, turning it around, and watching the sparkling bubbles that moved from the bottom to the top.

"Well, let's see what else is in there, if you guys don't mind us knowing?" Adaida looked at Olivia, Rald, and her sister.

"No, of course not. Let's see." Rald nodded and pulled out a package.

"This one has my name on it—it's Grobak's prize." He yanked the ribbon off and pulled the paper away, revealing a pale wooden box. He lifted the lid off and set the box down, whistling to himself. Sitting in a plush depression in the box was a faintly luminous piece of fruit that reminded Olivia of a mango. It was yellow, darkening to orange at the bottom, and she could feel the Energy contained in the fruit from where she sat. Her mouth started to water. Rald picked up the little card sitting in the box next to the fruit and read aloud, "Trivian Sun Pear, known for toughening the skin and bones of those who eat it. Expect a large boost to vitality."

"That's incredible, Rald! Congratulations," Hanwol said, eyeing the fruit with his mouth slightly open. Rald looked around at his salivating roommates and quickly slapped the lid back on his box.

"I'll just set this right here," he said, placing the box by his side near his knee. He reached into the basket and pulled out another package. "Olivia," he said, handing her the bright blue bundle. She took it from him, her hand dipping with the significant weight. The object under the tissue was hard and round. She removed the ribbon and peeled the tissue away, revealing a deep blue glass or crystal ball. A small card was tucked against it inside the wrapping, and she lifted it out to read the label out loud, "Heart Crystal Core Breaker—use this at Core rank nine."

"Whoa, nice, Olivia! Some people never break through rank nine because Cores build up a resistance that takes a lot of effort and Energy to break through. Oh, did you already know that?" Adaida asked, looking a little embarrassed.

"No, I didn't, Adaida! Thank you!" Olivia set the crystal on her bed next to her little vial. "What's next, Rald? This feels like Christmas morning!" Everyone looked at her in confusion, and she clarified, "Um, where I come from, some people give gifts to each other once a year to celebrate a religious holiday." Everyone nodded or said something like, "Ahh." Then they turned to Rald expectantly. He reached into the basket, lifted out another green-wrapped package, and handed it to Shani; then, he lifted out an identical one and gave it to Veena.

"From Ghall." Veena and Shani opened their packages together. Olivia watched Shani and saw, as she peeled away the paper, another vial, this one made of ceramic, so the contents weren't visible. At first, Shani read the label to herself, her eyes brightening with excitement.

"It's a mental boosting elixir! It says it will help with intelligence and will!" Veena announced, and Shani nodded.

"Congratulations!" Rald said, though he seemed a little bored. He reached into the basket and handed the last wrapped item to Olivia. It was, like the others, wrapped in tissue, but this time the tissue was black with a silver ribbon.

"From Alyss." Olivia felt the shape of a small box under the tissue, and the item wasn't nearly as heavy as the Heart Crystal. She set it on her lap and carefully untied the silver ribbon, and then she peeled the tissue down to reveal a black wooden box. She lifted the lid off the box and caught her breath. Nestled in the felt interior was a pulsating orange gem about the size of her thumbnail. It throbbed like a living thing, glowing with a bright fiery shimmer and then dimming down like an ember. A card was wedged into the crease of the lining, and she lifted it out to read it:

Olivia,

This gem has been infused with a fire elemental's soul fragment. If you absorb the Energy within this gem into your pathways, they will expand to allow for the broader passage of elemental Energy. In short, you'll become part elemental, a very small part, but still worth going into with your eyes open. This might sound extreme, and it would be if you didn't have such high elemental affinity, but you should come through the process just fine. Additionally, I am confident that this process will provoke the System to offer you a more rare class selection.

Be sure that you are outside, away from flammable materials, when you absorb this gem.

Best regards,

-Alyss

"Jesus," Olivia muttered as she read the card.

"You only say that word when you're freaking out," Adaida said, leaning over to look into the black box. "What in Nature is that?"

"It's . . ." Olivia paused to gather some saliva in her dry mouth, "It's part of an elemental's soul. Alyss thinks I should absorb it."

"Woah, that can't have been easy to come by," Rald said.

"No, it's quite a difficult task to capture part of any creature's soul, let alone a furious, ethereal being like an elemental. Then there's the matter of processing it into an absorbable condition like that. That's an extraordinary item," Hanwol said.

"It sounds suicidal to me," Shani said, "Do you really have elemental affinities that high?" Olivia just nodded, deep in thought. She felt both excited and strange about the idea. Would anything else about her change if she absorbed part of another entity's soul? She decided to turn to her cohort, who were all still staring at her and speculating, for advice.

"Do you think Alyss would encourage me to do something that could harm me or change me in some strange way? It seems extreme to absorb part of another creature's soul."

"I feel like Alyss cares about us. I don't think she'd have you do something bad, Olivia," Adaida said right away. Most of the others agreed though Veena seemed a little troubled.

"What, Veena?" Olivia prodded.

"Well, if your will isn't high enough, I think it could affect your personality. Sure, it's just a small soul fragment, but elementals are powerful beings. Do you mind telling us what your will stat is?"

"No, I don't mind. I have twenty will, but I still have five free points. Should I put them into will as well?"

"Twenty isn't bad for level nine, Olivia. Still, yes, I'd put the other five into it. Yes, it never hurts to have a high will when you're casting spells. Don't you all agree?" Veena asked.

"I agree—your strength is your spellcasting, Liv." Adaida nodded encouragingly. Nobody seemed to disagree, so Olivia applied the points to her will stat.

"Well, in for a penny, in for a pound." They looked at her with blank faces, and Olivia laughed. "I mean, no going back from here. I'll do it. First, though, we should drink our elixirs, don't you all think? Alyss says I need to go outside to use this gem; maybe you guys can come and watch over me afterward?"

"If everyone else is going to drink it, then I am," Rald said.

"Has anyone improved their race before? What will it be like?" Veena asked.

"I have, but only to base two," Shani said, looking at her sister, "We had a lottery in my town for a natural treasure. My father won, then he gave it to me. Adaida was on his bad side back then."

"You're oversharing, sister." Adaida didn't really look upset, though. "Truth is, my mother likes me better, so it's okay."

"She most certainly does not!" Shani sat up and leaned in close to Adaida, outrage on her face.

"It looks like you know the right buttons to push," Olivia laughed, but everyone, again, looked at her in confusion. "I mean, you know how to get to each other." She indicated Shani and Adaida, and they laughed.

"Anyway, we should all go to our beds to take the elixir. If it's as potent as it sounds, we might be out of it for a little while." Everyone gathered up their things and dispersed to lie down on their own beds. Olivia stretched out and took several deep breaths, then she broke the wax seal on her vial with her thumbnail and tilted it to her lips. At first, she was surprised by the lack of flavor—it almost seemed like she was pouring thick, syrupy water into her mouth. Still, as she swallowed the ounce or two of liquid, her entire body started to tingle, starting with her mouth and throat and rapidly spreading through to the very tips of her fingers and toes. Buzzing filled her ears, and her vision grew blurry with tiny pinpricks of light filling her view. A sense of euphoria flooded her mind, and for the first time in recent memory, she exhaled all of her problems and inhaled a sense of peace and pure pleasure. The scientist in her reasoned that the potion had triggered a massive dopamine dump.

Dimly, she was aware that her body was vibrating and that some sort of steam was rising from her, but she couldn't be bothered with it. Her vision continued to cloud and darken, and then she felt like she was flying among stars, a comet on an intergalactic tour. She lost sense of herself, at one point turning away from the stars to see her body lying on her bed and having the strangest sensation of looking at "Olivia" and thinking about how she was so much more than her. Then the feeling started to fade, and the pinpricks of light dissipated, replaced with the usual ambient light of their dormitory, and Olivia came back to reality.

Olivia sat up, feeling like she'd just slept a solid night through, noting how she was not sore in any way, and in fact, her body felt strong and limber like it hadn't in quite a while. Remembering Bronwyn's gleaming red hair, she pulled some of her hair up from her shoulder to look at it. It felt heavy and thick, and when she let the strands splay across her palm, she noticed that the black strands flowed like silky fibers that gleamed and glistened in the yellow-orange light of the dormitory. "I gained three ranks!" Rald shouted from the far end of the dormitory. Olivia smiled and called up her status sheet, noting that she'd also gained three racial ranks, up to base four.

Olivia examined her hands and nails, noting the smooth luster of her pale skin and the hard, perfect ovals of her nails. As far as she could remember, her hands hadn't ever looked that good, not even after a manicure. "Do I look different?" Veena asked from the next bed. "I gained two ranks." Olivia sat up and looked at her.

"Yeah, you look taller, and your hair is beautiful, Veena. My god, your eyes are glowing a little, and they look like they have little crystal facets in them!"

"Uh!" Veena grunted as she sat up, "You're taller, too. Your scar is faded but still there, and you also still have a silver eye, but it gleams in the light. Your blue eye is brighter, too. Olivia, your hair is stunning!" For the next few minutes, the cohort spent time looking at each other and exclaiming about how they'd changed. All in all, Olivia felt like they'd just grown a bit and gotten better looking. She wondered what exactly the effects the racial evolutions were having other than cosmetic.

"I wonder if there's a text I could read about racial evolutions. I'm curious what changes are going on under the skin, if you know what I mean."

"There's got to be. I know of a few things that happen, but I'd also be interested in knowing more," Veena said.

"Yeah, for one, you can't get very high level if you never evolve your race. A normal body can't handle that much Energy." Hanwol said.

"I'd say let's go to the library, but we need to go outside so you can absorb that crystal. I mean, unless you want to put it off? I recommend doing it, though, Olivia—you want to have it done before your demonstration tomorrow, don't you?" Adaida looked at her earnestly, and Olivia knew she was right.

"Yeah. If all goes well, my demonstration will level me, and then I'll be ten—I need to have this done before that if I want to gain the benefit for class selection." With that, her entire cohort escorted her through the hallways and out onto the commons. The whole while, Olivia was contemplating the prospect of absorbing part of another creature's soul, and she could only wonder if she was making a mistake.

↔ OLIVIA ↔

"Why did Alyss write that you shouldn't be near anything flammable? Are you going to burst into flames?" Rald asked, as they looked around the commons for a good spot for Olivia to absorb the elemental fragment.

"I don't know, but you're not helping my nerves!" Olivia frowned and pointed across the grass to the wrought iron fence that bordered the flower garden adjoining the commons. "Let's go in there; I'd like to be a bit out of sight," she said, gesturing to the various groups of students using the commons for recreation.

"Yeah, there's a little fountain square in there. It should be perfect." Veena took the lead, and they all followed her.

"Seriously, though, maybe you shouldn't wear any clothes you care about." Rald didn't want to let it go, and Olivia had to concede he had a point.

"I left my old clothes in my satchel back in the dorm." She shrugged.

"Well, I guess you could take off your clothes altogether . . ." He choked off his words as Adaida shoved his shoulder with a growl.

"Rald, maybe you should wait outside the garden and quit trying to stress Olivia out!"

"I'm not! I'm just being practical!"

Olivia tuned them out and took deep breaths, picking up her pace to walk past Veena and into the garden. She turned right, then followed the little brickwork path between large flowering shrubs. She'd explored the garden before and found it a lovely and relaxing place. She knew exactly where the little fountain was that Veena had mentioned. After a few more turns, she came upon the little babbling marble fountain shaped like four large fish jumping out of a wave. The water burbled out of the fish's mouths in a pleasant burble. Three marble benches surrounded the fountain, and thick shrubs bordered the brickwork square. It was about as private a place as they'd find on the academy grounds.

"Alright, I'm going to sit on the bricks on the far side of the fountain, please keep watch over me, but maybe Rald should watch the path in case my clothes burn off." She laughed as his eyes bugged out, and he started to protest. Then, she walked to the brick area beyond the fountain and sat down with her legs crossed. Veena, Shani, and Adaida sat on the bench on the near side of the fountain, their backs to the burbling fish, facing Olivia.

Hanwol and Rald just kind of paced around, looking awkward. Olivia tried to keep a smile on her face as she took the box with the elemental shard out of her ring. She opened it on the ground before her, then took up the lotus position, trying to clear her mind. Rald and Hanwol were whispering, but Adaida or Shani shushed them; Olivia couldn't quite tell which. She turned her mind inward and focused on her Core, watching the rings of elemental Energy rotating around the pulsing white center. When her mind felt calm and was aware of every inch of her pathways, she reached forward, felt for the box, and lifted out the little angular gem.

It was warm in her fingers, and she placed it carefully into her left hand, resting the palm of her right hand on top of it. Olivia reached out with her inner "Sight" to the gem and became aware of a roiling sea of burning Energy within it. It was like looking through a porthole on a ship and seeing the tossing waves of the ocean outside. Could she possibly contain this force? Was she meant to contain it?

Before self-doubt could creep into her consciousness, she reached into the gem and gave the Energy a gentle tug. At first, a thin tendril of the warm Energy poured into her through the pathway on her right hand, slowly coursing toward her Core. Then it began to pick up pace and volume, from a trickle to a stream to a river and finally to a raging torrent. At first, it was exhilarating, but the warm sensation quickly grew to a hot frenzy, almost like something was digging at her, pushing into her, and she began to feel a swell of panic rise in her mind.

Accept me! Do not struggle!

The voice was sibilant and multi-layered, like the voice of a storm or a fire. Olivia heard it in her mind, and then true panic raged through her. Was this fragment of a soul still alive? Would it take over her body? Her mind?

No! Open yourself to me; we will join!

Would Alyss have given her something that would destroy her mind? Olivia forced herself to calm and breathe, turning her will to the stream of burning Energy coursing through her pathways and holding it in place. In her head, she thought, *"Join with me but become a part of me. I am me and will always be so."*

Yes! Open yourself!

Olivia relaxed and stopped resisting, letting the fiery Energy surge through her pathways. It flowed in and around her Core and back out again in a cycle that picked up speed. The burning, painful sensation she'd begun to feel as the Energy filled her started to subside, and she realized her pathways had grown to accommodate the torrent. They resisted the heat and allowed the Energy to flow more quickly. Soon the Energy began to siphon off—some going into her Core but most bleeding out through her body and into the air. She didn't hear the voice again, but she felt the connection to the elemental within her and knew that something about her had fundamentally changed.

Congratulations! You have gained a new Feat: Elemental Heritage.

Elemental Heritage: Your very being has merged with the essence of a powerful, primal elemental. This heritage will be reflected in your racial evolutions and in your ability to harness and utilize elementally-attuned Energies. Elemental Energy that you wield through spells has increased efficacy.

Slowly, Olivia opened her eyes and noted the warm yellow-orange glow that suffused the very air in the garden. She focused on her classmates and saw that Veena, Adaida, and Shani were staring at her slack-jawed. Rald and Hanwol were pointedly looking the other way. Olivia looked down and saw a blackened circle stretching away from her body for about a foot in all directions, and then she noted her bare legs and, as she looked up, her naked body. She folded her arms over her breasts, and Adaida jumped into action, producing a cloak and pulling it around her.

"I hate to say I told you so," Rald said, but the others were talking at the same time.

"Olivia, your eyes are burning like there's a fire in them," Adaida muttered, pulling the cloak tight.

"That was so amazing!" Hanwol exclaimed. Veena and Shani said something too, but Olivia couldn't make it out in the chaos. She slowly stood up, pulling Adaida's cloak tight around her thin body. She noticed the orange-yellow glow in the air was starting to fade, and she reached up a hand to her eye, wondering what they looked like.

"The flames are fading," Shani said. "Your eyes are starting to look normal again." Olivia smiled and nodded to her, then looked at her status sheet. She saw her new feat listed and noticed that she'd gained yet another rank to her Core.

"Well, that was something else! You were sure right, Rald. How am I going to explain one of my uniforms turning to ash?" She wondered at herself; she didn't feel embarrassed at all. She still felt a sense of warmth and energy within her chest, and amusement was the only thing she felt about her clothes burning off. "God, I'm glad I wasn't wearing my satchel! I'd be devastated if that had burned up! What if I'd been wearing one of my nice outfits!" Adaida giggled, and her cohort crowded around her, blocking the view of strangers that might catch sight of a bit too much leg as Olivia walked back to the dormitory.

"Well, what's the story? Do you know how the absorption has affected you?" Veena asked as they all walked in a cluster across the commons.

"Yes! I have a greater connection to my elemental affinities, and I even have a feat called 'elemental heritage.' It should affect me as I continue to evolve my race. I hope it's nothing freakish. Were my eyes really on fire before?" Her vision had entirely returned to normal while they walked.

"Yes!" Shani replied. "You had smoldering flames inside those eye sockets, sweetie, and it was both scary and magnificent!" Olivia almost blushed at the compliment, but instead, she just grinned and winked at Shani. "Something's definitely different about you, Olivia."

"I like it, Liv," Adaida added, squeezing Olivia's arm through her silky blue cloak. "Roots, but you are a lot taller. You grew more than the rest of us, I think. Well, maybe not as much as Rald." Rald turned to grin but quickly looked away as Olivia took another step, and her long, pale leg slipped free of the cloak. Adaida and Olivia giggled, glancing at each other.

When they returned to the dormitory, Olivia went into the bathroom to soak in the tub. Rald announced that he was going to eat his fruit, and Veena and Shani said they would drink their second elixirs. Olivia didn't hear what the others were doing because she was in the bathroom, slipping into the big brass bathtub and letting the warm water pour down over her feet as it filled up.

She was absolutely exhausted, but in a good way—like how you feel after a long workout and a successful day. She leaned back against the curved slope of the tub and closed her eyes, turning her attention to her Core. Everything seemed in order; maybe her fire ring was a little brighter than before, and maybe her Core was a little more vibrant. Her pathways were more robust, that was for sure. She was excited to give her demonstration to the assembled students tomorrow. Olivia stopped cold and thought about that: she was excited—not anxious, not trepidatious, excited.

A soft knock sounded on the door, and Olivia heard it creak open. She turned to it and saw Adaida poking her head through. "Mind if I come in for a bit? I'm bored." Olivia smiled and scooted down in the tub a bit more.

"Sure, but sit over there," she nodded to the little chair next to the sink counter, a good six feet from the tub. Adaida nodded and walked over there. On the way, she stooped to scoop up her cloak that Olivia had let fall onto the little woven rug. "Hey, thanks for letting me borrow that!" Flustered, Olivia said, "I don't even remember dropping it on the floor; I'm sorry! I should have hung it up."

"Nothing to worry about. I think your mind was pretty frazzled from that experience, wasn't it?" Adaida sat on the chair and leaned back, looking at Olivia's face.

"For sure! First the elixir and that crazy trip, then the elemental absorption; my head's still spinning!"

"You look good, though. Like, vibrant."

"You're not too shabby, yourself. How many racial ranks did you get, again? I think Veena only got two, but I don't remember what you said."

"I also got two. Shani, of course, got three."

"Ugh! That's not fair! She already had one, right?"

"Yeah, but life isn't fair. I learned that a long time ago. My parents have always favored Shani. I'm fine, though—I've had plenty of people love me, don't worry."

"Still, I'm sorry about that. I was an only child, so I don't know the feeling of having to compete with a sibling."

"Yeah. She's always been just a little better at things than I have. Not just academically but socially. She always had the right thing to say to adults—parents, teachers, and neighbors. If there were an attribute for charm, she'd have a much higher one than me."

"I don't think that's true. You've been great to me, and Shani was cold to me for a long time."

"Well, that's because she didn't think she needed to impress you." She paused and gathered her thoughts, then continued, "She's not really fake if that's what it sounds like I'm saying. She's just good at impressing people she thinks she needs to impress." Adaida shrugged and sighed. "Anyway, I didn't come in here to talk about my sister!"

"Sorry! Well, why did you come in here?" Olivia felt her heart rate pick up a little.

"I was just bored, and I like your company." Adaida's lips curved up unevenly, the right corner of her mouth lifting a bit in a crooked smile.

"Well, it shouldn't matter what we talk about, then, right?" Olivia grinned back at her.

"Tell me about your home. What's the human settlement like?" Olivia hadn't expected that question, but she did her best to describe First Landing to Adaida. They talked for a long time about each other's homes, friends, and families. Olivia told Adaida a little about her life back on Earth. When she described her latest apartment in San Jose, Adaida had a lot of questions for her, mostly about the internet and VR. After a while, Olivia decided it was time to get out of the tub.

"Hey, I'm getting wrinkly here. You mind turning around while I get out?"

"Nothing I haven't seen before, you know," Adaida said as she sighed and stood.

"That may be, but . . ." Olivia gestured for Adaida to turn.

"I'll wait for you by the couches. Let's go get some food when you're ready."

"Alright, thanks for the company, Adaida."

"Sure. Thank you, too." Adaida gave her a funny little wave and then walked out. Olivia stood and dried off, getting dressed in one of her other uniforms.

She'd felt Adaida was crushing on her in the past, but this little conversation seemed to confirm things. Olivia liked her, for sure, but she wasn't sure she wanted Adaida like that. She wasn't really sure who she wanted, "Like that," which she knew was strange for someone her age.

The truth was, Olivia had never been in a really serious relationship. She'd always been too busy. Well, that was always her excuse. She knew she felt affection for certain people, and it wasn't always women. She'd been with men before, but she just believed in letting her feelings speak for themselves, and so far, she hadn't ever really felt that strongly about anyone. At least not as strongly as her mom, and books she'd read, made it sound like she'd feel. She knew she felt something for Bronwyn, but it was hard to read her, and Olivia had never gotten a solid feeling that Bronwyn thought of her as anything more than a close friend. Adaida was certainly pretty, though, she thought. And sweet; she was definitely sweet.

Olivia hummed a little to herself while she brushed her hair and looked at herself in the mirror. For a moment, she was confused about what she saw, and then she remembered the racial enhancements. She'd changed in ways she hadn't expected: her lips were fuller and more red, her cheekbones seemed more prominent, her entire face seemed slightly longer, a bit less oval. She had a hard time putting the differences into words, but there was definitely more to her now.

Her friends and family had always described her as pretty, and she'd never had anything to complain about in that department, but now, if she were honest with herself, she looked beautiful. As she stared at her reflection, she saw a slight flicker in her eyes, and when she moved closer to really stare into the mirror, she saw a brief image of a flame dancing before her iris. When she blinked, it was gone. "Yeah, something's definitely different about me," Olivia laughed, running her fingers through her smooth, shimmery black hair. She walked to the door and opened it, calling, "Adaida! Let's go; I'm starving!"

⚭ OLIVIA ⚯

Olivia was disturbed to see that more upper-class students and professors had shown up for her demonstration than had for the awards assembly. She was standing on stage next to Alyss, wearing her gray first-year robes and nervously wringing her hands behind her back. The confidence she'd felt the previous night seemed to have departed her, and she was back to her old, anxious self. That wasn't entirely true—she didn't like the crowd of quiet faces staring at her, but she still felt confident in her ability. She'd practiced her meta-element weaves for several hours before sleep and had gotten so fast that she couldn't count past two while constructing one. Considering her first attempts had taken minutes and unraveled before she could complete them, she was rather pleased with herself.

"Well, I'm impressed that so many of you have given up part of your Saturday to come and see a demonstration from one of my students!" Alyss said, affecting a bit of a showman's voice. The crowd was mostly quiet, though Copper gave a few hoots, and Olivia heard Rald call out, "Olivia!" She hadn't felt worried prior to that, but something about the way her cohort seemed to believe in her brought a sliver of doubt into her mind, and she began to worry about letting them down. "Just a moment while I get the stage ready for you, Olivia," Alyss said, loud enough for the audience to hear.

Alyss walked to the left side of the stage and produced a shiny metal stand that looked a lot like a chrome pole. She must have taken it from a dimensional container because it seemed pretty heavy. Alyss grunted as she rolled the broad base into position, then she stepped a few feet to the right and produced another one, rolling it ponderously in line with the first. Then, she put one hand on each shiny pole and concentrated for a moment. A bright flash erupted between the poles, and a wide, swirling maelstrom of Energy appeared between them. It looked like a colorful, spinning whirlpool suspended sideways in midair. Alyss turned back to Olivia and paced ten steps, then motioned for Olivia to stand next to her. "Please aim your spells at the portal; it will harmlessly disperse the Energy."

"Alright, thank you, Alyss." Olivia nodded and began concentrating on the swirling portal, glad to have something to grab her attention.

"Please maintain your decorum and keep quiet! Olivia hasn't been able to enact these workings before for fear of leveling too soon," Alyss announced as she moved behind Olivia and closer to the audience. For her part, Olivia closed her eyes and turned her mind inward, looking at her Core, instantly feeling calmer as she watched her spinning rings of attuned Energy gyrate around her inner heart of pure Energy. She knew what she was going to do; she'd run it over in her mind a million times. She'd studied her other spells and the way they spun her attuned Energy into a pattern and launched them. Now, she just had to manually do the same with her new meta-elements.

Olivia had decided to replicate the effect of her Fiery Burst spell—it had the simplest pattern that poured almost pure fire-attuned Energy out of her channel into the air. She took three deep, steady breaths, in through her nose, out through her mouth. Delicately, with precision she could only have imagined a month ago, Olivia pulled a thread of air-attuned Energy out of her Core and matched it with a thread of water-attuned Energy. When she had them next to each other in her pathway, she took another deep breath, held her right palm out toward the spinning portal, then rapidly formed the pattern for arcfrost and pushed the completed weave through her pathway into the pattern of Fiery Burst.

She felt a chilling, tingling sensation in her palm and a deep rush of Energy through her pathways. A buzzing, crackling torrent of frosty air arcing with jagged bolts of electricity howled through the air in front of her palm, pouring into the portal. The moisture in the air around the torrent of arcfrost seemed crystallized, and flakes of frost drifted to the stage. A collective intake of breath spread through the audience as the flood faded and Olivia let her hand fall and a surge of golden motes coalesced in the air pouring into her.

Congratulations! You have learned the spell: Arcfrost Cascade—Basic.

Arcfrost Cascade—Basic: Prerequisite: Affinity—Water, Affinity—Air. You conjure forth a torrent of raw arcfrost. Energy cost: 200, Cooldown: Minimal.

Congratulations! You have achieved level 10 base human and have 10 attribute points to allocate. Your first Class selection is available to you.

"Well done, Olivia," Alyss said from behind her, then she continued, more loudly, "Please quiet yourselves, everyone. Olivia has only just begun. If you're wondering, that was a meta-element that she just conjured; its destructive force actually put a strain on my portal." More buzzing conversations started up at that comment, and Alyss had to raise her voice even more. "Again, please be quiet. Allow Olivia to concentrate!" Olivia glanced at the audience, and suddenly they hushed. A few students pointed at her and whispered, and Olivia turned to Alyss, concerned that something was wrong. "It's alright, Olivia. Your eyes reflect the meta-element you just conjured; frosty storm clouds are hiding your pupils." More hushed conversations started up as Olivia absorbed Alyss's comment. She felt fine; the only change in her vision was that the room seemed a little brighter.

Once again, Olivia held her palm toward the portal, and the assembled students grew quiet. Olivia prepared a thread of fire-attuned Energy, a thread of earth-attuned Energy, and then took a deep breath. When her mind was set, she quickly formed her magma weave and pushed it into the pattern for Fiery Burst. A surge of hot Energy poured through her pathways and erupted from her palm. A veritable column of roaring magma surged through the air into the portal. The heat from the meta-element caused waves of distortion to appear in the air on the stage, and Olivia heard a high-pitched ringing sound come from one of the pedestals that Alyss had used to create the portal. After just a couple of seconds, the beam of magma halted, and, again, Olivia leaned forward, absorbing a surge of Energy motes that coalesced out of thin air.

Congratulations! You have learned the spell: Magma Ray—Basic.

Magma Ray—Basic: Prerequisite: Affinity—Fire, Affinity—Earth. You conjure forth a beam of raw magma. Energy cost: 200, Cooldown: Minimal.

Congratulations! You have achieved level 11 base human and have 10 attribute points to allocate. Your first Class selection is available to you. Warning! Your advancement is being held until you select your first class. Should you sleep or lose consciousness before selecting your Class, this advancement will be lost.

"Excellent, Olivia; are you doing okay? Can you continue?" Alyss asked, but she didn't wait for an answer; she stepped up to the portal and carefully inspected the shiny pedestals, a slight frown on her face. "Actually, I think we might have to pause for now, Olivia. You can demonstrate your other spells to me later." Alyss turned to the audience while Olivia absorbed what she'd just said. "Everyone, I think Olivia has more than earned her prize, don't you?" The audience gave a rather hearty cheer, and Olivia felt a surge of pride, but then a shout rang out.

"What? Two offensive blast spells? Not very nuanced, is it?" Professor ap'Gravin stood and approached the stage. "Sure, it requires some luck with affinities and some raw power to make a meta-element, but I still don't see how she warrants the top prize. It's most definitely not clear-cut enough for me to offer up another award." Olivia turned to the professor, a surge of heat rising in her, making her pulse pound in her ears. He almost took a step back when he saw her gaze, for a fiery roiling storm raged under her brows.

"I have something I could show the good professor," Olivia said calmly, her voice ringing out over the audience.

"Olivia, you've done enough, and my portal might not contain another blast," Alyss said quietly, turning her back to the audience.

"It shouldn't cause any damage. I'm feeling fine, Alyss."

"Well? I'm waiting," ap'Gravin said, glancing to the side where some of his students sat. Chuckles and sniggers sounded from the group. Olivia felt such an urge to conjure a bolt of magma and hurl it at them that she had to close her eyes and take stock of her mental state. She usually didn't react to threats or teasing with violent thoughts, and she knew the elemental shard was influencing her. Forcefully, she concentrated on her Core with her eyes closed and took two deep breaths; then, she opened her eyes and nodded to Alyss. Alyss stepped back and turned to the audience.

"Olivia has another spell she'd like to demonstrate that should put to rest your doubts." Alyss walked over to the portal and touched the shiny pedestal on the right; the swirling maelstrom winked out of existence with a pop. Olivia turned to the audience and held out her right hand, palm facing upward. She closed her eyes and looked into her Core, calmly pulling out one thread of attuned Energy after another, lining them up in her pathways. All in all, she had eight threads ready to weave, and then she took one deep, steadying breath and began. First, she weaved together the pattern for arcfrost, finishing in less than two seconds. Then, setting a new record for herself, she wove the pattern for magma in the space of one heartbeat. Holding those two patterns together in her pathway with an effort of will, she did something she'd never done before: she wove together a third meta-element: plasma. It took her nearly four seconds and sweat began to bead on her brow as she concentrated on holding those three weaves together. Still, she didn't stop and started the arduous process of weaving together a thread of pyrosteam.

Olivia wasn't aware of the murmurs breaking out in the audience or of ap'Gravin's huff of impatience. To everyone else, it looked like she was standing with her eyes closed, scrunching her brow down in concentration, but nothing was happening. Deep inside her, though, a furious effort of will was taking place while Olivia strained to hold together the three completed meta-elements as she laboriously crafted the pattern for pyrosteam. It was the hardest of the four, with the fire-attuned Energy fighting her every step of the way as she bent it around the water-attuned Energy. Still, she was doing it. She was halfway through the pattern by the fifth heartbeat, the other meta-elements still holding solid. She took a huge breath, and, letting her instincts take over, she flew through the second half.

Olivia opened her eyes, and they blazed with the fury of a white-hot sun— some kind of mixture of all her meta-elements. She looked directly at Professor ap'Gravin, and then four orbs burst into existence, orbiting each other in a complicated pattern over her extended palm. A ball of white, crackling arc-frost, one of shifting bubbling magma, another blue, roiling orb of superheated plasma, and finally, a cloudy globe of pyrosteam that pulsed with a fury reminiscent of a thermite reaction.

Each sphere was about the size of a baseball, and the Energy seeping out from the combined forces was palpable. Some in the front row of the audience stood and scrambled backward among the exclamations and cheers that began to break out. Olivia closed her eyes and stopped the flow of Energy. The orbs dimmed and winked out but were replaced by a new light—extremely bright motes of Energy coalesced out of the air and surged into Olivia.

*****Congratulations! You have learned the spell: Orb Manipulation—Epic.*****

*****Orb Manipulation—Epic: Prerequisite: Affinity—Fire, Affinity—Earth, Affinity—Air, Affinity—Water. You are able to conjure and manipulate orbs of pure meta-elemental force. Energy cost: 100 base (scalable), Cooldown: Minimal.*****

*****Congratulations! You have achieved level 12 and have 10 attribute points to allocate. Your first Class selection is available to you. Warning! Your advancement is being held until you select your first class. Should you sleep or lose consciousness before selecting your Class, this advancement will be lost.*****

Olivia ignored the notifications in front of her and watched ap'Gravin. His face had blanched a little, but he didn't speak. He simply turned on his heel and marched out of the auditorium. Olivia glanced toward her cohort and saw them standing and cheering loudly. Most of the crowd was cheering—even novices understood, or rather couldn't understand, what Olivia had done, and were caught up in the excitement that seemed to be infectious. Olivia scanned the crowd for the glowing blue eyes of Gwinna. When she finally spotted them, she stared at her rival, her own eyes still flaming, only very gradually cooling toward normal. Olivia grinned, teeth bared, as Gwinna broke first and stood to leave, turning away from her.

". . . Incredible, Olivia!" Alyss was saying. Olivia had missed the first part of what she'd said, but she smiled, her face flushed, and reached out to take Alyss's offered hand.

"Thank you!" Olivia couldn't stop grinning.

"You didn't mention that one! Do you realize what this means? I can't think of anyone that can hold together four meta-elements like that. Don't get me wrong; you still have a lot to learn, but your raw talent is exceptional. Word of this is going to spread. Oh, I hope . . ." She cut herself off and motioned for Olivia to follow her. "Come with me, Olivia. Let's go to my office so you can have some peace while you select your class. I'm assuming you leveled?"

"Three times!" Olivia laughed, and so did Alyss. Then, still holding Olivia's hand, she turned to the audience and held Olivia's arm high. Again, the crowd cheered. Olivia, acting on an impulse foreign to her, bowed with a flourish, then followed Alyss off the stage and through a side door.

⊰ BRONWYN ⊱

Bronwyn stepped into the throne room and found herself facing the far end where the two massive doors stood closed. She turned around to see the queen standing before her throne, smiling at her. "Come, child, let me embrace you; I couldn't be more proud!" The queen stepped forward to wrap her arms around her, and Bronwyn might have resisted if she wanted to, but she didn't want to. Warmth radiated from the queen in sync with the heat pulsing at Bronwyn's Core, and she leaned her head into the tall fae's bosom, soaking in the pleasure of her approval. "Now," the queen stepped back, still resting her hands on Bronwyn's shoulders, "Let me answer the questions buzzing in your mind."

"I didn't know I'd be losing my class!" Bronwyn blurted the first thing that popped into her mind.

"Oh, it wasn't a certainty, but, Bronwyn, what you've gained is far greater. Do you trust me?"

"I don't know why, but yes, I do." The queen smiled at this small insolence and gently squeezed Bronwyn's shoulders.

"Good. Now, I see you've not chosen your new class. Before the System infiltrated our prospects, there wouldn't be a choice. Those who survived their encounter with the Summer Heart would be granted their class, and I'd teach them about it. Now the System neatly informs you of what's happening behind the scenes. Well, some of it."

"But the selection says that it's not a 'System-curated class.'"

"Correct! Classes existed before the System, but they weren't so neat or straightforward. The System does provide a service; for the Energy it leeches, it helps Energy and its boons to be accessible to nearly everyone. The lack of a System didn't hamper the fae; we knew how to organize skills and spells that utilize Energy to create our own classes. All of the elder races could do this, and many members of the younger races learned some of it as well. The System knows that the Summer Heart has gifted you with the patterns for a class; it's forced to show it to you, but I'm sure it's offered you other tempting options, no?"

"Yes," Bronwyn said softly, her mind whirling with the idea that the System couldn't dominate the fae or even remove what they'd done to her; it was forced to try to lure her away with other options. "Does everyone who finishes the trial end up with this class?"

"Oh, no! Why do you think I'm so pleased with you? Your choices, your resilience, and the way you melded with the Summer Heart all led to the Summer Banneret. Some of my agents who've survived with three boons failed to come away from the Summer Heart with anything more than a closer connection to my Realms." Bronwyn noticed that the queen used her physical voice to speak with her; her lips moved, and she smiled with emotion. Was this a result of her feeling closer to Bronwyn?

"I don't," Bronwyn struggled with how to phrase her words, "I don't appreciate how the swarm almost killed me. Was it bad luck that they found me? Why couldn't you warn me about something like that happening?" The queen didn't answer right away; she let go of Bronwyn's shoulders and backed up to her throne, taking a seat. She regarded her for a moment, still smiling.

"I don't think it was bad luck. The Blessing of the Swarm will serve you well, and though it was traumatic, I was sure that you'd survive. You have a fierce spirit, Bronwyn. I couldn't warn you for two reasons—it's customary not to, and there are hundreds of variables that could change the encounters and outcomes in the trial. I didn't want to interfere. I wish I could say it would be the last time I send you into danger and cause you suffering, but you must understand that I would never do so without cause nor with a callous heart." Bronwyn couldn't muster any anger at the queen. Something had changed in her since coming to the Fae Realm, and she was aware of it, but finding words to describe it was difficult. She felt like her old self would have raged about the things that happened to her in the trial, but she wasn't so sure her change in attitude was all due to the fae; she'd experienced a lot in the last months, not least of which was traveling around fighting and making friends with Urghat.

"Alright, so, I assume you think I should take the fae class? The Summer Banneret?" The queen didn't speak, just smiled more broadly. Bronwyn took that as a yes and opened her status sheet to make the selection.

WARNING! The selection you have made is a non-System-curated class. Your refinement options may be limited. This selection is not reversible! Are you sure? YES/NO

Bronwyn touched the "YES," and more System messages expanded before her eyes:

Congratulations! You have gained the Class: Summer Banneret. Class spell gained: Solar Shell—Basic. Class spell gained: Wrath of Summer—Basic.

Solar Shell—Basic: Prerequisite: Solar Affinity. You surround your body with a barrier of solar Energy for a short time, protecting your physical form from harm and causing heat and light damage to beings and objects that you touch. Energy cost: 200, Cooldown: Medium.

Wrath of Summer—Basic: Prerequisite: Summer Banneret Class. Call upon the Summer Court to lay waste to a target area. Energy cost: 400, Cooldown: Very Long.

"Wow, um, I got some powerful sounding new spells, but I don't even have enough Energy to cast the second one."

"Take a look at your attributes, child," the Queen responded, and Bronwyn did so, calling up her status sheet:

Status				
Name:	Bronwyn Tallow			
Race:	Human - Base 2			
Class:	Summer Banneret			
Level:	15			
Core:	Summer Class - Base 3			
Energy Affinity:	5.6, Solar - 7.6	Energy:	337/337	
Strength:	72	Vitality:	39	
Dexterity:	19	Agility:	44	
Intelligence:	9	Will:	26	
Points Available:	0			
Titles & Feats:	First Colonist, Underclaw 10, Agent of Summer, Blessing of the Swarm, Blessing of the Herd, Blessing of the Summer Storm			
Skills:	• System Language Integration - Not Upgradeable • Unarmed Mastery - Basic • Tracking - Basic • Cartography - Basic		• Solar Shell - Basic • Wrath of Summer - Basic	

"When you look at your attributes, what stands out?" the queen asked, and Bronwyn knew where this was going.

"My intelligence is a lot lower than the others."

"Lucky for you, the class you've just taken isn't bound by the System to give you an increase in specific attributes; you'll be able to assign your points where you want, and if you want your maximum Energy to increase faster, you should put some of your growth into intelligence." Bronwyn nodded along with the queen's words. "You can also gain more Energy by improving your Core."

"Alright, but in the meantime, I can cast one of my spells one time before running dry?" Bronwyn wasn't trying to sound petulant, but a little sulkiness leaked into her voice.

"Well, I think you'd do fine with your fighting ability, but I do have a dangerous task for you. I'll grant you one more boon. Lean forward, Banneret." The queen held out her right hand, and Bronwyn leaned forward into her touch. She felt the warm, deep well of power beneath those fingertips as they rested on her forehead. An explosion of light went off behind her eyes, and then, as if frantically trying to catch up, a System message appeared:

Congratulations! You have gained the spell: Solar Arms—Basic.

Solar Arms—Basic: Prerequisite: Solar Affinity. Your weapons, wielded or natural, are imbued with solar Energy, causing extra heat and light damage to those you strike. Energy cost: 5 per second, Cooldown: Minimal.

"Thank you, um, Your Majesty." Bronwyn didn't know the queen's name, but she knew how to address one in general terms, at least in the human courts.

"You're welcome, Bronwyn."

"Will that work with my fists? Is that what 'natural' weapons means?"

"Yes, though I encourage you to learn to fight with other weapons as well. You will face some foes that might require a powerful weapon to harm. Now, as I mentioned, I have need of your services before I can release you to work with your people for a while."

"Um, okay, what can I do for you?"

"You might not be aware of this, but an agent of the Winter Court has already raised a hand against your people on Fanwath."

"No, I wasn't aware of that!"

"During the recent Urghat incursion against your settlement, a powerful Cadwalli named Thun influenced one of your citizens. Thun forced him to help the Urghat breach your walls."

"So, the Winter Court wants to destroy my people?"

"I think not. I think they'd rather use your people. Thun was acting selfishly;

he wanted something from the Urghat and bargained for it by offering to help them with your people."

"Is he still a threat to us?"

"Not presently; he's gone north to commune with the Winter Queen, and then he intends to seclude for a while to process the item he acquired from the Urghat. As I said, he's powerful, but he'll be vulnerable for a time following the full moon of Belintide; I'd like you to follow him, lie in wait, gather your strength, and then strike at dawn following the full moon. You have just over two weeks."

"Um, how will I find him? How will I know when the moon is full? I mean, I know what a full moon looks like, but doesn't it look full for a few days?" Bronwyn sputtered the first questions that sprang to her mind, and the queen smiled at her.

"I'll send you to where my scouts last saw him, and you'll be able to pick up his tracks. As for the moon," she held out her hand, and a small black stone sat in her palm, "Take this; when the morning of action is nigh, it will change from black to white."

"Just to be clear, you want me to kill him?"

"Yes, Bronwyn. He's not a good soul, and he will harm your people given time. Do you trust me yet?"

"I do, Queen . . ." she trailed off, wanting to say her name, but wondering if she should ask what it was.

"I've had many names over the millennia, Bronwyn. You may call me Queen Aestasia."

"Thank you, Queen Aestasia. I don't like acting as an assassin, but if this guy is evil and caused the deaths of hundreds of my people already, then I'll do what I must to stop him."

"He is certainly indirectly responsible for the deaths that occurred after the Urghat breached your walls. Are you ready, Champion of Summer?" the queen asked, smiling down at her. Bronwyn nodded. "Very well, I have one more parting gift." Again, the queen held out her palm, and a delicate silver ring sat on it. It was crafted into the shape of a winding band of vines adorned with tiny flowers made from other precious metals that shone in the bright light of the hall.

"It's beautiful," Bronwyn said, reaching for it.

"It's a dimensional container, and I've filled it with provisions for you."

"Oh, thank you again!" Bronwyn slipped the ring onto her right-hand ring finger and bonded with it, immediately sensing the considerable space it contained and the neatly packaged provisions within. Light flared to her left, and Bronwyn turned to see that the queen had created another portal.

"Step through now, Bronwyn. You'll find Thun's tracks near the glade where this portal opens. I'll be in contact with you through my kinfolk that dwell on Fanwath. Good luck, daughter." Bronwyn felt a slight lurch in her stomach when the queen called her daughter, and she smiled and nodded, not trusting her voice. She stepped through the portal into a twilit meadow and shivered at the lack of warmth.

⧼ OLIVIA ⧽

"Should I assign my five points from level ten before looking at my class choices?" Olivia asked Alyss. They were sitting in Alyss's office, which would have made a fully tenured Harvard professor envious. They sat near a wide bank of windows that overlooked the back gardens of the academy on two warmly upholstered sofas that faced each other. Built-in bookcases lined the walls, overflowing with leather-bound volumes and rolled scrolls. And that was just half of the office—a sizable shiny meeting table surrounded by chairs, a huge desk, and more bookcases filled the other half. The room was richly appointed with plush rugs, paintings in gold leaf frames, stained-glass lamps, and even little figurines of people and animals displayed on glass-shelved cases. Alyss had fancy tastes.

"It won't make a difference; your choices are already set. Go ahead and pull up the menu and have a look," Alyss replied, leaning forward on the edge of her seat, watching Olivia with her hands clasped on her knees.

"Alright, here goes." Olivia pulled up her status menu and selected the option for class selection:

Class selection option 1: Mage—Improved. Your intellect and strength of will make the shaping of Energy seem easy. This path will help you to further broaden and strengthen those abilities. Class attributes: Will and Intelligence.

"Mage is my first choice; it says it's improved."

"Your first choice is improved? That's good—you're definitely getting above-average selections. Usually, students are offered a couple of basic classes before seeing an improved one. Keep going; tell me what your next offer is. I'm familiar with the mage class, and it's not a bad option at all, but let's see what else there is. Olivia nodded and touched the little symbol to move to the following option:

Class selection option 2: Elementalist—Advanced. Prerequisite: Affinity with two or more elementally aligned Energies. Your affinities have shaped you and your abilities. Bending the elements to your will turns you into a veritable force of nature. Continue down this path to enhance your affinities and become further entwined with these primal forces. Class attributes: Will, Intelligence, and Vitality.

"Elementalist, and it's advanced."

"Oh, fantastic! Hold on just a moment," Alyss said, then stood and rummaged through a bookcase, pulling out a thin, red, leather-bound book. She sat down with it, flipping through the pages, then said, "Aha! Here we go." She read for a few moments, then continued, "Elementalist has strong attribute benefits, and there are several known refinements at twenty that are quite intriguing."

"You can see what refinements I'll get?"

"Some of them. Let me see here." Alyss read from the text she'd opened, then continued, "If you took Elementalist, improved your intelligence and will to more than one hundred, and learned a few spells using air-attuned Energy, you'd be offered a Stormcaster class. There are other refinements based on the other elements. I'd wager there would be more rare offerings if you met the requirements for more than one. Let's keep going, though—see what your other options are."

"Alright. It's lucky for me that I have you to help me, Alyss. No one in my community has resources like that." Olivia smiled at Alyss, then looked at her next option:

Class selection option 3: Energy Weaver—Advanced. Energy and its peculiarities are second nature to you. Weaving new spells, manipulating natural forces, and dominating the will of lesser Weavers are your hallmarks. Class attributes: Intelligence and Will.

"Energy Weaver, another advanced class. It sounds fascinating, though the Elementalist did, too. Is there any reason I would choose the Mage class over one of these advanced classes?"

"I've heard of that one! It's very uncommon, Olivia! I'll look it up; just a moment," she stood and looked through her bookcase again, but continued speaking, "As for why you'd want to choose an improved class over an advanced option, there are a few reasons: You might want to level more quickly—the higher-tier classes take more Energy to advance. You could probably hit level twenty in an improved class in the amount of time it took to get to level fourteen or fifteen in an advanced class. Another reason would be to aim for a certain class refinement. Some paths are well known, and to get to a certain known class refinement might mean starting with a basic or improved class. Finally, it might simply be the best fit for what you want. Just because a class is advanced or epic, even, doesn't mean it's what you want to do with your life. Hmm, aha!" She lifted out a thick, squat, black book and returned to her seat.

"So, the benefits of advanced classes come with an increased cost in Energy." Olivia nodded along, feeling like she had a pretty good grasp of things.

"Not exactly. I mean, yes, you have an increased cost in cultivation or earned Energy in order to level, but the cost of abilities or spells isn't increased. Hmm, yep, here it is, Energy Weaver. 'Known to require very high Energy Affinity.' Mmhmm, ahh, 'one of four known prerequisite classes to gain the Archmage refinement.'"

"Wow, sounds like a good option!" Olivia didn't really know what an Archmage was, but it sounded good to her.

"Very good, but the Archmage refinement wouldn't come at twenty. You'd need to refine into a more specialized class and then again at level thirty. If you did everything right, increased your attributes, and learned the right spells, you should be able to gain that refinement by level forty, and the number of people who reach tier four is vanishingly small." She gave Olivia a long look, then said, "But I think you'll do it, provided you get ahold of enough racial advancements. Any other options?"

"Yes, one second," Olivia replied, advancing the selection screen to the next option:

*****Class selection option 4: Elemental Archon—Epic. You have entwined your spirit with a being born of the elements. Elemental Energies are your lifeblood, part of your being as much as your mortal flesh. Nurture this side of yourself, building your elemental abilities to suit your design. Class attributes: Intelligence, Will, Unbound.*****

"Umm, it's an 'epic' class," Olivia paused as Alyss leaned forward to grab her hands.

"What is it?" Her eyes were wide open, staring at Olivia in earnest excitement.

"Elemental Archon?" Olivia couldn't help how she answered with her voice rising in a question.

"What exactly does it say?" Alyss didn't betray any emotion other than pure interest, so Olivia read her the full description.

"Ancestors! I knew that gem would influence your class choice, but I didn't imagine something like this! Are there any more options?"

"No, that's the last one," Olivia replied.

"Alright, alright. Hmm, let's think about this. Let me see." Alyss thumbed through the thick black book again but then set it down and returned to her bookcase. Olivia sat, part of her mind watching Alyss, but part of it racing through the mental images her class choices evoked. She read through the description of Elemental Archon again and felt warring emotions clash within her. She was excited by the prospect, but part of her was afraid. It said that elemental Energies would be her "Lifeblood," that she'd nurture that part of her that was elemental. Did it mean she'd lose some of her humanity?

"What does it mean when it says 'unbound' after class attributes?" Olivia asked Alyss while she rummaged through another bookcase.

"Some very rare classes give you attribute points to distribute as you level, just like you were given when you didn't have a class. Let me stress: it's very uncommon at level ten." Alyss huffed in frustration and moved to another bookcase.

"Do you think that epic class will change me? I mean, who I am? It says I'll be nurturing the elemental part of me." Alyss had given Olivia good advice up to now, and she felt she could trust Alyss, so she decided to voice her concern. The professor stopped rooting around for books, looked at Olivia gravely, and then responded.

"Olivia, I really don't know. I don't think so, but I can't promise that. Most classes, when they grant abilities beyond what someone can do naturally, offer them as something the person can control, like activating a spell. I have heard stories of people changing drastically as they gain powers or spells that encourage certain behavior. Necromancers communing with the dead is an example, or Blood Ragers seeking fights and gaining power through the carnage. I'm not sure what this Elemental Archon class will inspire in you, but I feel like you wouldn't have this option if it weren't already part of you in some way. It might just bring forth certain aspects of your personality or physicality that are dormant or quiet now." She turned back to the bookcase, "I'm trying to find some information for you, though. Give me a couple of minutes."

"Alright, thanks, Alyss." Olivia's impulse, strangely, was to select the simple Elementalist class. When she examined that urge, she realized she was responding out of fear. Something about the Elemental Archon class and the fact that it was "Epic" made her feel pressured, and her instinct was to balk. She'd never enjoyed classes in school when she didn't choose them. Of course, no one was telling her to pick the Elemental Archon class; it was just an imagined pressure—the idea that everyone would think she was stupid if she didn't choose it. Alyss tossed down another book and moved to the bookcases behind her desk. "Alyss," Olivia said, though the woman didn't seem to hear. "Alyss!"

"Hmm?" Alyss paused and looked back at her.

"I'm going to pick the Elemental Archon," Olivia said firmly.

"Are you sure? If I can't find any information in my books, I'll go ask some of my colleagues. Odds are we can find something."

"I'm sure. I feel like I want to pick it based on my feelings, not because you find some information that makes it the 'smart' choice. I know that sounds ridiculous, but . . ." Olivia trailed off, and Alyss walked back toward her.

"It doesn't sound ridiculous, Olivia. You're gifted, and I think you feel pushed into things because of your talents and what people expect of you. If you feel like you want to do this without someone telling you it's the right thing to do, then I can respect that. I'll be here to help. I don't think you can go wrong with any of your choices." She sat down across from Olivia and smiled warmly. "Take your time. Think it through and make your choice. You'll be fine."

Olivia nodded and closed her eyes, really thinking about her feelings. If she chose the improved class, she could level quickly and get a different refinement at twenty. One of the advanced options would be a nice middle ground, allowing her to level more easily than the epic class but giving her a good start on gaining power, leading to some interesting refinement options. The epic class, however, scared her. She'd level more slowly; she might lose something of herself as she grew in power as an "Elemental Archon," whatever that was exactly. That fear, though, that fear made her want to choose it. Was that childish? Or was it her listening to her instincts and not crumbling to do what everyone else would call "Smart"?

When she'd been young, Olivia had wanted to explore space. The idea was fascinating to her but also terrifying. Despite the scarier aspects, she'd always had that goal in her mind when planning and going through with her education, earning degrees in engineering and biology and then doctorates in math and physics. When she'd had the idea that led to her perfecting the cryo-tech that made interstellar travel possible, she'd wondered if she'd have to give up her dream; her research and development took more time than she could spare. Only when she'd gained enough clout through her shares in Vynatek had she been able to dictate her terms—she wanted aboard one of the *Pilgrim* missions.

Now, as she reminisced about those times, she asked herself what was the point? Why had her mind gone there? Then she remembered the teachers and family members that laughed when she shared her dreams. Slight, smart, pretty Olivia, exploring the solar system? What a joke. But she'd never seen it as a joke, and she'd never listened to even one of them. She'd known what she wanted, and she'd made it happen, despite her fear and despite what others thought she should do.

Now she sat there contemplating a decision that was potentially just as impactful as anything she'd ever decided. She was scared, but she was also fascinated by the idea. So, she decided to, once again, move into her fear. She flipped through the menu to the Elemental Archon page and touched the button that selected it.

Congratulations! You have gained your first Class: Elemental Archon. Class skill gained: Elemental Form—Basic.

Congratulations! World-first Elemental Archon! Feat awarded.

First Elemental Archon: Feat granted: Elemental Resistance—the basic elements are a part of you, and thus, you resist their extremes far more easily than others of your race.

Elemental Form—Basic: You are able to take on some of the physical attributes of specific primal elemental beings. Energy cost: 500, Cooldown: Long.

Congratulations! You have achieved level 11 Elemental Archon and have gained 10 Intelligence, 10 Will, and have 18 attribute points to allocate.

Congratulations! You have achieved level 12 Elemental Archon and have gained 10 Intelligence, 10 Will, and have 26 attribute points to allocate.

Olivia sat back on the couch, reading through and then dismissing each of the notifications that she'd gotten. "Well, I get ten will and intelligence per level and eight free points. I'm sitting on twenty-six points now because I still had five from level nine and five from level ten."

"Do you feel any different?" Alyss asked quietly. Something about her voice made Olivia look at her more closely, and she saw Alyss's carefully neutral expression.

"I feel fine." When Alyss didn't say anything, she said, "What?"

"Your, um, your eyes are smoldering again, though it's a bit different this time—like the flames are inside your irises, and they're kind of blue and white. Here," she said, pulling a small mirror out of a dimensional container and holding it out to Olivia. Olivia took the polished wooden handle and held the mirror in front of her face, bracing herself for what she'd see. She sighed with relief when she saw herself. Her eyes still looked like eyes, but they were luminescent with flickering silvery-blue flames where her irises used to be. Gingerly, she held her eyelids open with one hand and touched her eye with her other hand. It felt the same as ever, and she blinked rapidly to restore moisture.

"Whatever it is, it's on the inside."

"Olivia, can you summon your orbs again?" Alyss asked, leaning even more toward her.

"Yeah, just a sec." Olivia held out her hand, and, just as she had in the auditorium, she built her four meta-elements and channeled them into her Orb Manipulation spell. It was easier than before, and not just because she'd done it once—her ability to hold the meta-elements as she quickly created them all seemed almost effortless, and she was much faster about it. The orbs sprang to life, and Olivia felt warm and strong, and she couldn't help the laugh that bubbled out of her.

"Ancestors!" Alyss exclaimed, standing up and taking a step back. Olivia looked at her, a question behind her eyes. Alyss smiled, stepped closer, and then reached out a hand, touching Olivia on the shoulder. "It's not hot." Olivia didn't know what she was talking about, so she looked down at her shoulder and was startled to see blue, flickering flames lining her shoulder. She picked up the mirror from her lap and angled it to see her profile. An aura of blue flames was flickering along her shoulders and head like she was a living butane torch. She stood up, allowing her orbs to continue rotating around each other over her outstretched hand.

"It feels good, and this spell is a lot easier now."

"Well, once you create a spell, it's always easier, but I bet your connection to the elemental essences has improved your ability even more. That's a fascinating effect, Olivia. One day, I'm going to be writing a textbook about you, I'm sure."

"Thank you, Alyss. Thank you for your kindness and your support. I can't wait to see what comes next in my education here." Olivia allowed her orbs to wink out, watching as the flames limning her head and shoulders flickered and faded.

"Well, I have some news in that regard, Olivia. Before we left the auditorium, Professor Oylla-dak let me know that she was very impressed by you and wanted me to set up a meeting between you two. I think she might have a special opportunity for you."

❧ MORGAN ☙

After Morgan released all of the former prisoners of Gunther and Blake, he and Issa explored up the spiral stairs, looking for where Blake had stashed her dimensional bags and gear. If he were honest, Morgan was also hoping to find some treasure or clues as to who Blake had been. One of the people he rescued, a tall Shadeni man named Brel, said he'd lead some other survivors to free the women in the maternity cells.

The upper floor of the central wing was mostly unused and abandoned like the rest of the keep. Several chambers, however, had seen a lot of recent use. One large room was filled with open barrels half-full of various malodorous fluids. Alchemy paraphernalia littered the tabletops, and Morgan found a dimensional chest the size of a shoebox filled with ingredients from bales of grass, to pouches of sand, to wax-sealed boxes stuffed with fresh flower petals. There were literally hundreds of different components in the chest, and Morgan knew he'd need an expert to take stock of everything.

They also found evidence of Blake's less than savory experiments—a cast-iron incinerator, fueled by large Energy crystals, had been built into a huge stone fireplace. Issa, out of curiosity, had sifted through some of the ashes and found fragments of tiny bones. She cursed darkly, and when Morgan put a hand on her shoulder in comfort, she'd leaned into him, blinking back tears.

They found Issa's sword stuck into the top of a table in what must have been Blake's bedchamber. The room was a mess, with discarded clothing and bedding strewn on the floor and plates of half-finished meals piled on most furniture surfaces. Issa snatched up her sword, and when Morgan kicked open the big wooden linen chest, she jumped forward, grabbing her belt with her three different dimensional bags still strung on it. They found a lot of other dimensional bags filled with various camping and travel supplies. Dozens of weapons were in one of the bags, and yet another held clothing of all types.

"Most of this stuff probably belongs to the people we freed."

"You mean that you freed," Issa replied, squeezing his arm.

"Hush, you'd have done the same." He moved to open the big armoire in the room while Issa worked on getting dressed. When he pulled it open, piled laundry fell out at his feet, exposing a black pouch hanging from a peg on the back panel. Morgan lifted the pouch and saw the tell-tale runes of a dimensional container. He bonded with it and, as he looked within, let out a low whistle. "There's, like, fifty thousand Energy beads in here."

"Good! That evil bastard owes those people!" The way she said it, so matter-of-factly, Morgan didn't even consider arguing. They finished ransacking the room but found little of any value, though Morgan noticed scrape marks near the legs of the large bed. He kicked the bed aside along the path of the scrape marks, and then he tapped the exposed floorboards with his sword. The third board he pressed his blade into rattled and popped up on the opposite corner.

"Not exactly a great hiding spot," he said, kneeling to lift the loose board free. Within, he found a small, green-glass bottle with a wax-sealed cork and a plain, leather-bound journal. Watching over his shoulder, Issa bent to pick up the journal, and Morgan took out the bottle. It was heavy, filled with a liquid that made the glass warm to the touch.

"This is Blake's journal," Issa said, looking at the front page and then flipping slowly forward. "It details his experiments. Ancestors, Morgan! He did some vile things." She handed him the book. "Here, I don't want to touch it." Morgan took the book and put it and the bottle into his storage ring.

"Alright, let's go bring these bags of clothes and supplies to the people below, then we can share out some of Blake's fortune." When Issa didn't reply right away, he slipped his sword into the ring on his belt and took her hand, leading her back down the stairs. Keiry and the people he'd sedated with the stew had come to join the rest of the survivors, and when Morgan and Issa arrived, the assembled group of huddled, naked people gave out a tremulous yet heartfelt cheer. Some people hunched behind pieces of furniture or covered themselves with their hands, yet others stood proudly, seemingly not wanting to be cowed, even after the hell they'd been through. Morgan saw that some of the gathered women were visibly pregnant. His heart ached as he looked into their wan, bruised faces, and bloodshot eyes, and he wanted to reach out to comfort them.

Morgan knew better than to start grabbing onto victims of violence, though, so he instead took the dimensional containers containing clothes and supplies and dumped them into piles in the middle of the room. All in all, there were thirty-two survivors, and six of them were pregnant women. When they started sorting through the piles of belongings, finding their own things, and putting on some clothes, Morgan was astounded to see smiles and hear laughter coming from some of them. It was amazing what a change could occur just by giving someone back a bit of their dignity.

He and Issa had no way of knowing how much of the wealth in the bag had once belonged to the kidnapped people they'd freed, so they agreed to give everyone a thousand Energy beads and an extra five hundred to the pregnant women. "I know money won't make up for what happened to you here, but at least this might help you get back on your feet. Issa and I are traveling to Tarn's Crossing, and we'll be happy to escort you that way. Alternatively, my people have a new community a few days' travel from here, and I'll be happy to give you directions. There are a lot of opportunities there for industrious people."

"What about Lovely?" Keiry asked, glancing toward the hallway that led to the courtyard.

"That big damn bird?"

"Yes, that bird captured most of us!"

"Is it intelligent? Does it know what it was doing, or is it just a pet? Like a big cat bringing its owner a mouse?" Morgan immediately regretted his words, comparing these people to mice. When he saw the frowns and angry glares, he tried to smooth things over, "I mean, it's clearly a dangerous creature, and I'm not saying what it did to you is harmless; I'm just trying to see if I should try to kill it or if it might just leave on its own now that Blake is dead."

"It has a taste for people! It can't be let free!" a stout Cadwalli man growled.

"Oh? It didn't just grab people? It also ate them?" Issa asked.

"Well . . ." the Cadwalli trailed off.

"I don't think it ever ate anyone. As wicked as Blake was, I only ever was made to cook animals, and Lovely usually ate some of each animal it brought back," Keiry said, looking around.

"I have advanced Animal Taming," a willowy Ghelli woman with a badly broken wing said. "I could try to communicate with it. I'm able to sense animals' intentions a lot of the time.

"Alright, come with me," Morgan said, and he, Issa, and the Ghelli woman moved into the hallway leading to the courtyard. "I want you to stay behind me and be ready to run, though. Don't take any risks."

"I won't," she said softly. Issa put a hand on her shoulder as they walked, and Morgan felt thankful to have her and that she hadn't suffered more at Blake's hands. When they opened the door to the courtyard, Morgan stepped out first and, in the darkness of night, saw the bird-moth's big round eyes reflecting the light from the moons at him. He activated Azure Sight and looked around the courtyard, noting the broken masonry, rubble, and massive nest. Lovely sat quietly, unmoving, watching them as they stepped down onto the courtyard's flagstones.

"We need to get closer," the woman said.

"What's your name?" Morgan asked, stepping forward.

"Rillia," she responded, following close behind him. Morgan kept a hand on his sword hilt and stared at the nest, watching for any movement. The birdmoth's big head twitched slightly as it tracked their movement, but it held its massive beak closed and didn't stir otherwise. "I don't sense any hostility."

"Can you communicate with it at all?"

"I'm trying; let's get a little closer." When they were just ten or so paces from the nest, the huge creature uttered its "Cwooo, cwooo" sound, but softly, not the triumphant trumpet it had made when it dropped off prey to Blake. "It doesn't want to eat us. It knows the difference between people and prey."

"You can tell that?" Issa asked, impressed.

"Yes, it's smart, though. It knew it made Blake happy when it brought people here. I'm trying to give it the impression that Blake is gone." Rillia concentrated on the bird for a few moments of silence, and Morgan realized he'd let his guard down when the bird suddenly leaned forward, lowering its huge beak toward Rillia, and he almost jumped out of his boots. "It's alright; she's trying to communicate. She wants to do something for me; she wants to please. She's tame! She won't be any danger to people now that Blake isn't here to ask her to grab them." Suddenly, Rillia stepped forward and rested a hand on the bird's huge, gray-feathered head, right between its big round eyes. "Good girl, Lovely. That's right; he's gone." She turned to Morgan and flashed him a smile that made her seem a completely different person.

"Well, I'm glad of that," Morgan said.

"Me, too," Issa added, "I never saw her coming when she grabbed me, and I'd hate to think she'll still be a menace to travelers."

"She won't be. I'm imprinting some commands right now. She's going to avoid people and only eat holbyis and huldii."

"Wow, that's a cool ability."

"He means it's really useful," Issa said, squeezing Morgan's hand.

"Yeah." He nodded.

"It is, but it took me a long time to get my taming skill this high, and not many people have a class that allows for it. I was the only Tamer in my village." Rillia let go of Lovely's head and turned back to the keep. "We should let the others know it's safe. I can't speak for everyone, but I want to get away from this place as soon as possible." Morgan couldn't argue with that sentiment, and they returned to the hall to give the news to the other survivors.

That night, Morgan and Issa set up camp outside the keep on the grassy area between it and the cliffside. Most of the people he'd rescued from Blake joined them, and they built a large bonfire. A few of the former captives raided the keep's pantry before coming out, and among the supplies they found were several dozen bottles of wine. The bonfire turned into an impromptu celebration, at least among some of the people. Some were still shell-shocked or clearly had mental trauma, and they sat quietly in the grass or curled up in blankets waiting for the dawn.

"Sorry I lost the tent," Morgan said to Issa as they sat quietly, sharing a bottle of rich burgundy wine.

"You mean when you discovered me missing, you didn't take time to pack up the tent? I'm shocked!"

"Hah, no. I almost ran poor Munch to death, to be honest. I hope they're still where I left them, the roladii, I mean."

"I do, also. Hopefully, Lovely doesn't have any relatives nearby. I've never seen a bird like her, though. What a strange creature."

"Maybe Blake brought her from wherever he was from. He looked human but definitely wasn't." Morgan described how he'd had to burn Blake before he actually died.

"If you can stomach reading it, you might find clues in his journal." Issa shuddered and moved in closer to Morgan.

"I'll probably give it a try at some point but not tonight. Definitely not tonight." He lay back in the grass, pulling Issa with him, so her head rested in the crook of his arm. As he lay there looking at the stars and admiring the sister moons' beauty, he felt her breathing grow slow and steady, and he knew she was sleeping. He tried to plan for the next part of their journey to Tarn's Crossing, figuring it would take them a couple of days of hard riding to get there, but then he remembered his promise to let these people travel with them, and he added another two or three days to his estimate. Even knowing that, he couldn't help feeling good—he'd gotten Issa back, had managed to rescue all of these people, and rid the world of another evil. All in all, he felt more satisfied and accomplished than he ever had back on Earth.

◎ OLIVIA ◎

Olivia sat on the stone bench, hands folded in her lap, and did her best not to feel like a mouse under the predatory gaze of Professor Oylla-dak. Something in her didn't shrink away, though, and she felt a heat start to rise in her chest; she sat up straight and looked into the professor's dark, star-filled eyes. There weren't literal stars in her eyes, but something about the advanced race of the Shadeni woman had made her eyes look like the depths of space. It was beautiful and unnerving at the same time. Olivia almost chuckled at the irony of her saying someone's eyes were unnerving. She, with the blue flames licking at the insides of her irises, shouldn't be one to cast stones.

"Thank you for meeting me on your weekend, Olivia." Oylla-dak sat, legs crossed with one slender red knee escaping her tight black robes. Her hands were folded in her lap, and a warm smile exposed one of her long fangs. Olivia wanted to ask her about her wings—her cohort had told her that the woman could actually fly with them, and she desperately wanted to know more about it. Still, she restrained herself and answered her politely.

"It's my pleasure, Professor."

"That was quite a display you put on yesterday. I can't remember the last time a first-year student displayed such control and power. In fact, your control rivals some of our journeyman students, even some of our professors. You've a long way to come in terms of raw power, but I think your potential is astounding."

"Um, thank you, Professor." This was starting to feel a bit too familiar to Olivia. She'd had this talk with more than one teacher and, later, professors.

"I'm happy Professor Gan-dak awarded you a full scholarship and stipend. Are you aware of the value of such?"

"Only in terms of opportunity. I'm afraid I'm not terribly clear on the relative wealth of the peoples of this world or how much of that wealth would be required to attend the academy here."

"What an intriguing answer; I'm pleased to see that you're aware of the value of this opportunity, aside from the monetary investment we've placed in you." Oylla-dak leaned closer to Olivia and spoke mock-conspiratorially, "I have a pretty big budget, but people expect me to make the ledger balance at the end of the day."

"I thought I was given a scholarship without a service indenture?" Olivia could feel the way this conversation was going, and her pleasant mood was starting to sour.

"Oh, that's quite correct, Olivia. I don't intend to force you into anything, I just have an opportunity that you could help me with, and I was trying to remind you of what you've been given so that you'll have it in your mind when you consider your answer."

"Well, that's very forthright of you, I suppose."

"Yes, I'm not one to wheedle with my words. Let me get to the point: Fainhallow is not the only academy in this world or the closely connected worlds."

"Closely connected?"

"Yes, there are a few worlds that are relatively inexpensive to teleport to, given an adequately advanced City Stone. Let me get to my point, though: these schools, along with Fainhallow, have access to a few dungeons that open at certain times of the year . . ."

"Dungeons?" Olivia couldn't help interrupting again.

"Ah, yes, I forget how new your people are to the System, which is another topic I'd like to discuss with you at length, but not right now. Dungeons. Hmm, I'm sure that, in your mind, the word conjures up something like a prison? The System, when it integrates languages, tends to find a word like that, something that means prison, but in an archaic sense." Olivia nodded along, and Oylla-dak continued, "Well, a dungeon isn't a prison in the literal sense. They can be natural or made by powerful Energy users, and they exist in a sort of dimensional space. Perhaps the term was first used to describe them because the older, natural dungeons contained beings that were unable to leave and became mad with the strange, unnatural passage of time and movement of space. People would find the entrance and fight the denizens, often emerging with powerful natural treasures."

"I'm getting the picture," Olivia said. "My friend, Morgan, was put into a place that sounds similar when we arrived in this solar system."

"Oh? I'd like to hear about that sometime. Well, the dungeons I'm referring to aren't wholly natural. They're curated by the various academies and also by the System. We have access to four differently tiered dungeons, first, second, third, and fifth."

"Tiers?"

"Yes. Most of the races of Fanwath receive their first class at level ten and have a refinement option every ten levels, at least up to level fifty. We consider levels ten through twenty to be tier one, level twenty to thirty, tier two, etc."

"Okay, so I'd be considered tier one?"

"Correct, Olivia. You may have an idea where I'm going now, hmm? I'd like you to enter the tier one dungeon at the designated date and compete for Fainhallow."

"What sort of competition are we talking about?"

"The dungeon has various levels, and you'll have a certain amount of time to get as deep as possible." Oylla-dak glanced to the side while she spoke, and Olivia could see she wasn't being entirely forthcoming.

"And it's dangerous?" she pressed.

"Yes, there are denizens of the dungeon to contend with, and, of course, there's the risk of running into a student from the other academies. They aren't guaranteed to be violent, but it's not against the rules. I suppose I should say there are very few rules once you're in the dungeon."

"Um, this doesn't really sound like my sort of thing. I've never been physically competitive, and I can't imagine fighting other students to win some sort of competition." Olivia spoke firmly; she was sure about this.

"I wouldn't expect you to attack anyone. I will help you learn to defend yourself, though, and I think you have an excellent chance of winning, going further than anyone in some time. I haven't yet told you why this would be a good idea for you, not just the school." She leaned forward, and her starfield eyes squinted with sincerity.

"I'm listening," Olivia offered, forcing her mind to open to the idea.

"Olivia, this world is enormous, and the worlds neighboring us in the System's teleportation network are just as large. Some of those worlds have been part of the System for thousands of years and have very powerful people living on them. Your people are new, and I'm sure the System tried to place you in an area where you can thrive, but all it would take is one powerful Energy user with malevolence in their heart to annihilate your race. This dungeon is an opportunity for you to learn and grow. It's a chance for you to gain the skills and knowledge you'll need to help protect your people. Can I ask, how many of your people are here on Fanwath?"

"Well, between four and five thousand. We lost a few hundred fighting an Urghat invasion when we first arrived." Olivia saw no point in lying.

"Do you see how fragile that makes you as a race? My people, the Shadeni, are all over Fanwath. We tend not to build large cities, but even so, we are numbered in the hundreds of millions. The Ardeni are even more numerous. Now, if you aren't some sort of anomaly among your people, then I'd wager that your kind has a naturally high Energy affinity. That will make you, as a race, interesting to many people. Some of those people don't have good intentions. Are you starting to understand me?"

Olivia did see the point she was making, eliciting a slight panic attack in her. She'd thought about how few humans were here, and she knew, intellectually, that they barely had enough variation in their gene pool to propagate their race. They'd lost five times as many embryos as they had colonists when the System took them away from their ship. The idea of one of the native peoples deciding that humanity was a threat and wiping them out was, indeed, disturbing. "I understand," she said quietly.

"Now, take heart—there are good people as well as bad, and, though it's probably something an evil person would say, I want you to know that I have good intentions for you. I wouldn't send you as a representative for Fainhallow if I didn't think you'd do well or, being honest, if I didn't think you had the potential to do well." She paused and looked into Olivia's eyes again, waiting for her to nod. "There are many potential rewards in this dungeon—racial upgrades, Energy orbs, artifacts, and, most importantly, the opportunity to improve yourself through challenge."

Olivia barely heard Oylla's words; she was still thinking about the fledgling community of First Landing. She was imagining a titanic figure descending from the sky and unleashing armageddon. She didn't know where the image came from—probably too many bad VRs when she was a teen. Still, it reminded her of her real responsibilities. "As long as I won't have to kill anyone, I'll do it." Olivia wondered if she would have changed her mind so quickly as her old self when she'd just been a normal human before she'd bonded with an elemental's soul and earned a class that literally put fire in her. Oylla-dak smiled at her, a big, genuine smile that exposed her beautiful white teeth and two long fangs.

"I'm personally going to teach you to use your spells more effectively, Olivia. We have a week or so to prepare. I'll be pulling you from your classes for the time being, but what I teach you and your experience in the dungeon will more than make up for what you miss."

"Thank you, Professor." Olivia sat up straight and nodded her head politely.

"Call me Oylla, Olivia, at least when we're alone. Hmm, our names sound similar when you use the short form, don't they? How auspicious! Now, take the rest of the weekend to celebrate what you've accomplished during the last month, and we'll begin your training on Monday. Oh, one more thing: I have a package for you from Professor ap'Gravin. It's the award he owes you for proving him wrong during your demonstration." She had a wide grin on her face as she produced a small box wrapped in black paper with a delicate yellow ribbon.

"Oh, thank you. I didn't expect him to pay up!" Olivia took the package and held it gently between her hands.

"Nonsense. If he's going to attempt to malign you and Professor ap'Rall, then I'll make sure he settles his debt. Goodbye, for now, Olivia. Meet me in the library Monday morning." Oylla-dak smoothly stood, and with one hand on the hilt of the sword she had at her waist, she strode across the commons and into the academy. Olivia watched her go, and only when she was out of sight, did she blow out the breath she'd been inadvertently holding.

"Well? What was that about?" Adaida came up behind Olivia and sat next to her on the bench. "What? She gave you a present?"

"No! This is from Professor ap'Gravin. Oylla-dak made him pay up for challenging Alyss."

"Oh, open it! While you're at it, tell me what Oylla-dak wanted!"

"Well," Olivia traced a finger along the yellow ribbon on the package, wondering if Oylla had wrapped it or if ap'Gravin had actually given it to her like this. "It seems she wants me to go to a dungeon for the academy and compete with some other schools."

"What?" Adaida grabbed her by the shoulders and put her face about two inches from Olivia's. "She's sending you to the Proving Grounds?"

"Um, I don't know; she didn't say the dungeon's name."

"Trust me; it's the Proving Grounds. It's well known that the academies compete in them. Nature! I don't know if I should be excited or worried! Let me think about it while you open that present!" Adaida yanked the yellow ribbon, untying it, for emphasis. Olivia giggled, feeling infected by Adaida's energy, and she pulled the wrapping paper away from a small wooden box.

The box had a dozen seams cut in its top, creating little triangles that met in the middle where a round, brass button sat. Olivia glanced at Adaida, and she nodded encouragement. She pressed the button, and the wooden lid unfolded like a flower, the burgundy silk lining opening up to reveal a small round vial with a black wax plug on the top. Inside the vial was a bright red liquid. A small card was nestled in the silky interior, and Adaida snatched it to read aloud, "Botnor's Tincture of Racial Evolution. Olivia, it's another racial advancement mixture, and Botnor's potions are known to be strong."

"Wow, I guess Oylla-dak wouldn't let ap'Gravin slide with a cheap reward."

"Let's go to the dorm, so you can have some privacy while you take it! I can't wait to see what happens next! Maybe you'll grow a flaming tail or something!" She laughed and grabbed Olivia's hand, pulling her to her feet.

"Alright, alright! I'm coming!" Olivia allowed Adaida to pull her by the hand, though, happy to have a friend and happy not to be thinking about her entire race being wiped off the face of the world.

OLIVIA

Olivia waved her hand before her face while looking into the mirror. She didn't quite know how to feel about what was happening to her. To his credit, Professor ap'Gravin hadn't skimped on his award. The Botner's tincture had been even more potent than Radasheen's Hereditary Delver, at least for Olivia, giving her four full racial ranks. Some of her improvements were superficial, though nice—she'd gained about an inch in height, her hair was thicker, more lustrous, her skin had gained a certain luminosity that she would have said was impossible without digital special effects, and her scars and blemishes were almost totally faded. Even the scar over her eye was just a very faint line. These changes were welcome, but the bright flames in her eyes and the phantom flames that seemed to limn her body whenever she moved were a little disturbing.

It was like she had a fiery aura that rested when she was still but sprang to life whenever she moved. When she walked, when she waved her hand, every movement was accompanied by flickering blue flames that bore no heat. She had no control over it, and though it seemed harmless, what it portended for the future worried her. Would she grow more and more like an elemental as she advanced her race?

Adaida, sitting next to Veena on the counter behind Olivia, said, "It's rather incredible, isn't it?"

"I guess so, but I don't like the idea that I'm becoming less human," Olivia replied.

"You aren't, though. You bonded with a small part of an elemental, and that's growing in proportion with your original race. Your human portion has changed and grown just as much. Some are visible on the surface, but much of what's changed is under your skin," Veena said.

"So, you think that my human portion will always stay dominant as I advance my race?"

"Yes, silly, you're mostly human, and that won't change—not without you knowing it." Adaida moved forward and took Olivia's hand, waving it up and down, so the flames sprang to life. "They're so pretty! I can't feel them at all, though."

"Well, that's good; I wouldn't want to go around lighting everything on fire," Olivia laughed. "I can't imagine racial upgrades are cheap, and the ap'Gravin didn't skimp—why wouldn't he use this tincture instead of giving it up?"

"He's probably at the improved rank, and strong tinctures for base rankers like us wouldn't do much for him," Veena replied.

"He's not particularly handsome or 'improved' looking, though," Adaida said, echoing Olivia's thoughts.

"True. He must have been a real toad before he got started." Veena laughed wickedly, and the others joined in.

"Alright, alright, we better get going. You'll be late for class, and I need to hurry to the library. Thanks for keeping me company, though." Olivia smoothed her uniform straight, and the three of them hurried out of the bathroom and through the now-empty dormitory to the hallway. The rest of her cohort had already left, and Veena and Adaida hurried off to catch them. Olivia moved through the hallways to the library, self-conscious about the flickering flames that limned her body as she walked.

At that time of day, the hallways were busy, and she garnered a lot of sidelong glances from the people she met. Part of her wanted to shrink away from the attention, but that fiery sliver of her soul relished in the scrutiny, and she felt that familiar heat in her chest, urging her to stand up straight and meet their glances with her fiery glare. A shiver of excitement ran through her, almost like she'd won a competition as she did so, and her smile grew with each person that looked away from her and hurried by.

Oylla was in the library, though she didn't seem peeved at having waited. Olivia didn't think she was late, so she didn't apologize. "Good morning, Professor," Olivia said, aware that other students were nearby.

"Good morning, Olivia. Follow me; let's go out to the commons. It's a beautiful morning." Oylla led the way through the library to a doorway that Olivia had never been through. It led to a short hallway that stretched into a glass-walled sunroom. The sunroom had doors that opened onto the commons, and Olivia followed Oylla out. They walked around the academy building until they were in a far corner of the manicured lawns, devoid of other people. Still, not too far away, Olivia could see some student cohorts exercising together and, here and there, people lounged in the morning sun, drinking tea or eating breakfast.

"Alright, Olivia, tell me, have you any unassigned attribute points?"

"Yes. I had ten from levels nine and ten and gained sixteen more after leveling to twelve."

"Very good. What are your intelligence, will, and vitality attribute scores?"

"Um," Olivia called up her status sheet:

Status			
Name:	Olivia Bennet		
Race:	Human - Base 8		
Class:	Elemental Archon		
Level:	12		
Core:	Prisma Class - Base 6		
Energy Affinity:	9.1, Fire 9.6, Earth 9.6, Water 9.6, Air 9.6	Energy:	1744/1744
Strength:	6	Vitality:	12
Dexterity:	8	Agility:	6
Intelligence:	55	Will:	45
Points Available:	26		
Titles & Feats:	Elemental Heritage, First Elemental Archon		
Skills:	• System Language Integration - Not Upgradeable • Animal Taming - Basic • Stealthy Maneuvers - Basic • Prisma Core Cultivation Drill - Basic	• Orb Manipulation - Epic • Icy Shards - Basic • Fiery Burst - Basic • Stunning Ice Shards - Basic • Wind Gust - Basic • Arcfrost Cascade - Basic • Magma Ray - Basic • Elemental Form - Basic	

"Fifty-five, forty-five, and twelve."

"Outstanding! And you're only level twelve! Hmm, I know you'll want to improve some of your other attributes, but for now, at your level and with your ability with Energy, I think you should focus on those three attributes. You'll have the most immediate increase in power that way. I will help you practice spells that will make your other physical attributes less important."

"So, should I put all my free points in vitality?"

"No, no. Perhaps bring your vitality up to twenty, then split the remainder between intelligence and will. At level twelve, twenty is an excellent vitality for a mage." Olivia nodded, happy to have some solid advice, and did as Oylla suggested. She put eight points into vitality, eleven points into intelligence, and seven points into will.

"Wow, that gave me more than two-hundred Energy," Olivia said, but then she caught her breath, feeling a ripple of Energy or something related to it that pulsed through her body.

"It feels good, doesn't it? Gaining such a boost to your vitality all at once?" Oylla smiled knowingly. "Your Energy attribute is derived from your will, intelligence, and Core strength. Improving any of those will increase your pool."

"I knew that was the case but didn't expect such a jump. I wonder, has anyone figured out the exact formula?"

"It seems to vary a bit from race to race, but yes, there's a pretty solid understanding of the mechanism. I can lend you a relevant text if you'd like to do some experimenting."

"Thank you, Oylla, that would be nice." Standing before the woman, Olivia felt her usual awe and urge to be polite, but she couldn't help noticing that she wasn't as imposing as she had been just a few days ago. Olivia felt like it was a combination of her own physical growth and her growing familiarity with the tall Shadeni woman that made her feel more relaxed in her presence.

"My pleasure. Now, I've seen you perform some interesting feats with meta-elements. Your demonstrated spells will be very effective offensive abilities, but do you have any defensive spells?"

"No, I haven't learned any yet. I have my Orb Manipulation spell, which allows me to perform many useful actions, but nothing specifically defensive."

"Hmm," Oylla nodded, tapping her chin with one long, black nail. "I think that will be a good place to start. Please summon forth your orbs."

"Actually, Professor, I just thought of something. When I got my class, I learned a spell called Elemental Form, and I haven't tried it yet."

"Oh? By all means, let's see what it does." Oylla stepped back a couple of paces and watched Olivia intently. Olivia, for her part, nodded and concentrated on her Elemental Form spell, activating it. Something strange happened then, something she hadn't experienced with her other spells: she felt the pattern of Energy start to build in her pathways near her Core, but she felt an anticipation like the pattern was waiting for her input, and she knew it wanted her to choose an element to direct into it. She quickly pulled a thread of fire-attuned Energy from her Core and fed it into the pattern, and the spell took shape.

Olivia had never cast a spell with such a high Energy cost before, and she felt the surge of power flood out of her Core and into her body. Her vision was the first noticeable thing to change—everything she saw was washed out in bright shades of sepia. She held a hand in front of her face, and rather than flesh and blood, her limb seemed to be made of licking, seething, red-yellow flames. She made a fist and saw that there were digits under those flames, but they looked like smoldering embers. Oylla had taken another step back and held a hand up to shield her face. Olivia looked down and saw that the grass had blackened under her feet, and the blue-green blades were wilting, turning brown, and smoking in an ever-widening circle around her.

"Hold still, Olivia; I'd like to try something," Oylla said, pulling her sword free from its scabbard. It was a lovely silvery weapon with a long, slender blade. "Hold out your arm, Olivia; I won't harm you more than a scratch. Tell me what this feels like." Olivia lifted her arm, enthralled by the waves of heat that shimmered into the morning air. Oylla gingerly stepped forward, and then, quick as a serpent's tongue, her sword flicked out and sliced along the top of Olivia's forearm.

"Ouch!" Olivia yanked her arm back, reaching with her other hand to rub at the wound, but she couldn't feel anything that hurt when she touched it. In fact, she hadn't experienced pain so much as surprise when Oylla's sword had touched her. "Huh, I don't know if it really cut me." Olivia's voice sounded strange in her ears; it was loud and poured forth like it was carried on a hot wind. She was about to ask Oylla if she should allow the spell to drop when it began to fade on its own. She had a sense that she could extend the life of the spell by pouring more Energy into it, but she let it die out, and the flames began to dissipate; her pale flesh began to reclaim her limbs as the black and orange embers faded away. Soon, she stood, her usual self, none of her clothes or belongings any worse for the wear. When she looked at her arm where Oylla had cut her, there was a thin, white scar.

"I did hurt you, but your regeneration is much greater when in your fire elemental form. We need to try your other elements. You can take other forms, yes?"

"I think so; I just need to feed the spell differently attuned Energy."

"Do you need to rest?"

"No, I have enough Energy to cast the spell a few times, and I've already regenerated half the cost of the last casting."

"You're going to utterly dominate the Proving Grounds, dear." Oylla had such a grin on her face that Olivia couldn't help smiling back. Something in the back of her mind set off little alarm bells, though, and she had to voice her fear.

"I don't want to kill other students, Oylla. Even if it helps me to become more powerful."

"I know, Olivia! That's why I'm helping you; you're not a monster. You're humble, kind, and willing to listen despite your potential. I know you care for your people, and that sense of duty makes me want to support you. I'm not trying to say I have altruistic motivations, though. Of course, it will result in a lot of esteem and funding for Fainhallow if you perform as well as I'm hoping. Now, listen to me: I'm not sending you there to kill all the competition! I want you to defend yourself and hopefully display such power that you can make aggressive entrants back down. With any luck, though, you'll move so much more quickly through the challenges that you'll never run into any other students."

Olivia nodded and swallowed her objections. It wasn't really an option to not go to the dungeon, and the best way to avoid hurting other students was to make sure they knew they shouldn't mess with her. She concentrated and began to cast her Elemental Form spell, but when nothing happened, she said, "Oh, it's on cooldown. It feels like I need to wait a little while still."

"It's a powerful spell, so I'm not surprised it has a cooldown. Let's see if we can work out another defensive spell while we wait. Let's see here; go ahead and conjure your earth orb." Olivia nodded and complied, effortlessly summoning a softball-sized ball of stone to float above her outstretched palm. "Good, you can manipulate its movement and size, right?"

"Yes, it's pretty easy when I have only one orb out."

"How quickly can you move it? Do you have to have your hand out like that?"

"I've never really tried," Olivia said, frowning in concentration. She lowered her hand, and the orb wavered for a minute, but she just concentrated, focused her will, and it stabilized. Oylla nodded and moved to stand in front of Olivia, holding her two hands about a yard apart in front of her.

"Move the orb to my left hand," she said and waited while Olivia complied, slowly moving the spinning orb of rock to Oylla's outstretched hand. "Good, now to my right hand." Olivia pushed the orb with her mind, sending it to Oylla's other hand. "Yes, now back and forth as quickly as you can." Olivia, slowly at first but then with greater and greater speed, sent the sphere of stone back and forth between Oylla's hands. After a while, when the stone was a blur in the air, Oylla started moving either hand up or down, and Olivia had to adjust the stone's trajectory.

"This is fun!" Olivia laughed as Oylla kept spreading her arms further and moving her hands up and down more rapidly.

"You're a natural! Now, imagine knocking aside swords or thumping bandits on the head. You'll be fit to defend yourself in no time!"

MORGAN

It ended up taking Morgan, Issa, and the band of refugees from Blake's keep four days to get to the forest outside Tarn's Crossing. They'd burned through an entire day by the time they'd finally gotten everyone down the escarpment using ropes, makeshift platforms, and lots of patience. When they'd camped at the base of the rocky cliff that night, Morgan had drawn a map in the dirt, showing everyone roughly where they were in relation to Tarn's Crossing and First Landing. The following day, a few small groups of survivors had left to travel on their own, but more than twenty individuals, mostly Ardeni, had wanted to stay with Morgan and Issa and go to Tarn's Crossing with them.

They'd kept the pace easy and stretched a two-day trip into three and a half, and now a ragged cheer broke out among the men and women as they crested the slight rise in the forest road and saw the town sprawling out in the park-like vale. Issa reached over from Gopp's back and gave Morgan's hand a squeeze, a smile on her face. "Feels good to see smiles on their faces, doesn't it?" he asked her.

"Yes, Morgan. I was lucky you came after me, but they suffered for a long time in that place." Morgan nodded, holding her hand, and they rode toward the gates, garnering a lot of attention from the people moving along the road. When they came to the guards, one of them, a tall thin Ardeni woman with a huge, unstrung bow on her back, stepped forward.

"Hello, travelers, what's this?"

"I'm Issa ap'Roald. This is Morgan Hall, and the people with us are seeking refuge here—they were held captive by a criminal a few days from here." Issa gestured for one of the survivors, a man named Taern, to come forward. "This is Taern, he can speak for these people, and I think he should meet with the governor and the council. They're not going to be a burden here, they all have money, and some of them have relatives here."

"Alright, thank you, Issa. I thought I recognized you! You know your father isn't in town, right? I'm pretty sure he traveled upriver with the last caravan. Doing some trade, I suppose."

"Oh? Well, that's not lucky!" Issa sighed and looked at Morgan with a bit of a frown. "We can still stay at my home. I have a key."

"Alright," Morgan said, turning to Taern, "You'll all be okay now? The governor knows where to find us if you need anything, alright?"

"Aye, Morgan, and thank you! We all," he turned to the small throng of refugees gathered behind him, "Owe you a great debt." Mutters of agreement broke out among the people, and Morgan felt a warm rush of embarrassment at their gratitude.

"No, you don't. I only did what any decent person with the ability would do. Good luck, everyone, and remember: you're all welcome to come to First Landing if you can't find a spot for yourselves here." Not wanting to dwell on the goodbye, Morgan spurred Munch through the gate and rode a bit ahead while Issa said her farewells. He pulled Munch to the side of the road, allowing a cart pulled by two burly roladii with very few feathers to pass by. Were those a different breed of roladii? He supposed it made sense that some roladii would be bred for riding and others for draft-work.

"Ready?" Issa had ridden up beside him while he was musing.

"Yeah, where to, first?"

"Well, I don't see why we shouldn't meet with the alchemist right away. He's a family friend, and I know he'll be willing to help, but it might take some time to complete the recipe. Or, if he's unable, he'll hopefully point us in the right direction." When Morgan nodded, she rode Gopp ahead, and he followed. Tarn's Crossing wasn't a huge town, though it was a busy and growing trade hub for the region. That said, their ride through the crowded main street, the market square, and then through some side streets only took fifteen minutes or so. Issa hopped off Gopp and tied him in front of the little shop with a display-case window.

In the case, Morgan could see bottles and little pouches set out with large, boldly written signs proclaiming their efficacy. One large bottle with a bulbous bottom and fluted top had a sign that read, "Yorn's Draught of Laughter—Perfect for any celebration!" He chuckled to himself and tied Munch to the post.

"What's funny?" Issa asked.

"Oh, just that those potions and signs remind me of snake oil salesmen from my country's history."

"Snake oil?"

"Uh, yeah, it's what they called 'potions' and medicines that were supposed to work miracles but usually didn't do anything real."

"Oh, well, Yorn would lose his reputation quickly if he tried to sell fake alchemical products."

"Yeah, I know things are different here, don't worry." The two of them walked to the door, Morgan pulled it open for Issa, and they entered the shop.

Morgan's nose immediately informed him that many herbs and flowers were packed into the items displayed for sale around the small shop. Soaps, candles, vials, bottles of every size, little pouches, and wooden boxes were displayed with bold signs, just like in the window case. "Miracle hair growth!" one sign shouted, "Yorn's Poison Purifier," said another, "Celestial Life-Extension Cream!" caught Morgan's eye, but then a voice cut into his perusal, "Welcome, welcome! Is that Roald's girl, Issa?"

"Hi, Yorn!" Issa said, walking deeper into the shop to the little gray-haired Ardeni man leaning over his wooden counter. Morgan followed her, leaning sideways against the counter so he could see both of them as they spoke. "It's been too long!"

"Yes, indeed, Miss Issa! Who's this then? Is it that Morgan fellow I heard about? The one that put that rascal Swent in his place? Hah! His father sure has been quiet during council meetings lately!" Morgan didn't mean for his smile to fall off his face or for his brows to furrow, but when he thought of Swent, the pleasant day seemed to fall away, and he felt both angry and guilty at the same time. He certainly wasn't ready to laugh about killing the guy.

"Yes, Yorn, this is Morgan, and he's a sweet guy who doesn't like to dwell on killing young men, no matter how idiotic they were," Issa replied, reaching out a hand to squeeze Morgan's shoulder gently. Her touch brought Morgan back to himself, and he cleared his throat, looking down for a moment, then he smiled at Yorn.

"Nice to meet you, sir." He reached out his hand to shake Yorn's, and the old man smiled, though his unkempt white beard entirely hid his mouth.

"Well, let's talk business then! I'm sure you aren't here just to visit an old friend of your dad's, are ya?" He winked at Issa.

"We are here for business, but we came to you because you're a friend! There are other alchemists in town, you know!" Issa smiled, leaning forward toward Yorn earnestly, and Morgan admired her ability to charm.

"Oh, of course, of course! Thank you for thinking of me! Hey, while we're doing business, I have some sweetbread the missus sent with me. Can I share with you?" He turned and rummaged through a large leather briefcase on the counter behind him, turning back with a wax-paper-wrapped package.

"Oh, I can already smell it!" Issa said, leaning even further forward and making a show of smelling the package. Yorn laughed and gently unwrapped the loaf of moist bread. Morgan wasn't hungry, but the bread looked good, and Issa was playing along, so he figured it might be important not to rush their transaction. He gamely ate a slice of the bread, which was still warm in the center, and made exclamations about how delicious and rich it was.

"Now, tell me, what services can this master alchemist provide?" Yorn asked, and Issa looked to Morgan, raising an eyebrow as if to ask, "Shall I explain, or do you want to?" Morgan swallowed the rich bite of bread filled with chunks of candied fruit he'd been chewing.

"Well," he said, clearing his throat, "I have an advanced alchemical recipe and most of the reagents for it, but no one in First Landing yet has the skill or equipment to make it. Issa thinks you might be able to help."

"Oh? How intriguing. Where did you get the recipe, if you don't mind me asking?"

"From a dungeon. It comes from the personal recipe book of a self-styled master alchemist. We got it as a reward from the System."

"Oh, hmm, very interesting, indeed. Well, could I look at the recipe?"

"Well," Morgan glanced at Issa, ensuring she didn't have any objections to him going through with their agreed-upon negotiating tactic. She nodded encouragingly, and he continued, "I think the recipe is probably quite valuable, and you might learn a lot by simply reading it. Could we agree upon a fee assuming you can perform the mixture?"

"Oh, I see, I see." Yorn nodded knowingly, tapping his chin as though he were mulling over a problem. "Well, if you provide the ingredients and allow me to copy the recipe, I would simply charge you my daily labor fee." Morgan was about to respond, but Issa jumped in.

"What if we let you copy another two recipes from the book we got? You can choose them."

"Oh, well, I'd need to at least glance through the book to see if any of them are useful to me, but if they are, then I can waive my fee for, oh, for three of them." Morgan looked at Issa, and she nodded, so he pulled the recipe book from his ring and laid it on the counter.

"Alright, let me show you the recipe we need, first." He flipped the book to the page with the racial enhancement recipe and turned the book so Yorn could read it. His bright blue eyes scanned back and forth, and Morgan noticed that he slowly inhaled the whole while, not breathing out. Something about the recipe excited him.

"And you have the ingredients?" Morgan thought about the bag with hundreds of ingredients he'd taken from Blake's tower. In addition to what he'd already gathered from the Yovashi lair and his atrium, those should cover what he needed.

"Yeah, I do."

"Even the 'petals of the Threen Sun Rose'?"

"Yes, we got them as an award from the same dungeon."

"Well, the only difficulty I can see is that this recipe requires an arcfire distillation process."

"Arcfire?" Issa asked.

"Yes, it's a powerful meta-element, and a distiller like that is quite expensive. My old friend, Ulria, has one, though, and I think she'd let me borrow it. I'm sure I can bribe her off with one of the recipes I copy from your book here."

"So, you're interested in the recipes, then?" Morgan couldn't stop the slow smile spreading on his face.

"Oh yes; I won't play coy—this recipe is remarkable, and I have a feeling I'll find at least three more good ones in here. Shall we make it official with a toast?" Yorn reached under his counter and pulled out a tall, slender green bottle with a cork stopper. Then he brought up a fistful of little shot glasses. He poured three servings of bubbly, amber liquid into the glasses and pushed one, each, in front of Morgan and Issa. They raised their glasses, clinked them together, and drained their contents. Morgan and Issa sputtered and coughed, the harsh brew instantly going to their heads, and Yorn guffawed with laughter. "Good, good, now let's see those ingredients!"

Morgan took more than half an hour to pull out all the correct ingredients from his bags. Several times he had to show different bundles of similar-looking components to Yorn in order to have him select the correct one. When they were done, the afternoon had grown late, and Issa wanted to go to her home to settle in and have dinner. On their way out the door, Yorn called, "I'll need a day or three to get this done. I'll come 'round your father's house when I'm finished, alright?"

"That will be perfect. Thank you, Yorn!" Issa replied, and then they were outside, mounting their roladii and wending their way toward Issa's home.

MORGAN

"Do you think your father would be annoyed?" Morgan asked Issa.

"About what?" She stretched out, pushing her pillow back and turning to face him.

"That I've been sleeping in your room with you in his house for the last week?" He yawned and stretched, enjoying the tingles that spread through his tight muscles after a long night's sleep.

"Annoyed? No. Dismayed? Horrified? Yes!" She laughed, crawling over to him, holding his chin in her hands, and kissing him. Then she scurried out of bed and yanked the curtains back, letting in the bright morning light. "Today's the day! Yorn will be here any time now."

"Ugh, yep," Morgan grunted, sitting up on the side of the bed. He started pulling on his pants while Issa moved around the room, tidying up. Yorn had taken about twice as long as he'd expected to make the potion, but the missives he sent them over the last few days had insisted it would be worth it. "I haven't seen anything like this!" one message had said, elaborating that the Threen Sun Rose petals had been the "Most potent ingredient he'd ever distilled."

"Are you nervous?" Issa asked.

"About what? Taking the potion? I've advanced my race before, and it's never been a bad thing."

"I don't mean that it will be bad, but if it's as potent as Yorn hopes, you'll pass into improved. No one from your race has done that yet. What do you think might happen?"

"Alright, I know what you're doing. No, I don't think I'll grow a tail!" Morgan laughed and pulled on his boots.

"Can you help me with my buttons, please?" He stood and held up his shirt. Issa helped him on with it and buttoned the front for him.

"I'm not really joking around, though. I'm curious. Some Ardeni with improved races start to access hidden bloodlines and develop things like markings on their skin, harder claws, and even longer leg bones and extra tendons that allow them to leap really far. Did you know that some Shadeni even sprout wings when they reach advanced racial status? I mean real wings that allow them to fly, not like little fluttery Ghelli wings."

"Really? So, there's a chance you'll get longer legs eventually?" Morgan grinned and bent to kiss her, but she pushed him away.

"Jokester! I'm serious! What if your people grow a creepy third eye or something?" She backed away, hiding a grin, and Morgan chased after her. She turned and ran, squealing, through the house. He caught up to her in the kitchen and, after extracting payment in kisses, helped her make breakfast. They were finishing up when a knock sounded on the door, and Issa opened it to find Yorn waiting outside, a wooden box in his hands.

"As promised!" He said, holding out the box, which Issa took. Then he reached into his vest and produced the little recipe book. "On my honor, I only copied three additional recipes." Morgan leaned around Issa and took the book.

"Thanks, Yorn! I hope they serve you well," he said, slipping the book into his storage ring.

"Are you, ahem, are you going to drink it right away?" He glanced from Issa to Morgan, eyes hopeful. Morgan knew what he wanted, to see how the potion worked, but he didn't like the idea of Yorn watching him as he lay helpless, undergoing the "Metamorphosis" he'd been promised.

"Well, to be honest, we're not exactly sure. We've got some talking and planning to do. If we use it soon, I'll be sure to let you know what it's like and how it worked, okay?"

"Oh, yes, I suppose that's as much as I should expect. I'll look forward to hearing from you," Yorn said, starting to turn.

"Thank you, Yorn! I'll tell my father how kind and helpful you were!" Issa reached out to him but stopped short of grabbing his shoulder.

"Thank you, Miss Issa. Good luck, Morgan." With that, the little man wandered down the path to the road and was gone.

"You didn't want him watching you go through it, did you?" Issa asked, turning to Morgan. "So, you are nervous!" She held the smooth wooden box out to him. Morgan sighed and took the box.

"Yes, I'm fucking nervous." He chuckled and turned back into the house while Issa closed the door.

"Alright, big baby. Don't worry; I've only heard good things about racial evolutions. Let's go out to the back garden. There's a nice, sunny patch of grass you can lie down on." She led Morgan through the house and out through a sunroom into a lovely fenced-in garden. Morgan saw the little lawn she'd meant right away, and he sat down on the soft blue grass, holding the box in his lap. Issa sat down in front of him in the same pose she used for cultivating. They'd spent a lot of time over the last week cultivating; he'd even leveled his Core in the process.

The box had a seam where the lid could be slid off, so he did so, revealing a slender, amber-colored bottle nestled in some fluffy, dry hay. Morgan lifted out the bottle and set the box aside. "You know, we both earned this. Just because I'm missing an arm doesn't mean I have to drink this."

"Ugh! Not this again! You took the beating. Your skill won the fight; you drink the reward. I got plenty out of that dungeon!" Issa huffed in exasperation.

"Alright, alright." Morgan picked up the little card in the box and read aloud the note Yorn had written in lovely, looping calligraphy, "Once the cork is removed, be sure to imbibe within one minute." He glanced at Issa, and she nodded reassuringly. He held the bottle out toward her, "Will you pull the cork for me?" She reached out and ran her thumbnail around the wax seal, then gently pried the cork loose. Morgan tilted the bottle to his lips and poured the contents into his mouth, swallowing several gulps. It wasn't thick like he'd thought it would be; it was more like drinking a soda and tasted almost like grapes. When he'd drained the whole bottle, he set it down then looked at Issa, about to ask when something would happen, and then his vision exploded like a solar flare had gone off right in front of him.

Unlike in the past, when Morgan had experienced visions of flying or soaring in space, he was utterly insensate this time. One moment the world was exploding in his eyes, and then he was opening his eyes, groggily groaning and reaching up to rub his face. "God, that shit hit me like a Mack truck." The lighting was different than when he'd drunk the potion, and when he moved his hand to look around, he realized he was indoors. Grunting, he pushed himself up on his elbows, and that's when it hit him—his left arm was back. As he scooted up, he found that he was in a bed. Looking around groggily, he recognized Issa's room. He'd been out for a while, then, and she'd moved him in here.

The light coming in between the curtains was dim, so it was early evening or morning, but Issa wasn't anywhere to be seen. Sitting up, leaning against the headboard, Morgan held up his new left hand and squeezed it into a fist. It felt good. Frowning, he held both his hands out in front of him and wiggled his fingers. They were long and elegant, finer than he remembered them, yet strong. He inspected his arms, noting their lack of scars and the wiry muscles under the smooth skin. Well, his skin was nicer, and his limbs a little longer, but he was still human, right? He yanked the covers off and looked down at his body. Nothing alarming confronted him other than that he was completely nude. A surge of panic hit him when he realized even his storage ring was missing, but then he calmed when he saw it on the nightstand beside the bed.

Morgan stood, slipped his ring on his finger, and looked around, seeing his clothes folded neatly on the chest at the foot of the bed. He let out his breath, and that's when he realized he'd been holding it since he'd first noticed his new arm. His heart wasn't even racing. He took another deep breath, then felt on his wrist for his pulse. It took him a long while to find it because his heart rate was very slow, something like ten beats a minute. "This'll give Doctor Kerns something to talk about." He paused for a moment and looked at his status sheet:

Status			
Name:	Morgan Hall		
Race:	Human - Improved 2		
Class:	Vortex Duelist - Epic		
Level:	28		
Core:	Vortex Class - Base 8		
Energy Affinity:	9.2, Void 9.2	Energy:	5003/5003
Strength:	65	Vitality:	60
Dexterity:	56 (76)	Agility:	109
Intelligence:	132	Will:	113
Points Available:	0		
Titles & Feats:	Human Champion, First Hollow Guard, Ardeni Friend, Mark of Loyalty, Yovashi Bane, Legacy of the Azure Paladin, First Vortex Duelist		
Skills:	• System Language Integration - Not Upgradeable • Animal Taming - Basic • Stealthy Maneuvers - Basic • Melee Weapon Mastery - Basic • Fighting Crane Style - Basic • Sword Mastery - Improved Vortex Core Cultivation Drill - Basic	• Backstab - Basic Energy Drain - Advanced • Circle of Combat - Improved • Guard Ally - Basic Hollow Charge - Improved • Azure Burst - Basic • Azure Sight - Basic • Vortex Lance - Basic	

It looked like the potion had given him five ranks to his racial stat which seemed pretty incredible. He bent to pick up his clothes and get dressed and was so happy to have two hands again that he almost teared up. He'd tried to keep a brave face about his injury, but it really had been a considerable adjustment. As he tied his boots, he felt a twinge of guilt, thinking of the countless people on Earth who had similar or worse injuries with no chance of a recovery like he'd just made. He shook his head—that wasn't his fault.

He'd noticed that when he put on his clothes, they'd had to adjust themselves to his frame again. He wasn't much taller, but he'd become leaner, his limbs longer, and his torso more V-shaped. People might mistake him for an Olympic swimmer if he were on Earth. He opened the door and listened, and he swore he could hear the wind rustling the flowers outside and the clicking, scratching sound of a small animal moving on the roof, but he didn't hear Issa.

As he walked into the hallway, he caught the scent of cooked pork and eggs, but when he walked into the kitchen, the stove was cold, and the pan on top of it had been scraped clean. Still, he picked it up and smelled the old meal like it was sitting on a plate in front of him. "So, my senses are stronger now, too, huh?" He set the pan down, walked to the front door, and stepped into the cool evening air.

When he was out on the front porch, he listened to the sounds in the night, and, after a moment, he caught the sound of a familiar voice chatting happily and another female voice responding. They talked about food, and Issa told the other person how she liked to make travel packets of her favorite recipes. The voices were getting louder, so Morgan sat down on the stoop and waited. Soon he could hear their feet scraping on the loose gravel, and then he saw her coming up the path, her bright yellow eyes luminous in the twilight. She paused for a second, staring into the shadows where he sat, and then she broke into a run. "Morgan!" He stood and caught her, and she charged into him, wrapping her arms around his waist, and he hugged her back.

"Good to see you, too!" He said, chuckling at the ferocity of her hug.

"About time you woke up, you oaf! You've been sleeping for over a week!"

⚘ BRONWYN ⚘

Bronwyn circled the glade for the third time, moving out just a bit further, trying to find Thun's tracks. She'd picked up feyris tracks, a dozen pultii tracks, but not the ones she wanted. The night air was much chillier here than back in First Landing, and she wondered how far north the queen had sent her. She could feel that the air was thinner and had to assume that the reason for the chilly air was an increase in elevation. Thinking about it, Bronwyn realized she didn't have the first clue about where exactly on the planet First Landing was. Were they north of the equator? How far north? How long would she need to travel for temperatures to change significantly? The planet was massive; she knew that much, so she figured it would take a long journey to experience temperature extremes due to latitude changes. "So, we're climbing."

Having circled the glade four times now, Bronwyn still hadn't found Thun's tracks; she decided to climb one of the pine-like trees to see if she could spot any indication of what direction the Winter agent might have gone. The tree's needles were green and deepened to blue toward their tips, but otherwise reminded her a lot of the giant pines she'd seen from the highway driving through Washington state. Bronwyn found she could climb a hell of a lot better than she ever had back on Earth. She jumped up, grabbed a low limb, and hoisted herself effortlessly up. Sticking close to the broad trunk, she reached, grabbed, pulled, and clambered her way up the tree. When she'd climbed for several minutes, she found the branches obscuring her view had grown thinner, and she could see out over the landscape from her perch.

With a cold wind blowing through her hair and causing the tree to sway gently, Bronwyn studied the landscape to the north. From this vantage, she could see a natural break in the tree line that a landslide might have caused; piles of gray stones tumbled down a slope that seemed gentle from her viewpoint but was probably steeper than it looked. More than that, though, she was able to see that several peaks rose in the distance beyond the forest and that a brown-gray trail or road ribboned its way up between two of them. "Aha!" She descended from the tree, far faster than was probably safe, but it seemed so easy that she couldn't help dropping through the air from branch to branch, catching herself with her hands. "Goddamn, I could be a professional rock climber back home!" She laughed as she landed on the turf under the tree and brushed her hands off against each other. "Ugh, sap."

She strode through the forest, scanning the ground as she went, moving purposefully toward the spot where she'd seen the break in the trees and the faint line of the road that led up through the pass. Thun hadn't known she'd be coming to follow him, so surely, he'd use the road to cross the mountains, right? She supposed he could have other enemies he was trying to avoid. She'd covered about a mile through the trees when she heard a grumbling rumble of a voice and saw trees shaking just ahead of her. Bronwyn froze and carefully started to make her way over behind one of the nearby trees. With a tremendous crack and a rustle of falling branches and leaves, a huge, misshapen man burst through the trees ahead of her.

Bronwyn stood like a deer in headlights, unsure if the creature had spotted her. It stood there, nostrils flaring in its giant, lumpy face. It had to be twelve feet tall, and, though it was humanoid in general shape, the naked, furry thing had as much in common with a bear or pig as it did a human. Patchy, black fur covered a lot of its form, with spots of lumpy pink skin poking out of it in random areas. Its "Hands" were three-fingered and ended in thick black claws. Most disturbing was its face, though, pink and lumpy with long, yellow-brown tusks sprouting from its lower, distended jaw. Its red, beady eyes surveyed the area while its wide, dripping nostrils flared and huffed.

Something about the creature made her think of the Urghat but comparing an Urghat to this thing would be like comparing a modern human to a neanderthal or sasquatch. The huge creature took another massive inhale and turned to look directly at the tree behind which Bronwyn was hiding. It opened its mouth and roared, saliva stringing out and flapping in its breath as the thunderous sound rolled through the forest. "Guess you found me," Bronwyn said, stepping out from behind the tree. Apparently, small talk wasn't in the monster's repertoire because it immediately charged at her, raking a set of four-inch black claws down toward her neck and shoulder.

Bronwyn rolled to her left, easily dodging the big, arcing swipe. She cast her Solar Arms spell and noticed that her hands started to glow with a bright golden light. As she finished her roll and sprang to her feet, she darted behind the lumbering giant and, not able to reach anything much higher, punched a fist into the meaty area above its huge, stinking rump. Her fist, buzzing with Energy, sizzled as it impacted the creature's flesh like a miniature wrecking ball, sending a shockwave rippling through the blubber hanging off its midriff. She gagged at the smell of feces that wafted off the burning, matted fur and had to jump back to avoid another swing of the claws as the monster whirled with an angry snarl to retaliate.

Bronwyn danced around the roaring, drooling, lumbering, stinking giant for an exhausting minute or two, running in for quick hits, then rolling away to avoid being pulverized. She dropped her Solar Arms spell whenever she was evading, trying to save her Energy and allow her natural recovery to keep her in the fight. The giant, while dense and slow, had incredible resilience, and though she'd smashed it a dozen times, scorching its fur and flesh and tenderizing its innards, it seemed to keep going on pure hatred or frenzied hunger. While she rolled away for the seventh or eighth time, Bronwyn began to appreciate the idea of carrying around something a bit more lethal than her fists; they'd worked great on creatures like Yeksa and Urghat, but this thing was another story.

Finally losing some of her caution to frustration, Bronwyn worked her way around behind the creature again and sprinted forward, grabbing fistfuls of scraggly, louse-ridden fur and pulling herself up onto its boulder-like shoulders. Her balance was precarious, but she channeled Energy into her Solar Arms spell and clapped both her hands as hard as she could against the outside of the giant's bulbous misshapen ears. Her glowing, buzzing palms connected with a tremendous crack, and Bronwyn thought she could sense the Energy from one hand stretching out to mingle with the Energy from the other. The giant grunted and wobbled, then toppled forward in slow motion to fall, face-first, with a thunderous rumble, almost like a tree coming down. Bronwyn rode down with it, balancing on her knees and then rolling off onto the forest floor.

She wasn't sure if the creature had just been stunned or if she'd given it enough brain damage to kill it, so Bronwyn rushed over to the beast and began to pummel its big, lumpy head, using her Solar Arms spell to send spikes of solar damage into the same spot repeatedly. After several punches, with the creature's flesh sizzling and the bone beneath growing fractured and mushy, large golden motes began to coalesce around its fallen form and surged into Bronwyn.

*****Congratulations! You have achieved level 16 Summer Banneret and have gained 28 attribute points to allocate.*****

"Wow, holy shit!" She hadn't expected to earn that many points per level with her new class, nor did she think this one creature would be enough to level her. She supposed she might have been nearing level 16 already from the fights during the Urghat invasion and the creatures she'd killed in the swarm during her trial. Still, she was excited to have so much freedom—twenty-eight points to distribute however she wanted. Before messing around with her attributes, she stood very still and listened, wondering if her battle with the forest giant monstrosity had brought any company. If anything, it seemed like it had had the opposite effect; it was silent. The birds, insects, and small animals must have fled the battle.

Bronwyn took one last look at the fallen, filthy giant and then jogged off through the trees, looking for a good spot to lay low for a few minutes. She stopped by a trio of tall trees with some fallen branches near their trunks. Pulling the branches together, she made a little blind for herself and sat down on the mulchy ground to contemplate her attributes. The queen had indicated that intelligence was essential if she wanted to use her spells more. She hadn't touched that attribute since coming to this world, so she began by adding ten points to it. That done, she looked at her Energy stats:

Energy Affinity:	5.6, Solar - 7.6	Energy:	337/488

She'd gained over a hundred maximum Energy from the intelligence bump. She could now comfortably cast Solar Shell twice and Wrath of Summer once. She contemplated for a few minutes and pulled up her attributes again:

Strength:	72	Vitality:	39
Dexterity:	19	Agility:	44
Intelligence:	19	Will:	26

She wondered if she should increase her intelligence, even more, considering how much ten points had helped. Thinking about it, she began to wonder what else she was missing with the attribute system. She'd neglected dexterity in comparison to her other physical attributes as well. Was that short-sighted? She had eighteen points left, so she decided to put nine into dexterity and nine into intelligence. Feeling the surge of well-being and energy that came with so many attribute points at once, she pulled up her Energy stats again:

Energy Affinity:	5.6, Solar - 7.6	Energy:	358/626

"Woah." She'd basically doubled her Energy with one level. Bronwyn was happy that she'd made such gains. Still, she was also frustrated with herself—she'd started out in this world treating herself like a character in a VR game, min-maxing her strength and agility, assuming it was all she'd need to keep fighting above her weight class. The forest giant she'd just fought was a good indicator that simple martial skills wouldn't be enough to make it to the heavyweights in this world; she'd need to keep honing her abilities, and Energy was a huge factor in that regard. She barked a short laugh as a funny thought struck her, "Am I thinking more clearly because I just jacked up my intelligence?"

Bronwyn took a few minutes to eat a quick meal. She hadn't touched the queen's rations yet; she still had plenty of sandwich material that she'd packed in First Landing. After wolfing down a sandwich of rye bread spread with butter and piled high with smoked ham, she stood up and decided to pick up the pace. She wanted to see how fast she could move through this forest without making a racket. "Time to put my blessing of the herd to work," she said, giving each of her thighs a good stretch by pulling her ankles up behind her butt, one at a time. Then, she took off through the trees, scanning the ground for tracks.

As she raced through the forest, leaping over undergrowth and dashing between trees, Bronwyn laughed with the pleasure of it. She loved the wind rushing through her hair and over her ears, she relished the challenge of having to leap obstacles, and she enjoyed the mental stimulation of noting and categorizing all the tracks she crossed. So far, the only dangerous seeming animal she found tracks for were those of the "Forest Ogre" that she supposed belonged to the ugly monster she'd just slain. In seemingly no time at all, Bronwyn broke free of the forest and continued to run along its edge, leaping over the loose rocky scree that had once, in her opinion, been a landslide. When she rounded a rocky spar that jutted out from the mountainside, she was slowly making her way around, she caught sight of an overgrown dirt road about half a mile downslope. She figured if she maintained her course at her current elevation, the road, which wound its way upward, would cross her path in about a mile or two.

Bronwyn kept a steady pace, slowing down a little now that she was out of the trees and making sure she didn't surprise any more dangerous monsters. She didn't encounter anything of note before she descended a slight, rocky slope and came upon a bend of the old, ill-maintained roadway. When she started walking along the packed dirt, she scanned for tracks, noting lots of holbyis and other animals, several Urghat, and one Cadwalli. "Gotcha," she said, zeroing in on the Cadwalli tracks. She could see they continued up the road, and Bronwyn took a moment to take in the lay of the land. Stretching ahead of her and gradually moving into switchbacks, the old road climbed the side of a steep craggy mountain and disappeared from her view around the shoulder of the rocky peak. She didn't see anything large moving around, though birds and small animals scurrying in the roadside scrub were all around her. Stretching and cracking her neck, she started the climb—time to find her quarry.

⚘ OLIVIA ⚘

"I can't believe it's been a week already," Olivia said, staring at the splatters of rain hitting the banked windows in their dorm. Her friends had just gotten back from the cafeteria, exhausted from a bout of instruction from an unusually grumpy and hostile Commander Grobak. Olivia had been on her own all afternoon, Oylla having given her "Time to reflect" before she had to step through the portal in the morning.

"Busy days make quick lives. Our mother always used to say that," Adaida said, glancing at Shani.

"My dad said the same thing. I could never tell if he was saying I should slow down and enjoy life more or if I should be busy so the weekend would come faster." Rald shrugged, flopping back on the couch and throwing his feet up on the arm.

"My people say, 'time flies when you're having fun.'" Olivia sighed wistfully, dragging a finger through the condensation on the window.

"So, they're sending you off in the morning?" Hanwol asked. "How long will you be gone? We've got a break in a couple of weeks."

"Oh, God. I'll be back before then, right?" Olivia turned to look at Hanwol. "I better be! I was thinking this might take a few days, not a few weeks!"

"Didn't Professor Oylla-dak give you any idea?" Shani asked.

"Well, yes. There are six levels to the proving grounds with five rooms per level. She talked to me about getting as far as possible before giving up but never really said how long it should take. I figured it would go quickly until I couldn't progress, and then I could teleport out. Oylla said she'd be happy if I could get to the fourth level."

"Hah, that's because no one's gotten past the third floor since Illia Tarn." Hanwol snorted.

"Illia Tarn?" Olivia asked.

"Kind of a famous alumnus of Fainhallow. She reached the fifth level if I recall. She went on to lead the Ridonne Empire to a few victories over the Vinduv. Last I heard, she had traveled off-world, though." Hanwol looked around at the other students to see if anyone wanted to correct him or add to his explanation. No one did.

"That was before my time," Shani yawned.

"Before all our time," Veena added. "I think it's been nearly a hundred years since she was here."

"Well, anyway, I hope I'm back long before break! Will you all be leaving? I hope I can find a way to get home for a visit, but it's not a sure thing." Everyone looked at each other, then back at her.

"Yeah, I think we're all heading home for the break. You're welcome to come with Shani and me if you can't get a teleport home," Adaida said after an awkward moment.

"Thanks, Adaida; I'm glad for the invitation. We'll see what happens. Well, team, I'm supposed to head down to administration soon. I guess there are some formalities I have to go through before I can port to the Proving Grounds. Oylla said that after they process me, I have to sleep in a 'clean' room before the portal opens in the morning."

"Yeah, they don't want you to cheat somehow. All the schools have to do the same," Hanwol said, and it made Olivia feel better to know it was normal.

"You're awfully well informed about these things," Shani said to Hanwol.

"He loves competitions and dungeons; he could probably list off the top earners in every dungeon within a thousand miles of Zancryst," Veena said, tousling Hanwol's hair. He slapped her hand away and snorted, turning to read his book, done with the conversation as far as he was concerned.

"Want us to walk you to the admin offices?" Adaida asked.

"No, that's alright. You all look beat, and I'll probably wander by the cafeteria on my way." Olivia turned and started to walk away, but they all stood and crowded around. Rald pulled her into a hug and thumped her on the back awkwardly.

"Sheesh, you're skinny," he said, pushing her back. "Good luck, alright?"

"Hey, I'm not skinny; you're just a gorilla!" Olivia laughed.

"I think that would be funnier if I knew what that was," he said, but he also laughed. Then Olivia was mobbed by the rest of her cohort, and she had to fight back tears as they all gave her sincere well-wishes. When Adaida pulled out of a long hug, she held out a length of blue string she'd woven into a little bracelet. Olivia held it up and admired the little hearts and stars she'd entwined between the two borders.

"Wow, I didn't know you were so artistic."

"They won't let you take any enchantments in there, but this should get through okay. If you feel alone, just look at it, and you'll remember us out here waiting for you." She tied it around Olivia's left wrist, and this time a tear did escape the flames of Olivia's eyes.

"Thank you, Adaida. Thank you, everyone. I'll try to make Copper proud!" She turned and hurried from the dorm before more could be said. It felt good to have friends; she'd had friends before, but never so close. Having a team, a cohort, whose success was tied to hers was something altogether new to Olivia. She'd always been a solo achiever in the past, and she quite liked having other people to look out for while they did the same for her. Even when she'd joined Vynatek, it had almost been a hostile merger—she'd given them her tech and ideas, but she'd very clearly spelled out what she wanted in return.

"Watch out, freak." Olivia had been just about to say, "Excuse me," when she'd brushed against the other student coming around the corner, but that voice and those words froze her vocal cords. She turned to face Gwinna, looking down her nose at the Bogoli. She was tall for her race but still two full heads shorter than Olivia. Heat rose in Olivia's chest, and she opened her mouth to speak, but then she thought better of it. She just smirked and turned, walking on toward the stairwell that would take her to the administration level.

When she'd looked into Gwinna's blue gemstone eyes, Olivia had felt almost nothing. There had been a surge of irritation but absolutely no fear—no intimidation. Gwinna didn't matter to her, and Olivia felt like dismissing her was probably the best way to get back at the girl for her rudeness. "I was talking to you!" Olivia kept walking, a jaunt in her step, and soon she was down the first flight of steps, and Gwinna was in the past.

When she arrived at the administration offices, it reminded her of her first day at the academy. She smiled, thinking about how she'd impressed the evaluator by sending different attuned Energies into that device. It seemed very trivial to her now. The receptionist gave her directions through the little maze of hallways to get to the Office of Games and Competitions, where another receptionist had her wait on a low sofa by a dusty potted fern. After about twenty minutes, a thin Bogoli man, his face and scalp painted a solid royal blue, opened a door and gestured for Olivia to follow him.

The man was silent, and Olivia just followed, not wanting to be the one to start the conversation. The ease with which she endured his silence surprised her; in the past, she'd probably have tried to start some small talk to make herself feel less awkward, but now she simply followed, understanding that any awkwardness was a result of his lack of communication, and she wasn't responsible for his actions. It wasn't confidence, per se, more like a sense of surety, ease. Was it a natural easiness that came with increased power? She'd describe it as a feeling like she could handle a situation regardless of what happened. Did the elemental she'd bonded with have something to do with it? Was it simply her training with Oylla? More likely, it was just a combination of everything she'd been through in the last few weeks.

"In here, please," the slight Bogoli said flatly.

"Thank you," Olivia said, stepping through the door he'd opened. She was in a stone-walled, closet-sized chamber with another door on the far wall. Two crystals were mounted above the far door; one was pulsing with a red light. A small table filled the center of the room, and atop the table was a metal box with an open lid. Olivia stepped to the table and looked in the box. A white garment was folded within, and atop that were a handwritten note and a small golden, circular pendant on a chain. Olivia read the letter quietly to herself, "Place all of your belongings in this box for safekeeping. Wear the recall pendant, don the jumpsuit, and proceed through the door when the light turns green."

Olivia looked around the room, subconsciously looking for one-way mirrors or cameras. Nothing but smooth stone met her scrutiny, so she shrugged and started to strip off her clothes. She lifted the garment out of the box and piled her clothing, satchel, and storage ring into the box. Standing naked, she contemplated putting the blue woven bracelet into the box, but the red crystal stopped pulsing, and the other started to throb with a green light. She shook out the white garment, revealing a jumpsuit that would cover her from neck to wrists to the bottom of her feet with sewn-in shoes.

Olivia slipped the thin golden chain around her neck, then pulled the loose-fitting jumpsuit on, snapping a dozen silvery buttons up the middle. It hung on her like it was made for someone Rald's size, so she tried trickling some Energy into it. It instantly bonded with her, snapping to fit snugly against her body, almost like a second skin. "Well, at least I'll be flexible in this thing," she chuckled, lifting the lid to the metal box and securing her belongings within.

Suitably attired, Olivia walked to the green-lit door, turned the handle, and pushed it open. She walked into another room, almost identical to the other, except it had a cot in its center, with two blankets folded on top. On the far wall was a rune-etched archway with smooth stone at its center. Olivia presumed that was where the portal to the Proving Grounds would open. While studying the archway and its runes, the door behind her clicked shut. "So, just wait here for the portal to light up. Got it," she said, feeling like she had an audience even though none was apparent.

The room was dimly lit, just a faint orange ambient glow coming from the stone of the ceiling. Olivia wasn't cold at all, so she spread the blankets on the cot and lay atop them. She closed her eyes and tried to will the time to move quickly—she didn't think she'd be able to sleep. For one thing, she didn't sleep as much as she used to. Her body seemed far more efficient than it used to be. She didn't eat as much, didn't drink as much, and three or four hours of sleep a night seemed plenty to make her feel rested. For another, she was too excited to sleep. She'd worked hard with Oylla to get better with her spells, using them more quickly and efficiently. Her cohort had done an excellent job of hyping her up, also. She was no longer a reluctant participant—Olivia wanted to compete, and she wanted to win. She'd heard plenty of stories over the last few evenings about the kinds of things she could win, and she intended to make a good showing of herself. If not for her own personal gain, then for the benefit of the people back in First Landing that were counting on her.

Olivia began to meditate and channel Energy into her cultivation drill. She lost herself in the rhythm of Energy flowing through her pathways, alternating her different affinities and straining to pull in the sparse ambient Energy. She'd gotten so wrapped up in the process that it almost startled her when the portal swirled into existence with a hum and a whoosh of air that fluttered her long, black hair.

OLIVIA

The portal was a swirling maelstrom of silver and black whorls. It wasn't passively sitting in the archway, either, but rather tugging at Olivia and the room's air. When she stepped toward it and reached a hand into the spinning plane, it yanked hungrily at her, and she found herself stumbling into a frigid torrent that pulled her, tumbling, into what felt like a dark, underground river. Subconsciously, Olivia channeled some fire-attuned Energy into her pathways, more than mitigating the freezing substance of the portal. Then she worked to right herself, so she could face the direction in which she was being pulled.

It felt very much like swimming, and Olivia realized she'd been holding her breath when, after a few moments of paddling and kicking, she managed to face the portal's flow. She could see a distant point of light that seemed to shift around, but Olivia realized the light wasn't moving; the river of portal Energy flowed and surged in a great spiral toward that distant pinprick of illumination.

She wasn't yet out of wind, but Olivia decided to try taking a breath, more out of curiosity than any perceived need. When she exhaled, she didn't note any bubbles, and when she breathed in, nothing triggered her gag reflex—it was just like breathing heavy, cold air. Judging by the rate at which she approached that distant point of light, she figured she'd be in the portal for another ten minutes or so. She wondered if teleportation duration was indicative of distance. She'd gotten from First Landing to Fainhallow almost instantly, which had been a journey of more than a thousand miles.

Her estimate of the trip's duration was off by about half because she started to accelerate shortly after she'd steadied herself and got her bearings. Soon she was whipping through the spiral of cold, thick air in an eye-watering blur, and then she found herself splashing into a pool of nearly freezing water. Olivia was instantly thankful for her Elemental Resistance; what would have ripped the wind from her lungs and sent her into hypothermic shivering in the past was merely a little inconvenient to her now.

She waded through the water and looked around at her new surroundings. The water she was in had a faint blue sheen, and Olivia had a sudden spike of adrenaline as she recalled the blue, frigid water in the Yovashi's lair. Swallowing a gasp that tried to escape her lips, she carefully swam, breaststroke, to the stone lip of the pool, trying to move as silently as possible.

The blue sheen of the water made it hard to discern any details in the dark space, but she could tell she was in some sort of a cavern. When she scrambled up onto the stone, she was relieved to see that the area immediately around the pool was just smooth, almost polished-looking rock and that it continued to a stone wall where a heavy black, iron door sat, closed. "At least I didn't get dumped into a Yovashi lair for a welcome."

Olivia stood and let the water drip from her jumpsuit and squeezed her hair until it was just damp and not soaking wet. She walked over to the door and saw that it was bolted shut—a large, heavy padlock was holding the bolt from sliding. "The first challenge?" She wondered aloud. She supposed popping a heavy metal lock might prove difficult for some, but Olivia conjured a ball of plasma and tossed it at the padlock. A brilliant white flare engulfed the lock, accompanied by a hissing sound and the pungent, bitter scent of metal made instantly liquid. "C'mon, Liv, no waiting around if we're going to take the lead." She reached out, yanked the hot metal bolt to the right, and pulled the door open.

Olivia knew that every contender from the various schools would start in a separate location, but some of the paths converged on larger rooms, and there she might run into aggressive, hostile competitors. She figured the best way to avoid those types of encounters would be to make it further than everyone else, faster than everyone else. They could fight over the scraps she left behind. The door opened onto a short stone-walled hallway that led to another, identical door. Olivia walked forward, plasma orb already hovering over her palm, and tossed it at the lock. She yanked aside the bolt when the flash subsided and pulled the door open.

The scene that unfolded before her was shocking in its departure from the quiet, simple stone hallway. An enormous cavern filled her view, and pitched battles were being fought all over the rubble-strewn stone floor. Gigantic spiders swarmed in surging mounds toward Olivia's open door and several other identical iron doors up and down this side of the cavern.

Olivia realized, instantly, that she hadn't been the first to break through her locks and that several students had paths leading to this room. Before she could get a look at any of her competitors, though, a mass of clicking, hissing spiders the size of German shepherds rushed her doorway. They had smooth black carapaces with bright yellow dots all over the backs of their abdomens. Olivia swore their four-inch-long fangs dripped with venom, though later, she might think it was her imagination.

Olivia glanced left and right, then backed up to the first iron door she'd opened, forcing the aggressive giant arachnids to funnel into the short hallway. She tried to hold steady, tried to wait as long as she could, but the primal urge to scream and run nearly overwhelmed her in the face of the tumbling mass of creepy, deadly creatures. When a dozen or more of them pushed their way through the doorway and into her hallway, she couldn't contain herself any longer, and she stretched out her arm, palm out, casting Magma Ray at the throng of surging creatures.

Superheated magma bored through their bodies, instantly heating their innards to the boiling point, causing carapaces to burst with steamy explosions. Olivia directed the ray of magma around, torching and slicing apart the piled arachnids. The hissing scream of popping spider bodies nearly drowned out the cries of the tortured arachnids, but not quite, and Olivia shuddered at the inhuman sound.

*****Congratulations! You have achieved level 13 Elemental Archon and have gained 10 Intelligence, 10 Will, and have 8 points to allocate.*****

The surge of Energy from the defeated spiders caught Olivia by surprise, but she didn't waste time. She trotted forward to her doorway, kicking aside the spiders' smoldering, smoking, steaming corpses, careful not to accidentally kick her shin into any fangs. When she reached the doorway, she saw that she'd been the first to vanquish her arachnid horde. Screams, flashes, clangs, hisses, and scrabbling erupted and echoed around the other doorways. Olivia briefly contemplated helping the other students, but then she remembered Oylla's admonishment to make haste and not interact with other students unless forced to. She glanced further into the chamber and saw the far wall and a doorway, maybe two-hundred paces distant. No spiders were between her and the distant exit, all of them having chosen an entrance to attack or defend. "Not very heroic, but here I go!"

She set off running over the open cavern floor. As she sprinted, the sounds of combat grew louder at first but then faded as she put more distance between herself and the swarming masses of spiders. Olivia kept panning her vision left and right, then up and down, ensuring she wasn't ambushed by more spiders.

While studying the cavern's vaulted ceiling, she noticed thick webbing that stretched in long, billowing arcs between rocky imperfections and the cavern walls. When she was more than halfway across the cavern, she spared a glance behind her and saw that none of the doorways were yet completely free of spiders. She had a good lead on the other academy students.

With renewed determination, Olivia refocused on the far door and pumped her legs into a sprint. She was less than thirty yards away when a massive shadowy form descended from the webs in the upper reaches of the cavern to hang before the door. Olivia gasped in shock and skidded to a halt, only fifteen paces or so from the huge spider.

Slowly, the monstrosity uncurled its long legs, releasing the strand of webbing it had descended on and transitioning to the cavern floor. Part of Olivia wanted to stand, dumbstruck by the massive arachnid and its sudden appearance, but another, more primal part of her screamed in disgust and unleashed a Magma Ray, hitting the creature dead center and carving away half of its abdomen. The spider convulsed, its legs catapulting it into the air like massive hydraulic pistons, and steaming magma and ichor sprayed in an arc as it flipped onto its back, thrashing in death throes.

Olivia didn't slow, running straight at the iron door and hurling a ball of plasma at the lock as it came into focus. She was just crossing the threshold when the golden motes from the dead spider queen slammed into her, filling her with Energy and thrilling euphoria. She'd entered another short hallway, and before she inspected the far door, she turned and pulled the one behind her shut, summoning a ball of magma to force into the seam between the iron door and doorjamb.

She pushed and pressed until the magma had filled a good ten inches of the gap, and then she let it cool, hoping it would harden and make it difficult for the other students to follow her. "How many rooms is that? Two? Does the starting room count?" she wondered aloud. Olivia turned and walked to the next door, noting that it was the first one she'd encountered without a heavy padlock. She pulled the latch, and it swung noiselessly open on well-oiled hinges.

Beyond the door, she found a small, dark room bordered by smooth stone walls. When she advanced, she realized she was badly mistaken—it wasn't a small room; it was a small ledge that hung over a vast, black abyss. Olivia summoned a regular orb of fire and tossed it out into the abyss. She watched it flare out into the darkness, revealing nothing other than how large the chasm was. As the orb fell, flickering into the darkness, she observed its flickering progress into darkness. Maybe three hundred feet down, it finally hit a stone floor with a burst of flames, briefly illuminating jumbled rocks and boulders.

"So, I need to descend three hundred feet into the darkness?" She would have been dismayed if it weren't for her training with Oylla. Seeing as she hadn't been allowed to bring any belongings into the place, she didn't know how she'd have overcome this obstacle without her magic, and maybe that was the point. She concentrated, feeding air-attuned Energy into her channels, and then cast Elemental Form.

Olivia felt a surge of energy and potential as her physical being lightened, and her flesh became translucent with swirls of air and electricity pulsing and flowing around her limbs. Knowing how costly the spell was to maintain, Olivia didn't waste time, stepping off the edge of the cliff into the abyss. She fell, but she fell slowly, and when she held her arms out, she fell even slower.

The little arcs of lightning that flickered along her limbs gave off just enough light to reveal the stone cliff behind her as she descended, allowing her to mark her progress in the darkness. She was falling at maybe five feet per second. She knew, from trial and error with Oylla, that her form would last about a minute before fading unless she poured more Energy into it.

Olivia held her arms in close and allowed herself to fall a bit faster, keeping alert for any other threats that might come out of the darkness. She took a moment to look at her status sheet, taking note of her Energy—so far, her passive recovery plus the Energy she'd gotten for killing spiders had almost kept up with her expenditures; she sat at 1403/1865.

The minute of her descent stretched into eternity in her mind, and then it was over as her air and lightning-wrapped feet touched down on stone. Olivia had held her knees slightly bent, and her air elemental form was very light, so the landing was gentle and produced little noise. Still, as the currents of air-attuned Energy suffusing her body drifted away, a tremendous roar and the clacking, crashing sound of boulders skittering over the rocky ground echoed out of the darkness. Something big had noticed her arrival.

◈ OLIVIA ◈

Olivia summoned a ball of fire and tossed it high into the air, using her will to hold it, hovering there, shedding light over a large area. She was at the base of the stone chasm wall, and an uneven rocky floor spread out before her, littered with rocks and boulders from tiny to cottage-sized. She didn't see the source of the roar at first, but then the ground shook, and a bear-shaped boulder bounded into view. It was as bulky as a mid-sized sedan and covered with jagged, flint-like stone spikes. It turned to Olivia and roared, its huge, stony maw opening to reveal rows of uneven, razor-sharp stone teeth.

"Shit!" Olivia screamed, turning and trying to put some distance between herself and the red-eyed rock bear. It was fast, though, and as she darted behind a large boulder, it rushed past, swiping its claws along behind her, ripping chunks of stone out and showering her with rock dust. Olivia backpedaled and fired a Magma Ray into the rear haunch of the bear. The beam of super-hot magma splashed into its stony hide, spraying over it in a shower, but the bear only roared and turned to face her, obviously unharmed.

"Shit, shit!" Olivia tried her other meta-element spell, Arcfrost Cascade, pouring a buzzing, crackling torrent of freezing, electrified air out of her outstretched palm directly into the bear's face. It roared and shuddered but continued to advance on her, albeit in slow-motion. Each of its steps was ponderous, and Olivia could see it strain with the effort of moving toward her. She didn't know how long the effect would last, so she began preparing her next spell. She gathered a thread of water-attuned Energy and a thread of fire-attuned Energy, and she performed the weave for pyrosteam, pushing it into the form of her Fiery Burst spell.

A jet of superheated steam tore out of her palm, straight into the chest of the heaving rock bear. It blasted through its rocky flesh like a firehose hitting mud, and as the blistering torrent penetrated the cold rock of the bear's body, a series of thunderous cracks echoed through the cavern. The bear didn't even have a chance to roar as its stony form crumbled to wet, steaming rubble. A tremendous torrent of Energy motes flooded into Olivia as System messages appeared in her vision:

Congratulations! You have achieved level 14 Elemental Archon and have gained 10 Intelligence, 10 Will, and have 16 points to allocate.

Congratulations! You have learned the spell: Pyrosteam Drill—Basic.

Pyrosteam Drill—Basic: Prerequisite: Affinity—Fire, Affinity—Water. You conjure forth a piercing ray of pure pyrosteam. Energy cost: 200, Cooldown: Minimal.

"Thank you, Mr. Bear," Olivia said, hurrying to move across the rocky chasm floor. She still had to find the next door and wanted to maintain her lead on her competitors. She moved quickly but cautiously, unsure if more rocky monsters waited to attack her or if they might come along, given enough time. She kept her fire orb floating in the air above her, shedding light in a wide circle. It was in this flickering orange light that she spotted the iron door after crossing another hundred feet or so of rocky floor.

The door was mounted in another rocky wall, and Olivia wondered if there were more doors along the length of this vast, deep chasm. She wondered just how many starting rooms there were, and if there were paths through doors she hadn't seen. Deciding she couldn't waste time wondering about the unknown, she melted the padlock off the door and walked into a short tunnel, surprised to see a little, square, silver chest waiting for her. She closed the door and did her best to weld it shut with a ball of magma, then knelt before the chest. There wasn't any sort of lock on the clasp, and, glancing over the chest, she couldn't see any dangerous-looking runes, so she lifted open the lid.

The chest was only about as big as a lunchbox, and even then, the interior was almost empty. A lovely silver ring sat nestled in the folds of gray, silken lining. Olivia picked up the ring, admiring how the silver band was carved to look like intertwining vines of ivy with tiny blossoms here and there. When she bonded with the ring, she found it was a spacious and sturdy dimensional container, though nothing was hidden within it. She wore the ring on her left hand, reserving the right hand for her Copper cohort ring when she got it back. "All these storage rings—my little blue satchel is going to grow jealous."

She advanced on the next iron door, noting that it was built exactly like the other ones she'd opened. For the second time, though, it wasn't locked, and she pulled the bolt sideways and pulled on the door. The room she revealed was about five paces by five, with a low stone ceiling and solid stone walls. She couldn't see any doors or objects in the small space.

Olivia wondered if she'd taken a dead-end path or if there was some sort of puzzle she needed to solve to progress. She walked around the small perimeter, tapping at the walls, wishing she had her belongings so she could tap with her staff instead of her knuckles. "I'm wasting time here." Olivia walked back to the door, closed it, and sealed it with magma; then, she turned and faced the far wall. She held out her hand and cast Pyrosteam Drill straight into the center of the wall.

The narrow cone of superheated steam shot forth from her palm and penetrated the stone with a thunderous crack. Olivia moved the focus around in a small circle, blasting rock away in a cloud of hissing steam, dust, and rubble. When the spell faded and the air cleared, she could see the remnants of the wall and a partially deformed iron door. The metal had heated to the melting point in parts, and where it had drooped away from the frame, she could see darkness beyond.

Judging by the door's deformity and how it was still partially blocked by stone, Olivia didn't think she'd be able to open it normally. Instead, she concentrated on her Core, pulling forth a thread of air-attuned Energy and a thread of fire-attuned Energy, weaving them into the shape of plasma, and then casting Fiery Burst but pushing the plasma Energy into the spell pattern.

Congratulations! You have learned the spell: Plasma Wave—Basic.
Plasma Wave—Basic: Prerequisite: Affinity—Fire, Affinity—Air. You conjure forth a surging wave of pure plasma. Energy cost: 200, Cooldown: Minimal.

When the wave of crackling blue superheated gas and electricity hit the iron door, a tremendous surging burst of white light flared forth. When the afterimage finally cleared from Olivia's vision, she saw that the iron door had been reduced to a pile of molten slag. With a running hop, she jumped the threshold and the still glowing pile of molten metal and found herself in yet another short hallway facing another iron door. She didn't even think about it; she just tossed a ball of plasma at the padlock, averting her eyes as it flared and melted away. Then, Olivia slammed the bolt open and pulled the door.

An enormous octagonal room lit with glowing red crystals high up on the walls confronted her as the door opened. Standing in the center of the room, unmoving for the moment, was an iron man-shaped construct with an axe blade for a right hand and a long smooth barrel where the left should be. As Olivia took in the sight, the dark eye sockets on the construct started to glow with red light and, with a creaking, groaning grind, it bent to stare at her.

Olivia had time to take a breath and wonder if she should step into the room, but before she could do anything else, the huge iron man thrust its left nozzle forward, and a torrent of liquid flame surged toward her. Olivia screamed and dove back into the hallway, trying to slam the door shut as she passed. The flame surged against the door and the wall, splashing through into the hallway and licking at her heels while she hopped toward the door she had previously melted.

She seemed to be out of the range of the blast where she hunkered before the molten, destroyed door, but she knew that wouldn't last if the automaton moved closer to the door and pointed the nozzle into the hallway. "It's just fire. You don't have to be worried about fire," she said, concentrating on her Elemental Form spell and casting the fire version. Soon, her vision took on the bright sepia tones that told her it was working, and she walked forward, directly into the surging flames pouring forth from the construct's arm. She didn't even feel them. When she passed through the doorway and into the large octagonal room, she stepped out of the flamethrower's arc of fire and faced the huge metal being.

It seemed to take the construct a moment to realize she had passed through its flamethrower, but as Olivia continued to circle toward the far side of the room, it took note of her, and its gout of fire sputtered out. It straightened up and lifted its axe hand, taking one step toward her. Olivia had been expecting a new kind of violence, and she was ready with her new Plasma Wave spell.

She unleashed the flood of crackling, hissing, blue plasma toward the construct, and it tried to dodge, but it was huge, ponderous, and slow. The wave of plasma splashed against its lower torso, left hip, and thigh with a tremendous flash of white light and sizzling pops. The construct seemed to groan as it twisted sideways, half its support base suddenly turned to molten slag.

With all the grace of a collapsing building, it fell, metal ripping and rivets popping as its one good leg tried to fight gravity. When it thundered down against the metal floor, Olivia had another wave of plasma primed, and she unleashed it directly into the construct's chest. Another flash of white light, popping sizzling arcs of electricity, and then all was still, save the dripping and pooling of molten slag. A torrential wave of Energy surged into Olivia.

Congratulations! You have achieved level 15 Elemental Archon and have gained 10 Intelligence, 10 Will, and have 24 points to allocate.

Olivia glanced around the chamber for any other threats and, finding none, decided to spend her accumulation of attribute points. Looking at her status sheet, she reasoned she should improve her base physical stats to something an average human wouldn't call deficient. She'd spoken with plenty of colonists, enough to know that a "Good" stat for a baseline human was around eight or nine, so she increased her strength, dexterity, and agility to nine.

Olivia put the remaining extra points into vitality, bringing it to thirty-seven. She felt a surge of Energy rush through her body, leaving her feeling giddy and lightheaded for a moment. It made her feel strong, vibrant even, and she purposefully strode across the room to the locked iron door on the far side. A crackling ball of plasma materialized over her left hand, and she tossed it at the lock. When she opened the door, she found herself in a square room with a stairway leading down into darkness and a shoebox-sized silver chest sitting on the floor at the top of the stairs. "Well, that's level one done."

As she knelt to open the chest, Olivia ran through what she'd done so far in the dungeon, estimating how long it had taken her to clear the first level. It didn't seem like very much time had passed at all, maybe an hour. She felt absolutely fresh, too, thanks to the Energy she absorbed after killing the monsters that had been in her path. She carefully opened the lid of the chest and found a potion bottle and a black hunk of very heavy ore about the size of her fist.

When Olivia lifted the ore, hefting its solid, satisfying mass, she felt the depths of its potential pulling at her, and she knew it was valuable. She put it into her new storage ring and picked up the bottle. "Tyra's Tears of Renewal," she read. "Hmm." She didn't feel like she needed renewing at the moment, so she slipped the potion into her ring and then stood. "Time to descend," she said, smiling at how she'd taken to talking to herself in this dungeon, then she began the descent to the next level.

MORGAN

Morgan and Issa sat together in her father's kitchen, enjoying a huge breakfast of biscuits, eggs, sausage, and greens cooked with something remarkably like garlic. Issa had been filling Morgan in on what he'd missed while his body went through its changes. It amounted to a lot of her visiting and catching up with friends she'd been missing over the last couple of months. Morgan was just starting to wrap his head around the various names of her friends when a loud knock sounded from the front door.

Issa stood and went to answer, and Morgan kept eating. He could hear the muffled conversation taking place as he crunched down some bacon, and then the door thudded shut, and Issa came back into the kitchen, a harried look on her face. "Morgan, we need to go to the council building. There's an emergency meeting."

"Ungh, alright," he said, swallowing. "What's it about?"

"The trade ship my father was on was ambushed passing through the Deep Down. Some survivors jumped overboard and rode the current to safety, and they're going to make a report to the council." Her face was wan, and Morgan could see she was trying to hold her emotions in check, but a tiny tremble in her lower lip brought him to his feet, and he pulled her into a hug.

"Alright, alright, let's go hear what they have to say." He held her tight, and one soft sob escaped her, but then she sniffed and straightened up.

"Right. Let's see what the report is. Maybe there's hope."

They didn't waste time after that, most of their belongings were in their dimensional storage containers, so they didn't need to grab any gear. Morgan made sure the stove was off, then they hustled out the door and along the path leading to the bridge. They walked in silence, Issa not in the mood for small talk, and Morgan worried he'd say something wrong. He knew she was close to her father, and she'd be devastated if he'd been taken or killed in the raid.

Morgan knew what it was like to lose parents and family, but her relationship with her father was different. He'd been just a kid when his parents died, and he felt mostly numb to their loss. Every now and then, when half asleep, he'd remember something his mom said or the smell of his dad's cologne, and it would be fresh for just a moment, but it never lasted long. He supposed his sister's death was a lot more like how Issa would feel if her father were dead, and he didn't want her to have to experience that loss. He desperately hoped the news they were about to hear wouldn't be all bad.

They passed through the market square, down the street toward the mayor's office, and up a side street that Morgan hadn't explored before. It led past a library, a small park, and then into a courtyard before the town hall. A crowd was gathering outside, and just as Morgan and Issa arrived, the doors to the hall opened.

The crowd surged for the doors, jostling to get in and secure good seats. Though, there were still quite a few available when Morgan and Issa finally made their way inside. It was a high-ceilinged room with a dozen rows of benches facing a raised dais where an oblong table sat. Seven people sat at the table, and Morgan recognized two of them: the governor and Swent's father.

Morgan sat next to Issa on a bench about halfway from the front row, and then they waited as more people arrived and the seats at the table gradually filled with council members. The crowd hushed, and conversations dropped to murmurs as two bedraggled, hollow-eyed, Ardeni youths were ushered into the hall from a rear door. They were brought before the table of council members and given seats in the open area between the table and the rows of the seated populace.

"Silence! Silence, please!" the governor said, loudly at first but then in a shout. When the conversations fully died down, he cleared his throat and continued, "Thank you. We have before us Gil ap'Yarl and Dav ap'Hon. They bring grave news of the merchant flotilla from Fevra City. Men, thank you for standing before us; I know you're exhausted. Everyone here needs to hear your news, though, to organize the appropriate response. Please, give us your report." With that, he sat down, and Gil and Dav looked at each other nervously. Finally, one of the men stood, nodded to the assembled council members, then turned to the audience and spoke.

"I'm Gil ap'Yarl, and my news is awful, indeed. As we passed through the deep canyons, our entire trade flotilla was taken." The audience erupted in exclamations and questions; even Issa hissed and grabbed Morgan's arm, squeezing so hard that her sharp nails began to dig into his flesh through his shirt sleeve. Questions were shouted like, "What do you mean taken?" or "Taken by who?" or "Is everyone dead?"

"Silence, please! Let the council ask the questions for now. We'll take public comments and questions afterward!" The governor slammed his open palm on the table several times to get the audience to quiet down. "Gil, please describe, in detail, what happened."

"Alright, well, as I told Constable Turg, we were making good time down the Rill, picking up speed down into the deep canyons. It was about noontime two days ago when we got to the wide part of the river outside the Deep Down. That's when we knew something was wrong—they were hanging all over the cliffs. Even hanging from ropes that'd been strung over the river."

"Who was hanging?" one of the council members asked.

"The Urghat. The Urghat from the Deep Down, thousands of them."

"They were dead?" Holis, the governor, asked.

"Oh, aye. Long dead—scraps of rotten flesh and fur hanging from bones. Some of the crews started cheering when they saw all the dead Urghat, but Captain Thillis on the *Paradise*, he shouted for everyone to shut up. The order went out among the other boats, and pretty soon, we were drifting through the wide section, death hanging all around us. It was quiet, not a sound on the flat water. We had our bows out, watching the caves along the cliffs, but we didn't see anything. When all fourteen ships and boats were through the narrows, and we broke out the oars, that's when they came."

"Who came?" the same council member that had spoken earlier prodded.

"They swooped out of the caves, up high—gray-skinned with wings and talons. Their eyes were like coals, black and flaming red. They breathed gouts of smoke, swung swords and clubs, and grabbed us with their claws. I saw dozens carried off into the caverns and dozens cut to pieces. We tried to fight, truly, but when our boat caught fire, most of us jumped into the river. They plucked us out like garwings taking fish.

Me and Dav here, we were the only ones that got through to the narrows, and the current pulled us away. It was only luck! I saw so many grabbed up out of the water; I don't know why I didn't get grabbed! It wasn't fair, just luck!" The young man collapsed into his chair, holding his head in his hands, and the crowd broke into chaotic conversations and shouted questions. Morgan was jostled as some people tried to get closer to the council table to call out their questions and concerns.

Morgan felt Issa stand next to him, then the familiar pulse of her Energy gathering as she prepared her Battle Chant. She stood up on her bench, and her voice rang out, discordant and harsh, impossible to ignore, "Silence! You, Gil, and Dav, I'll have an answer: do you know of my father's fate? Roald the Artificer?"

Issa's eyes were purple-black smoke, and the force of her voice bore down on his mind, making him wince. He looked around and saw that he was barely affected compared to the general populace; most of them held their hands to their ears and hunkered down, looking at Issa with alarm. "Answer me!" Gil and Dav shot to their feet, almost like she'd forced them to, and while Gil shook his head violently, Dav managed to croak out a response.

"No, no, Miss! I'm sorry, but we barely managed to keep from burning, drowning, or getting hacked to pieces. I don't even know if my captain lived or died!"

"Miss ap'Roald! Please stop this and maintain your dignity!" the governor shouted. Morgan stood, straight-backed with his arms folded, towering over the assembled Ardeni folk. He wanted Issa to know he was there to support her, but he didn't say anything. Slowly, Issa let the buzzing background noise of her War Chant fade away, though a purple light still shone in her eyes.

"I'm sorry, Governor. I let my emotions get ahold of me. That said, I don't see what we have to discuss. Time is of the essence. We need to organize a rescue party." Several shouts of agreement rose from the crowd, and the governor's face began to redden.

"That's a decision for the council! We need to weigh the risks and determine the logistics!" Morgan felt Issa's chant start to buzz again, and then her voice rang out.

"Morgan and I will be organizing a rescue party near the merchant docks. Spread the word. We'll take as many as can fit on whatever boat we secure. If you organize something else, then we'll welcome the backup." With that, Issa turned, hopped off the bench, and strode toward the door. People made way for her, and Morgan hurried after her, not sparing a glance for the dumbstruck council.

"I'm sorry, Morgan," Issa said as they walked to the market square.

"Why?"

"For assuming you'd be coming with me on the rescue."

"Nothing to be sorry for when you're a hundred percent right." Issa looked up at him and took his hand. As they walked, Morgan glanced over his shoulder and saw that quite a few people had followed them out of the town hall. Some were running off in different directions, but a good crowd had formed behind them.

"We have a crowd following us," he said to Issa.

"Good. The council will debate for a while, but they'll realize we're right. By the time they come around, we'll be ready to set out. Morgan, if no one volunteers a boat, we might have to buy one." She looked up at him, an eyebrow raised.

"It shouldn't be a problem. We have thousands of beads and quite a few other valuables we can trade."

"You won't have to worry about a boat, Issa!" A white-haired Ardeni woman strode forward from behind Morgan, and with a start, he realized he recognized her. It was Swent's mother. "Rua is among the missing; you can take one of our barges—it'll carry a hundred folk on its deck."

"Good, thank you, Lynna." Issa reached out a hand toward Lynna but then dropped it and kept walking. "We'll do everything we can to get her back."

A series of wooden ramps led down from the market square to the riverbank under the vast, sweeping arch of the bridge. When they finished descending and stood on the boardwalk that ran along the river, Issa turned to Lynna and said, "I'll gather the volunteers here. Can you have one of your captains bring the barge around? The sooner we're off, the better our chances."

"Yes, I'll have him bring it around. I'll offer all of our sailors hazard pay to crew the ship. I'm sure we can come up with enough hands from among them." She turned and made her way down the long boardwalk and around the bend where tall wooden warehouses and docks started to protrude into the river.

Issa's eyes flared purple, and the discordant buzz of her chant started up again, "Listen! All of you that followed us here. We need hunters. We need fighters. We're going into battle against something terrible, but if our missing loved ones are to have a chance, we need to hurry. Get your things and spread the word. In one hour, we leave with the best one hundred fighters that Tarn's Crossing can muster."

⚭ MORGAN ⚭

Morgan stood near the prow of the long flat cargo barge, looking over the assembled grim-faced warriors. By the time the barge had arrived at the central pier, Issa had selected thirty-two experienced hunters and fighters. Most of them were above level twenty, which they called tier two. As she evaluated other prospects, the governor had finally descended to the docks with an entourage of town guards and militia. He'd informed Issa, trying to save some face, that the council had agreed to allow her and Morgan to accompany the rescue mission. Issa had started to argue but contained herself when she saw that the governor was sending his guard captain and forty warriors. Captain Rorth was a huge Ardeni, only five or so inches shy of Morgan's height, and he was apparently tier three, so, somewhere between level thirty and forty.

Even so, Issa had wanted to get more volunteers, bringing their number up to an even hundred, but Captain Rorth had insisted that any more volunteers would just lead to chaos in battle, and he didn't see the point in further delay. That settled, they'd boarded the barge with five brave sailor volunteers and the seventy-two hunters and fighters and begun the journey upriver. Morgan had wondered how the long flat barge with no sails would move upriver, but he'd soon learned that it was a marvel of artificed ingenuity. It had four brass rings, each about five feet in diameter, that hung off the aft deck into the water. The rings somehow generated a current that pushed the boat along, even into the Rill Catcher's flow.

"So, Morgan," Captain Rorth said, walking along the rail of the barge toward him, "Do you have any idea what these creatures that attacked our trade flotilla are?"

"No, I sure don't." Morgan turned to Rorth and leaned back against the railing, folding his arms on his chest. Issa was talking to some hunters a dozen paces away, but she looked up and frowned as Rorth continued toward Morgan.

"Don't you think it's odd that these new beings arrived in caverns home to Urghat for hundreds of years around the same time your people arrived on our world?"

"Is it? Odd? As you said, I'm new here. I don't know how often hostile groups move to new territory in this world. Back on my homeworld people were fighting over space all the time."

"Fanwath is a big place, and perhaps we've been lucky in our little corner of it, but yes, this is quite unusual." Rorth now stood a few feet from Morgan, and he leaned against the rail, casually mimicking Morgan's posture.

"Huh. Well, what's the plan? Seems like fighting them from the barge will be rather stupid if they can fly and breathe fire. Is there a way into the caves where we don't have to approach them like sitting ducks?"

"Sitting ducks?" he scratched his short silver beard thoughtfully. "I'm not familiar with this term, but I think I take your meaning. Yes, we'll beach the barge a few miles from the Deep Down. There are tunnels we can enter downriver from the deep canyons that lead into their caves. I'm glad to see I'm not the only one that thought floating into their abattoir would be foolish."

"Sounds good," Morgan nodded and turned to survey the river, inhaling deeply of the fresh air. He was still getting used to his sharper senses; ever since he'd woken from his "Metamorphosis," colors popped more sharply, details stood out more clearly, sounds traveled further, and the smells, the smells were intoxicating. Standing there, leaning over the rail, he could smell the tang of algae on stone, the blossoms on the shrubs and trees along the banks, and the hint of ozone from the summer shower that had dampened the grass and dirt a few hours ago.

"Well? What kind of skills do you bring to the table, Morgan? I missed your duel with Swent, but I heard you had some powerful Energy attacks. Is that so?" Rorth had moved to his side and shared his view of the river.

"Yeah, that's right. I'm moderately skilled with the sword, but I can dish out some Energy attacks. What about you?"

"Oh, I'm a Beast Hunter. It's a refinement of the standard Hunter class. I have some abilities that help me to identify a beast's weaknesses, and I'm a very skilled bowman. I noticed that blade on your hip there. I'm assuming it's intelligent? That's why you don't store it in that ring?"

"Mmhmm," Morgan said, looking down at the captain. What was he fishing for? Maybe he just wanted to assess an unknown asset, but something about his haughty tone rubbed him the wrong way. "Yeah, it's a decent sword. I'll be using it if the spaces are cramped. Otherwise, I have some other options."

"I'm not trying to pry, friend. I just want to know if I should put you near the front of the column as we enter the tunnels. The Deep Down is a big place. We've fought with the Urghat for more than a century, and we've never explored all the way in, even when we mounted major offensives."

"Oh, Issa and I will be near the front, yes." Morgan glanced over at Issa while he spoke, wondering if he could use her as an excuse to step away from the captain.

"She's still in tier one, though, correct?"

"Almost tier two, and she's got a powerful class. You'll want her near me."

"Hmm," Rorth said, stroking his silvery beard, his equally silver eyes looking into the distance while he contemplated. "Very well. Thanks for the dialogue, Morgan. Here's hoping we don't lose more people than we're trying to save in there." He turned and strode toward the barge's stern, calling to one of his men.

"I think he's trying to sniff out the other alpha in the party," Issa said quietly, walking up to him.

"Well, he's barking up the wrong tree; can't he see that you're the boss around here?" Morgan chuckled, draping an arm over Issa's shoulders.

"Funny, but he won't respect me until I'm a lot closer to his level." Her voice didn't sound amused, and Morgan knew her mind was on her father. Things didn't look good for him; Morgan had to admit. If these flying assholes had killed all the Urghat, why would they keep the captured Ardeni alive? That was assuming he'd been captured and wasn't one of the Ardeni slaughtered in the attack.

"Hey, I won't promise your dad is going to be ok, but we're going to do everything possible to get him out. Listen, I know it's a terrible thought, but if he's dead, at least you know he died loving you and on good terms. God, I know I'm probably saying all the wrong things, but I guess I'm trying to say that you always were good to him. He was proud of you, and there's no bad blood between you two. No unfinished business. Does that make any sense?" Issa was silent, looking out over the water, and Morgan suddenly wished his mouth had a rewind function. The silence stretched into an uncomfortable minute, and Morgan was frantically thinking of something to say when she finally sighed and turned into him, pulling him into a tight hug.

"It makes sense, Morgan. Thank you; I know I have a lot to be thankful for, and I know how harsh life can be. I hope we can save him, though." Morgan felt his racing heart start to slow, and he stroked Issa's hair, watching the banks of the wide, slow river drift past. The barge continued up the river for another two hours before Morgan heard Rorth calling orders to the volunteer crew, and it started to veer toward a wide tributary that branched away between some hills to the south.

"Gear up! Be ready!" one of Rorth's sergeants called out. Morgan was content to let the soldiers take care of the logistics of organizing the party and drew his sword in one hand, standing near the prow, keeping an eye on the shore ahead of the boat. After only thirty minutes or so, the tributary became too narrow and shallow for the big barge to continue, and Rorth called for the soldiers and volunteers to descend to the bank down one of a dozen rope ladders they threw out. Morgan looked down the fifteen-foot drop to the grassy bank and hopped over the rail. He was pleased with how gracefully he sailed through the air to land lightly, barely having to bend his knees to catch his momentum. He'd felt like something unseen was different about his body, and though he felt more robust than ever, he'd noticed that he moved more lightly with greater precision.

Not to be outdone, Issa hopped down to join him, though she stumbled a step, and he reached out to catch her shoulder. She nodded to him, drew her rapier, and moved to where Rorth was organizing the column. Morgan followed close behind. As they approached, Rorth nodded and said, "Morgan, Issa, up front with me. Sergeants, count out your squads and get in formation." Morgan moved to where he indicated, and soon the column of soldiers and hunters was moving through the brush up a narrow canyon, searching for a cave that Rorth supposedly had seen before. They didn't encounter anything other than an aggressive boar analog that charged and was filled with arrows before taking more than two steps. The sun was sinking in the west when they came to the end of a narrow box canyon where a tangle of dead trees and scrub obscured a wide, dark tunnel that descended at a gentle grade to the east. After they'd cut away a narrow path, the column continued into the darkness. Morgan walked in the front, Bloodfang in his hand and Azure Sight turning the darkness to shades of bright gray and blue. Further back in the column, some soldiers ignited light stones and held them aloft, ready to rush forward in the event of an ambush.

Morgan could feel Issa's Battle Chant buzzing just behind her teeth, ready to flow out and saturate the space with her power. Rather than narrowing and becoming more challenging to navigate as Morgan expected, the tunnel continued to widen. Soon they were walking in a tunnel with a ceiling nearly out of view above their heads and walls that were easily forty yards apart. "What the fuck made this tunnel?"

"Nobody knows what race crafted the Deep Down, but this is nothing," Rorth said from his left. "When we get really deep, you'll see halls that all of Tarn's Crossing could sit within." In his enhanced vision, Morgan studied the walls and ceiling and saw that they were incredibly smooth, not like something that tectonic activity would create. He supposed the tunnel could have been carved by a massive river or maybe volcanic flow, but he couldn't imagine the kind of cataclysm that would result from such a vast flow of magma. He was trying to imagine the source of the smooth-carved stone when he saw a shadow move along the top of the tunnel about fifty yards downslope. He hissed and raised his sword, pointing.

"What?" Rorth whispered.

"Movement. Get ready!" Suddenly he felt a buzzing in his bones, and his muscles ignited with Energy as Issa started to hum her Battle Chant. Rorth yelled for his sergeants to ready their men, then he moved next to Morgan, a huge black spear with a bright, shining tip held in both his hands. Morgan studied the spot where he'd seen the shadow, and then he caught another one moving just a bit to the left. As he followed its movement, he saw another and another start to move; soon, the ceiling was crawling with shadows. "There're dozens of them. Get ready!" he said again.

As he strained to see the details of the shadows, one of them detached from the ceiling, falling into the air in the center of the tunnel, and massive wings blossomed from its narrow form. With a horrible shriek, the creature pumped its wings and sped directly toward Morgan. Morgan wasn't standing twiddling his thumbs, though; he'd primed a Vortex Lance, and, without waiting for an invitation, he unleashed it. With a concussive blast, the projectile of Energy ripped out of his outstretched sword, a spiral of ripped air following in its wake as it struck the flying shadow dead center with a wet, cracking impact that echoed in the tunnel. The winged creature's flight path arced up into a backflip, and then it streaked to the ground, landing with a wet, reverberating thud.

"Nice shot," Rorth said, but he'd barely gotten the words out before another shriek tore through the air, then another and another, until the air was echoing with hundreds of them. Accompanying the shrieks were the sounds of hundreds of flapping wings as the shadows clinging to the ceiling took flight toward the column of would-be rescuers.

⊗ MORGAN ⊗

Morgan charged into a clump of the gargoyles, as he'd dubbed them in his own mind, and fired off another Azure Burst just as it came off cooldown. Six or so of the creatures tumbled through the air and over the rocky ground, supernatural flames clinging to their thick, clay-like hide. They screamed in agony or became still, depending on the severity of their burns and secondary wounds. The soldier they'd been hacking at was beyond help—most of his neck severed and massive punctures and contusions liberally covering his battered corpse. Morgan heard Issa's Hexing Shriek and the resultant wail of the creatures she'd targeted.

Arrows were streaming through the air, some of them flaming and some exploding. One of the hunters could paralyze the creatures his arrows hit, which helped immensely, but it didn't stop the swarm of shadows descending on the narrow column of rescuers. Morgan was at a loss with so many targets, his sword was coated in blood, and he could feel the Rager within it sending furious waves of Energy into his arm. He didn't even need to use his Energy-imbued forms to slash through limbs and bones, so furiously did Bloodfang strike. For a while, he'd stood back-to-back with Rorth and Issa, and they'd slain more than a dozen of the creatures, but as the battle wore on and fresh waves of flying combatants fell upon them, they grew separated.

Morgan could see over the heads of the fighting, surging, screaming melee, and was fairly sure Issa was still with Rorth about fifty yards downslope in the tunnel. He'd inadvertently carried himself away from them by charging clumps of gargoyles. Had they made any progress? Gray bodies were lying strewn all over the tunnel floor, but Morgan also saw the torn and broken bodies of a dozen or more Ardeni. Rorth's sergeants were shouting for order, trying to rally men and women into defensive lines and coordinate their fire, but their shouts seemed to add to the chaos. Many of the hunters had never worked with the garrisoned troops of Tarn's before and didn't respond the way the sergeants expected.

Morgan charged into another cluster of the gargoyles that had started to overwhelm a line of archers and reached out with his Energy Drain, targeting as many creatures as possible. He still had thousands of Energy points available to him, so he tore a stream of Energy out of eleven creatures; a massive influx of dark, bloody Energy poured into his channels. He surged forward into the cluster, hacking and kicking, breaking them apart as they scrabbled at the ground and flapped their wings in terror. A few of the creatures managed to break free and flee, floundering through the air to disappear into the deep shadows of the tunnel ceiling. The rest, Morgan left broken and torn on the cavern floor. Relieved of the pressure, the hunters began a new assault on the gargoyles that harried their comrades.

Some sort of cry broke out among the gargoyles, an ululating howl that spread from one pack to the next, and then they were airborne and flying away, some of them clutching the limp forms of Ardeni. Flaming and crackling arrows soared after the retreating horde, and Morgan launched a Vortex Lance into a clump of them, savagely roaring when it struck home, sending a limp gargoyle tumbling to crack up on the boulder-strewn ground. Morgan ran back to the head of the column, where he could see Issa and Rorth standing in a circle with another ten or so Ardeni. Suddenly the air filled with golden motes of Energy as it coalesced and streamed into the hunters, fighters, and Morgan. To Morgan's shock, a massive ribbon of Energy shot forth into the air, following the path of the gargoyles that had flown away into the shadows.

Congratulations! You have achieved level 29 Vortex Duelist and have gained 8 Intelligence, 8 Agility, 6 Will, 6 Dexterity.

He opened his mouth to call out to Issa, but then crackling blue light filled his vision, and he was no longer standing in the corpse-strewn tunnel; he was in a serene ancient vault with Gareth Tohlemay, the Azure Paladin. "Student! You've grown in both stature and power. I'm surprised to see you again so soon!"

"Gareth, um, sir, I was in a perilous situation with friends who'd just been attacked; I'm not sure I can be here right now." Morgan gestured to his blood-soaked sword, but then he noticed that he wasn't holding it—it was on his belt, and it and he were perfectly clean. "I'm not really here, am I?"

"Correct, student. You should know this by now. We're meeting with our minds! I'll be brief; just know: any time you spend here will only be fractionally reflected in reality."

"Oh, I wasn't sure because I didn't wake up for nearly a day last time. I was wounded, though." Morgan shrugged and walked forward toward the paladin.

"Yes, well, I can see that you've gone through much since then. The fact you're here tells me that you're ready to receive another impartment of my legacy. I'd like you to make a choice this time."

"A choice?"

"Yes, we'll be taking one of two paths with your training today. Nothing will stop you from expanding your abilities without me; after all, I learned all of my spells and skills without a mentor's help, but I'll be guiding you down one of two roads. Are you interested in learning more of my mastery over Energy, or would you like me to help you make my abilities your own? Your Core's Energy does not match mine, and I can only imagine that when you use my 'azure' abilities, they aren't nearly as effective as they could be if you learned to modify and create your own spells that utilize your Core's affinity."

"Do you mean the void-attuned Energy I have at the center of my Core now?"

"Precisely. When I taught you before, you didn't have any attunement. My own spells made sense. Now you have an attunement, and I believe if you can make some tweaks to my spells, they'll be far more effective in your hands."

"What about your legacy?"

"What I teach you is my legacy. What you teach others about me and my lessons is my legacy." He reached forward and laid a hand on Morgan's shoulder, a friendly smile revealing straight white teeth.

"Alright, understood. In that case, I'd like to learn how to modify your abilities to better suit my Core."

"Very good. Now listen and do as I say; as you've told me, time is short." Morgan nodded. "Good. Now close your eyes and turn your attention inward to your Core. I want you to concentrate on your Energy and watch what it does when you prime an Azure Burst." Morgan did as he was told, watching the spinning maelstrom of pure Energy orbiting the pulsing, throbbing vortex of his void-attuned Energy. Then he thought about his Azure Burst ability and began to activate it. Strands of Energy rushed out of his Core into the pathways surrounding it, weaving together into an elaborate pattern, sitting there, primed for him to release the spell. "Do you see it? Do you see the pattern?"

"Yes," Morgan said softly, amazed that he'd never watched his spell take form before.

"Now release the Energy and send it back to your Core. I want you to pull forth some strands of your void Energy. I want you to hold them ready, and then, as you prime Azure Burst again, I want you to feed the void-attuned Energy to the pattern." Morgan did as the paladin instructed, pulling forth some strands of void-attuned Energy, almost like he was about to perform his cultivation drill, but he held the strands poised near his Core and began the Azure Burst spell. As soon as he felt the pattern pulling Energy from his Core, he pushed the void-attuned Energy toward it. The pattern hungrily pulled the Energy, and he felt the spell was ready. "Good! Finish the spell. Release it!"

Morgan cast his Azure Burst, but instead of a crackling blue pulse of fire rolling out of him, a black, hungry wave of darkness surged out, engulfing the Azure Paladin and a good portion of his sanctuary. Just as the darkness came though, it faded away, everything it touched, including the paladin, unharmed.

Congratulations! You have learned the spell: Void Wave—Improved.
Void Wave—Improved: A true paladin wades into the thick of the battle, fearing not the surrounding hordes. Channel your Energy to release a wave of void Energy, dealing void-based damage and demoralizing your enemies that fail to resist your will. Energy Cost: 250, Cooldown: Long.

"Void Wave? Why not Void Burst?" He looked at the paladin.

"That's the question you have? Ahh, the flightiness of youth. Morgan, the System has named your spell for you because you didn't create the pattern. I imagine it chose the term 'wave' because that's how void Energy propagates, as opposed to Azure Fire, which tends to burst or explode outward. However, my student, what's more important is that you saw the pattern and changed the spell. Now, if you can learn to weave your Energy into patterns of your own, you can start to learn how to make spells without relying on the System or me to grant them to you. Do you see what you've learned?" Morgan did understand the value of the lesson, and he tried to grasp the implications. He understood the idea that Energy moving in patterns through his pathways is what made the spells, but how would one learn the patterns?

"I see the confusion behind your eyes. Patterns for spells like Azure Burst are quite complex, but there are much simpler spells. I'd start studying those; as you learn what sorts of patterns create what sorts of effects, you can start to combine and alter them to see what happens. I'd recommend doing it in a safe area, away from things and people you care about."

"Why did my new void spell come out as improved?"

"No doubt because of your strong affinity with void Energy. You subconsciously optimized the passage the Energy took into the pattern. Take what I've taught you and practice it, Morgan. When you return to me, I'd like to see you wielding more spells of your own. Goodbye for now, student."

"Goodbye and thank . . ." Morgan was cut off as his vision crackled with blue light again, and then he was stumbling forward, suddenly mid-step in the cavern where the battle had taken place. He looked around and found that everything was as it had been when his consciousness had been snatched away to meet with Gareth. He saw Issa and the clump of Ardeni and charged toward them. "Issa! Are you alright?"

"Morgan! Yes, we are, but we need to regroup; we need to get out or get deeper where we can't be ambushed from above!"

"This huge tunnel narrows and opens onto smaller pathways a few miles ahead. I think we should make haste to it," Rorth added, walking around the group to stare past Morgan to the field of battle. "Soldiers, gather up the fallen in your containers! Make a count of the dead. We move in five." While the soldiers moved to follow Rorth's directive, Morgan went to stand next to Issa, and he did an informal count on the survivors. He counted forty-seven Ardeni besides Issa and Rorth. They'd lost almost half their numbers.

"We can't afford many more battles like that. We've already lost as many people as we're hoping to rescue," Rorth said quietly.

"I won't be turning back," Issa said, glancing at Morgan. He nodded, and she continued, "If you want to take your men home, Rorth, I understand, but Morgan and I will continue until we know the fate of the people taken on the river."

"We'll continue for now." Rorth didn't say more, just walked to the center of the passage and scanned the ceiling, presumably looking out for more attackers.

"Those creatures didn't seem very intelligent to me. Less than Yeksa, even, though a lot tougher," Morgan said to Issa.

"Yes, much tougher. They were smart enough to ambush us and smart enough to cut their losses. Don't underestimate them, Morgan."

"I won't, but I'm just saying—I think there might be more to them. Like, they came off as mindless minions to me. Maybe I'm reading too much into it, maybe I'm thinking of too many movies, but I feel like something worse than those gargoyles is calling the shots." Issa, used to Morgan mentioning things from Earth that she had no understanding of, looked at him and frowned.

"I worry that you might be right," she said, lifting her rapier and walking toward where the much-shortened line of hunters and soldiers was reassembling.

◈ BRONWYN ◈

Bronwyn trudged through the light dusting of snow, climbing yet another ancient rockslide that had buried a portion of the old road. Whatever civilization that had built the road had long ago stopped using or maintaining it, and as she moved ever northward and into higher and higher elevations, the going had gradually become rougher. Over the last week or so, she felt like she'd covered a few dozens of miles, and her quarry didn't seem any closer. Twice she'd been set upon by packs of boyii hounds or their cousins; they had similar shapes and tails, but their coloring wasn't as bright as the ones down on the plains. These creatures were a bit larger, and shades of red, black, and gray dominated their fur.

The first time a pack had come out of the hills and surrounded her, Bronwyn had tried out her Solar Shell spell. A bright nimbus of yellow light had wrapped her, clinging to her flesh, and she'd been able to rebuff all but the strongest, most direct bites from the beasts. While they nipped and bit at her, yelping with pain from the glowing shell that seemed to scorch their mouths, Bronwyn had gone to work kicking and punching, driving them off in a matter of minutes. The second pack hadn't caught her by surprise, and when she sensed them coming out of the hills, she'd taken the attack to their alpha, a huge black and rust spotted male with three tails. She saw him coming up over a rocky outcropping and charged, summoning her Solar Shell and Solar Arms. When she pummeled him into a yelping submission, running with his tails tucked, the other boyii had turned and slunk away into the hills.

Bronwyn slid down the rocky scree back on the road and picked up her pace, jogging down the old highway, constantly scanning for those "Cadwalli" tracks she'd been doggedly following day and night. She only slept for a few hours each night, tucking herself in under fallen logs, between boulders, or, on one lucky night, in a shallow cave. The peaks had grown larger and more numerous over the days, dwarfing what she remembered of the Rockies from a camping excursion she'd gone on with a few friends in Colorado. One particular peak, off to the north and east, loomed over the others like a giant white claw protruding from the earth. It had to be twice as tall as any of the surrounding peaks, and the way it rose up and hooked over the range made it seem almost sinister and domineering. "I hope this guy isn't headed there," she huffed, but it didn't seem like he was; the road had a westerly veer, and the Cadwalli seemed to be following it.

It was another four days of hard travel before the tracks veered off the road, moving more directly north through a high, frost-covered valley. Tall, scraggly, pine-like trees grew there, though they were sparsely scattered through the valley, almost like the place had been forested before. Bronwyn's suspicions proved true when she tripped and fell on her face, having jammed her foot into a snow-buried stump. She slowed her pace, then, realizing that though the dusting of snow was new, there were older drifts scattered throughout the windblown vale. Her tracking ability was strange; though the Cadwalli had passed through before the latest snow, and his tracks were buried, she still saw them highlighted on top of the snow. They glowed brightly in her vision, more so as the days passed, and she gained ground on him. "Well, I think that's why they're getting brighter," she chuckled, talking to her imaginary audience. She hadn't done that in a long time, but out here, alone in the strange mountains, she'd taken to imagining she was live-streaming again.

Halfway through the valley, Bronwyn crested a small hill and froze in her tracks. Half a mile or so further into the valley, she saw a long tendril of smoke drifting into the gray sky. "Ahh, is it you at last?" She crouched down and moved quickly down the hill to obscure herself among a stand of trees. She was wearing her spiked leather armor over a double layer of her Contribution Store clothes. Even with a pair of thick leather gloves on her hands and a heavy cloak around her neck, she was chilly. "Not the best environment for a child of Summer, wouldn't you agree, chat?" She spoke softly, creeping through the trees, trying to get closer to the source of the smoke without making any noise.

The layer of snow on the mulchy, dormant grass of the valley made it easy to move quietly, so it wasn't with any great difficulty that she found herself peering from behind the broad bole of a tree into a clearing at a bizarre spectacle. A dozen or more braziers had been set up in an elaborate pattern in the center of the clearing, and they smoldered with the red light of coals. In the center of the spiraling pattern was a stone slab, round and perfectly flat, and a larger brazier sat at its center, flickering with blue, smokey flames. A very large goat-like man sat in front of the brazier, pouring over a thick black tome, one hand tracing lines on the page, the other shaking a strangely tinny-sounding little bell. Bronwyn had heard descriptions of Cadwalli before, and she'd always pictured them as smaller than humans, but this guy was hulking with black fur, red-orange eyes, and long, black spiraling horns coming out of the top of his head.

She almost started talking to her imaginary audience but pressed her lips together to stifle herself. With the noise the Cadwalli was making and the way he was intently staring at the book, Bronwyn didn't think there was much chance he'd notice her. Still, she carefully backed away, moving twenty paces or so back through the trees, until she came to a large tree with thick, heavy boughs of needles hanging down, heavy with snow. She clambered up among the branches, finding a nice, wide V where she could comfortably sit and bide her time. She'd found the mysterious Thun, and now she just had to wait until the right moment to strike. She fished her magical stone out of her ring and held it in her palm. Had the moon looked full last night? It was definitely big, but the clouds hadn't made studying it easy. The stone was still black, and it didn't give any hint that it was getting ready to change colors anytime soon. She tucked it into her belt, then leaned back against the tree's trunk, closing her eyes and catching fitful winks while she waited.

She spent the night, uncomfortable and cramped, up in that tree. When the black night faded to gray dawn, she looked at her stone, and it was still black. Very carefully, Bronwyn shifted and pulled herself to a standing position on her perch, allowing the blood to flow through her numb butt and legs. She stood there, leaning against the trunk, listening with everything she had, hoping for some clue as to what Thun was doing down there in the clearing. After a long while, the wind brought with it a faint, droning hum, and she realized he was chanting something. Betting on his preoccupation, Bronwyn took the opportunity to climb down from the tree and sneak up toward the clearing again, hoping to catch another glimpse of the strange Cadwalli's activities. His droning hum became louder, and when she got back to the tree she'd hidden behind before, she peered around to see the goat-like man kneeling in the center of the stone, a bloodied knife in his right hand and his left wrist held over the brazier, dribbling blood into the flames. His weird buzzing hum set her teeth on edge, and she involuntarily shivered.

Bronwyn carefully padded away from the clearing, dragging her cloak behind her to obscure her snowy prints, then reluctantly clambered back up into her tree. She badly wanted to run around and stretch her limbs, but she couldn't risk tipping the Cadwalli off. It seemed like his preparations were approaching some sort of crescendo, and she hoped that tonight would be the night, and in the morning, she'd be able to end this hunt once and for all. She paused to contemplate what that meant: she'd be trying to kill another person in the morning, all because the Summer Queen had told her that he was a bad guy. "I really must trust her, hmm?" Either that, she reasoned, or she'd been totally brainwashed while in the Fae Realms. "Maybe a little bit of both?"

There was no denying that Bronwyn felt different than she did prior to touching that crystal token that Hops had offered her. She was happier, less doubt-ridden, and filled with the sense of purpose that her task provided her. Even after a week or more of hiking through chilly temperatures, she felt good. She'd always liked hiking, though, and the fresh air and majesty of the mountains hadn't hurt her mood one bit. What a task, though! For her first job, she was sent to assassinate a being that was, ostensibly, far more powerful than she. Just how weak would this ritual make him in order to give Bronwyn a chance at defeating him come dawn?

As she sat back against the hard tree trunk, Bronwyn marveled at the idea that she'd been hiding in this tree for a day and planned to for at least another night. How strange her life had become on this new planet! She'd gone from helping to settle a colony, to hunting around the plains and dueling Urghat, to visiting mythical fairy people, to hunting through the mountains to kill an evil goat-man. She hoped he was evil. A slight frown twisted the corners of her lips down, but she shook her head to clear the thought; she had to be committed, serious, and one hundred percent game-ready. There wasn't room for doubt, not if she wanted a chance to survive. Bronwyn wasn't sure why she felt so confident that she'd need everything she had to win, but she did, and she'd learned to trust her gut when it came to judging competition.

Bronwyn fell into a fitful sleep as darkness settled on the valley, the little black stone clutched in her hand, and an extra cloak wrapped around her to provide some more cushion against the hard bark. Sometime in the middle of the night, she was woken by an uncomfortable sensation in her hand. She was startled awake with her eyes wide open, listening for what had disturbed her before realizing it was the stone. She carefully extracted her hand from her wrapped cloaks and held the stone out in the dim moonlight. Sure enough, it was gleaming white in the darkness—her time had come. Bronwyn carefully stowed away the extra cloaks wrapping her, then slid down the tree, slowing her descent by holding onto one branch and then another.

She crept through the powdery snow toward the clearing, aiming for her usual watching tree, glancing up between the treetops to see that the moons were more than halfway through the sky. Dawn would be upon her in an hour or so. She approached the tree, pressing her body against the bark, and then slowly slid to the side, peering around to see what Thun was up to in the clearing. The braziers were dimly glowing in the dark, faint wisps of smoke drifting up to the moonlit sky, but the central stone was empty save for the larger brazier. Eyes wide, Bronwyn scanned the clearing, looking for any sign of the Cadwalli. Something was wrong: before, when she'd watched him, her tracking ability had exposed dozens of sets of his tracks around the clearing and braziers. Now, the snow was pristine, without any highlighted footprints. Suddenly the hairs at the nape of her neck tingled, and Bronwyn spun around.

Thun smirked from the shadows, his orange-red eyes gleaming down at her from beneath his horned brow. "I thought I smelled the taint of Summer nearby. You came too soon, whelp; had the sun been in the sky, things might have gone differently for you." Then, he began to laugh, a deep, wet sound that originated down in his chest. Bronwyn stood up and edged sideways, ready to slip behind the tree.

"I thought you were doing some kind of ritual?"

"Oh, I did, I did. I see your Lady sent you with some intelligence, hmm? Pity, she didn't warn you that the weakness she promised I'd be stricken with wouldn't come until the night was gone. I'm going to enjoy this, Summerling. My Lady will reward me for what I'm about to do to you; I'll savor this night for many decades. Hah, if only I could thank the Summer Bitch myself! Sadly, she's not likely to invite me to her court."

"You're awfully full of yourself," Bronwyn couldn't hide the false note in her bravado, though she tried.

"With good reason, whelp. Now *come forward!*" When he said those words, Bronwyn felt her muscles start to respond without her bidding. Her left leg took a step, but she scowled and yanked it back as soon as she realized it.

"Fuck you," she said, a little more steel in her voice.

"Ahh, so there are some humans with spines, hmm? No wonder the Bitch recruited you."

"Watch your mouth, asshole!"

"Did I touch a soft spot?"

"Nah, but how 'bout I beat that smirk off your ugly face? Give you a chance to apologize."

"Insolence, too? Wonderful!" Suddenly Thun moved; his body blurred, and a booming crunch sounded as his left hoof stomped forward, rippling the ground and sending Bronwyn flying to bounce off the tree trunk and roll into the brazier-lit meadow. She felt dazed but also pissed off, tumbling with the momentum of her fall to bounce to her feet, crouched and ready, facing into the shadows of the trees where Thun's lantern-like eyes regarded her.

"C'mon, then. I heard the Winter agents were all chicken-shit anyway." She taunted, backing further into the clearing. She didn't want to give away her thoughts, so she forced herself not to look at the slightly lighter sky limning the eastern horizon.

◈ OLIVIA ◈

Olivia stepped off the stairway onto a polished marble floor the color of a pale pink rose. Warm light suffused the air, making the small chamber feel welcoming and restful. Opposite the stairs, about five paces away, a cherrywood door with a crystal doorknob awaited her. She glanced around the room, ensuring she hadn't missed anything, then walked up to the door and tried the handle. It opened easily, swinging toward her and revealing a short hallway that led to a similar door. "Hmm, not locked on this level?"

The next door also opened easily, revealing a room just like the one she'd come from but lacking a stairway. Five or six strides should take her to the next door, so she walked into the room, took two steps, and smashed her face into an invisible wall. "Ow! Damnit!" She backed away, holding her nose, to see if it was bleeding, but it wasn't—just sore. She looked more closely at the barrier she'd smashed into and realized it wasn't invisible—just perfectly clear glass or crystal. She tapped it, eliciting a clicking chime as her nails bounced off. Was she supposed to break the barrier somehow or circumvent it?

Olivia contemplated trying to blast the wall with pyrosteam or magma, then wondered if it was designed to be reflective. Out of caution, she stood to one side and aimed her hand at an angle toward the wall, then cast Pyrosteam Drill. A narrow cone of superheated steam erupted from her palm, hit the crystalline barrier, and reflected cleanly away to smash into the marble wall opposite her, gouging away the rose-colored stone and boring into whatever lay beyond. Olivia halted the spell and held a hand to the crystalline barrier; it was perfectly cool to the touch.

Olivia changed tactics, aiming her hands at the barrier again and casting Wind Gust, but instead of feeding the spell pattern the air-attuned Energy it wanted, she pushed out a thread of water-attuned Energy, twisted into the form of ice. A torrent of frost sprayed out of her palm, coating the barrier.

Congratulations! You have learned the spell: Frost Blast—Basic.

Olivia didn't bother reading the spell description; she just kept pouring Energy into the spell, watching as frost and then hunks of ice began to coat the barrier. She continued until she'd burnt half her Energy, and a good third of the barrier was encased entirely in a thick sheet of ice. Then she stopped the spell, summoned the heavy, dense hunk of ore from her ring, and threw it with all her might at the center of the iced-over barrier. The lump of ore hit the barrier with a resounding crunch, and thin fracture lines spread out in a spiderweb from the impact site. The ore fell to the ground, so Olivia picked it up and threw it again. This time the ore punched through the barrier, and the spiderweb of cracks expanded, with hundreds of tiny shards falling to the ground in a tinkling cascade. The barrier was broken, and the hole just big enough to step through if she were very careful.

Olivia picked up her ore and walked to the next door. When she opened it, revealing another short hallway ending in an identical door, she moved forward. She was more cautious now, not wanting to bump her nose into another barrier or something worse. Nothing assailed her before the door, though, and she pulled it open to reveal the next room. Once again, the room looked like it was empty, and it seemed identically sized to the first two. Olivia stepped forward and cautiously approached the other door. She was halfway across the room when the floor simply vanished. Olivia began to plummet downward, and panic almost proved to be her undoing. She looked around, started to tumble, and saw a marble floor, maybe a hundred feet below her, fast approaching. Finally, her startled mind got ahold of itself, and she cast Elemental Form, taking her air shape. Her body suddenly lurched upward as the gusts of wind wrapped around her limbs, and she became much lighter. As she slowly descended the last few dozen feet, she studied the ground below her and saw piles of bones and discarded, rotten scraps of clothing. When she landed, she looked up the long, square shaft lined with smooth marble to the faint opening two hundred feet above her. There didn't appear to be any other exit from the pit.

Olivia looked around the bottom of the pit. It wasn't as bright down there as in the top room, but she could see well enough. She counted four skulls among the scattered bones and two complete, mummified corpses. She knew the bones and corpses were old because there was no odor associated with them, and they looked extremely dry. She wondered at the lack of clothing and flesh on most of the bones and then at their age. Didn't this dungeon open every year? Had it been decades since someone fell in this pit? There was more to this story, and she didn't think it would be wise to stick around to see it unfold. How could she scale two hundred feet of smooth marble? Was she even supposed to climb out? Maybe there was a hidden passage.

Olivia decided that spending time down in this pit of bones looking for a hidden passage should be her last option. The bones were either evidence of other peoples' failure to find an exit or some sort of macabre warning, so she figured it would be best to get up and out as soon as possible. She was still in her air elemental form, so she decided to try out an idea she'd had: she pointed her palms at the ground by her sides and cast Wind Gust. A strong gust of air shot out of her palms, and, not appropriately braced, her left arm was pushed to the side with the force of the wind, and her brief upward trajectory turned to a sideways slide through the air. She slammed into the marble wall about ten feet off the ground and slid slowly back to the floor. "Oof, time to revise that plan a bit."

Olivia moved to stand in one of the corners of the deep pit, putting her back into the corner. This time, she held her hands in front of her, angling them toward the ground. Carefully locking her elbows and bracing her shoulders for the pressure, she cast Wind Gust again. This time she managed to keep her arms straight when the air began to stream out of her palms, and the force of it on her light, buoyant air elemental form pushed her slowly up the smooth marble walls, her back sliding along, wedged in the corner. Her spell started to sputter out when she was about a third of the way up, so she recast it, pushing Energy into it as quickly as possible. She dropped a few feet but then started to surge upward again. When she had recast the spell for the fourth time, she found herself bumping up against the marble ceiling. She was about five feet away from the closed door, with no floor to stand on.

As carefully as she could, Olivia angled her left palm so that she started to slide along the ceiling toward the closed door. When she was just above it, she ended her spell, turned, and grabbed out with both hands for the doorknob. She fell slowly, thanks to her form, and was easily able to get her hands around the knob. Face scrunched with effort, she twisted the knob and pushed against the wall with a foot, pulling the door open to flop back and forth over the pit trap. Olivia pushed against the wall again, making the door swing wide, and as it flopped back to close, she thrust her feet into the tunnel beyond, sliding on the marble, panting from the exertion.

Despite how worn and tired she felt from the effort, Olivia couldn't help laughing as she lay on her back, catching her breath: she'd actually flown! She lay there thinking of the possibilities; what if she combined the effects of the Elemental Form spell with a variant of the Wind Gust spell? Could she make a spell designed to truly allow flight? Not to mention, she only had the basic form of both those spells. She definitely had some experimenting and learning to do when she got out of this place. That said, she flopped over and looked down the hallway, noting the identical cherrywood door. She scrambled to her feet, made sure her Energy stores were well above half full, walked to the door, and opened it.

When Olivia saw the interior of the next room, she smirked; here was a challenge she was meant for. The entire floor of the next room was covered in flaming hot coals. Thick smoke rose from the flames, carried on a draft up through a narrow ventilation hole in the center of the ceiling. Olivia used her Elemental Form spell to take on the aspect of fire, and she strode through the coals, crunching them under her feet, not even noticing their temperature. She held her breath going through the room—she didn't know what sorts of fumes her Elemental Form protected her from, and she didn't think it was a good idea to experiment in the middle of a dungeon. Trying to tamp down her smugness, she pulled open the next door and stepped into the hallway. If her count were correct, the door just ahead of her should open to the last room on this floor.

Olivia let her Elemental Form wear off, then she sat down in the middle of the short hallway and rested. She wanted her entire Energy pool, and she wanted her Form to be off cooldown before she went through that door. So far, she hadn't seen any sign of her competition on this floor. She wondered how many made it through that first room with the spiders, and once again, she wondered if there were other starting rooms. Was it possible that some other students were ahead of her using parallel paths? "Nothing I can do about it right now. Just gotta keep moving!" She stood, stretched, and opened the door.

The final room was shaped exactly like the previous four, the only difference being that it was four times the size. Smooth, rose-colored marble surrounded a large, low-ceilinged space, and at its center, coiled around a large wooden chest, was a giant serpent. Olivia entertained trying to slip past the thick snake, but it lifted its head and stared at her, malevolence, real or imagined, lurking behind its eyes. The snake was probably as wide around as one of her thighs, and it had to be twenty or thirty feet long. It didn't look docile, though, and its coloring worried Olivia; it had shiny black scales with vibrant yellow circles evenly spaced down its spine.

Olivia took a step into the room, still a good ten paces from the snake, but its head rose from its coiled body and hissed at her, revealing a bright red mouth with a set of long, dripping fangs. She froze in place, and the snake didn't move; it just stared at her. Objectively, the snake didn't seem as significant a threat as some of the other things she'd already killed in the dungeon. The fact that it was the final guardian of this level gave Olivia pause, though. Perhaps it was exceptionally fast, and its poison was deadly. Did she have any defense against poison? The fire Elemental Form allowed her to heal quickly, but would it extend to poison or internal damage? She'd rather not find out.

One thing that had worked for her so far was the old adage, "The best defense is a good offense." Olivia knew snakes were cold-blooded, at least on Earth, so she primed her Arcfrost Cascade, put one foot out the door into the hallway behind her, ready to flee, and raised her hands to the guardian. Just as she launched a crackling torrent of freezing, electrified air, the Snake erupted, dodging to her left. She tried to track it with her blast, but it was so fast that she only caught the last couple of feet of its tail. It was enough to elicit a shrieking hiss from the creature, though, as the electricity of her cascade surged through its flesh. The colossal serpent spasmed, and though it thrashed and convulsed, it couldn't straighten itself out to strike at Olivia. She stepped forward, re-aimed her hands, and fired another Arcfrost Cascade, fully engulfing the upper half of the snake. Frost formed along its scales, and electricity buzzed and zapped along its length, and though the unfrozen portion of its body continued to twitch, the snake's mouth widened in a death gasp, and its tongue, flash-frozen, broke and shattered on the marble floor.

Olivia cautiously approached the snake, pressing one foot against the frozen portion of its neck, just below the head. Tiny cracks spread through the icy flesh, and a remnant surge of electricity tickled her foot, almost making her stumble backward. She was thinking of throwing some fire at the frozen creature, just to make sure, when motes of golden Energy erupted from the corpse, swirling into a stream that poured into Olivia.

Congratulations! You have achieved level 16 Elemental Archon and have gained 10 Intelligence, 10 Will, and have 8 points to allocate.

Olivia didn't know if she was leveling fast, but it sure seemed like it. According to everyone she'd spoken to, she'd have a chance to refine her class at level twenty and be considered "Tier-two." What would happen if she advanced to tier-two while still in this dungeon meant for tier-one students? Surely, they'd thought of such a possibility, and it wouldn't be a problem. "At least I hope so," she muttered as she walked over to the big wooden chest the snake had been guarding.

◈ OLIVIA ◈

The chest had a light coating of frost on its smooth cherrywood surface, but it opened noiselessly on polished brass hinges. It was about the size of Olivia's father's old red toolbox, but its contents wouldn't have gone well in anyone's garage. Laid out neatly, lined up next to each other in the bottom of the chest were a yellow, cloth-bound book, a fat, blue candle, a shiny, silver pocket watch, and a long, bright-red feather. "Four items, hmm?" She reached in and picked up the book, and the other three items shimmered and dissolved into blue and yellow smoke. "Oh, damn it!" Olivia hadn't considered that the chest had been offering her a choice. She supposed the book was a good honest choice, though—somewhere in her mind, she'd been most interested in it, or she wouldn't have grabbed it first.

She looked at the book's title and read it aloud, "Tuzrenstil's Basic Primer for the Efficient Use of Energy to Manipulate Spatial Connections. That's a mouthful." She flipped through the little book's pages and found that it seemed to have far more than met the eye. Looking at it, she'd guess it had a hundred or so pages, but as she thumbed the pages in a fan, they just kept coming. She stopped after a while and saw that she was looking at page 672. "More and more interesting!" Olivia tucked the book into her ring, a warm wave of pleasure washing over her at the thought of digging into it with a big cup of something hot and sweet when she got back to the dormitory.

Olivia walked through the last cherrywood door, through a short hallway, and entered a round, rose-colored marble room with a smooth, matching marble stair leading downward. Feeling the pressure of having to beat the other entrants, Olivia didn't waste time and began the descent to the third level. The rose-colored, smooth marble stairs only continued for about twenty steps, and then they abruptly transitioned to rough gray stone with patches of damp moss speckling them. Olivia was careful not to step on the moss, unsure if it held toxic spores or was slippery. After another twenty or so steps, she came out into a tight gray stone room, a rough wooden door opposite the stairway. So far, each floor had consisted of similar rooms connected via short hallways, so she wasn't surprised when she opened the damp, swollen door to reveal a hallway lined with dripping, wet stone. The door grated along the stone floor, its old iron hinges hanging loose in the frame.

Olivia walked through the tight hallway, not quite having to duck her head but still feeling the closeness of the ceiling. Drips of moisture tickled the top of her head and shoulders, and she was glad for her long black hair covering the nape of her neck. The next door was so swollen that she had to wrestle it out of its frame, dragging it along the stone floor, leaving splinters and chunks of rotten wood in its wake. When she'd finished yanking the door open and ceased her own grunting and grinding noise, she became aware of a muffled moaning sound coming from the next room. Cautiously she moved up to the doorjamb and peered inside.

The room was much like the one with the stairs in it behind her, but in the center of the damp, stone floor, an Ardeni girl was stretched out, softly weeping as she scrabbled against the stone, trying to get purchase to pull her leg free from what looked like a blob of pale green ooze. The ooze was large enough to fill a fifty-gallon drum, and it pulsed and throbbed in a disgusting, quivering undulation as it hugged the girl's leg from the hip down. When Olivia stepped into the room, alarmed for the girl, a long, thick tendril sprouted from the back of the ooze and seemed to regard her, weaving back and forth in the air. She circled it and tried to get around so she could see the face of the Ardeni girl. The tendril from the ooze followed her movement, looking very much like a serpent ready to strike.

Finally, she was around to the side enough to see the girl's face, and Olivia saw agony writ there. Whatever the ooze was doing to her leg, it wasn't pleasant. "Hold on; I'll help you."

"Ung," the girl grunted, "Don't let it touch you!"

"I've got to get it off you before I destroy it." The girl might have tried to answer her, but whatever she said was lost in her choking sobs, so Olivia turned her attention to the ooze. It was green, it was wet, and it seemed to like a damp environment. Perhaps fire was the answer. Olivia took a breath and cast her Elemental Form, taking on a fire aspect. Hot blue-yellow flames sprouted along her body, and her flesh became like red-hot embers. In the yellow sepia tones of her fire elemental vision, the ooze seemed to look more yellow than green, and it was much brighter than in her normal vision's color spectrum. She approached the slime, and when she was within a couple of paces, it lunged out with the tendril that had been "Watching" her. It seemed like the tendril tried to recoil at the last moment, but it was committed, and when it hit her arm, it sizzled and thrashed and then snapped back into the main body of the ooze.

When it touched her fiery arm, Olivia hadn't felt any discomfort, so she continued to advance, and the ooze quivered and shrank back from her. She reached forward, pushing the palms of her hands against the ooze where it hugged the girl's leg. The ooze seemed to hiss, and the surface bubbled a little as her hands got close enough to touch, and it shrank back further, pulling away from the girl's leg. Olivia kept advancing, driving the ooze completely off its victim, and when the girl sobbed and pulled her leg up to her chest, Olivia stood up, held out her right palm, and unleashed a Plasma Wave at the creature. Crackling, bubbling, blue plasma washed over the ooze, and it bubbled and popped and screamed and sizzled and then ceased to exist, nothing but a boiling, sizzling puddle left on the stone floor.

As golden motes gathered up from the cracks between the stone blocks of the floor, surging into Olivia, she turned to the girl and regarded her injury. She wore a black jumpsuit, much like Olivia's white one, but the material on her left leg was mostly dissolved, and the flesh beneath was red and blistered. The ooze had been digesting her, it seemed. Olivia let her Elemental Form drop and then knelt to look into the girl's orange-red eyes. "Are you going to be alright?"

"I, I'm not sure. My leg's on fire." The girl had tears streaming out of her eyes, and Olivia instinctively reached forward to brush her bedraggled bright-red hair out of her face.

"Do you have any means of healing?" Olivia had a tender heart, but she wasn't naive. She knew this woman had to be either a test or one of her competitors, so she wasn't quite ready to disclose her potion of renewal, not that she was sure it would heal the girl.

"I have a salve," the girl grunted, reaching a hand into the bosom of her jumper and withdrawing a small glass jar. "Is the ooze gone? Are there any more?" She glanced around the room with wide eyes, letting her gaze linger on the wet, slimy spot where Olivia had killed the creature.

"Seems like we're alone. Here, let me see that." Olivia held out her hand, and the girl, hesitant at first, reached out and put the jar in her hand. Olivia opened the jar and began to spread the buttery yellow cream on the most badly damaged parts of the girl's leg. "What's your name?"

"Jaliss. Thank you for saving me." She stretched out her leg so that Olivia could see more of it and had to suck air through her teeth to stifle a cry.

"I'm Olivia. What school are you from, Jaliss?"

"Archelide College. What about you?"

"Fainhallow; have you heard of it?"

"Yes," the girl said through gritted teeth. "Ahh, that stuff burns! I'm glad I got it, though."

"Sorry it burns, but yeah, it's mending the worst of it. I've covered the most burned bits, but I'll use it up if I spread it all over the leg. Do you want me to?"

"Yes, please. Even the parts where it barely started to dissolve the skin feel like they're on fire."

Olivia complied, gently smearing the oily substance all over Jaliss's leg. "Ahh, that's feeling so much better now."

"Good. Now," Olivia looked around the room, noting that each wall had a door. "I'm assuming you took a different route to this room than I did?"

"Yeah. I've not seen you or any rooms you've been through, that's for certain."

"Didn't you have a spell that could hurt that ooze? No fire?"

"I have an air affinity, and it didn't even flinch at my strongest lightning bolt." Olivia nodded, once again realizing just how lucky she was to have her considerable arsenal of affinities at her disposal.

"Alright, well, I'm glad to have helped you, but we are in a competition, right? How about we each continue through a different closed door?"

"Um, could I follow you for a little while? I promise I won't get in your way. I can't defend myself from these slimes." Olivia was torn by the request. She knew Oylla would tell her to stun the girl, tie her up and move on, but she couldn't be that ruthless, could she? What if an ooze came along and dissolved her? What would she do if the girl followed her all the way to the next level, though?

"Jaliss, I'm sorry to seem harsh, but I have a duty to my school and my people to try to win this competition. You have a necklace you can use to escape the dungeon, right?" Jaliss reached up and touched the thin golden chain visible above her jumpsuit.

"Yes." She frowned, a distant look in her eyes.

"Alright, well, I'm sorry, but I'm going to advance alone. Please don't follow me. If you're worried about the oozes, maybe it's best for you to use that pendant now. Good luck." Olivia stood and picked the closed door opposite the one she entered through to open. She had to yank it over the stone tiles like the last one, and she glanced over her shoulder once to see Jaliss watching her from the floor where she still lay, a slight furrow in her bright red brows. Olivia stepped through the door and pulled it shut behind her. Maybe it was harsh, but she had to be serious right now. "Time to pick up the pace again."

Olivia strode to the next door, yanked it open, and looked into another room with two big blobs of ooze quivering in the center. Without pause, she held up her hand and fired a Plasma Wave at the one on the left, utterly obliterating it. Sizzling beads of plasma-covered slime broke off the ooze and splashed the other one, causing it to convulse and shudder, hastily quivering across the floor to huddle in a corner. Olivia stepped into the room and launched a simple Fiery Burst at the quivery ooze, wondering if plain old fire would do the trick. She held the stream of fire against the hissing, shuddering mass of ooze, watching black smoke rise from the blob until it was just a blackened hunk of something that resembled burnt rubber. Once again, motes of Energy poured into Olivia, but she didn't gain a level. Still, not wanting to slow, she pushed through the next door, through the hallway, and opened the next chamber.

The third room had, predictably, three oozes in it, though one of them was red. "Could it be so simple? Are you immune to fire, Mr. Red Ooze?" Without waiting for an answer, Olivia assumed her fire Elemental Form, worried that they might get an attack off before she could finish three of them. She knew that while she was in her fire form, her ice spells were less effective, but she didn't care—the form afforded her immunity from at least the two green oozes, so she held up a palm and fired a somewhat weakened Arcfrost Cascade at the red ooze. A torrent of frost crackling with electricity tore into the fat, sluggish creature, and it seemed to scream as its surface bubbled, popped, and then burst apart with an electrical explosion. The two green oozes rushed toward Olivia, but they'd barely started probing toward her with long tendrils when she turned a palm to the one on the left and torched it with a stream of white-hot flames. When the radiant heat from the stream of fire reached it, the second ooze started to squelch away from her, but she chased it down, burning it to a blackened lump. This time, as the Energy motes from her three victims poured into her, she got a message:

*****Congratulations! You have achieved level 17 Elemental Archon and have gained 10 Intelligence, 10 Will, and have 16 points to allocate.*****

Before charging on to the next room, Olivia took a moment to allocate her sixteen free points. She put thirteen into vitality, then put one into each of her other physical stats, raising them to ten. "Two more rooms, then I'm onto the fourth level," she said to herself as she strode across the room, pulled open the door, and continued her rampage.

⚘ MORGAN ⚘

The rescue party, much diminished, continued down the gargantuan tunnel, ever descending, until they started to notice smaller tunnels branching off to the left and right. Still, the enormous central tunnel continued, but Rorth called a halt and turned to Issa and Morgan to consult. "I'm reasonably sure the left-hand tunnels lead down toward the Rill Catcher and the part of the Deep Down where the attackers originated. It's been many years since I was here, though, so I could be mistaken."

"Well, I'd like to get out of this big tunnel where we can get attacked from the air. Let's explore down that way," Morgan said. Issa nodded and started walking to the first tunnel on the left. Rorth looked at Morgan, and he shrugged, following after Issa. He could hear Rorth directing the rest of the column's marching orders. He caught up to Issa and said, "Hey, I know you're in a hurry to get to your dad, but don't get out ahead of the rest of us, please."

"I won't. I just want to get a look around. You're right here, anyway." She didn't sound irritated, exactly, but Morgan could tell she was riding on raw nerves. He followed close behind her, Bloodfang held in his hand, always hungry for more action. As they walked in the dim tunnel, he let his Azure Sight fade, and the true gloom of the depths hit him. If not for the yellow globes of light some of the soldiers held along the column, he knew they'd be wading through impenetrable darkness. On a whim, he tried to follow the Azure Paladin's guidance by recasting Azure Sight but funneling the void-attuned Energy in his Core into the spell. Suddenly, everything in his vision flared into shades of brilliant white and gray. He could see every detail in the tunnel, every strand of Issa's hair, and she stood out in the darkness like a phosphorescent light in a dim room. Looking around the tunnel, Morgan could see bright white shapes of slugs and beetles. He saw a dozen little luminous bodies resembling bats or rodents up a narrow crevice that he'd thought was just a dark shadow before.

Congratulations!Youhavelearnedthespell:VoidVision—Improved.
***Void Vision—Improved: Just as the void lacks light, so too does a master of the void eschew the need for it. Shadows, illusions, and even

material obstructions cannot hide your foes from you. You can read a person's emotions, and as your mastery of this skill advances, you will learn to see the truth of beings and items around you. Energy Cost: 75 per minute while active.****

Morgan waved the notifications away and looked at Issa. He saw within her bright, luminescent form tiny pulses of blue and red that rose from her chest and went through her head. Instinctually, he knew they indicated that she was anxious and under a heavy mental strain. He reached forward and rested his free hand on her shoulder, giving her a gentle squeeze, and he saw a little pink burst of emotion in Issa's chest. "This skill is fucking cool."

"You got a new skill?" she asked.

"Yeah, an upgraded vision spell. I can see everything." He scanned ahead in the dark, narrow tunnel and knew that nothing larger than a rat was within a hundred feet of them. "I should walk in front. I can see anything bigger than a fly for a hundred feet or more." She slowed down and let him walk up beside her, but then she matched his stride.

"We'll walk together." Morgan couldn't argue with that, so they continued that way, the tunnel plenty wide for them to walk side by side. This tunnel had a much steeper rate of descent, and they seemed to be wending from left to right, never more than a hundred feet of tunnel visible before a curve obscured Morgan's view. After about thirty minutes of traversal, they came around a bend, and Morgan saw three large, nearly incandescently bright beings in his Void Vision about fifty paces ahead. He grabbed Issa's shoulder and stopped her.

"Shh," he hissed, "Three up ahead. Do you see them?"

"No," she whispered, "Even my night vision spell can't see that far without more light." The column was a ways behind them around the curve, so the tunnel ahead was still very dark, Morgan guessed. He could see the shapes of the creatures, and they were reminiscent of the "Gargoyles" from above, though they seemed bigger, with longer arms, and he didn't see wings.

"They look like monsters. Let's not let them get the jump on us," Morgan whispered. "Go tell Rorth to hold the column behind the bend for a minute." Issa looked at him, a wave of purple-red emotion jumping up from her chest, and he said, "I'll wait for you." She nodded and slipped around the corner. Morgan studied the creatures while she was gone, ensuring they didn't move or notice him. When Issa slid back around the corner, she smiled to see him waiting, and he nodded, starting forward, and he felt the buzzing Energy of Issa's Battle Chant start up as just a low hum that wouldn't travel far. He watched their heads closely, waiting for them to look his way and notice him or Issa. The two of them glided through the darkness, carefully stepping over loose rocks, their basic ability to move silently once again proving invaluable. When they were only twenty paces away from the creatures, and they still hadn't noticed him or Issa, Morgan decided to take the attack to them. The creatures were definitely related to the gargoyles—larger, more heavily built, with heavy claws that looked like they could scoop through rock as easily as bisect a person.

Morgan squeezed Issa's shoulder, and he used Hollow Charge to close the distance. Holding his sword in a guard position, Morgan cast Void Wave, eager to see its effectiveness.

Things were different in the real world than in the reality that existed in his or the Azure Paladin's mind. When he released the wave of void-attuned Energy, the essence of light and sound and air being consumed was something like a god tearing the fabric of reality—the wave spread out from Morgan, devouring everything in its path until it hit the three large gargoyles. Then, with his Void Vision, Morgan followed the struggles of their individual wills and Energy versus his attack. The consumption of their matter slowed significantly, but didn't stop. The creatures shrieked in agony and surprise, but the Void Wave swallowed their cries in another hair-raising anti-sound. They tried to flee and nearly escaped the radius of the wave, but only because of their momentum; partially dissolved splashes of organs and bones fell to the tunnel floor.

As Energy streamed into Morgan from the destroyed creatures, Issa came up behind him, looking around at the slightly wider section of the tunnel expanded by his Void Wave. The stone had been eaten away by a few inches. Morgan wondered if casting void Energy as a persistent stream or torrent could have destroyed more stone. He thought it likely.

"Was that a new spell?"

"Yes, when I leveled up in the tunnel above, I had a meeting with the Azure Paladin again. He showed me how to use my void-attuned Energy in some of my spells." Morgan looked down the tunnel in both directions, noting the light of the soldiers' orbs growing brighter as they came around the bend. Nothing moved or appeared to be lurking the other way.

"I wish you'd left more of them for us to examine." Issa held her nose as she used her boot to prod the remains of one of the creatures, trying to see if anything useful could be gleaned from the corpse.

"Well, to be honest, I didn't know how effective that spell was. See anything of note?" Morgan went to look with Issa, noting the sound of running feet indicating at least some of the soldiers were rushing forward to see what had happened. As more light filled the tunnel, he let his Void Vision fall for a moment to see the natural color around him. The slaughtered gargoyles, stinking of raw entrails and their contents, hadn't managed to keep much flesh on their bones, but he did see a few patches of their skin along their forearms and lower legs. They were gray but a much darker shade than those flying up above.

"Not much left," Issa said.

"Ancestors! What did you do to them?" Rorth asked as he came running up.

"Void Wave. Let's keep moving." Morgan refreshed his Void Vision and walked ahead, letting the others sort out how they'd follow. Issa didn't waste any words, just falling into step beside him again. Morgan wasn't trying to be rude, but he felt stressed out by the mountains of dirt over his head and the growing feeling that these weren't the types of creatures to keep prisoners. They rounded a bend, and suddenly Morgan threw his hand out to stop Issa. Not thirty paces further down the tunnel, he could see the luminescent signature of a dozen more of the large gargoyle creatures. "Shh, I think a cavern is ahead with," he counted again carefully, "Eleven more of those big guys in it."

The creatures were active, milling about, some moving quickly to and fro and others just kind of shambling around. Morgan gestured back toward the soldiers and raised his eyebrows questioningly. "Yes, let's wait for them," Issa whispered. They slinked back around the bend and then waited while Rorth and the others approached, motioning for them to be quiet as they came into view.

"What is it?"

"A cavern with at least eleven of the big guys in it. We should hit them together, try to overwhelm them," Issa said. Rorth nodded and passed the word down the line—they'd sneak up as close as possible then charge them en masse. Morgan and Issa took the lead but didn't extend away from the main column; they moved together, slowly, lights out, walking inch by inch, with Morgan in front and then Issa, all the way down the line, holding onto the person's shoulder in front of them. They'd agreed to ignite their lights when they heard Morgan charge.

Morgan carefully watched the luminescent forms of the gargoyles as he approached, taking one slow step after another. When he was only ten paces from the cavern opening, he picked a cluster of three nearby creatures and charged. This time he didn't use his Void Wave; he reached out with an Energy Drain, yanking on the dark, toxic power he felt in their Cores, and then laid about himself with Bloodfang. The sword's solar steel cut through their flesh like paper, notching their bones and sliding out as Morgan stepped, lunged, slashed, parried some claws, then thrust again. He liberally used his sword styles, and as he finished the first trio, he ran to another pair of gargoyles that came in from a side tunnel. All the while, he was aware of Issa's screeching hexes and the yells, clamor, and bright lights of the other soldiers and hunters engaging in combat.

Just as he'd downed his fifth gargoyle, Morgan turned to survey the battle, and his pulse quickened—the cavern they were in was massive, and a wave of luminescent gargoyle shapes was surging toward them from a vast tunnel at the far end. There had to be more than a hundred of the creatures and, lumbering in the midst of the horde, were three distinctly larger, brighter forms—gargoyles that dwarfed the "Big" ones that Morgan had already killed. "Pull back!" he yelled. "Pull to the tunnel entrance!" He tried to be as loud as he could, but the sounds of combat made his voice seem small. He needed Issa. Frantically he looked around, trying to spot her, and when he did, his heart sank. She was on the far side of the cavern, further toward the horde, pushing a group of gargoyles up a steep tunnel.

He started to run toward her, looking for a target to use Hollow Charge on, but the screaming, hissing throng of gargoyles passed in front of the tunnel she was in, and Morgan knew he'd have to fight through them to get to her. He tried, charging at their flank, trying to push his way through. He unleashed his Void Wave, then an Azure Burst, and finally an Energy Drain targeting more than twenty nearby gargoyles. He'd made an enormous crater in their numbers, but they swarmed over their dead and pushed at him. Morgan, his big attacks on cooldown and his Energy running down near fifty percent, struggled to hold them off with his sword alone. One of the lumbering, massive gargoyles charged him then, smashing into him with a boulder-like horned shoulder, throwing him back, tumbling over the rocky cavern floor. Morgan nimbly found his feet and scanned the scene.

Many of the Ardeni were dead, scores of gargoyles still swarmed over the cavern floor, and he could no longer see Issa in the tunnel on the other side. He'd rolled to a stop near a tunnel entrance, and when he looked up into it, he didn't see any signs of enemies. He had to get across the cavern to Issa, but could he kill that many gargoyles? Not all at once, he decided. He'd need to keep them from surrounding him and bunch them up. He looked around again and said, "Like in the mouth of a tunnel." He backed up so the tunnel walls were on either side of him, then he began to shout, forming a Vortex Lance and firing it into the side of the hulking gargoyle that had thrown him. The shot reverberated through the cavern, and the supersonic bolt of Energy tore the hulk's arm off at the shoulder. It screamed with its wide, dagger-filled maw lifted to the ceiling and charged toward Morgan, a good portion of the host of gargoyles following behind. "Come on, then! Come and get it!" Morgan roared.

MORGAN

Morgan fought like a man possessed. Perhaps he was, for the spirit in his sword had come calling, and he methodically cut and clawed at the creatures swarming him. He wielded his sword in his right hand, slicing and stabbing, and his left hand, surrounded by the ghostly remnant of whatever kind of creature the Corran Blood Rager had been, slashed, tore, and ripped the monsters apart if they came within a yard of him. He'd rush forward whenever Void Wave was off cooldown, allowing the gargoyles to pack tight around him and unleash it to devastating effect. The Void Wave obliterated the hulk-type gargoyles nearly as easily as the smaller ones, and whenever one of the giants came in close enough, he'd use it to keep them from bowling him over. Knowing this fight would take a while, Morgan didn't use Energy on other attacks; his Void Wave was the most devastating and gave him the biggest bang for the buck, Energy-wise.

The creatures seemed to have no regard for their own safety and didn't learn any lessons from the piled corpses of their brethren. Now and then, a gargoyle would crowd through, overwhelming Morgan's guard, and land a crunching or slashing blow, and Morgan's wounds began to accumulate. When he felt his arms growing heavy, his wind coming harshly through his throat, and his vision starting to dim, Morgan reached out and drained the Energy from a handful of the creatures, restoring his flesh and invigorating his muscles. He came to realize that he would be able to keep this battle going almost indefinitely so long as he didn't let himself run out of Energy or become overwhelmed. Unlike their flying kin up above, these creatures either never figured out the futility of their actions or didn't care, and after what seemed an eternity to Morgan, he was standing in a tunnel, upslope from a long trail of slaughtered corpses, heaving for breath, but alone.

He was reaching out for Issa with Guardian's Senses when a river of Energy poured into him larger than he'd ever experienced. He barely had time to register that she was still in the direction he'd last seen her, maybe half a kilometer distant, when a series of messages filled his vision:

Congratulations! You have achieved level 30 Vortex Duelist and have gained 8 Intelligence, 8 Agility, 6 Will, 6 Dexterity. Congratulations! You have gained the skill: Sword Mastery—Advanced.
Level 30 Class refinement. Class refinement is permanent. Human Energy cultivators will next be offered a Class refinement selection at level 40. To view your options and make your selection, access the menu through your status page.
Congratulations! You have achieved level 31—Attribute advancement is being banked until you have completed your level 30 refinement selection. Should you sleep or lose consciousness before making the selection, any progress beyond level 30 will be lost.

Morgan waved the notifications away and ran down the slope, nearly gagging as he passed the remnants left by his Void Waves. He held a sleeve to his mouth and ran out into the enormous cavern where his epic battle had begun. It was quiet save for the scrabbling and hissing of a few gargoyles that hadn't quite figured out they were dead. Morgan scanned the cavern floor for Ardeni survivors—with his Void Vision, he was able to see that there wasn't any Energy pulsing within the bodies that lay strewn about. He wanted to pick them up for delivery to their families, but his need to get to Issa as urgently as possible didn't allow it.

Morgan charged across the cavern and up the tunnel where he'd last seen her, leaping over gargoyle corpses and the occasional dead Ardeni as he advanced. She'd not been alone, then, Morgan reasoned; hopefully, they'd been able to fight to someplace they could hole up. Morgan kept feeling with Guardian's Senses as he charged up the tunnel, a smile spreading on his blood-covered face as he realized he was getting closer. He picked up speed, charging up the tunnel, blazing past side tunnels, trusting his Guardian's Senses to guide him.

Moments later, Morgan could feel Issa less than a hundred yards away, and he began to hear the sounds of battle. He burst out of a tunnel opening into a four-way intersection where a small throng of gargoyles pushed, hissing and clawing, against a determined line of Ardeni fighters, including Issa. Her Battle Chant was going full-tilt, and as soon as Morgan got within ten feet or so, it buoyed his muscles and spirits, and he began to lay into the rear line of gargoyles, cutting them to pieces before they realized they'd been flanked. Looking over the shoulders of the gargoyles he was chopping at, Morgan counted three Ardeni fighting with Issa. By the time he'd cut down two of the rear gargoyles, they'd managed to subdue or kill two of the remaining five.

As one of the final three gargoyles turned to strike at Morgan, Issa slipped her rapier into its back, stabbing and freezing some vital organ, causing it to shriek in agony and stumble; Morgan finished it. The final two were easy to mop up after that. "Where's Rorth? The others?" Issa asked, leaning to catch her breath. Morgan surveyed the battered and bloody Ardeni, then shook his head.

"I'm not sure. I think they retreated down the tunnel we came in through. I got caught fighting a big fucking horde of these things."

"Glad you got away," Issa said, straightening and stretching her shoulder. Morgan could see dark purple bruises spreading down her arm from the top of her vest.

"Hmm, yeah, that's one way to put it. Anyway, what do you want to do now?" The three Ardeni with Issa had hollowed eyes and sported many minor cuts, bruises, and torn clothing and armor. "What about you guys?"

"We should go find Rorth and the rest," one of them said, starting to walk the way Morgan had come.

"Is it safe to go back that way, Morgan?" Issa asked.

"Should be; unless another horde came up from the depths."

"Let's go then; let's hurry." Issa started into a jog down the tunnel, and Morgan fell in behind her, the other three Ardeni bringing up the rear. They didn't encounter any enemies down the long tunnel, when they got to the big cavern where the battle had started; they were greeted with only corpses. "Please collect the Ardeni corpses," Issa said, moving about, checking for survivors, though Morgan was sure there weren't any. "Can you feel Rorth, Morgan?"

"I hadn't thought of that!" Morgan slapped himself on the head and concentrated on Rorth with Guardian's Senses. "He's not far, maybe a few hundred yards back the way we first came in." Issa nodded and looked at the three Ardeni.

"You three go back, find Rorth. Tell him Morgan and I are advancing down this big tunnel. Depending on his casualties, we won't blame him if you all make your way back outside. Ancestors watch you." She didn't wait for a reply, starting down the enormous cavern toward where the horde had come rushing in. Morgan caught up to her, waving briefly to the Ardeni soldiers as he jogged past.

"Hey, you sure that's smart?"

"I've figured out that you didn't exactly get away from the horde. You killed them, right?" Issa said, looking sidelong at Morgan.

"Well, yeah. I had to, so I could get past them to where you were."

"So, I doubt there's another horde lurking right down here. Let's see what all those things were guarding." She gestured down the slight slope to the big tunnel opening at the cavern's end.

"Yeah, alright. Let's move along the side, though; try to be sneaky." Morgan moved to the shadowy edge of the cavern, and Issa followed. Soon, they'd gotten to the far end and crept up to the edge of the big tunnel entrance. The stone was smooth and looked formed, not something natural. Morgan, his Void Vision active, peered around and looked down the steeper slope of the tunnel. He couldn't see anything moving, but there was a pulsing light about a hundred feet down, where the tunnel seemed to level off. Morgan briefly dropped his Void Vision to see that the light had a distinct red hue. He motioned for Issa to follow, and the two of them advanced, slinking in the shadows as much as possible.

When they'd made it about halfway down the tunnel, Morgan began to hear the hissing and growling he'd come to associate with the gargoyles. He paused, and Issa did as well, and she whispered, "I think I hear words in that." Morgan nodded, straining his ears.

"Hurry! Reinforcements are..." He couldn't make out the rest of the sentence; the accent or guttural nature of the creature's voice made it too hard to understand. He nodded to Issa, and they continued to advance. When the slope of the tunnel brought them low enough to see ahead into the next cavern, Morgan froze in his tracks, and Issa hugged tightly against the wall behind him.

Red light filled an enormous cavern with a ceiling lost in a smoky haze hundreds of feet from the ground. The light was pulsing forth from a twenty-foot-tall, shimmering oval of red light that looked, in Morgan's limited experience, like a portal. It stood in the center of the room with seven long, spindly stone spires surrounding it, little streams of Energy flowing from their tips into the red light, seemingly feeding or creating the strange gateway. Standing about halfway between the tunnel mouth and the portal were several gargoyles who seemed to be listening to a single, odd-looking creature. Morgan could see an unmistakable resemblance between the creature and the gargoyles, but it was kind of like comparing an orangutan to a human. This creature had the same gray skin, long limbs, and black talons, but it stood straighter, wore a shimmering red robe, and had much softer facial features. This was an evolved species of gargoyle, Morgan figured.

Some movement near the portal drew Morgan's eye away from what he'd started thinking of as the gargoyle leader. He looked and felt Issa tense behind him as she saw the same thing—several gargoyles were dragging bound, humanoid figures with hoods over their heads toward the portal. Morgan counted eleven gargoyles and five prisoners in the room and decided the odds were good enough to try to stop whatever was happening. He hissed, "C'mon, let's stop this shit." Issa's Battle Chant immediately began to buzz in the bones of his skull, and he stood up, Bloodfang at the ready, and charged toward the clump of gargoyles around their "Leader."

Just as in his battles before, he primed a Void Wave while ripping over the ground with Hollow Charge and managed to catch the gargoyles with their proverbial pants down. His surging wave of void-attuned Energy utterly destroyed the lesser gargoyles, but when it hit the leader, his red robe flared with brilliant light, and the spell passed over him without any harm. "Ungh!" the creature hissed, "Insolence!" The exclamation caught Morgan off guard—it was clearly spoken and not the guttural hissing voice he'd overheard from up in the tunnel. He didn't let his spell's ineffectiveness stop him, launching into an attack with his sword as the creature backpedaled.

Morgan hacked furiously, but the gargoyle leader deflected the strikes with its hands, bright pulses of red Energy accompanying each impact. "Who the fuck are you assholes?" Morgan asked through gritted teeth, watching over the creature's shoulder as Issa charged toward the gargoyles and prisoners near the portal. He could see that one of the prisoners had already been pushed through the portal, and the gargoyle that had been escorting him or her was watching Morgan's battle and Issa's approach. It shrieked and ran toward Issa. Morgan had to turn his attention back to the intelligent gargoyle as it, or he, judging by its voice, began to emanate a dangerous-feeling amount of Energy. Morgan quickly fired off an Azure Burst, hoping to throw the creature's attack or spell or whatever it was out of whack. The wave of crackling blue fire rolled out of him, washing into the gargoyle leader, and his robe flared again, blocking out the heat of the spell, but the force of its shockwave carried on, knocking him back, sprawling on the stone floor.

Morgan didn't waste any time, launching forward with his form, the Crane Flutters its Wings, and the fury and force of his blows proved too much for the gargoyle leader. While he struggled to get his feet under him, he lifted one hand to deflect Morgan's cleaves, but he couldn't keep up with the ferocious strikes, and one of Morgan's downward cuts got through, chopping into his shoulder, slicing through flesh and bone, and sending a spray of dark blood arcing out over the cavern floor. "Ahhh! Fool! The Starlight Empire will reap terrible vengeance!" He reached to his chest and touched something as Morgan lifted his sword for another strike. As his sword cut downward, the gargoyle leader burst apart into a cloud of red dust, right before Morgan's eyes. Morgan's sword arced through the cloud, scattering some red motes but not harming anything. The red haze, all that was left of the creature, began to flow away and stream toward the portal.

"Morgan! Stop them!" Issa called, her voice ringing through the air in her Battle Chant. Morgan looked and saw that she was fighting off two gargoyles, and the others were pushing their humanoid captives into the red light of the portal. Was the portal pulsing more rapidly? Morgan ran toward the gargoyles, watching helplessly while they shoved one, then another captive through the red light. When he was halfway there, the portal seemed to strobe and pulse more frantically, and he ran even harder, staring at one of the gargoyles near the portal and activating Hollow Charge. He streaked over the ground, smashing into the gargoyle, and then the portal pulsed one last time, so brightly that Morgan had to shield his eyes. He felt like he was caught on the edge of a tornado, wind pulling at him and roaring in his ears. He stumbled blindly, and when the wind stopped, and he lowered his arm, he was floating in darkness.

⧉ BRONWYN ⧉

Bronwyn rolled away from the rippling ground as Thun performed another one of his stomp attacks. When she came to her feet, she felt a shivering sense of danger to her left, and she dove again to her right, narrowly dodging a spray of razor-sharp ice shards. Thun laughed as he stamped his foot, sending another ripple her way. Bronwyn, already in a dive, was caught by the rippling wave of grassy soil and sent tumbling further into the meadow, where she smashed into one of the smoldering braziers. The hot coals rolled off her thick leather armor, though one of them sizzled as it plopped into the crook of her left elbow. "Ahh, dammit!" Bronwyn brushed it away as she bounced to her feet, dodging away, hoping to avoid whatever follow-up attack Thun launched.

It seemed her instincts were good because she'd only taken one jumping step when the ground exploded in a geyser where she'd been standing. Moist soil and rocks showered down into the clearing, and Bronwyn jumped, dove, and rolled her way to the far side, trying to distance herself from Thun. "Running already, Summer cub?" Bronwyn didn't answer, just pushed harder in her sprint, randomly dodging from side to side. Another spray of sharp icicles tore through the air, though much more widely spread than before, and one of them pierced her armor, burying itself an inch into her left shoulder. Bronwyn spun to face Thun, hoping she could avoid his attacks more easily with her eyes on him and some distance between them.

Thun stared at her from across the clearing, perhaps gauging whether it would be easier to kill her from a distance or to give chase. Bronwyn could feel the power in his attacks, and she wasn't feeling very confident about her chances when it came to killing him. She'd only been dodging him for a minute or so and was feeling the strain; could she keep it up for another thirty minutes or so? The eastern sky was definitely lighter than the rest of the sky, but thirty minutes was a long time to be fighting for your life. "Maybe another tactic," she muttered to her audience. "Hey, asshole. I don't even know who you are; why are you attacking me? Just because I'm working for the Summer Court?"

"Hah," Thun choked out the laugh, then spread his arms and stomped a hoof back into the soil as though he was bracing himself for something. His face twisted into a grimace, and he pointed both palms at Bronwyn and shouted, "Don't try to toy with me, welp!" Bronwyn knew better than to stand still while he readied some mega-attack, so she took two running leaps to her left and dove into a somersaulting roll. She felt and heard the rumbling crack of the earth behind her, and when she landed and rolled, the ground heaved her into another diving roll. She landed among the trees, which swayed and lurched, branches and needles showering down onto the snowy ground. Bronwyn took the opportunity to sprint deeper into the tree cover, dodging behind tree trunks and leaping over the undergrowth.

Thun laughed and gave chase, stopping to stomp on the ground, rippling the earth, and sending trees falling left and right. He didn't seem to know exactly where she was because he often sent tremors in directions perpendicular to the path she'd taken to flee. Bronwyn smiled and continued to put distance between them. Once he howled in frustration and launched another of his massive ground ripping quakes, but he destroyed a copse of trees several hundred feet behind Bronwyn, and she almost laughed as she watched the trees fall away from the cleaved soil. Briefly, she worried he'd give up the chase and retreat somewhere before the dawn, but he seemed single-minded in his desire to catch and kill her.

As she gained ground on him, he screamed several more times and performed that massive attack, splitting the ground and upending trees. Only as he did it for the fourth time did Bronwyn realize what was happening; she'd been luring him around in a loose circle, trying to bide time until the dawn, but he'd been using that spell to box her in. Each time he cast it, he created a fissure in the ground lined with fallen trees. "Ugh, penning me in," she grunted, turning to run toward a still-open area in the wooded vale. Bronwyn glanced to the east and saw the distinctive gray sky tinged with orange that told her the right moment was coming up.

Bronwyn sprinted flat-out, giving it everything she had, racing for the rocky hills that led up out of the western side of the valley into the gray stony peaks. She could hear Thun roaring and tearing apart the landscape for a few seconds, but then it stopped, and the tingles on the back of her neck told her he'd decided to try to close the distance between them. She'd just broken from the trees and was starting to pound up the loose dirt and rocks of the hillside when she heard the staccato crunch of Thun's hooves tearing into the earth behind her. She jumped to the side, expecting a charge. Still, Thun wasn't so easily avoided, and she felt, to her horror, his horns as they smashed into her lower back, rending her armor, gouging her flesh, and sending her flying with an explosive exhalation.

Bronwyn rolled and tumbled along the slope of the hill, sharp stone chips tearing at her exposed flesh. She tried to catch her breath, gasping and pressing a hand to her lower back where it felt like something had ruptured. "A merry chase, human. To no avail, I'm afraid. I'll have my pound of flesh and send the scraps back to your *Lady*." He sneered and drew out the word "Lady" mockingly.

"Please, I can't fight you. Why do you hate the Summer Lady so much?" Bronwyn struggled to her hands and knees, still pressing against her back where she'd been hit.

"So soft, truly?" He stepped forward and kicked at her with one of his hooves, and Bronwyn weakly put out a hand, catching the brunt of the blow on her forearm and sliding backward with its force. She groaned and cringed, frantically scooting further back on her butt, scrabbling through the loose dirt and gravel.

"Stop, please! I don't know what's happening here; why are you so angry?" Bronwyn kept scooting back, pushing herself up the hill, facing out over the valley, and at the far horizon. Thun stalked forward, the ground seeming to wince with each of his hoof steps.

"You stupid child. Fell right into her games without a thought as to what was happening? What did she offer you? Power? Wealth? Praise? Just a dumb pawn, but now you'll have to pay for the sins of your master." He stood over Bronwyn, his towering bulk throwing her into shadow, though she could see between his leather-clad legs, and, as a sliver of light erupted from between two of the eastern peaks, she grinned and lowered her cringing arms.

"Am I stupid? I have to confess: I'm feeling sort of clever." Her smile broadened as her flesh erupted in the brilliant white-yellow light of her Solar Shell, then she surged upward, channeling Energy into her Solar Arms spell. As she exploded off the ground, she brought her left fist up in a massive haymaker, but Thun wasn't slow; he lifted his arm to knock hers away, and that's when the expression on his face changed. His eyes widened, and his leathery lips parted in an almost comical "O" as Bronwyn's pulsing, vibrating fist blasted through his guard and connected just under his broad barrel of a chest. Thun wore a thick leather vest with a dozen buttoned pockets on the breasts, and Bronwyn felt it absorb some of her attack's force, though she still saw the power of her strike ripple through his body. He uttered a loud, air-filled, "Oof!" then stumbled several steps back down the slope, and then Bronwyn, for the first time, cast Wrath of Summer.

A perfect circle of light, ten feet in diameter, appeared on the ground around Thun, and then it erupted upward into a blazing column. Bronwyn could see Thun's shadowy form at the center of the column of light, and she observed little fragments of shadow detach from the figure and stream upward, dissipating into tiny particles. She had to shield her eyes after a moment, and then, a few heartbeats later, the light winked out. She looked up to see a perfectly delineated black circle on the side of the hill with Thun kneeling at its center.

The Cadwalli wasn't the imposing specimen he'd once been. Steam and smoke rose from his withered form, and he twitched as Bronwyn stood, hands out and ready. Thun's armor and fur were mostly gone, and his left arm had been dissolved down to a stump. His horns were shortened and round, and his ears and nose were oozing holes in his skull. Thun's breath rasped out of the ruin of his mouth, and to Bronwyn's horror, he began to chuckle, a sicky, gurgling sound filled with fluid. "Oh, fool I am." He ground out the words, spitting bloody phlegm onto the blackened hillside. He looked up, twisting his head left to right, and Bronwyn realized he was blind.

Bronwyn almost let her Solar Arms spell drop and tried to talk to the Cadwalli, but then a large red bottle appeared in his hand, and he tilted it to his charred lips. Bronwyn said, "Shit!" and launched forward, stepping past him, aiming a devastating straight-handed chop at the Cadwalli's throat. She felt her hand crunch through his esophagus, shattering the tiny bones and tendons in his voice box, and sending his weakened, blasted body tumbling down the slope. The bottle fell, clattering onto the scree, its thick purple contents dissolving into steam as it poured out. Bronwyn didn't risk him pulling another Hail Mary out of some dimensional container; she stomped down the slope, picked up a jagged gray rock the size of a basketball, and smashed it onto Thun's skull as he struggled to find purchase. His body jerked, but he kept scrabbling at the ground, gasping for air, and she had to pick it up and smash it down again.

Finally, the goat-like man stopped his struggles and fell to his face, but Bronwyn smashed him again, and then one final time before golden motes with flecks of purple began to coalesce around his form and then stream into her. When the surge of Energy hit her, it was unlike anything she'd experienced. She lost control of her body and stood transfixed as it poured into her, lifting her several inches off the ground.

Congratulations! You have achieved level 17 Summer Banneret and have gained 28 attribute points to allocate.

Congratulations! You have achieved level 18 Summer Banneret and have gained 56 attribute points to allocate.

"Well, Thun, I have to say I appreciate you being an absolute asshole and making this job more palatable." Bronwyn pushed Thun's still-smoldering corpse over with her boot, looking for any sign of the dimensional container from which he'd pulled the potion. Most of his clothes and armor were destroyed, but a gold-colored chain gleamed on his neck, and she reached down to pull it up from the remnants of his charred vest. It was a thick, twisted braid of metal with a jade disc affixed to it. She spun it to find the catch and, opening it, pulled it free from Thun's corpse.

The necklace was heavy, and she wondered if it was gold. "I suppose if it's magical enough, it might resist getting melted," she muttered while channeling a little Energy into it. She instantly became aware of another dimensional space, much larger than even the ring she'd gotten from Queen Aestasia. At first glance, she saw that it held a disturbing number of animal and humanoid corpses, as well as camping supplies, packaged food, bottles of liquor, and a score of small sacks filled with Energy beads—there had to be thousands of them. Looking past the corpses, she saw a black hammer and summoned it forth. It was about the size of a small, one-handed sledgehammer, but the handle and hammerhead were all crafted from one piece of black metal. As she held it up in the dawn light, black smoke drifted from the hammer's two heads, and palpable warmth drifted out from it.

Bronwyn shrugged and sent a trickle of Energy into the weapon:

*****Singe: Artificed Weapon. This weapon is crafted from dragon-ore and is nearly impervious to damage. Enchantments: 1. Smoldering—This weapon has been enchanted with primal fire, allowing it to destroy materials and damage flesh more easily. 2. Felicitous wielding—This weapon moves with the wielder in a symbiotic relationship, smoothly adding momentum to any motions. 3. Returning—Given the wielder has a strong enough will, this weapon will return to the wielder's hand after being thrown.**

"Not bad!" Bronwyn gave the hammer a toss, flipping it into the air and catching the handle. It seemed to slap into her hand effortlessly. She turned to look down the slope, eyeing a half-fallen tree trunk. She hurled the hammer through the air at the trunk, and it flew with a whistling screech and a trail of embers and ash. The hammer smacked into the trunk with a loud crack, and Bronwyn saw embers fly as the tree began to smoke. She held out her hand, concentrating on the hammer, and felt it out there, buzzing and rattling in the broken tree. She narrowed her eyes and willed it to come back, and it struggled for a moment, then burst out of the cracked, smoldering tree and tumbled back toward her to slap into her palm with a satisfying thwap. "Awesome!"

Bronwyn put the hammer back into the necklace and then examined its contents once more, looking for anything she missed. Behind the pile of corpses, she found a stack of large potion flasks, but none of them had a label when she pulled them out. She put them away, figuring she could ask Queen Aestasia about them when she returned. "Speaking of returning . . ." Bronwyn trailed off, looking back toward the mouth of the valley where she'd come in. She didn't like the vibes she felt in this valley, even after killing Thun, so she decided to get moving back the way she'd come. She fastened her new necklace around her neck and started jogging away from Thun's corpse.

ॐ OLIVIA ॐ

Olivia strode through the slime puddles and chunks of frozen ooze, moving toward the door that should take her to the final room of the third level. She'd had to fight, predictably, four oozes in the fourth room, so she figured there'd be five in the final room. She didn't want to be overconfident, though, so she paused in front of the door, leaning with her back against the stone wall, and waited for her Energy to top off and for her Elemental Form to be ready. So far, she didn't think this dungeon had been that challenging, but when she thought of the swarms of spiders, the giant rock bear, the barriers she'd had to bypass, and the girl caught in the ooze, she had to conclude that she was simply lucky to have a powerful skill set.

When she felt ready, Olivia pulled open the heavy, water-logged door and looked into the fifth room of the third floor. She'd been right on one count; there were five creatures within, but they weren't all oozes. She saw three green oozes, one red ooze, and a smooth, humanoid-shaped black, slimy creature. It was a bizarre and disconcerting thing to see: a walking slime, pacing around the far wall, shaking its smooth, bendy arms and grunting out weird noises. Olivia couldn't study it any longer, though; the nearest two green oozes had noticed her pulling the door open and surged toward her. She pointed her right palm at the advancing oozes and poured forth a Fiery Burst spraying the flames liberally over the two creatures. They hissed, popped, and shriveled into black sludge, and Olivia stepped between their bubbling corpses to fire Arcfrost Cascade at the red ooze that had started to surge toward her.

The spray of crackling white-blue ice first petrified, then exploded the red ooze, sending chunks of flash-frozen slime slithering over the stony, mossy floor. Olivia turned to face the final green ooze and the strange shambling ooze-man but was alarmed to see the black, shimmery, jiggling form trudging toward her with a rictus grin on its otherwise smooth, featureless face. Olivia saw rows of sharp needle-like teeth within its mouth, and she stumbled back in fear. This creature was much faster than the oozes. She backpedaled, holding her hands up, and firing the first spell that came to mind, Fiery Burst. The ooze-man waded through her flames, its grinning maw spreading further, and the fire seemed to roll over its jiggling body. Olivia's spell had just sputtered out when it reached forward and smashed a jiggly fist into her stomach.

Olivia grunted in pain, stumbling back, breathless. She knew that if she'd taken a hit like that when she first came to this world, it would have sent her sprawling, convulsed in pain, and unable to act. As it was, her much higher vitality seemed to be paying off. She quickly straightened and ran a few steps from the ooze-man, calling on her Elemental Form spell, but this time she fueled it with earth-attuned Energy. Olivia felt her skin stiffen and her sense of mass increase. She knew from practicing with Oylla that her body was now much denser and more resistant to physical damage. In her haste to get away from the ooze-man, she'd run close to the last green slime, so she summoned a ball of plasma and dropped it into the center of the probing creature. It writhed and contorted, bubbling and hissing as her plasma cooked it from the inside.

She felt an impact on her upper back, but it didn't hurt. Olivia turned and saw that the shimmering ooze-man was right behind her, and swinging its balled up, slimy fists at her. She held up her left arm, knocking aside the blows, pleased to see that the jiggly flesh of the ooze-man was ineffectual against her gray, stony flesh. Olivia fired one spell after another at the creature, trying to find a weakness in its resistances, but nothing seemed to work; even her Pyro-steam Drill simply slid along the surface of his body and tore into the far wall. Whatever this creature was, it was designed to thwart spells.

Frustration started to turn toward worry when Olivia realized how much Energy she'd burned and how long she'd been holding onto her Elemental Form. Once again, she blocked the creature's quivering fist, and the thought occurred to her that it seemed very weak against the sturdy earthen form; why not try to give it a good bludgeoning of her own? She called up a sphere of earth-attuned Energy, basically, a rocky orb the size of a bowling ball, and, just as she'd practiced with Oylla, sent it whipping through the air to crash into the oily ooze-man's body. The concussion of the stone into its jiggling chest sent a satisfying ripple through its body, and it tumbled back, sliding along the mossy stone to crash into the wall. Olivia followed up with an arcing barrage of strikes. She sent her stony orb forward again and again to pummel the creature. Sometime during her attack, her Elemental Form wore off, but she didn't panic; the ooze monster was starting to deform, and a piteous wheezing, wailing sound gurgled out of its smashed maw when she directed her orb of stone to crash into its rows of needle-like teeth.

Something inside the creature must have been solid because as she broke it apart, the creature lost what rigidity it had and became a quivering mound of black slime. Her attacks never breached its jiggling skin, but a viscous fluid started to leak from its mouth, and it seemed to cease its attempts to move or rise. Olivia whooped and let her rocky orb dissipate into a cloud of green-tinted Energy that faded into nothing. She just started to turn when her body went stiff, and a jolt of electricity passed through her.

The current was so strong that Olivia felt herself lose control of her muscles and fell to the ground spasming. She couldn't form a coherent thought as pulse after pulse of electricity wracked through her, and then she felt her consciousness start to slip. She fought against it, squeezing her eyes shut but forcing herself to focus inward on her Core, shutting out her spasming body and maintaining her consciousness with an act of will. "Poor thing," a familiar voice said. "She did a good job, though. Too bad she emptied her bag of tricks on that thing." It was Jaliss. Olivia couldn't believe it, couldn't wrap her mind around it; Jaliss had attacked her after Olivia had gone out of her way to help her.

Through the agony of electric pulses, Olivia suddenly felt a surge of Energy pour into her; the ooze-man must have finally died. "Oh no, you don't!" Jaliss said from somewhere behind her, and a fresh surge of electricity wracked through Olivia's body, making her spasm and lose control of her bladder. Red waves of embarrassment and rage surged around her Core, and Olivia knew the sliver of her soul born from a primal elemental was waking up and urging action. For once, she didn't try to hold it back. Her Elemental Form was still on cooldown, but she knew the pattern for it. Once again, turning her mind away from her spasming body, she focused on her Core and nearby pathways. She formed the pattern for Elemental Form, then removed almost all of it, just keeping the part that caused attuned Energy to form around her body, then she added the pattern for Fiery Burst. She wasn't doing anything all that complicated, just changing the way Fiery Burst was produced; instead of firing a burst of fire from one pathway through her hand, she was allowing it to propagate through all her pathways and out through her flesh. It was a quick hack, but she had to do something; she had no control of her body and couldn't move to focus a spell on her assailant. She was thinking fast, bending and twisting strands of Energy into the clumsy pattern, but once it was set, she fired it off, pushing all the fire-attuned Energy in her Core out to fuel it.

If Olivia were able to see, she'd have witnessed a ball of fire erupt from her prone, spasming form, billowing out with tremendous force, scorching the ground, the ceiling, and even the room's walls. Jaliss, who'd been standing a few paces from Olivia pouring electricity into her, was instantly scorched and flung back to slam into the stone wall. With the source of her torture knocked aside, Olivia's body stopped thrashing and spasming, and she was able to see the notifications that had appeared in her vision:

Congratulations! You have learned the spell: Elemental Bomb—Improved.

Elemental Bomb—Improved: Prerequisite: Elemental Affinity. You create an explosion originating from your body that unleashes 100 percent of an elementally-attuned Energy from your Core. Energy cost: Varied, Cooldown: Long.

Congratulations! You have achieved level 18 Elemental Archon and have gained 10 Intelligence, 10 Will, and have 8 points to allocate.

Olivia groaned and flopped onto her stomach, looking around the room with bloodshot eyes. A layer of ash coated everything, and the sickly odor of burnt fungus filled the air. She scrambled to her hands and knees and caught sight of Jaliss against the wall. She was twitching and scrabbling weakly with her left hand. Olivia struggled to her feet and staggered over to her. Jaliss was slumped against the wall, her skin covered with char, and parts of her face looked painfully blistered. Her hair had been burnt off save for a few patches, and Olivia saw that her right hand was missing some fingers. "Probably the hand you were pointing at me while you electrocuted me, hmm?" She knelt by the girl and poked her chest. Her eyes popped open, startlingly white in her soot-covered face. She started to cry and whispered hoarsely, "It hurts so bad! Oh, Ancestors, it hurts."

Olivia didn't listen to her or respond. She grabbed the girl's undamaged hand and lifted it, flattening it against the little round pendant hanging from Jaliss's neck. "Activate it. You're done." Jaliss struggled weakly for a moment, trying to pull her hand down, but Olivia just pressed harder. The girl sobbed, but she closed her eyes, and Olivia felt the heat of Energy pulse into the amulet. She let go of her hand and stood up, watching as the girl seemed to dissolve in front of her. She stood and sighed, looking around at the destruction she'd wrought. Even with the Energy from the enemies she'd killed, she was running on fumes. She moved stiffly over to what was hopefully the last of the soggy wooden doors and began the process of yanking the swollen wood over the stone floor. When she'd gotten it open enough to squeeze through, she peered into a square stone room with a matching stone staircase leading straight down from the opposite wall. A large, mold-covered chest sat in the center of the room.

Olivia squeezed through the doorway, turned, and dragged it shut behind her; she'd decided she would rather not have any more surprise visitors. Then, she walked over to the chest and lifted the heavy, soggy lid. She saw four items at the bottom of the chest and held her hand back in case she'd only be allowed to select one. The four items couldn't be more different; from left to right, she saw a shiny double-bladed axe, a floppy-looking black hat, a pair of shiny black boots, and a leather bandolier or belt holding seven glass tubes.

She thought any of the items could prove very valuable, but she looked down at her white jumper and the thin cloth pads under her feet and impulsively picked up the shiny black boots. Just as she'd expected, the other items seemed to burst into yellow and blue motes and then simply faded from existence. She wondered at the mechanic the System used to do that. Were the items being absorbed by the ambient Energy? Were they being transported into a bank in an alternate universe? She shrugged and looked at her new boots. They had sturdy thick soles and rounded toes, and the uppers would comfortably cover her feet and ankles. She set them down and slipped her feet into them; they were a size or two too large.

Olivia had learned by now how magical items in this world worked, so she trickled some Energy into the boots, and they instantly hugged her feet, and a System message popped up:

*****Boots of Steady Striding: Artificed Footwear. These boots have been made to help the wearer keep their footing on any sort of surface, and be very difficult to knock down. Enchantment: Self-repair and self-cleaning.*****

"Lovely!" Olivia said, walking in a circle and getting a feel for the boots. They felt better than any footwear she'd ever owned, even her favorite sneakers back home. Olivia took stock of herself, checking that her Energy was rapidly recovering and her big spells were off cooldown, then she started walking down the steps. She made it about twenty steps when she lowered her foot onto a partially submerged step. The stairway was dim, and visibility wasn't great, but she could clearly see that further progress down would require her to swim. "That's a new twist," she said to herself.

OLIVIA

Looking at the cold, dark water, Olivia debated whether to go back to the room where she'd first met Jaliss to try one of the other doors. She supposed there could be another path forward, but would she have to fight through four more rooms? There was also the chance that the doors only led to different routes up to the second floor. "Forward it is." She concentrated and cast Elemental Form, fueling it with water-attuned Energy. She felt a cool wave rush through her, originating from her Core, and when she looked down at her hands, they were shimmery and blue. She'd tested this form with Oylla and found that she could move quickly through water, ignoring all but the most frigid temperatures, but she still had to breathe. Not wanting to waste any time or Energy, she took a deep breath and walked down into the murky depths of the sunken stairway.

The water wasn't any colder than her water form flesh, so it didn't feel uncomfortable, and as soon as her head was submerged, she saw that the murky depths were liberally spotted with faintly glowing lichen. She could easily see where she was going, so she pushed off with her feet and began to slide through the water faster than any person on Earth could swim. It was almost like flying, and a wide grin spread on her shimmery, blue face. She reached the bottom of the stairs in just a moment and still felt fine with regard to her air reserves; she might not be able to breathe water, but her racial advancements allowed her to hold her breath for a very long time.

The room at the foot of the stairs was small, and the only exit was on the opposite wall. A few fragments of wood were all that remained of a door. She slipped past the broken timber and, fluttering her feet, raced up the short hallway to another doorway, this one with no door remnants at all. She saw movement in the water ahead, so she slowed down and glided to a stop at the doorway, peering ahead. Several dark shapes were flitting around in the water. They resembled snakes or maybe eels, but their heads were much larger than anything she'd seen in nature videos. She was trying to determine if they were hostile when one meandered in such a way that it faced directly at her. She caught her breath, which she'd already been holding when she saw that it had a strange humanoid head with flat, black, fishy eyes. Its wide maw gaped open and closed, sort of chomping at the water, and she saw that it was filled with triangular, pointed teeth.

Olivia ducked back behind the corner, just peering around with one eye to see how many of the weird eels were in the room, and she counted four. She thought about attacking them, but some of her spells were useless underwater, like her fire-based spells, and her lightning spells might even be dangerous to her. Could she freeze them? Would her Icy Shards have enough velocity if shot through water? She was thinking of a way to attack when their meandering movement took them all toward the far corners of the room, and she impulsively shot forward toward the far doorway. She kicked as fast as she could and didn't look back until she was well into the next hallway; none of them pursued her. She was glad she avoided the fight, but she was also starting to worry about air.

Floating before the next doorway, Olivia decided to try something: she floated up to the ceiling and channeled Wind Gust out of her palm at the corner where the two walls met. Prodigious air bubbles gushed out of her hand and collected in the corner, starting to slide off to the sides. She quickly poked her head into the most prominent air pocket and gulped a deep breath, grinning at her ingenuity. She dropped down and looked through the next doorway and wasn't surprised to see the same weird eels. She was trying to time their movements to slip through again when a larger shape suddenly rushed out of a hole in the floor that she'd taken for a patch of dark fungus. It streamed right toward her, and she caught a glimpse of a giant, gaping maw and spindly hooked arms with three claws grasping before she raised her hand in a panic and fired off her Icy Shards spell, hoping for the best.

A dozen or so shards of ice jetted through the water, and with the creature advancing rapidly, they didn't have to travel far before they sank into its face. The shards pierced its eyes, embedded in its open mouth, and ripped at its cheeks and forehead. Olivia watched the large eel creature thrash and begin to sink, wisps of blood rising in the dark water. She knew that fish were sensitive to smell in water and that this blood would possibly draw the other creatures, so Olivia darted forward through it and tried to make a run for the next doorway. Once again, she was pleasantly surprised to find that she wasn't followed; when she looked back, she saw a flurry of activity near the dead eel creature and realized that the smaller ones were eating the big one's corpse. Not wanting to waste time, Olivia turned and hurried to the next room.

A different sight waited for her through the next doorway. She could see into the next room and didn't note any movement, but she also couldn't see another doorway. When she moved a bit closer and peered into the submerged room, she caught a shimmer of light in the corner of her eye, and when she looked up at it, she realized there was open air above, about three feet higher than the door. She'd already had to renew the Energy flowing to her Elemental Form twice. Each time, it was more difficult and seemed to take more Energy, so she was both glad and trepidatious about this new development. Deciding to err on the side of caution, she hurried through the doorway and glided to the farthest, darkest corner, and then she very slowly rose up, so just the top of her head poked out of the water.

She was in a dark pool with a strangely sandy beach on the far side. A lantern burned very dimly from a hook in the wall next to a closed door, and an enormous lizard reclined in the sand near the gently lapping water. Anywhere Olivia chose to emerge from the pool would be three or four paces at most from the lizard. Bracing herself for the chill, she let her water Elemental Form drop; she wanted to hide here and wait for it to come back off cooldown so she could use a different one to face the lizard. The water was cold, but not enough to steal her breath, and though she began to shiver, she treaded water there in the dark corner for several minutes. When she felt her spell come off cooldown, she very slowly, carefully swam to the far corner of the little beach, trying to keep from splashing the water. When her hands and knees bumped into the sandy stone, she pulled herself up, keeping her eyes on the lizard. So far, it hadn't reacted to her and seemed to have its eyes closed. This close, she could see that it was gray-green overall, with tiny yellow and orange nodules all along its snout, neck, and back.

Olivia didn't fancy herself a violent person nor a killer, but she didn't want to give the lizard a chance to leap up and snap her leg off in its huge maw. Whispering softly, "I'm sorry about this," Olivia held out her palm and went for broke with a Plasma Wave. The superheated electrical plasma arched out of her palm in a wave of crackling blue devastation. It widened as it gained distance, and by the time the wave of plasma hit the lizard, it was three feet wide. It vaporized the lizard's flesh and boiled the muscle and blood beneath it. The lizard reflexively bounded into the air, its mouth open in a hideous shrieking hiss. Olivia tracked its movement with her hand and finished cooking it as it hissed and rolled and thrashed back from her. When her spell ended, the creature was a blackened, steaming husk. Olivia felt very guilty about killing the lizard. Something about it was different from the other monsters she'd slain in the dungeon. It seemed more natural, perhaps. It hadn't been a swarm of aggressive spiders, an ooze, or a ghastly fish with a humanoid head. It had seemed to suffer real pain and terror at her attack. Shaking her head and pushing the thoughts to the back of her mind, Olivia moved toward the door. She was about to reach for the handle when she caught sight of something out of the corner of her eye.

She walked over to where the big lizard had been sleeping and saw the curve of something pale yellow poking out of the sand. She gently pushed the sand aside with her boot toe and revealed a large yellow egg with pale brown speckles. Olivia knelt down and gently smoothed away the sand with her hands, and by the time she was done, she'd revealed five of the rubbery, round eggs. Not knowing what else to do with them, she put them into her storage ring. That accomplished, she stood and walked over to the door. It wasn't waterlogged or broken, and when she pulled on it, it smoothly glided over the sandy ground. She stepped through into a stone corridor about fifteen paces long and ending in another, identical door.

She wasn't sure what to expect beyond this door; was it the fourth or fifth room? She didn't know if the submerged room leading up to the sandy beach room was one space or two. Her Elemental Form was ready, and she had plenty of Energy, so she pulled open the door a few inches and peeked through. This room gave the impression of being much larger than any of the others on this level of the dungeon. That wasn't what stood out to Olivia, though; rather, it was the vegetation and the high ceiling with a light resembling a noonday sun. Moisture hung in the air like a tropical jungle, and the ferns and undergrowth crowded a narrow dirt-covered trail that led away from the door. Olivia didn't like that there was so much foliage around; how could she know if something was about to jump out at her? She was tempted to take on her earth-attuned Elemental Form but decided to hold it at the ready; instead, she summoned a ball of rock and willed it to orbit her body, prepared to intercept any attacks.

Damp fern leaves left trails of moisture on her hands, sleeves, and face as she pushed through the narrow path, trying to avoid making a ruckus. She'd traversed about thirty yards when she saw a break in the dense undergrowth and something colorful darted past the spot where the trail broke through. She tiptoed up to the last solid-looking tree before the open space and tried to peer around the trunk. She'd just poked one eye around the rough, green and yellow bark when a tremendous trumpeting roar sounded, and a feathered, horn-covered head bulldozed into the tree. It split the wood down the middle and launched Olivia, who'd been leaning against it, flying through the air to smash into another tree. She crashed through the branches, painfully scratching her back and arms, even through her tough jumper. When she landed, she was almost upside down, and her head and shoulders dug a furrow in the soft dirt as she finally slid to a stop. She could feel the ground shaking as something big stomped toward her, so Olivia, still slightly dazed, cast her earth Elemental Form. Her skin had just hardened to gray-brown rocky flesh when a massive beak snatched her up and, shaking her about like a ragdoll, carried her through the trees and into the big clearing.

Olivia could feel the huge, sharp edge of the beak grinding into her, but it wasn't terribly painful, and she didn't think it was making much progress through her hardened flesh. She wondered if the creature was trying to kill her or just carry her; it certainly hadn't held back when it smashed into the tree she'd been hiding behind. Maybe it already thought she was dead. She tried to look around, but the creature seemed to be trotting around the clearing in a way that made Olivia think of her old retriever when she pranced around proudly with her favorite chew toy. She began to grow dizzy, trying to focus on the details of the clearing, and instead just let her eyes move with the creature's bouncing gait. She was in a clearing maybe fifty yards wide, surrounded by ferns and trees, and she thought she caught a glimpse of a small pool of water at one end.

"Hey, how long are you going to shake me around? Are you trying to kill me?" Olivia didn't expect an answer, and she was starting to get worried; she couldn't maintain her earth form forever, and this thing would cut her in half if she let it drop. Every now and then, it would shake her in such a way that she'd see part of its body: long red and yellow talons, bright red, blue, and yellow tail feathers; was this thing a giant rooster? Olivia decided she couldn't delay anymore and triggered her Elemental Bomb spell, using fire Energy like before, because she knew what to expect from it. Her vision went orange and red for a moment, and she felt the warm wave of Energy pour through her stony flesh, then she was falling to the soft turf, the roaring of flames, and the thud of a colossal body accompanying her.

Olivia sat up, shaking her head to clear the ringing from her ears, and looked over her shoulder. A giant, brightly feathered, headless corpse was lying not five feet from her, its truncated neck smoldering and black. Bits of feather, bone, flesh, and blood began to shower down on her then, and she covered her head, though she still wore her rocky earth form. Olivia stood and scampered away a few feet, just as a torrent of Energy flooded into her.

"That had to bring me close to a level," she said, savoring the exuberance and positive emotions that always came with an influx of Energy. Olivia walked around the giant, colorful corpse toward the little pond on one end of the clearing. There, nestled among some intertwined branches, she spotted a bronze metal chest about the size of a big shoebox. "I guess that settles it; this was the fifth room."

◈ OLIVIA ◈

Like the last two chests, the bronze chest offered her different rewards, and when Olivia touched one of them, the other two disappeared. This time there were only three choices: a crystal orb, a red metal ring, and another book. She'd already taken one book, so this time she reached for the ring, not sure why it called to her more than the orb, but she wasn't disappointed when she bonded with it:

Ring of Thick Blood—The wearer of this ring will bleed much more slowly from wounds than normal, allowing more time to recover and heal before succumbing to death's icy grasp.

"Colorful," Olivia said, wondering who or what created the description for some items while others seemed to have none. It was a dull, red-colored metal that was warm to the touch. She wore it on the hand opposite her new storage ring and briefly wondered if they'd conflict with each other if they were on the same hand. I'll experiment with that later," she said as she fought through the foliage hanging over the path, trying to find the next door or stairway. She didn't have to go far; pushing through just a few feet of overgrown trail, she came to another clearing with a long, rectangular stone platform that housed a set of descending steps.

Standing at the top of the steps, looking down into the dark, dusty, cobweb-covered stairwell, Olivia took a moment to take stock of her situation. She was about to descend into the fifth level. Hadn't her friends said no one had gotten that far in a long while? Or had they said the sixth level? Either way, she'd made good progress, and she'd only been at it a few hours if her perception of the time was correct. She didn't feel particularly tired, thanks to the Energy she kept getting infused with, and her spells were off cooldown. Nodding to herself, Olivia summoned an orb of fire Energy and began to climb down the steps.

Her smoldering orb of orange flames cast the gloomy stairwell into shadows that leaped and jittered with each of her steps. The descent took a while, and unlike previous levels, the type of stairs didn't change midway; she came out into a cramped, dusty stone room with thick bunches of cobwebs in all the corners and even long strands extending from the open stairwell to the doorless archway leading out of the room.

Olivia willed her orb out ahead of her to melt away the cobwebs in her path and slowly started to advance into the tunnel. On previous levels, she'd found the next doorway just a dozen steps or so down each little hallway. This one seemed to stretch into darkness, even when she pushed her orb out so far that she began to lose control of it. She continued, though, and was comforted in the cramped, creepy depths by the fact that she hadn't passed any doorways and, so far, seemed to be quite alone; no other footsteps marred the thick dust on the stones.

After walking for many minutes, she encountered something new: a T junction. To her left and right, the hallway stretched into darkness. She didn't know if this was going to be some sort of maze, so she decided to take a right-hand turn and maintain that pattern on further junctions, if there were any. She walked for a hundred feet or so, then she started to make out an end to the tunnel; a wooden door barred further progress.

When she approached the door, she saw that it had a handle, but when she tried to push or pull on it, it wouldn't move. "We can't let a little thing like a doorway stop us, now, can we?" Olivia asked, and had to pause for a moment to wonder who she was talking about with the "We." She decided to chalk it up to being alone in a deep dungeon for too long. She stepped back a few paces and then fired a Pyrosteam Drill at the wooden door, obliterating the wood around the handle and along the doorjamb. When she dropped her hand and the steam in the air cleared, the door hung loosely open.

She took one step toward the door when it smashed open against the wall, and a throng of clattering bones and rusty armor surged into the hallway. Olivia had time to register what she saw and utter one word, "Skeletons!" Then, they were on her, and she frantically pushed her fire orb at the pack, pushing as much Energy into it as she could. Flames erupted on the first two or three skeletons, igniting their crusty, dry clothing and armor, but it didn't slow them. Just as the lead skeleton was bringing a heavy, rusty mace down toward her, she cast her earth-attuned Elemental Form and held up her arm, blocking the blow. Even with her thick, stony skin, the impact hurt, and she took another step back.

"Enough!" She shouted, holding out a hand and unleashing a Plasma Wave. This attack, the skeletons didn't shrug off. The force of the crackling plasma tore into the bunch of silent, grasping, clacking creatures, ripping apart their bones, melting their armor and weapons, and reducing the mob of skeletons to twitching, smoldering wreckage. She worked her way through the smoking battlefield and peered through the doorway. Nothing but a plain, square room waited for her with a matching doorway on the left-hand wall. Olivia destroyed the lock on the door with a plasma orb and then continued forward, down another long, dusty hallway.

She ended up having to clear three more rooms of mini-hordes of skeletons before Olivia found anything different. The last room she'd gone through had housed at least twenty skeletons in various states of decomposition, some of them with large portions of their bodies still covered with rotting flesh. When she'd gone through and down another long, dusty hallway, she'd come to a different sort of door; this one was banded with iron and had thick, rectangular bars of steel barring it shut as though to keep something inside from smashing its way through. Olivia could see that the bars were resting in steel brackets and could be lifted free on this side of the door, so the idea that they were there to keep her out didn't bear much weight.

Olivia pressed her ear to the metal, resting her head between two thick steel bars, and thought she heard the sound of a bellows pumping air and the grind of stone against stone. She'd already determined to go forward, so the only thing she needed to do was overcome her nerves and pull the bars down. She leaned back against the wall and glanced down the hallway from which she'd come. Nothing moved; nothing stirred the dust or cobwebs still clinging to the ceiling. The air was dry and musty, and as she rested her head against the stone wall, she felt webs sticking to her hair. She could always use her recall token. She touched the cool little disc of metal hanging from her neck. She could recall and say she ran into something near the end of the fifth floor that she couldn't handle. Surely, she'd made it far enough to do the school proud.

Her rewards so far were nothing to sneeze at; she'd gotten quite a few nice magical items and several levels. Was it worth risking an encounter with whatever was behind this door just for bragging rights and a chance at more loot? She remembered what Oylla had told her about how fragile humanity was in this world. She might not owe the people at First Landing much, but she nonetheless felt a sense of duty. They were going to need someone to stand up for them sooner or later, and Olivia had been gifted with the ability to manipulate Energy to such a degree that this "Proving Grounds" dungeon hadn't really been a challenge thus far. If she backed away now, on the verge of going further than anyone from Fainhallow in recent memory, what did that say about her? "That I value my skin? I really need to stop talking to myself."

She hoisted the first of the big metal bars out of its bracket, grunting at the weight. She'd just gotten it out of the brackets and was straining from the effort when an idea came to her. She accessed her storage ring with her mind and stowed the bar inside. Grinning, she reached out, slightly lifted the next bar, and stored it as well. She repeated the process three more times, and the door was exposed, ready for her to open it and see what horror the designer of this dungeon had locked within. "Maybe I'm building this up too much in my head. Maybe it's just another pack of skeletons." Olivia reached out, grasped the handle, and pulled, careful not to open the door more than an inch so that she could peek within.

The space beyond the door was similar in construction to the rest of the fifth floor, with low ceilings and neatly mortared stone blocks making up the flooring, but there wasn't much dust, and she didn't see any cobwebs. Looking further into the room, she saw why: a creature that looked like a cross between a rhinoceros and a rotting human was stalking around the room's perimeter, dragging an enormous stone maul along behind it. Each step it took was ponderous, and its breathing was the source of the bellows sound Olivia had heard through the door.

The room was about twenty feet wide but more than a hundred long, and at that moment, the creature was stalking away from Olivia down the long wall to her right. Briefly, Olivia entertained the idea of trying to sneak or run past the monstrosity. She didn't know what the other door was like, though, and didn't fancy the idea of trying to monkey with it while this two-thousand-pound creature bore down on her. No, better to deal with this thing on her terms.

Olivia gently closed the door, then, in a fit of paranoia, she spun around and cast Fiery Burst down the hallway behind her. Dust billowed off the floor ahead of the jet of flames, and cobwebs shriveled into smoke, but no lurking attackers were exposed. "Shit!" she hissed, "That little bitch really messed with my mind." It wasn't the first time Olivia had whirled around, expecting another Jaliss incident with a rival student sneaking up to knife her in the back or something.

Gathering herself, Olivia ran through her plan of attack several times, making sure she had an idea for every kind of contingency she could think of: what would she do if it ignored her spells? What would she do if it charged her and swung that massive maul her way? How would she react if more monsters came out of the shadows? How would she retreat if it became necessary? She thought of these and myriad other possible outcomes, and then she took three deep breaths and cracked the door open again.

The monster was coming toward her, so she closed the door and waited. When she felt the ground vibrate with the passage of the dragging maul, she pulled the door open and watched the creature's back as it proceeded away from her in its strange circuit. She quietly pulled the door open, stepped through, and closed it. Still worried about people sneaking up on her, Olivia used her will to press an orb of magma into the crack between the jamb and the door, then quickly turned her attention back to the colossal creature still continuing its shambling, crunching gait away from her. She didn't see any point in holding back, so she fired a Pyrosteam Drill at the retreating back, choosing that spell simply because it moved through the air the fastest. The beam of superheated steam blasted straight through the creature from its lower left back and out through its chest, throwing rotten flesh, hunks of bone, and splatters of black blood out in a shower in front of it.

With a thunderous roar, the undead rhino-man spun around, oblivious to the damage she'd done to it, lifting its maul over its head and smashing it into the stone ceiling in the process. Then it charged, and it moved faster than Olivia felt something that size had a right to do. She dove to the side, rolling over her left shoulder, and offered up a silent thank-you to Commander Grobak. Unable to see if the monstrosity had turned quickly enough to follow up with a swing of its cudgel, Olivia cast her earth-attuned Elemental Form and scrambled to her feet. Luckily, the laws of physics still somewhat applied to the giant monster, and it had continued past where she'd stood to smash into the wall. It had just turned to face her again when she gained her feet.

Olivia saw it tense at the knees and knew she was about to be charged again, so she held out both hands and let loose the most enormous Plasma Wave she'd ever cast. She knew she scored a solid hit, even though she couldn't see through the glare of the crackling blue spray because the monster screamed much differently than it had roared moments earlier. Before she could celebrate, though, the flaming, melting bulk of the rhino-man abomination came barreling into her, driving her backward into the wall, where she smacked her stony, dense skull with a crack that would have opened a coconut. She slipped into darkness, oblivious to the fate of her physical form.

⚜ MORGAN ⚜

Morgan had been teleported before, and he was pretty sure that was happening to him now. As the darkness seemed to rush past him, he wondered why teleportation seemed different based on who or what was causing it. He'd seen kaleidoscopic lights with the Token of Travel; when the Yovashi had teleported him by accident, he'd felt the tug of dimensional magic and a sense of timelessness. Now he was rushing through the darkness but very much aware of the time.

After five minutes or so, and not knowing how long this unexpected journey would take, Morgan turned his attention inward, calling up his class refinement options and scanning through each of them:

Class refinement option 1: Hollow Dreadnought—Epic. Prerequisite: Vortex Class Core. Confronting danger and savagely destroying threats, you have the means to absorb damage and recover from blows that would defeat lesser beings, all while dealing tremendous blows to your foes. Class attributes: Vitality, Strength, and Will.

Class refinement option 2: Void Adept—Epic. Prerequisites: Vortex Class Core and Void Affinity. You embrace the nature of your Core and Energy, learning to wield powerful magics to both manipulate space and lay waste to those that challenge you. Class attributes: Intelligence, Will, Unbound.

Class refinement option 3: No Refinement—You are pleased with the path on which you find yourself and choose to continue until your next refinement option.

Morgan tried to say how surprised he was only to see two options, but no words came out of his mouth. He figured talking wasn't something one did while teleporting. Both options were epic ranked, and so was his current class, so that didn't play a part in his decision-making. The Dreadnought class sounded very strong, but Morgan had to accept that the Void Adept class was perfectly tailored to him; it required both his vortex Core and void attunement. On top of that, it gave some "Unbound" attribute points; did that mean he could assign them wherever he wanted?

What really clinched the decision for him was that he'd already learned advanced swordsmanship, and though it was useful, nothing had been more effective in his more difficult battles than his Energy abilities. He decided it was time to try embracing the fact that intelligence was his highest ability score, and he was gifted with Energy use. With butterflies tumbling around in his stomach, he touched the option for Void Adept.

Congratulations! You have refined your class: Void Adept. Class spell gained: Void Step—Basic.

Congratulations! World-first Void Adept! Feat awarded.

World-first Void Adept: Feat granted: One with the Void—the harsh physical realities of existing in a vacuum are much less pronounced on you.

Void Step—Basic: You are able to instantly travel between two points in space, provided you can see your destination. Energy cost: 1000 Cooldown: Medium.

Congratulations! You have achieved level 31 Void Adept and have gained 8 Intelligence, 8 Will, and have 12 points to allocate.

Morgan had almost forgotten that the System was holding a level for him. He supposed he was lucky that being forcibly teleported didn't count as losing consciousness with regard to the banked Energy. He was very excited to try out his new spell, and he hoped it was a portent of the skills to come with his new class. Being able to teleport would be a massive boon in many ways. He felt a surge in his Core as his body accommodated the changes his new class and level had wrought, and he looked at his attributes:

Core:	Vortex Class - Base 8		
Energy Affinity:	9.2, Void 9.2	Energy:	6630/6630
Strength:	65	Vitality:	60
Dexterity:	74 (95)	Agility:	133
Intelligence:	162	Will:	133
Points Available:	12		

His Energy levels were truly growing massive, at least in his opinion, and even with the high cost of some of his abilities, his pool and regeneration hadn't had any trouble keeping up. He wanted to hold onto the twelve attribute points for now, but he was all too aware that something terrible could be waiting at the other end of the portal, so he dumped them all into vitality.

Morgan was just starting to wonder if he could get out the scrolls he'd been holding that contained advanced Fighting Crane forms when something changed; a pinpoint of light appeared in the darkness. He still gripped Bloodfang in his right hand and began to ready a Void Burst, pushing void-attuned Energy into his pathways. He watched as the pinpoint became a nickel, became a basketball, became a window of orange light, and then he was standing in a bright open space, a smoldering orange sun high overhead, with a screaming, howling mob of gargoyles charging at him with spears, clubs, and axes.

Morgan took one step and then unleashed his Void Burst; a dark wave of Energy rolled out from him, ripping reality with a crackling, mind-rending screech. The gargoyles in front tried to pull back, but the mob behind them mindlessly drove forward, and the entire pack was caught by the full force of the terrible Energy. As the wave of torn reality faded, chunks of partially obliterated bodies and the fluids within them piled and puddled around Morgan in a circle of devastation.

Morgan whirled around, waving his sword, ready for something else to attack, but nothing came, and his mind was having trouble grasping the reality of his situation. Where the hell was he? He stood in a valley that resembled what he'd imagine a crater on Mars would look like. The soil was red-orange, and not a single plant grew within sight. What's more, the orange, shimmering sun hanging in the sky was very different from the bright yellow-white sun of Fanwath. "What the fuck?" He'd known he was being teleported, but not to an entirely different world. Panicking slightly, he reached out with Guardian's Senses for Issa and found absolutely no hint of her. That's when he realized the portal was gone. He was standing among a pile of dead gargoyles in a blasted hellscape with no idea how to get home.

As he spun around again, he saw furtive movement in a narrow gap of the crater wall and realized some gargoyles were hurrying in that direction. Were they running from him? "The prisoners!" he said aloud as he started trotting up a hard-packed path toward the gap. While he was running, his mind was busy trying to solve his predicament, and he remembered the Token of Travel. "Will that work to teleport between worlds?" The description hadn't said anything about him having to be on his home world for it to work. He powered up the dusty slope to the gap in the crater wall, and when he peered out between the two sides of the cleft, he saw a dirt road running out over a desert-like landscape.

Five of the large gargoyles were dragging a string of six bound Ardeni, stumbling and flailing, along the road. Morgan couldn't see their destination; the dirt road ran through the empty landscape for as far as he could see. Morgan began to run toward them, then stopped. He'd nearly forgotten about his new spell; staring at a point not far in front of the gargoyles, he concentrated and cast Void Step. With a rush, a large wave of Void Energy pulsed through his pathways and out, ripping space around him with a terrible, strange cracking sound, and suddenly he was standing on the road in front of the running, growling creatures. He reached out with an Energy Drain, pulling a torrent of black and red Energy from each of the gargoyles, and then began to lay about with his sword, hacking, cleaving, and stabbing.

The gargoyles tried to fight back, to their credit, but they were surprised and weakened by his Energy Drain, and the minor cuts and bruises they managed to dish out were healed when Morgan drained the last three of them as soon as his ability was ready again. As he finished off the last gargoyle, he looked at the line of hooded, tied-up Ardeni and shouted, "Don't worry, I'm freeing you!" He supposed it must have been nerve-wracking hearing the combat but not knowing what all the screaming, stabbing, and hacking was about.

Morgan pulled a scrap of leather from his storage pouch and cleaned off his sword, sheathing it before moving over to the prisoners. The first thing he did was untie the burlap sack-like hoods that they had on over their heads, noting the deep purple bruises on most of their faces as he worked to untie the ropes around their wrists. They all uttered things like, "Thank you," or "Thank the Ancestors!" and Morgan nodded, trying to reassure them that things would be okay.

He noticed that, along with the ropes, they each had a strip of leather strung through a heavy pewter disc around their wrists. He snapped the cords on one and held it up, noticing the strange little runes stamped into it. "They using these to control you somehow?"

"That's right," a round-faced older man responded. Morgan moved among them, breaking the cords and stowing the little discs in his pouch. He didn't recognize any of the Ardeni; four of the six were darkly "Tanned" men, their blue skin almost purple, but the two women were just as swarthy, and all wore loose, cottony trousers and shirts. "Are you all from the trading flotilla that was raided?"

"Yes!" one of the women replied, rubbing at her chaffed wrists.

"Are you the only ones? Do you think they brought others through that portal?"

"A portal? Was that what that was? I knew something strange had happened!" The tall, bald man who spoke looked around, squinting at the strange purple-blue sky and the throbbing orange sun. "This isn't Fanwath!" The other Ardeni burst into distressed chatter, looking around, shock and fear on their faces.

"That's right. I got sucked in trying to stop the gargoyles that dragged you all through."

"Gargoyles?"

"Those creatures," Morgan gestured to the corpses, "I don't know what they're really called, but they look like something called gargoyles from stories I've heard."

"They had us in huge pens, and yes, they took many others before us. I didn't know they were putting them through a portal, though. They had Urghat penned up also; just a dozen or so." A different woman answered. She was shorter and older and had lots of gray in her amber-colored hair.

"Well, my name's Morgan, and I'm a friend to the Ardeni in Tarn's Crossing. I'm not sure how we're all going to get home, but we'll figure something out." Morgan looked around, squinting into the harsh light. "I wish there was some shelter nearby. I want to scout ahead and see if I can figure out where they were taking you, but I'd like to leave you someplace a little more secure."

"Please don't leave us!" the younger woman said, reaching out to grip Morgan's armored forearm.

"I'm not planning to. Hmm, let's just follow this road a bit; see what comes up." Morgan didn't wait for a response, turning to walk past the dead gargoyles and briskly along the hard-packed road. The light was harsh, the air was dry, and he began to sweat in his heavy metal armor. After hiking down the road for another twenty minutes or so, he glanced over his shoulder and saw the drooping, exhausted Ardeni, and he realized his improved racial traits were allowing him to weather the extremes of this world far better than those poor souls, so he called for a break and produced water and fruit from his storage pouch.

While they sat hunched on the dirt road, drinking and slurping at the fruit, Morgan tried looking around with his Void Vision. To his surprise, the ability cut back much of the sun's orange glare, reducing the haze in the air, and he was able to see that a few miles down the road, some hills began to rise up out of the barren desert. He saw the faint outline of sparse plant life on the hills and turned back to the little group of Ardeni, "Hey, there are some hills ahead with plants growing on them. Hopefully, we'll find some answers up there."

Once again, they set out, Morgan setting an easier pace this time, and after hiking for about an hour, they began to pass between low rolling hills with fat, cactus-like plants growing sporadically here and there. They reminded Morgan a little of barrel cacti, though they were shaped more like inverted cones than barrels. "Keep walking on the road; I'm going to climb this hill and see what I can see."

Morgan jogged up the smooth slope of the nearest hill, and when he reached its crest, he stared off in the direction the road was taking them. He activated his Void Vision again and took in a sharp breath. Maybe five miles away, he saw, rising into the strange, hazy sky, a tall, pyramidal structure the color of dried mud. On the one hand, it looked kind of like an ancient ziggurat, but on the other, it resembled nothing so much as an insect hive. He jogged back down the hillside to the group of Ardeni who were slowly trudging along the road and called out, "Hey, we need to cut into the hills. I have a feeling we'll run into a lot of company on this road pretty soon."

"I'm so tired and hot!" a grizzled older man said. Briefly, Morgan thought about getting all their names, but he knew he'd probably forget them before they stopped to rest and decided to put it off a while.

"Yeah, I know. I'm sorry, but we're too exposed on the road. If we move into these hills, we might find a good spot to rest." They didn't argue further, and, though it took a while, they all trudged up the hillside and followed the gullies between the hills. All the while, they edged their way toward where Morgan had seen the hive-like ziggurat. The huge, pulsing orange sun slowly moved across the sky, and, as it began to descend toward the horizon, Morgan wondered what night would be like in this weird alien world.

᯽ MORGAN ᯽

Morgan looked down at the little hollow and then out over the rough hillsides. He didn't see any better options, so he led the six Ardeni down into the rocky, scree-covered space between two hillsides. The slope was fairly steep, and the gully was well hidden from casual observation. "I want you all to rest here while I go and try to get eyes on the gargoyles and their operation here. I want to see if I can spot the other captives they brought through."

"What will we do if you don't come back?" the tall, bald man asked.

"Alright, hold on, what's your name?"

"Sento."

"Alright, Sento, listen. I'm not planning to abandon you guys. We can't just sit here and twiddle our thumbs, though, and you all can't keep up with me, right? I'll leave you with food and water, and I'll try not to be gone very long." Morgan looked over the whole group standing hunched together in the hollow. "I need you all to stay strong. Others need our help now, and if we're going to get out of this mess, we have to work together."

Morgan pulled a water barrel that he used to fill his roladii's bucket from his pouch and set it on the ground. Then he pulled several meals worth of bread, cheese, and dried meats out and piled them on top. He handed Sento and one of the women who stepped forward long hunting knives that he'd stowed away from somewhere, and then he said, "Alright. I'll be back soon. Don't light a fire." He glanced around, "Not that there's any wood around here." Morgan could see by their faces that they had more questions and things to object about, but he didn't give them a chance. He turned and jogged up the hillside and was out of their line of sight in just a few seconds.

He debated taking off his armor but decided to wait until he'd seen what was waiting near the mud-covered ziggurat. He was amazed at how tireless his "Improved" body was; he'd hardly had to drink water and hadn't eaten anything, and with the sun pounding down on his heavy armor, he was sure his old self would have been begging for a reprieve. Still, he moved like a stalking cat over the hillside, loping easily up and down the ridges. Within just a few short minutes, he was coming up on the rocky ridgeline that overlooked the flat expanse where he'd seen the massive structure.

Morgan lowered himself to a low crouch, and, when he topped the crest of the hill, he laid down on his belly to look out over the flat land beyond. He sucked air through his teeth when his mind registered what he was seeing. A brown, mud-covered pyramid rose from the hot desert soil about a mile distant from the ridgeline he was observing from. It was huge, with the sides of the base probably three hundred yards long, and it rose several hundred feet into the air at its narrow top step. It was crudely constructed, with sloping edges on the steps and yawning round tunnels peppering its various levels. Swarming in and out of the tunnels and around the base of the ziggurat were hundreds of gargoyles—some were hulking and wingless, while others were small and flew in short bursts with their broad gray wings.

Morgan didn't see any of the clothed gargoyle "Leaders" like he'd fought in the cavern, but as he drew his eyes back from the pyramid, he realized there was a lot more to the gargoyle settlement than just the muddy hive. The source of the water for the mud was a small lake, maybe half a mile across, that sat between the hills and the ziggurat, and, on both sides of the lake were huge "Pens" with mud-brick walls. There were dozens or hundreds of Ardeni and many other races represented in smaller numbers inside the circular pens. One of the pens held a huddled, pitiful-looking throng of Urghat.

The prisoners all looked miserable and, as he watched, Morgan could see large gargoyles driving small groups of prisoners into the largest tunnel at the base of the ziggurat. "What the hell are they doing with them?" He lay there watching for a while, wondering if he should risk attacking. The number of gargoyles in his line of sight was roughly the same as the horde he'd defeated in the tunnels beneath the Rill Catcher, but he had no idea what was waiting inside the hive. While he was thinking about it, he saw some movement off to his right, which he figured was the east, and he turned to focus on it. A long line of bound prisoners was being led in by a force of twenty or so gargoyles.

Morgan activated his Void Vision and studied the line of prisoners, surprised to see that they didn't look like any people he'd ever seen before. They walked on taloned feet, and they had ropes looped around their slender bodies pinning colorful wings to their backs. He couldn't see their heads because they were covered with sacks, but he didn't think they were denizens of Fanwath. "Are there more portals around this place?" The procession moved over the rough ground toward the lake and the mud-walled pens, and then the gargoyles pushed their prisoners into the one with the twenty or so, mud-covered, bedraggled Urghat.

Observing the movements below, Morgan's mind kept going back to the scrolls he'd gotten in the Swordmaster's Citadel. He decided to take the opportunity to study the scrolls while he waited for something different to happen down there. He pulled one of the scrolls out, and while he lay there on this stomach, he unfurled it before his eyes. Once again, he studied the strange, shifting runes, and they began to move more and more and then stream into his eyes. This time, he wasn't stopped by a System warning, and the symbols flooded into his mind, giving him a deep understanding of a new way to use his weapon.

Congratulations! Your understanding of the Fighting Crane style has increased! You have learned the form, the Crane Takes Flight. Your style is now—Improved.

When Morgan had seen the form's title back in the citadel, he'd been very optimistic about what it would do for him; would he really be able to fly? Now that he understood the form, he realized it wasn't quite so incredible, but it was still a powerful utility; using his weapon's momentum and a surge of Energy in the correct pattern, he'd be able to launch himself in any direction, almost as though he could fly a short distance, certainly farther than a normal person could jump.

He turned back to the gargoyle settlement, watching for anything that had changed while he'd been distracted, but didn't notice anything. After slowly scanning his field of vision from left to right, he reached into his ring, drew out the other scroll, and repeated the process. When the stream of runes finished flooding into his mind, another message appeared in his vision:

Congratulations! Your understanding of The Fighting Crane style has increased! You have learned the form, the Crane Lances Forth. Your style is now—Advanced.

The form seemed to be exactly what he'd hoped it was—it was basically another charge ability that allowed him to lead with his weapon's point encased in Energy and driven with tremendous force. "Figures, as soon as I get my fighting style up to advanced, I happen to take a class that doesn't focus on physical fighting," he muttered, once again looking out over the flat, sinister oasis below.

He immediately noticed another procession of bound prisoners being led in, this time from the west. When they got close enough for Morgan to study their physical make-up a little, he concluded that this group was not from Fanwath either; they had green-scaled legs and arms with long webbed feet. The poor creatures, hooded and bound as they were, seemed terribly lethargic and weak in the pulsing orange sunlight.

Morgan counted forty-three of the new prisoners and watched as the gargoyles led them to a muddy pen very near the shore of the little brown-green lake. As they pushed them into the enclosure, yanking their hoods off, Morgan saw that they were, indeed, some sort of amphibious people with neckless heads and bulging yellow eyes. Their loud croaks carried over the water and up the hillside as they scurried over to the wet mud and rolled in it, possibly seeking some sort of reprieve from the heat.

While Morgan observed the scene below, he began to try to formulate ideas about what was going on. Were the gargoyles just raiding other worlds? What for? Slaves? Food? Conscripted soldiers? As he imagined other portals to other worlds, Morgan caught himself in an assumption. The truth of the matter was, he had no idea if these strange prisoners were from worlds other than Fanwath. He'd really only seen a small part of his new homeworld. Did that mean there might be other portals home? Was there another way to get these prisoners out of here? Then he had to wonder if this was the only gargoyle installation. What if there were hundreds or thousands of these mud ziggurats around this strange, unpleasant world?

Morgan shook his head and started to scoot backward. There were too many unknowns. What he needed to do was get closer and try to find out some more information. He slid down the hill and loped his way back, up and down the other hills, to the little gully where'd he'd left the six Ardeni. When he came sliding down the hill into the shadow cast by the sinking orange sun, Sento scrambled to his feet, brandishing the knife. "Relax, it's just me."

"Oh, thank the Ancestors. What did you find out?" The other Ardeni stood up and came closer, all but one of the older men, who was sound asleep in the shade.

"Well, the gargoyles have a lot of prisoners tied up, and they bring a few into their big pyramid-shaped hive every half hour or so. Hey, are there bird-people on Fanwath? What about amphibious frog-like people?" The Ardeni looked at each in confusion and then shook their heads. The older woman cleared her throat.

"I'm not sure. There are other continents on Fanwath that we have minimal contact with. It's possible. They might not be advanced races; they could be like Yeksa."

"Mmhmm. Well, I need to get more information, and I've devised a bit of a plan. You all are going to have to sit tight for a while longer; I'm going to pose as a prisoner and sneak into one of those pens. I'll let them drag me into that ziggurat, and then I'll get some answers."

"Are you insane?" Sento took a step back, like whatever was wrong with Morgan might be contagious.

"No, don't worry. I'll deface one of those wrist things and wear it; I don't think it will work if I ruin the runes, right?"

"Well, yes, I suppose that would render it harmless." Sento shrugged.

"And I'll keep my gear in my ring. I've killed a lot of gargoyles; I'm not too worried about them, but if I do get in trouble, I can move pretty fast. Anyway, it's got to be done; I'm not leaving all those people to God-knows-what fate those gargoyles have in store for them."

"And what about us?" the younger woman asked.

"Well, you don't want to live on this world forever, do you? I need to get in there and figure out how they opened that portal or something. Just sit tight and stay in the shade. There's enough food and water here for a few days." Morgan began to unbuckle his heavy scale armor. "Here, help me with this, will you?"

After he'd stowed most of his gear in his ring and handed off his dimensional pouch with all of his camping supplies and most of his rations to Sento, Morgan took out one of the pewter disks and, using a knife, scraped away most of the runes. When he tied it around his wrist, he found that it did nothing to suppress his Energy. He still had Bloodfang hooked to his belt, determined not to put the sword into his dimensional container until the very last minute. He knew it was hard on conscious items, but what was he supposed to do in an emergency? Hopefully, he'd be able to take it out after just a short time. "Alright, I'm going to go watch that settlement until it's dark, then I'll sneak into the Ardeni enclosure. Don't worry; I'm not going to forget about you guys."

OLIVIA

The darkness only gripped Olivia for a few seconds because a sudden surge of Energy brought her back to wakefulness. She opened her eyes and scrambled away from the smoldering, disgusting mess of the partially obliterated rhino-man. Her chest, stomach, and legs were covered in smoldering gore, and as she scrambled out of the stinking mess, she retched, dry heaving over the stone floor. While she heaved, she continued to crawl away from the reeking mounds of gore, finally breaking free enough to get a breath of air that wasn't tainted by the putrid innards of the monster. When her spasming stomach finally settled, Olivia noticed she had a notification waiting:

Congratulations! You have achieved level 19 Elemental Archon and have gained 10 Intelligence, 10 Will, and have 16 points to allocate.

She waved it away, vowing to deal with her pool of attribute points before leaving the room. She staggered up to her feet and stumbled further away from the noxious corpse, approaching the far door. When she got close, she saw that it was slightly ajar, hopefully, triggered to open when the monster died. She looked over her shoulder to ensure she hadn't missed anything in the monster's lair. Not seeing anything, she pushed the door open and looked out.

A short hallway opened into a circular room with a descending stairwell. Sitting at the top of the stairs was a large, white chest with no visible clasp or metal tooling. "Alright, just a minute." Olivia pulled up her attributes:

Strength:	10	Vitality:	50
Dexterity:	10	Agility:	10
Intelligence:	136	Will:	122
Points Available:	16		

She felt like her mental attributes were doing just fine. Still, she could probably use a little more speed on her feet, and more vitality never seemed to hurt, so Olivia decided to put eight points into agility and vitality. That done, she took a deep breath, savoring the rush of Energy that flooded her body, and then she walked toward the large, white chest.

At first, Olivia thought the chest was painted white, but the wood was finely grained, and she could see that it had that color naturally. There was no clasp, but she could see the seam where the top met the bottom half, so she gently lifted it, and it smoothly opened on hidden, interior hinges. Folded neatly within the bottom half was a black, shimmering garment embroidered with borders of fine, silver thread. Olivia lifted the garment, and when she held the dense, rich cloth out in front of her, she saw that it was a multi-layered set of robes, complete with a silvery silken sash.

Curiosity left no room for caution, and Olivia sent a trickle of Energy into the robe, bonding with it:

Robe of Shielding: Artificed Clothing: This robe mitigates the effects of physical damage that would otherwise harm the wearer. Enchantment: Self-repair and self-cleaning.

Olivia looked down at her soiled, charred, stained white jumper and began to peel it off. She kicked off her new boots to complete the process and then began to wrap her fresh robes around herself. The black, silken inner layer was form-fitting, the outer layer with the metallic silver threading hung more loosely around her arms and torso, and when she pulled the sash tight, she couldn't imagine a more comfortable garment. Olivia pulled on her black boots and nodded, smiling at the improvement.

"Well, I don't know if they want to collect this when I get back, so . . ." She bent to stuff the filthy jumper into her storage ring. Olivia looked down at the empty chest and once again admired the beautiful craftsmanship. On a whim, she tried to put it into her storage ring, and it worked, vanishing into the container without a trace.

Nothing else keeping her there, she started down the dusty stone steps to the sixth floor. She strode down the steps confidently; she'd never been attacked in one of the rooms with stairs, and she'd stopped worrying about someone following her. If they planned to move against her, they'd have done so when she was knocked down by the undead rhino thing. So, she hurried down the shallow steps, two at a time, until she came out into a well-lit, white marble room.

The light seemed to emanate from the walls themselves. Nothing was present in the perfectly square room, not even a door. She saw something on the far wall, and took three strides into the room, to look more closely; a small white crystal shaped like an eye was mounted directly in its center. The white crystal was perfectly carved into a classic almond-shaped eye, with fine lines delineating the iris and pupil. Olivia took another step to peer more closely at the eye. It started to glow and sparkle when she did so, and she felt a warm tingle in her own eye.

Olivia felt like something was being measured; she wasn't sure what, but it seemed like she passed because the wall suddenly sank into the floor, allowing further progress. When the wall was completely gone, she saw that the room had simply doubled in size and that another wall barred her progress, this one with a flickering red archway in its center. Olivia walked up to the archway, and as she got close, she saw that the shimmering red light was hanging in the air. Looking through the red haze, she saw a short hallway between this room and another. "So, what am I supposed to do, walk through this red light?"

When she passed one hand under the arch and into the red light, terrible pain exploded in the limb, and Olivia yanked it back. Shaking it and wincing, she looked to see that no damage had occurred; it had been pain and nothing more. "Some sort of pain tolerance test?" She wondered what exactly that would accomplish, perhaps some sort of test of her will? Olivia tried to peer through the red haze to see if the next door was locked or had a handle. She was relieved when she managed to pierce the haze for a moment and saw that it was just another open archway.

The pain Olivia had felt in her hand had been bad, like picking up a hot frying pan bad, but it had faded almost instantly. Still, could she bear that kind of pain all over her body? What would it feel like in her eyes or her head and organs? She scratched her chin and shook her head; she was looking at this the wrong way. If they wanted to test her will, they wouldn't give her a simple pain tolerance test. This place wasn't run by Commander Grobak, after all. No, she needed to think about this like a spellcaster. "Is that red stuff Energy?"

Olivia reached out with her will and pushed against the red haze and was immediately rewarded by a large eddy moving through the haze, carrying away some of it. She grinned and redoubled her efforts, but this time she shoved a torrent of her own unattuned Energy out through her pathways and against the heavy haze of red, painful Energy. She created a void big enough to step into, so she did, and then she pushed out more Energy, making a capsule around herself to keep the red Energy at bay. Safely surrounded by a bubble of her own Energy, Olivia strode through the short hallway and into the next room.

Once again, Olivia found herself in a square, brightly lit room with an archway on the far wall. She approached it and saw another short hallway, but this one had a half dozen giant axe blades swinging like pendulums across it. "Oh, very action VR-like. How exciting!" She imagined this test was meant to see if she was agile and dexterous enough to slip between the blades as they swung at different times. "No, that's too obvious. Well, maybe there is meant to be more than one way to solve these little obstacles." Surely all great spellcasters weren't meant to be as nimble as cats. No, she could think of a few ways to get past these blades.

Olivia summoned a stone globe and hurled it against the closest axe blade with her will. With a deafening clang, the stone smashed into the flat, swinging blade, and it swung back and forth along the wrong axis, causing it to crash into the blade next to it. The two blades got caught up together, and something in the ceiling started to grind, and then they stopped moving, hanging together against the left-hand wall. Olivia smiled and began to hurl more stone globes at the other axes. It took her eight or ten shots to damage all the axes enough to allow safe passage, but the stone globes were easy to summon, and she rather enjoyed the effort.

The next room opened to another hallway with another test; this time, she had to walk through a veritable inferno with jets of scorching flame randomly spraying the walkway from the ceiling, the walls, and the floor. Once again, Olivia thanked her luck with the Core and class combination she had; she cast Elemental Form, took the fire form, and strode through the hallway without any difficulty.

When she emerged from the fire-filled hallway, she stood in a huge garden complete with a blue sky and a green, grassy hill. Rather than walls, the grassy knoll was bordered by tall hedges covered with blue and white trumpet-shaped flowers. Olivia stood on the grass before the hill, looking around with wonder and enjoying the fresh air and warm sun. As she started to wonder what she should do next, if she should climb the hill or not, a gust of wind, accompanied by a heavy, deep flapping sound, began to stir the leaves of the hedges and make her long dark hair swirl out behind her.

Olivia covered, held her hand up to shield her eyes from the sun, and glared into the sky. While she peered into the blue sky over the hill, a dark shape swooped into the garden from behind her and landed on the slope in front of her. Olivia staggered as the ground shook, and the colossal creature turned to regard her, folding its immense, leathery, green wings on its back. Extending a long, emerald-colored, shimmering neck, the dragon peered at Olivia with an enormous yellow saucer of an eye.

Olivia stood transfixed, her legs quivering and a voice in her head screaming at her to run and hide. Suddenly a husky woman's voice sounded in her head, echoing and booming as though it bounced around in her skull, "You've made it to the final room of the Proving Grounds. It's time for your final challenge! Are you ready to face me?"

Olivia's mind was racing in a hundred different directions. Half of her mental faculties were trying to figure out how to flee, but enough of her was cognizant of the question posed to her, and she tried to calm her mind and think about the creature's question. Was she ready to face it? Before she could think about it anymore, Olivia blurted, "No!"

Suddenly the palpably thick fear that hung around her faded away, and the dragon lifted its head to gaze down at her with both eyes. "Correct," sounded the enormous voice, and the wings flapped; the dragon was gone, and Olivia could breathe again.

She leaned over, resting her hands on her knees, and took a few deep breaths. She'd never been in the presence of anything so palpably powerful; she'd felt like she was standing next to a nuclear reactor on the verge of melting down. Had it been real? Was there a real dragon here in the Proving Grounds, or was the dungeon or System playing with her mind?

When she straightened up and looked around, she saw that the path she'd taken to the weird garden was gone; another tall hedge rose behind her. Seeing no other option, Olivia started walking up the grassy slope to the top of the hill. As she gained the crest, she could see down the far slope and, there, shimmering in the shadow of the tall hedge, was an oscillating, mirror-like portal. A small pedestal stood in the grass before the portal with something small sitting atop it.

Had that really been it? To her, the sixth floor seemed like it was the easiest of all the levels, just a few tricky hallways to traverse and a dragon asking if she wanted to fight. What if she'd said yes? Would it have killed her? Maybe it would have rewarded her for being brave. It had said, "Correct," though when she'd said she wasn't ready to face it, and that had been the honest truth. She couldn't imagine being able to harm something so massive, so dense with power. Was it a lesson in humility? The final stage of the Proving Grounds was meant to show the young mage powerful enough to get there that they were like an ant compared to some things in the universe?

Olivia walked down the slope to the pedestal, noting the shapes of a round, purple fruit and a silver-embossed scroll case sitting atop it. She reflexively reached toward the fruit as she caught a scent of its cloying, spicy, sugary odor, but she yanked her hand back before touching it. She leaned closer, sniffing it, and feeling almost intoxicated by the aroma. Then, she closed her eyes, steeled her will, and looked at the scroll case. It looked to be made from a polished black horn and tooled fancifully in silvery whorls.

Was she being offered both prizes, or was this another choice? It almost felt like another test of will; she'd nearly grabbed the fruit reflexively; was it meant to tempt her away from the scroll? Perhaps both prizes were fantastic, and it was an honest choice, but she couldn't help thinking in terms of tests. If the fruit was like other powerful natural treasures that she'd been given as awards at the academy, then it probably did something to improve her physically; perhaps it would advance her race or improve an attribute. The scroll, on the other hand, undoubtedly held knowledge. Which did she want more? Olivia stretched out a hand, and, as it started to sway toward the fruit, she jerked it to the scroll case and grabbed it.

As she'd feared, the pedestal and fruit faded into glittering blue smoke, and she was left standing before the portal with the scroll case in her hand. Olivia slipped a thumbnail under the clasp and opened the case, revealing a tightly bound, ivory-colored roll of paper. She took the paper from the case and unraveled it, stretching out a sheet about a foot long packed with System runes. As she stared at the runes, they began to shift and move about, and then they slowly started to lift off the paper and float toward her eyes. As the first characters seeped into her mind, Olivia was aware of vague notions and ideas, though she could never focus on one long enough to form a concrete perception of what it was. The runes moved faster and faster, and then, with a stream of light and firework-like bursts, it was over, and the sheet was blank.

*****Congratulations! You have gained deeper perspectives about your chosen path, and, at your next class refinement opportunity, you will have at least one selection from a higher tier.*****

Olivia let her hands drop to her sides, and she reached up to scratch at her head, "Well, shoot. What comes after epic?"

⚜ OLIVIA ⚜

With no other options that she could see, Olivia stepped through the portal. This one was either more powerful or more cleverly designed than the one that brought her to the dungeon because she found herself stepping onto the platform on the mountain outside Fainhallow Academy almost instantly. She was briefly disoriented, but when she realized where she was, Olivia smiled and savored the difference between her current self and the person she was when she'd first come to the academy. She'd grown so much, not just in terms of raw power and ability, but as a person.

Striding confidently down the steps to the impressive archway that connected the mountaintop to the academy grounds, Olivia inhaled deeply of the crisp mountain air and looked around. Just as before, no one else was about, and this time, there was no Yunsha to greet her on the bridge. Wearing her beautiful new robes, her wonderful, magical boots, and with faint blue flames limning her person, she approached the gates to Fainhallow. The guards on duty straightened, and the larger, Vodkin guard said, "Business in Fainhallow, ma'am?"

"I'm a student; I've just finished with the Proving Grounds dungeon."

"Uh, you were in the Proving Grounds?"

"That's right."

"Oh, erm, sorry to question you, ma'am, but don't those recall tokens bring you back to the academy portal room?"

"Oh, I'm not sure. I finished the dungeon; I didn't use the recall token." Olivia reached up and held out the little recall charm around her neck.

"What? Oh, erm, congratulations. Nester, run ahead and let the administration know that Miss, um, what was your name again, ma'am?"

"I'm Olivia Bennet."

"Right, run ahead and let them know that Miss Bennet is on her way in." The small, young, Ghelli man turned and ran up the street, not giving any sort of reply. "Welcome home, Miss Bennet. Congratulations!"

"Thank you kindly, sir!" Olivia smiled and gave a silly curtsey, then walked through the gatehouse. She was in a good mood and found the huge Vodkin's attempt at formality funny. She strode through the busy streets of Fainhallow, past the market, and up the main avenue to the academy; no one else gave her a second glance until she came to the huge, open doors of the academy proper. There, looking harried and flustered, several black-robed academy officials stood looking down the steps, excitedly waving and clapping as Olivia began to climb them. Olivia didn't recognize any of them and wondered what they expected of her when Oylla-dak landed at the top of the steps with a crack of flapping wings.

"Olivia! You finished! Come here, come here!" Oylla waved her forward, and Olivia hurried up the steps, unable to contain her beaming smile.

"We were all watching for your return in the portal room! It's been so long since anyone finished the dungeon that we didn't know you'd be sent to the academy portal stone!"

"Well, here I am!" Olivia waved around at the growing crowd.

"Wonderful! We're so proud of you, Olivia! This is fabulous news for the school. I trust the experience was valuable for you? Come, come! You'll have to give me a full accounting of it!" Oylla motioned for people to move aside and reached out for Olivia's hand, pulling her into the main hall of the academy. All around her, Olivia could watch the news of her return and what she'd done spread, and more and more students turned and regarded her with wide eyes. Something in her enjoyed the attention and encouraged her to stand up straight and smile. She loved the way her new robes flowed out behind her as she strode along, with the flames of her elemental heritage softly wisping in the breeze of her progress.

They'd almost made it to the stairway leading to the administration offices when someone crashed into Olivia from behind, wrapping arms around her and squeezing. "Oh, by the Tree! Olivia! You look amazing!" Olivia struggled in Adaida's grip, turning to face her with a laugh.

"Thanks! I missed you, too!" She finally managed to turn enough to put her arms around Adaida and return the squeeze. Oylla paused and turned to regard them with a crooked smile.

"We were so worried, but Professor Oylla-dak told us that she'd be informed if you died, so we just hoped you were still progressing!" Adaida looked up at Oylla and gave her a smile and a nod. "You were right!"

"Why were you so worried? I haven't even been gone a day!"

"Oh, no. Olivia, time moves differently in the Proving Grounds. To us, you've been gone almost two weeks," Oylla said from behind her.

"What? Really? How strange!"

"Well, the longer you were gone, the more I was sure you were doing well, don't worry. The last of the other schools reported their entrant's return or demise almost a week ago."

"Wow! Well, it all went very quickly for me. Sorry to keep you worrying!" Olivia gave Adaida another squeeze, then let go. "Where are the others?"

"Still in Grobak's class; I ran out," she gestured to her exercise robes. "I'm sure I'll be in trouble, but when I heard Grobak gossiping with the runner that told him you'd just returned, I couldn't contain myself," she looked at Oylla, "I'm sorry!"

"Don't worry, dear. This is cause for celebration. Go tell Grobak I said to give the students the afternoon off! We'll have a feast tonight; Melonfest break starts in two days anyway."

"Melonfest?"

"Yes, Olivia! I'll answer your questions, but first, I want to debrief your time in the Proving Grounds. Run along, Adaida! Come, Olivia," Oylla turned and started walking, and Olivia smiled at Adaida, then turned and followed.

Soon, they were in Oylla's office, Olivia sitting in a comfortable leather chair across from Oylla and a heavy door keeping out any sort of distraction. "Well, let's start at the beginning; tell me about what you encountered and how you overcame your obstacles." Olivia nodded and began to describe to Oylla all the things she fought, the doors she opened, and the barriers she overcame. When she got to the part about Jaliss ambushing her, Oylla hissed in frustration. "You were kind and right to make her recall."

"I felt sorry that she was so badly hurt, but I think she was going to kill me or force me to recall."

"Don't you dare feel guilty. Pity is ok, but not guilt. You did nothing wrong and were far more merciful than most would have been."

"Understood. Don't worry; her betrayal didn't leave room for much more than sympathy in my heart."

"Now, tell me what was next." Olivia finished the story of her time in the dungeon, Oylla interjecting with questions from time to time, especially about the rhino monstrosity. When she told her about the dragon, Oylla sat back and stared at the ceiling for a moment. "Do you think it was real?"

"It seemed very real. I could feel its power, and it left me with the impression that I was still quite insignificant in the greater world."

"Perhaps in the wider universe, yes, but Olivia, your potential and progress are already remarkable for this world."

"Well, thank you, but I honestly just feel like I got lucky. I happen to have a strong Core, and I have a gift for manipulating Energy. On top of that, the academy has showered me with gifts."

"It's true; some people are born with more gifts than others. You've done a good job applying your natural talents, though, Olivia. You should be proud. I'm happy that you want to give the academy some credit for your success, though. You know, the last person to complete the Proving Grounds was Asyr-dak. He became the second emperor of the Ridonne Empire, and he left this world over a hundred years ago. We should talk about what's next for you."

"What do you mean? Shouldn't I go back to class, like normal?" Olivia had a sinking feeling in the pit of her stomach.

"No, not like normal. I'm afraid you've outpaced your classmates by a great deal, and I think that a normal curriculum would be a waste of your time."

"But I have a lot left to learn! I really enjoy cultivating and learning about spellcraft!"

"Yes, yes. You do have a lot to learn, and I think professors ap'Rall and ap'Rek have more to teach you." Olivia had to wrack her brain for a minute to realize she was talking about Alyss and Sange. "Aside from those teachers, though, I think I will modify your schedule; we'll be dropping your other courses, and you will be apprenticed to one of the graduate professors."

"Um," Olivia didn't know exactly how to feel about this. On the one hand, she was glad that she'd still have a couple of classes with her friends and get some advanced instruction. On the other, she was having flashbacks of being forced to skip grades and leave her friends behind in high school. "Well, I like learning, and if you think this is the best path, I trust you, Oylla."

"It is; you've proven that you can handle yourself, and I think your time is wasted in the other three classes. If you have a passion for enchanting or alchemy, you can take those up as a hobby someday. For now, we should focus on your spellcrafting and Core development. Your new instructor will be able to fill in the gaps and then some."

"Who will I be apprenticed to?"

"Well, when you get back, you and I will sit down with a few of them for interviews, then we'll make the right decision together."

"When I get back?"

"Oh, I haven't told you about your reward yet, have I?"

"Reward?"

"Naturally! You represented the academy so well that we all agreed you deserved this." Oylla stood and walked over to her desk, picking up a small wooden box. She carried it over to Olivia and said, "Congratulations!" Olivia gingerly took the box in both hands and set it on her lap. Then she lifted the lid; inside were a ring and a necklace. She recognized the ring; it was her Copper cohort ring. She slipped it onto a finger next to the dimensional storage ring she'd gotten in the dungeon and lifted the necklace.

"It's beautiful," she said, letting it dangle in front of her eyes. It was a silver chain with a round silver pendant about the size of a quarter hanging from it. In the center of the pendant was a clear, egg-shaped crystal with a hundred glittering facets. Olivia could see hundreds or thousands of tiny runes carved into the silver around the crystal.

"It's a teleportation token, a re-usable one. It allows travel between the Fainhallow teleportation stone and your home City Stone. It holds enough of a charge to travel there and back, but then it will need a couple of weeks to recharge."

"Oh, thank you! Does this mean I can visit home? Oh, but we only have a Town Stone."

"Oh, that's nothing; I said City Stone, but any System Settlement Stone will work. And yes, you can visit home! Like I said earlier, we have a break coming up, and I expect you to go home and take a much-deserved rest!" Oylla held out a hand, "You can give me that recall necklace from the dungeon; you won't be needing it."

"Right," Olivia lifted the chain off her head and handed it to Oylla, then she slipped her new pendant around her neck. "Thank you so much, Oylla. I really needed this."

"You're welcome, Olivia. It's not as expensive as it could be. It requires that you're standing on our teleportation stone, out on the mountain, to activate. Still, its reusable nature makes it quite valuable. Protect it!"

"I will!" Olivia stuffed the charm down into her robes.

"You've gained quite a few valuable items from the dungeon, Olivia. You may continue to wear those robes when you return. You've earned the right. I'm going to require that you have Professor Brince add a small enchantment to change their color, though. I still want you in gray until next year."

"Yes, ma'am." Olivia was thrilled; she thought she'd have to remove the robes at the academy. It hadn't occurred to her that their color could be altered.

"Now, let's get you a bath, and then we can begin the celebration!" Oylla said, and Olivia smiled, warmth filling her heart. She'd truly earned her place at the academy, and there seemed to be people here who genuinely cared about her, and not just because of what she could do.

"And I get to visit home," she softly said as she followed Oylla out of her office and turned to make her way to the Copper cohort dorm.

⊱ BRONWYN ⊰

On the fourth night after Bronwyn killed Thun, she was camping along the mountain road staring into the brilliant expanse of stars, letting the embers of her fire warm her, when a twig snapped from the direction of the road. She jumped up and readied her Solar Shell spell, but when she looked in the direction of the sound, she saw the outline of a child in the shadows. "Who's there?" she asked, trying not to sound agitated.

"Hello, Bronwyn," replied the small shape, but it wasn't with a child's voice. Rather, it sounded like a young man with a rich rumble of bass chasing his words.

"Hello. Mind sharing your name?"

"You know me all too well, my friend; 'tis I, Coraignon, but I prefer the name with which you dubbed me." He moved closer, and Bronwyn's eyes picked out some details as the weak embers of the fire illuminated him. Coraignon was a thin, tanned little man about the size of a nine-year-old human. He had honey-colored hair and big eyes that glinted in the ember light. His teeth shone white as his smile spread.

"Hops?"

"Aye, sweet Bronwyn!" He took another step forward, but Bronwyn held out a hand.

"Hops! You tricked me! I can't believe you took a bath with me!"

"I'm sorry, Boldheart!"

"Oh, Boldheart, is it? Trying to be sweet since you kidnapped me?" She sat back down and motioned for Coraignon to sit as well. He strode forward lightly, and Bronwyn almost giggled when she saw that he was wearing green tights and had bare feet. His vest and tiny cloak looked warm, though, lined with fox fur.

"I've always thought you bold, and your heart is so big; it's my nickname for you," he said, sitting across the firepit from her. He dug a small clay pipe out of his pocket and began to fiddle with it.

"Why didn't you ever talk to me, Hops? So many times, I could've used a friend to sound things out."

"Well, because I was embarrassed and also afraid. You spent so much time with Urghat, and they love to eat my kind!"

"Hmph. Well, why were you embarrassed?" She frowned as he gestured to his small frame, and his thin lips quirked up in a smile.

"I'm a Brownie. Humans always dismiss us or fear us, but they never love us."

"Oh, Hops!" Bronwyn suppressed an urge to laugh at his dramatic statement, realizing he'd take it as his feelings being dismissed. "I do love you! You kept me company despite pretending to be a strange little animal, and I'll never forget that."

"Well, I loved spending time with you! I wasn't born when the fae had access to Earth, so you're the first human I've met. You're just like the heroes from our stories! You stood against evil, protected your people, and loved with all your heart! My cousins were so jealous when I told them of our times together."

"Well, I hope we can still spend time together!"

"Oh, me too! The queen doesn't often have much for us Brownies to do, but I begged her to let me bring you this message."

"Message?"

"Yes! I'm supposed to show you to a Way Tree; the Queen knows about your success and about the revered dead you carry in that amulet; she wants you home as quickly as possible to give you your reward and to pay homage to Thun's victims."

"These corpses; they're fae?" Bronwyn touched the necklace hanging just below her throat.

"Summer fae, aye. Thun collected us when he caught us out."

"Oh God, that's awful."

"Queen Aestasia asked that we make haste; she says she has important news for you."

"Now? Or should we wait for the sun?" Bronwyn glanced up at the brilliant stars and the two moons—the big and little sisters.

"I can see fine; come, the tree isn't far." Coraignon stood and held out a hand for her. Bronwyn took his warm little hand in hers and stood up.

"All right, let's go, Hops." She allowed him to pull her at a brisk walk a short way up the road, and then off through a moonlit meadow. They passed into the cool shadow of tall, blue needled fir trees and approached a huge, ancient trunk, clearly struck by lightning once upon a time. Bronwyn looked up at the towering, mostly barren forest lord and let out a low whistle. "Quite a tree."

"You should have met him before the lightning stole his beauty. He gained some special magic from the bolt, though. He can send you to the Summer Court if you stand inside that hollow between his branches there."

"Really?"

"Oh, yes; his spirit is strong."

"Are you coming with me?"

"Not yet; I have another task for the queen. I'll miss you, Bronwyn. I hope we can meet again soon." Bronwyn squeezed his little hand tightly and knelt on one knee so that she could pull him into a tight hug. His thin little body felt very light and small, but he was warm like a tiny furnace.

"Be careful, Hops! I miss you already!"

After she stopped squeezing him and stood up, Coraignan waved to her and pointed at the blackened hollow between the lowest of the tree's huge branches. Bronwyn nodded and leapt up, grabbing the bottom edge of the hole and hauling herself up. She stood on the edge and turned to wave one more time, and then she walked into the hollow. It was dark at first, but then warm light filled the hollow, and when she turned around, she could see out into a sunlit, flower-filled meadow.

The smell of charred, musty wood was gone, and when she stepped to the edge of the tree's hollow, she saw that its bark, here in the Fae Realm, was vibrant and alive, and the tree's massive branches were heavy with leaves. "Thank you, old one," she said softly, then hopped down into the meadow. A fluttering, winged figure flew into her vision, shedding tiny motes of light or Energy. "Hello, miss," Bronwyn said when she saw the little fairy's face.

"Agent of Summer! Welcome home! The queen awaits." She flitted in a small circle and sped off, pausing to see that Bronwyn followed. She hurried after the little fairy, savoring the warmth of summer and the sun on her skin that had been exposed to chilly night air only moments ago.

Bronwyn was surprised to find the fairy leading her through forest paths and into another meadow, this one surrounded by tall, white-barked birch trees. The ground in the clearing was soft and springy, rich dark soil showing between the clumps of grass. Queen Aestasia was standing alone in the center of the meadow, the sun causing her skin to glow with a rich, honeyed gleam. "Daughter! Come, we have sad business to attend to before speaking of other things."

"I'm sorry; I didn't know the bodies in this necklace were your people," Bronwyn said, stepping closer and holding a hand to the necklace.

"When I sensed your conflict, I scried your battle and briefly saw what you saw. I'm sorry for the intrusion, my agent, but I feel the need to see what I can in such harrowing situations. I'm not always successful, but my connection to you during your battle with Thun was very strong." She reached out a hand when Bronwyn stepped close, running her fingers lightly over Bronwyn's auburn-red curls. "I was so proud and so worried when you fought. Your cleverness and tenacity were a good match for Thun's pride."

"Thank you; I almost failed, going to the clearing too early."

"It all worked out, thanks to your fleet feet. Now, walk with me, and allow me to make a space for our fallen kin." She reached down, and the earth simply parted before her hand, making a body-sized hole. "Place the first of our kin here, please, Bronwyn." Bronwyn reached into the ring and selected the first body, pulling it forth into the rich black soil. The body was that of a tall man, similar in size and appearance to those that stood guard outside the queen's throne room. "Seraile, welcome home. Your service was great, and the Realms welcome your spirit." The soil closed over the body, and tiny shoots of grass and dandelions sprouted from the dark dirt.

They walked all around the meadow, planting the corpses of the fallen fae and even the dead animals. The queen spoke just as fondly of the dead animals, and Bronwyn wondered if they had been fae in animal form. All in all, they buried over seventy bodies in the warm, sunny meadow, and when they were done, it was covered in flower patches, and not an inch of black soil could be seen through the dark, green grass.

"Thank you for honoring the dead with me, daughter."

"Of course," was all Bronwyn could think of to say.

"I have important news for you about your people and, in particular, your friend Morgan." She paused, perhaps for effect or perhaps to make sure Bronwyn was paying attention. "My agents on Fanwath reported an invasion taking place near the location of your settlement. Energy users from another world had created a portal and were kidnapping natives by the hundreds. I was debating a response when it seems your friend, Morgan, became involved and caused the invaders to retreat."

"Oh, that's good!"

"That was my feeling until my agents informed me that the hero who closed the portal had gone through beforehand and is now trapped on the other side."

"What? Morgan is on another world?"

"That's correct, and it's quite a distant world, one where I have very little influence; the Realms don't touch it."

"Oh, no," Bronwyn frowned, imagining being the only person on a hostile world.

"All is not lost, however. I've devised a plan with the help of your friend, Coraignon."

"Really? You'll help Morgan?"

"Not precisely; I'll help you because I know you'll want to help him, and I think it will benefit humanity on Fanwath to have all of their heroes on the same world. At least for now."

"Thank you, then, and thank you for your honesty."

"I'll always be honest with you, child, even when it hurts. Now, I was able to briefly scry your friend, thanks to some help from Coraignon, who has met him several times. I found Morgan resting in a barren landscape with a few other people from Fanwath. Using that knowledge, I created this," she produced a triangular block of stone about the size of Bronwyn's hand. It was densely inscribed with flowing, looping runes of silvery metal. "This is a teleportation keystone, and I believe it will work perfectly with one of the portals in your friend's tower." She held it out, and Bronwyn took it, marveling at its dense weight and the sense of thrumming Energy within it.

"So, I can open a portal to the world where Morgan is?"

"Yes, and, in the interest of being transparent with you, I'd like you to know that those that invaded from that world are not native to it; they hail from yet another world and are heavily influenced by the Winter Court. It is in my interest to see you rescue your friend and thwart them further." Bronwyn narrowed her eyes and regarded her queen, whom she'd grown so fond of so quickly. She noticed that she wasn't feeling the overwhelming emotion that had stricken her while speaking to the queen in her throne room.

"Is something different? Your aura isn't overwhelming me with emotion anymore."

"I'm trying harder to restrain it, Bronwyn, and I have less influence in this place than in my seat of power."

"Well, thank you for helping me and for telling me all of your motives. That's all of them, right?"

"No. I also wanted to reward you for your service against Thun. You struck a great blow against the Winter Court, Bronwyn."

"Should I get going then? It sounds like time is of the essence."

"Yes, but Bronwyn, there's one more thing. Your friend Morgan currently holds a powerful boon granted to him by the System upon your people arriving through space. Coraignon noticed it right away, and though he seems a good person and tries to stop evil when confronted with it, I'm not sure he's the right person to hold it. He has a title that makes his already powerful Energy use vastly more so; the System has designated him as Humanity's Champion. Perhaps you should discuss with him if he's the right one to hold it; it can be transferred."

"Oh, really? He never mentioned that to me."

"Indeed."

"Well, alright, I'll talk to him." Bronwyn didn't quite know how to feel; she did want to confront Morgan about the title, but she also felt like this was the first time the queen had tried to manipulate her. Obviously, she was implying that Bronwyn should try to take the title or, in a best-case scenario, get Morgan to give it to her.

A breeze fluttering through her hair broke Bronwyn's internal dialogue, and she saw that the queen had summoned a portal. "This will take you to a meadow near your people's settlement. Good luck, daughter! I know you'll be successful." Bronwyn smiled, feeling awkward with her mind whirling in a dozen directions, but she managed a wave and a smile.

"Thank you," she said and stepped through the portal. The air changed in quality immediately, and though it was still summer, everything smelled different. The light was different, and she felt instantly more isolated. Bronwyn hadn't realized how at home she felt in the Fae Realms now, and she wondered what that said about the changes that had occurred in her. Movement from the corner of her eye caught her attention, and she looked up at the blue sky, gasping when she saw the unmistakable sight of a dirigible airship. It was hanging in the sky, attached to a long tether, over the long, dun-colored wall of First Landing.

MORGAN

As the huge, sweltering orange orb of the planet's sun slipped beyond the western horizon, Morgan began his descent into the gargoyle settlement. The night was very dark, with no moon in the sky, but Morgan's Void Vision made traversing the terrain easy, and when he got down near the captive enclosures, he moved stealthily in the even deeper shadows of the high, mud-brick walls. When he followed one wall to a point where the small lake's muddy shore met with its corner, Morgan took a moment to smear some mud over his exposed, pale flesh, hoping to aid in his deception.

At ground level, the walls were much larger than they appeared from up on the ridge, and he got disoriented a few times trying to find the correct enclosure. He had to leap up to grab the high wall, pulling himself up to peek over, only to discover that he was looking down at strange creatures and not the Ardeni he was trying to join. Still, he went unnoticed, and his third attempt brought him to the correct pen, and he quietly mounted the wall, sliding over on his belly to fall nimbly to the hard-packed dirt ground.

He landed near a sleeping Ardeni, who didn't notice his arrival, but another younger man was sitting near the wall and gasped when Morgan landed. "Shh," Morgan said, holding a finger to his muddy face.

"Who are you?" the man whispered.

"I'm a friend. I'm going to figure out what these guys are doing, then try to figure a way to get you all out of here."

"What do you mean? They're kidnapping us. Isn't that obvious?" another voice asked from behind Morgan. He whirled to see a white-haired female Ardeni, dressed like a sailor.

"Yeah, but what's going on in that pyramid? Why are they bringing captives here? How do they open the portals? I can't get you out of here until I understand more." Morgan whispered, glancing around furtively.

"They can't hear you, and if they could, the big brutes probably wouldn't understand." She gestured to the disc on her wrist. "They don't worry about us as long as we're wearing these."

"Why not break them off? I thought they had to keep an eye on you to keep you from removing them."

"Well, why didn't you break yours off?" She asked defensively, looking at Morgan's wrist.

"This? It's fake." He showed her the scratched-out runes.

"Oh! We can't remove them. When we think about trying it, we feel burning pain in our heads."

"Ahh, now it makes sense. I took this and some others off some people I rescued. I'll take them off you. No, wait. I'll scratch out the runes like on mine; then you can defend yourselves if the time comes, but you won't draw suspicion in the meantime." Morgan summoned one of his knives from his storage ring, which he'd put on a leather string around his neck. Then, he scratched out the runes on the woman's pewter bracelet. He handed her the knife, "You should be able to do the same for the others now. How often do they come to take prisoners into their hive?"

"It seems random. I don't know."

"Alright," Morgan noticed that their conversation had drawn more of the Ardeni over, and he whispered, more loudly, "Hey, don't make a scene; I'm trying to help you all. Has anyone seen Roald, the artificer from Tarn's Crossing?"

"Yes! He was here; they took him earlier today."

"Dammit! How do I make sure they take me when they come for prisoners again?"

"Just be near the gate; they just grab the first of us they see," one of the new arrivals said, a short, stout, green-haired fellow.

"Look, when you get your bracelet fixed, don't start attacking gargoyles or trying to run. We aren't on Fanwath, and I don't know where a portal to get us home is. I'm going to try to scout out the gargoyle nest to figure out what's up, but I need you guys to play cool until something changes or I return with some news." Morgan had raised his voice slightly, making sure all the Ardeni heard him, and then he nodded and moved over by the bamboo-like gate. None of the Ardeni were resting near it, probably to avoid being taken, so he had a lot of space to himself while he waited. The woman he'd been talking to came up behind him.

"What will you do in there?"

"I don't know. Watch what they do; figure things out. That kind of thing."

"What if they're killing the people that they bring in there? They never come back."

"Then I'll have to resort to violence. I've slain my share of these creatures." He spoke matter-of-factly, and the woman took another look at him.

"You're big; that's for sure. Are you a high enough level?"

"We'll find out." Morgan shrugged and sat down in the dirt in front of the gate. She moved away, taking his short response for lack of interest in the conversation, and he felt a little bad for seeming rude, but he had some things on his mind. He had a bad feeling about Roald, and he didn't know how he would break it to Issa if he found Roald was dead. For the hundredth time that day, he wondered if Issa was okay. Had she gotten out of the Deep Down after he got sucked into the portal? Had she continued searching through those tunnels all alone, looking for a sign of him or her father? Was she still alive? He'd tried Guardian's Senses, again and again, never getting any sign of her, and he knew that was normal with him being on another world, but it still stressed him out.

He forced himself to meditate and work on cultivating his Core while he waited for the gargoyles to come. He noticed right away that the Energy in this world was sparse compared to Fanwath, and he made very little progress over the course of two full cultivation drills. He was about to start a third when the gate rattled, and a guttural snarl signaled the arrival of some gargoyles. He stood up, waiting for them.

The gate was jerked open by the lead gargoyle, and it strode forward to Morgan with no hesitation, holding out a length of rope. It slipped the looped rope around Morgan's head, pulling the scratchy cord uncomfortably tight, and then it and another gargoyle walked back into the pen, hunting for more people to add to their harvest. The Ardeni crowded into the far corner, trying to avoid them, but the gargoyles were relentless and began to drag two others toward Morgan and the gate.

At one point, Morgan heard the voice of the woman he'd been talking to raise in a shout, saying, "Don't you dare! You'll blow our chance!" Morgan silently thanked her; he figured she was stopping one of the Ardeni from using Energy to attack the gargoyles. Soon the other two captives were hooked to the rope, and the gargoyles were dragging them out of the pen, Morgan in the lead. He walked quickly, so there was slack in the rope; he didn't like the feeling of being tugged around by the neck.

As they were led through the muddy paths between holding pens, Morgan could hear the wails of the captives and smell the decay of death. Clearly, some of the prisoners were in worse shape than those in the Ardeni pen. The gargoyles didn't say anything, just breathed heavily, grunting or growling at each other as they progressed. At one point, another string of captives passed in front of them, the gargoyles leading them in a bigger hurry than the ones pulling Morgan and the two Ardeni along. Morgan saw that the captives hooked to that other line were the bird-people he'd spied from above. There were five of them, and they spoke in a strange cooing warble that reminded him of quail.

"Why doesn't the System Language Integration work on those people," one of the Ardeni behind him asked.

"I don't know. Maybe they're like Yeksa," the other replied. Morgan thought about that; why didn't the language integration work with Yeksa? Were they too low with regard to Energy affinity for the System to bother with them? His thoughts were interrupted as the gargoyles began to mount a long, muddy staircase leading to the bottom tier of the ziggurat. Up close, the hive-like structure seemed to tower over him, far more than he'd thought it would, and the tunnel on the first tier yawned widely, smoothly constructed of compressed mud.

As they finished the climb and began to move into the wide tunnel, the air grew damp with humidity, and hot air seemed to waft from within. Groups of gargoyles moved about in the tunnel, passing by Morgan's slow-moving group on both sides. Morgan counted a hundred or more gargoyles as they traversed through the big tunnel; most of them were the large, walking creatures, but now and then, a group of the thinner, flying gargoyles would swoop past. They turned from the central tunnel about a hundred feet in, taking another side tunnel, narrower in construction but angled upward.

The side tunnel began to bend and climb more steeply, and Morgan grew convinced that it was spiral in nature, moving up through the levels of the ziggurat. Other tunnels opened in different directions at occasional intervals, but the gargoyles leading them stayed on the main, upward-climbing, curving path. After a ten-minute climb, the tunnel finally leveled out and opened into a massive, oval chamber buzzing with activity.

Morgan saw a double row of bubbling green-crystal tanks shaped very much like the cryo-pods on the *Pilgrim*. A line of twenty or more gargoyles stood to one side of the room, and a string of bound captives was on the other. As they were led over to the line of prisoners, Morgan watched as one of the robe-wearing "Evolved" gargoyles led a captive frog-person to one of the tanks and forced it to get it. It didn't scream or thrash, just laid down in the roiling liquid. Then the gargoyle leader hissed something at one of the hulking gargoyles, and it strode forward to submerge itself in the adjoining tank.

While he watched, wide-eyed, Morgan and the Ardeni were added to the end of the prisoner queue. The two tanks roiled and hissed, green steam rising into the air, and then the shadowy form of the frog-person that Morgan could just make out through the green crystal of the tank seemed to dissipate and fade away. The gargoyle burst out of the other tank a few moments later, no longer hulking and bipedal but taller, with wings. It screeched triumphantly, and the robed leader hissed at it, subduing its outburst and chasing it out of the chamber with shrieks and clicks. "What the fuck?"

"Ancestors! Are they using people to advance their race?" the Ardeni next to him asked.

"I think so, but this shit needs to stop right now." Morgan produced another of the knives he'd taken from the Swordmaster's Citadel and handed it to the Ardeni. "Start working on cutting these others free. I'm going to start killing gargoyles." Morgan snapped the cord holding his ring around his neck and slipped it onto his finger, summoning his Umbral Razor. He slashed through the rope around his neck, focused on the gargoyle leader, and cast Void Step.

With a crackling rip in reality, he faded from existence and reappeared directly behind the gargoyle leader, his black, smoking sword already swinging toward its neck. The creature didn't have a chance to react, caught completely by surprise as it was screeching at another gargoyle. Its high-pitched command cut off as its gray, hairless head thudded to the ground. For a moment, the room was silent, and then the massed gargoyles burst into frenzied action, howling and charging at Morgan.

BRONWYN

Bronwyn loped easily through the trees and across the meadow leading to the eastern gate of First Landing. Quite a lot of activity buzzed around the entrance; people were going in with loads of timber and other bulging sacks and loads. A flock of weird little sheep-like creatures was being driven out into the meadow, and a regular crowd was waiting for the guards to allow them through into the town.

When she got to the back of the line to wait, she noticed that many of the people going in and out were of the native races, and she felt some comfort seeing that the locals seemed to be accepting the new human settlement. She stood head and shoulders above most of the people in line, and as the line shrank, one of the guards caught sight of her and shouted, "Is that you, Bronwyn?" She recognized him but couldn't remember his name.

"Yes," she replied, smiling broadly.

"Shit, come in! The council will want to see you! Where have you been?" Bronwyn pushed up past the others in the line. Some grumbled and muttered, but they let her past when they got a good look at her. She wasn't wearing her spiked armor, but she had a sense of confidence and an aura of Energy that, when added to her natural size and her beautiful face, gave people pause when their first instinct was to be unpleasant.

"I had to take care of some far-away business, it seems. I would've let the council know, but it kind of took me by surprise. What's going on? What's with the airship?"

"Oh, this crowd at the gate is typical; we've got a lot of trade going with nearby communities, but the airship is new. Some explorer or traders or something came out of the north on it and made contact. They're Ardeni but also have little painted people called Bogoli on board."

"Huh! Any idea where I can find Arthur Ballard?"

"Yeah, the new council building; follow the road to the hill. You can see it from the Stone."

"Right, thanks," Bronwyn said, pushing through the gate. When she laid eyes on the interior of First Landing, Bronwyn had her first clue that she might have been gone a little longer than she'd subjectively felt. Nothing terribly drastic had changed, but there were enough new things that she wondered if she'd been gone longer than the few weeks it seemed to her. Shops lined both sides of the boulevard, and the crowds, while still predominantly human, were quite diverse.

She passed by an alchemist's shop, a tailor, a butcher, and an actual inn called "The Sleepy Hare," which had sprung up across from the bathhouse. Terraced flower gardens had been installed on the Colony Stone hill, wrapping it in tiered layers of vibrant color. Quite a few people called out greetings to her as she climbed up the steps to the top of the hill. Queues delineated with polished wooden handrails had been installed on each side of the Stone, and quite a few people were in line to interact with it.

She looked down the hill toward the original tavern, saw that it was swarming with activity, then looked beyond it to a large, square, stone block building with an actual, honest-to-goodness clock tower rising out of the steepled roof. She could see from where she stood that it was 1:35 in the afternoon.

She strode down the steps, followed the cobbled path around the pond next to the inn, and then approached the stone building with the clock. Another sign of growth or progress that had a more negative connotation was the rifle-wielding guard standing next to the big wooden door. He wore neat uniform pants with a matching button-up, navy shirt, and a conical metal helmet. "What's your business?" he asked, barely glancing at her.

"I need to talk to Arthur or any other council members here. I'm Bronwyn Tallow." That woke him up, his eyes snapped in her direction, and he cleared his throat, moving to pull the door open.

"Sorry, ma'am! Welcome home!"

"Thanks," she said, walking through the open door. She'd been welcomed home to two different places today, and it felt kind of good. The inside of the administrative building was cool, with high ceilings and big banks of windows letting in plenty of light. There was no secretary or receptionist, at least not yet; the foyer opened into a large room with a big meeting table at its center. Several people sat around chatting. Bronwyn saw Arthur, Maria, and Alec Green talking to a tall woman with long black hair and a gorgeous gray and silver robe. She could only see the woman's back, but she swore little blue flames were flickering along her shoulders.

Arthur's eyes turned toward her, and his face broke into a huge smile, "Bronwyn! We were so worried about you!"

"Heya, Arthur. Hi, everyone," just then, the tall woman turned, and Bronwyn just about fell over; it was Olivia, and she looked amazing. Her red lips spread in a bright smile, lighting up her face, and Bronwyn immediately noticed that her eyes were different; they were both blue now, but they seemed to smolder with flickering light. Her scar was nearly gone, as well, though Bronwyn could see it, knowing what to look for.

"Holy shit!" She strode forward, and Olivia met her halfway, and they grabbed each other up in a tight embrace. She was so much bigger! Olivia felt substantial and tall and incredibly warm. She tucked her chin down into the crook of Olivia's neck, savoring the scent of her, then she pushed her out to arm's length and took a good look at her face, "What happened? You look amazing!"

"You too, Bron! You seem lighter, happier; where have you been?"

"Hey, I asked first!"

"Well, we have a lot of catching up to do! I'm here for a week!"

"Yeah, we definitely do. Um, I hate to bring bad news to a happy reunion, but I have some information about Morgan." She let go of Olivia's shoulders and turned to the other council members, "You guys know where Morgan's been?"

"Last we heard, he was traveling to Tarn's Crossing to speak with an alchemist about something to do with his arm," Arthur said.

"His arm?"

"Oh, hmm, yes, he had one of his arms cut off in a fight."

"Oh, jeez," Olivia said.

"Well, I have information that he was pulled into a fight with some people invading from another world. I guess there was a portal, and he managed to get it closed, but he got stuck on the other side somehow."

"What?" Maria gasped. "Another world? Invaders?"

"Yeah, I guess with portals and teleportation and whatnot, things like that happen. From what I gather, the invaders were kidnapping people near Tarn's Crossing." Bronwyn shrugged.

"What can we do?" Arthur asked, almost at the same time as Olivia.

"I might have a way to open a portal to where Morgan is. I think we need to help him."

"Of course, we do!" Olivia blurted. "What about Issa? Is she with him?"

"I don't know. What I know, I've told you, other than how we can get a portal open, which is with this," Bronwyn pulled the portal stone out of her necklace and held it up. "We need to put it into one of the portals in Morgan's tower, and it should work." Olivia reached out for the stone, and Bronwyn handed it to her, though she felt reluctant to let go. What was that about? If she could trust anyone, it was Olivia, right? She shook her head, realizing she'd missed what Olivia said. "What?"

"I said, where did you get this? Who told you about Morgan?"

"I," she paused—how much should she share about the fae? Did the queen want her to mention their relationship? She hadn't said anything to the contrary; still, Bronwyn felt some hesitation. "I made friends with a very powerful being, a member of an elder race. She gave me the information and made this stone."

"Hmm," Olivia ran a thumb along the silvery runes. "You trust her?"

"Yeah, but we can be careful; we should bring soldiers with your new rifles. We'll take some through and leave some to guard this end of the portal."

"An excellent idea," Arthur said. "I don't like the idea of opening a portal to a hostile world from inside the walls of First Landing, but I can't condone leaving Morgan and perhaps Issa stranded. Not after all they did during the Urghat invasion."

"Right," Maria added.

"Well, we have five council votes here," Alec piped in, finally joining the conversation. If we're all in agreement, I think you should act sooner rather than later."

"Yes, go make your preparations. I'll pick some militia with the new rifles and send them to the tower." Maria started walking to the door.

"Let's go get this portal working, Bron," Olivia said, also starting toward the door.

"Wait! You don't have to come, Olivia! It's going to be dangerous." She reached out a hand to grab Olivia's arm, but the other woman took another step, pulling away.

"You don't have to worry about me," she turned and grinned at Bronwyn, fire dancing in her eyes, "I've learned a thing or two that might be helpful."

"Right..." Bronwyn trailed off as Olivia continued through the door, striding purposefully in her shiny, ankle-high black boots. Bronwyn followed after, throwing a final glance at Arthur and Alec.

"Good luck! Please keep us informed of developments," Arthur said in parting. Bronwyn nodded and slipped through the door, hustling to catch up to Olivia's long strides.

"Hey, wait up!" she called as she came up behind her. "Damn, Olivia, what's with all the flames flickering behind you?"

"Oh, they're not hot, don't worry. They seem to spring up more when I'm agitated or hurrying."

"Yeah, but like, what's the deal with them?"

"I absorbed part of a primal elemental's spirit. Plus, I have a class that enhances my elemental affinities."

"Well, shit. That's cool. You're still you, though, right?"

"Yes, silly. I'm still me, though I should maybe ask you the same question. Seems like you have a few secrets of your own."

"Right, well, like I said, we need to spend some time chatting. Right now, I think we should hurry, though."

"Why do you think I'm walking so fast?" Olivia laughed, and Bronwyn grinned along, happy to hear the sound again.

When they arrived at Morgan's tower, the door opened easily for them, and Tiladia was waiting inside, her twinkling lights bouncing agitatedly. Her voice, sounding like falling glass on a metal floor, came across as strained, "Lady Olivia, Lady Bronwyn, welcome to Morgan's tower. Have you word of him?"

"Actually, yes," Olivia said, "We do. We need to visit the portal hub he has in this tower because he's been trapped on another world." She hefted the portal key that she still held, "Does this look like it will work with his portals?"

"Hmm," Tiladia swished through the air to the outstretched stone, swirling around it. "Yes, it looks much like the ones that Vormendion used. Is Morgan alright?"

"We don't know," Bronwyn said, moving past the other two toward the stairs. "Is there a trick to getting to the portal hub on these steps?"

"It's the fourth floor. Just think of it as you mount the steps, and you should arrive where you desire. If not, I'll find you." Bronwyn nodded and started up the steps, trusting that Olivia would be close behind. She took three steps and then found her fourth, bringing her out onto a landing. Looking around, she saw that she was in the right place; six stone archways lined the round room around the stairwell, each densely covered in runes. When she finished looking around the room, Olivia stepped onto the landing next to her and immediately approached the archway directly ahead of them.

"Let's see here, Tiladia; where's the keystone fit?"

"Directly in the center of the arch; do you see that gap between the stones?" Tiladia's voice answered immediately, and Bronwyn turned to see her floating, flickering form hovering at the top of the stairs. "Do be careful, though; the portal will require a large influx of Energy to activate, and I'll have to close it if hostiles come through."

"You can do that?" Olivia turned to regard Tiladia.

"Oh, yes."

"Alright, well, we're waiting for some militia to come and help out," Bronwyn said.

"Oh! I'm terribly sorry, but Morgan has not extended guest privileges to any of the militia. The only other person, other than Issa, that has permission is Maria Rios so that she can tutor Ykleedra."

"And we can't give anyone else permission?" Bronwyn asked with a sigh.

"No, I'm sorry; Morgan hasn't extended those rights."

"Alright, Tiladia, what about through the portal? If we rescue others, can they come through? You mentioned 'hostiles' coming through," Olivia asked.

"The portals are unable to distinguish friend from foe, which is why they're not to be left unattended while active." Tiladia's tone had grown higher and higher during their conversation, and Bronwyn realized that she was experiencing something like panic.

"Relax, Tiladia. It's okay! Olivia and I will go through and find Morgan, but if we send other people we rescue through this portal, I need you to let them through the tower to the outside. Maria will be coming along; tell her what's happened and that she's in charge of anyone that comes through before Morgan or us."

"I will, but there's one more concern, ladies," Tiladia spun about between the two of them.

"Yes?" Olivia asked.

"Though I sense you have enough Energy to open the portal, if you go through, it will only remain open for a few dozen minutes. I can guarantee that Maria does not have the Energy stores to re-open it."

"Alright, so if we don't find Morgan right away, we need to keep our explorations short; we can come back through, wait, and then reopen it, right?" Olivia rubbed her chin thoughtfully as she spoke.

"That should work, yes," Tiladia said, sounding calmer. Olivia nodded, then reached up with the stone between her hands, slipping it into the gap at the top of the arch. It sank in with a satisfying *snick*, and she took a step back.

"Any tips on how to activate it, Tiladia?" Olivia asked.

"Simply channel Energy into the stone you just placed. Once you've reached the threshold, the portal will open."

"Give me your hand, Bron; here goes nothing," Olivia said, holding one hand back for Bronwyn and the other out toward the stone. Bronwyn reached forward to hold onto Olivia's warm hand, and then her friend suddenly flared with bright blue flames. The stone at the center of the arch began to glow with an orange luminescence, and a vibrating hum emanated from the arch. Olivia only concentrated for a few seconds before a red, swirling pane of Energy sprang to life in the archway, opening a window into nothing and everything all at once.

◈ OLIVIA ◈

Opening the portal had taken more than two thousand Energy, which was probably a significant amount. Still, Olivia could have done it almost three times in a row with her Energy stores. Squeezing tightly to Bronwyn's hand, she stepped into the portal and felt her friend coming in after her. Though darkness enveloped her, and there was no feeling of air or movement, she felt like she was being thrust through inter-dimensional space with incredible power. She couldn't say whether it was an effect of Morgan's tower amplifying her Energy or the keystone that Bronwyn had obtained, but the teleportation through the portal was swift. One minute they were in the tower; the next, she was stepping onto hard-packed, sandy dirt under a moonless, star-filled sky.

"Who's there?" A panicked voice hissed. Olivia looked toward the speaker, seeing a huddled group of Ardeni limned in the red light of the portal.

"We're friends. Where's Morgan?" Bronwyn said, stepping up next to Olivia.

"Morgan? The big fellow who rescued us? He's insane; he went to sneak into the invader's base." A taller, smooth-headed man said, standing up and moving a bit closer.

"I've got his tracks," Bronwyn said, moving around the portal and pointing up the side of a nearby hill.

"Wow! That makes things easier," Olivia said. She turned to the huddled Ardeni. "Are there more people in need of help? Why did Morgan go to sneak into their base?"

"Yes! He said he saw lots of captives in pens. He wanted to sneak in to try to figure out a way to get us out of here," a woman replied, moving up next to the taller, bald man.

"Alright, well, we've got a way out, but we're on a time crunch. I need one of you to step up and come with us; if we find people that need rescuing, I'll want someone to lead them back to the portal." The huddled Ardeni looked at each other, eyes wide as they glanced at the portal. The first man who had spoken to them shrugged and stepped closer to Bronwyn.

"My name's Sento. I'll come."

"Great," Olivia said, pointing at the portal. "The rest of you through there. You'll be safely back on Fanwath. Lead the way, Bron." She gestured up the slope, and Bronwyn didn't wait for any second-guessing; she just trotted right up the side of the hill, and Olivia had to hustle after her. She was thankful for her new boots; no matter how the gravel and sandy dirt tried to slip out from under her, she never lost her footing. She could hear Sento panting behind her as he scrabbled up.

Bronwyn didn't slow, loping easily up and down the sandy hills, avoiding the strange cacti that looked like triangular shadows in the darkness. After a short while, Bronwyn scrambled up a steep ridgeline, and Olivia had to strain to keep up. She took her eyes off Bronwyn to look for handholds, and when she finally scrabbled to the top, with Sento grunting quite a ways behind her, she was surprised to find Bronwyn laying on her belly looking out over a settlement of some sort.

"Get down," Bronwyn hissed. Olivia dropped to her hands and knees, scooting up to lay next to Bronwyn.

"What do we have here?" Olivia whispered, looking out over the strange scene. A small lake, illuminated by scattered light posts and reflecting the stars above, sat at the base of the ridgeline. All around it were dark, rounded walls made into the shapes of pens, and Olivia could see huddled people lying, pacing, or sitting within them. A squat pyramid rose above the desert floor at the far end of the lake, dark openings on several of its tiers yawning into dimly lit tunnels.

"Look," Bronwyn said, pointing to an oversized shape that seemed to be patrolling up and down one of the lanes between pens. From there, it looked like a giant, hunched man, bathed in shadow, but when it stepped into the light of one of the posts, Olivia saw that it was unclothed and dark gray. Now that she'd seen one, she spotted dozens more of the creatures pacing around the pens.

"Guards?" she asked as Sento finally gained the top of the ridge and fell down onto all fours, panting. "Sento, are those big gray guys walking around the ones that kidnapped you all?"

"Yes," he said, finally gathering his breath. "Your friend called them garboils or something."

"Gargoyles?" Bronwyn asked.

"That's it." He nodded, grunting as he tried to scoot forward on his belly.

"Well, should we try to get these captives moving back to the portal? We'll have to fight those guards at least, but if we can get everyone running, we might be able to hold them off." Bronwyn fidgeted, then added, "We only have around half an hour 'til that portal closes."

"I don't know; what if there're thousands of those things in that pyramid?" Olivia asked, frowning. "I hate to say this, but maybe I should go back through the portal, so I can keep it open while you try to figure out where Morgan is."

"Yeah, that might be the best move . . ." Bronwyn was cut off as a loud, reverberating klaxon blared forth from the pyramid. It sounded like a dozen discordant horns being blown at once, and it instantly changed the scene below: captives jumped to their feet, jostling to see what was going on, and the gargoyles on patrol all started running toward the pyramid. "What the fuck?" Bronwyn stood up, squatting down, ready for action.

"I feel like this might be the time to move; this feels like Morgan is up to something," Olivia said, also climbing to her feet.

"If the number of gargoyles charging into that big tunnel is any indication, he's going to have his hands full. We better move!" Bronwyn yelled, already starting down the slope.

"Come on, Sento! You've got to let these prisoners out and get them back to the portal! Bronwyn and I are going to find our friend." Olivia charged down the slope after Bronwyn, trusting her boots to keep her from slipping. Soon they were racing around the edge of the little lake, running full tilt toward the pyramid; there weren't any of the "Gargoyles" in sight, having all run into the big tunnel on the first tier of the structure. "Can you still see Morgan's tracks?" she called to Bronwyn. Damn, but she was fast!

"Yes! I can see where he climbed the wall!" She ran around the pen where, presumably, Morgan had climbed in, but she didn't turn back to the gate when she circled the corner, charging ahead toward the steps leading up to the tunnel. "I saw his tracks coming out of that pen," she called back. "He's gone up the steps!" Bronwyn was pulling ahead of Olivia, and she didn't show any sign of slowing. Olivia dug deep, running as hard as she could, wishing she'd learned some spells that would allow her to move faster. She couldn't stop her mind from theorizing ways to utilize wind spells with her air Elemental Form to make her run faster, but she shook her head, focusing on the moment.

When they gained the top of the steps and Bronwyn charged into the tunnel, Olivia paused to look back. She could already see people streaming out of some of the pens; Sento had done as she asked. Hopefully, they'd all work together to release as many as possible. She didn't know who all was held in those pens, but anyone kidnapped and living in captivity deserved to be freed as far as she was concerned. She turned and charged after Bronwyn. The dark tunnel gave her pause, for the first time fearing she might lose Bronwyn. She yelled ahead, "Bronwyn, wait! I can't track!"

The tunnel was lit with weird chunks of red-range crystal that shone periodically out of the mud-caked ceiling or high on the walls. In the dim, creepy light, she was relieved to see Bronwyn slow down and turn to look at her, waving her forward impatiently. "I'm running as fast as I can," she softly called as she got closer.

"Yeah, I'm sorry, look, I can see Morgan's tracks cause they're tons brighter than the gargoyle tracks, which, by the way, the System calls Rakeyda tracks, but there are fucking shit loads of those things. I mean, I can't count them all cause they're piled on top of each other, but it's in the hundreds."

"Well, we need to hurry, not just for Morgan, but for the portal! I'll try to keep up." Olivia started jogging, and Bronwyn hurried past her, leading the way. She took a sloping tunnel to the right, and Olivia could see that the dried-mud ground had seen a lot of traffic, even without Bronwyn's tracking skill.

"His tracks go this way, but so do all the Rakeyda tracks. Some look really old and faint, but hundreds are bright and fresh." They continued, jogging up the tunnel, ever climbing as the tunnel wound upward through the gargoyle, or Rakeyda lair. Their spiral climb had grown tighter, and Olivia felt like they must be nearing the top when some figures charged around the corner, racing toward them.

A tall Ardeni man, followed by a dozen or so other types of people from a burly Urghat, to several bird-like people, to a diminutive, little lady with the features of a rodent, came charging toward them, eyes wide with panic. They were covered with mud and gore, and they slid to a halt when they saw Bronwyn and Olivia. "Run! The invaders are busy fighting a madman!" the Ardeni hollered as he got close.

"We're going to help him! How many invaders?"

"Hundreds! You won't get to him; he's fighting a retreating battle up another tunnel; the invaders are between you and him! Run!" He didn't listen to their protestations or to Olivia when she shouted about the portal. The crowd of escaped prisoners rushed past them, taking little care not to jostle or shove the two women.

"Can't blame them; they look like they've been through hell," Bronwyn said, starting up her jog again. Olivia followed her wordlessly. After a short while, they came to a large chamber littered with Rakeyda corpses. Olivia saw a handful of other dead people, but the gray gargoyle-like corpses made up the vast majority. Bronwyn stopped in her tracks, pulling her collar up over her nose, and Olivia held a sleeve over her own mouth when the scent hit her—the air was warm and damp, and the overpowering stench of spilled guts and bile made it very difficult to breathe.

"Good grief!" she hissed, scanning the room for any sign of Morgan.

"Did he do all this?" Bronwyn walked into the room, careful not to step in the puddles of blood and gore. Empty, bubbling, green-crystal vats occupied the center of the big room. Some of them were cracked with their contents dripping down into large, pungent puddles. They were working their way through the room, scanning for signs of Morgan, when a terrible screaming roar cut through the distant sound of the alarm klaxon. Bronwyn turned toward the sound; it had emanated from the mouth of a narrower tunnel that led away from the room, up into further heights.

"We should . . ." Olivia cut herself off as Bronwyn started sprinting toward the tunnel. "Here's hoping one of us can get back to the portal in time," she sighed, running after her. She figured they still had twenty minutes or so before the portal collapsed, and she was pretty sure Morgan or Bronwyn could make it back in less than ten. Hopefully, one of them would be able to get it open again if Olivia couldn't make it.

When she entered the tunnel, she saw that it had a door that had been slammed into the wall so hard that the hinges had broken, and the mud-caked wall had cracked and crumbled into a pile around it. She charged up the narrower tunnel after Bronwyn, hopping over bloody, broken, gray corpses with every few steps. This new tunnel was very steep, and, once again, Olivia thanked her new boots; she made several missteps into puddles of gore and was sure she'd have slipped onto her face had it not been for the magical footwear.

She had to scrabble over a small pile of corpses to catch up to Bronwyn, but when she did, the other woman held her back. "Get ready; they're just ahead, around this corner; are you sure you can fight?"

"Oh, I can do better than fight," Olivia said. "Just don't stand in front of me when things go sideways." With that, the two women stepped around the final corner to look into a high ceilinged, square room about forty feet across. A small horde of gray, roiling, thrashing beings, some tall and hulking, others thin with wings, and still others, standing near the back, wearing robes and wielding beams of scarlet Energy, had cornered a familiar figure. Morgan stood with his back to the room's corner, his long, black sword sweeping left to right, keeping the creatures at bay.

His eyes were wild, and his tall, black-clad body was surging with stolen red Energy. When the gargoyles in the front were pushed into a charge, they seemed to overwhelm him for a second, and then a rip in reality made Olivia doubt her senses for a moment; was she losing consciousness? Then the sound came to her—a rending of light and space and time, a sound so strange and so against nature that her hackles rose and her mouth filled with saliva as though her body was preparing to purge a poison. A black globe of nothing spread out from Morgan, decimating the front row of Rakeyda, causing them to turn and try to flee in panic. When the bubble faded, Morgan was standing among a pile of broken corpses, brandishing his sword, waiting for the next wave.

"Look!" Bronwyn said, pointing to the other side of the room. Another Rakeyda variant was standing on a platform, hurriedly flipping levers and moving crystals around on a control panel of some sort. Tubes ran from the control panel to several large vats lining the wall, where Olivia could see humanoid shapes floating in green bubbling liquid. The Rakeyda on the platform was enormously tall with massive wings and wearing a shimmering silver robe.

"I'll help Morgan! You go try to deal with that guy!" Olivia shouted. Bronwyn nodded and charged forward, and that's when the entire pyramid shuddered, vibrating like it was on top of a giant snare drum. The klaxon, still droning away outside, cut off, and a different sound commenced; something like a giant jet engine or train. Olivia kept her feet, thanks to her boots, but nearly everyone else in the room stumbled when the rapid vibrations rolled through the chamber.

"Stop him!" Morgan roared, and Olivia turned to see him pointing his sword at the tall, silver-robed Rakeyda.

⊱ MORGAN ⊰

Morgan was exhausted, and the strain of sustaining himself via Energy Drain was starting to show; his pathways were burning, his Core throbbing, and his mind felt frayed, like he couldn't focus properly on a given thought. Still, he persisted, and now, against all hope, he saw Bronwyn and Olivia standing on the other side of the throng of gargoyles. Was his mind playing tricks on him? Had the gargoyle leader created some sort of illusion to throw him off? How could they be here?

He saw them hesitating at the entrance as if wondering if they should help him or deal with the big wizard gargoyle that was messing around with that big control panel. He menaced the encroaching gargoyles with his sword, trying to keep them back until his Energy Drain was ready again, and then the world started to vibrate. The alarm that had gone off when he began smashing the green crystal tanks faded away, but a new sound took its place—something like a whooshing rattling freight train or, as Morgan had experienced once in his life, a tornado.

The ground shook more violently for a moment, and he stumbled back into the corner, bracing himself against the wall. Most of the gargoyles fell down, so he wasn't overwhelmed immediately. He looked toward the big, robed gargoyle and saw its hands glowing bright red, and some sort of Energy was pouring out of it into the bank of crystals it had been messing with. Morgan turned to where Olivia stood with wide eyes and shouted, "Stop him!"

He watched as Bronwyn leaped to her feet and then charged the robed gargoyle with her fists suddenly limned in golden light. Olivia saw Bronwyn's action, and she turned to Morgan, striding toward the rear of the jostling, grunting, hissing mini-horde of gargoyles. "Damnit!" Morgan hissed, worried that she was about to become gargoyle food. Then she burst into blue flames, and a torrent of lightning-wrapped fire that hurt his eyes to look upon sprayed out of her hands, completely annihilating the back third of the gargoyle throng. "Holy shit!"

Olivia didn't stop there; she took another step forward and sprayed a stream of orange, smoking magma over the next clump of gargoyles in her path. They fell away, either instantly dead or so incapacitated by pain or injury that they might as well have been. There were only twenty or so gargoyles left between Morgan and Olivia, and she shouted, "Move out of the way!" He didn't have to be told twice; he turned to where Bronwyn was fighting the big winged and robed gargoyle and activated Void Step. With a crackling rip in space, he was gone, and Olivia unleashed another torrent of plasma, spraying it over the screaming, mewling gargoyles.

Morgan appeared behind the robed gargoyle as it fired a beam of red light at Bronwyn. She'd encased herself in a layer of shimmering, glowing light that seemed to be deflecting the majority of the beam's damage. Morgan swung his two-handed blade with all his might at the gargoyle's exposed back, slicing away a large chunk of one of its wings. It screamed and whirled, the beam of Energy sputtering in its hands. Morgan swung again, but the gargoyle grabbed his blade, stopping it with a red-glowing hand, and wrenched it sideways. Morgan wasn't weak, but that gargoyle pulled him around like he was a child.

He stumbled sideways as the gargoyle yanked his sword again, then the creature brought its other, glowing-red fist down on the flat of his blade, and it shattered into a thousand little pieces. "You asshole!" Morgan roared. At the same time, Bronwyn leaped backward, avoiding a swipe of the gargoyle's long, spiny tail.

"Did I break your toy, fleshling?" the gargoyle growled, a deep chuckle following its words. Morgan summoned Bloodfang and launched into the Crane Flutters its Wings, refusing to give in to the urge to bandy words with the gargoyle. The creature, once again, thrust its red, glowing hands out, intercepting Morgan's cleaves, though it seemed some strain started to show in its alien face. It hissed angrily, but Morgan kept pressing the attack, activating Azure Burst as the last of his cleaves was deflected.

Crackling blue flame erupted from Morgan, rolling out in a dome around him. Bronwyn's eyes widened, and she kept scrambling backward. The creature held up its hands, holding them out with red Energy flaring against the onslaught of azure flames. For a moment, it held them back, but then the fire rolled through its barrier, and it howled in agony as they washed over its silvery robe and flesh, reducing much of the material to ash. As it staggered back, Bronwyn was there with a wild, glowing haymaker that she delivered to the center of the creature's back, directly beneath its wings.

Something cracked loudly with the impact of Bronwyn's fist, and Morgan dove forward, thrusting his sword into the creature's gut. The gargoyle coughed up a gout of blood, and, to Morgan's horror, it reached a glowing, red hand out to grab Bloodfang. Just as it started to pull, the ziggurat shook again, vibrating rapidly, and Morgan stumbled. Bronwyn, who'd been coming in for another attack, also stumbled. The gargoyle laughed again, even as it fell to a knee, "Fools, you're too late. Better to run and hope I'm too busy to seek vengeance."

Morgan fell back onto his butt as the ziggurat shook again, violently. What was happening? Something to do with the control panel the gargoyle leader had been interacting with. Still sitting on the vibrating ground, Morgan pointed his sword at the crystal and wood control panel and primed a Vortex Lance. The gargoyle saw what he was doing and screamed, "No, you idiot!" Just then, a white, steaming streak of superheated water vapor tore through the gargoyle's face, obliterating half its head, and Morgan's Vortex Lance blasted forth to shatter the crystal face of the control panel.

"Got him!" Olivia crowed, running over the vibrating ground. "What's going on with this place? Is it going to blow?" she hollered over the roaring, freight-train sound that accompanied the shaking. Morgan was about to try to answer when the world suddenly turned inside out. The light became darkness, and darkness became blinding light. Bronwyn, who'd been struggling to her feet, suddenly lost her physical aspect and looked like a wispy, vaporous being of pure Energy. Morgan strained to look at Olivia and saw her also reduced to a flickering, multi-colored walking torch.

"Whaaaaaaaaaaaa . . ." He tried to ask what was going on, but his voice turned into a long, quaking warble that echoed in his head. Then with a buzzing zap and an avalanche of silence, everything reverted to normal, and Morgan was left lying on the ground, dumbstruck by the lack of noise and normal aspect of his vision. "What the hell?" He grunted, just to see if sound still existed, and he noticed Olivia's heavy breathing and Bronwyn's muffled curses like a spell had been broken.

"Something just happened; we weren't in normal space," Olivia said, her words coming out thick and slurred.

"Ungh," Morgan grunted, struggling to his feet. He looked around the upper chamber of the ziggurat, noting the mangled remains of the gargoyles that Olivia had finished for him. Then he realized the lights that had been glowing orange-red the whole time he'd been inside the mud-caked interior of the gargoyle base were dead, but a pale white-yellow shaft of light was streaming through a door behind where the control panel had been. "Let's see what's going on," he gestured toward the door.

"Right," Bronwyn said, fully recovered from her fall. She took two steps toward the door, and then the light suddenly changed from dim shadows illuminated by the shaft of light to an omnipresent golden glow. Morgan looked around to see a tremendous haze of golden motes rising from the defeated gargoyles. Suddenly a broad river of Energy was transfixing Morgan, lifting him into the air, and something similar was happening to Olivia. Bronwyn's stream of Energy was significantly smaller, though her share from the gargoyle leader alone was enough to stop her in her tracks.

Congratulations! You have achieved level 32 Void Adept and have gained 8 Intelligence, 8 Will, and have 12 points to allocate.

"Level!" Morgan said as a reflex when he'd recovered.

"Same," Olivia said, "And I can make my first refinement!"

"Huh, I didn't level yet," Bronwyn said with a shrug. Then, she strode through the door, Morgan close behind, and he saw her mount some stone steps. He glanced back to see Olivia right behind him, still limned in pale blue flames.

"You need to explain what's going on, Olivia; seems you learned a thing or two at that school."

"Yep," she winked at him, "But you have some explaining to do first, my friend."

"Yeah, just tell me: have you heard from Issa?" Her grin fell away, and she shook her head.

"Sorry, Morgan. I just got back from the academy yesterday, and then Bronwyn brought news of your predicament. I'm not sure where Issa is." They'd nearly reached the top of the steps, and the bright light was now accompanied by crisp, cool air. Morgan took a deep breath; he hadn't realized how terribly dank the air in the ziggurat had become. When he and Olivia stepped out of the stairwell onto what had to be the top of the square ziggurat peak, Bronwyn was standing, looking out over a rampart, and she turned to them.

"We might be fucked," she dead-panned. Morgan stepped toward her, noticing how their breath plumed out in the chilly air. When he got to the rampart and looked out, expecting to see the small lake and the mud wattle captive pens, he was shocked to find a broad expanse of white. Snow blanketed the flat plains for nearly as far as he could see, ending only at the horizon where purple, jagged peaks rose into the pale blue sky. Looking at the sky, Morgan was further disturbed to see two suns rising toward the zenith—one was pale and white, the other larger and yellow.

"We're not in Kansas anymore."

"Yeah, and I forgot my ruby slippers," Olivia said, walking up beside him.

Arthur Ballard surveyed the sprawling refugee camp that had taken shape around the western wall of First Landing. He wanted to be annoyed at Olivia, Morgan, and Bronwyn for sending him all these mouths to feed, but the truth was, most of the refugees hadn't been any trouble at all. Even the Urghat, though unwilling to stay in First Landing, had disappeared into the northern plains without any violence, seemingly happy to just be back on Fanwath. The Ardeni were recovering nicely, and when they'd figured out where they were, they'd celebrated enthusiastically; they'd be back in Tarn's Crossing with just a few days of travel when they were ready.

The stranger folk, the frog people, and bird people, whose languages weren't translated by the System, were keeping to themselves, but the linguists and astrobiologists were having a field day trying to learn their languages and about their home biomes. All in all, Arthur had high hopes for their ability to add to the diversity and productivity of First Landing. If only he hadn't had to trade his best three Energy users for them all, he'd consider himself a happy man.

Captain Gella stood on the observation deck of his airship, *Shrike*, and watched the strange humans deal with this bizarre crisis. He'd been sitting in one of their taverns tasting one of their foreign delicacies, some sort of grilled sandwich with a smokey cheese and a tart pickled slice of vegetable when the wild low-affinity creatures had streamed out of that incredible iron tower. He'd thought the humans would massacre them; instead, they sheltered them and were trying to learn to speak with them. Bizarre indeed. He supposed the creatures didn't seem hostile like Yeksa, but if the System found them worthless, why waste the time and effort?

"They're strange people, aren't they?" Falia asked, her eyes tracking the movements of a wagon bringing foodstuffs to the refugee camp.

"Very strange, but very valuable. When Lord ap'Gravin learns about our Energy affinity surveys, he's going to reward us handsomely. I'm hoping he'll choose *Shrike* to lead the 'recruitment' efforts."

"Mmhmm. So many of them were so open and willing to share the details of their ability. Truly a naive people. It's lucky we came upon them before they learned more or allied with an established faction."

"Luck had little to do with it. Lord ap'Gravin has sources all over the continent. Well, sound the last call; we're shipping off with the sunset."

"Aye, Captain!"

Professor Oylla-dak calmly walked to her study door, refusing to hurry despite the frantic nature of the tapping. When she opened it, she was surprised to see Professor Somhairle; the reclusive professor usually kept to himself, studying his strange brand of magic that he claimed to have inherited from fae ancestors. "May I help you, Professor Somhairle?"

"Where have you sent Olivia Bennet?" He sounded strangely flustered, and the lack of niceties was quite out of character.

"What do you mean?"

"Olivia Bennet. The human student? Where is she?"

"Why are you so concerned?" Oylla found this man's urgency rather alarming.

"She is no longer on this world, Professor. Did you send her elsewhere?"

"How strange that you would know that, Professor! Her whereabouts are privileged information, I'm afraid. Did you have some need of her?"

"So, you're aware of her departure?" He seemed to calm visibly, taking a deep breath. "Very well, please let her know that I require a meeting with her when she returns. Thank you, Professor." He didn't wait for any sort of response; he simply turned and strode away on his impossibly long legs. Oylla closed the door, and when the latch clicked, her smile curved down into a frown.

"How very strange," she said quietly. She did not know where Olivia was; she was meant to be visiting her home settlement. She strode over to her desk and took out the shiny black slate that gave her access to her students' information. Holding her thumb against the cool, smooth surface, she thought of Olivia. Her information came up—Copper cohort, first year, enrollment status, course marks, known affinities, and health status. The last line was of particular interest. It didn't show Olivia's current status, but it didn't show any trauma or death, either. "If she's not tracking, then Somhairle was right; she left this world."

Oylla touched the opaque white sphere on the corner of her desk, and it glowed a soft orange as a woman's voice drifted out of it, "Yes, Professor?"

"Bring me Professor ap'Rall and the auburn-haired Ghelli girl from Copper cohort. I'll need them for a scrying."

Ykleedra ducked under the thick ferns of her new home, the beautiful atrium in Morgan's tower. She'd made a nice, dark burrow in the rich earth, surrounded by ferns and a few flowering, broad-leafed plants. She loved the damp nature of the air and the rich smell of all the plants. When she sat in her little burrow, whiling away the time, she could easily daydream with the brook's tinkling sound playing in the background. Today, as she came into the den and gently moved aside the soft, dark loam, she smiled especially broadly. Her brother and sisters would be with her soon.

She felt a little guilty about deceiving Morgan; she didn't think he'd destroy the eggs, but she couldn't trust him completely—not after he'd killed her mother and grandmother. If she wasn't mistaken, Morgan had also killed her father. He seemed regretful, but did that make it alright? Did that mean he wouldn't lose his temper and kill again? No, she had to be careful with him, and a little deceit was warranted when it came to the safety of her kin.

She looked lovingly upon the five eggs but most of all on the larger, red-flecked egg. Here was her baby brother, and he was already proving himself something special, growing nearly twice as fast as her little sisters.

ABOUT THE AUTHOR

Plum Parrot is the pen name of author Miles Gallup, who grew up in Southern Arizona and spent much of his youth wandering around the Sonoran Desert, hunting imaginary monsters and building forts. He studied creative writing at the University of Arizona and, for a number of years, attempted to teach middle schoolers to love literature and write their own stories. If he's not out enjoying the beach, you can find Gallup writing, reading his favorite authors, or playing *D&D* with friends and family.

DISCOVER
STORIES UNBOUND

PodiumAudio.com

www.ingramcontent.com/pod-product-compliance
Ingram Content Group UK Ltd.
Pitfield, Milton Keynes, MK11 3LW, UK
UKHW041304180426
11947UKWH00009B/671